The Rogue

By

Jeff Rienstra

Library of Congress Control Number: 2020907118

ISBN: 9798650974628

Special Thanks

I would like to give special thanks to the following people who kept me motivated during this "very" lengthy project. First, to my wife and daughter who let me sit out on the deck with a cigar and a laptop avoiding chores for hours on end. To my talented niece for putting together the cover. To my dentist who kept bugging me to read the book, and then providing his personal editing recommendations when I finally conceded (after many years). To my sister, Amy, who helped with editing. To my Captiva fishing buddy who read an unfinished version and encouraged me to continue. To my brother-in-law, the first who was ever allowed to read it during the early stages, and telling me that I might have something worth pursuing. To my childhood buddies who shared this same infatuation (Jim & Reed) – remembering those camping trips and adventures in Michigan's great outdoors. We had fun with some wild imaginations (i.e., *"The Boogie-Wamp Swamp Monster Climbing up a Tree..."*) For all others who have pursued this passion. And finally, to my mother who always said that I should be a writer.

TABLE OF CONTENTS

PROLOGUE

"In a time before cell phones and social media ..."

The leaves in Michigan's Upper Peninsula had begun to turn early in the fall of 1998, the end result of an unnaturally hot and dry summer season. The calendar marked only the first weekend in September and already travelers could spot dense pockets of spectacular color amidst the hardwoods populating the northern soil. Oaks, sugar maple, beech, basswood and birch produced a conglomeration of flaming reds, magnificent yellows, and luscious greens, transforming the highlands and valleys into a vast sea of heavenly beauty. Fall was the season where Mother Nature unharnessed her true potential with breathtaking scenery that could compete with any that the Midwest had to offer.

In the north woods, outdoor sports weren't just spotty pastimes handed down to a select few. Hunting and fishing was a way of life ... a mechanism for survival, as well as a pleasuring indulgence. The sportsman's personality transformed into that of a five-year-old child on Christmas morning when hunting season knocked on the door. Northerners, speaking their Yooper English, a dialect influenced by Finnish immigrants, tolerated the invasion of *flatlanders* into their territory as a means to their own economic survival. The *Trolls*, as they were often called, from beneath the Mackinaw Bridge, stimulated an economy dependent on seasonal draws. Real cash flow had a way of washing aside cynical dispositions born from seeing those countless "toys" with manufacturer's suggested retail prices surpassing what an average working man might earn in a year. Specialty stores would feed droves of giddy husbands with inventive excuses to purchase the latest and greatest in outdoor equipment. If a man failed to own some form of weaponry related to *"the Hunt,"* then his peers might deem him to have something genuinely wrong with his persona. For the hoard of aliens that would make the annual pilgrimage to the U.P., jobs and families were forgotten. Soldiers of the fall sought solace where there were no traffic jams or annoying beepers. Left behind were all elements of chaos that formed their hectic societies. Hunting was an escape, and escape is what they did into the nineteen million acres of federal and state lands accessible to the public. A man could disappear and not cross tracks with another if he so desired. But solitude was a dangerous fate to tempt.

The wilderness acreage of Northern Michigan houses a variety of creatures thriving in uncultured habitats, most of which have been mercifully denied the destructive forces of Man's civilized expansion. For those who venture into this land with respect to its discreet but volatile personality, the experience could be both enlightening and fulfilling. But for those ignorant souls who fail to understand barriers that should not be crossed or abused, fate no longer becomes a product of their own self-control. Nature has her little secrets that the human race, with all of its sciences and abilities to reason, was neither meant to discover nor comprehend. From the impenetrable jungles of the Amazon to the towering peaks of the Himalayas, strange forms of life have remained hidden from human eyes since the beginning of time. Humanity's fear of the unknown is what gives birth to legends that persevere through generations. Many believe in stories of large beasts stalking the forests of Oregon, or serpents lurking in the depths of Lochness. Ignorance is the idea that Man must explain only that which presents itself in true form rather than in theory. When a new life form is discovered, the thought process automatically makes one visualize remote corners of the globe. Folks find comfort in believing that their own backyards are void of such revelations. In truth, Michigan possesses her own pockets of impenetrable swamplands where Man has never walked. The creatures that dwell there have remained in seclusion ... until now.

***

The Upper Peninsula had experienced a summer unlike most in '98. Some would say that it was due to the El Niño phenomenon. An abnormally wet spring saw the region pounded by torrential rains that flooded many of the western lowland areas. With the jet stream pushing in warm air from the southern plains, rain took the place of what would have been late winter and early spring snows. Rivers quickly overflowed their banks. Thousands of creeks sprouted new veins with the surplus of water draining down from the highlands. Animals were displaced from their natural habitat as maneuverable land mass in the swamps deteriorated. Deer and bear climbed to higher ground in search of food. Coyote and bobcat were seen more frequently, as they, too, were driven from cover. The regularity of wildlife sightings left a false sense of security that the weather had not upset the balance of nature. Unbeknownst to those who tracked such things, nothing could have been further from the truth. Nature simply brought more animals together to compete for less space. Incidents involving a black bear wandering down *Main Street* became old news. The surging number of nuisance-animal complaints saw law enforcement agencies allocating more resources to critter relocation. As luck would have it, the anomaly did catch the eye of tourists. People loved to see the bears, so long as they weren't opening hatchbacks or raiding picnic baskets at campsites.

But just as the rains came, so sudden and harsh, so did they go. Spring fell into summer, which proved to be just as bizarre. When the rain ceased in mid-June, it stopped seemingly for good. Intense heat followed. Lowlands that had so recently driven out the animals, sucked them right back in as the food supply in the timber dwindled. A dismal crop of acorns sent the whitetail in search of cedar. July and August experienced record temperatures averaging in the mid to upper 90s, sometimes peaking above the century mark. The drought had gripped the entire Midwest. From May to late August, rains came in small, insignificant amounts.

While the crops lay parched in the fields of America's heartland, the tall timbers of the north woods showed that they, too, were affected by the drought of '98. Fires soon blazed throughout Minnesota, Wisconsin, and Michigan, scorching thousands of acres of forest. It didn't take long for that summer to be labeled as the worse fire season in history, rivaling the extreme droughts that had plagued western states like California for years.

What frustrated the firefighting community most was what little spark was needed to ignite the infernos. They would start from the ineptitude of careless campers, a cigarette butt tossed out the window of a car, or kids playing with fireworks left over from the 4th. The results were always the same in the end ... habitat lost. State parks were closed from state to state as *Smokey the Bear* indicators signaled *high* fire danger at park entrances. The unstable weather, coupled with the park closings, took a major divot out of an economy that lived on the almighty tourist dollar. People stayed home or spent their hard-earned money elsewhere.

In early August there was one fire that seemed to surpass all others in terms of magnitude. It occurred in the western portion of the Upper Peninsula in an area spotted by only a few small communities. This particular fire had left the experts utterly perplexed because of the peculiar center of the burn. About forty miles south of Houghton-Hancock there begins one of the largest cedar swamps in the entire Midwest. The tangle of thick conifers takes form just south of State Route 38 running between Ontonogon on the western coast of the peninsula, to Baraga, a quaint settlement in the southern-most tip of Keweenau Bay. Ranging between ten and fifteen miles in width, the swamp snakes its way south until making an abrupt turn to the west just north of State Route 28, where it then extends through the Middle and East branches of the Ontonogon River. There had once been a logging road dissecting the center of the swamp, but the two-track had long since closed after being washed out by rains and melting snows through the years. The only real access is by way of canoe down the Ontonogon, a route rarely taken by paddlers. The threat of being stranded kept most sportsmen with any wits about them searching for other avenues of enjoyment.

The fire began somewhere in the middle of the great swamp. Black smoke billowed so high that it could be seen for twenty miles in any direction. Most believed the blaze was caused by a lightning strike from a rare summer thunderstorm. The environmentalists were caught completely off guard because they had no idea that the drought had affected the lowlands to such a degree that would allow a normally saturated area to burn with such fervor. It was soon discovered that the problem with battling a swamp fire was gaining access to it. There was really no safe mechanism for getting firefighters and their equipment into the major cell. The brunt of the battle was waged from the sky with planes and helicopters dumping water and fire retardant chemicals. The intense heat proved to be too much for the men and women who fought it. Bordering towns became their priority. Local units of the National Guard were mobilized by the Governor, along with a mass of volunteers, digging trenches to stop it from spreading into the highlands. Many would say that it was divine intervention that prevented an all-out breach. Dry winds brought a cool storm front down from Canada and dumped four inches of rain in less than twenty-four hours. The flames were doused and the swamp's invader had been checked at the door.

It had been a glorious day when the last spark fizzled out on the great swamp fire of '98, but the ordeal did not pass without cost. The Devil had collected his toll in the form of fifteen firefighters who sacrificed their lives. Nearly every town within a thirty mile radius was quick to establish memorials for the brave souls that put themselves in harm's way and paid the ultimate price. The firefighting community grieved in their own way. A county park was reserved for a day allowing 480 men and women to reunite and ponder the fight they had endured together. There were no families ... no news cameras or journalists ... just firefighters and a few Guardsmen who stood by their sides. At the center of the gathering were fifteen two-by-fours pounded firmly into the ground. Sitting atop each stake was an empty helmet, still black from soot and ash. And at the base of each post sat a keg of beer as a monument to each fallen comrade.

Aside from the long-lasting effects on surrounding communities, there were enormous consequences to the ecosystem. As happens with most forest fires, animals became disoriented in their attempt to evade the virulent threat. Having been driven out of the large swamp in the preceding spring by the unforgiving rains, they were cast out a second time by the heat and destruction of the fires. It was first thought by so-called experts from local universities like Michigan Tech, Northern and Lake State surveying the region that natural habitat had been altered to such a degree that life would have to regenerate from within before most creatures would return to its sanctuary. After numerous aerial surveys, it was discovered that the majority of the swamp affected by the fire had been its most impenetrable, central region. It was a tract of land so dense that it might never have witnessed a man's presence. Though many of the creatures that dwelled there had perished, there were others that instinctively and cautiously followed the food sources to higher ground, remaining undetected by their own desire. These creatures were forced from their natural habitat into a territory that would quickly jeopardize their existence. The encounters with Man began soon after the Amen fire of '98.

CHAPTER ONE

"Okay kids, settle down back there. Why don't we play a little game?" James Carmichael made his attempt to restore order in the overloaded station wagon. Lori, his wife of ten years, briefly lifted her head from the nook between the car seat and the window. James noticed a red line indented in the meat of her forehead where the chrome trim from the door had pressed against her skin. He wondered how she could sleep with such a racket coming from the back seat. It was inevitable, an eight-year-old boy with a six-year-old little brother getting bored on a long road trip. *What the hell else were they going to do*?

"What kind of game, daddy?" inquired Jody, the eldest of the two Carmichael boys. Jody's blond head eagerly popped through the gap between the bucket seats. His brother Robby, always trying to keep pace, tugged at Jody's shirt from behind. The older brother kept the six-year-old at bay with a sharp elbow to the chest. Robby's wail reverberated throughout the car.

"Daaaaadeeee!" cried the emotionally injured adolescent. "Jody hit me!" James heard a crisp slap of retaliation from Robby's hand making contact with the back of Jody's neck.

"Oh boy, that really hurt," responded the older sibling matter-of-factly. "You hit like a girl," he teased.

"Daaaaaadeeee!" The youngest boy's voice climbed another octave.

It was time for the father to step in. A small headache had evolved into a real humdinger during the past twenty minutes, and James' nerves were beginning to fray. The endless verses of *Row-Row-Row Your Boat* and One Hundred *Bottles of Beer on the Wall* could cause a man's head to explode. On more than one occasion, James almost wished that his throbbing noggin would go ahead and disintegrate, ending his current state of suffering for good.

"Alright, that's enough from you guys." James reached back and grabbed Jody's collar before another assault. He almost chuckled aloud when he heard himself utter those infamous words ... "Do you want me to stop this car right now?" *Boy, if that didn't bring back some memories,* he thought. Only there had been four hyper-active boys in the back seat of his dad's old Chrysler. *Christ, the headaches that pop must have had.*

"Ha, ha!" hooted Robby, witnessing his brother's plight.

"That goes for you, too, Rob" added James. Robby sank back dejectedly in his seat, teetering on the verge of a crying spell. His pale white cheeks began to turn red, camouflaging the tiny freckles that were sprinkled across his pudgy face. James knew that both boys were tired. They were all tired. "Now, do you two want to play a game or not?" he asked, trying to recondition the atmosphere. He released Jody's collar. Lori had barely twitched through all of the commotion. The attitude in his boys instantly changed to that of excitement. James was amused by how a child's focus could turn 180 degrees with the use of just a few choice words. With the enormous work load that had been dumped into his lap over the past few months, he could use a tangent from reality himself.

James Carmichael had closed a big deal that afternoon in Chicago. The Yagazuki Corporation had finally accepted his bid to landscape a new facility in Naperville. He smiled with pride at the thought of receiving his next commission check. It would be a nice boost to his family's cash flow. James had been working on the deal with the lift-truck manufacturer since the initial announcement that the company was investigating the Chicago area for development of a three-tiered facility that would ultimately sit atop sixty acres of prime real estate. Yagazuki was the second largest manufacturer of material handling equipment in the world, and when James Carmichael closed the deal his resume became that much more appealing. He worked for Grow-Tech Industries, a landscaping firm specializing in industrial park development. Yagazuki had been his first major score in a profession that saw only short-lived moments of glory. "There was always more business to be gotten," was the motto of an idealistic boss who was an arrogant east-coast transplant five years his junior.

But James could at least relish in the moment for now, even though the moment saw him taking a painstakingly long drive to visit his wife's Aunt Edna in Houghton. Lori had driven the first four hours of the trip, giving James just enough time to unwind from the day's activities in the city. After passing through Green Bay, the weary father took over the driving detail, and that's when the boredom began to unravel in the kids. *If only they knew what awaited them at Edna's,* James smirked inwardly. James began to wonder what the hell he was supposed to do all weekend. The only two activities that seemed to be available that time of year were fishing and looking at trees. Since James wasn't the outdoor type, having been raised in the confines of Cincinnati, Ohio, he was not too keen on pursuing either. He could care less about the changing leaves, the northern air, or the tug of a steely at the end of a fishing line. He looked forward to the possibility of slipping into town to visit a pub or two while the kids explored the wooded acreage around Edna's estate. There would be some major butt-kissing before Lori would release him. He'd become quite proficient in that category. He had done a lot of coddling with the Japanese over the past few months.

"What game are we going to play, daddy?" expressed Jody impatiently.

James adjusted his visor to block the evening sun. A silent belch escaped his mouth allowing him to taste the Big Mac he had eaten two hours earlier.

"We're going to play the *deer game,* boys," replied the senior Carmichael.

An inquisitive expression crossed Jody's face. "What's that game, daddy? Have we played that game before?"

James smiled at the curiosity exhibited in his son's voice. Robby's head broke through a small space that his brother had inadvertently left unoccupied. A moment of opportunity grasped.

"Can I play too, daddy?" asked Robby, anxious to join in on any form of activity that presented itself.

"Yes, Robby, you can play too. The game works like this ..." explained the sly father, capturing the interest of four eager ears, "both of you look out your windows for deer. If you see one before the other spots it, I'll give you a whole dollar."

"Oh wow, big whoop," replied Jody as he rolled his eyes. He let his father know that he was less than impressed with the prize money that had just been placed on the table.

Times sure have changed, thought James. *A buck must not have the buying power as it once did in a child's world.* "Okay, how about two bucks?" James gave the counter-offer, having fun negotiating with his oldest boy. He was determined not to go any higher than five.

"Five bucks and I'll play." Jody made the offer final as if he was reading his father's mind, folding his arms firmly across his chest with a look of stubborn resolve.

The father gazed at his son through the rear view mirror. He wanted to laugh, but refrained. *That boy's going to be a good negotiator someday.* He was suddenly gripped by a feeling of pride that only a father could understand. "Alright, Jody, five bucks it is."

"Oh wow! A whole five bucks," injected Robby with great ebullience. He had been closely monitoring the exchange between his dad and his brother. Five bucks would buy a ton of Power Ranger comic books. Both boys split to their separate sides of the car with faces plastered to the chilled glass of the windows.

Lori stirred in the front seat. She reached over and softly caressed her husband's wrist. "You okay, honey?" she asked while letting out a wide yawn. She slowly arched her back to work out the kinks from the short, but effective nap.

"I'm doing fine now that the boys are on a little mission," replied James, gesturing toward the back seat.

Lori smiled and stole a quick glance at her sons, each engrossed with the task of winning the money. "Are you sure we can afford this little game of yours?" she asked with a grin, once again focusing her attention to her husband.

"After today, Lor, I may have been able to afford ten bucks." They both laughed.

"My husband the child psychologist."

Lori glanced out the window, searching for some hint as to their location. "Where are we?" she finally asked after detecting no apparent signs of civilization.

"We've got about another hour to Houghton," replied James, squeezing his wife's hand.

"It sure is a pretty evening. And those colors are absolutely gorgeous," noted Lori, referring to the sea of trees ascending up a steep ridge on the eastern side of the two-lane highway. The other side fell off into what looked to be a swamp. "Didn't they have some big fire around here?" asked Lori, recalling some footage that she had seen a month or so ago on CNN.

"Yeah, I think so, but not exactly sure where." James noticed a turkey buzzard picking at the carcass of a dead raccoon on the side of the road. *Stupid animals,* he thought. "I believe it might have been around these parts."

James Carmichael didn't realize how close to the burn site they actually were – less than a mile from one of the endangered perimeters to be exact. The two of them gazed forward, enjoying the peace that had overcome the car.

"There's one, daddy! I see one! I see one!" cried Robby in the back seat, bouncing up and down like a turbo-powered jack-in-the-box. He spotted two does preparing to cross the scarcely traveled hardtop.

"Goddammit!" was the response of the shocked father as the car swerved slightly onto the shoulder. "Robby, don't you ever yell like that in the car!" he scolded.

"But daddy, I saw two deers! I won the game!"

James tipped his head forward to stretch his tight neck. He took a few seconds to allow his nerves to settle. He heard a light chuckle from his wife as she continued her stare out the window at the passing trees. "Alright, Rob, you won the game," he finally conceded.

"Yay! I won! I won!" bragged the boy.

Jody refused to let his brother's poor gamesmanship provoke him. He tried to remain relaxed, even though he was seething with envy inside.

James began to feel pressure on his bladder. He hadn't taken a leak since the stop in Green Bay, and those two Cokes were taking their toll. "I've got to make a pit-stop, hon," he declared to his wife. "Does anyone else have to go to the bathroom?"

"Where you going to find a bathroom, daddy?" asked Robby, taking a short break from mulling over how his new financial fortune should be invested.

"You're so stupid," responded Jody, trying to get a rise from his brother. "Behind the trees, dorkhead."

"Don't call me a dorkhead. You're a ... a ... stupidhead." Robby's comeback didn't seem to have quite the hitting power that he had hoped for.

"That's enough, boys." Lori finally spoke up. "I could use a quick stop too, dear."

James smiled. “Just don’t squat in any poison ivy,” he jested. He pulled the car over and slowed to a stop on the gravel. Traffic had been unusually sparse for a Friday evening. The sun was just beginning to dip over a rise on the far western horizon. James opened his door and was greeted by a brisk rush of cool September air. Lori followed his lead.

James slowly rose to his feet, crinkling his nose at the stabbing pain in his stiff knees. He took a deep breath and felt the fresh air fill his lungs. He then looked around and noticed the color in the trees, whiffing at the sweet fragrance of the pines. *It is beautiful,* he thought. There were no horns blasting or sirens wailing. He could actually see himself enjoying that type of setting. *Oh the hell with that,* he decided. There wasn’t any money to be earned up in those parts.

“Come on, Jimmy.” Lori interrupted his moment of meditation. She turned away from the car and walked up a sandy embankment to the edge of the forest. Tall ferns brushed against her thighs as she made her way to a hidden spot amongst the trees. Lori loosened her belt, dropped her jeans, and squatted next to a pretty birch. She could barely make out the top of the station wagon on the road below. Her ears detected James struggling to make his way up the embankment and then shuffling through the foliage to his own secluded potty-place a short distance away.

The boys remained in the car with neither claiming to possess the need to go. Jody figured that it was his turn to be in control, him being the oldest and all. He did have that unwritten right of seniority. And his first order of business to establish that inherent power would be to change seats with his little toad of a brother. Not because he wanted to ... just to prove a point. “Okay, Robby, I want to sit on that side now,” declared the new leader of the automobile.

“This is my seat and you can’t have it,” protested Robby.

“I’m going to hit you if you don’t move.” Jody leaned forward with an intense look to validate his threat. Robby tried to push him back, but didn’t have much luck. He was pinned against the door.

“Leave me alone, I’m going to tell mom,” cried Robby. His cheeks began to turn red again.

"You tell and I'll push you out of the car ... and mom and dad won't even care." Older brothers had a way of being so cruel. Jody grabbed Robby by the front of his shirt and shook him hard. And then Robby screamed. It was an awful scream, certainly not the product of a simple tease. Jody released his grip, knowing that he hadn't shaken him *that* hard. He looked into Robby's eyes and noticed something different about them. They were not filled with the typical anger and frustration of a bullied little boy. They were wide ... with fear. His younger brother cried out again, nearly forcing Jody to cover his ears. Robby raised his arms and pointed a quaking finger to something behind his brother ... something that was outside the window.

"What's wrong, Rob?" There was now genuine concern in Jody's voice. But Robby didn't respond. He only stared with terrified eyes fixed in space ... outside the window.

Some strange force began to turn Jody's head against his will. He did not want to see what had frightened his brother so, but Jody knew that he didn't have a choice. He cautiously turned around. At first he was blinded by the bright rays of sunlight. There was nothing else ... only trees descending down the embankment on the far side of the road. He began to believe that either Robby was pulling a fast one in response to the earlier threats of physical abuse, or that the dorkhead's imagination was running wild again. He was always waking the family in the middle of the night, besieged by childish nightmares, usually involving the werewolf or some other icon of evil. He was such a baby sometimes. Jody thought about how he himself hadn't experienced those types of nightmares since he was ... and then he saw something at the edge of the road. It wasn't immediately visible because it had blended with the trees. But now he saw it ... standing there ... looking at him. Jody's body instantly went rigid. He could barely hear his own uncontrolled screams mixing with those of his brother. The two boys clutched each other tight and rolled to the floor.

Jody wanted to believe that his father had heard them, but then his mind drew a ghastly vision. *Oh please ... please ... no,* he cried to himself, too scared to speak out loud. He couldn't control the trembling. Jody then detected Robby's sudden silence. His brother's limp body just laid there in his arms. His eyes stared blankly to the ceiling.

"Robby!" Jody was now more scared than ever. The swelling tears began to stream down his cheeks. "Robby!" he shouted, trying to pull his brother out of his state of shock. Robby would not move or acknowledge that he had heard anything. "Robby!" Jody cried again and again.

Jody suddenly ceased his attempt to revive his little brother. The inside of the car had changed somehow. The Taurus had become darker, as if something had cast a shadow over it. He glanced upward and noticed that sunlight was no longer reflecting off the inner door where Robby had been sitting. He turned his head, hoping that that his father had finally returned. Jody was unprepared for what he saw next. His mouth could make no more sound as he stared in horror at what filled the window's glass. The hideous face spread from side to side, top to bottom. Its eyes searched the interior of the car until they finally settled on the two boys. Had he looked more closely, Jody may have been able to detect the curiosity written in the creature's expression, perhaps similar shock to what he was experiencing. But in the youngster's mind his worst nightmare had come true, and he was about to be slaughtered by the most grotesque monster that ever lurked in a child's closet at night. Jody Carmichael's world went dark as he collapsed on top of his brother.

At first, James determined that the screams emanating from the car to be the product of another sibling battle. He zipped up his fly and pulled his belt snug around his waist.

"Jim?" It was Lori calling from behind some trees. "Can you see the kids?" There was concern in her voice.

As he took a step in the direction of the road, James stopped. The screams had quieted. *Hmmmm,* he thought, *the fight must be over.* He decided that the boys would receive some minor punishment in an attempt to hush them for the remainder of the trip.

Lori finished her business in swift fashion and peeked through the trees in the direction of the car. "Oh my God! My boys!"

Her cry sent Jim sprinting to the edge of the tree line. When he looked to the car he couldn't see the boys inside. Panic rippled through his body. *How could I be so stupid to leave them alone?* He'd heard the stories of abductions in supermarket parking lots.

Why should things be different up there? "Where the hell are they?" he yelled.

"I don't know!" answered Lori.

"Jody! Robby!" cried the anxious father. There was movement in the brush on the far side of the road. For a brief instance James thought he spotted a dark patch of hair pass through a gap in the trees. But he was more concerned now with the fate of his boys. James slid recklessly down the embankment and performed a full body roll in the gravel at the bottom. Loose stones dug into his skin. When he got to his feet, James raced to the car, the worst possible scenarios fumbling through his scattered brain. Lori had made her own way to the vehicle.

"I saw it ... I saw it cross the road!" she screamed. "Where are my babies?"

James had no idea where the kids were. He could not see them through the window. In two hasty strides he was at the rear door. When he swung it open he saw both boys cowering on the floor.

"Oh Christ!" James bent down to Jody who straddled his younger brother. Both boys lay motionless in each other's arms. Jody appeared to be unconscious, while Robby's eyes were wide open. His little face was white as a ghost's. Robby would not acknowledge his father's presence. "Jesus Christ, what the hell happened?" asked the disheveled father to nobody in particular.

Lori ran around to the opposite side of the car and opened the door. Her hand covered her mouth as if holding back another scream. "My babies!" she sobbed.

James gently picked up Jody while Lori tended to Robby. He uttered his eldest son's name, invoking no response. Jody's eyes remained closed, his complexion pale and clammy. "I think they're both in shock. We've got to get them to a hospital, now!"

The Ford station wagon sped down the highway, well exceeding the posted speed limits. Lori sat in the back seat with one son propped up under each arm. She gently caressed their foreheads.

James finally broke the long stretch of silence. "Lori, what did you see back there? You said you saw something."

His wife, who had been staring down in a daze, looked up to meet her husband's eyes in the rear view mirror. "I don't know.

I...I just don't know," she answered weakly, her voice crackling with every word. "I just saw this big ... something ... run across the road. Running ... on two legs! My God, I don't know what it was! It was after my babies. That's all I know, Jim. It was after my babies." More tears streamed down her face. There would be no more conversation in the car.

James silently pondered his wife's words. He had been kicking himself for failing to protect his family in the way a father should. But he, too, had seen something. The only reasonable explanation was a bear. The part about running on two legs didn't quite fit, but who was he to tell what a bear could or couldn't do. He had no fucking clue! The one fact that he did know was that Jody and Robby had the living shit scared out of them.

***

Peter Brummeister opened his tired eyes to darkness. His dream had been disturbed. He had been young again, fishing with his little brother Mikey down by the old mill pond. "By God," he whispered. It was as if he and Mikey had actually been there. That smile, he could remember it clear as the morning sunrise. *Mike was always a good kid,* thought the aged man. *Always full of piss and vinegar, that one.* It was seventy years since he'd last seen him. It was just before his brother had been stricken down by polio at the premature age of seven. "Poor bastard."

Reality quickly settled in and the dream vanished. He was old again. There was a noise outside. It was a heavy clanking sound followed by a chorus of frenzied squawks. Something was stirring the birds in the henhouse. Brummeister reached for the lamp on the nightstand. *Probably those damned coyotes,* he figured. When he found the switch, the lamp clicked on with a less than adequate lighting effect. He glanced over to his wife, Mildred, who lay still on her side of the bed. A string of drool hung from the corner of her mouth, ready to drop to the wet spot on her pillow.

Strange, thought the old man. *Usually those critters didn't have to worry about breaking down doors to get at my cluckers.* Peter looked at the alarm clock on the nightstand. It read 3:36 A.M. He'd be up in about an hour anyway. He couldn't sleep much anymore.

He swung his white legs over the side of the featherbed and pushed himself up off the mattress until his bare feet made contact with the cold, wooden floor. "Yikes," he whispered softly as a shiver darted up his humped spine. Peter stood up as straight as his curved back would allow, and then stepped into the moccasin slippers that had been a gift from a granddaughter last Christmas. He walked over to the closet and reached inside, feeling his way up the side wall for the flannel robe that traditionally hung on an old brass hook. The robe had also been a gift from a grandchild, but he couldn't recall which one. There were so many anymore. He gingerly made his way into the kitchen without the aid of any lights. He didn't want to chance scaring away any critters just yet. He'd much rather say "how-do" with a dose of buckshot.

Brummeister had gone through this routine before. The coyotes would wander in every now and then and try to pick off a few chickens for a cheap meal. There were just too damn many of them ever since they repealed the bounty on their pelts. "State idiots," he scorned, "got their heads up their asses." People had lost interest in trapping the mangy dogs when the profit was taken out of it. He had sure shot his share through the years. The general rule of thumb in the U.P. was, if you saw one you shot it and let it lay.

Peter raised himself up on his toes and peeped out the kitchen window centered squarely over the large porcelain sink. It was too dark to make out any shapes in the yard. His cataracts prevented him from seeing much in the daylight, let alone at night. There was no moon to speak of to illuminate the two acres of land that made up his homestead. But that was the one good thing about buckshot ... you didn't *have* to see much.

He next went over to the closet in the walkway between the backdoor and the kitchen. Inside he found his Ithaca propped up in the corner. There was a box of shells on the top shelf. The rounds slid easily into the well-oiled twelve-gauge that had been handed down to him from his own father. After the sixth shell slid snugly into place, the old man returned the half-empty box. Peter had always taken good care of his guns. The Brummeister sons would appreciate his efforts one day when it was their turn to inherit the family heirlooms.

He racked the first round into the chamber, making more noise than he would have preferred. He half expected his wife to scamper out into the kitchen ready to clobber him over the head with a rolling pin. Mildred was always getting after her husband for not realizing his age when he went off like this. "Call the neighbor, you old goat," she would say. "You'll drop dead one of these days, Peter, and I'll let you rot where you lay."

The hell with that, thought the feisty old German. *I'll bake my own bread. Nobody's gonna piss for me.*

Peter took one last look out the window. There was still nothing visible to the naked eye. The sounds from the yard had quieted. In fact, the chickens were now completely silent. He contemplated as to whether or not that was a good sign. *They must have nabbed a quick meal and skeedaddled,* he concluded. "Lordy, but them dogs couldn't have gotten all them birds." A thin smile curled across his lips. Deep down, he enjoyed the playful game of cat and mouse. Sometimes the coyotes won ... sometimes Peter won.

The back porch was slick with a layer of early morning frost. The old man eased his way forward, cringing at a moaning board underneath his feet. He'd stalked like this a thousand times before, usually after deer. But age had finally caught up to the native Yooper, confining him to his ground blind over the past few seasons. Doc Turner had warned him that it was time to give up hunting altogether. His heart had showed some abnormalities at the last checkup, and until they located the root of the problem, the physical exertion of meandering through the woods was put on hold.

The night air was painfully brisk, and there was no breeze to conceal any noise. He knew that coyotes had sharp senses, and they would be doubly alert during a chicken coup raid. "Just give me one good shot, you damned nuisances," he muttered. One shot from the Ithaca could easily take out two or three at once. "Just have to line them up proper."

Peter squinted toward the henhouse, attempting to make out movement in the shadows. There was only darkness. Suddenly, he picked up on a rather distinct noise from inside the run-down shanty. It sounded almost like ... chewing. *Chewing? Chewing what?* He hesitated and listened for a moment longer. There was a definitive crunching sound. *Damned wild dogs,* he swore under his breath. His thick German temper took hold of his emotions. Just the notion of the coyotes having their way with his birds made his blood boil. He was now furious with the realization that his entire flock might have been destroyed. The necessity for a silent approach evaporated as Peter's anger drove him to march straight across the frozen dirt between the house and the chicken coup.

As he neared the small structure, he clicked off the shotgun's safety and positioned his finger on the trigger guard. He propped the gun up into the crook of his shoulder, pointing it at the open door. Peter held back the temptation to start blasting into the night. *Hell,* he thought, *it wouldn't do them birds no harm now.* Then he noticed something that caused him to hesitate. He never left the door to the coup open. It may have happened once or twice following an afternoon feeding, but never at night. Peter was starting to feel a bit jittery as he advanced gingerly to the entryway. The continuing sound inside told him that he had not yet been detected. When he looked to the ground he saw the door. It hadn't just been opened. It had been torn away, right off its hinges. Black bears had wandered in now and again, more often than not ever since that nasty fire had burned half of that godforsaken swamp off to the west. There seemed to be quite an abundance of animals roaming the hardwoods ever since. But the bears had never been so bold as to go after his chickens. Usually they were too shy to come within a mile of a man's home. It just didn't make any sense.

As Peter worked out the scenarios in his head, the sound from within subsided and silence engulfed the yard. Peter refused to look away from the doorway that stood invitingly before him less than five feet away. His finger twitched on the trigger. *There ain't no reason to be nervous, gosh darnit.* He cursed himself for acting like a child. After all, he was the one yielding the scattergun. Bear or no bear, whatever was in that coup was going to be in for a world of hurt when he threw some buckshot at it. Peter took a confident step forward, and that's when he heard another very distinct sound. *Breathing!* It was deep, heavy breathing, not like the quick panting of a small dog. He kept the barrel of the gun pointed forward as he stepped around the battered door. His left arm slowly reached around the corner for the switch. His plan was to flick on the inside light and get a good glimpse of whatever the heck that henhouse was holding. Then, he'd let loose with the twelve-gauge.

Peter moved as silently as his aged body would allow, knowing all too well that the animal must be aware of his presence. He fumbled for the switch through the cobwebs. The heavy breathing did not stammer. It was directly in front of him. His finger found the dusty switch. He steadied the gun with one hand, ready for a snap-shot reaction.

"Peter! You out there?" It was Mildred calling for him from the front porch. Peter swung around, signaling for her to quiet when his foot got caught underneath the dismembered door. He lost his balance and watched as the barrel of the gun point skyward. The German landed on his behind with a loud thud.

"Ohhhhh ..." he moaned from the excruciating pain in his tailbone. The backyard was suddenly doused in light after Mildred activated the floodlights. For a brief moment, Peter found himself blinded. As his eyes acclimated, a terrifying cry arose from just inside the chicken coup. It was a chilling howl unlike any he'd heard before. Peter quickly spun his head and peered in. His knees knocked together beneath the robe as he sat frightened and dumbfounded on the cold ground.

Then it came, a dark, towering shape advancing on him through the murky light. It was only a few feet away. A blast of flame shot out the end of the Ithaca. Peter was knocked backward when the twelve-gauge sent a round of buckshot at the charging animal. A hoarse scream followed the shot. Peter was hit hard on the side of his head. He vaguely saw the shadowy figure pass. Course hair brushed against his cheek, leaving warm moisture on his skin. His balding head hit the ground as the escaping creature stormed past him. It darted for the trees beyond the fenced perimeter of the yard. For a moment, Peter actually thought he saw two shapes, but his mind was racing in circles. He instinctively swiveled the barrel of the gun around to where he thought the animal, or animals, had gone off to. He racked another shell into the chamber and let another round fly ... and then another. The gun bucked in his hands. Then the old man thought he heard the *twang* of barbed wire snapping. He couldn't see a damn thing. His eyes were clouded.

"Oh my!" It was Mildred reaching down for her husband's arm.

"I'm alright", he proclaimed sternly, brushing her arm away, infuriated that he hadn't gotten off a clean shot.

"Your face, Peter! It's covered in blood." Mildred wiped away a large smudge from his cheek as he rose to his feet. "You're hurt," she cried.

"That ain't my blood, Millie. I think I got a piece of him before he got out." Peter's wrinkled lips formed a wide grin. "Did you see what it was?" he asked, searching the tree line where the creature disappeared. He turned to his wife, feeling the adrenaline flow through his veins. It felt good. It made him feel young.

"I couldn't see too clear. I don't have my glasses on, but I think there were two of them. They must have been bears ... big ones." Mildred's eyesight was worse than her husband's. Her driver's license had been taken away four years earlier for that very reason.

"I knew it," responded Peter. He bent down and picked the shotgun up off the ground. *Better keep it handy ... just in case.* There was nothing more dangerous than a wounded bear in the area. His head was sore from the collision with the retreating animal. He was already looking forward to reliving this story with the boys down at the café on his daily visit into town for coffee.

Peter then turned his attention back to the henhouse. He sidestepped the fallen door and walked inside. What he saw after clicking on the light caused his heart to skip a few beats. Mildred gasped and had to look away. Every chicken had been slaughtered, some half-eaten, some just torn to pieces. Wings ... legs ... heads ... scattered everywhere. It was a bloody mess.

Brummeister took an unsteady step backward. "Why don't you go back to the house and make us a pot of coffee, Millie," he told his wife, gently patting her on the back in an attempt to comfort. She nodded her head and walked slowly back to the house, careful not to let the long housecoat drag across the dirt. Peter, in the meantime, began to search the ground for some form of clue as to how severely the bear had been hit. *Strange,* he thought, shaking his head. Bears just didn't do that sort of thing. Peter really wished he would have gotten a better idea on the animal's size, too. A quick blur was all he could manage.

When the old man looked to the far wall, he noticed a sizable hole. It had obviously taken the brunt of the buckshot load.

"Musta just nicked him with that first shot," he deduced. His eyes drew a line across the blood-stained floor to his own two feet in an attempt to pick the spot where the bear had taken the pellets. He saw a black mat of fur in a slot where two slabs of concrete formed together. Peter knelt down, hearing the numerous cracks ripple through his knees. He scooped up a chunk of meat with calloused fingers. It was a good inch thick with a smattering of long, black strands of hair. Peter brought the evidence closer to his eyes for a more thorough examination. *It sure looks like bear hide,* he thought. He tossed the tissue to the frozen ground outside, not giving the matter another thought. As far as Peter Brummeister was concerned, the case was closed. He figured that he must have hit the animal in the thigh or some other meaty part of the body.

There was no blood trail outside the shack ... only a few meaningless drops before it stopped altogether. He'd fix the fencing in the afternoon when it warmed up. Besides, it was time for Peter's coffee, and on the off chance that the wounded bear did decide to return, he would rather be inside the house with something that had a little more "pop" than the Ithaca. The .30-06 would remain uncased on the kitchen table for the remainder of the morning.

***

Birdy MacIntosh kicked the Jeep into neutral, pumping the gas twice to clear the black smoke from the tailpipe. She reached into her half-empty mail pouch and withdrew four items addressed to Mr. and Mrs. Benjamin R. Tucker of 23400 Bear's Den Highway – Jessup, Michigan. Birdy passed the envelopes through the open window and deposited them into the bill of a wooden duck, a product of Ben Tucker's woodworking talents. Ben was a retired autoworker, transplanted from the Lower Peninsula. He had become quite the crafty souvenir maker, preying upon wayward tourists. Many a Ben Tucker genuine *Injun Tomahawk* had found its way into the eager mitts of a raucous juvenile. In Birdy's eyes, Ben's birdhouses were his greatest creations. She would see them strewn along her route at various households, as well as in her own backyard. Birdy loved to watch the larks and swallows peck at the seed in the summer months. Her favorites were the colorful cardinals against the white backdrop of winter. Birdwatching was Birdy's passion, hence the nickname that stuck for over twenty years. But her interests were not limited to the winged animals. Seldom did she pass up an opportunity to stop and take notice whenever one of God's creatures presented itself. She collected hundreds of books and magazines about wildlife, and read them over and over. She digested the information as though it were more critical for her survival than the very air she breathed. Birdy was ever so close to convincing her husband to buy a computer that would allow her access to the endless world of knowledge now available on the Internet. Convincing him to spend fifty bucks on a set of radials was like trying to pry a bear cub from its mother.

Birdy closed the protruding duck bill that served as the mail receptacle's lid. She half expected to hear a "quack" in response. "Hoo-hee," she giggled. "Now that would be a hoot." She rolled up the window a few inches. Even though the afternoon sun was in full shine, the cool September air still put a nice nip on the nose. She left the window cracked just enough to allow a touch of fresh air circulating through the interior. She would do whatever it took to drown out that nasty pipe stench, a sign that her husband had recently used the four-by-four.

Just the thought of that awful smoke poisoning the lungs was nearly enough to make her gag. Birdy shook her head in distaste. She could almost feel the aroma permeating her clothing, seeping into her thick skin. Although she would not hesitate to display her revulsion for tobacco smoke, Birdy had no qualms about smokeless tobacco. In fact, she rather enjoyed a little snuff in her lip while out on the route. It was sort of a tradition in her family. Her Grandpa and Grandma Janks both chewed snuff. Her parents chewed snuff. And now she was keeping the custom alive with her own little snuff habit. *At least it isn't bothering other people,* she justified, *unlike the second-hand smoke from those darn cigarettes.* The snuff tradition that trickled through the limbs of the family tree paralleled another "inherited" trait ... significant tooth loss at early ages. "Ith's a heredithary thang," was a common phrase mumbled from the stained lips of her Grandpa Joseph in an attempt to explain the attribute that mysteriously plagued the Janks clan.

Birdy snatched a tin of Skoal from the breast pocket of her Mail Carrier's vest, an award for fifteen years of service from the small community she served. With two chunky fingers, she took a pinch from the small canister and skillfully packed it between her lip and receding gumline. Yup, Birdy McIntosh enjoyed her snuff. *One of the true pleasures in life,* she thought as the wintergreen flavor filled her mouth. Most folks around town didn't give it a second thought. But then again, most folks nearly passed Birdy off as a man anyway. She had always been quite stocky, standing five feet eight inches tall in her boots, and gracing the scales at two hundred and twenty pounds. In reality, Birdy was a dear, sweet lady with a heart of gold.

The aging Jeep rumbled into motion as Birdy shoved the gearshift into first and released the clutch. After a couple of awkward jerks, it was off to the next house three miles up the road. Birdy knew most of her "customers," as she called them, personally. She would stop periodically to collect local gossip, always willing to lend an open ear to someone's misfortunes. *A day like today will certainly bring them out,* she thought to herself. They would be working in their yards and preparing homes for the coming winter. Those "cold nasties" were just around the corner. Birdy had been after her own husband to cut up three limbs that had fallen from the big oak in their backyard after a windstorm that hit the area a few weeks back. She heard him say all too often ... "there will always be time tomorrow."

Birdy eased the rusty Jeep around a slow curve. As the vehicle made its turn, she glanced at the sunlight glimmering off a small pond. Two Canadian Geese swam lazily across the rippleless water. "Must be locals," she said to herself. The migrating birds had already started their descent to warmer climates. A thought then crossed Birdy's mind. "This would be a great day to get that recipe from Mabel." She would probably be outside working on her garden. Birdy concocted her excuse ... a minor problem with the Jeep. "Yes sir," she said with cunning intention, "I'm gonna get that banana bread recipe yet." Mabel Sanders had the most delectable banana bread recipe in the entire U.P., and Birdy had just been dying to get her hands on it. Mabel had taken the first prize ribbon at the Founders Fair in Appleton seven years straight and was hesitant to allow any competition into the mix. But Birdy had been charming the widow for years. She was always helping her out with errands around town and transporting emergency shipments of groceries when the weather was bad. Mabel, after all, was eighty-six, and when the roads got hairy in the winter months, Birdy was there with her Jeep. Heck, it was on her route anyway. That's what neighbors were for.

As Birdie drove around another bend, she detected motion out of the corner of her eye. *A deer!* The balding tires skidded subtly on the loose gravel as the Jeep came to a stop. The deer bounded onto the road, halting abruptly in the mail carrier's path. It was a magnificent buck with a rack that would cause any hunter to quake with *the fever*. Birdy eyed the animal closely, counting the lengthy tines atop its head. "Eight ... nine ... ten ... eleven," she whispered, careful not to produce any motion that might spook the buck. "Good golly, sweet molly," she uttered, "a twelve-point." *Too bad Phil isn't here to see this. His pumper would jump right to the moon.*

The animal stood in the middle of the road as if it were confused. Birdy was not about to let this opportunity slip through her fingers. She kept the Cannon Sureshot in the glove box loaded with a full clip of film at all times. She was always snapping wildlife photos while working. Deer were her favorite subjects, too. They were so graceful and pure. She especially enjoyed the fawns in the spring as they struggled to walk under the protective presence of a doe. But never had she scored a picture of a buck of this magnitude. She judged the glare on the windshield. The bright sun had a way of distorting a good shot. She decided that there was nothing to lose by giving it a try. "If it turns out ... it turns out. If it doesn't, well Phil will just have to take my word for it."

Keeping her head frozen in place, Birdy's right arm slowly reached toward the glove box. Her hand stopped before finding its destination. Only an outdoor observer such as herself could have detected the abnormality in the buck's behavior, and Birdy knew whitetails. The animal's thick chest heaved, taking in air, and then exhaling dense clouds of steam through its black, flaring nostrils. Birdy studied the eyes as they searched past the Jeep like it wasn't even there.

"What's going on, here?" she uttered silently, trying to figure out what bothered her about the deer. "Why doesn't he run?" She would have thought differently had the deer been a doe ... but such a mature buck ... well, they didn't get that big by standing around watching cars.

The buck swung its massive rack around and peered back in the direction from which it came with its nose held high to scent the winds. It then spun its head toward the Jeep, but it wasn't looking directly at the Jeep. *Something sure has that thing buggered,* thought Birdy. *It has to see me right smack dab in the middle of the friggin road.* The road darkened as the sun slipped behind a high cloud. Without moving her head, Birdy shifted her gaze to the trees in the direction of where the buck was focusing its attention.

There! Movement! She saw a shape for a brief instant before it disappeared in the foliage. She hadn't seen enough of the shape to determine what it was. Birdy directed her eyes back to the deer. There was something odd happening, but she just could not put her finger on it. As the sun reappeared, Birdy spotted a sparkle underneath the deer's midsection. It was a bead of moisture dripping to the ground. She watched that single drop fall, almost as if in slow motion, to a sizeable puddle that had formed on the gravel beneath it.

"My God ... blood!" she gasped, this time not so quietly. The realization struck her like a jolt of electricity. She brought her hand to her mouth. But the buck still paid no attention to the occupant of the vehicle. It continued to scan both sides of the road, jerking its head from side to side, becoming more anxious with each passing second.

This poor deer is wounded. But what would attack a buck like that? Birdy knew that bears wouldn't ordinarily go after such an animal. *Or would they? A fawn, yes, but a buck ... no way!* Birdy questioned her knowledge of Michigan's wildlife hierarchy. "Heck, that buck might just run down a bear and stick its behind with that rack." She almost chuckled at the notion, but the potential seriousness of the situation overrode that urge. She pondered the question with every tidbit of trivial knowledge stored in the archives of her brain. Then another concept presented itself ... *Wolves!* Though she hadn't seen any in the wild personally, she did know that the DNR had reintroduced them into the U.P. And judging by the articles in the local papers, they had done quite well. What Birdy didn't know was that the wolves had been released some fifty miles from her current location and had not yet spread to the outlying Jessup area. She knew that it couldn't be poachers. Poachers did their dirty work at night, lighting up the fields with million watt spots, and then picking off defenseless animals with high-powered rifles. *Ugly people*, thought the mail lady, sidestepping the issue for a brief moment.

Without warning, the buck shifted its body into such a position that allowed Birdy to see the wound. There was a wide, jagged gash across one of the hind quarters. It was so deep that she thought her eyes caught a glimpse of bone. One of the rear legs was coated entirely in red. "My word!" she exclaimed, keeping her hand over her mouth. The buck had been attacked, alright ... but by what? The animal took three steps toward the side of the road, stumbling a bit as though it were becoming sluggish from blood loss. "What could do such a thing?" she asked herself again. The deer ducked its head low to the ground when it reached the edge, cautiously marking each step. Birdy watched as it slowly advanced to a group of small pines. But the deer did not proceed into the cover of the swamp. It stopped and brought its mighty head around to face the rear yet again, taking one last look at the road. A dark blur appeared in the corner of Birdy's eye some fifty yards in front of the Jeep. Her first notion was that an animal had crossed, but she hadn't gotten a good look. It appeared to be something with girth.

Birdy did not yet fear for her own safety, but a nervous sensation was slowly creeping into her body. Evidently the buck had detected the same motion, because it had turned its head and froze. Birdy then began to look around, sensing that something was about to go down directly in front of her. "This buck is being hunted, and it darn well knows it." She was witnessing something that few humans had ever encountered in the wild. As she was shifting her attention back to the deer she caught movement in the rear view mirror. Something had just crossed behind the Jeep. Birdy quickly spun around to scan the road. Nothing! Common sense would have sent most people packing. But Birdy McIntosh was unlike most people. Her curiosity and keenness for wildlife kept her in place. She reached toward the glove box a second time to retrieve the camera. *This could be interesting,* she decided, forcing her nerves to settle a bit.

Birdy scooped up the camera and checked the number on the digital readout verifying the number of remaining exposures. Twenty-four pictures were available. She aimed the Cannon at the buck and waited to see what transpired. Birdy brought the camera to her right eye and peeped through the sight to line up the shot. Once in view, she played with the zoom to bring the animal closer. Birdy depressed the button to take a picture. The film advanced inside the camera. As she was just about to snap another, the deer vanished in a cloud of darkness. Birdy nearly fell into the passenger seat as her body jerked. It was the gear shift that stopped her movement. There was nothing there ... no deer ... nothing. The attack had come without warning. The buck was gone.

Birdy continued to gaze into the swamp, but the cover was too thick. She was not about to get out of the Jeep for a closer look. Whatever would take a buck like that would likely not hesitate to go after a human. She continued to assure herself that she was safe inside the vehicle, even if the attacker did happen to appear. And she would be ready with the camera should that indeed happen. Birdy was beginning to wish that she had heeded her husband's ongoing advice to stow his .357 magnum revolver under the seat. "There be a lot of crazies in this world, Bird, and you ain't exactly out there within screamin distance of any help." She shrugged off the idea. Guns were not her cup of tea. She could never shoot a living creature.

Birdy wiggled a bit, shifting her body away from the gear shift that was pinching her plump bottom. The shadow of a lone crow danced across the road. She sat there for a few minutes, hoping to catch a glimpse of the animal that had seemingly overtaken the deer. When nothing happened, she began to think that maybe the buck didn't get nabbed after all. Perhaps it had somehow gotten away and the pursuit was ongoing somewhere in the swamp. She weighed the possibilities. At least the deer would have a better chance of surviving in the thicket if it *was* being pursued by predators.

Finally, Birdy decided that enough was enough. The day wasn't getting any longer, and there was more mail to be delivered. Mabel Sanders' banana bread recipe once again became her motivation for the day. Birdy hoped that she would still be able to catch the widow outside. She was also eager to relinquish her tale to the townsfolk later that evening.

As Birdy began to let up on the clutch, her world seemed to collapse around her. A tremendous shockwave reverberated through the Jeep when a large tree limb came crashing down on the hood and careened onto the road in front. The scare caused Birdy's left foot to slip off the pedal. The vehicle lurched forward and stalled out. There was another "crash" on the roof. Now Birdy was truly frightened after noticing the substantial dent on the hood. The other limb remained on top of the Jeep with smaller branches covering windows on both sides like a large toupee. Both limbs were about ten feet long, and ten to twelve inches in diameter. The base of the one in front of the Jeep pointing up toward the sky indicated that it had been freshly broken.

The recognition that she was now under attack sent her into a panic. Birdy fumbled for the key while keeping her eyes up searching for or whatever had ... Suddenly, a third branch shattered the back window. The violent impact sent shards of glass clear into the front seat. Birdy felt a few hit the back of her head. She turned the key in the ignition and in one smooth motion popped the clutch. The Jeep spun forward and bounced violently over the limb that had been blocking her path. A cloud of dust followed. All Birdy wanted then was to get out of there as quickly as possible. Had she been able to see through the dust in the rearview mirror, Birdy may have seen the creatures crossing the road advancing on the fresh kill on the other side. But she didn't. She kept driving with her eyes focused on the road ahead.

Although Birdy McIntosh relayed her story to the local Sherriff and a good number of townsfolk with curious ears, the ordeal would be written off as a band of poachers harassing a potential witness to their crime. "Must have pushed that buck right to the edge of the swamp, Birdy," they said. And as for the flash that she had seen through the lens of her camera ... well, she didn't have the zoom on, and she really hadn't seen anything to speak of. Birdy McIntosh had been victimized, and then scared off quite effectively so that they could claim their prize. As for the supposed gash in the animal's side ... she really only saw blood, so it could have been a draining bullet wound. There seemed to be an answer for every question. And with the passage of time, even Birdy began to think that she had overreacted. But some of those skeptics would later learn for themselves what she had actually crossed paths with that day.

CHAPTER TWO

The general consensus around town was that Ole' Ned Crosby was more than a few dimes short of a dollar. He was a squirrely gomer with a thick, wavy mop of bone white hair atop an oddly pointed crown. Ned's spindly arms protruded from a frame that was barely one hundred and thirty pounds soaking wet. He glided across the earth on gangly legs in an awkward gait that resembled that of an erratic robot from a black and white sci-fi movie from the fifties. What intimidated people most were his deep-set, hollow eyes that had a tendency to cut through to the back of a gawker's skull like hot iron prodders. His gaunt face reflected years of bitter endurance to the trials of his life.

The old man was as eccentric as they came, and the people of Jessup made valiant efforts to stay clear of the path he walked. His clothes were old and ragged, and he aired a stale aroma from an endless stream of cigarettes and what most people believed to be an IV of liquor. The rambunctious children in town would laugh and holler behind his back ...

Ned, Ned
Kill you dead,
Eat your heart,
Cut off your head!

Johnny Jones disappeared one day,
Went walkin in the woods and lost his way,
Saw Ned's cave and went right in,
Carved to pieces and served with gin.

Children could be such vicious and unforgiving beasts when playing with the emotions of the weak. Over and over he would hear those words sprouting from their chocolate-stained mouths ... grinning ... laughing ... all at his expense. They would gang up on him like a pack of coyotes on a gut pile when parents were out of site, and unleash their relentless verbal assaults. The chant, in fact, had become so commonplace that even the adults would share a laugh or two, behind his back of course.

Ned had gained legendary status in the eyes of the youngsters who resided in Jessup. He was the evil troll that lurked in the dark woods, awaiting little kiddies who lost their way. And parents would often use his example as a reason why it was so important to veer from strangers. "You might fall into Ole' Ned Crosby's dinner pot, Becky." Just the sight of the scary old codger was enough to motivate any curious lad to stay his distance.

The taunting never really bothered Ned too much. He often played along in the childish games, periodically stopping to scowl at the persistent hecklers. It actually gave him enjoyment watching the little *bastards* scatter as if the boogeyman himself had just licked his bloody chops. Truth was, Ned Crosby didn't give a good goddamn about what anybody thought of him. He had been a loner his entire life and would remain so until the day they buried his shriveled body in some shithole for a cemetery.

He lived in a remote cabin seven miles west of town. The place seldom saw visitors. There would be one or two lost hunters every year stumbling up to his doorstep in need of help. Only one word could define a visitor on his property ... "Trespasser!" He had created his own little fortress of solitary confinement, which was the life that he preferred. Ned made day trips into town about twice a month to gather supplies, but every other Friday when the sun went down, he would make an appearance at the local pub to tie one on. Charlie Perkins, the town mechanic, was really the only human being who had ever taken any time to get to know Crosby. Charlie was also the only man that Ned allowed to set foot on his land for more than two minutes.

The old man had resided in Jessup, Michigan nearly all of his seventy-three years. The only meaningful time spent away from the community was when Uncle Sam sent him on a four year vacation to Italy during WWII. His stint in the army brought the only claim to fame that he would capture in life, a chunk of shrapnel embedded in his buttocks from a German mortar round. The same explosion had killed two of Ned's best buddies ... "Big Eddie" Demarco and Sammy "Sly" Stewart. Ned often thought about the guys from his outfit, men who had confided and trusted in one another while facing death every rotten second of every rotten day and night. He would see their grungy faces in his sleep, sometimes appearing in peaceful, reminiscent dreams ... like the time "Big Eddie" had taken a crap in their Sergeant's helmet, or the time when "Sly" shot the canteen out of the mitts of a German Captain. It was the best shot that Ned had ever witnessed. Four hundred yards with the Springfield, and by golly, they didn't use those fancy super powered scopes back then. The next shot went through the Kraut's ear of course.

Most of Ned's dreams did not resurrect peaceful memories. His head was often clouded by the horrible visions that soldiers brought back from war. The blood and guts of brutal combat haunted him whenever he closed his tired eyes. Although those men were long gone in the physical sense, they would never be forgotten. Ned's return to the States had been as uneventful as his departure. His parents died early in life, and there were no immediate relatives to celebrate his homecoming. The young loner began his new life as a saw-man in the local pulp mill at a point in time when the timber industry continued to harvest booming crops. Jobs were available for those who had no qualms about putting in an honest day's work. In the Upper Peninsula, one did not require much of an income to sustain a comfortable life. The forests and waters provided what the stores could not.

Michigan held the title as the nation's leading producer of lumber for a quarter of a century before 1900, with a peak harvest of 5.5 billion board feet in 1890. After the majority of virgin stands were depleted in the Lower Peninsula by 1900, the lumber companies moved north into the State's untouched territory. Harvesting progressed steadily for thirty years between '10 and '40. Ned Crosby hired on with the Jessup Lumber Company just as the industry began to take a downward turn.

The JLC was established in 1919 by a man named Zachariah Jessup, a very astute businessman with an eye for opportunity. "Mister Zach," as he was labeled by those who worked for him, had settled in Michigan's northern territory after making the journey from Boston where he was known for his uncanny ability to turn a penny into a buck. Although he had achieved success as a print-shop owner out east, he was engrossed by a personal void that needed to be filled. Jessup had read about the wilderness territories of the United States since early childhood, and his craving to settle unchartered lands stayed with him until he was able to realize his dream. Jessup's keen eye for opportunity zeroed in on the timber industry. It was by no means as glamourous or adventurous as searching for gold or silver in California, or as exciting as playing with the stock market like he'd done with creative marksmanship. Jessup viewed the timber industry as a crucial resource to civilized man's continued expansion. The Upper Peninsula of Michigan provided plenty of valuable hardwood.

The entrepreneur sold his Boston-based business for a decent profit, and with some financial backing from a few Bostonians who were anxious to invest in his ideas, he packed up his two sons and hauled them off to the northern country. There was no wife in the picture. Marie Jessup had passed after giving birth to their youngest. The Jessup clan first stepped foot on Michigan soil in 1907. By 1929, he and his two sons had built a small empire. The Jessup Lumber Company's annual output of timber ranked third amongst its closest competitors in the Midwest, and was on the upswing with plans for further development. A small community sprang up around the thriving lumber mill bringing families in search of the opportunities that Jessup offered. The business owner acquired the reputation of being a fair and generous boss who took great pride in his work.

In 1934, the community's population peaked at nine hundred inhabitants. "Mister Zach's" greatest achievement then came in 1936 when Jessup, Michigan was given official town status and rewarded with its own position on the State map. Zachariah Jessup was the unanimous choice as the first Mayor, and he practiced with the same moral obligation as he did his business. His unequivocal popularity saw him become the godfather to over twenty babies of grateful employees through the years.

In 1947, the aging entrepreneur passed on, leaving the business to his two sons, Benjamin and James. Ben was the younger of the two heirs and had a passion for wagering enormous sums of money in high-stakes card games. He would travel to Chicago for weeks at a time, returning home only to replenish his pockets from the company till. James, on the other hand, was more like his father and ran the operation with the same zeal. James ignored his brother's frivolous antics and concentrated on the lumber business at hand. Unbeknownst to

James, Ben was vamping around the Windy City accumulating staggering debts with the wrong sorts of people.

The elder Jessup boy contracted pneumonia in 1954 and died shortly thereafter. His passing forced Ben into the company's head seat, a place that didn't suit his nature. The pressures and obligations of running the business did not fare well with the remaining Jessup son as the timber industry started to decline. Ben's drinking and gambling excursions worsened to dangerous levels until he was finally forced to sell off all ownership rights to the JLC in order to make good on personal debts. Coincidentally, once the final transaction had been completed, Ben Jessup, the only remaining member of the Jessup family, mysteriously vanished forever. Rumors of Ben's demise quickly circulated the town, all of which seemed to focus on his affiliations in Chicago. There was always speculation about cement shoes and a November fishing trip on Lake Superior.

The name of the men who took over the failing lumber mill never became known to the people of Jessup. The townsfolk looked on as fancy automobiles bearing out-of-state tags, primarily from Illinois, drove in and out of the small office complex next to the mill. They dared not ask too many questions. The business was in a slow decline and began issuing pink slips to employees who at one time were considered to hold iron-clad jobs. In 1972, the town's population had been cut in half, and Jessup became just another small, Midwestern burg breathing on welfare fumes. Only those businesses providing everyday essentials were able to hang on.

Ned Crosby saw his hometown pass through good times and bad. When times went hard, he was not affected like most. Ned knew how to survive off the land. It was easier for a loner with no dependents ... no other mouths to feed but his own. Ned Crosby collected his last paycheck from the JLC on June 4, 1972 after a major workforce reduction that preceded the closing of the mill. With no family to support and minimal expenses, he had been frugal with his earnings. Ned had stashed enough away to live out his "golden years." After his departure from the mill, he would take a drive down to Appleton, a mining town ten miles to the south, and collect his monthly unemployment compensation until his age allowed him to start receiving social security.

The country's welfare program kept Jessup afloat until 1980, when a paper company acquired the lumber mill and converted it into a small pulp processing operation. This reprieve brought some locals back to work and provided Jessup with a livable economy and a second wind. A few small businesses popped up in 1985, like Eckardly Tool and Die, and of all things, an ice-cream plant that served specialty flavors to Midwestern grocery stores. Ned was too old to get back to work at that point in his life. Arthritis had crept into his joints and prevented him from performing much physical work. He faced the plague of the elderly with great frustration, cursing the moments when he could barely open a can of beer, or turn the doorknob to his own home.

Aside from the arthritis, Ned Crosby was in pretty fair shape for a man of seventy-three. The sharp pains in his hands and legs usually came and went with the weather. Even though his pointy knees and calloused knuckles were beginning to show significant signs of swelling, his stubborn demeanor kept him walking tall. Damned if he couldn't still get out in the woods and drag a buck home, even if he did have to stop and rest more often. If hungry, he would walk outdoors and harvest a deer regardless of whether or not they were in season. "It ain't as if the damned things were short on supply," he would say to himself. Ned's third-hand box freezer that hummed away in his make-shift pantry was always stocked full of meat. Alongside the venison were squirrels, opossums, raccoons, and even a porcupine. And every last bit of it would be consumed in time.

Charlie Perkins, the town mechanic and local handyman, was the only Jessup resident close enough to be considered a friend. Charlie was an easy-going, happy-go-lucky fellow who could have befriended a water buffalo suffering from a nasty case of hemorrhoids. Charlie would drive out to Ned's place every so often and check up on the reclusive hermit. Although Ned would never openly admit it, he did enjoy their chats. He really appreciated the fact that Charlie would help him out with some of the more difficult odd-jobs around his home. Charlie would occasionally repair loose shingles on the cabin's faltering roof, or split a cord of wood for Ned's stove. Other than Charlie Perkins, Ned's only other source of companionship came from Duff, his eleven year old black lab.

The Jessup Inn was the regular Friday night hangout for many. The community's lone watering hole doubled as a boarding house for visiting sportsmen and travelers. The building was not much to look at on the outside, but the interior provided a warm, cozy atmosphere expressing authentic northern traditions. There were mounted deer heads hanging across each wall. A bear skin was nailed over the mantel above the fireplace that was always occupied by a roaring fire. A montage of faded snapshots featuring local hunters parading their trophies adorned the knotty pine paneling. A single pool table with a withering felt top filled a tight corner allowing players barely enough space to steady their warped sticks.

That night had been no exception to Ned Crosby's uneventful life as he drained more than the necessary amount of Budweisers to fulfill his quest for all-out inebriation. As had become customary for Ned's Friday night binges, the alcohol fogged his brain and he began to reel on about the "good ole days" crawling across the fields of Italy with "Big Eddie" and "Sly". The amused patrons laughed, not at the humorous anecdotes, but at the man's obnoxious behavior while he rambled on and on.

They would always laugh at "Crazy Ned," the way insecure observers might make fun of a mentally challenged person walking down the street. Ned Crosby had no competition to challenge him for the title of "Town Drunk." The truth to the matter was that he seldom touched the stuff throughout the rest of the week. But because the people of Jessup rarely saw him anywhere else but perched atop one of the Inn's cedar bar stools crocked out of his mind, the label stuck. If those same people had ever taken the time to stop and study their own drinking habits they may have found that their personal indulgences far outweighed those of Ned Crosby. But every town needed its dupe, and Ned was a good target who rarely defended himself against their ruthless jabs.

Charlie Perkins had wandered into the crowded bar that night and pulled a stool up alongside the animated war veteran. They caught up a bit on each other's activities of late while drinking a few more Budweisers. Ned hadn't talked to Charlie in two weeks and was pleased to see the man's bearded face. He felt that Charlie was the only person in town who really seemed to understand him. The affable mechanic would always nod in approval at Ned's pessimistic theories on where the country was headed. "Right down the shitter!" he often said. Charlie just smiled, trying to be sincere in his responses, and listened the way a child would listen to his grandfather spin off on how good times once had been.

When Ned finally proclaimed that it was time for his Friday night vigil to end, he slammed his fist on the counter like a judge adjourning a court, and sprang to his feet. Charlie implored him to give up his keys, knowing that the old man was in no shape to drive. Ned quickly became irritated.

"I been drinkin here fer ten years and I ain't had no reason fer someone to drive my ass home yet!" he stammered, reaching for the key chain in his breast pocket. With those words of wisdom, Ned Crosby left the tavern.

Charlie merely sank back in his stool and rested against the brim of the bar. He shook his head. There was no stopping the old fool. *Poor guy,* he thought quietly to himself. His moment of silent meditation ended with a loud shout from across the room. Charlie swiveled his torso and saw Brian Donaldson raising a half empty schooner in his direction.

"Over here, Charlie!" yelled Donaldson over the other voices of the bar that were growing louder with each passing hour. Springsteen was singing *Glory Days* on the jukebox.

Charlie smiled, grabbed his glass from the bar, and headed toward his long-time friend who worked at the local power company. He looked to the exit one last time. Ned Crosby was gone. "Be good, Ned" he whispered to himself.

***

The Friday night routine was sentenced to end as it always did ... a simple drive back to the cabin, a ham sandwich and one last bottle of Bud for good measure. After all that excitement, he would then pass out in bed. Ned drove the back roads home in order to avoid the two men who tried to pass themselves off as local law. Every now and then a Trooper would cruise by for the sake of protocol, but not at that hour.

Ned piled into his '73 Plymouth outside the Jessup Inn. He kicked the beer cans on the floor, an indicator that the night's festivities had started prior to his visit in town. The engine roared to life and the automobile rumbled off northbound. His extended stay at the bar that night, coupled with the added rounds of drink with Charlie was making the journey somewhat more difficult. To top things off, a mid-September rainstorm had been raging since early afternoon. The driver soon felt the effects of the alcohol as he struggled to focus on the wet road. Large bomblets of water exploded on the windshield while the less-than-adequate wipers worked frantically to keep pace. They squeaked like rodents with each labored pass. The Plymouth, a goliath of a car, grumbled down Townsend Road, occasionally fishtailing from side to side in the thickening mud.

Ned leaned forward in the driver's seat, straining to see the road ahead. "Christ, but dis wedder is bad tonight, eh," he murmured to himself. About another solid month and it would be one dilly of a snow storm. He'd have Charlie come out and help him put the chains on the tires when that time came. Ned smiled, thinking of his friend Charlie. "One good man in a world of assholes." It sure had been nice to see Charlie. Ned found himself wishing for that snowfall to come sooner rather than later. Any excuse to have his friend come out for a visit was a welcome opportunity.

Approximately two miles from Ned's home, the Plymouth slashed around a sharp bend in the road that seemed to pop out of nowhere. Ned had driven that same route a thousand times before, but somehow had forgotten about that one bend. The balding Good Years spun wildly in the mud, kicking up a cascade of stones as they gripped for traction. Ned was able to straighten the car with the ease of an experienced NASCAR driver, but as he corrected the vehicle's direction, the single working headlight illuminated a set of glowing eyes in the center of the road. Seconds later came the full shape of the paralyzed deer, and a good sized one at that. Though his reflexes were still somewhat lax from the alcohol buzz, Ned managed to brake the Plymouth and steer hard to the right to avoid the collision. The car banked off of a short mound on the side of the road before gently rolling back onto the muddy surface. No longer a prisoner in the hypnotizing force of the headlights, the doe bolted into the brushy cover on the other side. The Plymouth nestled to a complete stop.

"Jeezuz H. Christ," cried the startled old man, slamming a balled fist into the torn dashboard. Pain knifed through his arthritic hand. "Awe shit!" He massaged the throbbing joints with his thumb and index finger. "Next time I'll run yer fat ass over, ya stupid bitch!" he cursed. But the doe was no longer present to hear his slander.

A bead of sweat had formed on Ned's wrinkled brow. It endured on a single flap of skin for a brief moment before gravity sent it rolling down the bridge of his pocked nose. *Goddamned animals,* he thought, *just standin dare in da middle of da road like dey was just waitin fer a car ta spladder dem. Stupid bastards, dey are!* It was as if they were convinced that they were invisible to traffic.

"Invisible! Yeah, dat's it!" Ned joked. "You stupid fuckers are invisible, ain't ya," he slurred. Ned had his share of run-ins with deer crossing paths with the Plymouth. An impish grin crossed his face as he deliberated over the number of animals he'd managed to mangle through the years. "Was it six ... or was it seven ... maybe eight of dem bastards bouncin off da steel horse like tennis balls." *The old girl could take a hit, sure as hell,* he giggled to himself.

The stretch of road that Ned Crosby was traveling was one of the more popular deer crossing areas in the county. The animals would funnel in and out of the big swamp that ran along the western edge of Townsend Road. The higher ground to the east provided acorn-producing hardwoods, an important staple of the whitetail's diet. The swamp was a tangle of dense cedars, tamaracks, and other conifers that were virtually impenetrable to humans in many parts. Obsessed locals thought the quagmire to be a haven for evil spirits and menacing demons. Superstitions were derived from stories passed on through the generations. The stories told of men entering the swamp never to be seen again alive. One such story even led to the swamp's unofficial name. The tale went – over thirty years ago, two eager, young sportsmen from down state had traveled north to the area in search of trophy whitetails during the firearm deer season. Both were knowledgeable in the ways of the woods, having logged countless hours in remote regions of the United States and abroad. They had set out into the swamp one day, each carrying their rifle and a pack holding a few days of rations. When neither man returned after a week's time, desperate wives initiated a search and rescue with the State Police. Over fifty Troopers, conservation officers and volunteers scoured the outer boundaries of the swamp as best they could. Dogs were brought in to pick up on the scents, but nothing was found. After five long days of crawling through the mangle of brush and trees, the party disbanded and the two hunters were written off as dead.

The exhausted search team had encountered nothing but trouble throughout their ordeal. One volunteer fell through a clump of moss and sank to his waist in muck, necessitating his immediate extraction and return to safety before hypothermia could set in. Another volunteer broke an ankle on a buried tree root and had to be air-lifted out. A full day had been wasted with that casualty. But with the rescue attempt came stories of strange sounds during the night hours. Sounds, that as one Trooper put it, were neither human nor from any animal he'd ever heard before.

Two days after the search had been terminated, one of the missing hunters miraculously appeared. He had managed to crawl out of the swamp onto a bordering road where a passing Trooper happened by. The man was lying face down in the snow, his clothing torn to shreds ... his body near death from frostbite and exposure. The officer claimed that when he knelt down to the man and rolled him onto his back, his blue lips uttered but one word before the last breath escaped his mouth. Very faintly, the man said ... "Amen." The Trooper claimed that the man said it as though his prayers had been answered.

And from that point on, the swamp became known as the "Amen," a true contradictory of terms if there ever was one.

The bucks grow large,
With antlered trees,
Go forth brave man,
And pay yer fee.

If you will the courage,
To face the demons within,
Then pray with pure heart,
The journey ends with Amen.

Although the rhymes and legends played as trivial superstitions to some, the majority of the local population believed them to be true. Only a few courageous souls ever entered into the purgatory known as the Amen ... men with a certain kind of grit who ignored their own common senses. Even the most experienced woodsman had lost his bearings, only to be overcome by utter helplessness. Since that fateful day some thirty years earlier, eleven more people on record had disappeared within the confines of the Amen. Those whose fate would never be revealed fueled a legacy for years to come. The Amen Swamp became known as the Upper Peninsula's own little Bermuda Triangle.

Ned Crosby knew enough to stay clear of that God-forsaken hellhole, especially at his age. *Fifty years earlier ... well, maybe, just to spite the pussy-faced critics.* But that was a long time ago. He didn't believe in all of that hocus-pocus bullshit. Ned believed in reality, and reality told him that the Amen was nothing more than a treacherous plot of ground where a man could easily lose his sense of direction. Besides, there were plenty of big bucks on the outskirts of the swamp if that's what fancied a man's appetite. He always said ... "You can't eat dem horns, unless you was a porcupine." Ned was somewhat familiar with the Amen Swamp in that his cabin sat on sixty acres of hardwoods that fed down into the lowlands. His porch overlooked a clearing that carved a path through the trees to the Amen's front door.

Ned brought his thin arm to his forehead and wiped away a streak of sweat. The pain in his hand finally subsided from the spontaneous blow to the dashboard. He took a deep breath, grasped the steering wheel, and placed his weathered boot on the accelerator. The car lurched forward once again. He was now only two miles from home.

"Come on, you old girl. Let's git me home and sleep dis one off," he said to the Plymouth, chuckling silently. The rainstorm continued to pour buckets of water from the black northern Michigan sky. The car's rusty muffler, speckled with nickel-sized holes, moaned louder as more gas was fed through the cylinders. Ned figured that one more Budweiser would sure ease the tension from the stressful trip. He was sure that there was at least one more in the icebox from the twelve-pack he'd purchased a week earlier at McKrueter's Market. That familiar wry smile crossed his thin lips. "Yep ... one more Bud and I'll be out like a ..."

"Jeezuz H. Christ!" he hollered for the second time that night. As the car fishtailed around another winding curve, an odd pair of glowering eyes hovered high above the road ahead. Ned slowed the Plymouth until it slid to a halt some distance from the frozen animal. "What da hell?" he asked himself, squinting through the smeared windshield as a queer sensation swept over his body. The eyes appeared to be standing too tall to belong to a deer, and the road was as flat as a fourth grader's chest. They did not move ... nor did they blink. The eyes just sat there ... floating ... staring at the Plymouth as though it were coaxing the vehicle into a duel.

"Awe hell," he gruffed. Ned shook his head and passed the crazy notion off as an alcohol-induced trick being played on his weary head. "You wanna stand in my way, huh?" There was cockiness to his tone now. He gunned the big engine and the seven working cylinders urged the car into motion, picking up speed on a collision course straight toward the creature before him. The driver had no intentions of swerving this time. His mind was hell-bent on putting some more venison in the freezer. A buck knife was conveniently stored in the glove box for just such an occasion. Just a little slicing and dicing and he would be home free.

"I'm gonna take you out, you sonuvabitch!" Ned cried, as if he were making a final charge on Hitler's bunker. His knuckles turned white from the pressure of his fingernails digging into the plastic casing around the steering wheel. He strained his eyes to see through the obscure windshield, ignoring the rapid motion of the wipers. Then, as the charging Plymouth closed the distance, the large body began to materialize. It wasn't a deer at all. It was as black as the night air ... and standing upright on two ...

"Shit!" Ned was so consumed in determining what the creature was that he nearly hit it head on. He veered hard to the left at the last second, catching the animal on the right front fender. There was a tremendous crunching sound as metal and flesh joined together. Ned heard a high-pitched scream as the animal was tossed to the opposite side of the road. He made a futile attempt to regain control of the skidding car. The front end was already sliding down into a deep culvert feeding into the swamp. Momentum carried the rear end completely around until the Plymouth came to an immediate stop after slamming into a tree at the bottom of the ditch. Ned's body was thrust forward.

His head smashed into the windshield with a sickening thud. The old man's limp body slumped back into the seat as an eerie silence engulfed the night.

"Eddie ... Eddie!" Ned Crosby regained consciousness, uttering the name of his war buddy. *It was Eddie,* he thought, *sittin right next ta me, jawing about Sammy and dat hooker he picked up dat night in ...* Then his eyes opened, allowing a moment for reality to sink in. He looked around slowly. Eddie was not there. Nobody was there. He was by himself in the Plymouth. Ned's first thought was that he must be dead, but he hurt too damned much. His head felt like it had been split open with a dull axe. Raindrops pelted his cold, wet face through the hole in the windshield. Ned tried to move, but stopped after a bolt of pain rifled through his side. He gently touched the wounded area, feeling an instant burning sensation. He concluded that a few ribs were broken. His head was thumping with the emphatic rhythm of a bass drum. The severe concussion was causing lightheadedness and nausea. Ned desperately fought the urge to vomit.

"What da hell happened?" he asked himself. "Where am I?" Those questions circulated through his cluttered mind, but everything was dark. He rolled his head and licked the roof of his mouth. There was a salty taste on his tongue. Blood! Ned carefully raised his arm and probed his crown. His hair was warm and moist. Shards of broken glass littered his scalp. He looked at the hole in the windshield. "Oh God!" he muttered as two fingers inadvertently pulled back the loose flap of flesh hanging from his head. "Oh Jeezuz!" The urge to puke appeared again, and this time he was unable to hold back.

After spilling the contents of his stomach onto the seat, Ned closed his blurred eyes and sighed deeply. *Ain't dis a damned mess,* he cursed to himself. Then he began to remember the collision ... the eyes ... the thing. At first, the accident was little more than a fuzzy blip, but after concentrating for a few minutes, it came back to him. He recalled seeing those eyes ... and then the body. It had been standing ... on two legs ... like a man. *But it weren't no man. Too big. Jeezuz!* He hardly had time to make a clear analysis before losing control of the car. *Poor girl,* he thought, knowing that the Plymouth had more than likely seen its last road trip. Just the effort to think clearly was clouding his vision.

"Bear!" The word fluttered from his bleeding mouth. "I hit a goddamned bear." *And big one, too,* he figured. "Served dat bastard right," he scowled. *Screwed up my baby like dis.* Ned was referring, of course to his battered car. He was genuinely sorry for the loss, like he had just parted with a life-long friend. "Looks like you won't be boucin no more deer off da road, girl." Then another thought crossed his mind. Ned smiled under the pain, remembering the animal's scream ... like its balls were caught in a vise. Ned Crosby began to laugh and cry at the same time. The needles in his ribs flared with each spasm, but for a few previous seconds, he didn't care. "We got em good, didn't we!" he bellowed.

***

As Ned Crosby basked in his moment of vengeance, the victim's dead body lay stretched out in the sloppy mud that was Townsend Road. Raindrops peppered the lifeless corpse, matting the thick hide of black hair. Its head blocked the flow of a small stream cutting through the gravel to lower ground. Water began to pool by its open offset jaws. The body was similar in size to that of an adult bear, just as Ned had rationalized. A wide gash in its abdomen had opened upon impact. The cause of its untimely death, however, was a snapped neck from impact with the ground. Ned Crosby was unaware that the stricken animal was not a bear at all. In fact, it was barely a juvenile ... and it had not been traveling alone.

The adult female bounded off into the cover of the brush with two lengthy strides. She recognized the distinctive whine of the strange machines from previous journeys to the boundaries. It meant only one thing to her kind ... danger! The smaller, hairless creatures were plentiful where the trees thinned ... and there were many of them. She had been taught to travel only at night when venturing this far, when the threat of the hairless creatures was small. Her only reason for drifting from the clan was to search for food. Their supply had deteriorated when the fires came, driving her kind closer to the shrinking boundaries. She was also teaching her young one. It was just as she had been taught, and others like her for generations. Stay away from the hairless ones and their powerful machines.

The female had sounded a warning to her trailing juvenile to let it know that danger was near. They needed to hide quickly and avoid detection. But the young one failed to heed the mother's warning for the sole purpose of satisfying its immature curiosity. The female, thinking that the young one had stayed with her, crouched behind a growth of thick brambles. The constant growling of the big machine grew. Suddenly, her ears were invaded by a wailing cry of pain. She swiveled just in time to see the machine disappear down the slope on the other side of the clearing. Her eyes quickly found the juvenile's body lying motionless in the mud only a few paces away. The female tilted back her bulky head, bringing her nose into the cool, wet breeze. Her broad nostrils flared as she scented the air.

Cautiously, the female crept out to the young one, feeling her way with the padded souls of her immense feet ... one step at a time ... prepared for any form of assault. Although there was no movement or sound from the ditch, instinct told her that the threat was still present. When she finally reached the fallen juvenile, she scented the wet air again, this time inhaling deeply. Her eyes darted up and down the road, carefully analyzing the situation. Two short, guttural grunts were uttered to warn the young one that they should move from that place. Other hairless creatures were sure to come. No response was generated. The female hunched down and ran her nose along the full length of the body. She lowered her head further, discovering the wound in the juvenile's side. She lapped up blood still oozing from the fresh gash with her wide, sandpaper-like tongue. The female then whimpered solemnly and started pawing at the corpse as a cat would play with a ball of yarn, trying to inspire life. The jabs provoked nothing but silence. Finally, she hefted the limp body with great ease and proceeded to shake it out of desperation. The young one's head flopped from side to side like a rag doll as though it were attached only by the skin of its neck.

The female was faced with the grim reality of a mother who had just lost her child. Her whimpering became more pronounced as she cradled her dead juvenile in her massive arms. She held the body close to her bosom with sorrowful commitment. The recognizable scent of death was now apparent. She had never experienced such a loss before. This had been the offspring of her first reproductive season. She would be deemed a failure in the eyes of the clan, perhaps never to mate again. Mistakes were not acceptable to her kind, a race that survived by maintaining its distance from such dangers.

A faint sound emanated from the ditch. The female swung around in a defensive posture, still clutching her dead. The juvenile's head flopped against her elbow, but she paid no attention. The disturbance was repeated. Although she could not see the source of the noise, she knew it came from the machine that had just killed her juvenile ... the machine that held the responsible hairless one. It was the hairless one that destroyed her young one. It was not her fault. The clan would have to understand.

A rage began to boil inside her nine foot body ... a burning hatred for the creature responsible for causing death. A menacing growl escaped her cavernous throat. The corpse was gently laid to rest on the muddy surface of the road. The female then erected her towering frame to full extension and flailed her powerful, hate-driven arms in the darkness. Her quiet snarl erupted into a bellowing roar of fierce determination that communicated her intentions to every living creature within earshot ... including Ned Crosby. She was now on the offensive.

***

His eyes opened wide with terror as the animalistic scream pierced the night, punishing him for what seemed like an eternity. He pressed his palms tightly against his ears. The pain in Ned's side was ignored while his frail body quaked with fear. It was a cry unlike any he'd ever heard. What frightened the old man most was that he didn't just hear it ... he could feel it vibrating through his seventy-three year old bones, a chain reaction that ignited in his fingers and spread to his toes.

He was able to regain some composure as the roar trailed off into silence. Ned's heart raced in his chest while his mind was consumed with constructing a lifeform that could have produced such a wretched sound. He slowly motioned his body across the rain-soaked vinyl of the bench seat, wincing at the reappearing pain in his side. He wanted to scream himself. He wanted to cry out. And for some reason ... he wanted to look. *Don't look goddammit!* He tried to convince himself. *It's all in my head.* But Ned knew there was no argument in that lie. The awful scream had been real, and the source was lurking just beyond the protective shell of the Plymouth. He *had* to look. He *forced* himself to look.

Ned reached the passenger side window, and with his soaked shirt sleeve, he wiped away the condensation on the cold glass. At first he saw nothing but pure darkness giving him a short-lived reprieve from his fears. But the false sense of security was washed away when his eyes cut through the darkness and made out the monstrous silhouette on the road above. The figure stood still as if sizing up the car. Ned's body convulsed. He sat with his eyes transfixed on the form. It was no bear.

"M...m...mother...of...g...g...god," he whispered with a quivering voice. His words were gargled from the large lump swelling in his throat. Ned's chest began to heave as he fought to take air into his burning lungs.

Then it happened, so sudden that Ned barely had time to react. The creature lunged at the car with astounding speed. Ned summoned just enough energy from his drained muscles and recoiled to the opposite side of the car. His head banged into the driver door. He felt the Plymouth shutter as the raging beast slammed into its exterior. The forces of hell were seemingly unleashed with a thundering onslaught of hammering fists. The creature pummeled the sinking roof. Ned's heart beat faster as each blast shook his soul. His breaths came in short gasps. The roof caved closer and closer toward his cowering face.

And then the hammering ceased. Once again there was stillness in the night, disrupted only by a gentler rain. Ned managed to drop down to the candy-wrapper infested floor of the Plymouth. He could feel the empty beer cans collapsing under his weight. Fearful of what lay ahead, he ducked underneath the steering column and curled into a fetal position. His heart was on the brink of exploding. A dull ache had formed in his right arm and was gaining slowly on his shoulder.

"Please...go...away. Please!" He pleaded through bloodied lips and begged for salvation between labored wheezes. Breathing became more difficult. Tears streamed down the wrinkled sides of his wounded face. The world was spinning. Though he had always looked forward to the day when he rejoined “Big Eddie” and “Sly”, he did not want to greet them like this. He wasn’t ready. Ned balled like a scolded child and clutched his chest.

When a few seconds ticked by without an encore attack, Ned laboriously lifted his head. It was difficult for him to focus. He was losing what little strength he had left. Ned grabbed the steering wheel and hoisted himself upward, just a little, and looked toward the window. Regardless of how hard he prayed for the nightmare to end, he discovered that the horror had only just begun.

Ned found himself staring directly into the most horrid face that even the cruelest of all nightmares could not manufacture. The skin was riddled with snake-like creases from the sloping forehead to its pointed chin. The glass fogged with each steamy breath. The eyes bore directly into Ned’s own, communicating the hatred that was about to be unveiled. The corners of the monster’s mouth curled back to reveal its jagged teeth.

The creature reared back its gigantic head, disappeared for a brief moment, and then shot forward with a vengeful roar that signaled no mercy for the human within. Ned Crosby let out one final gasp before his world went black.

CHAPTER THREE

Tyrone Pullman had been stationed in the Cadillac for over an hour. A trail of smoke snaked upward to the ceiling from the half-burned joint in the ashtray. He needed a little buzz to get the adrenaline pumping. Snoop Dog boomed out a rap on the CD player, a little too loudly for some who passed by. A black kid with a fancy car always seemed to spark interest in a community where an African-American was a sparse commodity.

Fuck all of you, thought the calm and collected sentry. *You wish you was able to afford this car, you white pieces of shit.* He could feel their stares, dissecting his life with one quick glance. That was all it really took. "The brother's up to something ... he's on crack ... must have a gun." Well, they were right with two of the three assumptions. Although Tyrone's financial success relied heavily upon the cocaine trade, he never touched the shit. It wasn't good for business. But he *was* up to something, and he *was* packing some heavy equipment.

Tyrone continued to watch with some amusement as hands clutched purses a little tighter or reached around to the backside to secure a wallet. ... all on his account. *I'll give you a thing or two to talk about,* he thought. *Just hang around a little longer.* Tyrone Pullman had been stationed in his current location for a reason. Lord knew he would much rather have been back home in Flint with his own people. *But Gerald had to go and do what he did,* he thought. It didn't necessarily make any sense ... his world. People got whacked every day, and for what? The white people were the ones who ended up with the coin in the long run. The brothers were simply the pawns, playing the game for their masters. Tyrone figured that his day would eventually come at the hands of someone smarter ... someone with a thirst for the green. It was a game of survival where the strongest ruled and the weak were snuffed out of existence. You had to watch your back with every step. Those who got fat and careless did not last. Bam! Bam! It's over!

It wasn't too long ago when he and Gerald were the ones on the upstart. He lost his only two real brothers in the battle for supremacy on the streets of Flint. When the smoke cleared, it was Tyrone Pullman and Gerald Johnson running the show. The coke trade was more than just a lucrative business in their world. It was a means of gaining respect. A young black man's avenues were limited when growing up in the poverty-stricken city, and cocaine provided the only light at the end of a long and dark tunnel. He and Gerald had earned their respect, and the only method of keeping it was through intimidation. Trespassers had to be taught harsh lessons. Tyrone considered himself to be the brains of the operation, even though Gerald was the so-called "boss." But Gerald had always been one to act on emotion rather than reason, and that's why he was in his current predicament.

"We can't let that motherfucker get away with it!" That was Gerald's proclamation earlier in the spring. The "motherfucker" who Gerald was referring to sold out his top lieutenant from Lansing, and the heat was sure to spread to the Flint connection. The disagreement centered on whether or not Daniel Stubbs, the man from Lansing, would in turn sell the two of them out in order to save his own ass. Gerald was under the impression that he would. Tyrone, on the other hand, had known Stubbs since high school and thought differently. Gerald was the kingpin in that particular organization, so his decision was final. The "boss" concluded that the only way of getting his lieutenant out of his cell would be to eliminate the prosecution's star witness ... the Narc. Besides, having Danny Stubbs shut down was severely dampening the northern traffic.

Gerald and Tyrone made the short drive up to the State's capital on a warm, April evening. The Narc actually lived in Potterville, a small town just south of Lansing. It was a perfect setup for a hit, two miles from the highway, the closest neighbor a quarter mile down the road. Nothing could go wrong ... but it did. Gerald had indulged in a large stash of coke before reaching their destination that night. Tyrone remembered becoming nervous with his partner's increasingly erratic behavior throughout the trip.

"I'm gonna waste that mothafucker!" cried Gerald over and over again, carelessly waving a 9mm Glock around his sweaty face. Tyrone had seen cocaine do some weird shit to people, and he knew that dealing with doped-up idiots was an extremely delicate matter. Even the subtlest remark could unleash unpredictable consequences. So, he just sat back and drove, thinking about how his own ass was riding on such a thin edge.

The two hitmen pulled up to the rural residence. It was a peaceful setting, a decent sized tri-level house with a barn in the front yard. Two horses ran freely in a pasture. Tyrone's common sense allowed him to see the red flags right away. It was not the typical setting for a Narc. But Gerald was beyond any form of persuasion. He was too keyed up to make it happen right then and there. Tyrone could only sit back and keep a watchful eye out for unexpected trouble.

The plan had been a simple one. Gerald was going to walk right up to the front door and politely ring the doorbell. When the Narc answered ... two slugs ... one through each eye. That was the trademark of Gerald Johnson.

"Wait here, homes. Be right back." With a mischievous grin, Gerald exited the car and strolled nonchalantly up to the door as if he were a salesman making a house call. Tyrone looked on from the stolen Camaro parked in the wide driveway. He anxiously glanced up and down the road, searching for headlights. There was only darkness. Although he'd been involved with hits since he was twelve, Tyrone Pullman was nervous. There had always been that distant voice questioning whether or not he was doing right. He supposed that his conscience was attempting to speak to him. *Fuck it,* he thought. *I was born into this shit. I might as well play it out.* Besides, the coin was incredible.

Gerald, in the meantime, calmly rang the doorbell just like he said he was going to do. He held the Glock behind his back, looking as though he were prepared to make a sales pitch for a new line of vacuum cleaners. His orange Nike's glistened in the light from the front porch. Tyrone almost snickered, seeing how out of place his partner looked.

When the door opened, Tyrone did not see a man standing in the foyer. His lower jaw dropped. "Oh Shit! Don't do it, man!" Tyrone contemplated jumping out of the car to stop his partner, but contemplation did not provide a quick enough reaction. He watched in horror as Gerald's arm moved from behind his back, swinging the gun around. The intended target had not answered the door. It was a little girl ... a blond-haired little girl ... maybe five or six. "Don't do it, Gerald," repeated the distressed driver of the car. But the only person who could hear Tyrone was Tyrone.

The little girl didn't know what hit her. *Pop!* Tyrone saw the 9mm recoil in Gerald's hand, and then the child tumbling backward across the floor until she disappeared from sight.

"You dumb nigger!" This time he screamed his distaste. He looked on as Gerald stepped over the child and entered the house. A dog began to howl a short distance away. The horses in the pasture scampered off to the far corner of the property. Tyrone could only listen through the open window to what followed. A woman screamed ... a shrill scream. *Pop! Pop!* The woman was silent. *Pop! Pop! Pop!* And then there was a different sound that was louder. *Boom! Pop! Pop! Pop! Pop!* It sounded like Gerald emptying his clip. Silence then engulfed the household and the yard outside. *Where the fuck is Gerald,* he thought. Someone else had shot. He was sure of it.

Tyrone's peripheral vision picked up a flicker. He turned to his right, seeing the headlights approaching from up the road. He looked back to the open door. Gerald was there, but something was noticeably wrong. His partner was propping himself up against a white pillar, grasping his side. Tyrone then saw the blood. He'd been shot. Gerald attempted to step down to the sidewalk. He stumbled and fell hard to the ground. He lay still on a slab of cement some thirty yards from the Camaro. The headlights were nearly to the driveway. Tyrone turned his attention from his fallen comrade to the approaching vehicle.

"Keep going," he whispered beneath his breath. Everything was all fucked up now. His heart stopped when he noticed the car beginning to slow. There was a flashing light. "Shit!" *A turn signal!* When the car turned off the road and into the driveway, Tyrone panicked. He could not save his friend now. Gerald was probably dead anyway. Tyrone turned the ignition, jammed the car in reverse, and hit the gas. The rear tires shrieked and left a black patch of rubber as the car motored backward. The startled visitor, fearing a collision, turned off the drive and into the grass. The Camaro flew right past the newcomer and tore into the road. Tyrone put the car in drive and sped off without looking back. Knowing there would be a swarm of cops in the area within a matter of minutes, he had to escape the scene as quickly as possible. A black man in a cherry red Camaro would not be hard to find. The highways would be too dangerous, so he figured that his best bet was to ditch the car in Lansing and shack up for a few days with one of his "associates." The car was stolen so it couldn't be traced to him. But they already had Gerald. If Gerald was still alive, he wouldn't sell out his friend ... or would he?

Tyrone slipped his way into Lansing that night, first ditching the car in a woodlot, and then lifting a pickup from a deserted farmhouse. He holed up in a friend's apartment for a week, watching as the story unfolded on the local news channels every day and night. Headlines in the morning paper the next day read ... "Gang-Related Execution Leaves Police Officer and Family Dead." The Narc had been a cop, and there were a lot of pissed off white people reading about a little girl getting her head blown off. Tyrone read the editorials as residents of Lansing expressed their rage. Perhaps if the cop had been black things may have been different. But the cop was white, sending inner-city relations into turmoil. The kicker to the story was that Gerald, the murdering thug, had lived. *Damn*, thought Tyrone, knowing all too well that his life was now hanging by a burning thread. His friend who rented the apartment was the only person in Lansing, or Flint for that matter, who knew of his whereabouts.

Seven days after the incident, Tyrone Pullman emerged from his seclusion and headed home. There had been nothing in the media indicating that the accomplice had been pegged. He was then certain that Gerald hadn't sold him out. Tyrone was able to follow the story in the Flint papers as well, careful not to express too much interest. Only a select few trusted crewmembers held his secret. Gerald's arraignment was swiftly funneled through the justice system. Lansing's Mayor and a smattering of local and State officials became heavily involved with the case, grabbing valuable press during the election year. One interesting facet of the case was that jurisdiction went to the county seat due to the locale of the crime. Though city politicians screamed for extradition, Gerald was held in Eaton County to be tried *and* convicted by a predominantly white jury. He was royally fucked. Tyrone could only wait and see how the fate of his partner played out. In the meantime, he became "boss" by default and ran the business with his own flat style, mostly through subordinates to keep his name clean. That was the smart way of conducting business in the drug game. The days of the hardline gangster were over.

The trial took only four days to reach its conclusion. Guilty! Gerald's counsel could not offer any logical form of defense, and a plea bargain was out of the question. Even the judge had lost his composure at the "self-defense" argument. Mandatory life with no possibility of parole. Gerald *was* fucked! Throughout the proceedings, Gerald had been in contact with Tyrone through a number of runners. It was mainly Gerald initiating the communication. All of those messages attested to one common theme ... "Get me the fuck out this or I'll let them know who was with me that night!" Tyrone's alternatives dwindled with the plight of his partner. Gerald had forced him to take action or jeopardize his own freedom.

So Tyrone Pullman now sat in the big Caddy, a plan of action prepared, and nerves of steel to carry it out. He had no choice. The prisoner was going to be transported down to Jackson that afternoon to live out his days at the expense of the taxpayers. Two guards would drive him down. He would be shackled from head to toe in a Ford Econoline van bearing government plates. The van would leave the jail in Charlotte at approximately three o'clock, head out to I-69, drive north toward Lansing where it would merge onto 96, and then ultimately turn south onto 27 for another 30 miles to its final destination. There would be no other cars in tow. The information had been expensive. Fifty thousand dollars to be exact. Fifty thousand for a chance at freedom. But Tyrone wondered how much freedom they would actually have if by some miracle they did succeed. He had thought long and hard on that topic, realizing that his world might be just a little bit safer without Gerald Johnson to impede his advancement. The decision was not going to be an easy one, but he would have some time to mull it over. Some difficult business decisions just had to be made, even if it meant offing a long-time partner.

When Tyrone saw the van, his blood began pumping "Showtime," he said under his breath. He picked up the smoldering joint and stuck it between his lips, inhaling deeply. He held the smoke in his lungs for five seconds and then exhaled a cloud of smoke. Though he would never touch the white powder, he considered marijuana to have the necessary calming ingredients for just such an occasion. Tyrone snuffed out the remainder of the joint in the ashtray. It was time to roll. He steered the Caddy into the road behind the Ford as it passed by. A quick peek into his rearview mirror verified that his "rammer" was in the game, a beat-up Grand Marquis. The small caravan drove out of Charlotte and jumped on the highway. Traffic was not too heavy even though rush hour was quickly approaching.

It was a nice day, thought Tyrone, taking in the mid-afternoon sunshine through his Oakleys. But it wasn't the type of day that he would have preferred for the task at hand. Not in the middle of the afternoon with people watching in plain sight. It was a *dumbshit* plan that would more than likely take him down. The purpose of the joint was to defeat those worries and ease the tension.

A State Trooper passed in the south-bound lane going in the opposite direction. Tyrone cringed. He figured that the cop was on his way to set up a speed trap for impatient commuters. The problem with tailing a government vehicle was that they never seemed to follow the speed limit. That small oversight could put the entire plan at risk. If some county-mounty insisted that he was taking advantage of the Ford's apparent immunity ... well, it could put a definitive end to all that he had worked so hard to achieve. Gerald would go to prison, and he would go into hiding again. Tyrone stole a glance at the speedometer. It hovered around seventy-eight. *Not too bad,* he thought. The Grand Marquis was close on his bumper. *So far, so good.*

The three vehicles skirted the southern edge of Lansing before turning south on US 27 where traffic was lighter yet. "Good deal," muttered Tyrone. The moment of truth was quickly approaching. After passing the Mason exit, Tyrone opened his window. He stuck out his slender arm that was always adorned in expensive gold, and casually waved to the trailer. The signal sent the Grand Marquis steaming past him. He did not make eye contact with JC or Billy ... merely a twitch of his forefinger, motioning them to go ahead and advance on their prey. Tyrone faded back a bit, allowing the larger car to gain on the van. A sign told him that it was two miles to the exit ... the drop ... the extraction. It was time to act. The Grand Marquis pulled back into the passing lane, as if reading Tyrone's mind. He watched the window on the passenger's side slide down. The big car rolled on past the van and then settled back into the slower lane. They were in position. Tyrone checked the rearview mirror. No cars in sight. Although there were a few in the north-bound lane, they posed no immediate threat. He was gambling that a cop wouldn't happen by. It would be a hit and run. Go in, grab the cargo, and get the fuck out. Easy?

Satisfied that they had the advantage he wanted, Tyrone flipped on his lights. It was the final signal. The driver of Grand Marquis jammed on his brakes, allowing no time for the van to react. The collision was instantaneous ... metal slamming against metal. Both vehicles skidded sideways across the asphalt like battling rams with their bumpers locked. Tyrone stayed close until they finally came to rest just off the shoulder. The two men in the Grand Marquis opened their doors and exited the mangled car, each yielding a sawed off shotgun. Billy and JC ran toward the inert truck and began pumping buckshot into the cab. Tyrone hesitated, fearing that a loose shot might stray in his direction. The two guards in the van had disappeared from sight. The hitmen then stepped back from the Ford and began to reload. Tyrone swiftly jumped from the Caddy and raced to the fight on foot. He drew his H&K and held it at the ready. Cars in the north-bound lane were slowing to gawk at the assault in progress. He noticed one man making a call on a cellular phone. That was okay. He had counted on that. This had to be quick. There was still time.

As his two soldiers began to raise their weapons again, shots rang out from inside the truck. JC's chest evaporated into a cloud of red mist. He careened backward and fell down dead with his fingers still clutching his weapon. Billy began to fire more rounds toward the van, but then Tyrone saw his kneecap explode. Billy rolled into the ditch to escape the slugs peppering the pavement around him. Tyrone silently crept up along the side of the van, keeping his eyes on the driver's mirror, watching for movement. He felt his way along the riddled side-panels with an outstretched hand. When he reached the cockpit, he heard a voice on the radio.

"Keep your head down! Help is on the way."

"Get the fuck out here, now!" was the distressed reply of the guard inside. "My partner's dead! I got two of them!"

Tyrone slid his head toward the shattered window, stealing a quick peek inside the compartment. The driver was slumped across the steering wheel with half of his head spilled onto the dashboard. It was a gruesome scene, but not unlike any that Tyrone had witnessed on the streets of Flint. He gently maneuvered under the driver's window and raised his gun into the opening. The 9mm spit a volley of fifteen rounds into the cab until the chamber was empty. He popped in another clip and brought his head up to the window. His shots had found their mark. The guard was curled in a sickly ball on the floor of the vehicle. His eyes stared vacantly to the ceiling. There was no life left in him.

"Yes!" The cry came from the rear of the truck. Tyrone changed his aim to find the source. Gerald's sweaty head popped up from behind the steel grate. "You are one sweet nigger!"

Tyrone then jogged to the back of the van. A siren wailed in the distance. "Get down!" He fired five shots into the lock. The door swung open. Gerald bounced out of the van, careful to avoid tripping over his shackled feet.

"Get these fucking things off me!" pleaded the prisoner.

Tyrone ran back around to the front of the van and opened the driver's door. He frantically searched the two bodies for a set of keys. He eventually found them on the passenger's belt. His own shirt was now covered in blood. He tossed the keys back to his friend. "Get in the car. I've got to check out Billy." Gerald fiddled with the keys as he hopped clumsily to the parked Cadillac. Tyrone ran to the top of the ditch and looked down. Billy smiled back up at him, his teeth chattering from shock.

"Is ... is ... it over?" he gasped, cradling the part of his leg that was now minus a kneecap. The sirens were getting closer. Cars had now stopped in the south-bound lane about 100 yards back. That was also good. It might slow the progress of the advancing police. Tyrone knew he didn't have time for Billy. There was only one solution to the problem. Tyrone raised his gun and fired a single shot through Billy's forehead. His friend rocked back, and then fell forward into a patch of weeds. Although Tyrone felt sorrow for the loss, he also found comfort in knowing that Billy didn't have time to realize his fate. He then ran back to the Caddy, got in, and squealed off down the highway heading south.

Both men remained silent. Each knew that luck would now play a significant role in achieving success. Tyrone made a ninety-five mile an hour sprint to the exit and swerved off the highway. He turned right on the county road, and then made a quick left. It was a wooded area holding sufficient cover. It was perfect for dumping a hot car. Gerald, confident with his friend's plan, silently looked on as Tyrone turned off the narrow road and onto a two-track that wound down into a small, wooded ravine. Gerald then saw the second vehicle, an older pickup. It was nothing flashy, just an early-90s Chevy.

"You's good, Tye," said Gerald. "Real good." The Caddy slowed to a stop and the two men got out. Gerald had already unshackled himself from the binding chains. He picked up the rattling pieces of steel and threw them into some tall grass. "I don't ever want to have those motherfuckers on me again!" he screamed.

Tyrone had wandered behind a stand of short pines and reappeared with a roll of camouflage netting. "Help me out with this," he told the fugitive.

"Damn," replied Gerald. "This keeps gettin better and better, don't' it?" The two men spread the fabric across the Cadillac until the car was completely covered in camo. It was intended to give them a little extra time. Tyrone next moved to the Chevy truck and opened up the spacious tool compartment nestled inside the bed against the cab. He withdrew a bag containing clothes.

"Put these on." He tossed a pair of coveralls to Gerald who seized them out of the air. Tyrone tore off his bloody shirt and shoved it in the bag along with Gerald's prison garb. He then slipped into his own set of faded Carhartts. Tyrone stuffed the bag of clothes underneath the Cadillac. Every movement had been calculated ... practiced ... every second accounted for. When Gerald walked around to the passenger side of the pickup, preparing to get in, his partner stopped him. "No, homes. Back here." Tyrone motioned to the tool compartment.

A smile formed across Gerald's startled face. "Fuck you, man. I been sittin in a steel box for the last four months."

Tyrone didn't have any time for this bullshit. He could hear sirens in the distance. "Look, G, if you go sittin up there in front, someone's bound to recognize your black ass. Then we're both fucked." He tried to remain calm.

"I ain't gettin in no fuckin box, man!" Gerald responded, as if he had forgotten about what had just gone down. After all, he was still "the boss" and his call would be followed.

Tyrone matter-of-factly stuck his hand inside his front pocket. He caressed the cold metal of a concealed .32. *It would be real easy,* he thought, *to end it right here and now. I'd be a helluva lot better off alone. I could go home.* But the tone in Gerald's voice deflated. He raised his hands in retreat. *Always the emotions,* thought Tyrone.

"Alright, bro," said Gerald. "You right, man. It's just that I been cooped up in that shithole so long." He was now cool. "Let's get the fuck outta here."

Tyrone released his grip on the handgun. "Okay, G." He opened the side-lid to the tool compartment. Gerald was impressed that his friend had taken the time to make his stay in the box as comfortable as possible. Tyrone had thrown in a small mattress, a sleeping bag, a cooler stocked with beer and sandwiches, and a bag of pretzels. There was even a Sony Walkman to drown out the noise of the road. An AK-47 was mounted on two brackets against the thin, steel wall. Tyrone had covered all of the bases. He helped Gerald up into the small shell and then gently closed the lid until it locked in place. He could hear Gerald shuffling around inside trying to get situated in the tight quarters. *He'll be alright,* he figured.

Tyrone then opened the door to the Chevy and crawled inside. He took a bag from underneath the seat that contained a cheap disguise ... a beard and mustache that he carefully glued to his face. There was also some talcum powder that he spread throughout his cropped hair. He masterfully transformed himself into a fifty-five year old black man within a matter of seconds. It was time to move out.

Tyrone drove back onto the main road, circumventing some deep ruts in the two-track to keep Gerald comfortable in his little cave. He made his way back to the highway and headed north on 27, right back to the scene of the crime. It was risky, but necessary. All part of the master plan.

Four police cars passed him before he reached the buzzing battleground. He slowed with the line of traffic to watch the activity in the south-bound lane. At least twenty police cars lined both sides of the highway while two ambulances and a firetruck were parked next to the Government van. There were a bunch of cops hovering over JC's body spread out on the asphalt. Only his weapon had been removed. The pool of blood in his chest still glistened in the afternoon sun. Two other officers were hauling Billy's corpse up out of the ditch. A body bag had been placed on the shoulder of the road, unzipped and ready to be occupied. For a brief moment, Tyrone thought he could see a smile on his dead friend's face. He quickly shook the image from his head. "Poor brother," he muttered solemnly to himself. He was only seventeen ... barely a man. Recruited from the playground only a year ago.

Tyrone shifted his gaze forward. He watched a family of four in the vehicle ahead covering their mouths in horror at the sight he had caused. Children's visions forever tainted. Tyrone looked on as a lone female Trooper lazily waved the cars through the checkpoint. As he passed the woman, Tyrone gave her a nod with an innocent smile. The officer's face did not change its serious expression. She just glanced at his face, made a quick scan of the interior of the truck, and then waved him through while shifting her gaze to the next car in line. Tyrone drove on, increasing his speed with the rest of traffic. He and Gerald were heading north.

***

The woman took the initiative and began walking toward him, her face shadowed by the early morning darkness. The sun had not yet risen in the eastern sky. Her feet pranced gracefully across the smooth rocks that served as miniature islands in the narrow stream. He listened to the soothing sound of the trickling waters.

Her face remained hidden in the shadows as she drew nearer. He waited on the bank, watching her toes testing the frigid water. Did she shudder? He wondered. Perhaps she was smiling. He longed to see her smile with happy heart again. She was so beautiful. Her long slender legs stretched to the high slit in her silk skirt. Golden hair danced in the mild summer breeze. It was all just as he remembered from the short time he had with her.

He looked away for a brief moment, questioning whether the vision was real ... if *she* was real ... if he was with her ... again. His eyes scanned the dense trees. He surveyed the green meadow accented by droves of blossoming daisies. It *was* real! They *were* together again. They would always be together.

He turned his attention back toward the woman, now ready to accept her. His strong arms reached outward to hold the woman he had loved so dearly ... so long ago. His head tilted sideways in an anxious attempt to steal that first glimpse of her tender blue eyes. From behind, the sun made its morning presence, finally casting its light over the piece of hallowed ground that the two lovers had once shared. But he found himself momentarily blinded by the shimmer off the brook. She was there, but he could not see.

The woman's body floated into his arms and he could feel the warm flesh of her hands grasp his own. She whispered his name as her hair brushed against his face. But her voice was distant. It was her ... yet it was not. An odd sensation began to unfold inside him. There was a disturbance off to his left ... a snarling growl. He turned and looked to the tree line as a large, black wolf stepped into the clearing. Its eyes glowed. The charcoal-nose curled back. Blood flowed from the corners of its mouth as if it had just come from a fresh kill. He began to tremble. Movement from his right forced him to turn again. Another wolf, identical to the first, crawled out from the high grass of the meadow as if it were stalking them. He tried to pull away from the woman's clutches, but she would not let go. He tried to scream ... to warn her of the impending danger, but no sound would escape his throat. The wolves came closer. The woman's hold tightened. The sky suddenly went dark as thick storm clouds rolled across the horizon. Bolts of lightning began to strike in all directions, shaking the ground as thunder exploded. What was happening?

And then the warm sensation of her skin turned icy cold to the point that it burned. He felt the pain enveloping his entire body. He looked down in agony at the hands that were now torturing his wrists. But they were not human hands. They were the hands of a skeleton ... bones! But how could that be? When he rolled his head back, he saw the face of the woman who had once stolen his heart. The wolves were now by her side, but he paid them no attention. For a split second it was her. She was real. Everything would be okay. And then the pale skin on her face began to melt away in layers, dropping in slabs to the ground where the wild dogs lapped them up. Her smile dissolved as teeth fell from blackening gums. The eyes sagged back into the dark, hollow sockets of her rotting skull. He stared in shock as they ignited into flames and then turned to puss. And then the wretched mouth began to form words.

"Come with me, Ross. Come with me. We can be together again."

When he tried to pull away, he found that his feet had been shackled with heavy chains. He tripped and fell to the ground. The wolves converged and began nipping at his feet. He kicked wildly at them while the demon hovered above. A bolt of lightning reached down from the sky and struck the figure, blasting it into a thousand pieces. The taste of death bit at his tongue as he fought to escape.

"Nooooooooooo!"

Ross Pickett awoke to the blaring ring of the telephone on the nightstand next to his bed. For a moment, he thought that he was still consumed in the nightmare that continued to plague him. *How many years has it been?* he asked himself. *Christ, it was horrible.* He could feel the sweat dripping off his body. It had been *too* real. It was happening too often.

The phone rang again with the ironic sound of an alarm clock. He reached to the table and fumbled for the receiver. "Yeahllo," he mumbled, rubbing the sleep from his tired eyes.

"Sheriff?" The voice on the other end was gruff.

"Yeah, I'm here. What is it?" Sheriff Ross Picket let out a wide yawn and then stretched his long legs. When his feet popped out from under the covers of the king-sized bed, the cold air tickled his toes.

"Pickett?" The voice questioned again.

"Yes! I'm here! What is it?" Ross raised the tone of his own voice, expressing his irritation. *Damn phone,* he thought. Maggie was supposed to either get it fixed or pick up a new one.

"Can barely hear ya, Sheriff. Didn't wake ya did I?"

Hell yes, you woke me, dumbass, the Sheriff cursed inwardly. "No, you didn't wake me," he lied to the caller. "Who is this? And what can I do for you?"

"What was that? Didn't quite catch that last remark."

This is turning into a regular Abbott and Costello routine, he thought. *Yeah ... who's on first?* Ross took a deep breath to calm his growing impatience. Two years earlier and there would have been a bottle handy in the drawer of the nightstand to help him soothe his nerves. *Heck,* he remembered, *two years ago and I wouldn't have even heard the damn phone ring. Old ghosts.* "No, you didn't wake me. Now who is this?" He repeated his inquiry in more measured voice.

"Hey Ross, this here's Ralph Corner."

Ralph Corner? The Sheriff registered the name to a face. A grin stretched across his unshaven face. "What's up, Ralph? Gotta bear in your barn again?" he asked jokingly. Last fall, Ralph had called him out to his home claiming that a malicious black bear was tearing up his pole barn. Ross went out to the Corner farm only to discover an ornery little badger that had somehow managed to lock itself inside. When the Sheriff opened the door with his 30-30 in hand, the feisty animal charged right out past him, straight toward old Ralph Corner. Ross had never seen an old man move so fast. He shimmied up a tree like his hind end was on fire. The badger, unable to continue its pursuit, just strutted off like it was king of the world, leaving a very shaken and embarrassed Ralph Corner in its wake. Ross couldn't remember ever laughing as hard as he did that day.

"What was that, eh? Your phone isn't working so good."

"Nothing, Ralph." He peeked at the digital alarm clock next to the phone. Three-thirty A.M. *Nice,* he thought sarcastically. "Ralph, do you know what time it is?" *This better be good. And where the heck was Maggie? She should have been home by now. Probably a big crowd at the bar,* he reasoned. Ross shifted his concentration back to the caller.

"Well, sorry to disturb you, Sheriff, but when I see the law being broken, I report it." It was Ralph Corner's turn to display some sarcasm.

Touché, thought Ross. "Okay, Ralph. Sorry about jumping your back like that. What's going on?"

"I seen a pickup go by bout fifteen minutes ago doing some shining."

Ross detected a trace of triumph in the man's voice.

"The bastards lit up my darn bedroom and nearly sent Mertyl to her grave."

Mertyl was his wife of thirty-nine years. *A sweet woman,* thought Ross. He remembered that she had baked a lasagna casserole after the funeral. Ross shook off the thought.

"I'm sure it was the Jones boys," exclaimed the old man. "Never were no good, the both of them. Probably all liquored up and raising hell. You know, I knew their daddy? He was just like them."

Ross knew the Jones boys well ... Frank and Jesse. There was some irony in those names. The Sheriff had hauled them in a few times for drunk and disorderly, but never on a poaching violation. Although every man and woman who lived in the county knew they did most of their hunting at night with a spotlight, they were slippery enough not to get caught. Besides, half the population of Jessup was apt to be guilty of that very same crime at one time or another, including Ralph Corner.

"Anyways," he continued, "bout five minutes after they was by here, I heard two shots. If you're gonna catch them, and you should," he stressed, "they're probably still close by."

Ross massaged his eyes again with his thumb. He glanced out the window at the pouring rain. *Shit!* They most likely had the deer skinned and quartered already. *Well, I am the Sheriff. Lucky friggin me.* "Alright, Ralph, I'm on it. Maybe I'll check your freezer while I'm out that way." He couldn't resist the jab.

"You just leave us be and go on about your job," rebutted the old man, much too hastily to hide his innocence.

"Yeah, right. I'm out the door. See ya, Ralph." Ross hung up the phone and sat up in the toasty bed. The sheets slid off his naked body causing him to shiver. Ross picked up the phone again and dialed the number to the Jessup Inn. Maggie answered on the second ring.

"Hey, babe. Just wondering where you were."

"Is everything okay?" replied his live-in lover. "It's three-thirty, Ross."

"I gotta take a drive and check on some possible poachers."

"Oh, that's all? I thought you might be missing a certain someone tonight," she said seductively.

"Only in your most perverted dreams," he responded. Ross heard the girlish giggle on the other end of the line. That giggle usually started a sexual frenzy when they were alone together. He craved Maggie's giggle. He craved her warm body lying next to his following a long night of love making. Ross considered himself extremely fortunate to have her in his company. At forty-five, men still drooled over Maggie Barnes' curvy figure. But more importantly, Maggie had a mind of her own. She certainly hadn't traveled any streets paved with gold. Maggie had worked her knuckles to the bone for everything she had in life, including Ross Pickett. She began her life downstate in Canton Township on the outskirts of Detroit. At age sixteen, she moved to Jessup with her father, Paul Barnes, a retired Ford autoworker. He had made the journey with his teenaged daughter to escape the city that had a tendency to swallow people up. With his retirement, Paul Barnes purchased a small market to provide for the two of them. Although it didn't make them rich by any means, the market did allow them a comfortable life, which was all that he really hoped for.

Maggie had been a very gifted student in school, graduating from Appleton High at the top of her class. Even though she wanted to stay with her father and help him operate the market, Paul insisted that she continue her education at a higher level. He sent her off to Northern Michigan University in Marquette where she studied education in hopes of one day becoming a teacher. Maggie knew that money was tight, but the pride exhibited in her father's eyes motivated her to excel. She would return to Jessup nearly every weekend to help with the store.

Then, in her third year of classes, Paul Barnes suffered a stroke and died unexpectedly. Maggie blamed herself for years. He had worked so hard, and she had abandoned him to carry the tedious workload on his own two shoulders. Instead of finishing her education, Maggie decided to run the market herself, forgetting the dreams that had once driven her. She did okay with the business that catered to the needs of the nine hundred locals residing in the northern Michigan town. But as time passed, so did the development of larger food chains expanding into the area. When she heard of plans for a Walmart to be built in Appleton, Maggie realized that she couldn't complete with bulk prices. People would drive ten miles just to save a dime on a pound of bananas. Reluctantly, she sold the market, and so went the last remaining tie of her life with Paul Barnes.

At that point in time, Maggie was faced with the task of finding a new means to make a living. There was an old schoolhouse at the end of Main Street that had been deserted for years. Her sharp business sense, learned from first-hand experience, found a need for the abandoned building. She stopped and gave it a thorough look-see one day. A bar! The idea struck her like a pie in the face. Of all things, Jessup did not have a town tavern. Though there had been a few attempts through the years, none of them took hold. Within a week's time, Maggie Barnes purchased the schoolhouse with money from the sale of the market. With a loan from the bank, she converted the building into a respectable bar and boarding house with five rooms in the top level. "Jessup Inn" seemed to fit. Nothing fancy.

Jessup was far off the beaten path to attract much of a tourist flow, but the rooms did fill up during the hunting seasons. Maggie also found that her town was located on one of the more popular snowmobile trails that stretched across the U.P. There were always sleds parked in the deep snow outside the tavern on weekends throughout the winter months. Over time, her menu evolved into an attractive assortment of northern cuisine, like fresh pasties and whitefish. Maggie enjoyed mingling with the patrons who frequented the bar on a regular basis. She found the erotic thoughts embedded in their eyes to be amusing, and flattering, as they undressed her in their dirty thoughts. Maggie would flirt with them, and laugh at the jokes they told, most of which could not be repeated to their mothers. Overall, they were a decent bunch. She worked the counter and helped out in the kitchen. The Jessup Inn experienced fame in 1985 for serving up the U.P.'s best burger, something she took great pride in.

Maggie Barnes never married. However, she did conceive a wonderful son who adored her dearly. Chuck Barnes was the by-product of a brief affair with a food vendor out of Houghton. It took only one night of passion, not love, to change her life forever. When she had finally summoned enough courage to inform the man of his part in the pregnancy, he had slapped her hard across the mouth, drawing blood from her lip. After calling her a "fucking whore," he left her life forever. The words stung with the venom of a pit-viper, much more than the unnecessary slap. Her self-esteem had taken a nose dive. But when Chuck was born, the sun seemed to shine upon her once again. The boy was a wondrous gift from God that filled a void in her lonesome life. Charles Paul Barnes meant the world to her, and she would do everything in her power to give him a promising life. It was what her father had tried to do for her. Their household was one of love and understanding.

"We were a little busy, so I kept the bar open for another half-hour," continued Maggie over the phone. Ordinarily, she would close at one, but there were a few boarders who were intent on tying one on. It was the opening weekend for grouse and woodcock, the first round of the fall hunting seasons. The rooms upstairs were filled with anxious bird hunters. One of the Inn's drawing powers was that Maggie allowed them to keep their dogs in the rooms, something that most roadside motels frowned upon.

"I just had a call from Ralph Corner. Looks like the Jones brothers may be out doing a little night shopping." Ross cradled the phone between his chin and shoulder as he pulled the Levis up around his waist. He noticed that they were feeling a little snug. *Better start working on the spare tire*, he thought.

"Isn't Mark on call tonight?" replied Maggie. Mark Bennington was Ross' sole Deputy on the Jessup police force.

"Naw, I gave him the night off. His little girl's still pretty sick." The Sheriff looped his leather belt and then latched it securely in place.

"Oh that's right. Poor dear. I saw her mother yesterday and she seemed to think that Jenny might need to get her tonsils out." There was genuine motherly concern in Maggie's voice.

"I'm going to take a quick drive and check this out." His muscular arm ducked into the flannel shirt sleeve.

"Nice night for a drive, Ross," she said sarcastically, not wanting the conversation to end. The night had been a long one and she couldn't wait to return home and snuggle with her lover. "You be careful of Frank and Jesse. They can get a little rough." She had them tossed out of her place on a few occasions.

"Don't I know it. I shouldn't be too long. I'll try not to wake you when I get back." He buttoned up the comfortable shirt and tucked the tails into the jeans around his waist.

"Nonsense. I'm just getting ready to lock up. I'll have coffee on when you get home. And the bed will be nice and warm, too," she teased, once again with that erotic giggle.

Ross was aware of just how deliciously warm their bed could get. He hoped that the Jones boys had done their dirty work and went on home. "God, I love you, Maggs," he then said with sincerity.

"You better, big boy."

"See you later." He hung up the phone. Ross then walked halfway to the bedroom door before stopping. He stepped to the dresser and opened the top drawer containing his holstered Colt .357 magnum revolver. *Just to be on the safe side,* he said to himself. The Jones boys *could* get a little rough at times just like Maggie had warned. Ross strapped on the weapon, entered the hallway and plucked his insulated rain parka from the coat rack. Hopefully, his time would be spent inside the truck and not out in the weather. But it was better to be prepared for the worst. He sat down on the sofa in the living room and slipped his size fourteen feet into his Timberlands, a gift from Eevie a lifetime ago. *When was that? Five ... six years?* It was just a few weeks before she had been diagnosed with ovarian cancer. He could see that Doctor's face vividly in his mind telling the two of them that his wife had only one month to live. They had cried hard together on that cursed day. But Eevie, God rest her soul, had been strong ... for him. She would not share her agony while deteriorating on the hospital bed. She knew that her pain would utterly destroy her husband.

Ross dispelled the somber thought that would all too often creep into his head. It was always sparked by simple things ... experiences they shared. "Old ghosts," he said as a drop of moisture formed in the corner of his eye. It didn't take much to trigger the sad memories. Ross often wondered how she had been so brave to hide her anguish from him. At times, he felt guilty about his relationship with Maggie. But deep down inside, he knew that Eevie would be happy for him. She had been that type of person. He had loved his wife with utmost devotion, and now he loved Maggie with equal commitment. Though there would always exist some sense of jealousy, Maggie understood his past. He would not hide his inner thoughts out of respect for her. Life must go on, and for Ross Pickett, life was now moving in the right direction.

Ross laced up his boots and then strolled back down the hallway, halting at the door to Chuck's room. He opened it, careful not to make any sound, and peered inside to check on the boy that would one day be his son. Chuck was snoring soundly underneath an action poster of Joe Montana throwing a touchdown pass to Dwight Clark. *He is a damn good kid,* Ross thought. At sixteen, Chuck Barnes was the starting quarterback for Appleton High ... and a talented one, too. But aside from the boy's athletic prowess, he was smart as the dickens in the classroom. If by chance he didn't get an athletic scholarship, Ross figured there would be ample opportunity with his academic standing.

Ross had a couple of connections with some scouts from a few of the major colleges. He himself had been an All-American tight end at the University of Wisconsin. His hopes for a professional career evaporated when he blew his knee out in a game against Michigan State back in the day. The doctors told him that he would never play again. *Another old ghost,* he thought. Though he and Chuck were not of the same blood, Ross saw a lot of himself in the young athlete and looked forward to raising him as his own. Maggie had done a damn good job of it, but the boy was in need of a father figure.

Chuck had thrown for three touchdowns earlier in the night, with over two hundred and fifty yards in terrible weather conditions. Ross was unable to attend the game with arch rival Iron Mountain, but he did catch the clips on the eleven o'clock news The primary obstacle that gifted, young athletes from the remote North suffered was exposure. The media in those parts was miniscule in comparison to coverage of the larger programs downstate. But Ross would see to it that the kid had a shot. He owed him that much.

The Sheriff closed the bedroom door, thinking that the two of them should get out and do some hunting over the weekend. Added to Chuck's many talents was his marksmanship with a gun. He had recorded three doubles on grouse last year, which was an exceptional feat. Ross planned on picking up a dog that the two of them could train together ... a Brittany.

Ross opened the back door to the quaint home and shivered at the sight of the rain. *This is gonna suck big time.* He pulled the hood over his head and jogged out to the Chevy Tahoe that was getting a free car wash in the drive. He felt that flaring dull ache in his knee caused by the staples that still remained from his reconstructive surgery. There was no time to work out the kinks.

Age was showing as the pains frequented his joints more often. Old injuries had a way of catching up on an old athlete.

Ross climbed inside the big truck and turned the ignition. The heat was set to the highest mark, but it took a moment for the warm air to circulate through the vents. The Sheriff then switched on the police radio. Sharon Cooper would be monitoring the night watch at the Town Hall. Sharon was one of three gals who worked part-time shifts for the miniature police force. The girls were rotated regularly to keep their hours down so that they wouldn't be considered full-time and become eligible for benefits. Everything was a budgetary matter when it came to town finances and the people who controlled them. Ross keyed his mike and spoke.

"Hey Sharon, you awake over there?"

"Howdy, howdy, Sheriff. Wattcha doing working at this hour?" Her adolescent mannerisms resounded over the airwaves. Ross had always thought that she and Maggie could have been sisters. Although Sharon was twenty-five years younger and a little on the ditsy side, each shared that same appealing giggle. But Sharon Cooper performed her duties competently and Ross rather enjoyed her youthful antics. He told Maggie once that he thought Sharon had a crush on him. After all, he was fairly fit for a man of fifty. Ross Pickett was a brawny, lumberjack type who kept himself in decent physical condition, a discipline learned from his gridiron days. It was getting more and more difficult to keep that spare tire in check. Ross stood six feet four inches tall and displayed few signs of a typical man his age other than a few stands of graying hair over his ears. He tried some hair dye once, but quickly nixed it after Maggie expressed some jokes at his expense. His muscles were tone from regular workouts with a set of barbells in the basement. Ross was proud that he'd been able to maintain his athletic form. It allowed him to keep pace with Chuck in the woods, as well as around the yard when they were goofing off with the football.

"Sharon, Ralph Corner called and wants me to check out some possible poachers out to his place. Just wanted you to know that I'm out and about."

"Okey, dokey, Ross. Stay in touch."

Small town sophistication at its finest, he mused. The Sheriff backed the truck out of the drive and headed out into the night.

***

The man hunched over his personal computer in the dark room as images from the screen flashed across his eyeballs. He had been at it for a good three hours and his neck was beginning to stiffen. It seemed so long ago, but he was reminded each night when the nightmares sent his boys into uncontrollable screaming fits. James Carmichael and his wife had not slept alone in bed together since.

The frustrated father was out of ideas. He put an end to the lengthy appointments with the psychologist three days earlier after witnessing the pain in his sons' eyes while they were forced to relive the event in a hypnotic trance. Although Robby had shown some progress, it was Jody who was affected the most. The youngest Carmichael boy who had been so outgoing and carefree only a few weeks earlier, now clung to his parents like a toddler in a room full of strangers. James could see it written on his face ... the horror ... the fear of the dark. The new, introverted personality made James feel as if he were now raising a completely different child. He took a two-week leave of absence from work just to be with his family and try to regain their lives.

The Carmichaels rarely discussed their ordeal in Michigan to outsiders other than the doctors. James, did, however, speak to Bob Wentz who was a long-time family friend from South Bend. He and Bob had attended college together at Northern Illinois. Wentz listened to the distraught father's story with great interest, more so than the authorities who performed the half-assed investigation. Bob was an unconventional sort who believed in things that sounded absurd to most. From the infamous U.F.O. sightings around Area 51, to the Government's cover-up of the JFK assassination, Bob Wentz was a believer in tabloid headlines. Bob was also a top-notch attorney with a very astute law firm, so credibility of character had never been an issue. Wentz had already formed an opinion before James finished. Without revealing too much information, he offered the name of a web site that might provide some answers to his friend's dilemma.

James checked the clock at the bottom corner of the screen. It was two-thirty A.M. and he was alone. Lori was in bed with the kids. He was relieved that there had been no screams that night.

Probably only a matter of time, he figured. James had been surfing through various web sites, searching for clues as to what they might have encountered on that road. He remembered the details as told by his wife ... how the animal "sprinted" across the pavement on two legs. For some unexplained reason, Robby and Jody could only see the source of their terror when asleep. When awakened, neither could ever remember the reasons for their screaming. "Post-Traumatic Stress Syndrome" was the terminology used by the professionals.

James visited a number of sites covering North American wildlife in order to gain a better understanding of the black bear. He looked at pictures and read articles. He even went so far as to submit a few questions in a chat room occupied by a rotating group of zoologists.

"A bear does not run on two legs," he said aloud in the quiet den. "What the hell else could it have been?" Even the zoologist had found humor in the inquiry. James was not about to give up. He had to understand. He couldn't sleep anyways. Then he remembered Bob's advice to visit that one particular web-site. He reached around his backside and withdrew the wallet from his pant pocket. Inside the fold was a small, crumpled piece of paper with some scribble.

"At least give it a try, buddy," said Wentz earlier in the week. Oddly enough, he would not reveal the contents of the site. James was reluctant to proceed, given Bob's personal beliefs, but he felt as though he was at the end of his rope.

James unfolded the paper and set it down next to the keyboard. He then typed in the address ... WWW.EXISTENCE.COM. When his index finger tapped the "Enter" key, the computer began its search. It took a few moments for the slow processor to open the picture. As the visuals for the web-site appeared across the screen, James Carmichael sank back in his chair.

"Oh my God."

A scream erupted down the hall.

***

Ross Pickett had been Sheriff of Jessup, Michigan for two full years. He was originally from St. Ignace where he served as a conservation officer for the Department of Natural Resources following the abrupt end to his football career. He was raised in the Upper Peninsula and never had much of a desire to leave once those football dreams dissolved. He met Evelyn Bowden in the town nestled at the northern foot of the Mackinaw Bridge. She had been sightseeing on Mackinaw Island with her family on a long weekend trip. As chance would have it, Ross had taken a trip to the island himself that day to bike its perimeter. The two met in a bar and hit it off instantly. Eevie was from Ludington, a city along Lake Michigan in the Lower Peninsula. The courtship was short and sweet as each made weekend drives to share in the other's company. In just three months, the two were married.

Ross thoroughly enjoyed his life as a C.O. His duties ranged from patrolling the back roads for violators to relocating nuisance animals. But Eevie was his life. Never had he felt so much love and admiration for someone as he did for his wife. She was a dedicated and understanding woman who willingly bowed to his every need. Not that Ross ever took advantage of her servitude. He did the same, in fact, for her. They traveled together, played together, and prayed together. Eevie had been raised a devout Catholic and was not afraid to express her faith in public. Ross had never been exposed much to religion, but he found Eevie's open faith to be refreshing. The Picketts tried to have children, but couldn't for reasons that doctors could not explain. Each wanted to share in the birth of a son or daughter, but when it didn't happen there was no animosity felt toward the other. They were happy and that's all that really mattered.

Ross retired from the DNR in 1990 after twenty years of service. He became fed up with the growing bureaucracy and politics within the department. He saw long-time friends being relocated to unwanted posts in an effort to force them into early retirement so the State could replace them with younger men and women at lower salaries. So Ross bailed with his small pension before his turn came to get bumped. Times were changing and he did not want to change with them. Ross had an uncle who passed away and left him a fifty acre plot of land in a small western U.P. town called Jessup. He had never before heard of the town mentioned in the letter from the Estate's executor. He had barely known the uncle from his mother's side of the family. But Ross was eager to get a look at his newly acquired inheritance, so he and Eevie took a drive west one day. They fell in love with the piece of land as soon as they laid eyes upon it. It was autumn and the leaves were in full color. The couple was mesmerized by the beauty of the picturesque backdrop of the surrounding forest. There was a cozy little cabin perched atop a ravine with a tranquil stream. The couple agreed that this would be their own little paradise to live out the remainder of their days together.

But just like the unpredictable weather of the Upper Peninsula, so went those seemingly unbreakable plans for the future. Eevie became gravely ill. It happened so fast that they barely had time to react. One day they were sharing moments in the green foliage of their beautiful homestead, and the next day Eevie was lying in a hospital bed undergoing extensive tests with tubes covering her frail body. While Eevie withered away to little more than skin and bones, her faith remained strong. Eevie knew where she was headed and was prepared for the journey. Ross stayed with his wife to the end, fighting back tears as his own faith plummeted. Eevie passed two and a half months following the initial diagnosis. Ross cursed God for decreeing such a horrible fate upon them. He buried Eevie in the town's cemetery on a gloomy, overcast October day. Other than his wife's family from downstate, only a handful of townsfolk had showed up to pay their respects to the woman they hardly knew. Maggie Barnes had been one of those people.

Ross was suddenly alone in the world and quickly cowered into a tight shell. He was unable to face life without the companionship of his soulmate. It didn't take long before the bottle became his best and worst friend. Time passed in a blur. He began to drink himself to sleep to ensure that his dead wife's face would not reappear in his nightmares. There was nobody to comfort him or serve as an outlet. Ross began to detach himself from society altogether.

It was when Ross Pickett began to frequent the Jessup Inn that he met Maggie. She had taken an interest in the anguished man against her better judgement. Maggie began to initiate conversation with him. Though it had been more out of pity at first, there was something about Ross that intrigued her. Perhaps it was the fact that unlike most of the regulars, Ross showed no sexual interest in her. In the beginning, he would simply brush her off. He did not wish to confide in anyone, particularly someone of the opposite sex. But eventually his personal prison began to crumble and Maggie's efforts were rewarded. Ross did begin to open up. Maggie was finally able to get the dejected man to talk of his misfortunes, and for the first time, about Eevie's death. Ross was able to release the misery that had been eating up his insides. Together, they sat in the deserted bar after the doors had been locked, and shared in their lives. As it turned out, they were both lonely souls in need of someone to confide in. It was Maggie who first suggested they go on a date. Ross was discouraged by the idea, thinking that it would somehow be an act of betrayal to the love he continued to feel for Eevie. But Maggie convinced him that they would just go as good friends with no commitments. Ross agreed to dinner and a movie in Appleton. The outing quickly evolved into a real debacle as both participants seemed to lack coordination. Neither had been on an official date for some time and their nerves made simple tasks seem like mind-bending brainteasers. Conversation had been small and meaningless. Ross managed to spill an entire cup of coffee down the front of his white dress shirt, while Maggie clumsily tipped over a large carton of buttered popcorn in her lap during the movie. Although an outsider looking in might have seen the affair as a comical sideshow, neither Ross nor Maggie found it very amusing. They were pressing too hard.

When the evening finally ended, Ross courteously walked Maggie to her front door where they both stood for a moment fumbling for words. Ross politely said "good night," condemning himself for his lack of speech when no other words would come. He then turned away and walked back in the direction of his truck, thirsting for the bottle secured beneath the front seat. It was a cold March evening and there was a fresh ten inches of snow on the ground. As Ross approached his vehicle, his foot hit a concealed patch of ice. Both feet slid out from underneath him. His arms grasped at the air as he tried to maintain his balance. His body landed hard and the powdery snow encased him. He just lay there, embarrassed beyond belief ... angered by his childish stupidity. He thought his actions to be inexcusable ... the ultimate betrayal to the woman he loved who lay not far away in her cold grave. He wished for the night to end there and then. He wished for the bottle.

Then, after a long silent minute, he heard a faint giggle. It was subtle at first, as if the person behind it were trying to hold back. The giggle then exploded into uproarious laughter. He sat up, brushed off some snow, and saw Maggie Barnes doubling over, cackling hysterically at his expense. And that was all it took ... just one silly, innocent act to break the tension that had mounted the entire night. Ross' first opinion was that her behavior had been rude and distasteful. But then he began to look at himself. He *did* look like an idiot and realized that it *was* funny. Ross started in, clutching his own belly. *Hell yes, it was funny*, he thought. Maggie bounded down the steps of the porch and literally dove on top of him. They rolled over and over in the cold snow like school children in a wrestling match at recess. That night they laughed, they danced, and they embraced each other as two people who were miraculously saved from the cloud of seclusion that had swallowed them up.

Ross Pickett and Maggie Barnes fell in love as the weeks and months passed. Maggie became the pillar of strength that Ross so desperately needed to break his dependency. At first, it had been like ripping a sucking leech from his skin, a task that required both delicate ease and cruel force. But Maggie was there when the demons appeared on their nightly visits. Without her, he would have been lost forever. Maggie was his savior, a gift that would eventually be attributed to his former wife. He came to view his newfound love as a message ... "Get on with your life, Ross. Get on with your life and live."

Ross became a new man after breaking his addiction. He became fit, toning his body into condition with determination and sweat. He became respectable again, spending time in town amongst the people and getting to know them personally. And most importantly, Ross Pickett was well-liked. He was an easy going man when the bottle wasn't dictating his life. Then, an opportunity presented itself. Earl Bevins, the town Sheriff, had decided to call it quits after twenty-eight years of service to the community. Maggie talked her man into running for the elected position. There were others who urged him on as well, regardless of his somewhat clouded past. So he did run ... more on a whim really ... just to see what might happen. Before he knew it, he was wearing the badge that declared him Sheriff of Jessup, Michigan.

He had made the transition back to law enforcement, even if it was on a much smaller scale.

The job in Jessup wasn't the most demanding of positions; however, it gave Ross something to do while Maggie operated the bar. He wanted no part of that atmosphere. Crimes were few and far between around Jessup. An occasional speeder from out of state or a disruptive drunk and the Inn provoking confrontations was more or less the extent of the local crime wave. Jessup was generally a quiet town where the people were wholesome and good. There were a few who blemished the private society, like the Jones boys ... but not many. Even Frank and Jesse were not all that corrupt in their ways. They were just a couple of kids needing a kick in that ass once in a while. Ross really enjoyed his work.

The Sheriff moved in with Maggie and Chuck in May of that year. He had already managed to establish a firm, father-son relationship with the boy ... another void in his life that had gone unfulfilled. They meshed like "Frick and Frack," debating over critical matters of the world such as which teams would be in the Super Bowl, or what scent was more productive for luring in a nice buck. They became the best of friends. Ross shared a great deal of common ground with the young man. They would often travel to Marquette or Houghton together and take in a college hockey or football game. Ross and Maggie talked about getting married on numerous occasions, and had even gone so far as to look at some rings. Ross was anxious to make the family legal and proper. Life was good again for Ross Pickett and he felt as though there was nothing blocking him from a future of happiness.

He had been out driving in the storm for a good forty-five minutes. The rain hadn't let up a speck and the roads were getting nasty. Mud was often worse than snow, creating a greasy film that could easily send a vehicle spinning out of control. Some areas remained nice and level while others were almost completely washed out. He drove along Woodland Road past Ralph Corner's place. *Ralph must have gone back to sleep,* he figured. There were no lights visible inside the house. *He's probably peeking out his window just to make sure I made the effort.* He smiled, picturing the old man's eyes peering out between creases in the shades. If anybody had been out there in that crap, they were most likely long gone.

"The hell with this!" The Sheriff made a U-turn in the road and headed back toward town. He would drive out to the Jones' place in the morning and ask a few questions to put a little scare in them. Ross turned onto Townsend Road just in case Frank and Jesse had taken the long way home. Besides, he was warm in the truck ... and awake. This route would also allow him to swing by the bar and make sure Maggie had everything closed up. He would then make a quick visit to the office to see Sharon. *That would make her day,* he thought. Ross chuckled. "Aren't we the conceited one, tonight," he beamed. The thought caused him to flex his biceps a few times.

The Tahoe was now cruising at a slow pace. The surface was much softer from the drainage into the lower land on the east side. Ross reached down and locked the transmission into four-wheel. The effect was immediate as all four heavily treaded tires gripped the road. It induced a sense of superiority over the elements.

The Sheriff looked out the rain-streaked window at the swamp lurking beside the road. The place had always given him the creeps. He'd heard the stories of the men who disappeared. There was the one tale in particular ... the two hunters getting lost with only one finding his way out. Ross remembered that both of the men had eventually died. It was all before his time, but the people still spoke of it. "Dumb shits," he said. *Nobody belongs in that mess of a swamp.* Then he recalled a piece to that eerie rhyme that some of the old timers would chant around town, primarily to frighten the listening ears of gullible youngsters.

The bucks grow large,
With antlered trees,
Go forth yon sportsman,
And pay yer fee.

If you will the courage,
To face the demons within,
Then pray with pure heart.
The journey ends with Amen.

"Nice," uttered the Sheriff with a slight tingle riding down his neck. *Nice and spooky that is.* There was nothing like a good, scary fable to keep the kids up at night.

Ross diverted his attention back to the road. He was a capable outdoorsman who'd lived in the north nearly all of his life. He was privy to the basic skills of survival, including the ability to track nearly every type of game animal in the State. When it came to picking a hunting location, Ross knew enough to avoid certain places. That swamp, in his view, was one of those places.

***

The enraged female grew frustrated by the machine's failure to resist her brutal assault. It would not fight back as she hoped it would. She became even more infuriated that it would not cry out in agony as her young one had cried out while being slaughtered. The hairless one's machine had killed her juvenile and so she would destroy it purely out of revenge. But as the relentless attack progressed, she began to tire. When her fists began to ache from pounding on the hard shell, she finally ceased altogether.

The female scented the machine, keeping her ears alert for alien sounds. Her enormous head leaned forward and dipped to the level of the opening. As she gazed in, she saw something move. There was a noise. She saw it ... the small, hairless one hiding within. She thought of how easy it would be to crush this inferior creature, but instinct forced her to hesitate. She had been taught not to act without gathering information. The wetness still fell from the sky and her hair was matted from the night's travels.

The female crouched into a readied position, keeping her eyes focused on the target of her hatred. The anger began to boil once again as she envisioned her slain juvenile lying in the road above. There would be no mercy for this one. There would only be death. The hairless creature inside the car made a sudden motion. The female reared back and screamed her intention. The provocations did not generate the outcome she hoped to achieve. The hairless one's body fell from sight and into the darkness of the machine.

Her ears detected a noise from the path somewhere in the distance. She lifted her head high and scented the air. The gaping nostrils flared. Danger! She had to hide. The sound was growing louder. More hairless creatures approached. With one giant leap she was back on the surface of the road next to the young one. Her feet sank deep into the soft mud. She effortlessly hoisted the lifeless body from the ground and sprinted off into the cover of the swamp. She did not stop for several hundred yards, side-stepping stumps and trees with incredible grace for a creature of her size. The juvenile dangled from her mammoth arms.

***

He steered the truck around a curve, purposefully punching the gas to reaffirm his superiority over the slippery track. He was getting bored and there was nothing else to do at the moment. "I might just as well have a little fun while I'm out here." Then he saw a reflection off the side of the road ahead ... a car's reflector ... in the ditch. "What the ...?" Ross brought the Chevy to a stop parallel to the culvert and switched on the spotlight. He aimed the beam down toward the car.

"Jesus!" It was Ned Crosby's car. He was sure of it. The car was wrapped around a thick tree. The metal in the front portion of the vehicle was mangled, and the roof ... "Christ!" exclaimed Ross. It was a gruesome sight that depicted only the worst possible outcome. Crosby had to be dead.

The Sheriff put the truck in park and depressed the emergency break with his left foot, leaving the spotlight on to illuminate the scene below. He opened the door and leaped out into the cold rain. When Ross reached the top of the culvert, he first tested the ground with his boot for traction. He then heedfully made his descent, slow and sure. His boots lost their grip in the muddy weeds roughly halfway to the bottom causing him to slide on his rear until his feet slammed into the front tire. Ross pulled himself up with the aid of the deformed fender. It had been smashed beyond recognition. He quickly calculated that the tree couldn't have caused the damage based on the angle of the car. He was sure of it.

Ross felt something strange on his hand as he released the ruined piece of metal. The substance was mushy and littered with course strands of hair. He brought his hand out of the shadows and into the light. Ross wiped away the mud to reveal the foreign matter. There was fresh blood ... warm blood that was not his own. A hunk of sticky animal flesh clung to his palm. It was matted with long strands of dark fur. The obvious answer told him that it had come from the hide of a bear.

Not knowing what else to do with the specimen, Ross stuffed it into the side pocket of his parka. He then knelt down and studied the rest of the fender. It was bent inward. Strong metal displaced that much indicated that Ned must have nailed a pretty good sized animal. The rain pinged off of the crumpled hood. Ross' scalp was already soaked to the skin.

"Ned!" he blurted after realizing that he had not yet located a body. Ross slid across the soft earth to the passenger side window and looked in. Nothing! He tried the door but it was locked. He didn't try to maneuver around to the other side because it appeared to be pinned against a wall of cedars. Instead, the Sheriff shattered the glass with his elbow. A sharp pain rolled up his arm as particles of glass sprayed over the front seat. Ross reached through the opening, careful not to slice his arm on the shards that remained in the window's frame, and unlocked the door. It swung open with a loud grinding noise. When he stuck his head inside, he heard a faint moan over the pounding rain. It was coming from the floor. It was Ned Crosby ... alive. He dove onto the seat, now ignoring the glass, and grabbed the old man's arm. Ned was lying in a fetal position, almost childlike, with an innocent expression forged on his pale face. A chunk of Ned's scalp seemed to be missing. There was blood everywhere. The Sheriff reached for his neck and felt for a pulse. Though faint, there was a soft rhythm. Ned Crosby was alive, but barely. Ross knew that he could not wait for an ambulance. Appleton rescue was a good twenty minutes response time, and probably more given the weather. He had to risk moving the injured man.

Ross placed a hand under each shoulder and gently extracted the old man from the tangled wreckage. He was surprised at how light Ned's body actually was. Ross figured it was the adrenaline. He hoisted Ned's body over his shoulder, circumvented the car, and fought his way up the embankment. He kept his toes pointed outward, allowing his heels to dig into the mud. Once he made his way to the top, Ross carried Ned to the rear of the Tahoe and opened the hatch. He laid him carefully onto the carpeted floor, pushing away the various pieces of equipment to make room. A duffel bag was used as a make-shift pillow. He took off his Gortex parka and converted it into a blanket. Next, he raced to the passenger door and withdrew a safety kit from the glove compartment. He had no time to feel the chilling effects of the hard rain drenching his body.

Ned's head had a terrible gash that was bleeding profusely. It would need immediate attention. Returning to the rear of the truck, Ross snatched a handful of gauze and wrapped it securely around Crosby's head. He watched the gauze turn bright red as the blood quickly soaked through the material. Ross slammed the hatch, confident that he had done all the he could for the man to that point. He jumped back into the truck behind the steering wheel. The heater was kicking out a steady stream of warm air. That was good, for the both of them. All four tires simultaneously spun into action as he gunned the engine. He flipped on the flashers and then reached for the mike.

"Sharon! This is Ross!" His breathing was labored.

"Well howdy, howdy, Sheriff. Did you catch ..." The dispatcher was cut off before she could finish her sentence.

"Listen goddammit! Ned Crosby's been in a bad wreck out on Townsend Road. I've got him in the truck and I'm on my way back to town. He needs help, pronto! I want you to call Appleton Fire and Rescue and have them meet me in front of the Post Office. Should get there about the same time.

"Got it, Ross. See you in a bit." Sharon Cooper's response reflected that she understood the gravity of the situation.

The Tahoe skirted the edge of the road. Ross drove as fast as he could possibly go without endangering the injured man in back. He could ill-afford to make a stupid mistake now. The big tires proved their worth by carrying the big truck across the mud with ease. Ross found himself thankful that the town had scraped up the funds to purchase the lease earlier in the year. An ordinary patrol car would not have performed well.

Fifteen minutes later the Tahoe rolled into the deserted streets of Jessup. The Sheriff saw the ambulance's red and blue flashers approaching from the south. County Road 16 was the main artery that dissected Jessup and shot straight on down to Appleton. After finessing the truck to a subtle stop on the wet pavement, he got out and ran around to the back to check on his ailing passenger. The ambulance's wailing siren awakened those who lived in and around Main Street. Porch lights began to flicker on like fireflies commencing their nightly ballet. Doors opened as curiosity seekers peered out to see the commotion disturbing their night's slumber.

The ambulance pulled up to where Ross was waiting. He was holding Ned's motionless head in his large hands. The old man looked like death warmed over. His face was ghostly white, and his skin was cold and clammy. Two paramedics rushed from the emergency transport. One carried a case that Ross thought to resemble a large tackle box.

"What do you have?" inquired the man with the box.

"His name is Ned Crosby. Car wreck. He's pretty messed up," answered the Sheriff. That was about the best medical diagnosis that he could offer. He allowed the professionals to take over and do their jobs. One of them tilted Crosby's head forward and undid the gauze wrapping.

"Trauma to the head, Jack. Lost a lot of blood." The medic that Ross assumed to be "Jack" was now checking Ned's pulse.

"Pulse is weak. Possible cardiac arrest. We're going to have to get him north right away."

"North" meant that Ned truly was in bad shape. The Appleton Medical facility was only equipped to handle minor ailments, and a heart problem was not one of them. Ned was going to a real hospital in Houghton with access to a more specialized medical staff. The paramedics performed their well-rehearsed roles admirably. After they put a collar around Ned's neck for support, Ross helped them carry him to the ambulance where he was loaded onto a stretcher and then pushed inside. The doors were shut, and in less than a minute, the vehicle disappeared from sight. Ross was left alone standing in the rain. He listened to the siren fade in the distance. His waterlogged shirt and jeans clung to his chilled skin. He was damn cold. Ross looked about the street, noticing the gawkers who hung around like buzzards awaiting the death of a diseased animal.

A blinding light caused the Sheriff to cover his eyes. Mark Bennington dimmed the brights of the squad car and pulled up next to his superior. The window rolled down and the Deputy's boyish face appeared. "Golly, Ross. You look like shit. What happened? Sharon called and said you might need some help."

Ross placed both hands on top of the car and leaned forward. He was exhausted. "Old Ned Crosby had one hell of a wreck over on Townsend, Mark. It doesn't look too good for him."

"Geez." Mark sounded dumbfounded, not quite sure of what else he should say.

"Yeah," continued the Sheriff, "he's gonna need the Big Fella tonight." He motioned up toward the dark sky with his eyes. "There's nothing we can do now. Go ahead and get on home." Mark looked almost hurt, as if he had expected some action. *Not in this town, boy,* thought Ross to himself. "Why don't you meet me out to my place in the morning ... say around nine. I want to check this thing out. I'll call the hospital before we leave to check on Ned's condition."

"Sure thing," replied the eager, young Deputy. "Just call if you need anything else. And get yourself into a hot shower."

It was sound advice. The Sheriff gave the roof a stiff pat. "You bet, Mark. Be good." The Deputy drove off.

Ross meandered back to the Tahoe with the engine still running, taking one last look at the people shuffling back into their warm houses. Unbeknownst to Ross and the people of Jessup, it was only the beginning of what would be an eventful fall season.

CHAPTER FOUR

History has proven that gossip in a small town is capable of spreading faster than an incurable plague in a third-world nation. The same could be said for the very active rumor mill in Jessup. Like the old telephone game played by children, the story is shared between two friends, who in turn tell two more friends ... and so on, until the final receiver hears a completely different account of the initial tale. The variances depended predominantly on the imaginations of the conspirators, and Jessup held its share of imaginative dullards who craved a slice of good gossip to free them from their daily boredom.

The mouth-watering feature story at Arlene's Café that next morning had been the big accident on Townsend Road. Although none of the town's inhabitants knew what had actually transpired during the early morning hours, the void of detail was conveniently filled by their own best guesses. Peter Brummeister passed the wreck on his drive into Jessup for his customary morning coffee. "Damnedest thing I ever seen," he said to the spirited patrons of the establishment. Brummeister went on to describe how the car had been all twisted up like an empty beer can. He then managed to sway the conversation back to how he had fought off the two black bears with his "good ole" Ithaca. But that was old news, and nobody really cared to see the scab on the old man's wrinkled head again.

Arlene Tunnison, the diner's owner, heard the story firsthand from Sharon Cooper. They shared a cup of coffee after Sharon finished her shift. Arlene had been holding the attention of a few listeners at the food bar. Francis Mecklinberg, along with a slew of other witnesses, was awakened in the night by the sirens and had actually seen the "body" being loaded into the ambulance. Francis swore on her dead mother's grave in front of three ladies from the Auxiliary that ... "the old drunk looked dead as a stump."

The restaurant was buzzing like a rustled hornet's nest. They sat in their booths and tables dissecting the case with methods of deductive reasoning that would have impressed Sherlock Holmes himself. Even Birdy McIntosh made a rare appearance before her morning route. Nobody really cared about the fate of Ned Crosby. They fed only on portions of the story that led to his predicament.

Charlie Perkins sat on a stool at the bar, gulping down the remaining morsels of a Denver omelet. A long strand of cheese hung from the corner of his mouth. He swiped it up with a fork and then shoved the remnants between his teeth. Charlie had been quietly observing the talk circulating the café. He was apparently the only occupant who was genuinely concerned with Ned's wellbeing. His fellow townsfolk and their cheap gossip made his full stomach churn. They could care less whether Ned lived or died. They were ecstatic in their own deviant ways, simply by the fact that something had stimulated what would have been just another pitiful day in their useless lives. Charlie threw six bucks on the counter, situated the hat atop his grease-stained head, and walked out of the restaurant. He shook his head in disgust. Charlie figured that the Sheriff would be calling on him soon enough to fetch Ned's car. He had some pressing work awaiting him at the shop in the meantime.

***

Ross awoke to the sound of Willie Nelson crooning a version of Patsy Cline's classic ... "Crazy." The clock radio kicked on the music at seven A.M. sharp. He opened his eyes and stared at the plaster ceiling, trying to make out shapes in the circular grooves. The musical notes danced through his ears with a soothing effect. He was still exhausted from the night's activities. The muscles in his arms and legs ached. "Sign of the times," he quirked to himself.

The light from the rising sun in the east shimmered through the half-opened blinds. Rays of sunshine cast long, vertical lines on the far wall. As the song came to an end, Ross found himself humming along with the country-western singer. It was one of those tunes that would stick with him for the rest of the day. And this was going to be one humdinger of a day. He had finally crawled under the sheets at five-thirty following a twenty minute shower. Maggie had a pot of coffee on as promised when Ross returned home, but it went untouched. He needed rest ... not caffeine to keep him from it. Maggie received a brief rundown of Ned Crosby's crash before he collapsed in her arms.

"Ross? Are you awake, hon?" It was Maggie calling from the kitchen. The Sheriff's nose smelled the bacon and eggs on the griddle. His stomach rumbled with hunger. He was ravenous, having not eaten a bite of food since a light tuna sandwich for lunch the day before.

"Yep," he answered with a hoarse voice. His mouth stretched to its maximum limits as he partook in a nice, long yawn. His arms reached high above his shoulders to stretch out tightness in his joints. He heard the soft patter of bare feet on the hallway floor.

"Food's ready." Maggie poked her head through the doorway with a caring smile painted on her face. Her long brown hair, with not a speck of gray to show her age, was combed back over her ears, still wet from the morning shower. There was something about wet hair that Ross found to be stimulating ... the way it glistened in the sun. Maggie glided through the doorway as if she had interpreted her man's hopeful thoughts. She wore only a faded flannel nightshirt that hung loosely just below her trim waist. The top four buttons were unsecured, exposing the ample cleavage between her two breasts. Ross' eyes traced the long slender legs to the delicate bare feet supporting them.

Sensing the brewing temptation, Maggie lowered her dainty hand and undid the two remaining buttons holding her unfettered shirt in place, shedding sprinkles of sunlight on a pair of scarlet panties hugging her waist below her navel.

Ross eyed the creature before him as a goddess more beautiful than any swimsuit model he'd ever laid eyes on. His eyes craved her. His hungry hands longed for the feel of her silky skin. Maggie began to massage the inside of her wanting thighs with slow, circular motions. She was ever so careful not to rush so that Ross could gain its full magnitude. Her free hand gently pulled one side of the shirt down over her shoulder, just enough to prevent exposing the yearning breast underneath.

"Chucky's still asleep," she whispered softly. "See anything on the menu you'd like this morning?"

Ross said nothing. His expression spoke volumes. Maggie closed the door with a brush of her hand and strolled seductively to the king-sized bed. She climbed on and straddled his accepting body, lightly running her fingernails over his muscular chest. Ross eased the shirt from her torso and explored her naked body with wandering hands. Maggie's back arched as a subtle moan of pleasure escaped her lips. Ross could not wait any longer. He pulled her head to his and they kissed deeply.

***

Tyrone Pullman had been monitoring the radio throughout the three hour drive. The shootout was the hot topic with all of the Lansing stations, as well as those in surrounding areas. As the fugitives ventured further north, the story seemed to lose its luster. For the first time that day, Tyrone began to feel somewhat at ease. He had literally pulled off a miracle and he damn well knew it. He also realized that there was now a massive manhunt in progress. Cops would be scouring the state from top to bottom. Killing law enforcement officials was not a lucrative business to be in, and he had been involved in more than his share of late. Gerald, in the meantime, had no clue as to where his partner was taking him. They were headed away from the focus of the intense search ... away from the populated cities downstate.

Tyrone pictured Flint in his mind as he passed by the Gaylord exit on northbound I-75. He envisioned cops busting up the local hubs where Gerald was known to hang. Families' lives brutally disrupted as the heat broke down doors, smashed windows, kicking anyone and everyone's ass that stood in their way. *There ain't no stopping a determined cop,* he thought. Tyrone had witnessed police "search and destroy" missions before. Friends of his had died from their battering riot sticks, their skulls caved in and their faces mangled. He shook off those depressing thoughts and reached for the tuning dial on the radio. He turned from station to station, getting only pop, rock, country and more country. *Shit,* he thought, *not one rap station within a hundred fucking miles.* But Tyrone knew that he couldn't expect much less in those parts of the State. He was confident that his decision to take a northern route had been the safest option, but it was not without risk. They would stand out.

Tyrone Pullman's plan was to bypass the denser population of cops in the south and take his chances with the occasional speed trap up north. He would drive across the Mackinaw Bridge and then head west. The possibility of shacking up in some deserted cabin off the beaten path did cross his mind, but anxiety would probably push him to continue the trip down through Wisconsin and finally into Illinois where the two of them would hole up with some associates in Chicago. There were two effective places for a man to disappear for a period of time; one being the remote outdoors, and the other being in a poor urban neighborhood where even the police didn't feel comfortable. Tyrone now had both at his disposal. All he had to do now was make a decision and get there.

Aside from the police threat, there had been one other important factor plaguing his mind since the extraction. It was the man lying in the tool compartment in the back of the truck. If his partner began to show even the slightest signs of losing his composure, Gerald would have to be dealt with. Tyrone continued to ponder that issue with each passing mile marker. He would be better off on his own. But did he actually owe Gerald anything?

"Fuck no!" he cursed aloud. "The motherfucker threatened to take me down. That sure as hell ain't no sign of loyalty." It was an act of desperation. And Gerald had shown no signs of remorse when J.C. and Billy went down while helping him regain his freedom. "Fuck no!" He began to think that maybe he should just end the relationship with the help of the .32 in his pocket. Life would be a whole lot easier. Tyrone would have to wait for an opportune time if that was the action he chose to pursue. He then started to believe that it might just be safer to hide out in the sticks. That would give him time to study his passenger and determine whether or not he should live. He still had time to think it over. *Just give me an excuse, asshole.*

***

After the unexpected early morning workout, a hearty breakfast and his second shower in about three hours, Ross made a phone call to the Trauma Center in Houghton to get word on Ned's condition. He talked to five different people before finally being transferred to someone with any knowledge of the situation.

"Yes, Sheriff, we've been monitoring Mr. Crosby since he was brought in last night." The nurse in the intensive care unit seemed a little too abrupt for his liking. She resembled more of a frustrated customer service representative taking complaints in a department store. “He’s still in critical condition,” she continued.

“Has he said anything about the accident?”

“No sir. Mr. Crosby has not yet regained consciousness.”

“What’s the outlook? Ross asked the questions, knowing that it wouldn’t be too promising.

“I’m sorry, Sheriff, but I’m not a doctor. I could have someone give you a call if you give me a number where you may be reached.” Ross gave the nurse his home phone number as well as the number for the office. He politely thanked the nurse for her time and hung up the phone. *Well, that’s that,* he thought. He would have to wait for Ned’s prognosis. He glanced to the clock on the wall in the living room. It was approaching nine. Mark would be rolling in soon.

Chuck Barnes lumbered into the room, clad only in a pair of cotton shorts with a block “M” embroidered on one thigh. The boy’s lifelong dream was to play quarterback for the Michigan Wolverines in front of the one hundred thousand plus fans. Ross took him down to Ann Arbor last fall for a game with his alma mater. The contest had been a blowout by halftime, but the camaraderie was priceless. Chuck fell in love with the stadium as well as the campus. Ross’ hidden agenda was to encourage interest in the Badger program, but that had been a wrong move on his part. Chuck’s dream of wearing the Maize and Blue had been forever etched in his brain.

The boy had a rifle for an arm. And standing six feet two inches tall with a few more on the way, he was a damn good prospect. Speed was something to be desired. That could come with age and training. Some of the smaller schools were already showing interest, but Chuck had larger ambitions. Ross smiled, remembering his own young self when he had been ready to conquer the world.

“Well, look what the cat dragged in,” the Sheriff jested. “Jenna keep you up a little late last night?” Jenna was Chuck’s high school sweetheart ... a cheerleader. Ross occasionally had to kick himself in the rear when he caught himself staring with admiring eyes at the well-endowed high school junior. *Ah, to be sixteen again.* “I think it’s time we had a little talk about da birds and da bees, my boy.”

The comment drew a smirk from the teen as he clawed at his misplaced head of hair. "Whoa, old timer," he rebutted. "You forget that I come from the age of PG-13 and HBO. I think you have your roles reversed." Ross got up off the sofa and followed him into the tight-quartered kitchen. Chuck laughed as he reached into the refrigerator and retrieved a half-gallon jug of orange juice. They were constantly playing these little cat and mouse games.

If only you could have seen me in action this morning, thought Ross. "I ain't dead yet, limp-dick."

"Ross!" protested Maggie as she stepped into the room. The Sheriff's face turned two shades of red. "Nice language for you," she continued. "Chuck, quit drinking out of the container."

"Yes, mommy," replied her son in a childish manner. He found a glass in a cabinet and filled it.

"Ross, I think Mark's here. Should I make some more coffee?" asked Maggie, seeing the squad car pulling into the drive through the kitchen window.

"No, Maggs, we've gotta roll." The Sheriff grabbed his insulated Carhartt jacket draped over the back of a chair. He never wore the uniform provided by the town. He thought it to be too confining. Ross preferred to mesh with his surroundings. Mark, on the other hand, was the prudent Barney Fife sort who displayed great pride in portraying the image of a proper law enforcement official.

"Where are you going, Ross?" inquired Chuck.

The Sheriff stopped at the door and turned to answer him. "Ned Crosby had a bad wreck last night. Mark and I are going to check it out."

"Mind if I tag along?" The tone in the boy's voice revealed his eagerness to aid in some authentic police work.

"Not if you don't mind eating a little mud. Get some clothes on that wimpy body of yours." There was always room for one more dig.

"Any time, grandpa," challenged the teenager while retreating to his bedroom.

There was a knock on the door. Maggie greeted the Deputy and let him into the house. "Morning, Mark."

"Morning, Maggie ... Ross."

"How's Jenny doing?" questioned Maggie with concern.

The Deputy took off his hat and politely held it against his chest. "Huh? Oh, Jenny. She's doing all right," he answered shyly.

Odd, thought Ross. He raised an eyebrow, thinking Mark had been caught a little off guard by the question. "Chuck's going to come along," he added.

"Great!" Mark's eyes lit up. "The kid had a great game last night, Ross. Boy, has he got an arm."

"Just don't let him hear you say that. We might have trouble fitting his head through the door there." The two men laughed.

"Any word on Crosby yet?" Mark quickly turned serious.

"Still critical is all they could tell me." Ross shook his head. "Should hear something by this afternoon I would hope. By the way, Maggs, someone may be calling from the hospital."

"I'll be right here until two. Do you want me to give you a buzz if they do?" The house had been equipped with a police scanner and radio just in case Maggie ever had an emergency and needed to get in touch with him. Cell phones had not yet grown with much popularity in the north, primarily because of the poor cell coverage. They were still restricted to two-way radios and landlines.

"Yeah, we may be a few hours."

Chuck sprinted back into the room wearing a ragged pair of jeans and an old sweatshirt. He gave the Deputy a friendly pat on the shoulder. "Sup, Mark?"

"Good game last night, Junior. I think I saw a scout or two in the crowd, and they weren't watching that linebacker from Iron Mountain."

"Yeah, we did alright."

The three of them finally left the house after Ross and Chuck smacked lips with Maggie.

***

Roughly eleven miles from where the investigative team departed, the female sloshed through the mucky waters of the Amen Swamp until she reached the lair. The twigs and brambles twisted through her heavy hide. After the hairless one's vicious attack on her juvenile during the dark hours, the hate-driven beast had carried the corpse into the most isolated regions of the swamp. A proper burial was customary in the ways of the clan. When she arrived, the others looked on as the grieving female performed her ritualistic duties for the fallen one. For generations they had inhabited that plot of ground and were secure in the safety of its dense cover. When the fires pushed them away during the days when the sun grew hot, they had been forced into uncommon territory, compelled to wander closer to the perimeter of the swamp to follow their sources of food.

The clan's timeless history allowed them to elude detection from the world outside. Though there had been occasions when their existence had nearly been compromised, they had always managed to maintain stealth for the sake of their own survival. They were at the top of the food chain, but they were also intelligent and understood their place. The creatures were nocturnal in nature with superior senses and physical attributes that made them efficient hunters. They lived as a clan, grew as a clan ... and hunted in packs.

With this new revelation, the clan was sensing a cloud of danger hovering over them. Their safety had been compromised because of the female's reckless actions. She had broken the rules and would have to suffer consequences. Viewed as unworthy in their eyes, no male would ever mate with her again. It was customary ... for the survival of the species.

As the female buried her juvenile in her slow, methodical way, the others were anxiously milling about while sniffing the winds for fear that she had been followed. It was time for the punishment phase of the ritual. Once the corpse was sealed in the mucky pit, out of sight forever, the larger males began to make darting advances on her backside. They would scream their distaste before retreating to allow room for another. It was a taunting process that was repeated over and over again. The female was aware of the penalty that would be imposed upon her. She growled more out of frustration than anger. The vocal assaults preceded the physical acts.

The males began to make contact. Their bodies slammed into her with incredible force, enough to cause tremors on the swamp floor. The other females huddled together silently in the background with their own juveniles. They would only play witness to the odd ceremony. It was a lesson for all to learn. The rules would not allow the chastised one to fight back. An act of defiance would bring about certain death. The female could only erect herself and prepare for the next blow.

After countless assaults, the leader of the clan produced a thunderous cry that echoed through the trees. It was the signal for the ritual to end. The female crouched to the ground, feeling the effects of the painful blows to her body. She knew what was now to be. The leader, standing a full head taller, stepped into the forefront and pulled the female up to a standing position by the long fur on her head. He then pushed her backward with such force that she nearly toppled over. The male pushed her again ... and again, motioning her away from the protective lair. The female had been exiled from the group forever ... sent away to fend for herself. The ultimate punishment was decreed. She would now be alone.

As she made her way into the swamp, she could hear the other females protesting the actions of their leader. They jumped around, grunting with displeasure. But the rules were made to be followed, and there could be no exceptions. Those that could not follow the rules would be discharged to a life of solitude so that they could no longer jeopardize the safety of the clan. The female disappeared from sight, but she did not feel despondent toward her fate. She felt a sense of release. The anger began to grow within her once again ... not necessarily for her own kind that had forced her away, but rather for the hairless one that had destroyed the life of her juvenile. There was now only one purpose emerging ... vengeance! She would return to the scene and avenge the death of the young one. She would kill, and then feast upon the forbidden flesh of the hairless creature. The female vanished into the cedars.

***

Townsend Road was still in the same pathetic condition from the previous night's rainstorm. As the four-by-four crept toward the scene of the accident, the ascending sun had begun melting the heavy morning frost blanketing the northern landscape. It was a typical September morning in the U.P. The temperature hovered somewhere around the freezing mark. By mid-afternoon, it would climb to the mid forties ... cool, but comfortable. *Good day for a bird hunt,* thought the Sheriff while losing himself in the picturesque setting. There was no other place in the world that he would have preferred over the Upper Peninsula. Ned Crosby's had just been one of those bumps in the road that had to be endured now and again.

The trip out to the wreck had been a quiet one. Ross figured that everyone was a little tired, but the crisp morning air would give them a little jolt of life. Ross parked the Tahoe in the same spot as he had done only a few hours earlier. The three passengers all exited the vehicle and walked through the crunchy mud to the top of the ditch. The cold temperatures had sealed the muddy road with a very thin layer of ice. The surface was slightly firmer than Ross' first trip to the scene, but it was still extremely sloppy and difficult to maneuver on foot.

"That car sure ate a lot of tree," remarked the Deputy with eyes fixed on the Plymouth. They all hesitated a moment and surveyed the sight before them.

"Yeah," added the Sheriff, "drinking and driving sure don't pay, do it." It had been a statement, not a question. He hoped that Chuck was learning something from the experience. They were all privy to Ned's drinking binges down to the Jessup Inn. Everyone in town was. Ross remembered Maggie commenting that Ned had been pretty snockered before passing through the doors on his way out last night. *She must have said it before I fell asleep,* he thought. A pleasant recollection of the morning's activities entered his head. Another glance to the mess below instantly subdued those thoughts. It resurrected memories of his own bout with the bottle and how it had nearly defeated him. *Old ghosts. Christ, why can't they just leave me alone?*

Another thought suddenly popped into the Sheriff's wandering mind ... something from the previous night. He recalled the piece of flesh that he lifted from the car's fender. He wished he had brought his parka containing the specimen. "Mark," he said, turning to the Deputy. "I want you to check this out." The junior constable followed the Sheriff a little too closely down the embankment. The ground was still quite treacherous. Chuck decided to embark on his own little investigation and gracefully slid down the slope to the rear of the car. The boy didn't seem to mind dirtying his old clothes.

"Take a look at this fender." Ross was kneeling down next to the crumpled piece of metal. The Deputy followed his lead. "See how it's dented inward? It doesn't fit the point of impact. If anything, it should be pushed outward." He paused a moment to allow Mark to observe. "I think that Ned may have hit something up on the road ... an animal of some kind, before he lost control. It probably caused the accident. I found some hair and blood around this area." He circled a section of metal with his finger.

"I see what you're saying." The Deputy was studying the fender with the intensity of a meticulous pathologist.

Seeing the seriousness in his partner was humoring, but Ross sobered after remembering that someone nearly died there last night.

"There's some dried blood around the rim." Mark scraped off a sample with his fingernail. "What color hair?" he asked, holding the red flakes close to his eyes.

"Dark ... almost black. And long, too," Ross answered. "What are you thinking?"

"Well, it took a big animal to do that amount of damage, unless of course there was already a bruise on that fender. I doubt it," he continued thoughtfully. "They don't make fenders like this anymore. It's solid. You can also see that the break in the paint is fresh."

Ross noticed the peeled flakes that Mark was referring to. *This kid isn't bad,* he thought.

"Okay, first off, this was definitely not the result of the collision with the tree ... right?" Mark waited for Ross' acknowledgement. The Sheriff nodded. "Secondly, whatever Ned may have hit had some size to it ... right?"

Again, Ross nodded his acceptance to the Deputy's direction. He began to see Mark's theory taking shape. He had the same idea last night, but he wanted to hear it from someone else's mouth.

"Thirdly, you say you found some dark hair on the fender?"

"Yup," replied the Sheriff.

"And you don't think it could have been a deer or you would have said so by now." Mark hesitated briefly before revealing his summation. "How about a bear?" The Deputy's eyes showed a glint of accomplishment.

"Yeah, how 'bout a bear. That's what I was flirting with last night." The Sheriff straightened his body and arched his back to work out yet another one of those menacing kinks. "Just wanted you to feel it out before I put the idea in your head." He looked down and saw the mud caked against the front tire. *Tracks! There had to be tracks!* He rotated his head and searched the ground surrounding the wreck before realizing that the rain had already settled that issue. "Must have been a whale of a bear," he said out loud, stepping away from the car.

"Ross!" Chuck's call came from just inside swamp. "Come and take a look at this!"

The Sheriff walked through the brush and found the boy down on one knee holding something in his hands. Mark stayed at the car, continuing his investigative duties there.

***

The female stood completely still behind two rotting tree trunks rising from a pool of black swamp water. The crowns of the white pines had long since toppled over without support from their deadened bases. She had first scented the hairless creatures on her return journey to where her juvenile perished during the night. She carefully approached until she saw one of them moving toward her. The others remained outside the perimeter, milling around the machine like scavengers. She was no longer running from these hairless ones. She was now hunting them.

The female's breathing was relaxed and controlled so as not to make any compromising noise. She could easily detect their putrid stenches. Her nostrils flared as she took in each catch of air, tasting their pale flesh with her hungry tongue. She would kill on this day. There was nothing else to live for. When the lone hairless one separated from the group, the female formulated the plan in her head. The ways of the clan taught her that the hunter must be patient and allow the prey to present the opportunity for the kill. But her fueled anger was making it difficult to control emotion. She wanted to charge and taste blood.

Watchful eyes concentrated on the hairless creature as it advanced on her position. She opened and closed her enormous claws, twitching with anticipation. It was almost within striking distance. Then, the hairless one lowered itself to the swamp floor, acting as if it were examining something. Perhaps she had left a track. The female cocked her rear foot, ready to leap on the unsuspecting prey.

Suddenly, the creature produced a noise. Her target cried out to the others as if it were summoning them. She froze, wondering if she had been detected. Perhaps she failed to realize the skills that these creatures possessed. The hairless one cried out again. Was it a warning signal? She slowly ducked back behind the large stumps, blending with the backdrop of the swamp. She watched anxiously through a small gap in the deadfall. When the second hairless creature appeared, the female found herself faced with a choice. She would not attack more than one without knowing their capabilities. The clan had never hunted these creatures before. They had always been taught to avoid them ... but that was before they became destroyers of her kind. The female watched ... and waited.

***

Ross finally broke through the entanglement of brush, unaware that he could have followed a much easier path only a few feet away. Chuck was sitting on a downed log in a small opening, examining what looked to be a branch.

“What’s up?”

“Take a look at this,” answered the boy, looking up to the Sheriff. He raised a branch from a medium-sized spruce with a diameter about as thick as his wrist.

“What about it?” Ross took the branch in his own hands, looking it over from top to bottom. “Broken branch. So what?” He shrugged his shoulders.

Chuck looked to be somewhat surprised by the Sheriff’s failure to grasp the importance of his discovery. “Not broken, Ross. Cut ... or sliced.”

Ross looked at Chuck with a quizzical expression, and then back to the branch. He was right. The branch had been sheared off as if someone had used a sharp blade.

“Over there, more of the same.” Chuck pointed down a rough trail leading deeper into the swamp. “That’s your game trail.”

Ross took a few cautious steps down the path, observing the damage inflicted upon the small trees. Something big had moved through there. A number of limbs littered the ground. He also noticed brush on the swamp floor that had been kicked out of the way. "Jesus, you're right," he whispered, still holding the branch. "Something very large came through here in a hurry." But there was something else that didn't quite click. Most of the branches had been displaced from a height that a bear would have difficulty reaching on two legs let alone all four. *What the hell does this mean,* he asked himself. A sudden noise from his right made Ross flinch. He turned his head and peered through the thick trees. Something had moved. His nose then caught wind of a rank smell hanging in the swamp air. It seemed to be growing stronger, like a rotting animal on the side of the road baking in the hot summer sun. A bad feeling began to swell in his gut. His right hand instinctively probed his waist for the .357. It was not there. *Damn!* A twig snapped.

***

The female relaxed her muscles ever so slightly and rocked back on the balls of her heels. A hidden root suddenly cracked beneath her foot. The larger of the two hairless creatures turned in her direction. She had been careless. She would now have to risk attack. The thing appeared to be staring directly into her eyes, but it did not acknowledge her presence. When she quietly scented the air, she detected fear emanating from the alerted one. That would be to her advantage. She would kill the larger one first. It was clearly the Alpha of the two. She was still well hidden behind the deadfall, totally blended with the environment. Just a little closer and she would attack.

***

Ross contemplated as to whether or not he should move further into the swamp to investigate the noise. Intuition told him that something was out there ... watching him. He felt vulnerable and isolated, as if a line had been drawn in the sand and he was being dared to cross. *Could it be the bear!* He asked himself. It had taken a pretty tough hit from the car, and probably wasn't in the best of spirits. *But a black wouldn't hang around this long ... or would it?*

He asked himself those questions and more while peering through the trees for what seemed an eternity. His large body began to weaken. There was fear in him. It was a fear that he had never experienced before. He wished for his sidearm.

Suddenly there was movement in front of him. It was charging! Ross quickly bent to the wet ground and hauled up a large branch, his only means of defense. He would have to protect Chuck. He raised the limb high over his head and prepared for the assault. But where had the creature gone? He searched the foliage. *There! It's coming again!* As Ross tensed, a black squirrel darted out from underneath the branches of a cedar. He watched the tiny animal dive to the ground and then scurry up a taller pine, chattering incessantly. The Sheriff's head tilted to the side. He let the branch fall from his arms.

Chuck was rather amused by the Ross' antics. "What the heck are you doing?" he asked.

Ross turned, embarrassed for acting like such an imbecile in front of the boy. "Stupid rodents," he muttered, disgusted with himself. If he did have his gun, he would have popped the little bastard. But that stench still hung in the air. It was making his stomach roll. "Nothing," he lied to Chuck. "I was just trying to get a feel for the size of the bear that went through here last night." His shoulders slumped as he walked past the boy who seemed to be getting a good chuckle at his expense.

"Well you have a funny way of doing that. Hey, Ross, you smell that?" Chuck was wrinkling his nose from the pungent odor.

"Yeah, it's not pretty, whatever it is."

"Something died in there, man." The teenager grimaced from the intrusion on his nose.

"Ross!" Mark yelled from the car. The Sheriff wiped away a streak of nasal drippage and took one last look into the dark swamp. "Come on, Chuck. Let's get out of here." The two of them walked single file out of the bush, unaware of the eyes transfixed upon their backs.

***

The risk of attack was too great now. She had been ready to pounce on the unsuspecting creatures, but they retreated to the perimeter. The female glanced menacingly to the trees above, angered by the squirrel that was alerting the hairless ones of her presence. She wanted to scream out in frustration, but instinct forced her to remain calm. She would have another chance. She would have her revenge.

Other squirrels then erupted in the trees, joining together to form a chorus of chaotic heckling. The female turned and crept off to escape the torturous noises that had awakened the dark mire. Some of the little creatures followed as she withdrew from her ambush position. They scampered across the damp ground and rocketed between the limbs, relentlessly taunting her as she vanished into the trees.

***

It was incredible. The squirrels were everywhere ... in the swamp ... in the hardwoods ... chattering together in one massive onslaught of noise. As he and Chuck found their way to the swamp's edge, Ross saw his Deputy sitting on the hood of the car gazing skyward to the trees. The three of them silently stood together, each attempting to get a handle on what they were experiencing. There must have been a hundred squirrels ... black squirrels, gray squirrels, red squirrels ... everywhere ... peering down on them from their perches. What bothered the Sherriff most was that these were creatures that ordinarily kept silent when people were about. And here they were in plain view for all to see. It was almost as if they were echoing a warning ... not because of them ... but for them?

The Sheriff shielded his eyes from the sun that was beginning to peek through the taller pines shading the swamp. The noise was maddening. He was tempted to cup his hands over his ears to block out the cacophony. Then, as if ordered by the final stroke of a conductor's wand, the chattering ceased. The squirrels vanished from sight into the cover of the trees. A few faint heckles from a group of strays faded away in the distance. All was quiet again.

"I think I know where I'm going to make my next squirrel hunting trip." Chuck broke the silence with a shallow attempt at humor. But inside, he was experiencing the same nervous tension as his two companions.

"Never seen anything like it in all my life," added Mark with his eyes still fixed to the trees above. "Must have been 60 ... 80 ... I don't know."

Ross detected the edginess in his Deputy's soft voice. He could not shake the feeling of vulnerability that had overtaken him only minutes before while standing in the swamp. The Sheriff did not want to be there any longer. He wanted to be home with Eevie ... Maggie. *Goddammit, Ross,* he scolded himself. There was something about the Amen that wasn't right. He could feel it toying with his head. The Amen Swamp ... the spirits. The thought made him shudder. There was only one thing to do ... change the subject. "Well, the concert's over." Ross hoped that his behavior did not expose the concern he felt.

"Yeah ... ah ... well ..." Mark tried to reacquire his train of thought. "Oh! Take a peek at the roof of the car." He pointed toward the Plymouth after one last apprehensive glance to the trees. "I think you ought to see this."

Ross sauntered over to the vehicle and noticed right away what Mark was referring to. *Christ! How did I miss this?* Without uttering a word, the Sheriff ran his fingers over the smashed metal. It appeared as though someone had gone berserk with a sledgehammer, like at those carnivals where you pay a buck for a couple of whacks on some old rust-bucket. The entire roof was caved in as if it were a thin layer of aluminum foil.

"No chance the car rolled during the accident. Not that I can see anyway," said the Deputy, standing behind his boss. Chuck joined them for a closer look. "Check out these gouges." The Deputy motioned toward a series of deep grooves in the metal, each running parallel to one another in sets of five.

"Claws." Ross muttered the word, not necessarily for the others to hear.

"No way, Ross." Mark chuckled. "Spaced too wide for a bear claw."

There was truth in what the Deputy had said. The marks had a good six to seven inch gap between them. Ross could sense that eerie feeling trying to grip him yet again. *What the hell happened here?* One thing was certain, he wasn't about to come to any ridiculous conclusions in front of the others. Not now.

"If a bear made those marks, and did that to the roof, he sure wanted into that car in a bad way." Chuck added his two cents to the inquiry. "And he was one big fucker."

Ross almost commented on the boy's inappropriate choice of language, but decided against it. That was exactly what he had been thinking.

"You don't actually believe that a bear made those marks, do you?" Mark sounded confused. It seemed obvious to him. Though he had failed to inherit the same outdoor knowledge as most of his peers, he was a man of common sense.

"I don't know what the hell made them, Mark." Ross turned away from the car, caught off guard by this new revelation. This was supposed to be an easy job. He wanted to believe that he had been correct with his initial assessment. Ross prayed that he had been correct; however, common sense was now teasing him with the notion that maybe there was something else out there ... something that he had nearly confronted while standing alone in that swamp ... the Amen Swamp.

"Ross ... is ...gie ... out there? Ross?" Maggie's broken voice sounded over the radio in the Tahoe. Ross clawed his way up the slippery bank, wiped the mud from his hands onto his jeans, and reached into the truck to retrieve the mike. Chuck and Mark followed.

"Yeah, Maggs. Go ahead."

"Hi, Ross. A Doctor Blake called from Houghton and wanted to speak to you about Ned."

"Did he tell you anything?"

"No, he said that he wanted to talk to you personally. Says it's important. Sorry."

"Alright, Maggs. We're wrapping up here. Be home soon." *That was odd,* he thought. *Now what was so important that it couldn't be discussed over the phone?* The Sheriff replaced the mike and informed the other two that the investigation was over, at least for them.

CHAPTER FIVE

It didn't take long for details of the investigation to rip through the heart of Jessup a second time that day. Mark's first stop after the morning outing had been to Arlene's for some late breakfast. The questions were asked both direct and to the point. "What happened out there, Mark?" "What did the car look like?" "Was there a lot of blood?" "Is old Ned alive?" They came from all angles, men and women huddling around the defenseless Deputy like hawks surveying an open meadow in search of a meal. A part of him enjoyed the attention. It gave him a feeling of significance in the community. He was reluctant to give in to the minor inquisition at first, but as the minutes passed, words began slipping from his mouth. Mark never could keep a secret for long, and the people of Jessup knew it.

"What did you and the Sheriff find, Mark?" It was Arlene muscling her way through the crowd to serve the two plates of food ... eggs on Texas toast, Canadian bacon, and a double serving of hash browns. The popular dish was also known as the "Deer Hunter's Deluxe" on the café's morning menu. The restaurant's owner firmly held her position after setting the breakfast in front of the hungry Deputy.

"Not much, Arlene. Just a beat up car's all." Mark jabbed a chuck of meat with his fork. He did not look up to the wondering faces hovering over him.

"The boys who were at the Inn last night said the old coot was drunk as an Irishman on St Patty's Day."

"Yeah, well ..." continued the Deputy, "that's all hearsay at this point in the investigation." He sputtered out his answers between bites, attempting to use official police lingo to impress the onlookers. After all, he was a professional law enforcement officer.

"Did he just up and drive off the road? Peter Brummeister said he nailed a tree pretty darn good."

Gene Steubens, the town's astute Mayor, had entered the café and zig-zagged his way through the crowd. He stood next to Arlene who was holding her hands on her hips like a mother waiting for a child to fess up to spilling juice on the carpet.

"Oh! Hi, Mayor." Mark stood up from his booth, utilizing his crinkled napkin to wipe away a few specks of potato that dangled from his boyish mustache. He clumsily extended a hand to the dignified Mayor, nearly knocking over a cup of coffee in the process. Mark had always been intimidated by Jessup's leader, even though he stood a good ten inches taller. Steubens was an authoritative man with a flair for making others feel inferior while in his presence. His boisterous voice was no match for anyone who wished to enter into a debate. He had a skillful knack of forcing opponents to cower from his educated dialog that was filled with an array of hidden slander. Gene Steubens had his way with the unsophisticated residents of Jessup. He was a short, heavy-set man who made up for his dumpy looks by engineering a domineering personality.

Steubens came to Jessup from downstate where he had always been involved in community service so long as it served his own business purposes. His wife and two children were of the same mold. None of them missed many meals, and all seemed to display a level of arrogance unfitting of their environment. The Steubens kids were never at fault when disturbances erupted on the school playground, and Mrs. Steubens ordered the women about as if she were the First Lady.

Gene Steubens entered their lives with promises of transforming Jessup into a community of prosperity. He often bragged of close relationships to high government officials down in Lansing, who, for one reason or another, were indebted to him for the patronage that he so loyally bestowed upon them. The claim had not been a total fabrication. Gene Steubens had known a Senator once ... in kindergarten. But that young boy who was now established in the State's government hadn't actually been a close friend to little Eugene Steubens. In fact, the class bully had teased the overweight child to the brink of tears nearly every day in what had been the longest year of the small-time politician's life. But the people of Jessup did not need to know those details. His uncanny ability to pluck a name out of a hat to capture an ear was impressive enough, even if there was no merit in his words.

The Steubens family moved north in 1991 after spending ten years in Roscommon, a small community in the northern Lower Peninsula that was very similar to Jessup in size and make-up. Gene held the post of City Manager for five of those ten years, a testy period in his eventful life. One trait that managed to shadow Gene Steubens was his bad luck when it came to making personal business decisions. He and his wife had inherited a small fortune from his in-laws after they were killed in a car accident while vacationing in Florida. His in-laws had never cared for him, and he reciprocated the sentiment. But they tolerated him for the sake of their daughter.

Steubens would flaunt his fortunes in the faces of others. Even when he didn't have money, Gene would never think twice about overextending his credit so long as he and his wife could both drive Cadillacs around town and thumb their noses to the paupers who looked up to them. He had lived that life since his graduation from Michigan State University many years earlier. A marketing major with an emphasis in bullshit, his career stretched from one dead-end sales gig to the next ... from cars to life insurance ... from dog toys to shoes. They were all the same, lasting for only a few months before moving on to the next. What the man could not accept through his less than lucrative career was the simple fact that he knew he was a darn good salesman who was not worthy of failure.

Gene Steubens' enigma was his inability to hold onto a dollar. Any money that he did manage to stash away was eventually lost in the market on some dying stock. When his ship finally came in with the inheritance, Steubens had a time with it. It was a means for correcting previous failures and showing the world that he was a man with whom to be reckoned.

After turning forty, Steubens began to shy away from stocks and developed an interest for real estate, an industry where he would again experience bitter failures. Always possessing a thirst for more, Gene was eager to invest in properties that promised future wealth ... most of which were get rich quick scams established by fly-by-night salesmen with sharp tongues of their own. There were condominium projects that never seemed to evolve past the teasing brochures, and strip malls to be built on lands owned by unknowing participants. They all involved a witty salesman dangling the deal like a piece of cheese in front of a naïve mouse. They spoke in such a way that made Steubens feel as though he were an important business mogul. It was effective ammunition.

After a lengthy succession of fraudulent deals that deteriorated the family's inheritance to the brink of extinction, one very special opportunity came rolling into his lap. A "firm" from New York was looking for investors to sink funds into a golf resort to be constructed just north of Houghton Lake. A gorgeous blonde with mesmerizing blue eyes drew Gene Steubens into a tangled web. Her firm's venture extracted nearly eighty thousand dollars from the smitten man's bank account. In the end, Gene Steubens had been fooled by a very talented actress who allowed him to flirt with her until the final transfer had been completed. When the dust settled, the woman was gone, the "firm" out of business, and Gene Steubens was out eighty thousand dollars. Although most men would have been devastated by such misfortune, Gene considered it only a minor glitch on his road to success. There was always money to be found somewhere. But when the bills for the cars, the house, and the lifestyle began to pile up, Steubens began scrounging for cash. He soon became a product of his own miscarriages, devising personal scams to take advantage of other fools searching for the quick buck.

Gene was a natural born salesman who could sell a Japanese import to the President of the UAW. Like the numerous rip-off artists who had preyed upon him, Gene was now on the offensive, selling products and ideas with no inherent foundation or value. He became a master of the swindle, primarily targeting the elderly who were weak against the art of persuasion. With money funneling into his expanding bank account, Gene Steubens could set aside the past and show the world that he had made it.

Suddenly, without warning, a wrench was thrown into the spokes of his money wagon. With increasing pressure on the State government from family members of the countless seniors who were losing retirement funds, officials in the Attorney General's office took action. They began a crusade to ferret out the likes of Gene Steubens who had no ethical motives for financial advancement. Gene soon found himself running barefoot on a bed of hot coals, and he was not a fast runner. A State agent caught him in his own act, purchasing a sizeable portion of burial insurance, one of his many expensive, but useless products for the elderly. Steubens established the scam in the Traverse City area, a hotbed for aging retirees with money. The man had been seventy-five and resembled any number of his other victims. He purchased a plan that was intended to deliver widows and widowers the appropriate funds to provide proper funerals for their spouses. The double-cross was in the fine print that most people failed to recognize on the last page of the contract. The insurance would expire after the insured reached the ripe old age of sixty-five. He had been marketing a valueless product to people who had already surpassed the qualifying age upon purchase.

The Attorney General, himself a senior citizen, used the likes of Gene Steubens to heighten his own political gain. The hand of the State's top law dog came down hard. But a good lawyer, who would eventually suck the life out of Steubens' savings, was able to get the Roscommon resident off on a technicality. Gene remained free, but his questionable business ventures were finished. He was now on a watch list.

Standing with her husband through the entire ordeal was Gretchen Steubens, a hefty lady with an iron-clad fist for having her way. Her husband had provided before, and he would provide again. Gretchen Steubens was the only human being that intimidated Gene. He didn't really love her. It was more of a business arrangement for them to remain together. But they were friends, and they did face the trials of life on a mutual plane. Gene never associated his wife with any of his business dealings out of respect for her. If something were to happen that would force him to surrender his freedom, he would not drag Gretchen down with him. That was one promise he had made to himself when he made the transition from the hunted to the hunter.

The year following Gene Steubens' fall from grace had not passed unruffled. Their financial portfolio was non-existent and the "Repo Man" was knocking on the door. Gene did continue to hold his position as the Roscommon City Manager, the final wheel that would drive him out of the lower portion of the state for good. As City Manager, Steubens had access to city funds. Since his previous arraignment had been in Traverse City, the town was not privy to his suspect behavior. Steubens had managed to finagle a tale of a dying uncle that required him to spend a great deal of time away from town. It was a simple lie that took a long while before it was finally discovered. So Gene, with a till of money at his fingertips, began dipping his ladle. It had been just a little at first, enough to pay off the mounting bills. But as time passed, the act became easier. It was almost a sickness ... like a gambler who won big on the first pull of the slots. Hundreds turned into thousands from a budget that was modest to begin with.

Gene's dishonest actions progressed for six months before the first question was asked. A group of ladies requesting financial support for the revamping of the local park along the Au Sable River sent the community of Roscommon into an intense public scandal. A detailed audit showed that there were no funds available for the project. The Steubens' were once again the center of attention, facing legal prosecution for embezzlement. But once again, the slippery fox sidestepped his way out of the firefight with the aid of his well-versed counselor. His defense was to play dumb. There was nothing in his personal possession that could be tied to the city's account ... no receipts ... no transfer slips ... no canceled checks. The money had simply vanished into thin air. It was just coincidence that this occurred while Gene Steubens was in charge. There were others who had access as well, and the big-city attorney enacted a magnificent performance of pitting townsfolk against townsfolk, directing blame to other innocent faces. There had been reasonable doubt in the eyes of the jury and the defendant was acquitted on all charges. But there was no forgiveness in the community. A recall petition was formulated and the City Manager lost his seat, as well as the respect that he craved. Realizing that his life in Roscommon was over, Gene packed up his family and headed north.

Steubens settled in Jessup, a simple town where he figured his quick wit and verbal artistry could provide a suitable life. His mind was constantly working toward a solution to his personal recession. Since real estate had been one of his targeted markets down south, he tried his hand at selling properties once again, only this time with a more honest approach. Still holding a license to sell in Michigan, Gene opened up a private office and began showing properties primarily to out-of-staters who were looking for vacation homes. A large portion of his business revolved around hunt clubs searching for lands to privatize for their own use. These groups migrated from all over the Midwest. They were predominantly deer hunters who would occupy the clubs during the short firearm season. When he saved a little money, Gene began to purchase chunks of land from bank foreclosings and financially despondent locals looking for a means to bail themselves out of debt. He would then flip the tracts for significant profit to businessman, doctors and lawyers who had no time to search for bargains on their own. The business grew to a respectable level, and for the first time in his life, Gene Steubens felt that he had found his true niche in the world. Although he would have preferred a faster paced environment, Gene felt comfortable in Jessup and was determined to hold on to what he had built. He had finally earned a sense of respect that he so feverously desired since childhood.

One day while strolling down Main Street, Gene noticed a flyer tacked up on a telephone pole. It was a statement from Maury Paulsey, the local barber, requesting the support of the townsfolk in the upcoming Mayoral election. "Mayor!" The little man said it aloud. And then he said it again with the addition of his last name. "Mayor Steubens!" It was a fitting union of words. His brain set in motion a plan that would place him in command of a community that so desperately needed his talents. That day, Gene Steubens walked right down to city hall and put his name in the hat.

The platform was to tap the tourist trade. "It's a gold mine," he claimed. And he professed that the key to opening those locked doors was in his selfless possession. Maury Paulsey had no real pitch to the voters. It was later learned that he never really wanted to be Mayor in the first place. Some buddies had urged him to run when nobody else showed interest. Gene Steubens, on the other hand, wanted the seat in the worst way. He walked door to door explaining to the townsfolk how he planned to revive their community and create a greater cash flow for all who lived there. His aggressive approach to the campaign brought victory in the end. People now looked up to him as both leader and friend.

After three years in office, the town had yet to see those vast improvements that their leader had so adamantly promised. Although he did try, his deals to lure outside investors always found a way to fall through the cracks. Failure began to stare at him in the face again. But Steubens was determined to make things work this time. He traveled to Chicago, Detroit, and even as far as Cincinnati on one occasion drumming up plans for developments for his meager town of nine hundred. After countless rejections, one deal finally exploded from out of the blue. It was a peach that even he had trouble believing. Similar to his failed Houghton Lake venture, it involved a firm that built golf resorts. The difference was that this firm had actually followed through with their projects and opened them for business. Gene Steubens sold his community with astounding finesse, highlighting even the most insignificant features that Jessup had to offer. He sold the town's history, reviving the stories of Zachariah and the old lumber mill. He sold the remoteness for the vacationers who wished to escape their hectic lives in the cities. He sold the unparalleled scenery. Gene Steubens sold the fact that there was not a decent golf resort in the entire Upper Peninsula. The region had been overshadowed by the hundreds of fine courses downstate. A resort in the U.P. could draw thousands from Illinois, Wisconsin and other Midwest states. There was a casino only twenty miles to the east, with more in the works on nearby Indian reservations.

Gene sparked an interest and a marketing team traveled to Jessup to perform their analysis. After a month of non-stop information gathering, the firm from Chicago gave the green light and ground was broken on a complex that would be called "Hideaway Pines." The firm purchased two thousand and eighty acres just outside of Jessup from Steubens Real Estate, lining the Mayor's pocket with a nice little bonus. In Gene's mind, he had worked his tail off for the town and he was due a piece of the pie. Architects drew up plans for two eighteen hole championship courses. "The Diamond" would be the tract slashing through a section of land full of valleys and ridges, enchanted by northern hardwoods. The developers drew upon local lore and designated "Amen Basin" as the name of the course that would cut through the outer boundaries of the Amen Swamp. An enormous lodge and clubhouse would be situated between the two courses with future plans for condos. Things were happening in Jessup, and Gene Steubens was the man behind the scenes. The people would be thankful for the good paying jobs in both the construction and operational phases of the project. Everyone would prosper.

But Gene Steubens quickly discovered that he would not receive much credit for his efforts. Much to his surprise, the Mayor found that there were actually some who vehemently opposed the change that was taking place in their peaceful town. Most overlooked the entire development altogether as though it was some strange dream that would ultimately fade with the next sunrise. And most people from town hardly cared about the political structure of their local government that bared such little importance to their existence. This complacency was beyond the Mayor, whose only goal in life was to bring wealth to his family. But he knew the golf resort could provide for all.

Regardless of the town's apathy with Hideaway Pines, Steubens vowed to keep prying underneath their thick skins until he was appreciated. In the meantime, he would have to succumb to their lackluster ways and maintain the status quo in order to remain in their good graces. His method for accomplishing that objective was to push where there needed pushing, and finesse where there needed finessing. He would be patient, but the day would come when Jessup would look at him as its savior.

There was one mark on Gene Steubens' resume that would finally be attributed to the incessant politician's laborious struggles. Existing in many small town cultures is an event that brings the community together for one or two weeks out of the year allowing residents some much needed fellowship. Michigan had its Peach Festival, Mint Festival, Cherry Festival, a Fish Sandwich Festival, and countless other festivals. It was an avenue of escape for residents from the monotony of life, as well as a means to draw notice to their communities. In 1995, Jessup's feisty Mayor decided that his town should be no different than the rest. With the idea of providing a boost to local businesses and creating yet another avenue for the tourist dollar, the Rutt'n Buck Festival was born. Although Gene Steubens would have preferred a more subtle, sophisticated theme, he understood that anything was better than nothing at all. All of the town's councilmembers were avid deer hunters. All except for Gene Steubens, and none had ever heard of an event with a similar theme. It was a unique idea in their eyes, one that would perk the interest of out-of-towners and locals alike. The outcome was positive for the town as a whole. A few new businesses even found their way onto Main Street ... like Northern Antiques, which offered an impressive selection of "old stuff" ... and The Woman's Touch that sold a wide array of items handcrafted by the local Lady's Auxiliary.

With each passing year, the Rutt'n Buck Festival seemed to grow in strength. More and more people became involved with the planning. The Festival took place on the last weekend in September as a calling card to the upcoming deer season. The beer tent was always the main draw, offering a live band and cheap prices on liquid cheer. On Saturday afternoon, the tent was utilized for Vegas-style gaming where all proceeds went to local charities and fund raisers. This year, the event would sponsor the Ridenbauer family whose son Jonathan had been diagnosed with leukemia. A sizeable amount of cash would be donated to help pay for medical bills and family stays in Green Bay where the boy received treatment.

On Sunday morning there would be a parade with the Appleton High School Band and a number of floats built by resident youngsters. The clowns would throw candy to children lining Main Street and the Fire and Rescue vehicles would sound their high-pitched sirens. The "Queen Doe" would be presented to the masses with her court at the end of the parade. There were some who found the idea of having a "Queen Doe" in a Rutt'n Buck Festival to hold too many sexual innuendos, but their views were heavily outweighed by the majority. It was all done in good taste and in good fun. Each year, the Festival committee would attempt to rummage up some celebrity to act as Grand Marshall. This year they were excited to land Channel Seven news anchorman Dan Dorring from Houghton.

The town was enthusiastic. Even though they were still one week away from the ribbon-cutting ceremony when Gene Steubens would open Main Street, the preparations were in full swing. Banners were being strung across Main Street at both ends of town advertising the coming event. Volunteers were recruited by organizers to fill positions where help was needed. You could sense it in their mannerisms. It was a friendlier atmosphere that was all Gene Steubens' doing. Although the festival accounted for much of the change in personality, the one item that sat in the back of most locals' minds was the bow season opener. The festival was simply a sparkplug to the most festive season of the year ... fall.

"Well, speak up, boy. What happened out there?" This was a perfect opportunity for Steubens to splash some nobility over a crowd of voters. And what better target was there that a demure young Deputy who was barely old enough to buy liquor. It was obvious to the onlookers that Mark Bennington was intimidated. They enjoyed witnessing Steubens having his way with the boy. They enjoyed seeing him have his way with anyone so long as it wasn't one of them.

The Deputy shrugged his shoulders, searching for the proper words as the shorter man loomed unusually tall before him. He couldn't stand the sight of Gene Steubens let alone the blustering voice that overpowered and subdued so many. Steubens had always talked down to the Deputy as if he were a child, never taking him seriously at his job. *Someday,* thought Mark silently to himself. *Someday, I'll give you yours.* He was always conceiving little schemes on how he could get back at the Mayor for all of the grief he had caused him. Ross had repeatedly told Mark to stand his ground and be his own man. The Sheriff was the only person in town who ever stood up to the cocky, little tyrant. Ross never recoiled when the Mayor went off on one of his harangues. Mark envied the Sheriff, with his easy-going personality and his cache of common sense that he utilized so effectively. But Ross could also be bold and aggressive if the situation called for a different approach. Mark thought that he and Ross made a pretty good team. He hoped to wear the Sheriff's badge one day when his colleague decided to call it quits. Mark was confident that he would make a darn good Sheriff, too. But it would be a whole lot easier if Steubens wasn't around. In the meantime, the Deputy would have to work on building his own self-esteem.

"What was that, Deputy?" Steubens chided. "Did you say something?" The Mayor was efficiently working his magic for the crowd. He winked at Art Conley as if to say, "watch this." His chubby lips stretched into a grin.

Mark was backed into a corner. *What would Ross do?* He asked himself quietly. "Bear ... a bear," he whispered, caught in the Mayor's web like a struggling fly.

"What did you say?" Steubens inched closer to the Deputy's face. "I didn't quite catch that."

"Bear! It was a bear, okay!" *Oh shit,* thought Mark. Ross wasn't going to be too happy with him. The words just flowed from his mouth without the slightest hesitation as he caved under the pressure.

"A bear?" The Mayor backed away, contemplating the boy's words. A series of murmurs arose throughout the café.

"Well ... ah ... we're not quite certain. But ... it could ... it could have been a bear." Mark made a futile attempt to cover his statement and insert a sense of doubt. But the damage had been done and the word would spread. He already heard Art Conley speaking to John Talbert.

"Let's go have a look for ourselves, eh Johnny?" The two men pushed their way through the door and left the building.

"Guys!" Mark called out. "It's not a good idea." He tried to get up and go after them, but his path was blocked by the omnipresent Mayor.

"Just hold on, Deputy." Steubens grasped Mark's shoulder with surprising force. "What's all this about a bear?"

Goddammit! The Deputy cursed himself for being such an imbecile. Ross would be royally pissed. "We're not sure, sir." He saw Art's truck perform a U-turn in front of the café and then head off north toward the scene of the accident. "Some of the evidence suggests that Mr. Crosby may have hit a bear or something ... that's all." The Mayor gazed into his eyes as if he were waiting for the true story to be revealed. But he did tell the truth. They didn't know for sure. "I'm sorry, Mayor, but I've got to get back to work." Mark pulled away from the Mayor's hand and dropped a ten dollar bill on the table. "Keep the change, Arlene." He then brushed past the onlookers that had converged on him and hurried out the door to escape further questioning.

The beleaguered Deputy expelled a sigh of relief when he finally made his way into the street. Although Steubens had not tried to stop him, Mark Bennington was sure there were some sharp daggers being tossed into his backside right about then. Mark didn't care. He started thinking about taking a long nap. His only concern now was avoiding Ross for the rest of the day.

***

Tyrone Pullman found himself fascinated by the size of the mammoth structure connecting Michigan's two peninsulas. The tires hummed like a swarm of mellowed honey-bees on the steel grating. The transparency was a little unnerving as he watched the whitecaps of the straights hundreds of feet below. He smiled at the thought of Gerald's round eyes bugging out of their sockets. Gerald was outrageously afraid of heights. He remembered a few years back when the two of them had traveled to Texas to set up some business dealings, and how Gerald had insisted that they drive rather than fly. Tyrone also recalled Gerald's anger when he had laughed and call him a "chicken-livered motherfucker."

The driver gazed out the window toward the island to the east as the truck passed the halfway point on the arching suspension bridge. The sun was in full shine and boats of all sizes created bubbly wakes as they cut through the open water. There were ships, speed boats, sailed yachts, and even ferries carrying tourists to and from Mackinaw Island. It was a relaxing vision. Tyrone had never in his life traveled so far north. Although he had seen pictures of the various sights, they certainly did not do them justice. Seeing them in person provided a whole new perspective. The black man understood why so many white people spent money to make trips to that part of the state. It was nice, and he found himself wondering why his own people didn't take advantage of those surroundings. The answer could only be the obvious. "Because the white folk have all the fucking money, dumbass," he cursed out loud. The politicians sure wanted them to think that they were out there fighting for equal rights of the African-American, but they sure as hell weren't going to let them take over this little part of their country. Keep them in the cities and let them kill each other off quietly like animals. Let them live in the government housing projects like rats. That was the ultimate conspiracy in the eyes of Tyrone Pullman. And that's why he had embarked on a career in the drug trade like so many of his brothers before him ... to get a taste for the better life ... the white folk's life. If he couldn't do it the honest way, then he would grab it by whatever means necessary.

A loud rap in the back of the truck interrupted Tyrone's moment of peaceful meditation. *Gerald probably had to piss like a racehorse,* he thought. The driver smiled. Gerald would have to wait a while longer. He wasn't about to pull off to the side of the road on top of the Mackinaw Bridge. *Then again, that might not be a bad idea. Maybe Gerald would like to have a gander at the scenery for himself?* It was an enlightening vision, his companion diving back into the tool box like a scared rabbit. No, Gerald would have to wait.

Tyrone slowed with the line of traffic as he approached the toll booths. He chose a lane and stopped behind a Jeep pulling a small boat, three cars from the toll attendant. As he peered forward his heart fluttered.

"Shit!" he said without moving his lips. Standing with the toll attendant was a State Trooper checking faces inside cars. Tyrone looked to the other booths. Each held a cop performing the same task. He watched as the attendant would take money. The cop would then peek into the car and compare the faces to a picture that he was holding with a free hand It was no doubt a picture of Gerald Johnson. Maybe even a picture of Tyrone Pullman. There existed a very real possibility that he might have been implicated by now. If the cops discovered that his disappearance coincided with that of his business partner's ... well, two and two makes four.

The brake lights on the boat trailer in front of him turned off and the cars advanced one space. "Alright ... alright," he told himself. "Just relax." He nearly forgot about his disguise. His plan had been worked out to account for these little obstacles. Tyrone stole a quick glance into the rearview mirror without moving his head to analyze his appearance. It would be impossible for them to recognize him. *I look just like another fifty-year-old brother,* he told himself. The wildcard was Gerald. What if he banged on the sidewall of the toolbox? "Calm down, homes," he said aloud. "Play this cool."

Tyrone reached for his wallet as the Jeep pulled away from the toll booth. He eased the truck forward and stopped next to the attendant. "Afternoon, sir," he said with pleasant voice. He noticed the Trooper giving him a hard look, and then diverting his eyes to the picture he held. *Yeah ... because I'm black, cracker! We all look alike, don't we?* But Tyrone just sat there and smiled, not letting his emotions show on his face. He pulled two singles from his wallet and handed them to the attendant to pay the one dollar and fifty cent toll. "Sure is a beautiful day, ain't it?"

"Yeah, right." The attendant's response was less than enthusiastic.

Yeah, fuck you too, redneck. Tyrone continued to smile as he was handed the change. "Oh ... could I please get a receipt, sir?"

He thought that added a nice touch. The attendant smirked at the request, but complied and produced a printed receipt of the toll. "Have a nice day, sir." He used his sleeve to wipe a streak of sweat from his forehead. There was another rap on the metal behind his back. "Not yet, my friend," he said to himself as he basked in his small victory.

***

The sign along northbound 26 read five more miles to Houghton. It had been a seventy mile trip from Jessup that took close to one and a half hours. There had been some slow moving trucks blocking traffic. Ross needed to use his flashers on one occasion when an elderly man, barely large enough to see over the dash, insisted on turtling along at forty miles an hour. But he did politely pull off to the shoulder when he finally sighted the hurried police vehicle. Ross laughed when the old man made the effort to wave a shaky hand at the passing officer.

It was a simple drive to the northern city. The Sheriff's route took him up County Road 16, then west on 38, and finally north again on 26 for the stretch run. Jessup was actually located in the southwest corner of Houghton County. It was the result of some map-making philosophy that Ross never quite understood. The sun had begun its mid-afternoon descent into the western sky, preparing to end what had been another picturesque day in the U.P.

Throughout the trip, Ross dwelled on Dr. Blake's words during their brief conversation earlier in the day. The man had been reluctant to reveal much information over the phone. *Why would that be?* He thought. The Sheriff replayed the conversation in his mind. He had returned the call to Houghton General and was patched through to Dr. Henry Clark.

"Yes, Sheriff, I've been awaiting your call."

He sounded like an older, educated man. *Heck,* thought Ross, *he was a Doctor*. "Sorry it took so long, Doctor. I had some business to finish up," replied the Sheriff apologetically.

"That's quite alright, young man. Your wife was a pleasant conversationalist."

"Yeah," Ross continued, "Maggie likes to yap on the phone. Typical, huh?" He didn't feel the need to clarify his relationship with Maggie.

"My wife possesses that same attribute, Sheriff. I imagine the trait is a genetic one that has evolved within the species. But I better recant my last statement before I get myself into too much trouble." Both men laughed. It was time to get to the matter at hand.

"How's Ned Crosby doing, Doc?" Ross expected the worse, recollecting the sight of the old man as he was loaded into the ambulance ... the pale skin ... the limp body.

"Yes, of course. As you, I assume, are aware, the patient suffered a heart attack. I'll try to keep my terminology simple for your benefit."

"I'd appreciate that, Doc." Ross felt slightly degraded by Blake's comment. But the Doctor was right. He knew nothing about medicine other than general CPR and simple first aid from his training with the Department of Natural Resources. As the conversation continued, Mark and Chuck had gathered around him at the kitchen table.

"Of course," replied the wordy Doctor. "Mr. Crosby is still in critical condition and remains unconscious as we speak. I'll be up front with you, Sheriff. The prognosis is not promising. I'm sorry. If I was a betting man, and I'm not, I'd give him ... say a thirty percent chance of pulling through." Hearing the sigh from Sheriff, the Doctor continued. "But let me add that I have seen patients in much worse condition improve remarkably. Only time will tell in Mr. Crosby's case." Ross lowered his head and rubbed his eyes. "There is something else, Sheriff." Dr. Blake coughed hoarsely into the phone. Ross deducted that the man was either a smoker or had a nasty cold by the sound of the phlegmy spasm. "At one point Mr. Crosby did regain some sense of consciousness and that's what I really wanted to talk to you about."

"Why's that, Doctor?"

"Well, I'd rather we talk in person, face to face, if that would at all be possible."

He sounded peculiar, almost nervous. Ross wondered whether or not this would be something that he really wanted, or needed to hear. That feeling from earlier in the Amen Swamp began to tickle at his spine. He quickly stymied its menacing crawl. *Ridiculous,* he thought. "I can be there within a couple of hours." It was his job to pursue ... not retreat.

"That would be splendid. Maybe we'll know more regarding the patient's status by the time you arrive. I'll be here until six tonight."

I'm on my way, Doctor. And thanks for calling." The two men hung up in unison.

The streets of Houghton were busy on the colorful, autumn afternoon. Shoppers roamed the sloping streets in search of bargains, and kids played in yards speckled with the first wave of fallen leaves. It seemed that the seasons were changing quicker as the colors in the trees were much more pronounced than those surrounding his Jessup community. Ross thought about the next trip he would be making to the city in the not-too-distant future. He and Maggie always made at least one journey to Houghton before Christmas. They both preferred to dust off their shopping with one giant splurge. There would be a lot of snow on the ground by then. Traveling in the U.P. could become quite chaotic during the winter months.

Ross watched the cars travel over the expansion bridge connecting Houghton to Hancock, its sister city on the opposite shore. The water dividing the Keweenaw Peninsula was alive with fishing vessels. Most looked to be charters coming and going, loaded with anxious sportsmen in search of salmon and lake trout. The icy waters of Lake Superior, the greatest of the great lakes, were visible to the north. Ross enjoyed boats and hoped to own one someday. His father used to take him down to the shores of St. Ignace where they would admire the enormous barges passing beneath the "Mighty Mac." Ross smiled from the reflection of time spent with his father. He even recalled seeing the Edmund Fitzgerald on a few occasions before it met its demise up around Whitefish Bay back in '75.

Ross welcomed his trips to Houghton. It wasn't a big city in comparison to its southern counterparts, but it was comfortable. The people were pleasant enough and the atmosphere was very family-oriented, much like that of a smaller community. More and more money had been filtering into the region as wealthy out-of-staters erected summer castles along Superior's marketable coastline. Ross recalled a small blurb in a paper he once read about the public's outcry at the increased property taxes. High property taxes were one thing that Jessup would never have to worry about. Jessup was Jessup ... unless someone was to strike gold on Main Street. There were some with the impression that the Hideaway Pines Golf Resort might just be that deposit of gold at the end of the rainbow. Ross had his doubts on that issue and was not afraid to express them ... especially to that self-indulgent ass, Gene Steubens. That was a person he preferred to keep out of his thoughts for the time being.

Ross was tempted to make a quick detour when the Tahoe passed by a Burger King. He hadn't eaten since breakfast and he was getting hungry. He decided against the idea and proceeded on toward the hospital just east of town. His route took him through the campus of Michigan Tech University. Coeds paraded the grounds on foot, bikes, and roller-blades ... toting bookbags and other pieces of college paraphernalia. Seeing the students scurrying around the dorms and educational buildings resurrected fond memories of his days at Wisconsin ... a beautiful fall day ... preparing to do battle with the likes of the Hawkeyes or the Spartans ... the party-filled Saturday nights with a keg of beer under one arm and a warm coed under the other. *Damn, time goes by too fast,* he thought.

Just past campus, 41 traced the shoreline for another mile. Houghton General was situated in a peaceful milieu enveloped by a stand of tall oaks. Ross followed the signs to the Trauma Center, a recent addition to the older, main structure. He parked in a spot designated for visitors. As he sat there for a minute, a familiar feeling overtook him. He hated hospitals. There were too many bad memories of being cooped up in a small bed after reconstructive knee surgery, and worst of all, the endless days and nights waiting for Eevie to ... *Old ghosts,* he thought. He had no positive connections with hospitals in his lifetime, and now he would most likely hear similar words again sealing the fate of another human being. There was death in that place. He could now feel it pulsating within him.

The receptionist at the front desk directed him down the hallway to a set of double doors. The sterile smell that he knew all too well was making him nauseous. Each breath of air brought back Eevie's painful expressions. He stopped at the drinking fountain and took a sip from a less than adequately pressurized stream of water. A sign above the doors read "Nurses Station / I.C.U." *That's it,* he thought. *Let's get this over with.*

The center was small, but surprisingly modern for the U.P. in his mind. Ross shuffled through the doors like a gunslinger entering a saloon in an old western movie, unsure of what to expect on the other side. A large island desk caging a larger woman in nurse's whites sat in the middle of the room. She glanced up from a computer with a courteous smile. Ross caught hint of a mustache growing just above her lip. *You really ought to dye that thing, honey,* he joked to himself.

"Can I help you, sir?" Her voice was sweet and sensitive, not matching the face from which it came.

Her gentle demeanor caused Ross to feel guilty for the silent wisecrack. As Maggie would say, he could be an immature ass at times. "Yes, maam, I'm looking for a Dr. Blake. He should be expecting me." He tried his best to act like a gentleman.

"Ah! Sheriff Pickett, I presume."

Ross swiveled on his heels, startled by the voice that appeared from behind. Standing there was a very short man, probably in his late sixties, wearing a white smock. He wore standard scrubs underneath. An identification card was pinned on his breast pocket. Ross read the name over the picture ... "Henry C. Blake, M.D." The Doctor extended his little hand and grasped the Sheriff's with an astonishingly firm grip. He shook it vigorously. His full head of chalk-white hair was uncombed. He could have easily been mistaken for a miniature Einstein or a mad scientist. A broad smile stretched across his wrinkled face revealing two rows of uneven teeth that were brown in color.

"Henry Blake. Glad you could make it on such short notice, but there is a matter of importance that we need to discuss."

"It's nice to meet you, Doctor."

Dr. Blake turned to the nurse at her station. "Doris, please hold my calls. I'll be in conference. If Martin phones, tell him I took the month off or something to that effect." His comment drew a giggle from the nurse. The humor was beyond Ross' comprehension, but he smiled anyway as if he understood the apparent shenanigans in play. "And Doris, let me know if there's any change in 109." The Sheriff assumed that 109 was Ned Crosby. It was a morbid thought, referring to a patient by a number. But it did indicate that Crosby was still alive.

The energetic Doctor led Ross at a brisk pace down a hallway to a door with his name imprinted on a slab of brown plastic. "Damned administrators," he said. "It's budget time so they think we can just drop everything and crank out the numbers that they want to see within minutes."

Ross reasoned that the man referred to as Martin was one of those administrators. Ross remained patient.

Dr. Blake ushered him into the office and offered a chair. The Sheriff remained standing and folded his arms across his chest.

"Looks like we pulled you away from a little yard work," said Blake.

"Huh?" *What the hell is he talking about?* But then he saw him nod toward the dried mud on his worn jeans. "Oh ... yeah," replied the Sheriff with a grimace. "The mud ... not quite the proper dress code for a Sheriff, huh? Actually, I just returned home from investigating the accident before we spoke on the phone."

Dr. Blake plopped his fanny down into his heavily padded leather chair. His head was not tall enough to clear the high back rest. It was an amusing sight, like a child playing in his father's lounger. Ross smiled, fighting back the urge to chuckle.

"Is there something I missed?" inquired the Doctor, noticing the expression on his visitor's face.

Ross threw up his hands as if to block an oncoming hit. "Sorry, Doc. A funny thought just crossed my mind. Forgive me ... please."

"No harm done. Anyways, back to the accident." He leaned back and swiveled to look out the window. The Sheriff followed his gaze and saw a pair of squirrels collecting acorns in the freshly cut grass outside. "That's the reason I called you here this afternoon," continued the man. "I sincerely apologize if I've disrupted your day in any way, but I deemed it necessary that we discuss your Mr. Crosby." He rotated back to face the Sheriff with a serious look. He was no longer the jolly little leprechaun that greeted him in the nurses' station.

The change in expression made Ross feel ill-at-ease. *What's going on here?* he thought to himself. *This man acts like he is afraid of something.* Ross finally sat down on the edge of the offered chair in front of the Doctor's desk, careful not to rub off any dirt from his jeans. After a few seconds of silence, Blake leaned forward and rested his chin on folded hands. He began his speech, almost as if it had been rehearsed.

"Mr. Crosby was brought in last night after suffering a massive heart attack. He nearly died twice ... once in route to the hospital, and again while in the capable hands of our staff. He was successfully revived both times." Dr. Blake reached into his desk drawer and withdrew a pack of cigarettes.

Ross had been correct in that assumption after the coughing fit on the phone. It amazed him how someone could be allowed to smoke in a place where sterility was so important.

"Mind if I smoke?" he asked while passing the flame of his lighter to the tobacco.

"No, please continue."

Dr. Blake took a long drag from his cigarette and blew a steady stream of smoke to the ceiling. The satisfaction was evident in his face. "Anyway," he continued, "we analyzed the patient's physical condition and discovered that he had suffered a serious concussion as well, evidently the result of hitting the windshield. We came to that conclusion from the numerous particles of glass embedded in his scalp. Mr. Crosby required sixty-four sutures to repair his lacerations." Ross recalled the gash in Ned's head. "He also has three broken ribs, but that's not an immediate concern. The head wound is what concerns me most." The Doctor inhaled more smoke and then rested the cigarette on the edge of a clay ashtray made by the hands of a child ... a grandchild perhaps. Ross remained silently attentive. "Mr. Crosby is an older man, yet his body is in remarkable physical condition, for his age that is. That will play a critical role in whether or not he recovers from this ordeal. Now for a touch of the unusual."

The Doctor sank back in his chair once again with folded arms. Ross felt like he was in the principal's office and was about to be disciplined.

"After a careful examination of his heart, we found it to be quite sound. Fatty tissue and cholesterol levels were within normal ranges. He is a strong man, Sheriff."

Ross sensed that the main point to the lecture was ready to fly out of the Doctor's mouth.

"In fact, Mr. Crosby's heart could be compared to that of a man nearly thirty years his junior."

"Then how the heck did his heart go bad all of a sudden?" Ross didn't intend to raise his voice. It just happened. He was confused, and was now starting to lose his patience.

Blake help up his hands in retreat like the Sheriff had done only moments before. "Hold on. Hold on. Let me explain ... please." Ross forced himself to calm down and listen on. "Young, healthy people suffer heart attacks every day for one reason or another. It's just that the odds of it happening are greatly minimized." He paused again.

Here it comes, Ross. Get ready.

"My theory is derived more from intuition than medical fact. It is my personal opinion that Mr. Crosby's heart failure was rooted by some unnatural occurrence."

Ross was puzzled by the man's point. Now he was totally in the dark. "I'm sorry, Doc. I'm not quite on the same wavelength here."

Blake sighed heavily, as if he did not want to continue. "Okay, putting it bluntly." His eyes closed tight for a second, and then reopened.

Here it comes, thought the Sheriff.

"I believe Mr. Crosby had the living *bejesus* scared out of him." Blake paused, allowing for the bomb to strike its target.

Boom! There it was, like a ton of bricks landing on his head. Ross pulled himself up off the chair without a word and lumbered to the window, seeing the two squirrels now chasing each other around a tree.

"Sheriff." It was the Doctor's turn to stand. "Please hear me out before jumping to conclusions."

"This isn't quite what I expected to hear, Doctor." *Or was it,* he wondered. Ross leaned on his arms against the windowsill. He felt tired, and old.

Dr. Blake went on. "As I indicated in our phone conversation, there was a point where the patient did regain consciousness." Ross turned and faced him. "It was more of a daze really, but nevertheless, I believe that Mr. Crosby had some sense of awareness to his surroundings. His pulse-rate jumped to the moon, necessitating immediate sedation." The Doctor saw the interest in Ross' face as he walked back over to the front of his desk.

"Did he say anything ... anything at all?" Ross eyed the man's face closely, studying his expression, searching for any subtle changes that might provide a hint to what he was going to say.

"He did indeed. That's where this story becomes a little more complicated." Dr. Blake walked around to the front of the wide desk and hopped up onto its glistening surface next to the larger Sheriff. "On one occasion, Mr. Crosby opened his eyes, which I might add were bordering on wildish. It was as if he were looking at something that only he could see in his own little world if you will. Then he began to mutter on ... mostly unintelligible words. He did manage to blurt out something about this ... some horrifying creature. I believe *'Devil'* was the exact term he used to describe it. He would cover his face with his hands, as if he was trying to ward off the illusion. It took three orderlies and a good-sized nurse to restrain the poor fellow."

"And that's where your theory came from? That what Crosby saw last night may have caused his heart failure ... because he was scared shitless?" Ross shuddered.

"Yes, Sheriff. But allow me to add another pertinent clue to our little mystery. I'm certainly not proposing that Mr. Crosby was actually frightened by some monster that he just happened upon. That, of course, would be absurd." Dr. Blake produced a short chuckle. But Ross could not find that same humor in the little man's interpretations. He kept a somber expression and allowed the Doctor to continue. "You see, we did detect a high level of alcohol in his blood, and under the proper conditions, people might visualize almost anything stored within their own imaginations. The proper term would be ... hallucination. The human brain is a very complex organ, more so than Man may ever fully understand. Coupled with the head injury ..."

Ross abruptly cut the man off. "So what you're suggesting is that Ned may have seen something that was a product of his imagination." The Doctor nodded in agreement. "And that it was probably caused by the concussion, with the alcohol tossed in for added effect." Blake nodded a second time. It was now Ross' turn to play analyst. "Well, Doctor," the Sheriff now sat back down in his chair, this time without consideration for the mud on his jeans. "I know for a fact that Ned did see something last night." Ross noted the change in the Doctor's face. The eyebrows curled and his lips tightened. He was caught off guard. "My Deputy and

I found evidence that Ned might have hit a bear ... a big bear. And let me tell you, it made one hell of an effort to get at him by the looks of the car."

Blake smiled. "Well there you have it!" He beamed, jumping down from the desk. "The monster did exist after all." He raised his arms to the ceiling in praise. But the moment of jubilation was short-lived when he saw the Sheriff's annoyance. He lowered his arms to his sides. "I'm sorry, Sheriff Pickett. Forgive me ... it's been a long night. Is there something else?"

"I don't know, Doc. It's just that old Ned's lived in those parts all of his life. He's seen bears before. I just don't know." Ross shook his head, feeling another tremor building. He started pacing the room, contemplating what the Doctor had unloaded on him. Crosby must have seen hundreds of bears in his lifetime out near that swamp. *Hell, he lives right next to the Amen. What made this one so different than the rest? Sure ... it might have tried to get at him, but ... shit!* He needed some fresh air. His headache was growing with each passing second.

"Okay, Sheriff." Blake placed his hand on Ross Pickett's shoulder, sensing the man's frustration. He lowered his voice and spoke gently. "You see, the object of Mr. Crosby's apparent nightmare was nothing more than an act of deception. A trick, if you will, played on him, by him. Instead of seeing a bear, perhaps he visualized something more demonic, thus causing a state of panic."

There was merit in the Doctor's words. *What else could Ned have seen? It had to be a bear ... nothing else. It was a bear!* Ross began to feel more at ease. He jumped when the Doctor slapped his palm hard on the surface of the desk.

"I tell you, Sheriff, we make a good team don't we?" Blake was grinning from ear to ear, trying to add a positive spin on their meeting. Ross smiled in response. "That's the spirit, old boy."

A soft buzz emanated from the speakerphone next to the ashtray. Dr. Blake quickly reached over, punched a button, and plucked the receiver from its cradle. "Yes? Has he spoken? Did he? I'll be right there." He jarred the phone down and darted toward the door. "Follow me, Sheriff," he said without turning. "Our patient has just opened his eyes."

Ross followed the fleet-footed Doctor through three sets of doors, dodging hospital personnel like a skilled half-back. They came to a stop in front of room 109. Blake led him inside.

The room was illuminated with four large, fluorescent light fixtures hanging loosely from the ceiling. There was a clutter of bulky machines, each beeping and buzzing as if they were living beings. Wires reached out of the machines like tentacles converging on a lone bed at the center of the busy room. One end of each line was attached to a monitor, while the other was attached to a frail, old man's chest and arms. Other than a white hospital sheet covering his groin, Ned Crosby lay naked on a narrow mattress. Ross stared with sad eyes at the resident of his town. The man looked frightful ... his complexion that same pasty white color as when Ross had found him clinging to life in his mutilated car. It was almost as if the blood had drained from his body. Tubes protruded from a nose disguised by a deep purplish bruise. He looked so vulnerable laying there. Then he noticed Ned's eyes. They were open, and affixed to some spot on the ceiling. But they did not appear to be receptive to what was going on around him. They were blank ... dead-like. For a brief moment, Ross saw Eevie lying in the bed. It was her body dwindling down to a collection of bones, waiting for the inevitable. *Get those fucking ghosts out of your head,* he cursed silently. *Eevie is gone.*

Another Doctor was chatting with a nurse who was much prettier than the gal at the desk. This Doctor was a younger looking man that looked barely old enough to drive. He greeted Ross and Dr. Blake while the nurse hovered over the machines with a clipboard. She made a few markings after spot-checking various readings.

"He just opened his eyes five minutes ago. Heart rate started jumping again." The younger Doctor gave his brief to the senior physician.

"Is he responding at all?" Blake asked as he eased his way through the maze to the side of the bed.

"No, Doctor ... nothing." Ross stayed out of the way of the professionals and stood his ground at the door.

Blake extracted a penlight from a breast pocket and shined it into Ned's lost eyes. There was no response as the patient continued to stare aimlessly to nothing in particular. The Doctor straightened, placing both hands into the small of his back. He arched backwards, wincing from a slight rush of hidden pain. "Damn back," he whispered.

"Dr. Blake?" Ross spoke. He had an idea. *Maybe it's stupid,* he thought, *but who knows?* "What if I try ... a familiar voice I mean?"

Blake shrugged. For the first time since Ross' arrival, he showed signs of tiring. "It can't hurt, Mr. Pickett. At this point, we're running out of ideas." He backed away to allow room for Ross to take his position next to the ailing man. Ross took the cue and finessed his way around the monitors, careful not to touch anything. He took one last look at the three onlookers and then bent down to Ned's bandaged ear.

"Ned?" He spoke softly. "Ned? It's Ross ... Ross Picket, Ned. Can you hear me? It's Sheriff Pickett, Ned. Can you hear me?" Crosby's swollen lips moved slightly, generating a faint whisper. "Doctor!" Ross called out, causing an instant response from the medical team. They joined him at the bedside. "I think he's coming around." *By God, it worked,* thought Ross. He continued. "Ned!" This time he spoke louder. "Ned! Can you hear me, Ned?"

Dr. Blake occupied himself with Crosby's wrist when the patient's head slowly rolled toward the familiar voice. His eyes were no longer hollow. There was life in them. Ross felt his own heartrate jump with excitement. He would have answers after all. But then Ross noticed something else beyond the eyes. He could see it written on a disturbingly distraught face. Fear! It was a fear that Ross wanted no part of, but he had to push on. He was the Sheriff. He had to know, not only for his own selfish reasons, but for closure.

"Rossssss ...." Crosby mumbled with a weak, barely audible voice. His eyes managed to focus on the Sheriff. "It's ... out ... there." His words were staggered, but his conviction grew stronger. His body began to convulse, a repercussion of the terrifying nightmare.

"What's out there, Ned? What did you see?" Ross clutched Crosby's shoulders, feeling the contour of bone beneath the loose skin. He tried to prevent Ned from moving but the old man's spasms became too strong.

"It's ... out ... there ... Ross." He tried to sit up, but the Sheriff held him as still as he could. "I hit it square ... with ... with the ole girl ... and ... attacked ... me!" Crosby was suddenly shouting ... then screaming. His body was trembling uncontrollably as he fought to get his message out. His eyes were wild with fright. Tears swelled in his sagging ducts as he relived his accident.

Ross now found himself experiencing Ned Crosby's horror. It was as if their minds had joined and Ned was transmitting his emotions to the Sheriff. *What the hell could have done this? It was a bear, goddammit! A big fucking bear!* But Ross had to be sure. He began to press.

"What's out there, Ned? What did you hit with your car?"

Sheriff! Please!" It was Blake trying to intervene. Ross was pushing too hard. "This isn't the proper ..."

But Ross had to know. He lowered his tone to appease the Doctor. "Please, Ned. I've got to know what you hit on the road." *Christ! What's going on here?* He thought. He was begging for an answer to end this conundrum.

Sweat began streaming from Crosby's face. Blake showed signs of concern, but he hesitated before intervening a second time as if he, too, wished to know more.

"Weren't ... no ... bear!" Ned fought to sputter out his words. "Weren't ... no ... bear!" he repeated. "Devil! The ... Devil ... come ... git ... me." The words faded into silence as Ned's body fell limp. A sharp alarm filled the room as his eyes closed.

"He's crashing," said the younger Doctor.

Ross was thrown out of the way and stood in a catatonic state as the medical crew worked feverishly on Ned Crosby. He heard someone yell ... "Code Blue!" Seconds later, two men wheeled another machine into the crowded room. To Ross, it was as if he were watching an episode of "Rescue 911" with Chuck on a Saturday morning. It was all so surreal.

Blake slopped some sort of goop on the old man's sunken chest. "Clear!" He touched two circular paddles to the bare skin and the body convulsed violently. Blake then waited for a signal from the other Doctor who shook his head indicating a negative response. "Clear!" The torturous feat was repeated with the same conclusion. The steady tone of the heart monitor did not waver. Blake then released the paddles and leapt on top of the bed with striking grace. He proceeded to pound on Ned's chest with a balled fist. Blake gave five short pushes to Crosby's sternum while the nurse placed a mask over the old man's mouth. The valiant attempts to resuscitate the patient proved futile. Finally, after one last check, the Doctor climbed down from the bed.

"Time of death ..." Blake checked his watch and then looked up to the Sheriff. "One thirty-five P.M." Ned Crosby's nightmare had ended.

***

Trooper Ray Jackson ducked in behind the slowing Ford Probe. He touched the switch activating the flashers. "Got some balls there, boy. Doing eighty on my road. No way, no how," he said as the sporty car rolled to a stop on the shoulder of the two-lane highway. The Trooper had already radioed in the tag numbers. Dispatch informed him that the car was registered to one William J. Ferry. No outstanding warrants. It would be just a routine stop. Jackson pictured what was probably circulating through the youngster's head. It was no doubt a barrage of obscenities that would cease once the officer showed himself. He'd heard it all before. A wide grin formed on his dark face, exposing a large gold tooth that gleamed as if he were in a toothpaste commercial. *Damn, if this isn't a fun job,* he thought as he gathered his ticket pad and brimmed hat. Jackson was one of the few black cops on the north side of the Mackinaw Bridge, and he enjoyed every second of it.

"No sir," he jibed. "And this homeboy don't put up with no crap neither."

Ray Jackson had lived in the Appleton area for seven years with his wife Carol. Both were born and raised in St. Ignace and were members of a very small minority. Jackson's father had captained a ferry for the Arnold line, while his in-laws entrepreneured their way onto the Island with a small fudge shop. Though the color of his skin did cause him to stand out in a crowd, Ray Jackson made a pleasant life for himself in northern Michigan and worked his tail off to achieve respect within his profession. He scoffed at the "brothers" who thought that life in the big cities was difficult. At least down there, they had numbers and could always fall back on their own. But there were more redskins than blackskins in "hic-neck country," a term that he invented after years of firsthand experience.

The Trooper had been assigned to the Appleton post after giving ten loyal years of service to St. Ignace. There were times when the pressures of racism and bigotry nearly drove he and Carol out, but they dug in their heels and held strong. It wasn't as if there were rednecks in white sheets lurking around every corner. And really, the vast majority of the people were decent and accepting. It was the subtle things from those select few that crawled under his skin ... the quiet smirks of arrogance when he would take his wife out in the evening for a bite to eat ... the salesman ignoring his presence as he shopped. The ignorant idiots would not dare chance a remark directly to his face. Ray Jackson was a large man, standing six feet six inches tall, and topping the scales at nearly two hundred and fifty pounds. There was no fat on his boxy frame. He was a solid mass of muscle that could intimidate any common criminal, let alone any member of his own community. Most men in similar circumstances might have cracked, but not Ray Jackson. He had served two tours of combat as a Navy Seal in Vietnam, so this was a cake-walk.

The Trooper was not one to lie around and let life pass him by. He grasped opportunity. Being a black man in a region of such little color did offer certain advantages. Although he refused to accept his promotions within the force as a byproduct of State-sponsored affirmative action programs, he was realistic in knowing that some of his fortunes had resulted from '*political correctness*.' Jackson despised the term. He always referred to it as an excuse rather than a point of motivation. Whatever the case, he made damn well sure that his stripes were earned so that nobody could label him a "token" of the system.

Life in Appleton had been rough at first. By making the move, he and Carol had to start from square one, gaining respect and establishing friendships in a crowd of skeptics. But as the first few months passed, the tensions eased and the majority slowly accepted the newcomers. It took one heroic episode for Ray Jackson to firmly establish himself in the cynical eyes of the nonbelievers. It was in his second year of service when a nasty spring snowstorm shut down the city. A four-year old little girl who had been left unsupervised in her backyard had wandered off from a mother spending too much time catching up on soap operas. The girl ventured across the road and onto a thin layer of ice covering a swift tributary to the Muskeweenaw River. The hand of God must have been cradling the little girl's life that day because Ray Jackson was breaking trail through the mounded snow on his way to work just as she fell through. She immediately disappeared from sight as the current pulled her under. The State Trooper, acting more on instinct than common sense, jumped from his truck and sprinted toward a spot in the river downstream from where the girl had vanished. As he reached the bank, Jackson leaped as high into the air as he possibly could and formed a human cannonball with his large frame, much like he used to do in the pond behind his grandfather's house. There were no second thoughts or doubts. The little girl would die if he didn't find her.

Jackson's body crashed through the ice and entered the frigid waters of the deep stream. He forced himself under the water and ice, searching for the body with groping arms. Fortunately, destiny did not hold death in the little girl's hand that day. She miraculously floated right into his belly. Jackson clutched her tight, bringing her flaccid body to his chest as he fought off the onset of hypothermia. He gathered every last ounce of strength that his well-conditioned body could muster and shot upward through the ice like a missile. A group of onlookers had gathered near the bank. One man, having witnessed the dilemma progressing from his home, tossed a rope to the struggling Trooper. Five locals yanked the frozen man and child from the water. When the girl was brought to shore, she was not breathing. Jackson, disregarding his own well-being, performed C.P.R. until he was rewarded with a gargled cough. He rolled the little girl on her side and allowed the water to drain from her lungs. The people surrounding them cheered his bravery. There were "well-done" pats on the back, high-fives and many words of praise.

After spending the night in the Appleton Medical Facility, Ray Jackson was literally kidnapped by a hoard of gracious townsfolk who proceeded to toast him for three hours at a local tavern. From that moment on, the Trooper was not "the black cop" in their eyes. He was a member of the community. He was a hero who had saved the life of a little girl. Even the Governor, perhaps in an attempt to supplement his own minority support, bestowed upon him the Medal of Valor, MSP's highest award for bravery and merit.

The Trooper stepped out of the cruiser. He eyed the expensive car in front of him through mirrored sunglasses. Ray flexed his bulging biceps, more for his own self-satisfaction than for the driver in the car before him. His body was impressively sculpted, and he was not afraid to use it to his advantage. Life as a Seal had given him the motivation and mental fortitude to remain fit upon his discharge. Circumstances of war compelled him to attain maximum fitness for the sake of survival while he served with his team. Nam had been a hellish place ... fighting those little bastards that never seemed to have any quit in them. But he did go back a second time. He felt it his duty to return. Whether the war had been right or wrong didn't matter to Ray Jackson. He was a man who loved his country and the job he had protecting it. The Seal would not allow others to die in his place.

The Trooper straightened his burly frame, intent on putting a little scare into the white boy. He tipped his hat forward over his closely cropped scalp, sanctioning just enough room for his eyes to see. He systematically strutted to the driver's window, his right hand hovering over the grip of his Smith and Wesson 9mm. A cop could never be too careful. Even the most tranquil of settings was capable of exploding into mass chaos. The first rule of law enforcement was to be prepared for the unexpected. There were no second chances in his line of work. Jackson's Seal training had given him skills beyond that of a normal human being, and he used every last one of them. His eyes were constantly surveying for the hidden gun or the unseen accomplice. Jackson checked the rear of the car as he approached. The driver's window had already been rolled down.

"Afternoon, sir." His face showed no expression as he spoke in his deep, monotone voice. "License, registration and proof of insurance please." The young boy who the Trooper judged to be sixteen or seventeen looked up to him as if he were staring into the eyes of a hungry grizzly. In a way, that was exactly what he was doing.

"I ... I ... wasn't going too fast, was I, officer?" The boy whimpered like a lost puppy. His girlfriend sat impatiently in the passenger seat. She began searching through the glove box for the requested paperwork.

Jackson reasoned that the kid was probably doing a little showboating for his honey. *Hell, I used to pull the same shit with Carol back in the day.* The Trooper had already made the decision not to write the ticket, but a lesson needed to be taught in highway etiquette. Besides, his shift was almost over and Carol was cooking tenderloin for dinner.

"License ... registration ... insurance ... please!" boomed the officer, emphasizing each word very carefully. Luckily, the boy could not see the angry glare of Jackson's eyes through the mirrored glasses. His voice seemed to have the desired effect on little Willie Ferry. He sat up rigidly in the driver seat. Jackson began to wonder if he'd ever seen a black police officer before. Willie pushed back his girlfriend and fumbled through the glove box. He finally produced an envelope that he willingly surrendered. Jackson went through the paperwork, acting as if he were truly interested. "You know how fast you were going, boy?" He asked the question without looking away from the driver license.

"No, sir. I ... guess ... I wasn't paying much attention."

"Damn straight you weren't paying attention, William." He looked down to the frightened lad. Something told him that this kid was more concerned with how his father might receive his getting a ticket. Perhaps by taking the car away for a while. Kids had to have consequences. The lesson had to be taught and Jackson was a very capable educator. "When my boss sees people like you driving like hellfire down my road, well that makes me look bad. And when I look bad I get mad. You were pushing eighty, William. That makes me look *real* bad." The Trooper's speech was slow and methodical. He allowed each word to sink in. "What do you think I should do here, William?" He knew what the response would be. He just enjoyed hearing it over and over again. *I promise I won't ...*

"I ... I swear I won't do it again. Please ... my father will kill me." The boy appeared to be on the brink of tears.

"I don't know, William. If I let you go this time, how do I know you're not going to just shoot on out of here laughing you tail off?" The boy could only shrug his shoulders. He was out of answers. "You don't have any drugs in the car, do you?"

The question drew startled expressions from both kids in the Probe. "No, sir!" was the quick reply. It was almost too quick for Ray Jackson's liking.

Ah hell, he thought. *Carol's probably got that loin on the grill right now.* It was time to end this case. "Alright, William. Tell you what I'm going to do." He leaned real close to the window. The driver backed away slightly. "I'm gonna cut you a huge break and let you go ... this time." The relief in the boy's face was obvious. "But if I ever catch you haulin ass like that on my road again, I'm gonna burn your butt. You got that!"

"Yes, sir! Thank you, sir."

"Now, move on." The Trooper turned away from Willie Ferry and started back toward the cruiser. He stopped suddenly and swiveled around to face the boy who was in the process of rolling up his window. "Oh ... and Willie ... you have a nice afternoon." Jackson tipped his hat and offered his broadest smile. He walked back to his car and watched the Probe crawl away, nice and cautious like.

***

The drive home seemed to last twice as long. Ross cracked the window and allowed the chilly air to circulate through the truck as he made his way south. He needed the stimulation to clear his mind. The day had passed in a blur, like a shooting star streaking across the night sky to some unseen destination. There for a second ... and then gone ... forever.

The sun was merely a glowing orange ball descending upon the trees on the western horizon. Had the Sheriff taken the time to notice the scenic portrait that nature had painted, he might have pulled off the road as he often did just to watch and admire. But his thoughts were elsewhere, teetering back and forth like a playground toy. Ned Crosby was gone. Ross felt saddened by the loss even though he had never been very close with the old man. Death always produced such a bitter awakening into reality, but there was no time to mourn the loss of life. That would have to wait until later. There were still too many unanswered questions picking at his brain.

Throughout the drive, Ross tried to analyze each page of the story. He pieced together circumstantial evidence as well as cold, hard facts. There had to be a logical explanation for Ned's death. The one truth that kept sending the Sheriff's head into a tailspin was that Ned Crosby had been a Yooper nearly all of his life. He had seen as many bears in the woods as the next man, and he understood them ... how they lived ... how they moved. So what was so different about this encounter that made the old man believe that it was something else? It's size? *Possible,* thought Ross. Just as Chuck has surmised earlier on Townsend Road, *that would have to be one big motherfucker. It had to be a bear,* continued the Sherriff in his silent dissection of the day's events. *What else in God's name could it have been?* He figured that Dr. Blake must have been right. The combination of a concussion and the alcohol must have produced some pretty bizarre hallucinations. But there remained a frightening sense of doubt in the back of his head. It was a premonition that he would one day regret ever hearing of the Amen Swamp. Ross was beginning to feel a rekindling of the ghosts of old. There *was* something that would ease his nerves and allow him to just forget. The thirst was tempting his will. *Would a drink taste good right now?* he asked himself.

Ross slammed his fist against the dash to disperse the thought. "Goddammit!" he cursed out loud. "Get that out of your head right here and now!" Maggie was his life. Maggie and Chuck. He could not afford to lose himself again. He had to remain strong.

The Sheriff took the back roads to allow for some extra time to think, an idea that he was now regretting. He turned on to Townsend Road and drove past the ditch where Ned Crosby met his misfortune. The car was no longer an ornament on the tree below, but the scarred bark served as a reminder of its recent presence. *Charlie Perkins must have come out and towed it in,* he concluded. Ross mulled over the idea of calling Ray Jackson, an old friend from his D.N.R. days in St. Ignace. Ray had preceded the Sheriff in the move to the western U.P. and was stationed down in Appleton. The two men had been buddies for many years and often got together with their wives on weekends. Ray had been there when Eevie passed. He was a solid individual with a jubilant personality, and Ross could certainly use a touch of that at the moment. Ross looked one last time into the rearview mirror.

***

The startled eyes followed the path of the noisy machine until it disappeared. She waited patiently until both the familiar scent and sound had dissipated. The muscles in her powerful legs relaxed when the danger passed. Her dark figure emerged from its crouched position behind a grove of cedars.

The female was hunting again. She had returned to the place where her juvenile had bled during the dark hours only to discover that the hairless one's machine was gone. The discovery fueled her rage. The female would stalk the path where the machines traveled until she found it, using her superior sense of smell to detect the distinct odor. She would never forget that hairless one's scent. It was now embedded in her senses. If she happened upon another of its kind, she would destroy ... and feed. There existed nothing in her drive but evil intent for the inferior beings. The path was a good game trail. She knew that her prey would be plentiful there.

The female was alone in her quest for vengeance. Her clan was forgotten. She was forgotten. They had driven her out of their society to live amongst the hairless creatures. Slowly and deliberately she skirted the edge of the swamp, continuously scenting the air for the familiar odors. She would not stop until she tasted blood, drawn from her own claws and teeth. The light was fading rapidly from the sky. Receding rays of sun reflected off a small cloud front moving in from the west. The air grew colder. That would be good for the hunt. The scent was strong.

CHAPTER SIX

The job had not been a pushover by any means. Charlie Perkins had to sweat Ned's Plymouth out of the ditch, first tugging one way, and then pulling another. He initially surveyed the scene with his scientific eye, like a microbiologist formulating an opinion on a newly discovered organism. Charlie was the resident expert when it came to hauling out wrecks. He'd seen his share of some awful ones through the years. Drunks usually ... like old Ned.

"Darn," he said. "What a shameful mess. Poor, Ned." Charlie had been burdened with a sense of guilt for allowing his friend to leave the Jessup Inn when he knew how badly off he was. If only he had demanded those keys.

"Friends don't let friends drive drunk, you jackass," he muttered under his breath. It wasn't as if Ned could have overpowered him. The proper course of action would probably have been to notify the Sheriff. Ross could have gone to the Inn and picked him up, and Ned would have been his old cranky self the next day. "Oh well," he said with a sigh, "not too much I can do about it now." Ned was always whooping it up on Friday nights in town. Why should last night have been any different from the rest? He'd been his usual boastful self, recanting the war stories that Charlie had heard over and over again. His tales of combat were interesting to the mechanic, regardless of the repetition. *Darn!* There he was, sitting with the old man on a bar stool, and now ... Ned was lying in a hospital bed up in Houghton. Mark Bennington had filled Charlie in on the details of the wreck with a phone call to the station. Charlie told the Deputy that he'd haul the car into town when he got the chance. *Life just don't make sense,* he thought.

Charlie Perkins ran one of two service stations in town. He was a diligent workaholic who took great pride in his talents. He had fiddled with small engines since early childhood, taking them apart piece by piece and then restoring strictly from memory. His aunt, who raised him since his third birthday, would often find her vacuum disassembled in the middle of the living room floor. Practice spawned perfection, and soon people began to take lawnmowers and snowblowers to the young boy's home so that he could work his magic. The only resident of Jessup who didn't care much for Charlie Perkins was Floyd Merriweather, who at one time owned the local hardware store. Floyd's sales on new appliances and lawn equipment had taken quite a dive on account of Charlie's growing notoriety. Upon graduation from high school, Charlie opened a small repair shop. His business was steady, but with the passage of time his interests transitioned to more profitable items like cars. With no formal training, the self-educated entrepreneur turned into an outstanding mechanic. Charlie's reputation as an honest perfectionist was known throughout the county. He had a sixth sense that could pinpoint a problem simply by shutting his eyes and listening to the purr of an engine.

Charlie felt himself to be an important cog within the working structure of the community. At times he felt like a knight in shining armor, answering the call of damsels in distress. Day or night, if someone summoned his help, he would respond without hesitation. Charlie would cruise the roads after major snowfalls in search of stranded motorists. What motivated him most was the joy he saw on their faces when they first sighted his wrecker. The fifty dollar service fee was well worth the price of salvation. There were those who would argue the cost or try to negotiate him down. But Charlie would simply turn and walk the other way with a shrug. Attitudes quickly changed while out on a deserted road with no place to go. And there were those who occasionally did not have money handy. As long as they were likeable enough, Charlie would write up an invoice with his address and allow them to send him payment. Truth was, Charlie would never have really left anyone stranded regardless of the circumstance.

Everybody in Jessup was fond of Charlie Perkins. He became known as the "gentle giant." He was average in height, but about fifty pounds overweight. His jolly demeanor was appealing to the townsfolk, especially the children. He was always the unanimous choice to play the role of Santa Clause in the elementary school Christmas pageant. Charlie's smile was warm and friendly, and he always had a kind word for folks. Likewise, they always found a kind word for him. "Charlie's Pit Stop," his place of business, was a regular morning stop for a number of old cronies who would sit and chew the fat over a complementary cup of the host's bitter coffee. Charlie did sweat a bit when a Shell station opened at the other end of town. It was one of those fancy convenience stores that offered a lot more than just gasoline and a tune-up. But small-town loyalty kept his business afloat, and for that he was truly grateful. Charlie Perkins was everyone's friend.

With some expert mechanical choreography, the taut steel cable was finally able to yank the car free and drag it up the steep embankment. Had the rear tires been damaged, Charlie guessed that he would have had to borrow Tom Wohler's flat-bed, or replace them with some temps. As it turned out, they were fully functional, unlike the front two that were shredded. Charlie attached the chains to the front end and engaged the lift to hoist the car. He couldn't stop thinking about Ned Crosby sitting in the driver seat. He gazed at the hole in the windshield where the man's head must have hit. "Just awful," he said.

When he was satisfied with the height, Charlie shut off the winch and locked the car in place. He didn't bother attaching safety lights. There wouldn't be much traffic. Besides, he didn't have far to go. He walked around to the side of the Plymouth and peered inside. Charlie could see the red stains.

"Darn, Ned," he gasped, pulling himself away from the window. "Ya got yourself into a mess, didn't you?" Charlie shook his head. There was something else that caught his attention. For the first time since arriving on scene, he noticed the deep grooves in the dented roof of the Plymouth. "What the heck?" he said as he moved closer. Just as the Sheriff had done earlier in the day, Charlie ran his ringers down one of the claw marks. "What the heck did this?" He tugged at his thick beard as he studied the grooves. Charlie Perkins had not yet been privy to the rumors that were already funneling through town. He arrived on site just after Art Conley and John Talbert had performed their private inspection. If he had driven in ten minutes earlier, he would have listened to them reiterate Mark Bennington's bear theory. But Charlie was forced to make his own conclusions. Not being much of an outdoor enthusiast, which was highly unusual for a Yooper in his line of work, he did not think "bear." Charlie did, however, conclude that the car had not rolled. Something big had pounded on that roof ... something extremely strong. He looked away from the car and glanced toward the swamp as if he were searching for something. Then those haunting words from his childhood came back to him.

Things that howl,
Will curl your hair,
Come on in,
And see what's there.

If you will the courage,
To face the demons within,
Then pray with pure heart,
The journey ends with Amen.

Creepy! Charlie felt a faint shiver prickle his skin. Goosebumps popped up along his greasy arms. "Hmph!" He checked his watch and determined that it was time to move on. "Enough of that gibberish," he exclaimed. It was getting late and the light was fading fast. After a quick assessment to ensure that all was safe, Charlie piled into the wrecker and unzipped his Carhartt jacket.

His first order of business was to stop out to Ned's place and pick up Duff, the old man's black lab. Little things were often overlooked. With no close kin in the area, Charlie figured it was his duty to care for the dog while its owner recuperated. *Poor dog must be in a panic by now,* he thought as the big, Ford rolled out onto Townsend Road. It wasn't likely anyone else from town knew that Ned even had a dog. Charlie imagined what his wife would say when she saw that he brought the animal home. He would be facing one of her hairy conniptions, sure as heck. "Oh well," he mused. Rachel, like so many others in Jessup, didn't care too much for Ned Crosby. The mechanic supposed that it was as much Ned's fault. Ned never made much of an effort to get to know folks. *Too bad,* thought Charlie. Ned was a decent guy once you got to know him. Charlie planned to make a call to the hospital up in Houghton once he returned to the shop to check on his friend.

The mechanic turned off the main road onto a two-track that led to Ned's little oasis in the northern woods. The trail took him about eighty yards through a stand of hardwoods to the open gate. Next to some slats of rotting wood was a post with a crooked sign that read "Ned's Place." Charlie smiled. He had helped him install the sign last spring. His paranoid friend originally wanted to add ... "Trespassers Will Be Shot!" But Charlie convinced him that such a statement might not be appropriate. The beacon marked the entrance to Ned's cabin that was purposely secluded from society.

Night had cast its darkness beneath the canopy of trees as the wrecker with Plymouth in tow rolled down the rutted track. Fifty yards from the gate, the landscape opened up and the headlights illuminated the weather-worn shack. Red paint on the decaying walls peeled from years of neglect. Odd pieces of junk littered the ground around the front porch like tombstones marking graves in an old appliance cemetery. A rusted cast-iron oven that hadn't held a pot roast in over twenty years sat next a vinyl recliner that was chewed to bits by raccoons, porcupines and other creatures of the forest. It certainly was a unique landscaping theme.

Charlie parked the truck twenty feet from the front porch and turned off the ignition. He slid out of the cab and into the evening air that was getting a bit nippy. He immediately heard the hoarse barking from the anxious dog inside.

"Just a minute, boy. I'm a comin." He called out to the animal to let it hear his familiar voice. Five freshly cut cords of wood lined the east side of the porch, a sign that Ned must have been out with his chainsaw. Ned always made sure that there was a good supply of fuel for winter heat. "Too much is not enough," he would gloat to his friend, Charlie. But the man was getting up in years and the mechanic had tried to persuade him to hold off until he was able to come out and help. "Nonsense!" would be the gruff reply. Ned had a way of doing things, and that was that.

Charlie heard the exited dog scratching at the wooden door inside. When he opened it he was nearly bowled over by two large paws meeting his chest. Duff whimpered as he danced around the visitor. His bushy tail slapped at the air.

"Whoa, boy. Easy now." Charlie knelt down to the animal's level and received a few sloppy licks. He patted the dog on its graying head. Duff acknowledged the attention with a satisfying grin. "That's a good boy."

Charlie noticed a puddle on the floor just inside the doorway. The poor dog hadn't been outside in nearly twenty-four hours.

"Come on, boy. Let's get out." Charlie stood and held the door open. Duff uttered a short, gratifying yip, and then bolted out into the yard. After sniffing the ground for a few seconds, his bowels finally moved. The lab left his mark with an impressive pile, and then pranced back inside. Duff was ready to receive some more attention.

"I'll bet that's been storing up for a while, eh?" Charlie stroked Duff's bristly backside. "Let's see about getting you something in your stomach." He flicked on a table lamp, closed the door and strolled to the kitchen. The dog followed anxiously on his heels, knowing that food was in its future.

Crosby's cabin was actually quite comfortable inside. It had only four rooms; a kitchen, the main living area, a bedroom, and of course, the bathroom. The living room was small, but cozy, holding a sofa, a table with two chairs, and a large wood-burning stove to heat the structure. Charlie enjoyed his visits because of the paraphernalia that the old man had collected through the years. Hanging from the walls were numerous old photos from the war. There seemed to be a long story with each faded face. Charlie had become quite familiar with all of Ned's buddies from the past. He would listen to their stories while in the cabin with as much enthusiasm as he did while sharing a beer at the Jessup Inn.

There was an unspent mortar round on the mantel that the veteran had somehow managed to smuggle back from Italy. Next to the dead explosive, or so he hoped, sat an open box of shotgun shells for critters that roamed into the clearing out front. Ned was always taking out coons whenever they meandered too close. *To each, his own,* thought Charlie. Ned had a few other firearms tucked away in his little hideaway. The humming freezer in the pantry was certainly not filled with beef. Over the heavy mantle there hung a double-barreled scatter-gun on two deer hooves protruding from a wooden plank. It was quite fitting for the décor.

Charlie opened the refrigerator door. "Not too much to chaw on, boy," he said after seeing the near empty space inside. He then remembered Ned bragging about how Duff was partial to ham sandwiches with a dab of mustard. Sure enough, there was some shaved ham in a baggie from McKrueter's Market stashed in one of the bottom drawers. Duff sat patiently as his feast was prepared. The dog's tail vigorously dusted the linoleum on the kitchen floor. Charlie threw the contents of the baggie between two slices of stale wheat bread and looked back into the fridge. "There isn't any mustard in here, boy. Guess you'll have to eat it dry, eh?" Before surrendering the sandwich over to the drooling mouth, Charlie made Duff slap his hand with a paw. "Good boy." The meal was gone in three gulps. Charlie watched as Duff licked the floor for fallen morsels. The mechanic then snared a single Budweiser long-neck. It looked too lonely there in the refrigerator for him to pass up. He searched the cabinets until he located an open bag of chips. Duff followed him to the sofa where Charlie plopped down. After sharing the snack with his companion, the tired mechanic took a few long swigs from the beer, sat it down on the floor and closed his eyes. Duff hopped up on the couch next to him and rested his head on Charlie's soft belly.

***

The female crept silently through the trees that lined the path, following the familiar scent of her marked prey. The forest was quiet, as was the path that carried the hairless creatures in their machines. After twenty minutes of cautious hunting, she found the scent growing stronger, penetrating her nose like sharp thorns. She continued to follow, pursuing her revenge. She sidestepped the deadfalls and glided past the pools of water, leaving no trace of her presence, always prepared to dart into cover at the first hint of danger.

But as the female moved on, the scent began to fade. It was weakening, as if she had passed by her quarry. She lifted her magnificent head and inhaled long and deep through her nostrils, wondering if she had missed her target. The scent was there ... but faint. The female then began to walk back her steps, retracing her route. The scent began to grow stronger again. She could feel herself getting closer to the source. She stopped and searched for a bearing. After a careful glance in each direction, she bounded across the path with stunning quickness. She had passed by the scent because the prey had taken a different route ... into the trees at the other side ... farther from her domain. Anticipation was building again. She tasted the odor on her tongue with each lengthy stride. The female's pace quickened as she now followed the much smaller path.

When the trees opened up into a clearing, she saw light. The female hesitated, surveying her environment. She cocked her head, ready to retreat ... or attack. The scent was strong. The hairless one was there. Instinct prevailed and each step now became a cautious one. Her shadowy figure moved from tree to tree, skirting the clearing to gather information ... crouched and ready for the unexpected. Then she saw it, sitting by another of its kind near the dwelling with the light. Her nose probed the soft breeze that had moved in with the cloud front. To this point she had not yet been detected. She knew that her hunting skills were superior to the senses of these weak creatures, but there was still much to be learned from them. As she glared at the machine sitting idly in the clearing, the rage began to boil within her as the memories of the juvenile's death returned. She targeted the murderer and then planned her point of assault. She would not be retreating again to the cover of the swamp. Tonight, she would spill the blood of the one who had been the aggressor.

The female watched for movement as she drifted across the clearing. Her vision was sharp in the darkness, but she could be vulnerable in the open. Only the light emanating from the dwelling worried her. She wondered how many there might be, or more importantly, if they would fight. But she wanted them to fight. She wanted to hear their screams of pain as she slaughtered them for what they had done.

When she finally reached the machine, she let out two quiet grunts in an attempt to provoke hidden danger to expose itself. All was still. The female shifted her gaze once again to the dwelling a short distance away. The scent of another was present. It was much stronger than that of the one she was hunting. But that one would have to be dealt with later. She positioned her body over the hard shell and uttered two more soft grunts, trying to incite movement from inside. There was still no response. In one broad sweep, her curled fist slammed into the side panel of the machine. She felt the shell give way to her power. Her ears perked at the sound of an animal inside the dwelling. Her body immediately ducked into a defensive posture. But she did not run.

***

Charlie awoke to the sound of Duff barking at the front door. He looked at his watch, squinting as his eyes adjusted to the light. "Ah heck!" He'd been asleep for close to two hours. "Rachel's gonna tan my hide." He frowned at the thought of his angry wife greeting him at the door. She was always working her way into a tizzy whenever he wasn't where she thought he was. And tonight she would be meeting Duff ... doubly special. The dog continued its persistent yapping. Charlie took a moment to study the excited animal. There was something peculiar about his demeanor. Duff would charge the door with a loud bark, and then retreat a few paces with a low, nervy growl.

"Whatsamatter, boy? Gotta take another dump, eh?" But the old Labrador paid him no attention. His only concern was the door leading to the outside.

Charlie slipped off the sofa and stretched his stubby arms behind his back. He inadvertently kicked over the half-empty bottle of Budweiser sitting on the floor. Beer leaked out of the long-neck, spilling onto a ragged throw-rug. He made no attempt to clean up the mess. The dog's unstrung behavior was unsettling.

"Duff!" he yelled. "Duff! Come here!" The dog looked for a brief instance in Charlie's direction before returning its focus back to the door. Charlie's confusion soon turned to irritation. Duff's hysterics continued to intensify as he began to claw at the base of the door, ripping away large slivers of wood. He would stop periodically and plug his snout into the growing gap.

What the heck has that dog all riled, thought Charlie. "What is it, boy? Something out there?" He walked to the small window next to the entrance, pulled back the stained curtain and peered out into the dark yard. There was nothing out there that he could see. The array of junk loomed eerily on the grounds out front. He then let loose the curtain tail and grasped the brass doorknob. It was cool from the outer temperature. Charlie decided to get a better look from the porch. He did not intend to let the dog outside, but as he cracked the door to peak Duff squirmed through his legs and was gone.

"Darn it, Duff!" he sniped. "Get back here, now!" Duff disappeared into the night. Only the dog's rampant barking signaled its general location. Charlie's eyes could not penetrate the blackness at first. There was no moon to cast shadows. But as his eyes slowly acclimated, he thought he saw something not too far away. He heard a strange snarl that seemed to originate from the growing form. The outline of the shadowy figure gradually came into focus. "What the heck?" He then saw a much smaller shadow running in circles around it. *Duff!*

Suddenly, there was a high pitched yelp. "Duff!" he cried. The dog began to bark again with much more vivacity. Whatever that thing was, Charlie figured that Duff could get it moving on out of there. But his speculation was instantly diffused with a thunderous roar that echoed through the clearing. It wasn't a bear. God knew that it wasn't a bear. Duff and the creature tangled viciously in the yard, neither giving ground to the other. The commotion moved just out of Charlie's field of vision. He stepped back from the doorway, remembering the spotlight that Ned had installed that summer to illuminate the clearing for deer. Charlie fumbled for the switch on the wall, but before the lights flicked on he heard a pained squeal.

"Duff!" he cried again, knowing that he had been too late. The dog was silent. The power to the spots kicked in and shed light on the yard. Charlie's knees wobbled, nearly causing him to lose his balance. He clutched the doorframe to steady himself. Standing thirty yards from the porch was a monster of mammoth proportions that was not of this world. Its head hovered at least nine feet above the earth. It stood upright on two thick legs. The body was a medley of long, black hair matted with burrs, briars and whatever else it picked up from the terrain it traveled. Its right arm hung loosely below a knee, while the other held an object at the height of its shoulders. It took a moment for Charlie to register that the struggling animal within the creature's grasp was Duff, kicking for his life. The creature's massive hand was wrapped around the dog's suffocating neck. *It had a hand!*

The beast glared in the direction of the doorway, unable to see past the bright light of the spots. Although it could not see Charlie, he could see its face ... vividly. It was almost ... human like. *Oh God!* he shrieked inwardly, unable to utter a sound through his quivering lips. The creature raised its free limb to block the blinding light. It roared at the man it could not see with deafening ferocity. The mechanic trembled with fear, praying that it would not come at him. Then, the monster clutched the dog's hind quarters and effortlessly ripped it apart. The mutilation produced a sickening, cracking sound as the spinal column snapped. Charlie felt bile build in his throat. His feet felt as though they were permanently nailed to the wooden porch. They would not move. The beast held both ends of the dog, one in each hand, roaring as if gesturing its triumph over the inferior animal. It then threw the mangled pieces of bloody flesh to the ground like two sacks of garbage and began to approach the door where Charlie stood.

He finally snapped out of his trance upon realizing the creature's intentions. Charlie was the next target. The beast was within fifteen yards, still unable to see him through the light. It appeared cautious about its actions as if it didn't quite know what to expect. *The face,* thought Charlie. *The God-awful face!* The mechanic forced his body into motion, wheeling around and propelling himself into the false security of the cabin. The door slammed behind him. Charlie dead-bolted the lock knowing all too well that it could not hold back the evil outside. It was coming for him. His eyes darted desperately about the interior of the living room, seeking out some means of defense. He heard a board creak on the porch outside. *My God,* he thought, *it's at the door.* His pulse rate was soaring. Time was running short. Then his eyes zeroed in on the old shotgun hanging over the mantel.

"Thank you, Jesus," he uttered as he raced for the weapon. The creature unleashed another horrendous cry that seemed to shake the small cottage. Charlie snatched the gun from its resting place and then reached for the open box of number sixes on the mantel. As he brought it toward his chest he was startled by a loud rap on the cabin wall. The box slipped from his grasp and fell to the floor. Shells scattered in all directions. The hefty mechanic sat down on his rear, leaning against the wall facing the door only fifteen feet away. He scooped up a half dozen shells with one hand while holding the shotgun with the other. The barrel of the gun broke easily. He inserted a round into each chamber and snapped the barrel shut. Charlie put the remaining shells in his moist lap. His bladder had already released its contents. He switched the safety to the "off" position and aimed at the door with shaking hands ... and waited. There was no sound. ... no movement ... nothing. He just wanted to close his eyes and wake up from the nightmare.

Charlie Perkins was not a religious man, but praying seemed to be the proper action. He started reciting the Lord's prayer in his head. Then he saw movement in the window beside the locked door. Charlie adjusted his aim, swinging the weapon toward the glass. Two eyes were peering in at him. A white cloud of steamy breath flowed through the gaps in the beast's fangs. The misshapen nose touched the window pane as though it were probing. It was learning. The glass fogged as the nostrils flared. Two pointed ears protruded from the sides of its head where fur gave way to black skin. The hearing organs flexed with each controlled breath. It was the expression on the face that caught Charlie's undivided attention. It was almost an inquisitive look.

Boom! Charlie could stand it no longer. A shrill scream succeeded the loud report of the shotgun. Pellets from both rounds of birdshot destroyed the lamp on the table by the doorway as well as the glass in the window. The lamp had been the only source of light in the room. All was dark now. Charlie had let loose both barrels without taking aim. By the sound of the anguish outside, he knew that some of the pellets had found their mark. But Charlie also knew that birdshot was not going to do much damage to a creature of that size. He had to make his shots count ... the vitals ... the head. He ejected the spent casings and inserted two more into the smoking chamber. Charlie figured that if the thing wanted him bad enough, it would come regardless of what stood in its path.

But why? He thought. *Why is it doing this to me? What is it?* Charlie prayed that the first volley had frightened the beast enough to drive it away, back to the hell that raised it. His mind was racing for a means of escape. *The truck!* It was parked just outside. If only he could find a way of getting to it.

The cabin had fallen into a dark, gloomy pit of uncertainty. The creature was silent, no longer protesting the wounds received at the expense of the shotgun. Charlie was frozen to the wall with his eyes and ears alert for the faintest of sounds. He began to wonder if it had run off. He willed his body to move from the floor, but it wouldn't oblige. His only recourse was to wait it out until someone came for him. But there was nobody who knew where he was. His hopes for rescue were diminished by the sound of another creaking board. It was still out there ... coming ... again. Charlie began to feel droplets of sweat rolling down his cheeks. He could now hear the monster probing for a means of accessing the cabin. Its claws gouged at the walls like fingernails on a chalkboard ... until it found the door. Charlie's eyes were wide with anticipation, wondering what it was doing. The doorknob began to turn. He could not speak. His mind could not process. The creature was thinking its way into the building.

"Oh, God ... please ... please don't kill me," he finally began to blurt out. Charlie Perkins had never faced death before in his lifetime, and was not savoring the experience. The clearing outside was still aglow from the spotlights. Charlie could see the shadows of its feet in the narrow slot beneath the door. He raised the barrel of the gun, unable to hold it steady.

A tremendous blast from outside nearly buckled the door inward. It remained in one piece, but a few extra cracks in the wood had developed. The creature's power was astounding. When it pounded on the wood a second time, the top half of the door disintegrated, exposing only the broad midsection of the hairy beast. The head was high above the overhang, out of sight.

Boom! Boom! Each shot found the creature's torso, driving it backward only step. "Fucking birdshot!" roared the defeated man. "You stupid fucking birdshot!" He was babbling senselessly, knowing that he was not long for that world. He heard the growl, almost like that of a bear, but ten octaves lower. With a powerful kick, the remaining half of the door splintered into pieces. The monster ducked into the room, and in two quick strides it was on the man cowering against the wall. Charlie made one final defensive maneuver to halt the charge. He swung the butt of the gun at the charging creature with all of his remaining strength. The stock snapped like a twig on a surging forearm. Charlie felt himself being pulled up off the floor as razor-like claws stabbed into his shoulder, cracking bone as they tightened their grip. He felt warm blood oozing down his side. But there was no pain. There was only the pressure on his shattered arm. He dangled before the monster's wretched face with his eyes closed awaiting the inevitable. The air in the room was filled with a stench that rolled his already queasy stomach. Tears were streaming down Charlie Perkins' face.

"Please ... please!" he yelled with his eyes shut. He did not want to face the being. He now wished for death. "Get it over with." His voice was fading as he begged for a merciful ending.

But nothing happened. The creature just held him there. It was inspecting him. Charlie forced himself to open just one eye ... just a crack. The rank breath consumed his nose. It was hot and musty. But as he opened his eyes farther he saw a different expression on the face that had been so filled with hate only moments ago. He saw ... sympathy. Charlie wanted to believe that maybe the creature was contemplating whether or not it should set him free. That somehow this disfigured creation had feelings ... like a man. That maybe it didn't want to hurt him.

Then, the monster's expression abruptly changed, as if it remembered its true mission ... to kill. Charlie felt hot, filmy saliva saturate his face when the creature cried out. The pain in his ears was unbearable. A wisp of air preceded an odd feeling in the mechanic's gut, like he had just been relieved of thirty excess pounds. He was flung hard into the wall where he fell to the ground with a thud. The creature stood over him, its breathing heavy ... waiting for the man to make a move as if it wanted his to fight back. Charlie felt himself growing weak. The room began to spin. He reached to his stomach with his left arm. There was no feeling in his right. His hand slid into a mass of warm, slimy substance. He felt the rubbery matter until the excruciating pain traveled the complicated route of nerves to his brain. Charlie was holding onto his own intestines that were lying on the floor beside him. He let out a cry of agony and then vomited on his own face. The creature's foot slammed into his head, crushing his skull like an egg. Charlie Perkins finally found peace.

***

The Upper Peninsula had submerged into darkness when Tyrone Pullman decided that it was safe enough to allow his hidden companion some air. After the tense moments at the bridge, Tyrone exited the expressway and traveled west on Highway 2. He was pleasantly surprised by the lack of cars on what was one of the U.P.'s main arteries. He was finally starting to feel as though he had made a successful break from the dragnet. Tyrone figured that only a stupid mistake would cost them from this point forward, but with Gerald Johnson by his side, anything was possible.

The Chevy truck held two sixteen gallon fuel tanks. He was forced to switch over to the second just south of Grayling, and now the gauge was showing about a quarter of a tank remaining. Tyrone had not planned on making a gas stop so soon. He would have preferred to either get across the state line, or find that little hideaway nestled somewhere in the remote woods. It was a minor mistake, but one that could prove costly if he wasn't careful.

Tyrone assumed that the white folk would be finishing up dinner and sitting down to watch the evening news. He was well aware of what the lead story would be. Two brothers killing white cops had a tendency to warrant heavy media coverage. He would have to chance a gas stop, hopefully some little hole in the wall where they wouldn't be observed by too many. He'd been listening to Gerald's persistent pounding on the cab of the truck for over thirty minutes. It was time to let him out.

The driver eased the truck off the road, careful to use his turn signal ... watchful for that unseen cop. He checked the rearview mirror. There were no oncoming headlights in either direction. He got out and pulled the lever to release the hatch of the tool box.

"Motherfucker! What the fuck you doin, homes?"

Gerald's petulance irritated Tyrone to no end. There was no gratitude in him. *Just give me a reason,* he said to himself as he fondled the .32 with his pocketed hand.

Gerald emerged slowly from the metallic coffin, wincing from pain in his stiffened joints. Tyrone managed to smile as he backed up a step, just in case Gerald unraveled too far. Gerald looked like an old man suffering from a severe bout of arthritis as he hefted his legs from the small opening. Crumbs clung to his shirt and pants from the bountiful supply of snack foods. Had there been better lighting, Tyrone would have seen the large wet stain on Gerald's coveralls in the groin area. The beer had taken its toll.

The freed prisoner slid awkwardly down the sidewall of the Chevy. Tyrone kept a watchful eye on the man, unsure what would go down next. Gerald was a funny man. He could be your best friend one minute, and the next ... well he'd just wait and see. Tyrone judged that a shot from the small .32 would go virtually unnoticed in their current location should there be a confrontation.

While facing away from his partner, Gerald dusted off his shirt and turned around. His voice did not exhibit a complementary pitch. "What the fuck you doin, man! Fuck! I been pounding the fuck out of that goddamn box for an hour!" His arms waved in the air as he unleashed his discontent.

Tyrone let him say his peace. He figured that Gerald needed a chance to let off some steam. After all, he had been caged for a good six hours.

"See this, Tye?" Gerald pointed to his groin. "I pissed myself, motherfucker!"

The recipient of the tirade kept silent, caressing his hidden weapon.

"You're lucky I don't cap your ass."

He'd heard enough. "Listen, G." Tyrone decided it was time to put a stop to the childish tantrum. He leaned forward. "I saved your ass, homes. And as for the banging on the fucking truck ... I had to slick my way through a line of cops at the fucking bridge to get your sorry ass here." He spoke with confidence, unwilling to give ground to the ungrateful slob. It was his turn to be in charge. Tyrone pointed a steady and determined finger at Gerald's chest. "You done nothing but bitch since we got your ass out of those fucking chains. If it weren't for me, you'd be getting ass fucked right now by some Skinhead in Jackson. So shut the fuck up!" The harsh rebuttal was satisfying. Tyrone felt a sense of empowerment. He examined his friend's face, waiting for the reaction.

Gerald looked to be shocked by the outburst. He cocked his head sideways like a dog attempting to decipher the words of its master. He stood silent, caught off guard by his ordinarily passive partner's lecture. But the words did seem to sink in. His lips stretched into that familiar, easy-going smile. His intensity was gone for the moment. "You right, Tye." He was now speaking in a normal tone. "I owe you my life, man." He pointed to the back of the truck. "That box ... not knowing where I was ... just got me all fucked up is all." He extended his hand. "Thanks, brother."

Tyrone took his outstretched hand with a touch of caution, and they shook like friends. "We got a long way to go, G. And there's gonna be a lot of people lookin for our black asses."

Where we at?" Gerald took back his hand and looked around. He could see nothing but darkness.

"I drove north. We're in the U.P."

Gerald turned to his friend with a look of surprise. "The U-what?" he asked.

"The Upper Peninsula." The conversation was casual now. Tyrone released the weapon in his pocket. He would not have to use it ... yet.

"Why ..." Gerald was about to unleash another outburst, but decided against. It was a life-saving decision as far as Tyrone Pullman was concerned. "I don't want to know, Tye. You done pretty damn good so far." Gerald leaned back against the door of the Chevy and took in a deep breath of fresh air. He closed his eyes. "I don't even wanna fucking know, man."

***

Ross Pickett had just settled into his La-Z-Boy with a diet Coke in one hand and a steaming bag of microwave popcorn in the other. Saturday evening was routinely his one opportunity for some alone time. It was just him and the "Idiot-box." Maggie was working the bar, and Chuck was out with his girl. Since cable had civilized the northern community, it seemed that more people were hanging out in their own homes to admire the many channels of meaningless information. Ross was hoping to catch tonight's game on ESPN, but paperwork in the office kept him a little late. He got home just in time to see the final score. Nebraska had destroyed Oklahoma 55-10. It was shaping up to be another Husker run to the National Championship. But Michigan and Ohio State were staking some early claims of their own. Although the Big Ten powerhouses had been his worst nemesis while in college, he did enjoy seeing the league do well in national play. There was nothing like college football in the veteran athlete's eyes. It was kids playing solely for the fun of the game. And as for the fanatics that followed the teams ... well, their enthusiasm spoke for itself.

Ross looked to the clock on the wall. It was nearing eleven and time for his favorite show "Cops." He could relate to the documentary-style series that followed law enforcement personnel around the country. He was amazed at the war-like settings in some areas and the confrontations with the vermin of society. Ross had always thought that the show should produce a segment on the duties of conservation officers. Their lives could get just as hairy as their counterparts in blue.

Just as he shoveled a handful of buttery popcorn into his mouth, the phone rang on the end table. He looked at it with disgust and then muted the sound on the television. He took a quick slug from the soda and swallowed the food.

"Hello?"

"Hi, Sheriff, this is Rachel Perkins ... Charlie's wife."

The Sheriff was partly concentrating on an angry German Shepherd cornering some young punk while a deputy grinned in the background. Ross loved the dog pursuits.

"Yeah? Oh ... hi, Rachel. What can I do for you?" The kid on T.V. looked like he was about to crap his pants. *Serves you right, you little bastard,* Ross mused. He never did understand why people ran from the police. It never ended well.

"Have you seen Charlie around anywhere? He hasn't come home yet and I'm beginning to worry."

The concern in the woman's voice stung his ears. Ross now diverted his full attention to the phone. "Last I knew, Rachel, he was going to pick up Ned Crosby's car out on ... out on Townsend Road. It may have taken him a little longer than he anticipated. The car was in pretty bad shape." But then he remembered that the car wasn't there when he drove by earlier on his way home from Houghton. It wasn't like Charlie to just up and disappear like that.

"He always calls if he's going to be late. I checked the station and the bar. Maggie says she hasn't seen him all day." Rachel Perkins was on the verge of hysterics. She was known to have a flair for the dramatic. Everyone was aware of the tight leash she kept on her affable husband.

Ross liked Charlie Perkins. He was a good man. But if Rachel didn't know where he was, perhaps something was amiss. He attempted to comfort the woman on the phone, shutting off the T.V. in the process. "Well, I'm fairly certain there's nothing to worry about, Rachel. Like I said, that car was banged up pretty darn good. Charlie had his work cut out for him." He was lying without knowing why. He covered his mouth and burped quietly.

Ross began to feel the acid build-up in his stomach. Something told him that he was going to have another late night.

Rachel was rattling on about Charlie's predictable habits when he cut her off. "Tell you what, Rachael. I was going to take a drive out that way anyways," he lied again. His real plan was to get some much needed sleep by dozing off in the chair. That would now have to wait. It was time to play Sheriff again.

"Oh, and Sheriff, I just remembered something. Charlie was grumbling on about that old drunk's dog after hearing about the accident. Do you suppose he might have gone out to Mr. Crosby's place? Lord, he better not bring that thing home. You know we just don't have the ..."

"Okay, Rachel," he interjected. "I'll swing out there and see." *That had to be it,* he thought. *Charlie probably fell asleep or something.* Ross said good-bye to the worried wife and hung up.

Ross was suddenly engrossed by a powerful feeling of déjà vu as he suited up for the cold weather. The temperature had fallen drastically outside, and much to his surprise, a light snow was beginning to filter down from the night sky. As he stood in the doorway, he felt for the grip of the pistol holstered on his hip. This time the weapon was securely in place. The sidearm gave him added confidence. He was not looking forward to making another trip out to that swamp.

Ross trudged out to the Tahoe. The ground was still soft from the prior night's rain, but a thin layer of ice was again beginning to form. He climbed into the truck. He felt an eerie sensation that something evil was enveloping his town and that he would soon discover its source.

"Jesus!" he bellowed aloud with a crooked smile. "Don't start scaring yourself, Ross." He laughed nervously. *This is shit-town U.S.A. Nothing happens in places like this.* Ross didn't bother contacting Sharon Cooper at the office. He wasn't up for listening to her mousy voice tonight. He pulled out of the drive and headed north ... again.

***

"Ya bedder be careful wit dat spot, Jess. Dat Sherf almost caught up t'us lass night."

"Fuck em. I'll put a round right 'tween his eyes wit dis here rifle," replied the younger Jones brother, holding the powerful spotlight out the window of the pickup. A Remington 300 Win Mag with a 16 power scope rested between his scrawny legs.

"Christ amighty, if ya ain't a dumb shit! I don't ever wanna hear ya talkin like dat," scolded Frank Jones as he steered the vehicle slowly down the road.

Frank and Jesse were on the job that night. It was common practice for them to be out in weather that would cause the deer to move. A cold front was settling into the region and the light snowfall was growing in strength. The deer would be emerging from cover foraging for food in the open terrain. Neither man had tasted much beef in his lifetime. Venison was a means of survival for them, just as it was for their daddy, and his daddy before him. The Jones family had resided in the Jessup area darn near since the town's inception. Each generation felt it their God-given right to live off the land regardless of the game laws that governed it.

Frank and Jesse were a mean pair, a trait also passed down the family tree. Both were small, gangly men with exceptional strength when it came to bar-room brawling, an activity that had landed each in jail on more than one account. Each wore long brown hair tied back in a ponytail. Their clothes were old and stained with grease. Heavily bearded faces topped off the image depicting a rebellious defiance of modern society. They were both woodsmen in the truest definition, and pure redneck to those who made their acquaintance. The Jones boys lived as bachelors with their father, a decrepit old man who was dying from emphysema. Frank Sr. depended on his boys to provide for him. His wife had died ten years earlier in a freak accident involving the cleaning of a gun. It was a well-known fact that Frank Sr. never cared much for his wife. She had been a quiet lady who kept to herself. Many eyes witnessed the bruises on her distraught face when she traveled into town a few times a month to visit the market. She had been a battered woman, yet nobody ever lifted a hand to help. When word of her curious death spread, both local and state law enforcement personnel were out to investigate. As it turned out, Frank Jr. and Jesse were the only witnesses to the shooting and their well-formulated stories exonerated the father from any wrongdoing.

The Jones men stuck together like a pack of wild dogs, not allowing anyone to drive a wedge between them. Rumors arose of how it had not just been Frank Sr. roughing up Bernice Jones. Birdy McIntosh had seen Jesse push her to the ground on one occasion, but she didn't stop for fear of receiving the same treatment.

Clancy had been the youngest of the three Jones boys, and quite possibly the worst of the bunch. He was killed in a car chase following an armed robbery attempt in Ontonogon. Clancy had been only twenty-one when he met his untimely death.

The Jones clan had always been an intimidating lot. There was even talk of a working still somewhere on their eighty acre property. None dared to trespass for fear of being shot. The Jones' place consisted of a double-wide trailer that sat next to a dilapidated old cabin. There was quite an arsenal of hunting hounds, two or three for every form of prey in the North country. They had three beagles to run snowshoe hares in winter, a couple of German shorthairs for grouse and woodcock, and two of the best bear-treeing blueticks ever to run the Upper Peninsula.

Neither Frank nor Jesse had ever held a real job. To them, their job was survival. Selling animal pelts was one source of income. The other was the illegal sale of venison to restaurants. They would venture out onto the backroads under the cover of darkness and harvest as many animals as they could find. A contact from Newberry would make the trip to Jessup twice a month to purchase their frozen meat. Venison provided a steady source of income, just enough to buy needed supplies to continue their outlaw ways. To their delight, there had also been an increase in demand for trophy whitetail racks. The two brothers established a covert business relationship with a taxidermist in Escanaba to accommodate this growing market. Nice racks could fetch a chunk of change from the rich who were either too lazy or lacked the heart to hunt for themselves. Bar owners, in particular, would buy their impressive trophies to give ambiance to their establishments.

Frank and Jesse were a slippery pair, knowing when and where to hunt. There was a police scanner mounted inside the cab of their battered pickup. The C.O.s and State Troopers rarely made visits to their neck of the woods, but when they did, the boys were usually ready for them.

With the changing weather conditions, the brothers were hard at work that night and enjoying every second of it. Though they had killed too many animals to count in their lifetimes, there still existed the thrill of seeing a big deer drop.

"Hey, Frank. Hold on." Jesse placed his hand on his brother's arm as he shined the beam into an open field holding what looked to be about twenty skittish deer. Heads bobbed to the sudden change, but the powerful spotlight hypnotized their eyes and held them in place. Frank stopped the truck and leaned forward to look out his brother's window. There were two small bucks in the group, nothing of much value. Then he saw another deer wander into the clearing. It was a big deer with its head held low in the tall grass. Experience told him that it was probably a dominant buck hiding its horns. Then, as if on cue, the animal lifted its alert head and exposed the massive rack.

"Check out dem horns," Jesse whispered as he cut off the rumbling motor.

"Looks to be a ten, maybe twelve. Biggin alright." A wry, toothless grin stretched across Frank Jones' face. This buck was going to get them some serious cash. "Hold em dare, Jess."

His brother held the spot in place, careful not to invoke a reaction. Had the trophy buck not been with this group, Frank would have extracted the semi-auto .30-06 from behind the seat and dropped as many as he could with the expanded ten-round clip. But this was a special animal that called for the "big gun."

Frank quietly opened the door and snuck out of the cab. He snatched the rifle from between Jesse's legs and crept around to the rear, holding his head just high enough above the sidewall to keep an eye on the meadow. The big buck had ducked its head back into the cover of the grass, but its large body provided ample opportunity for a kill shot only eighty yards away. Frank slowly rose and rested the rifle against the truck. He peered through the Leupold, an investment well worth the money. The other deer, coming out of their trances, began walking towards the tree line to seek refuge. The tails on the does danced in the night air, sensing danger. The buck started to follow.

The intensifying snowfall made it difficult to pick out the animal in the lens. Frank steadied himself. He squeezed the trigger and the gun bucked in his hands. He saw the animal mule-kick, take two bounding leaps, and then disappear. Jesse trailed the buck's brief flight with the spotlight.

"Yeah, boy! Ya got em!" hollered the younger brother.

"Damn straight I got em," replied the shooter with a hint of conceit. He was the best goddamned shot in the county, bar none. "Let's go git 'im, Jess."

Jesse flicked off the spot and the two men jogged out into the field with flashlights in hand. It didn't take long to locate the buck. They'd been through this routine hundreds of times. When they walked up to the deer, each took a moment to admire the mass of its antlers. Jesse knelt down and counted the points out loud.

"Thirteen, Frank. Nice deer, eh. This bugger's worth some serious cash," he said, turning to his brother.

"Let's get em back to the truck." This was neither the time nor the place to gut the deer, or admire for that matter. There was always the possibility that someone may have heard the shot. Each brother grabbed hold of an antler and they dragged it back to the road. It was a professional hit and run operation. With a back-wrenching heave, the buck was loaded into the bed and covered with a plastic tarp. The head and hide would be driven down to Escanaba in the morning along with a nice eight-point that Jess had nailed the night before.

***

Ross' first stop was the scene of the accident on Townsend. He stayed there only a moment, knowing there would be nothing for him to find. The snow was beginning to fall with more emphasis and it was starting to stick on the freezing ground. He clicked on his spotlight and directed the beam down into the ditch. He saw the fresh gouges in the earth where Charlie had hauled the vehicle back up the embankment to the road. Ross switched off the spot and drove off toward Ned Crosby's place. His eyelids were hanging heavy from lack of sleep. The snowflakes streaking down in front of the headlights created a hypnotic illusion as if he were traveling through space. Ross' exhaustion was deep-felt and he now wished that he had gone straight to bed after returning from Houghton.

***

“Shit! Someone’s comin.” Jesse propped his body up in the passenger seat when he detected the oncoming headlights.

“Relax, Jess. We ain’t doin nothing now,” Frank answered calmly. He’d done this too many times to get jumpy over an approaching car. He was a pro. But as the car drew closer, he made out the inactive flashers on top. It wasn’t a car. It was the Sheriff’s truck. He felt a twinge of concern, but he did not let it show. There was no reason for Pickett to stop them. And if he did, he had no right to go snooping around under that tarp in back.

“Shee-it! It’s dat fuckin Sherf.” Jesse now recognized the vehicle. “I told ya we shouldn’t have come out two nights in a row!”

“Just relax. He ain’t lookin fer us,” said Frank, not knowing if his statement were true. He could see the Tahoe slowing. He peered into the passing truck as the two vehicles paralleled each other. The Sheriff’s face was hidden in the dark interior. Frank knew that the driver slowed for a reason. Pickett would easily recognize their truck. “Nothin to see, asshole,” he muttered. He watched the taillights disappear around a curve behind them.

Jess had turned completed around in his seat to assure himself that the cop was not going to wheel around and pursue. “Do ya tink he seen anything?”

“Naw,” replied the older brother. He thought about Jesse’s prior assertion. They *had* been pressing their luck. Two nights in a row was not good practice in their line of work. But the risk had been worth the reward. They dropped a nice buck that would command a handsome bounty.

***

Ross recognized the truck right away. It was the Jones boys. *What the hell are they doing out here at this time of night?* But his question didn’t really warrant an answer. He knew darn well what Frank and Jesse were up to. He slowed the Tahoe as their truck passed by, attempting to steal a glance at the contents of the bed. It was too dark. Ross thought about pulling them over just to satisfy his curiosity, but he decided against it.

"I'll catch up with you boys, later," he said to himself.

After three more miles, the Tahoe came to a stop at the open gate. Headlights illuminated the sign that read ... "Ned's Place." The crooked lettering made it obvious that the sign had been carved by hand. Ross let off the brake. The big truck rocked back and forth down the rutted two-track. Large roots bulged from the ground like long, curly fingers, making for effective speedbumps. Ross wondered how old Ned managed to get his car in and out of there, particularly with heavy snow.

Through the dense trees he spotted evidence of light. *Charlie must be here after all,* he reasoned. Someone was there. After another minute of careful maneuvering, the Sheriff finally steered into the brightly lit clearing that reminded him of a high school football field on a Friday night after the crowd had departed. Ross knew those glaring spotlights on the front porch weren't installed for shooting squirrels. He wondered just how many deer Ned had plugged out there through the years.

Ross saw the Plymouth attached to Charlie Perkins' wrecker parked in front of the run-down shack. *God, what an awful place,* he thought as he surveyed the structure. There couldn't have been much holding it together. But the general setting was rather pleasant, like a fairytale wonderland derived from a child's storybook ... with snowflakes floating softly to the earth onto a bright field of goodness ... the dark forest lurking beyond. The only thing removed from the peaceful portrait was a gingerbread house. The junk in the front yard didn't help its cause, though.

The Sheriff drove up alongside the wrecker and noticed right away there weren't any tracks behind the wheels in the freshly fallen snow. The truck had been sitting a while, he judged. At least since the snow started. *How long ago had that been?* The Sheriff tooted the horn once to let Charlie know that someone was outside. Sneaking up on people out in the sticks was not always a wise thing to do. Paranoia swept over him when there was no response. Something wasn't right. The cabin was completely dark, yet the spots were on. *Why?* Then he saw the door ... or lack of it. The entryway was open. Ross left the safety of the truck, keeping the engine idling just in case. *In case of what? Christ, Ross!*

The Sheriff's eyes scanned the clearing. The serenity was lost when he focused on a red object lying next to an old wash tub.

Red! Blood! He did the math and was horrified by what the answer might reveal. But it was too small to be an adult human, he assured himself. It was something else ... an animal maybe. Ross jogged cautiously to the carcass. Its black hide was white with snowflakes. As he side-stepped around an old appliance he saw the stained ground around it. Blood was everywhere, like a fresh gut-pile. He kicked the object lightly with his boot. The front half of Duff's stiffening body rolled free of the severed hind quarters. Ross tasted bile in his throat. It was Ned Crosby's dog. The broken spinal cord protruded from the animal like a cracked popsicle-stick, adorned with tattered threads of spaghetti-like intestines. Duff's blank eyes stared up at him, as if it were cursing the newcomer for failing to arrive sooner. Ross looked in disbelief, coming to the realization that the dog had literally been torn apart.

The Sheriff turned away from the obscenity with a hand covering his mouth. He had seen the insides of an animal before, but not like this. *The window!* "Jesus!" he cried after noticing the window next to the open doorway had been shattered. Now it wasn't just an eerie feeling overwhelming the Sheriff. He was truly frightened. Not a sound emanated from the dark cabin. Where was Charlie? The lack of sound coupled with Duff's shredded remains brought on a ghoulish aura over the clearing. Something evil had gripped this place. Ross stood dumbfounded while snow clung to his head and shoulders like a bad case of dandruff. For only the second time in his career as a law enforcement officer, Ross Pickett unholstered his weapon, anticipating imminent danger.

"Charlie?" he called to the silent home. His voice cracked like an adolescent in mid-puberty. "You in there, Charlie?" There was no response. His eyes surveyed each corner of the building, looking for clues as to what might have happened. There was no evidence offering a reasonable explanation. Ross then walked back to the Tahoe, observing all possible angles of attack. He felt the cold grip of the pistol in his palm, praying that he would not have to use it. He opened the door and picked up the mike.

"Sharon, this is Ross. You copy?" His mind was swirling with scenarios.

"Howdy, howdy, Sheriff." The perky voice blared over the local frequency. "Whatsamatter, ain't you sleeping again tonight? You know you really should ..."

Ross cut her off sharply for the second time in as many days. "Goddammit, Sharon! Shut up and listen." Though he felt sorry for the outburst, there was no time to apologize. "Now listen to me," he began again in a more controlled tone, "I want you to find Mark and have him hightail it out to Ned Crosby's place."

"But Sheriff," she replied, a little hurt from the scolding. "I think Mark's over at the bar tonight."

"I don't give a damn where he is! Just find him and tell him to get his ass out here!" His voice rose again. "And I want you to contact the State boys in Appleton. Have them send someone out here, pronto."

"What is it, Ross? What's going on?"

"I don't know yet. Please, just do it." Before he replaced the mike, Ross thought of something else. "Sharon?"

"Yeah, Ross?"

"Tell Mark to bring a couple of rifles."

"Alright, Sheriff. Be careful." Sharon expressed her concern and signed off.

***

Mark Bennington caught the gist of his boss' call as he listened to their conversation. It was definitely something important ... real police work ... with guns and everything. He zipped up his trousers when his lover signed off.

"Sounds bad," Sharon commented, watching the Deputy slip back into his shirt. She covered her bare chest with her arms, feeling somewhat embarrassed, as if they had been caught in the act.

"Where does Ross keep the key to the gun cabinet?" asked Mark, still perspiring from the second go-around of the evening.

"I think he keeps it in his top drawer." The switch-board operator turned away and slid her arms into her push-up bra. Mark took a moment to admire her naked body. Her skin was so smooth, her lips so soft and inviting. And most importantly, Sharon Cooper was a dynamo in the sack, something he hadn't experienced since high school. Unbeknownst to the town rumor mill, the two had been engaged in sexual relations for over three months. It was usually like this, after hours at the town hall or parked somewhere in the boonies. Together, they had written the book on how to make love in the back seat of a Cavalier. Mark did feel guilty about the affair. He loved his wife dearly, but the sexual spark just hadn't been there for the last year. Sharon gave him new meaning to life. It was both exciting and adventurous at the same time. They would make subtle suggestive gestures to one another whenever they passed on the street, careful to ensure nobody was noticing.

Mark dug through the assorted papers in the drawer until he located the key. He walked over to the steel-framed cabinet and opened the heavy door. It took him a minute to decide on the appropriate weaponry. He chose a .30-06 and a shotgun not knowing what sort of situation he would be facing. It was best to cover all bases. He picked up some boxes of ammunition and headed for the door.

Sharon stopped him in the hall, clad only in her bra and panties. "Be careful, baby." She wrapped her arms around his neck and inserted her moist tongue into his accepting mouth. She then grasped his rear end and pulled him closer. "Do you think you can come back when you're done?" She wanted more from her lover.

"We'll see what time it is, Sharon. My wife might think something's up if I'm out too late." The remark drew a frown from the mistress. He smiled. "Oops, sorry." He knew that Sharon didn't like him bringing up his wife. She was jealous and wanted Mark to leave Mary, but she also knew that his kids came first. Mark Bennington wasn't a faithful husband, but he was a dedicated father.

"I'll see what I can do, Sharon." With that, the Deputy gave her a peck on the cheek and left the office. Sharon quickly dressed and returned to her desk to make the call to Appleton.

***

Ross retrieved his Mag-Lite from the glove compartment. He clicked on the heavy-duty flashlight and stepped onto Ned Crosby's front porch. The boards creaked under his weight. With the beam of light, he traced the outer edges of the doorway. The door itself had been reduced to nothing more than a pile of kindling. The hinges, though slightly bent, remained in place. His light found three deep, parallel grooves in the outer wall. He had seen those marks before ... on the roof of Ned's Plymouth. The spacing was the same. *Claw marks! Had the bear been here?* he wondered. Ross scratched his head, puzzled by his own thoughts. He shuddered as he closely examined the marks, trying to visualize the size of the creature that made them as he had done earlier at the crash scene. He holstered the .357 and traced the grooves with a finger. It slipped easily into each crevice. *Must be a big mother,* he thought.

As the Sheriff took a step into the dark cabin, his boot slid forward as if he had stepped in butter. He followed the beam from the Mag-Lite to the floor and discovered that he was standing in a wide streak of blood. It looked as if someone had taken a large paintbrush to the wooden planks. It was thick blood indicating a bad wound ... a mortal wound. The trail stretched from about ten feet inside the living room to where it dissipated into a few tiny droplets on the front porch. Ross concluded that something had been dragged from there ... a body! *Charlie!* "Oh, God," he said, "don't let that be Charlie." But the facts were now painfully clear. After killing him, the bear must have dragged the corpse to the doorway, picked it up, and then hauled it off into the night. *But a bear wouldn't just take him away like that, would it?* Charlie Perkins was a good sized man. Ross had been in law enforcement for many years. He had never seen the result of an animal attack on a human. He had been lucky ... until tonight. He couldn't comprehend a bear killing a large man and then dragging him off. But maybe Charlie wasn't dead.

"Charlie?" Ross called out into the room, knowing all too well that there would be no answer. He turned to the broken window. The glass had been shattered outward. There was a broken lamp against the wall. The lampshade was speckled with tiny holes. *Shotgun!* The pattern was right. His light did not pick up any traces of blood at the window or around its perimeter. Ross walked to the far side of the room, concentrating on the other wall where the shot must have originated. As he passed the couch, he inadvertently stepped in a slick, rubbery substance that made a squishing sound as his boot mashed it into the floor. The Sheriff backed up a step. A sickening aroma emerged to his nose. He doubled over and vomited when the flashlight illuminated the heap of bloody intestines that had once belonged to Charlie Perkins. The contents of Ross' stomach spewed out onto the sofa as he clutched it for support. His head was spinning. The awful smell continued to cause dry-heaves even after his daily intake of food and drink had been lost.

Ross looked to the ceiling. The pounding in his head was unbearable. He could not conceive how a man could be gutted. The air in the room was thick with the stench of death. He regained as much composure as his traumatized body would allow and eased himself back up on unsteady legs, avoiding the grizzly sight on the floor beneath him. Ross forced himself to continue the investigation regardless of what he might find. It was his job. Charlie Perkins had been a friend. He had to find the rest of him.

The Sheriff stepped over the ugly mess and trained the light on an empty ammunition box lying next to several scattered shotgun shells at the base of the far wall. There was a pool of blood larger than that at the doorway. *The kill zone,* he thought. Ross knelt down on one knee, picked up a spent casing and brought it close to this face. "Birdshot," he whispered. *Charlie didn't have a chance.* After a quick glance around, he found three more spent casings, all stained with the mechanic's blood. He saw the scattergun, broken at the stock. Ross figured that Charlie put up quite a struggle.

Some blood from the casings had managed to get on his hands. Ross wiped it onto his jeans. He stood up once again and started re-examining the room. He froze in horror when his eyes honed in on the severed arm lying only five feet from where he stood. It was still encased in the sleeve with the initials C.E.P. embroidered on the cuff.

"Christ, Charlie," Ross said as he bowed his head in grief. "I'm so sorry. God, I'm so sorry."

The wailing of the approaching siren awoke the Sheriff from a quiet moment of contemplation. Ross crossed his forehead and shoulders with his right hand, an instinct from his catholic experiences with Eevie. He lumbered slowly outside, feeling exhausted. As he exited through the doorway he saw the Deputy's squad car roll into the clearing and fishtail sideways in the snow covered grass next to the Tahoe. The door swung open and Mark Bennington stumbled out toting a scoped rifle in one hand and a pistol-gripped shotgun with a folding stock in the other. He stomped up to the porch like a charging patriot, arms at the ready. It was the first time Ross had actually seen the young man out of uniform. Another siren screamed in the distance. That would be the Troopers from Appleton.

"Hey, Ross! What the heck's going on?" There was eagerness in the boy's voice.

You don't want to know, Ross thought to himself.

Mark noticed the Sheriff's odd expression. His unshaven face was pale. "Ross," asked Mark, "is everything okay?"

The Sheriff sat down on the porch step, avoiding the droplets of blood that Mark had failed to detect. He stared out into the snow-laden clearing, past the remains of Crosby's dog. He focused on a single snowflake making a slow, gentle plight to the white ground below. There he was, in a town where time was measured by the position of the sun rather than hands of a clock, and a speeding ticket was considered a "crime wave" ... and now this happens. Something had just bloodied the innocence of his peaceful community. It was something evil and two men were now dead because of it. *Two men and a dog,* Ross corrected his thought. *It's not supposed to be like this. This shit is over my head.* Ross suddenly felt that he was that single snowflake, falling helplessly, only to be swallowed up by obscurity until he was lost forever.

"Ross, you okay, buddy?" Mark leaned the guns against a warped six-by-six supporting the awning over the porch. He touched the Sheriff gently on the shoulder, sensing his tension. Ross flinched from the interruption. "What's the matter? You look like you seen a ghost."

Ross found himself wishing for one of his old ghosts. *Mr. Beam would make a fine companion right about now,* he thought. He could feel himself slipping into that abysmal void. It would be so easy. But like he had done a thousand times over, he forced the notion from his head. *Clean it up, buddy,* he told himself. "Yeah," replied the Sheriff, sounding as if he were a defeated man. "Ain't that the truth?"

"What's going on, Ross? That's Charlie's truck isn't it?" Mark motioned to the wrecker in front of the Plymouth.

"Sure is." He looked up to the Deputy. "It's Charlie's alright. But Charlie isn't going to be driving it anymore. He's dead." That last word hit hard.

"Geez," said the Deputy, glancing to the doorway. "Is he inside?"

"Part of him is. Don't really know about the rest." It was a morbid statement, but true. Mark took a step in the direction of the door before Ross stopped him. "Don't go in there, Mark. Believe me, if you've had dinner, you don't want to see. We're going to need a coroner out here. Go put a call in to Appleton."

The Deputy slowly backed away from the cabin at the request of his boss. His curiosity urged him to see for himself, but his faith in Ross told him to accept the advice. Mark returned to the squad car, leaving the weapons on the porch.

A blue State Police car rolled into the clearing with a large black man peering out from behind the steering wheel. Ross recognized the driver immediately by the ear to ear smile and the big gold tooth, as well as the color of his skin. The Trooper got out of his vehicle and put on his hat.

"What's up, homey? Some rednecks giving you trouble out here?" The officer skipped up to his long-time friend. He stopped short of the porch upon noticing that Ross was not quite in tune with his humor. "Damn, boy, you look like hell."

"Hi, Ray, how you doing?" Ross stood to greet his friend. Although Ray Jackson was slightly shorter, his girth gave him a much larger appearance. They shook hands, with Ross allowing the Trooper the firmer grip. He was in no mood for ego-inspired games. Ross was glad that Ray Jackson had taken the call. He needed some reassurance; something the Trooper was very capable of providing.

"Man, something's got your cage rattled." The booming voice mellowed when he looked past Ross and saw the blood in the doorway. Before the Sheriff could stop him, Jackson was inside the cabin. He heard a light click on, and then a heavy sigh. After a few minutes, the Trooper returned to the front porch and sat down next to the Sheriff who was fidgeting with a small twig. Jackson spoke as he stared out into the clearing just as Ross had been doing.

"Man, I haven't seen shit like that since the war." Ray shook his head, recalling the gruesome visions from his tours in the

Nam. He had also seen his share of some nasty accidents while on the force, but none compared to the sight inside the cabin. "What the hell happened in there?" He turned to his friend who appeared lost in his own world.

"Huh?" replied the Sheriff.

"What the hell did that, Ross?"

"Bear." His answer was quick and to the point. There was no doubt in his mind. *A goddamned black bear had decided to take out a little revenge on a man who clobbered it with a car. But that would mean the bear actually hunted ... pursued a man after the accident. Coincidentally, Ned's car was at the scene. Did it think Charlie had been Ned? Was it hunting Ned?*

"Ain't never heard of no bear chewing someone up like that," added the Trooper.

Ross proceeded to recount the events of the past twenty-four hours. He told him about the accident and the trip up to Houghton. The only thing he left out was the menacing thought in the back of his brain that something else was out there. *It was a bear!*

Jackson listened intently to every word, trying to conjecture each piece of the puzzle. When the Sheriff finished, the Trooper leaned back and remained silent. He sensed there was something still bothering his friend, but he wanted Ross to bring it out into the open without any prodding.

"Don't know, Ray." Ross leaned forward and looked at the Trooper. "Just seems awfully strange, doesn't it." It was not a question.

"Yeah, boy," was the simple response. Jackson watched as the man gazed out into the trees, seemingly detached from the outside world. He'd seen Ross take a psychological nose-dive before. It had been just as hard on Ray and Carol when Eevie died. They both watched as their long-time friend deteriorated before their eyes. Ray was well aware that it nearly killed Ross. The two had a few ugly confrontations during that testy period, some on the brink of getting physical. But then Maggie entered his lonely life. She was a God-send, and the Trooper loved her like a sister.

Suddenly, Ross woke up. "Ray?"

"Yeah, boy. What's up?"

"What if it wasn't a bear?" Ross studied his friend for a reaction. *Why am I doing this?* he thought.

Jackson smiled, and then the roar of laughter erupted from his thick throat. The humor lasted for only a few disturbing seconds when the Trooper finally realized that the Sheriff had been serious with the question. Ray coughed twice, playing down the outburst. "Ross, man, what the hell are you getting at?"

The Sheriff's mood remained solemn. "I don't know, but what if there was something else out there? Christ, look what it did to that man in there. You yourself admitted that bears don't do this kind of thing. And where's the body?"

"Yeah, Ross, but I was just ..." Ray hesitated, wondering where his friend was going. The Trooper didn't know the first thing about the animals. For all he knew it could have been a rabid bobcat.

"I don't know," continued the Sheriff. "It just doesn't add up. But, you're probably right. I'm just weirding out here. I've been up now for a good part of twenty-four hours without any sleep. Forgive me."

"Don't sweat it, buddy."

The two were interrupted by Mark Bennington. "The call's been made, Ross. Coroner will be out in about a half hour. Hey, Ray." He gestured toward the Trooper.

"Mark, good to see you again." They shook hands in front of Ross' tired face.

The Sheriff got to his feet. "Mark," he started, "we got us a big, bad bear running loose in that swamp. I don't know whether or not he'll come out again, but I want the word to spread. We need to tell folks to keep an eye out. This is something that we can't keep to ourselves. Just don't provide all of the shitty details. People up here are smart enough not to panic over this sort of thing. But he's killed once, and there's no reason to think he wouldn't do it again."

"Wow," was all the Deputy could say with a surprised look on his face.

Ray Jackson saw something building in the Sheriff's words that made him uneasy. Ross was acting strange as he searched for a truth that existed only in his mind.

"He's a mean sonuvabitch," continued Ross Pickett. "If somebody runs into that bastard, there's no telling what might happen." His voice grew stern as he stressed his next remark. Ross turned to face his Deputy, pointing a finger at his nose. "If you find any stupid asshole who takes it upon himself to go out on his own little bear hunt, you make an arrest on the spot. You clear on that?"

"Yes, sir. No problem." Mark nodded. He felt somewhat at ease now that the town was already aware of a bear's presence. At least he wouldn't receive the tongue lashing for sparking the rumor earlier in the day at Arlene's.

"Let the people know about this after I speak with Rachel Perkins." That was one visit he was not looking forward to. But it was necessary. He didn't want her hearing about her husband's death from anyone other than himself.

"Got it," replied the Deputy. "What are you going to do about this, Ross?"

The Sheriff thought a moment, as if he wasn't sure. But he knew exactly what his next step would be. "I'm going after it." That caused Ray to raise an eyebrow.

"Okay, Sheriff. I'll see you later. Seeya, Ray." Mark shook hands with the Trooper, piled into his car, and drove off. The two men now stood alone together, watching as the Deputy's lights disappeared in the trees.

"Ahhhh, Ross?" Jackson broke the silence. "How you figuring on finding that there bear? I know you're good in the woods and all, but there ain't gonna be any tracks to follow, and you ain't *that* good. That's a big swamp."

"You let me worry about that," he answered confidently. Ross had already started devising his plan. He would commission the Jones brothers and their blueticks. He'd heard them brag about their dogs before, and there was nobody better qualified to go on a hunt like this in the Amen. As much as he despised the idea, utilizing Frank and Jesse was his only option. Their payment would be the carcass. He figured it would be enough. "And Ray," he continued, "I'd like you to come along if you wouldn't mind." The Trooper looked stunned by the request, but Ross needed him. Although Jackson was not necessarily an outdoorsman-type, he had been trained to survive in nearly every form of terrain and climate. And Ross preferred not to be by himself in the middle of nowhere with Frank and Jesse.

"Are you sure we shouldn't let the DNR boys in on this, Ross? This is kind of their bag you know." Jackson had to question the legality of what his friend was proposing. It *was* a DNR matter and he didn't want to make waves between the two departments.

"Fuck the DNR," Ross answered angrily. "This is my problem and I'll handle it the way I see fit." He was determined now.

"Just wanted you to be prepared, my man. They may holler a bit if word spreads."

"I don't care, Ray." There were no second thoughts.

"Well, I've scheduled a vacation day tomorrow anyway. We haven't spent much time together lately ... so why not?" He shrugged his broad shoulders.

"Ray, do you think you can get your hands on three or four radios with good homing capabilities?

"Yeah, I should be able to manage that. Can I ask why? Are we planning on going our separate ways out there?"

"Naw," replied Ross, "I just have a feeling he might lead us right into the heart of that friggin swamp. I want to be in touch with the outside world just in case."

"Like in case we get our butts lost?" The Trooper smiled nervously.

"Yeah, something like that."

"Okay, Ross. If you don't need me here any longer, I've got some phone calls to make."

"Get going, Jackson." Ross patted his friend on the back and walked him to the squad car. "Give my love to Carol."

"Ha!" boomed the Trooper. "You ain't gonna wanna deal with that woman after dragging my black butt out of the house on a vacation day." Ray climbed into the vehicle. His massive frame barely fit.

"Ray ... one more thing," said Ross before the door shut.

"What's that?"

"Bring a big gun." The comment drew a nervous look from the Trooper. He smiled regardless. They decided on a time, and then Ray Jackson left.

***

The female rested from her journey. The night had brought success to her hunt and she savored in the victory. Ragged morsels of meat clung to the thick hair around her satisfied face. Her long tongue licked away some of those remnants caked with dried blood, allowing her to taste the sweetness of her special meal again. She had never hunted the hairless ones before. It was forbidden by the clan. But the meat had been more than satisfying. It had been fulfilling. The others did not know what they had missed for so long. The hairless ones were weak creatures and could be killed with considerable ease. And there were many of them dwelling beyond the boundaries of the lair.

The driving rage subsided when the hunger pains were gratified. She rested against the base of a tree, tired from the long trek back into the swamp. Her eyes closed, giving her peace of mind. But the death of her juvenile would continue to haunt her sleep. There was no dispelling the hatred that drove her. The small reprieve was short-lived. At one point in the night she screamed at the images in her head. Her roar sent the message that she would kill again until those visions were gone. She would survive to spite the others who had shunned her from their world ... and she would kill her enemies.

***

Tyrone Pullman finally located a gas station to his liking. It was a single pump beer store with a dimly lit parking lot. *Perfect,* thought the driver. No other businesses or homes in the immediate area. There was a dark trailer situated behind the store where Tyrone assumed the owner might live. He was running out of options with the gas gauge toggling the empty mark.

The Chevy pulled up next to the deserted pump and stopped. Tyrone saw a white man peep out the window to check on the new arrivals. He could also see flashes from a television screen against the shaded glass. He turned to his passenger who was preparing to open his door. "Wait a sec, G. I think it best if you stay put. I don't want no cracker recognizing your ugly face."

"Shit, Tye," replied Gerald, "these motherfuckers don't know nothin bout us." It was a subtle protest derived more out of habit than anything else. The somber tone in his friend's voice had not fallen on deaf ears. Gerald studied his partner and saw how tired he looked. Tyrone had been driving all day and into the night. "Okay, Tye."

Tyrone nodded, delighted that Gerald was finally showing signs of understanding their new reality. If anyone recognized him, who knows what might happen. He swiveled on his seat, unlatched the door and stepped out. The wave of cold air against his skin sent a stimulating rush throughout his stiff body. Tyrone bent over with straight legs and touched the cool asphalt, giving his hamstrings a good stretch. It felt good to be outside. He walked to the back of the truck, screwed off the two caps and inserted the nozzle into one of the orifices.

As the fuel began to flow, Tyrone glanced over to the window of the station thirty yards away. The white man inside was leaning up against a wall with his arms crossed. He pretended to watch the television screen, but Tyrone could see him sneaking a peek now and then to make sure that his customers were on the up and up. Tyrone figured the color of his skin was making the store owner nervous. Tyrone laughed inwardly at the display of ignorance. *Fucking redneck,* he thought. *Don't know nothin about me and you already think I'm gonna race outta here without paying.*

The nozzle clicked off. The first tank was full. Tyrone inserted it into the second opening and repeated the process. The chilly air caused him to cross his own arms. A breeze was building and a few snowflakes began to float out of the sky. Tyrone kept a watchful eye on the actions of the attendant inside. He formulated a plan in his mind should something go wrong. There was no other evidence of light in the general vicinity. He studied each direction of the road closely. They were alone. Had he been younger and the circumstances been different, Tyrone might have taken a crack at knocking off the little beer store. But those days were over. He hadn't taken money at gunpoint in years. He remembered the adrenaline rush from getting away with the crime. Although many of his brothers failed to escape capture at some point in their lives, Tyrone had managed to avoid getting busted. He had no criminal record whatsoever. Not even a speeding ticket. Tyrone was smart, and he planned on maintaining his clean status.

The pump clicked off again. Tyrone withdrew the nozzle and placed it back in its slot. He looked at the dollar amount. "Damn!

Sixty dollars?" The truck was a gas hog, but it had served their purpose well. He took one last look to the cab to satisfy himself that Gerald was out of sight. The passenger hadn't moved. Tyrone then casually strolled to the building, opened the door and entered to the sound of bells jingling on the doorknob. The man behind the counter did not change his expression. He looked the black man over from head to toe, like a butcher sizing up a piece of beef.

"Evening, sir," said Tyrone with a polite smile.

"Hmmph," followed by a curt nod was the unpleasant response.

Yeah, fuck you too, scolded the customer inwardly. But he simply smiled and walked on past the man, as if the rude behavior went unnoticed. Tyrone stymied his inner anger. It was clear to him that whitey's behavior would be the same wherever they went. *Fuck it! If that's the way they wanted it ... fuck it!* He walked to a cold storage unit filled with meat, feeling the perpetual stare on his back. He forced himself to remain calm. He would not fall to the idiot's level.

Tyrone opened up the cooler and grabbed a sampling of meat products. He took out some shaved turkey, roast beef, bologna, shaved ham, and a few turkey drumsticks. Cradling the chilled items in his arms, he then walked into another aisle and picked up three loaves of bread. Tyrone placed the groceries on the counter in front of the alert storeowner.

"Just a few more things, sir." Another smile, and then he walked to a different cold storage unit where he withdrew a case of Genuine Draft. He returned to the counter with the beer and four bags of Doritos. At first, the white man acted as though Tyrone were invisible. He stood motionless, staring at the final round of Jeopardy on the television.

"I got about sixty in gas, too." Tyrone reached for the large wad of money in his front pocket. The store owner turned and faced him with an expression that was still blank and cold. He eyed each item, ringing them up on the outdated cash register.

"Ninety three dollars and fifty three cents." Not even a hint of gratitude for the business. The white man just looked at Tyrone, mocking him for being less of a man simply because of skin color.

Tyrone put two fifties on the counter. "Keep the change, homes." He couldn't resist the slang just to make the man's skin crawl all the more. As the store owner was about to mutter a comment, a news bulletin appeared on the television. The man looked away from his customer to watch. A young anchorman's face came into view and he began to speak.

> "We interrupt the show in progress to bring you an update on the gangland style shootings that occurred just south of Mason earlier today. Three men brutally attacked a state prison van that had been transporting a drug kingpin to Jackson Federal Prison to serve out a mandatory life sentence for the murder of an undercover Lansing Police Officer and his family. Witnesses say three assailants forced the van off the road and began spraying the vehicle with gunfire. Both guards were killed in the gun battle, along with two of the assailants. Police say that one attacker apparently shot another in an execution-like manner. The prisoner and the unidentified accomplice escaped and have not yet been located. Police are urging anyone with information relating to this crime to contact authorities immediately. They are considered armed and extremely dangerous. The known fugitive is Gerald Johnson who committed the murders in Lansing last spring. If anyone recognizes this man, please maintain your distance. Once again, these men are considered to be armed and extremely dangerous. We now return you to your regularly scheduled programming."

Before the news bulletin cut away, Gerald's mugshot from the night of his arrest filled the screen. Tyrone was horrified.

Someone was bound to recognize Gerald if they remained visible. And then he wondered if the attendant had been able to see his passenger from the window. He watched the man closely as he stood with his eyes glued to the television screen. Tyrone tried to feel the man's thoughts through his body language.

The attendant turned, his face still brooding from the presence of a black man. Tyrone gazed into his eyes. They looked different. They were wider ... nervous. The man looked down at the money on the counter and finally picked it up. He punched a button on the cash register inducing the drawer to open. He then placed the bills in the proper compartments and extracted change. Tyrone turned away for a brief second and looked out the window toward the truck. He did not see Gerald's head through the cab window. *Awwww shit,* he thought. All he needed now was for the fugitive, whose face had been splashed all over the T.V. to come waltzing into the store.

Tyrone turned back to the attendant and froze. He was staring down the barrel of a large handgun. He heard the hammer cock back into firing position. The white man's face now displayed a smile, but he was frightened, too. Tyrone did not move. The man with the gun looked anxiously out the window to check on the passenger in the truck. Tyrone raised his arms, attempting to question the man's actions as if he truly did not understand what was happening.

"Sir? Is there a problem?" Tyrone tried to form a soothing grin.

"Shut up!" The man was incredibly nervous. Tyrone watched his finger caress the trigger. "Where's your friend?" he asked while scrutinizing his prisoner.

"I don't know what you're talking about. What's this all about? I just want some ..."

"I said shut the fuck up!" The man jammed the barrel of the gun hard into Tyrone's nose. I'll blow your goddamn head off right here and now!"

Tyrone believed him. The man was waiting for an excuse to kill him.

The storeowner backed away a step and retrieved a phone from underneath the counter where the gun had been hidden. He cradled the receiver between his shoulder and cheek and began to dial. He impatiently waited for the person on the other end to pick up. "Come on ... come on." The gun shook in his hand.

The report from the shot preceded the impact by only a millisecond. The store owner's lower jaw disintegrated into a spray of blood and bone fragments. As he was spun around from the hit, his gun discharged. Tyrone felt an excruciating pain in his left ear. Both men fell to the ground. As he clutched the side of his head, Tyrone could hear the man on the other side of the counter screaming in agony. He could feel his own blood flowing through his hands. "Fuck!" he cursed. He'd been shot. The ceiling overhead was spinning. He looked at the door and saw Gerald rush in holding the 9mm that had been stashed under the front seat of the truck. Gerald looked to Tyrone and then ducked as the loud report of another gunshot shattered the glass behind the door. He crept up to the counter, reached over and blindly emptied his clip into the floor on the other side. Spent casings peppered Tyrone's dazed face. He reached into his pocket, withdrew the .32 and tossed it to Gerald. The flopping sound on the other side of the counter told him that the attendant was still alive. Gerald checked to make sure there was a live round in the chamber and leaned over the counter again. Tyrone listened as eleven slugs silenced the white man for good. Gerald then turned to him with the smoking gun in hand. The smell of gunpowder was heavy in the air.

You all right, Tye?" Gerald leaned in close. "Take away your hand and let me have a look."

Tyrone let go the side of his head and saw the blood on his hands. He then noticed that Gerald was smiling. "What the fuck is so funny!" shouted the wounded man.

"Damn, Tye. That white motherfucker shot off half your ear."

"Awww, shit!"

Gerald helped him to his feet. He pulled a rag off the counter and applied pressure to the wounds. "Here, hold this."

When Tyrone stood he was overwhelmed with dizziness. He placed his hand on Gerald's shoulder to steady himself. His head throbbed.

"Guess we is even now, homes," said Gerald.

Tyrone thought about that statement. Gerald had just saved his life. But it didn't make them even, not by a longshot. Gerald was the reason he was in the mess to begin with. *No, Gerald,* he thought, *we are not even.* He stepped away from his partner and glanced around the corner of the counter. The white man's body was bent in odd angles in a pool of blood. Five slugs had found his legs and chest. His head was little more than a glob of hair and flesh. Then he saw the phone lying on the floor. He reached down and brought the receiver to his good ear. There was a voice on the other end.

"Hello ... hello." It was a woman ... a 911 dispatcher.

Tyrone yanked the cord from the wall. "We've gotta get the fuck outta here!" he cried. Gerald immediately understood why. Someone had heard the entire ordeal. There would be cops coming soon. Gerald gathered up the groceries and the two men bolted from the store. Since Tyrone was in no shape to drive, Gerald took the wheel with no argument and they squealed out of the parking lot. As they headed out into the darkness of the U.P., Tyrone could not help but ponder the consequences of what had just occurred. Did the dispatcher hear his name over the phone? Was there a camera in the store? If the cops linked the crime to Gerald, they would soon be scouring the area. His own blood and fingerprints were now at the crime-scene. Tyrone Pullman's life just became even more complicated.

Their first evasive action was to get off the main road. The cops would center their search there, and two black men would stand out. But Tyrone did not know the U.P. He had only memorized the direct route to Chicago. Regardless, he and Gerald would have to chance it. They would go by direction and take back roads.

"We need to get off this road, G", said Tyrone, sagging against the passenger window. He felt the cloth over his ear saturating with blood. "They'll be looking for us." Tyrone's voice was fading. His vision was blurred.

Gerald looked over to his friend and watched as he passed out. For a moment, he thought that Tyrone may have been dead. But he could see his breathing. Before Tyrone lost consciousness, Gerald was able to hear the last message. He saw the road sign ahead and turned north. They were going to have to hole up somewhere in order to give Tyrone some time to heal.

***

Joanne DeClerk heard each crisp shot echo through her ear piece as she sat helplessly in her chair. The dispatcher immediately relayed the emergency to all patrol cars near the scene as soon as she recognized the situation. Although the caller had not uttered a single word, she was able to make the trace. Once the shooting ceased, she listened as the two men conversed. Extensive training taught her to listen for every detail ... any clue as to the identities of the criminals. She heard a name ... "Tye." She scribbled it down on her note pad. Both men sounded African-American. She did pick up that one of them had been shot in the ear. That was written down as well. Joanne listened as the footsteps came closer to the phone. She spoke, attempting to provoke a response. But the line went dead. The men would be gone.

The dispatcher then directed the patrol cars to the store. Afterwards, she could only sit and listen as the officers described the discovery of the murder victim. Although she had heard it before, her heart always ached for the victims. She pictured families torn apart by such senseless tragedies ... little girls crying for fathers who would never come home again ... wives sleeping in lonely beds. Tears welled up in Joanne's eyes. The stress of the job was becoming too much for her. She found herself praying for justice to befall those who had just taken a human life. *And for what?* she asked herself. In the end, God would see them punished for their heathenistic ways. Joanne took off her headset. Her shift was over. She would go home to her family and love them.

***

Sheriff Ross Pickett collapsed into bed at three in the morning. His final stop that night had been to the home of Rachel Perkins to inform her that her husband was dead. Ross first picked up Trudy Benson, one of Rachel's close friends, to spend the night with her. He stayed about an hour at the Perkins home, allowing Rachel to cry out her emotions on his shoulder. Satisfied that she would be okay with Trudy at her side, Ross left and went on home.

Maggie demanded a quick synopsis of the day's events, so Ross obliged her. The doubts still hung in the back of his mind scratching at his conscience. The facts cried out "bear." However, there was another theory inching its way to the forefront suggesting that something else was out there in that swamp. As he shut his eyes that night, the claw marks reappeared in his mind. Even Dr. Blake had expressed his own intuition that Ned Crosby's experience had been anything but ordinary. Ross envisioned the old man staring up at him from his deathbed and the horror in his terrified eyes. And then there was Charlie Perkins. *Christ,* he thought. Sleep would not extricate the Sheriff from his anxiety that night. There was something unusual in the Amen Swamp, and Ross knew that he would soon face it on its own ground. Only then would he find truth.

Ross leaned toward the woman by his side. He caressed her smooth cheek with his callused hand and then prayed. For the first time in a long time, Ross gave thanks to God for bringing Maggie into his troubled life.

CHAPTER SEVEN

Beauty was a virgin snow on the birth of a northern Michigan sunrise. By daybreak, three inches of fresh powder had blanketed the western U.P. Farther north, Houghton and Marquette were slammed with an additional four. As snows accumulated across the region, the personality of the landscape changed from one stage of splendor to the next. The gentle, quiescent mark of white, combined with the turning colors in the trees, was an uplifting vision for the human spirit. The growing light in the clear blue sky sparkled off the fluffy snow as if it were a new beginning to life.

Ross Pickett felt invigorated by the scenic beauty of the hills as he drove the country roads on his way to Ned Crosby's that morning. The truck's heater had not yet generated enough warmth to prevent his lungs from exhaling clouds of steam. The eastern horizon glowed fiery red as the sun began its gradual ascent. Stars were still visible in the fading darkness, waiting for the sun's rays to wash them away.

Ross had been blessed with three hours of uninterrupted sleep. Although he certainly could have used more, a strong cup of coffee and a slap in the face from the dawn's cool air was enough to energize him for the day's events. He felt fresh and alive, ready to face the uncertainty plaguing him. The previous night's fears were replaced with enthusiasm towards the coming hunt. He cherished time spent in the woods, absorbing nature at its purist. The thought of tracking down the murderous creature that robbed Jessup of its town mechanic made the adrenaline pump through his veins. *This is my day,* he thought, glancing over to the .30-06 encased on the passenger seat. Today, he was the hunter.

It had been a far from perfect morning when he met Maggie in the kitchen prior to his departure. She was not so enthused with the idea of him venturing out into the Amen Swamp with the Jones brothers.

"It's a foolish idea if you ask me," she told him.

"Listen, Maggs," Ross answered, "it's my job and I'm not going to let someone else do it for me."

"It's not your job, Ross, and you darn well know it. The DNR handles these things. You should know better than anyone."

Maggie had hit a nerve. He knew that she was right, but there was more involved, and Maggie just wouldn't understand. "This is my town and those were my people! This is going to be my goddamned hunt!" Ross needed more support from his wife-to-be. It *was* his town and those *were* his people.

"Oh come off it, Sheriff. That's a bunch of bull and you know it."

Ross was somewhat befuddled by Maggie's conduct. It was the last thing he expected from her. He didn't need the grief that morning. "What are you trying to say, Maggs?" He stared hard into her eyes. "Do you think I'm incapable of succeeding?" *Nice one,* thought Ross as he tried to send her on a little guilt trip.

"Maybe I am, Ross!"

It was a stinging comment, one that could not be taken back. He saw her lack of confidence in him, and it hurt. "You still don't trust me after all these years, do you? You think that I'll go right back to the bottle and drink myself to death, don't you?"

Maggie just turned away and walked off into the bedroom. It had not been a pleasant fight. Both were injured by the others' remarks. Ross just figured it best if he left and allowed her time to settle.

The Sheriff steered the Tahoe into the clearing that still held Charlie Perkins' wrecker, a harsh reminder of the recent tragedy. The truck was covered with snow. Ross cringed as visions of Charlie's guts splattered on the cabin floor returned to him. The morning's serenity was lost.

A rusty Ford pickup truck was now parked next to the wrecker. It was the same truck that he had passed on his way out last night. Ross recognized the wooden siding protruding from the walls of the long bed. The tailgate had been removed to allow room for two homemade kennels sitting side by side. Each unit housed one very eager dog, both of which were alerting the owners of his presence. Frank and Jesse Jones stepped around the front of the truck when they heard the vehicle nearing. Ross studied the two men through the windshield, questioning his judgement to invite them on his safari. Mark had contacted them last night and told Ross that they both seemed anxious to run their animals. *Hell,* he thought, *they probably would have been out here running them anyway.*

The Sheriff watched as Frank Jones pulled up his sleeve and peeked at his watch. He appeared agitated. Frank's face was heavily bearded with a large bulge in one cheek from a sizable cud of chew. He chomped vigorously on the tobacco, working up the saliva until a steady stream of brown fluid spewed from his mouth. A small amount of spittle drooped from his chin. Jesse, the younger brother, also wearing a heavy beard, had a crooked grin on his face, exposing numerous dark gaps that had once been filled with teeth. Both men were lean and weathered from the outdoors. Their skin was tanned from the wind and sun. The Jones boys looked alike, thought alike, and even dressed alike, both wearing insulated denim coveralls faded and tethered from everyday use. Ross noted the blood stains, perhaps an indication of the previous night's activities. Each man had his hair tied back in a long ponytail. Jesse wore a camouflaged stocking cap while his older brother favored an old John Deere trucker hat.

"This is going to be interesting," Ross said to himself. He forced himself to smile as he exited the Tahoe.

"Nice ya could make er, Sherf," said Frank, blowing warm air into his clasped hands. "Jezzuz H., we wuz ready to git goin an hour ago."

Ross walked up to the two men. The pointed remark fell on deaf ears. He expected that type of behavior from the likes of them. "Well, Frank, sorry to keep you and Jesse there waiting, but I don't think an hour is going to make all that much difference." Ross knew he was late, but he needed the extra hour of sleep, and he wasn't about to let the Jones brothers patronize him for it.

It was Jesse's turn to speak up in a hoarse, throaty voice that only a mother could love. "This ain't no pettin bear we's chasin now, Sherf. This is a mean'un." His crooked grin was chiseled in stone, not shifting an inch even as he spoke.

These are two ugly bastards, Ross joked inwardly, while picturing each holding a banjo. "What makes you say that, Jesse?" He figured Mark must have filled them in with a few, unnecessary details. It was the one peeve he had with his Deputy. When backed into a corner, Mark was hard-pressed to hold anything back. He was weak, especially around that *piece of shit* Mayor. Ross had repeatedly told his Deputy that he should stand his ground when confronted by an aggressive personality. But he was still growing, and Ross' job was to coach him. Ross shivered, feeling the brisk air numbing his cheeks.

"We seen inside, Sherf," said Frank as he motioned toward the front door of Ned's cabin. "Nothin else ta do while watin fer yer lazy ass."

Nice dig, thought Ross. "Are you boys having second thoughts?" he chided, giving his own stab at their pride. A quarter of the sun now showed above the tree line. The snow wouldn't last the day. The temperature was supposed to reach fifty by mid-afternoon.

"Just want ya ta know what her up against, lawman," continued Frank in a less than friendly manner. "If dat fucker charges, I don't want no stupid sonuvabitch pissin his pants when he should be backin me up."

"You just worry about your dogs, Frank. I'll take care of myself." Ross scolded himself for allowing the man to scratch a nerve. He needed to find some common ground with those two in a hurry or the day would be a long one.

"Dat's what worries me, Sherf, you takin care of yer self. But as fer findin da trail, dat bear'll be leavin a fuckin highway. And when ma dawgs git on his ass, he's gonna take us inta dat hell swamp." The bearded man gazed into the trees that ascended down into the Amen.

Frank Jones painted a very realistic picture of the coming hunt. Ross knew his way around the woods, more so than most, but he also knew that he was outclassed by the two men gloating before him. He would never verbally admit as much in their company. The former conservation officer had dealt with bears before, but not to this extreme. His experience was limited to tranquilizing a few innocent blacks that had mistakenly wandered into a populated area and tore up some garbage cans. Never had he dealt with a man-killer. It just didn't happen in Michigan. He wasn't sure whether he should feel excited or frightened.

Ray Jackson's words stuck in his head regarding the legality of what he was about to do. Did he really have the legal or moral right to dispose of the animal? When he finally settled down after the shocking discovery of Charlie Perkins' remains, Ross did have a little time to think about potential repercussions from the environmentalist community. They would paint it as the destruction of an "innocent" animal that had unintentionally crossed paths with civilization. Word of his actions would certainly reach the general public downstate. *Well tough shit,* he clamored to himself. This was not your average run-of-the-mill bear encounter. If the "bunny-huggers" wanted to raise a fuss, then he would shove the Coroner's pictures of what was left of Charlie in their tender little faces. *Here, assholes, this is what your innocent little fucking bear is all about! This is my reason for killing the murderer!* Ross found himself hoping for a chance to do just that. He wanted to be the one to pull the trigger and put an end to the nightmare.

The Sheriff's self-debate over personal ethics ended abruptly when a blue Ford Ranger pulled into the clearing with Ray Jackson at the helm. Frank and Jesse looked at each other in disbelief as the big black man piled out of the truck and greeted Ross with his usual warm smile and hearty handshake. Ross led his bull of a friend to the two brothers. He was indeed a sight for the backwoods country boys. Ray was decked out in full battle gear from head to toe. He wore loose-fitting jungle pants and a field jacket with a hood that flopped when he walked. He toted an AR-15, .223 caliber rifle in his large hands, with a bandoleer holding five clips strapped across his bulging chest. Ross couldn't help but chuckle at his buddy's appearance. Although he didn't quite fit in with present company, he sure as hell lightened the mood. Ray Jackson made Rambo look like a cupcake.

"Jesus, Ray." Ross whispered into his ear with his back turned to Frank and Jesse. "We're not going to war today."

"Hey, buddy, I am ready to kick some black bear ass." The two men laughed aloud. "Sorry I'm late. Carol had a little goin away present for me this morning, and what a morning it was." Jackson gave the Sheriff a mild wink with his left eye.

"No problem, Ray."

Frank and Jesse continued to stare at the newcomer. “Holy crapper,” whispered Frank to his brother, “get a load of dat pisser.”

Ross made the formal introductions. “Gentlemen, this here is Trooper Ray Jackson from the Appleton State Police Post. He’ll be joining us this morning on our little outing.” Ross detected the disapproval in their eyes. “Ray, this is Frank and Jesse Jones, two of the best trackers in the U.P.” He added the compliment in an attempt to ease the tension.

Jackson extended his paw, but neither man took it. “What’s the matter boys,” boasted the Trooper, “ain’t you ever seen a brother before?”

Frank turned to his brother with a conniving smirk. “Ya know, Jess, I heered dat bears are partial to dark meat, eh.” Another brown stream of fluid gushed from his dirty mouth. It was the Jones brothers’ turn to laugh.

“Well boys,” answered the Trooper in good humor, “looks like you got yourself a nice prime piece of bear bait.” He turned to his friend. “You sure know how to pick em, Ross.”

The Sheriff simply lowered his head in embarrassment. This had not been a good start to his party. Before he had a chance to ward off any further damage, Frank opened his big mouth.

“What you mean by dat, boy?”

Jackson quickly pivoted toward the much smaller man. His facial expression turned to anger. He’d lived through enough bigotry and racism in his time. He’d been called all kinds of names, but the one label he absolutely could not stand was “boy.” His grin was replaced by a scowl. “Listen, you sheep-fucking asshole. Don’t you be standing there and calling me no boy or I’ll take your head off.” His finger was pointed at the unimpressed forehead of Frank Jones.

“Fuck you, boy!”

Oh shit. Ross caught Jackson by the arm and spun him around before he could advance on the instigator. The flustered Trooper shook off the hold.

“Listen to me!” shouted the Sheriff to his dysfunctional crew. “We don’t need this kind of bullshit today from either of you. We’ve got a killer bear out there and it isn’t getting any closer. If either of you wants to continue the crap later, that’s fine. But wait until the job is finished. Got it?" He directed the statement to all three.

Jackson relaxed. "Sorry, buddy." Frank and Jesse just nodded silently and then strolled back to their truck. Jesse opening up the kennels and fastened leashes to the collars of the hounds. Frank retrieved a large bore rifle from the cab and stuffed a box of shells into the front pocket of his coveralls. Jesse wore a Ruger .44 magnum holstered around his waist. He would be the dog handler. Ross walked back to the Tahoe and withdrew his own weapon, the Remington .30-06 Model 7400 semi-automatic, fitted with a 3x9 scope. The hunting party had more than enough fire power to dispose of one bear.

As Frank Jones chambered a very large cartridge into his gun, he called out to the Trooper. "Hey, gomer! You gonna shoot our bear wit dat pop gun ya got dare? Cuz if ya are, let me know where we can send yer belongins." Frank and Jesse roared over the joke.

Ray Jackson didn't say a word. His temper had already skyrocketed once to a dangerous level, and the two rednecks were at it again. It was time for a little lesson in northern hospitality. He pulled back the breech on the Colt and racked in a shell. He then calmly toggled the convert switch to 'full auto', pointing at the ground in a safe direction and squeezed the trigger. Snow and dirt danced on the earth as the rifle spit out thirty rounds in a matter of seconds. Jesse fought the taut leashes while the dogs jumped and retreated from the eruption of gunfire. Ross, whose back had been turned to the Trooper, nearly jumped out of his boots. When the smoke settled, Ray Jackson stood there grinning at the startled brothers, holding back a secret desire to shoot the bastards on the spot. "We'll see," he said softly.

***

Mark Bennington stumbled into Arlene's at eight that morning, tired from his own long night. He made his rounds as requested by the Sheriff, first spreading word to a few residents in town, and then visiting some folks who lived out near the kill site. Mark had knocked on twelve doors, disturbing most from their Sunday morning slumber. Four of those who weren't home were probably in town already for church, he guessed. They would learn of the previous day's events soon enough.

Mark's primary target was Birdy McIntosh. She played a crucial role in the Jessup grapevine. He knew that Birdie's job allowed her to effectively spread local gossip. Although she wouldn't be working that morning, the Deputy counted on her impatience to distribute a juicy story. Mark figured he could now tap the main pulse of the town at Arlene's. And besides, a nice big breakfast would sure hit the spot. What Mark didn't know when he entered the establishment was that the story had already ballooned into one barnburner of a tale. Locals were now talking of how Charlie Perkins had been eaten by a savage bear that was still on the loose.

Arlene was the first to notice him at the doorway. She waved with a dishtowel in her hand. Mark returned the gesture and then scoped out the café to see what faces he recognized. Fred Wentworth, owner of the Five and Dime that doubled as a smoked fish shop, was sitting with Erma Samuels enjoying a stack of pancakes. They had not yet detected his presence. Much to the Deputy's surprise, the café was not very busy during the breakfast hour. There were a few unfamiliar faces, too. Just as he was contemplating turning around to leave, the powerful voice of Gene Steubens exploded in his ear. The Mayor, who was sitting with John Talbert and Art Conley, had his back to the doorway, but when he saw Arlene motioning to someone he turned to investigate.

"Mark, my boy. Come over here. Talk to me, son." The Deputy's slender shoulders sagged. He walked dejectedly over to the threesome. The Mayor lifted his hefty frame from his chair to greet the young man. "Have a seat, Deputy. Please."

Mark sat down in the offered chair, knowing all too well that he was about to be drilled. "Morning, sir," he said, resting his head on cupped hands.

Steubens sat down next to him and placed his hand on Mark's back. "Seems we've had some trouble last night, huh?" said the Mayor.

Mark looked at his round face, questioning the legitimacy of the pleasantries. Surely he had something up his sleeve, anything to make him look like a fool. "We've got a bad bear running loose, sir. Apparently Charlie Perkins ran into it last night at Ned

Crosby's place. It killed the dog, too." Mark rubbed his fatigued eyes. He didn't want to participate in this conversation. Not now.

"Word has it that Charlie was actually eaten by a bear." The Mayor watched the Deputy's reaction closely.

Mark's eyes opened a little wider. "Ah ... well ... not exactly." He was careful with his response.

The Deputy's hesitation told the Mayor that there was something more to the story. "Well, what the heck happened, boy? There's this talk about a killer bear roaming the woods and nobody has come to me with any information yet. What's going on?"

Steubens was going off again, playing the all-important leader role. Mark found himself wishing that the Sheriff was there for support. Ross would have set him in his place. "Uh ... well," he sputtered, "Ross found Charlie's body last night at Crosby's, and ... uh ... well, it looks like a bear did him in." Mark noticed the other two gentlemen listening closely. He also saw Fred Wentworth approaching from the side. He was getting himself pickled again.

"Where's the Sheriff now?" questioned Steubens.

"He's gone after the bear with Frank and Jesse Jones. They were meeting at first light." Certainly that wasn't anything that should be kept under wraps. They would find out soon enough.

"So, our beloved Sheriff has put together his own little posse. Isn't that interesting?" Steubens looked off toward the far wall as if he were scheming.

Mark watched him. He could now sense Fred Wentworth standing directly behind him. He turned to greet the man. "Hey, Fred." Mark managed a tight smile.

"Hello, Mark. I heard about the bear. What's being done about it?" asked the storeowner.

"Pickett's out hunting down the animal with the Jones brothers as we speak," butted in the Mayor.

"Well, if anyone can find it, Frank and Jesse can," added Wentworth.

"If they can't, someone else certainly will run across it," Steubens interjected.

Mark quickly turned his attention to the Mayor. "What do you mean by that?" he asked.

"It seems that a few other interested parties have decided to go hunting as well after word spread through town. Some of the business owners have staked a little reward money."

Oh damn, thought Mark. *This is all I need. Ross will be pissed for sure.* "Who went out, Mayor? His voice expressed his building apprehension.

"I heard that Seth Jennings and his boy packed up this morning and trucked off into the Amen. Seth's a good man in the woods from what I hear. I believe there were a few others mulling over the idea." Steubens saw this as an opportunity to bring some free advertising to his town. He had already started formulating a marketing campaign. As the Deputy stood, Steubens' hand clutched his arm. "Where do you think you're going? I'm not done with you yet."

Mark shook off the Mayor's hold and zipped up his jacket. "You just don't get it do you ... you ... you jerk!" The words came easy for once. He was finally able to vent his anger toward the man who had continuously belittled him in front of the entire town. The Deputy's only wish was that the moment could have been conceived under other circumstances. Mark Bennington was upset, but he knew darn well that his feelings paled in comparison to what Ross would think.

Steubens sat in his chair, stunned by the sudden outburst from the Deputy.

"Do you realize what this bear has done?" continued an irate Mark Bennington. "It has killed people."

"What do you mean it has killed *people*?" asked the Mayor, quickly picking up on how the Deputy had pluralized the number of victims.

Mark cursed himself for running his mouth again. He had to end the conversation before digging a deeper hole. Mark turned and headed toward the door. All eyes in Arlene's Café followed his departure.

"You come back here, Deputy!" cried Steubens.

But Mark Bennington did not stop. He kept his back to the overpompous windbag and walked right out the door. He had to get in touch with Ross as soon as possible. Mark now understood the purpose for the walk-talkies that Ross had insisted upon. He trotted across the street to town hall.

***

The dogs were quick to pick up the trail at the steps of Crosby's cabin. Ross heard Jesse remark that it was unusual for a scent to be so strong after a new snow, but he eventually waved it off and credited the ability of the blueticks to sniff a mole out of a shit pile. The dogs were fine looking animals, thought Ross as he followed the brothers into the tree line. They were offspring from the finest bitch that ever ran the Upper Peninsula according to the oldest Jones brother. Both shared beautiful markings with toned bodies from years of running bobcat and bear.

The four men slowly fought their way through the tangles of the Amen Swamp. Jesse set the pace in front, holding tight leashes while the dogs struggled to advance. By ten o'clock, Ross felt his legs beginning to tire from the seemingly endless hump over the deadfalls and blackwater pits. The rifle grew heavy in his arms as he ducked under the cedar branches blocking his path. He already noticed a nice gouge in the shiny stock of the Remington. The braches were strong and sharp, and if he wasn't careful, he could easily lose an eye. But Ross felt confident with the weapon in his hands. The .30-06 was a powerful rifle that could knock down any species of big game in North America, or so he hoped.

The bear had no intentions of evading the protection of the Amen, just as Frank Jones has predicted earlier. The animal was luring them in a zig-zag pattern as if it knew it was being pursued. The blueticks had their noses buried to the ground. Occasionally they would lift their heads to scent the breeze. Ross knew the breed to possess incredible scenting instincts for the type of environment they were encroaching. He'd hunted behind talented bird dogs that would pattern themselves around the hunters. The blueticks, on the other hand, seemed to have minds of their own. They just continued to strain forward on the taut leather leashes, guided solely by their noses through the dense foliage. They would let out a howl every so often when a flash of strong scent filtered through their snouts. Ross asked Jesse when he would know if they were getting close. The dog handler scoffed at the question and responded by saying that "all hell would break loose."

Although the swamp was difficult to penetrate, the hunting party would intermittently stumble into a clearing that would give the Amen an entirely different appearance. It was during those merciful reprieves that Ross would stop and take notice of the hidden beauty that few had witnessed. The snow seemed to muffle all sounds, creating a peaceful, untouched aura. Only the baying dogs and a few agitated squirrels interrupted the pleasant silence. Rays of bright sunlight sliced through spotty holes in the umbrella of pines, yet underneath the false tranquility was a grim reality. *And here I am,* thought Ross, *chasing the thing on its home turf.*

The Sheriff's clothing was drenched with sweat, even though the outside temperature still hovered around the freezing point. Hunting was much more festive when there was game to be found. This type of chase was something else. He'd had easier workouts during the hot summer two-a-day sessions at Wisconsin. But the howling of the tracking dogs seemed to keep the adrenaline flowing just enough.

Ross caught sight of Ray Jackson maneuvering the terrain like a Seal on a recon mission. He carried his size with astounding grace. "How's ... it going, Ray?" he called to the Trooper between breaths.

"Fine and dandy," replied Jackson as he diverted his attention to a large stump in his path. He didn't sound the least bit winded. Ray performed a body roll over a heavy clump of rotting wood and landed skillfully on his feet, looking as if he were having the time of his life.

Ross stopped for a moment and reached into his fanny pack. He withdrew a Snickers bar, tore off the wrapper and took a healthy bite. His deprived body desperately needed the nourishment. The sugar would provide a boost of energy. Ross finished off the candy bar with a second bite and then took a few swigs of water from his canteen. He wiped away the spillage on his chin and then recapped the metal canister. He could see the others pulling away. The greatest danger of entering such a swamp was failing to maintain sense of direction. Ross never entered the woods without a compass pinned to his parka. He checked the heading ... due north. As he was about to move on he heard his radio squelch. The Jones brothers looked back, aggravated by the sudden halt to their progress.

“What da hell’s wrong wit you?” called Frank. “We gotta good scent.”

“It’s the radio. Someone’s trying to reach me. Just a minute. We need a break anyways.”

“Dat bear ain’t takin no breaks,” responded Jesse.

But Ross didn’t listen. He pulled the radio from his belt and turned up the volume. “Mark ... Mark, is that you?” The other three men took a knee.

“Ross ... Ross ... this ... Mark ... others ... there.” The reception was bad. Ross couldn’t make out what the Deputy was saying.

“Come again, Mark. A lot of static on this end.”

“There are some other ... out ... swamp ... after ... bear. Steubens ...” Ross did not need the Deputy to repeat himself a second time. The scattered message was now very clear to him. Word had gotten out and men were out there after his animal.

“Goddammit!” he cursed. *That dumbshit Deputy! I’m going to tan his friggin hide.* He brought the radio back to his mouth. “I copy, Mark. I’ll talk to you when I get out of here.” His tone told the man on the other end that the meeting would not be a cordial one.

“What’s up, buddy?” Ray Jackson had crept up behind him. Ross turned to his friend.

“That was my Deputy, Ray. It appears that some vigilantes might be joining us out here. Goddammit! I told Mark not to ...”

“Relax, Ross,” interrupted the Trooper. “That might work to our advantage. It might get the bear moving back toward us.”

“Ray, you don’t know how big this swamp really is, do you?” The Trooper shook his head. “Let’s just get moving. Maybe we can get the thing before it runs into someone else.”

The two men picked their way through some trees to where Frank and Jesse impatiently waited.

“Is yer little party over?” asked the younger of the two.

“Just get your dogs moving, Jesse. We’re running out of time.”

Jesse looked confused for a moment, but then heeded the Sheriff’s advice and sprang to his feet. “Let’s git, dawgs! Where dat bear at?” The dogs, sensing that the hunt was back in progress, shot forward and nearly yanked the handler to the ground. Jesse let out a wild “Yee-ha!”

The lack of physical exertion during the stop caused the Sheriff's body temperature to drop. The perspiration quickly turned cold, giving him chills. He had to keep moving and continue to hydrate. He also realized that the Jones boys would be more apt to just leave him lay if he were to collapse or get injured. He took another long swig from his canteen and set off after the others, shifting the weight of the heavy rifle to his other arm.

Up ahead, the baying suddenly grew more pronounced. One of the dogs really let loose. The other then followed suit when it too tasted the stronger scent. The dogs were barking wildly, dragging Jesse forward step by step. The handler had to lean back on the leash to hold them steady.

"What is it?" asked the Sheriff, fighting to catch his breath. The cold air burned his lungs.

"Frank stared at the hounds, studying them closely with his head cocked to the side. He nodded to his brother, who returned the signal. "It's him," he said softly, "and we're at his front door."

Ross thought that Frank was acting as if something had spooked him. He didn't understand the hesitation until Frank pointed to a tree at the edge of the clearing. The Sheriff followed the length of the trunk to a spot ten feet off the ground where the bark had been shredded. "Damn." It was the only word that Ross could think of to express what was going through his mind.

"Yeah," said Ray Jackson who stood by his side, "damn is right." There was uneasiness in the Trooper's voice.

"He's a biggin all righty," uttered Frank, peering off into the swamp ahead. His forefinger gingerly caressed the trigger guard on his rifle. "Bigger'n I ever seen."

Ross detected a nervous tension in the man's demeanor. He wondered if this was just Frank's way of tormenting his companions. But after examining his face more thoroughly, Ross decided that he had been telling the honest truth. The Sheriff's grip on the Remington tightened.

Jesse grabbed the blueticks by their collars and released them both. The dogs darted forward, howling at the scent. They understood the job at hand.

"Git em, Buck! Git em, Rip!" hollered the master after giving the dogs their freedom. The blueticks disappeared. The baying gradually drifted farther and farther away. The others followed in close pursuit.

***

The female heard the soft echoes of the animals far off in the distance. Initially, she thought nothing of the familiar sound. It was the season for the small four legged creatures. She had been taught to evade them because they hunted for the hairless ones. Lessons learned from long ago would forever be embedded in her intellect.

As the dogs came closer, the female raised her sloping head and sniffed the air. She was agitated. Never had they ventured so far into the clan's lair. But the howling persisted, coming closer and closer. She checked for wind direction. The female was angered with herself for making such a foolish mistake. It was an error that could prove costly. She had traveled upwind from the point of her kill, disregarding one of the most important lessons of all. For the first time in what seemed an eternity, the female felt vulnerable. Panic ensued. She was being hunted by the hairless creatures for what she had done. They were taking out their own vengeance. The small four legged animals would track her.

The female forced herself to calm and think out a solution to the problem. She still had the advantage. This was her domain and she knew how to move with stealth. The animals had to be thrown off her track. The answer would soon be delivered to her. She deliberately backtracked in the direction of the approaching animals. It was her only option. If she continued to run, they would pursue. She could stand and fight, but not without knowing the strength of the hairless creatures that were sure to follow.

***

Seth Jennings and his sixteen year old son, Bobby, heard the dogs. The elder Jennings realized the significance of the disturbance resonating through the swamp. There was a bear on the run. It was his bear.

"Come on, Bobby. Let's get after it," called out the father to his son. The two of them bounded off through the undergrowth.

Seth and Bobby Jennings had set out into the Amen Swamp after hearing of the two thousand dollar reward that the town had placed on the head of the bear that killed Charlie Perkins. Seth hadn't held a steady job in nearly three years. The thought of two thousand tax-free dollars in his pocket sounded pretty darn good. The Deputy said that the Sheriff had moved out with the Jones brothers and their dogs at daybreak. Seth knew the hounds would get the animal on the move. His plan was to put himself somewhere between them and the bear. Who knows, he might just get a lucky shot off and become two grand richer. There was a nice Jeep for sale in town that he had been eyeing.

Seth dragged his son out of bed that morning and hauled him off into the Amen Swamp where they spent the last three hours fighting their way through the dense cover. Young Bobby had done nothing but complain the entire way. He continuously lagged behind his father, clenching the .30-30 Winchester like a toddler holding a baton. Seth had to periodically stop and wait for his son, scolding the kid for his lack of effort.

"You get your butt in gear, boy," he'd yell, "or I'll bend you over right now and slap yer ass with a switch."

The threats were genuine, and really the only source of motivation for Bobby to continue the charade. He hated the outdoors. He hated guns. Bobby hated his father for bringing him to such a place. Seth Jennings was always trying to teach his son how to be responsible, typically with a beer in one hand and a sharp tree limb in the other. Bobby understood that he was an embarrassment in his father's eyes. They shared no common interests in life. Seth had wanted a son who would join him in the woods and kill animals. Bobby wanted a father who would share in his passion for literature and music.

"I don't know how the hell you could be my boy," was a phrase that his father often used. "We sure as hell didn't fall off the same tree."

Bobby Jennings could only sit, listen, and hope that time would pass by quickly to the point where he could eventually leave his home and see the wonders of the world outside. The Amen Swamp was by no means the world he craved.

The howling drew closer and Seth quickened his pace. His enlarged beer gut bounced up and down with each step. "Come on, boy!" he shouted. "We're gonna get us two thousand dollars worth of bear."

"But, dad," replied the son who was quickly tiring, "I can't keep up with you." He stopped momentarily, bending over and resting his hands on his knees. His father, after glancing back and noticing that his son had stopped, ran back to him.

"Now you listen to me!" cried Seth. Bobby erected himself and looked into his father's eyes. "You get your ass moving or I'll leave you out here!" A hand came out of nowhere and slapped the boy's face hard. Bobby's cheek stung from the blow against his skin. It wasn't the first time. "Now come on and act like a goddamned man for once." Seth turned and started off again. Bobby, with his feelings severely damaged, forced himself to follow. He ducked the limbs that whipped past his head.

The baying continued as Seth Jennings and his son closed the gap. Bobby kept pace with his father, his breathing heavy. He was physically exhausted. They struggled through a particularly thick stand of cedars and entered an open area feathered with tall sawgrass. Seth stopped when he heard the animal crashing through the brush ahead. He turned to his son. "It's coming, boy," he whispered. "Chamber a round and get ready. He's coming."

Bobby followed his father's lead and racked a shell into the chamber of the Model 94 lever action. He could hear the animal approaching, splashing through the water, busting through the high grass. His body trembled. He'd never been in this position before. Bobby wanted no part of it.

The bear was so close that they could hear its heavy grunts. It was running full tilt right at them, just out of sight.

"There," whispered Seth to his son. He pointed forward into the clearing. Bobby looked and saw the black object rising and falling above the brown blades of swamp grass. It was moving with terrific speed. He could see the water exploding as the swamp gave way to its massive size. Seth raised his gun. "Don't shoot till I say when," he said calmly, aiming in the direction of the charging animal.

Bobby held up his rifle and stared down the barrel with both eyes opened wide with fright. He had never in his life shot a living animal. He wanted to run and hide. He wanted to be home with his mother.

The bear was upon them before they knew it, firing out of the grass like a bull at a rodeo. “Shoot!” Seth yelled to his son, and then fired. The blast from his father’s weapon just inches from his head ruptured the boy’s eardrum. He released the Winchester and dropped to the ground, grasping the side of his head in pain. Seth’s shot caught the bear in the front shoulder, barely nudging the creature from it rampaging pace. The bear howled in pain, but kept coming, right for the man that had wounded it. Bobby rolled away and watched in horror as the beast tackled his father before he could chamber another round. Seth Jennings screamed in agony as two giant paws pounded on his caving chest.

“B ... B ... Bobby!” he cried. “Shoot ... shoot!” But the boy could not hear, nor could he move. He sat in a pool of frigid water, frozen with shock, witnessing the viscous mauling as if it wasn’t real. Seth gazed over to his son one last time before the bear clamped down on his skull and crushed it. He died instantly.

Sensing that the human was immobilized, the bear then turned to Bobby Jennings. It reached him in one lunge. The boy covered his head and then rolled onto his stomach as the weight of the bear landed on his back, pushing him deep into the thick mud below the waterline. He lay with his head submerged while claws sliced through his heavy clothing and ripped away at his skin. He turned his head from side to side, gasping for precious pockets of air. Bobby felt the blood spilling down his sides as the bear bit down on his right shoulder, crunching bones and tearing away at his flesh. The boy then screamed at the unbearable streak of pain rifling through his arm. The bear continued its savage assault, snapping down on his neck with vice-like jaws. Bobby’s last vision was the sight of a dog charging into the clearing and leaping toward the animal. When his neck snapped, he too was dead.

***

The baying of the blueticks tantalized the four men. Ross tried to distinguish whether they were ants discovering a picnic, or flies being drawn into a spider’s web. They stumbled and fell, trying to keep pace with racing animals ahead. Their exhausted bodies endured numerous scrapes and bruises. Ross felt blood trickling down his cheeks. The cedar limbs slapped against his face like steel wool. He envied Ray Jackson's panther-like ability to dodge the onslaught of obstacles as if they weren't even there. The Trooper was the only member of the party who hadn't yet taken a plunge to the swamp floor. Ross knew that Jackson had done this before, but back in those days his prey had been a different type of animal. Even Frank and Jesse exhibited weakness while sprinting through the difficult brush. All were soaked from head to toe.

Jesse would halt the charge every few minutes, put his hand in the air to silence the team, and then listen for the wailing in the distance. When the direction was noted, they would tear off again. For all Ross knew, they could have been running in circles. There hadn't been time to check for direction. The dogs would appear to be off to their left. Then, as if the earth had magically rotated, the baying arose to the right. The Sheriff had no choice but to have faith in the two brothers who guided him. His heart pumped in his chest like a steam engine.

Jesse halted the group yet again. He listened above the heavy panting of the tired party. The Trooper grabbed the back of his head and took in a deep breath. "Let your lungs ... get some ... air, buddy."

The Sheriff followed his advice. He recalled similar guidance from his trainers in college. It did feel better. His lungs expanded with much needed oxygen. He found himself wishing that he hadn't given up jogging. His knees were beginning to ache.

"Shhhh!" Jesse urged them to quiet as he concentrated on the changing pitch of the dogs. They appeared to be about a hundred yards out.

Ross' body flinched when a crisp rifle shot echoed through the trees. "Oh, no," he gasped. All four men stood together and listened to the ensuing screams of both bear and man.

"Who da fuck is dat?" chimed in Frank, irritated at the possibility that his prize might have been lost to another. "I'll kill any sonuvabitch who shoots dat bear."

Ross did not doubt his proclamation, but the next few seconds told the hunting party that the bear was alive and well. Another scream pierced the silence of the swamp. Ross' stomach churned. Another victim had fallen to the killer. Mark told him that others were hunting, and now they had chased the damned animal right to them. The Sheriff wanted to kill it ... now! He wanted to see it die in front of his eyes. Ross sprinted past the surprised men and hauled off after the creature, summoning every ounce of energy he could muster. He crashed through the brush, now welcoming the pain from the slashing branches.

Ross would fall, and then spring up again. Nothing was going to stop him. He cried out his fury. His lungs burned. The others lit out after him. It was Jesse who caught him first, reaching out in an effort to stop the futile charge. Finally, Jesse was able to grasp the Sheriff's collar from behind. He dove for the larger man, forcing him to the wet ground where they both landed with a large splash. Ross struggled to free himself from the scrawny but exceptionally strong redneck riding his back. His head was covered in black muck. The two men wrestled on the swamp floor until Frank and Ray appeared. The Trooper clutched his friend underneath the armpits and hauled him to his feet.

"Just what da fuck do ya tink yer doin!" boomed Frank.

Ross was shaking like an addict needing a needle. His muscles were tense. He was seriously thinking about taking a swing at the man who stood between him and his bear. "I'm going to kill it, asshole!" He wiggled his body free of Ray Jackson's grasp.

"You ain't gonna kill shit like dat!" yelled Jesse, who stood upright, wiping the muck from his own face.

"Easy, Ross," said Ray. "Just simmer down a bit. Those boys are right."

"We've gotta move, Ray. Goddammit!" cursed the Sheriff. "There's someone else out there!"

"Listen!" Jesse silenced the group with a wave of his hand. "The dawgs," he whispered.

They all stood a moment and listened as the barking evolved into a frenzied tirade. The battle ahead reverberated in and out of the cedars.

"Come on, I tink dey's got em!" cried Frank.

It took the men ten minutes to crawl through a nearly impenetrable thicket to close within fifty yards of the fight. They hesitated as a savage roar from the cornered animal split their eardrums. The dogs were badgering the animal, nipping at its rear while ducking the potentially fatal swipes of its claws. The peacefulness had exploded into pure pandemonium as the life and death struggle ensued.

Jesse huddled the group together and formulated the plan of attack. Ross suddenly felt fatigued. The emotional discharge had quickly drained his adrenaline. He mentally cursed himself for losing his head.

"Alrighty, boys," uttered Jesse in barely an audible voice. "Dawgs got em cornered. Dis here's da lass hoo-rah. We gotta git em b'fer he gits ma dawgs. Spread out bout twenty yards and keep an eye open. Dis bear's one pissed mother."

The four men formed a skirmish line with Jackson on one end, Ross in the middle and the Jones brothers taking up the slack on the far end closest to the bear. When they lost visual contact with one another, Ross suddenly felt alone. As he stepped quietly through the knee deep water, he pointed the muzzle of the rifle straight ahead. He cut in and out of the low-hanging limbs, knowing that this was the worst place to meet up with a bear.

The animals continued the viscous battle, now only twenty yards from the advancing men, but still out of site. Ross knew it was directly in front of him, somewhere in the shit, but he could not see any movement. He heard the bear bellowing with anger. The Sheriff's heartbeat quickened. The adrenaline that had been lost was now recycling though his pulsating veins. Sweat streamed down his blackened face, stinging his eyes. It would all come down to this one final stand. Man and dog versus killer bear. And man would win. Man had to win. There were no more doubts now. He was confident that they were doing right.

A high-pitched yelp stabbed his ears. A dog was down! The other bluetick persisted in its assault on the much larger animal. Then a shrill cry of pain erupted from the remaining hound. The commotion ceased. *Shit! What the hell do we do now?* Frank and Jesse were nowhere to be seen.

"He got ma dawgs!"

Ross heard Jesse off to his right, slightly ahead of him. He sensed the sorrow in the hoarse voice. Two close shots rang out. The first was a muffled ... *Pop!* It was Jesse's .44 magnum. The second was a thundering ... K*aboom!* The report of Frank's big bored rifle bounced from tree to tree.

"Comin yer way!" yelled one of the brothers.

Ross squatted into firing position, trying to see under the thick skirts of the cedars. His finger offed the safety on the .30-06 and probed the trigger. He had five shots and would use every last one. He could hear the bear crashing through the cover towards him like a herd of elephants. He steadied his aim on the approaching sound, cursing his chosen location. There was no room to shoot. If the bear broke through the trees it would be on top of him before he knew it. *Stay calm*, Ross told himself.

The animal came and then passed out of sight. Although it had only been a few yards out, he had not detected so much as a hair on its body. He dared not risk a blind shot for fear of hitting one of the others. *Damn!* "Ray!" he called off to his left. "He's coming to you!"

Ross then heard three short bursts of staccato gunfire spraying from the Trooper's Colt. The bear roared.

"Motherfucker!" cried Jackson. And then he screamed in pain. Ross busted his way through the swamp and fell flat on his stomach into a small clearing. The wind was briefly knocked out of him. When he finally raised his head, he was confronted with the morbid sight of the enormous black bear squeezing the life from his friend. Jackson's head was arched back. His hands gripped the thick throat of the creature to counter its snapping jaws. His legs kicked wildly at the bear's body. The animal was much too powerful for Jackson to hold it back. Its head lurched forward and clamped down on the man's shoulder. Blood spouted from the wound and the Trooper screamed again. His voice gargled and his eyes were wide with shock.

Ross grabbed the rifle that had slipped from his hands. Still lying on the ground, he leveled the cross-hairs on the animal's hind end. He couldn't chance hitting his friend. *Boom!* The gun jumped and Ross saw a clump of hair explode on the animal's thigh. The slug spun the bear sideways. Jackson fell from its hold and lay sprawled across a fallen log. He wasn't moving. The bear had tumbled onto its back and was clawing at the sky trying desperately to regain its feet. Ross looked toward his friend, wondering if he were still alive. Within seconds, the animal had bounced back up and began its charge on the new threat. It was only ten yards away. *Boom! Boom! Boom! Boom!* And then he heard the click of the empty chamber. Blood and fur spat from the fresh wounds. The creature staggered slightly, but momentum carried it closer. Ross' rifle was empty. The bear's progress had been slowed. It swaggered drunkenly back and forth on all fours. A bloody froth leaked from both sides of its chomping mouth. Red and white foam sprayed from the nose with each dying breath.

Ross couldn't move. His brain had cut off all functioning nerves that would allow him to escape death. He knew the beast was dying, but whether he would live to see it die was uncertain. With one final surge of incredible will, the great animal reared up on its hobbled hind legs. Its blood-stained head loomed eight feet off the swamp floor, wallowing from side to side with a violent passion. It was strange, but Ross found himself marveling at the enormity of the creature and its sheer power. They had tracked this animal into its home to kill it. And now he stood face to face with the monster. He could not blame this animal for the hatred it held for him. Man was the invader here.

The bear seemed to home in on the being that had caused it harm. Its gaping red jaws opened to reveal the rows of bone-crushing teeth ... the same teeth that had ripped Charlie Perkins to pieces. One final cry of dominance was unleashed, and that's when Ross Pickett figured he was going to die. He could only watch as it lunged for him.

The thunder exploded from behind. The bear's head snapped back as the body continued to fall forward. The animal was dead before its body thumped on the ground. A splash of warm blood splattered across Ross' electrified face. The bear's head lay no more than a foot from his own. A large portion of the back of its skull was missing from where the slug had exited. Ross lowered his head onto a clump of moss and closed his eyes.

"I got ya, you bitch!" hollered Frank. The elder Jones brother jumped over the sprawled out Sheriff to admire his prize.

"He's a monster, Frank!" Jesse joined the celebration, standing over the corpse of the huge boar. Neither man paid much attention to their two fallen comrades.

Ray! The realization that his friend might be dying brought Ross out of his fog. He pushed himself up off the ground, side-stepped Frank and Jess who were googling over their kill, and sprinted to the Trooper.

"Ray!" he cried as he sat down and cradled the man's head in his lap. He gently pulled away the torn fabric of the Trooper's field jacket to check on his wounds. Blood pumped from the gashes in Jackson's shoulder. Ross slipped out of his parka and ripped away the flannel shirt he wore underneath. He tied it snugly around the lacerations, converting it into a crude tourniquet. When he tightened the knot, a shallow moan escaped Ray Jackson's mouth.

"Stay with me, man! Don't you go dying on me now!" This was one death that Ross would not be able to handle. What would he say to Carol?

Jackson's eyes opened. They were groggy at first, but after a few seconds he was able to focus on the face above him.

"Don't you die on me, Ray," repeated Ross.

Jackson watched him with a feeble expression on his bloody face. A week smile formed on his lips. "Man," he gasped, "I thought ... you was never gonna shoot." The Trooper laughed and coughed at the same time.

"You possum-playing bastard, I thought you were dead," cried Ross with a soft smile of his own.

"Well ..." the Trooper coughed again between words. "I'd had enough of the homeboy. Figured it was your turn to wrestle with him." The two men laughed together, bound by a friendship that each cherished deeply. Ross held Jackson close. It was over.

Frank and Jesse stared at the pair lying on the ground. Frank elbowed his younger brother kiddingly. "Told ya dey like dark meat."

A lone black squirrel chattered high in a tree. Ross looked skyward to locate the small animal. He saw it perched on a limb, barking loudly at the clearing below. An uneasy feeling swept over him as he remembered the incident at the scene of Ned Crosby's accident. It seemed like a month ago. Ross searched the trees, sensing some strange presence. The lone squirrel was joined by three ... and then five more ... and then ten. They jabbered at the humans as if they had been caught trespassing. Ross reached for the sidearm on his hip. He was the only member of the party who seemed to take notice. Frank and Jesse concentrated their efforts on the task of skinning the dead bear.

And then, just like that, the chattering ceased and the swamp grew deathly quiet. The agitated rodents were gone, no longer visible in the trees. "Damn," Ross whispered to himself, "what the hell is wrong with this place?" Ray Jackson moaned in his lap. Ross looked down on his friend, the squirrels forgotten. He had to get the man out soon. He wanted to get as far away from the Amen as humanly possible. He wanted Maggie.

***

A short distance away, within sight of the clearing where the hunters rested, a dark, stump-like object sat in the middle of a deep pool. Only the tiny ripples in the water gave evidence that the object was not a stump at all. The female's head emerged with her heavy hide sagging from the wetness. The remainder of her bulky frame sat hidden beneath. She peered through the tangles of brush at the hairless creatures gathered in the clearing.

The female witnessed the fight with eyes and ears. The dogs had tracked her well into the swamp. Her initial intention was to lead them to a location that would give her the advantage for an attack. It would be thick with cover so they would spread themselves thin. First, she would kill the four legged animals to confuse the masters. Then she would pick them off, silently killing one while the others continued on unaware of her presence. But when the female crossed tracks with the bear, her mind devised another scheme. She traced the fresh tracks of the other creature, mixing two scents to confuse the pursuers. Her opportunity to separate from the bear's trail came when she encountered a stream. With one powerful leap, she was off the bear's track and standing in water. The female then backtracked up the creek. When they approached, she ducked underneath the water to shroud her own scent. The plan worked to perfection. The four legged creatures continued to follow the track of the bear with the hairless ones close behind. Now the female had taken the advantage. She was now pursuing from behind, and they knew nothing of her presence. She kept them in sight, studying their movements, waiting for the opportunity to present itself. Her massive body meshed with the trees whenever they glanced in her direction. She was invisible to their eyes.

When the thunder sounded, the female grew curious. She recognized the sound of the weapon. It had been used against her with little effect the previous night by the one she had killed. She had heard similar sounds when the weather grew cold, but never so close to the clan's lair. She shortened the distance, guided by her overwhelming curiosity. She listened with alert ears as the battle was fought. Instinct told her to disengage from the potential threat, but the need for revenge drove her to continue.

Their scent grew stronger as she slowly approached, as if their numbers had multiplied. There was death in the air. Then, as she crept even closer, the explosions seemed to erupt all around her. She hunkered low to the ground in an evasive posture and prepared for an assault.

The bear was on the run, attacking the hairless ones. At one point, she recognized that her curiosity had taken her too close. They had surrounded her position. To elude detection, the female slid into the pit and watched with her head just above the waterline. Again, she was invisible to their eyes. Her hide served as protection against the bitter cold temperature.

Through the brush, the female watched with interest as the bear charged out of the cover of the trees at one of the hairless ones who stood alone. It used the weapon, but the bear was not phased. It pounced on the defenseless creature. The female was learning. She watched every detail ... the defensive and offensive actions and reactions. Even the bear was able to easily kill the hairless one. Then, another charged out of the cover and fell to the ground. The thunder erupted again, this time louder than the first. The blaring noise momentarily obstructed her hearing. The sounds pounded against her highly sensitive eardrums. This hairless creature appeared to be more powerful than the first. The bear was in pain, but it continued to attack. Its pace was slowed when more of their weapons erupted. The female realized then that the bear was dying. She saw the wounds. But it fought to advance and kill. She admired its will. Another of the hairless ones appeared, and then another. After another clap of thunder, the bear finally died.

The female sniffed the winds, noting the familiar scent of their weapons. These were new lessons learned. The hairless ones were not as weak as she had thought. Although their weaknesses far outweighed their strengths, their power could not be underestimated. But this lesson would not detract from her ultimate quest for vengeance. It was all she had to live for. She would hunt another day, but not before she learned more about them.

A squirrel cried out in the trees high above. The female slowly tilted her head back and peered into the pines. More of them joined in, sounding the warning for the hairless ones. They hounded her. She wanted to scream and watch their puny bodies scatter. But that would alert her enemies who were dangerously close. The female slipped out of the black pool and slithered away into the quagmire. She had been careless to creep so close. Her safety was compromised. Light made her vulnerable to the hairless creatures. Only under the cover of darkness would she continue her mission. The squirrels could not detect her in the night hours. Neither could the hairless ones with their weak senses. The female retreated to her private sanctuary deep in the swamp, away from the clan that had once considered her one of their own.

CHAPTER EIGHT

Tyrone Pullman's fuzzy vision stalled his ability to ascertain where he was and how he had arrived there. Slowly, the definition of the small room began to sharpen around him. As he moved, the stabbing pain in his right ear quickly reminded him of what took place in the not too distant past. Tyrone attempted to sit up on the hard cot, but his spinning head produced a wave of nausea. He lay back down. He scanned the room and centered his eyes on something hanging over a fireplace. Tyrone squinted to bring the object into focus. It was a deer head staring down on him.

"What the hell?" The effort to focus caused an eruption of pain in his head. Tyrone closed his eyes and caressed the bridge of his nose. He wondered if death could deal such pain. Maybe, if that white man had aimed a few inches to the left ... the nightmare would be over. He felt the consequences of the last twenty-four hours throughout his body. His life seemed to be in an irreversible tailspin.

After a moment of quiet reflection, Tyrone conjured up enough strength to sit. He hoisted himself up on his elbows, allowing a few seconds for the surge of dizziness to pass. He was encased in an old, faded sleeping bag that smelled like mothballs. The air in the room was cold enough where he could see his own breath. There was nothing remotely familiar about the place. The last thing he remembered from the night before was getting into the truck and listening to Gerald ramble on ... something about backroads.

Gerald! Where is he? Tyrone's head swiveled around and saw that he was alone. He brought his hand up to shade his eyes from the bright sunshine gleaming through a window. Tyrone figured that he must have been out for some time. He reached up to his wounded ear and gently felt the tender area. The side off his head was plastered with strips of gauze held together by some sort of tape. The fabric was dry, which meant the he was no longer bleeding.

Once again, Tyrone looked about the interior of the rustic building and decided that it was some form of cottage. There was a sleeper bed pulled out of an ancient couch with a few loose sheets and blankets strewn over the top. He assumed that Gerald must have slept there. Again, he glanced up to the deer head peering down on him. He shook his head. Tyrone hated animals.

The wounded man forced his legs off the side of the cot. His feet, still enclosed in the sleeping bag, settled on the shag carpeting that looked as if it hadn't been washed in a decade. *That's some ugly shit,* he thought as he studied the pea-green coloring. It took a few more minutes for him to will his body to stand. When he did, his knees wobbled briefly under the weight of his body. Tyrone let the smelly sleeping bag fall to the ground. He then stepped out of it completely and took a deep breath, allowing the musty air to fill his lungs. The aroma of pine trees was strong. He noticed the Klashnikov propped up against the far wall next to the open doorway. Gerald must have put it there for a reason. The 7.62x39mm Assault Rifle was Tyrone's weapon of choice. He had three back home in Flint, all fully automatic. They were expensive, but well worth the money. He started wishing that he would have brought the others with him.

A noise from outside caught his attention. It was a melodic whistling sound ... a familiar tune. The name of the song was on the tip of his tongue, but he couldn't quite grasp it. He remembered it being something from his childhood. Gerald Johnson provided the answer as he waltzed through the doorway with an armload of wood.

"Zippity do dah, zippity day, my oh my, what a nice fucking day." A few pelvic gyrations and deep bass blasts were tossed in to taint the tune with a touch of hip-hop. "Hey, buddy!" he shouted. "How we feeling this morning?"

Tyrone watched curiously as Gerald walked to the fireplace and deposited the load of wood into some sort of holding device. He then brushed the bark from his hands as if he had performed the chore a hundred times before. Gerald was smiling and carrying on like everything was fine and dandy in the world. But that was the reality of Gerald Johnson.

"Where we at, G?" asked Tyrone.

"I don't know where the fuck we is, man. I do know that nobody gonna find us here."

Tyrone walked to the doorway and stared into the forest that crept to within twenty yards of the front porch. He listened to the gentle breeze stirring the branches. There were no cars, trucks, or sirens. It was nice. But not knowing where his feet were planted was discomforting. Tyrone was a man who required control over his environment. All control had dissolved when a slug from the storeowner's gun had ripped off half his ear. *But maybe Gerald had done good,* he thought. After all, he didn't wake up in a cell. He looked at his partner. Perhaps he *had* misjudged him.

"Do you have any idea where we're at, G?"

"Not really, Tye. I just did like you said last night and ditched the main road. Drove backroads for about an hour. Then this dirt road turned into a trail. Fuck, man, we are so far out in the sticks, ain't nobody gonna find us." Gerald closed the door. "Damn, if you ain't one heavy motherfucker. You was out cold all night and I had to carry your sorry ass all over hell. I hid the truck down a little hill out back. Nobody's gonna see it, not even from the air. Now, I'm gonna git a nice warm fire burning and have some suds."

Tyrone sank down into a torn recliner and kicked up the foot rest. It felt good to relax. Holing up for a few days would give him some time to heal, and hopefully regain some of that control. Tyrone figured that he might as well make the best of their current situation, but he wished they had brought some weed. He watched Gerald stoke up a fairly decent flame and then retire to the sofa with a Genuine Draft in hand. Tyrone felt like getting toasted himself, but he knew his stomach wouldn't settle much for beer. He sank back in the chair and shut his eyes. The half of his right ear that was still attached to his head pulsated with each heartbeat.

***

Ross Pickett slept in until ten on Monday morning. His muscles and joints ached from the strenuous romp through the Amen. He didn't get home until midnight after spending five long hours with Ray up at Houghton General. Maggie picked up Carol in Appleton and met him in the waiting room. The Trooper's wounds necessitated immediate surgery. Thankfully, when the procedure had ended, the Doctor informed the worried trio that the former Seal should be fine in five to six months. He had been extremely lucky. It was originally feared that Ray might lose partial use of his left arm as the result of extensive damage to the tendons and ligaments. But after a lengthy reconstructive procedure, all signs pointed in the positive and a full recovery was the prognosis. The Doctors did tell them that the rehabilitation process would be difficult. That didn't bother the Sheriff. Ray Jackson was a fighter, a trained professional, a man who had battled far worse odds. The jagged scars from the ninety-three stitches would give the Trooper something to brag about one day.

Ross' idea to pack the radios had saved Ray's life. After raising the State Police post in Appleton, a rescue chopper was dispatched to the swamp. The Troopers were quick to respond after realizing that one of their own was in peril. The airmen homed in on the beacon signal after the Sheriff provided the pilot with general coordinates. Ross then popped a canister of smoke when he heard the rotors in the distance. With no room to land, Jackson had to be hoisted in a caged stretcher. The Air-Med team then whisked the fallen Trooper away to the north, leaving Ross behind to search for and identify bodies of unseen victims.

Frank and Jesse had to be persuaded with two hundred dollars each to leave their previous prize for even a short period of time. The bear was gold in their eyes and they didn't care much for the idea of another staking claim to their kill. But the search lasted only twenty minutes. All they really had to do was walk back the wide path created by the bear as it had charged from victim to victim.

It was actually Ross who first stumbled onto the bodies of Seth and Bobby Jennings, lying in the dark water only yards apart. His heart sank when he recognized the pair. As Ross looked into the dead eyes of young Bobby, he could see Chuck's reflection. The boys were about the same age, and Ross had known Bobby quite well from town. The kid used to stop in the office and gawk at the police equipment, most likely to escape the threats of his belligerent father. *He was a nice enough kid*, thought Ross. It was such a waste of a promising life. The Sheriff chastised himself for failing to prevent the tragedy. His job was to serve and protect, and he had botched it miserably.

It took both Jones brothers to haul Seth Jennings to the clearing while Ross cradled the body of the teenager in his arms and carried him out. Ross' conscience would not find forgiveness. If he hadn't started his personal crusade perhaps the animal would have simply drifted off into obscurity ... and Bobby Jennings would still be alive. The guilt would reside inside him for a long time. In the past, he would have fought off those demons with the aid of the bottle. But that was the past. The new and improved Ross Pickett was forced to face the disturbing truth head on.

Frank and Jesse remained in the swamp to claim the hide and head of their trophy. The meat would be left to the coyotes and other scavengers roaming the Amen. The two woodsmen chose to make their way out on foot while Ross hitched a ride with the second chopper. He accompanied the two fresh corpses wrapped loosely in blankets. As he hung in the harness suspended over the canopy of trees, Ross wondered how such a place could look so beautiful from above, and be so brutal and unforgiving below. The day's victory had been bittersweet. He had entered the bowels of hell and walked out alive with his purpose attained. But the list of victims had grown longer that day.

The faces of the dead mercifully absconded from his slumber during the night. When Ross finally opened his eyes on Monday morning, the sun was halfway to its midday roost, but the blinds were closed tight preventing the day from penetrating the room. He figured that Maggie must have shut them to allow him more time to sleep.

Other than the typical aches and pains, the Sheriff felt surprisingly sound considering the workout he'd endured. The scratches covering his swollen hands and face served as a quick reminder of where he had been. It was not going to be an easy day, let alone an easy week for Ross Pickett. There would be funerals to attend. He guessed that the rumors would already be thriving in town. Amidst all the scuttlebutt would be an onslaught of queries, possibly doubting his judgement. Ross would have to face his peers like a possum playing chicken with a semi. He just wished the semi would swerve. He wondered how the locals would really perceive his actions. Would there be praise or blame? If he had the power to go back in time, would he have done things differently? His head was muddled with thoughts.

After dressing in jeans and a flannel shirt, Ross walked barefoot to the kitchen where he was greeted by a barrage of questions from a curious teenager. The Sheriff satisfied the boy's interest to the best of his ability, leaving out those details too gory for an adolescent's ears. Also missing from the abbreviated tale was the terror he felt when finally confronting the killer. Certain tidbits of information would forever be sealed in his personal vault. Even Maggie would be hard-pressed to unlock that door.

Maggie sensed that there were other things bothering her man. Ross sat at the table for a good part of an hour, stirring his untouched coffee as his eyes stared blankly at the cream making a spiraling pattern. He didn't talk, nor did he observe the newspaper on the table. He didn't even question why Chuck was home on a Monday morning. The high school was conducting parent-teacher conferences. Maggie knew Ross Pickett better than anyone and she could see that there was a battle ensuing in his thick head. Yesterday's spat before his little escapade was more or less forgotten. Neither wished to rekindle the argument, so they carried themselves as if the conversation never happened.

Maggie was hurt by the fact that Ross would not share his feelings. She realized he had experienced a form of trauma that she might not be able to comprehend. But Maggie wanted in regardless. She had already plucked him out of the gutter once. Maggie didn't know if she possessed the willpower or the character to do it all over again, and that truly frightened her.

Maggie pulled a meatloaf casserole out of the oven that was intended for Rachel Perkins. She was finally alone with Ross after Chuck had gone into the living room to watch T.V. Feeling that his silence had lingered long enough, she spoke out. She had to get him out of the house and maybe wake him up a little. "How about some breakfast at Arlene's?" She gently touched his neck.

"Huh?" Ross jumped a bit, as if he hadn't even known she was there.

"Come on, babe. Let's get out of here for a while. I'm buying."

"Oh, I don't think so, Maggs. I'm still sort of tired." The Sheriff fiddled with a spoon between two fingers.

"Come on, big boy. Get your butt off that chair. We're going into town." Maggie Barnes would not be cheated. She tugged kiddingly at his armpits. Ross smiled. *That was a positive sign*, she thought.

"Alright. You're a strong little wretch, aren't you?" He stood and faced her.

"Yeah, and I'll deck you right in the nose if you don't bow to my every whim." She curled her fist in jest and stuck it in front of his face.

Ross laughed and pulled her close to him. He stroked her wavy, brown hair. "I love you, Maggie Barnes. You have no idea how much I love you."

"I do know, Ross," she replied as their lips met.

***

Sergeant Jack Berkowski of the Michigan State Police looked on as the Coroner's black station wagon rolled out of the parking lot. Cars along Highway 2 rolled slowly on by as passengers gawked at the five police cruisers stationed in front of the store. Berkowski had been at the crime scene for two hours with his fellow investigators, collecting the many bits and pieces of evidence. This was a strange one in his experienced eyes. There were too many anomalies suggesting a grander story than a mere robbery.

"What went down here, Berky?" Trooper Samantha Godson joined her supervisor at the door. She had just arrived with her partner for the day, Mike Johanson.

"I don't know, Sammy. It's peculiar. Things just don't add up." The Sergeant surveyed the interior of the building. He closely examined the gelling pool of blood behind the counter where the victim's body was found. There was more blood in lesser amounts on the floor directly in front of the counter.

"Looks like a simple robbery-homicide. What's got you all flustered?" inquired the newcomer to the scene.

"Well," continued Berkowski, "for starters, it doesn't look like any money was taken from the till. Heck, there's over two hundred bills in there. If I were robbing someone out in the middle of nowhere like this, I don't think I'd leave the cash. The drawer was wide open."

"Well, maybe the perp panicked, or maybe someone drove by and saw what was happening."

The Sergeant turned to Godson and pointed toward the front of the counter. "See that blood there on the floor?"

She followed his finger. "Yes, so what?"

"We've got one .44 magnum behind the counter with the victim. Two shots were fired from his gun. We're assuming that's the perp's blood there in front of the counter." He pointed to the red splatters and then continued. "We found thirteen 9mm casings and eleven .32 casings over in that general area."

Godson walked up to the dried blood splashed on the floor, careful not to disturb the evidence. "Any prints?" she asked as her eyes studied the area.

"All over the counter. No match yet."

"What else?" Godson was now searching for something that the others might have missed.

"The victim was shot from the side. And the shot came through that window there." The Sergeant pointed to the small hole in the large storefront window. "Blew his lower jaw clean off. It looks like it was a hollow-point. Now this is where it gets interesting."

"Why's that?" asked the female Trooper, now examining the tiny hole.

Berkowski continued. "I don't know how he did it, but the victim was able to dial 911. Even though he wasn't able to talk to the dispatcher, the gal was able to hear everything that happened ... the gunfire, and then voices from what she believed to be two men."

"Two? Any names?"

"She heard one ... 'Tye' something."

Godson did some vocal calculations. "Tye ... Tye ... Tyree ... Tyus ... Tyrone?"

"Possibly," responded the Sergeant. It was the same name he had guessed. But the name meant nothing at this point in the investigation.

"Okay, we have a possible first name. Now what?" This was Godson's first homicide and she was eager to prove her competence.

"Well, the dispatcher believed the two men to be black."

"If that were true, then we shouldn't have much trouble locating them."

The comment drew a curious look from the superior. "I hear what you're saying, Sam, but be careful with that. We don't need to start a witch hunt." Berkowski had seen it happen before. A crime occurs, and the minorities are the first to be scrutinized. But times were changing ... for the better. People were changing.

She nodded, accepting of Berkowski's criticism. It was a dumb thing to say. Wearing the uniform brought on many forms of added responsibility. "Sorry, Berky. I'm just trying to put the pieces in place."

"Okay, we presumably have a man standing in front of the counter here." Berkowski positioned his body in front of the counter, sidestepping where spots of blood had been circled with chalk. "The victim shoots, and then gets shot himself from someone outside the building." He formed his fingers into a gun and pretended as if he were firing shots. "Why would the victim shoot in the first place?

Godson didn't have an answer for him.

"Perhaps the victim perceived that he was in danger."

"Do you think he got jumpy just because the assailant may have been black?"

The Sergeant didn't particularly agree with that explanation. He found it hard to believe that a man would pull a gun on another simply because of the color of his skin. There had to be something else. He had served fifteen years in the Upper Peninsula and had never encountered a race-related incident where firearms were involved. The victim must have had a reason. "Let's look at it from another angle, Sammy," he continued. "Let's say that these two men came here for gas, and maybe something to drink, eat ... whatever. Let's just say they were customers. One stays in the vehicle outside while the other comes inside to pay for whatever it is he's purchasing."

"Go on." Godson showed her undivided attention.

"Okay, now let's say the victim recognized the customer." Berkowski scratched his chin as he thought out the problem.

"What do you mean, like on '*America's Most Wanted*' or something?" joked the subordinate.

"Hey, Sammy, I've heard of crazier stories. The television *was* on." Berkowski motioned toward the T.V. sitting idly on a shelf behind the counter. One of the policemen had turned it off earlier. "The man works out here and lives out here. What else does he have to do between customers?" He didn't let on, but the very show that Godson mentioned had crossed his mind.

"Good point," she conceded. "Go on."

"Now, the victim recognizes the customer as someone who is a *bad guy* for whatever reason. The customer's partner see's the activity unfolding inside, sneaks close, and drops the man with a shot through the window. As the victim is shot, he then fires his own gun, hitting the man at the counter, hence the blood on the floor there." Berkowski then walked to the door. "The outside shooter comes into the store to help out his buddy." He returned to the counter. "The owner, still alive, manages to pop off another round. The first shooter and his accomplice unload their clips, one with a 9mm and the other with the .32, and kill the man." The Sergeant pretended to hold his hand over the counter and shoot to the ground on the other side. "The two perps take off ... end of story."

"Guess that's why you're the boss, eh," responded Godson, displaying her admiration for the Sergeant's well-honed skills.

"I've been at this a long time, Sammy." He smiled, acknowledging the flattery. "It's just speculative for the time being."

"But it's a start. Now we just have to figure out who those two men were."

Godson's partner, Mike Johanson, had wandered in after snooping around the pumps. He listened quietly as Berkowski presented his unproven theory. He too was an admirer of the man's talent for deductive reasoning. He could put together a jigsaw puzzle blindfolded. But when the Sergeant finished, it was Johanson who inserted the final piece. He immediately correlated the evidence with the story that had been humming over the airwaves for the past twelve hours. It all fit together. "Sergeant?"

"Hi, Mike." Berkowski turned to the Trooper. "Didn't see you come in. What's up?"

"I was just listening. I have an idea of my own."

"Well, what is it son? Speak up."

Johanson now had his Sergeant's full attention. "You've heard about that highway shooting downstate, right?"

"Yes, of course. What about ..." Berkowski's sentence trailed off as he contemplated what the Trooper had said. *Could it be?*

But why would they come north? "What makes you think this is related, Mike." Berkowski needed more than a guess.

"First of all," began the ardent young man, "we don't have too many ...," he hesitated a few seconds and then continued "... men of color." Johanson winced, wondering if he would be reprimanded. When Berkowski didn't change his expression, he relaxed and continued. "Secondly, you mentioned that maybe the store owner recognized the face of his customer. The prisoner who escaped near Jackson ... well, his picture has been plastered on every T.V. from here to Detroit. My wife and I were watching last night and saw it on the news." Now it was time for Johanson to bring it home for his captive audience. "What if the store owner placed that face on his customer, or the customer's partner?"

Damn, thought the seasoned veteran, *the kid is making sense.* It would certainly explain why a gun was pulled. But he had to be sure before issuing an all-points bulletin throughout the U.P. The two rookies looked on as their Sergeant strolled out of the building. They followed closely in his footsteps.

"Tom!" hollered Berkowski to a county Deputy who was just about to get into his squad car.

"Yeah, Berk?"

"Anyone check to see if he had any kind of surveillance equipment?"

The Deputy scratched his head. He, like Mike Johanson and Samantha Godson, was fairly new to law enforcement, and he certainly hadn't received the same level of training that the State Police give their cadets down at the Lansing complex.

"Heck, I don't know," he finally said.

"Come on, boys and girls," uttered Berkowski to his flock of students. "Let's go inside and have a look-see." All three officers trailed the older, experienced man back into the store like pupils preparing to receive the day's lesson. In many ways, Jack Berkowski's role *was* that of a teacher, providing wisdom that would further their careers. And he enjoyed playing the part very much.

The quartet gathered beside the counter. Berkowski scanned each wall carefully, first searching for the obvious, like monitors or a camera. He then looked for hidden devices. When nothing jumped out at him he pointed to the far wall. "Mike, go check out that wall. Look behind the pictures, anywhere. Look for a camera. With luck, we had a paranoid victim."

Mike Johanson did as he was told. The others were directed to do the same on opposite walls. Berkowski stepped behind the counter and studied the area closely. Although there were no cameras in plain sight, he knew that the latest in video surveillance technology saw cameras on the market with lenses no bigger than the tip of a pencil. If there was such a device, it could be anywhere. Berkowski felt underneath the counter for an activation switch. His hand roamed over a tiny button. After bending down to examine it further, he found the button taped against a piece of wood trim. Attached to the button was a wire that ran the length of the counter. Berkowski followed the wire until it disappeared into a piece of drywall, all hidden from plain site.

Interesting, he thought. *Now where do we go from here?* He looked at a narrow section of molding between the seams in the drywall in the ceiling. The Sergeant hopped up on a chair. He withdrew a small folding knife from his pocket and began to pry away at the molding. After loosening one end, he replaced the knife and gripped the wood between two fingers. The molding pulled away easily, exposing the concealed wire underneath.

Berkowski then traced the wire all the way to the back wall where, once again, it ran into a tiny hole. The other officers noticed his peculiar behavior and joined him again at the counter. Berkowski deduced that there must be some sort of camera on that back wall, most likely mounted with a wide angle lens to scan the entire store. The owner rigged the unit so he could activate it at his discretion. If they were lucky, the man had turned it on before he was shot. The Sergeant jumped down off the chair and proceeded to turn over the pictures of all shapes and sizes. Then he came to a large Budweiser mirror with a big buck etched on the glass. *Bingo!* It had to be it. Berkowski carefully removed the frame from where it was hanging and revealed a cut-out compartment in the drywall. Inside the small cubbyhole was a video monitor with a blinking light. It was a signal that the battery was low.

***

Ross and Maggie summoned Chuck and herded into the Tahoe for the trip into town. Maggie held the casserole in her lap. They would deliver it to Rachel Perkins following breakfast. There would be a steady stream of townsfolk following in their footsteps. Some might degrade small towns for one reason or another, but when someone was in need of help from a neighbor there was no place you'd rather be.

When Ross turned down Main Street he saw Julie Whitaker and Kyle Roaker preparing to hoist one of the banners for the upcoming Rutt'n Buck Festival. They both waved to the familiar truck. Ross offered a lethargic salute in return. "Nice timing for a festival," whispered the Sheriff under his breath. He wondered how they could actually go through with the damn thing after all that had happened.

"What's that, hon?" Maggie heard a few murmurs from the driver.

"Oh ... I don't know. It's just that festival ... and this bear thing. It doesn't fit. What will those families think?" He looked to his woman.

"Well, Ross, maybe the town needs this. A tangent can be a good thing sometimes. Take their minds off things."

"I don't know." Ross was dangerously close to whining. "I just don't think it's very respectful is all. Those people need time to mourn."

As Ross continued down Main, he noticed a large gathering at the steps of Town Hall. People were huddling around some dark object stretched out across the cement steps. Mark Bennington's squad car was parked directly across the street. The Deputy was speaking with a rather rotund gentleman who appeared to be jotting down notes on a scratch pad.

Ross then noticed another man, a stranger standing by himself away from the crowd. He stood next to an old V.W. van with Montana tags. *You're a little ways from home, buddy,* he thought. There was something peculiar about the man, as though he did not belong. Ross judged him to be somewhere between thirty-five and forty. He wasn't big, nor was he small ... just average in height ... tough to pick out of a crowd. He wore faded, denim jeans and a leather bomber-style jacket. His jet-black hair was shoulder length and graying at the sides. The man's lightly bearded face appeared cold. *Hell, you're from Montana,* thought

Ross. *You should be used to this weather, my friend.* For whatever reason, he was not partaking in the commotion across the street. The stranger just stood there, alone, watching the activity like a referee quietly judging a sporting event. His eyes were hidden behind a set of mirrored Ray Bans that followed the Tahoe's progress as it rolled on by. The man gently nodded in Ross' direction. The Sheriff returned the gesture and then focused his attention back to the crowd of locals.

"What the ..?" mumbled Ross as he parked the truck behind the Jones' pickup. The bed was laden with fresh blood. Although he had not yet gotten a good peak at the object on display, intuition told him to turn around and head back home.

"What's going on, Ross?" asked Maggie, peering over the dashboard.

"Maggs," he replied with a disturbed sigh, "your guess is as good as mine." Just the fact that Frank and Jesse were involved gave the Sheriff a bad feeling. Maggie and Chuck followed him into the street.

Fred Wentworth was the first to notice the Sheriff's arrival. "Hey, Ross!" he yelled over the excited voices. Some of those in the crowd turned their heads to look. Fred ran over to him, acting like a man who had just struck oil in his own backyard. The others quickly returned their attention back to the reason they were there.

"What's this all about, Fred?" The Sheriff shook the storeowner's extended hand, keeping his eyes forward. Maggie and Chuck rushed past him and wedged their way through the wall of people.

"Boy oh boy, Ross. That sure is a beauty. Let's hear ya tell the story. Frank there said it damn near tore you apart."

The hunger pains in Ross' stomach were rudely interrupted by a sickening roll. *Those stupid bastards,* he cursed inwardly. "Awwww Christ!" Ross stepped around the dumbfounded man and skipped up to the crowd.

"Howdy, Ross."

"Morning, Sheriff."

"Nice work, eh Ross?"

"By God, he's a monster, Ross. Was you pissin yer pants?"

Ross ignored the greetings, the idiotic questions, the pats on the back, and shuffled his way to the center of the circle.

"Unbelievable," he whispered when he finally laid eyes upon the object that had sparked so much interest that morning. Stretched across the cement steps was the bloody hide of the bear. The head, or rather half a head, was still attached to the cape, along with the four enormous paws. Men, women, and children daringly took turns goggling next to the trophy. They would pick up the clawed appendages and compare size to their own humbled hands.

A feeling of guilt swept over Ross. He actually felt pity for the slain creature that lay exposed to the public like a cheap carnival show. It was not a fitting end for such a magnificent beast. And what would happen if one of the town's newest widows were to happen by? *My God,* he thought, wondering if any of them had any sense of dignity.

Frank and Jesse were strutting around like peacocks at the top of the steps, both gleaming with pride. Their torn coveralls were stained red. The younger Jones brother noticed the disapproving glare of the Sheriff. He gave Ross a wink after reading his thoughts.

Chuck had knelt down and was holding up one of the paws, sizing up the lengthy claws. "Geez, Ross! He's twice as big as you said he was!"

The Sheriff did not acknowledge the statement. He pushed his way out of the crowd, needing room to breathe. He was utterly disgusted by it all. He had to get out of there before he got sick.

Gene Steubens noticed the Sheriff attempting his escape. He pulled himself away from a conversation with a few local business owners and trailed him into the street. Steubens closed the remaining five steps in a short trot and then grasped Ross' elbow. "That's a helluva job, Sheriff! Just a helluva job!" The fat, little man was out of breath from the twenty yard jog.

Ross swiveled and scowled at the Mayor. The sight of his pudgy, condescending face sickened him even more. In Ross Pickett's mind, the arrogant ass was about as pleasant as a perpetual enema. Gene Steubens had always been a patronizing fool, thinking that he had the upper hand on the inhabitants of Jessup. Running the town, in Gene Steuben's eyes, meant running the Sheriff, but Ross felt otherwise and was not afraid to tell him so. Ross thought it was humorous how the Mayor would spin his big-city ideas and visions for Jessup. Steubens seemed to be the only man in town actually interested in change. In the Sheriff's eyes, he was not from those parts and had no right messing with their perfectly non-eventful lives.

Ross rolled his eyes, anticipating another confrontation. He wasn't good at hiding his despise for the man. "Gene, you know we really don't need this crap. Not now." He casually motioned to the crowd that continued to buzz around the carcass.

"Don't need this? Don't need this?" The Mayor lifted his arms high like a traveling faith healer preparing to perform a miracle. "Ross, my blind friend, this is exactly what this town needs!"

"What the hell do you mean by that, Gene?" Ross was confused by the joyous outburst. He did not trust the man.

"Dollars, Sheriff! Big dollars! We have over there," he pointed a chunky finger to the bear, "a fascination, a tourist attraction if you will. It's another answer to this dullish town's prison of irrelevance. Just think, Ross, people will drive miles out of their way to see the great killer bear of Jessup, Michigan!" His obstreperous voice sang out like a ring announcer.

That's just what this is, thought Ross, *a friggin three-ring circus.* People had died, and now their Mayor wanted to celebrate that by putting the murderer on display. Had Ross not observed the sincerity in the man, he would have bust a gut laughing as if he had been pranked. As absurd as it was, Ross could actually picture Gene Steubens dressed in tails and top hat, drawing cheers from anxious crowds. It was time to set the record straight.

"Gene," the Sheriff placed his hand on the much smaller man's shoulder, "all we have there is the hide of a very unfortunate animal that had to be eliminated. I do not think it would be wise to brandish it with some outlandish form of sainthood." The Sheriff spoke in a steady, measured tone, as if he were telling a child that Santa Claus was not real.

"Hide ... hell!" boomed the Mayor. "That's where you're wrong, Sheriff. Frank Jones says he has an acquaintance in Escanaba who does some darn good taxidermy work. Frank believes that this friend of his can transform that hide back into the man-eating creature it once was. ... you know ... fangs bared ... and snarling." Steubens gave his best impression of an angry bear. He curled his upper lip and blurted out an amusing growl.

Ross thought the Mayor's impression more resembled that of a deranged beaver. *If only you had been there,* he thought.

The Mayor continued. "We'll put it up over in Fred Wentworth's store ... or better yet, have it encased in glass and stand it in front of the Hall. Who wouldn't want to see the bear that killed four men?"

"Four men? Who told you that, Gene?" Ross' attempt to control his emotions was rapidly failing. His voice was getting louder.

"Calm down, Ross." Steubens pressed his hands against Ross' firm chest. After a sharp look from the Sheriff, he withdrew them to his sides. "Your Deputy filled me in on Ned Crosby, and the Jones boys there told me about Seth Jennings and his boy. Poor lad." The Mayor bowed his head as if he was saying a short prayer, but Ross didn't buy it. "And I might add," continued Steubens, "that since I am the Mayor of this community, next time I will expect that sort of information to come directly from you."

Ross was now furious and could no longer hold back his ire. The line had been crossed. A pulsating vein bulged in his forehead. "Now you listen to me, you little prick! I don't have to tell you shit!" His voice rose above the hushed crowd. The people turned toward the disturbance as Ross carried on his verbal assault on the cowering man. "And as for your demented ideas about that fucking bear, why don't you pin up some pictures of Charlie Perkins' guts along with his left arm that decided to depart from the rest of his body." Ross' face grew red, unlike that of his counterpart which had turned pale. The tension between them had been building for a long time. Ross felt that it was finally time to put the man in his place, regardless of the consequences. "And why don't you have Bobby Jennings' mother sell tickets and popcorn, you sick little bastard. I don't know where you're coming from, mister, but how about letting us bury our dead and move on with our pitiful lives. Now, get out of my face."

Steubens' body quivered from the barrage of profanities. He was both frightened and furious at the same time.

Ross was startled by the silence that had befallen the street. He could hear a dog barking off in the distance. He scolded himself for losing control in such a public place, but the man had deserved every last word of it. Perhaps he had overstepped his boundaries. *Well tough shit!* All he wanted was for Jessup to retreat back into its nice, quiet mode of existence. They didn't need a killer bear on display or any other tourist attractions ... just peace and tranquility. It was inconceivable to him how the human mind could devise such a thoughtless scheme.

The Sheriff turned away as he was no longer able to stand the sight of Steubens. The bystanders began to chatter softly amongst themselves. After a few minutes, they had forgotten the disruption entirely and reverted back to their gawking.

The Mayor returned to his voters without a rebuttal and was quick to join in on the conversation. His job now was damage control. He would deal with Sheriff Ross Pickett in his own fashion. Gene Steubens immediately set his mind in motion on a plan that would oust his nemesis for good.

Ross, in the meantime, walked to the other side of the street. He noticed that the stranger who had previously drawn his attention was no longer present. The van was missing as well. *At least someone has some smarts in this world,* he thought. He then saw Mark Bennington still speaking to the man with the note pad. The Deputy had a mischievous smile written on his young face as the Sheriff approached.

"Hey, Ross. This is ..."

"Winston Lovells!" The large man finished the presentation, extending his hand to greet the Sheriff.

Ross took the man's hand hesitantly and gave it a quick shake. *What now?*

"I'm with the Detroit News, sir," goaded the reporter.

Oh boy, thought Ross. *Here's another headache in the making.*

The man continued, "I was passing through your quaint little village while on holiday with my family."

"Nice timing," Ross groaned.

"We happened upon your interesting town meeting over there, and let me say, Sheriff, you've got quite a story from what I've gathered from some of these nice people. Your fine Deputy included of course." Mark smirked, embarrassed by the compliment, but then looked away from Ross' hard stare. It was the '*wait until I see you later*' stare.

"Excuse me, Mr. Lovells is it?"

"That is correct, sir. Winston Lovells of the Detroit News."

"Fine, would you mind terribly if I had a few private moments with my *'fine'* Deputy here?" Mark suddenly looked worried, as if he knew what was coming.

"Not at all, Sheriff, but I would like your account of how you and your party hunted down the man-eating beast. It's not every day you see an eight hundred pound black bear in this state, or any state for that matter. This is big news."

Ross nodded politely to the journalist and watched him waddle off to the crowd while writing down some more notes. Mark exhibited the face of a kid who had just been caught with his hand in the cookie jar.

"Man-eater, Mark?" The Sheriff crossed his arms.

"Hold on there, Ross." The Deputy held his hands out in front of him. "Those weren't my words. Mr. Lovells was just asking a few questions," he answered defensively.

"Eight hundred pounds, Mark?" The question put the Deputy at a loss for words. "You know," continued the Sheriff, "I'm no zoologist or anything, but I find it hard to believe that a bear, especially a dead one, could put on about two hundred and fifty pounds overnight." The sarcasm in his voice was duly noted.

"Yeah, well, I guess parts of the story did get a little inflated. I think the reporter was talking to Frank and Jesse. You know how they like to boast about themselves."

Ross' expression relayed his disappointment. But he didn't feel up to disciplining the Deputy now. Out of respect for the boy, he would scold him in private. But he *would* teach him a lesson. Mark was careless in many ways. If he was to continue to pursue law enforcement as a career then he would have to show more poise while under fire.

"Sheriff!" The round man from Detroit had returned with his note pad at the ready. "Could I have those comments now?" He folded over a page of scribblings and revealed a fresh sheet of white paper.

"Okay, Mr. Lovells," said Ross, uncertain as to whether or not it was the proper thing to do. "I'll give you the truth and that's all. No dramatics."

"That's my job, sir. The truth and nothing but the truth."

Yeah right, thought Ross. He turned to his Deputy one last time. "Mark, see what you can do about dispersing those people over there. And have the dynamic duo get rid of that damn bear before I confiscate it."

"Sure thing, Ross." Mark eagerly left him alone with the reporter.

"Okay, Mr. Lovells, this is the story. First of all, three men were allegedly killed by the animal." The Sheriff hesitated, wondering why he used that term. The reporter was quick to pick up on the slip of the tongue.

"*Allegedly,* Sheriff? Is there some doubt as to whether or not that animal is the true culprit?" Lovells was probing like the master he was.

Goddammit, Ross scorned silently. It was time to bail. "No, Mr. Lovells, just a wrong choice of words is all. We are positive that we killed the right bear." *Nice work,* he thought, *why don't we start talking about evil spirits and monsters?* An image of Ray Jackson's amused face flashed past his eyes. *No,* Ross confirmed to himself, *there is no doubt.*

"Alright, Sheriff, if you say so. Now about the four men who were killed. Mr. Ned Crosby and ..."

This sonuvabitch won't stop, thought Ross. *This isn't an interview, it's a fucking interrogation.* Lovells was trying to play him ... force a blunder. The Sheriff would not allow himself to fall into his little trap. "As I said before, Mr. Lovells, three men died as a direct result of the bear. The other man, Ned Crosby, died Saturday night from heart failure in a hospital up in Houghton."

"Your Deputy mentioned that Mr. Crosby had a run-in with the bear on the eve of his so-called heart failure. Is there any truth to that?"

Ross eyed the overweight reporter as he wrote with penmanship that only a doctor could love ... or read. The man was relentless with his prodding and was becoming somewhat of a thorn in the Sheriff's side. "Mr. Lovells, let's get this straight since your ears are failing to operate properly. It *was* a heart attack. Ned Crosby had one genuine heart-stopper. I watched the man die before my eyes!" His voice was rising again. He forced himself to regress. He remembered some words that a close friend had once told him long ago ... '*never cross a reporter.*' It always had a way of backfiring. "Those are the facts. Do you wish me to continue?"

The reporter nodded and the story passed through Ross' mouth with blunt sincerity. He provided a complete account of the weekend's events that included Ned's accident, which may or may not have been caused by a bear. He told him about Charlie Perkins' death minus the gory details, and then the demise of the Jennings men. Ross figured that Rachel Perkins didn't need to read about how the Sheriff had stepped in her husband's guts on Crosby's floor.

When the reporter appeared content with the statement, he thanked Ross and returned to the disbanding crowd to snap a few pictures of the giant hide that Frank and Jesse were preparing to load into their truck. Ross loitered for a few moments in the street until he was satisfied that the majority of onlookers had gone on about their morning business. Gene Steubens gave him a nervous look and then followed Fred Wentworth toward the Five and Dime. The reporter performed his funny duck-like walk across the street to a Dodge minivan holding an equally enlarged woman and two young children. Winston Lovells waved to the Sheriff as he drove his family out of town. Ross smiled as he watched the man's wife barking in his ear. *Let him have it, missy,* he quietly thought to himself.

***

"That high strutter doesn't know his ass from a hole in the ground," complained the disgruntled Mayor behind closed doors at the Five and Dime. "I'm telling you, Freddy, this could be huge for us, and that man doesn't give a damn."

"I don't know, Gene. Ross may have a point. My wife went over to see Rachel this morning and said she wasn't doing too well." Helen Wentworth ended up staying with the distraught widow for three hours.

"Poppycock! Fred, my friend," said Steubens as he reached his arm around the man's neck, "I feel for the woman. Believe me I do. But we've got to move on. You yourself keep telling me how bad business has been lately. Look around, Fred. There's nobody in your store." Steubens paused a moment and allowed it to sink in. "And it isn't going to get any better unless we do something about it. This is a prime opportunity for Jessup. Things are happening ... the Festival this weekend ... the golf resort down the road ... and now this. Think about it, man."

The businessman still wasn't sold on the Mayor's plan. His moral sensitivity told him that it wouldn't be the proper thing to do. Ross' words in the street hit home. The Sheriff was well respected within the community. But Fred's store had been on the skids for a few months. He had three mouths to feed and profits had been steadily declining. His young son, Joey, was going to need braces next summer. He wondered where that money was going to come from.

When Fred Wentworth opened his small souvenir shop five years ago, he considered it to be a sound enough investment at the time. Even though Jessup was merely a blip on the State map that tourists blew through with barely a blink of an eye, he figured that a knickknack shop might offer tired families a suitable atmosphere to stretch cramped legs. Nearly every shelf in the Five and Dime was stuffed with an array of trinkets and toys. The favorites were the tomahawks that Ben Tucker made in his woodshop. He had a number of headdresses on display that were purchased from the Ojibwa tribe up near Baraga. Fred enjoyed watching the kids play Cowboys and Indians.

Customer flow had been well below the forecasted numbers written into Wentworth's business plan presented to the bank for the most recent loan. His uncle, and avid sportsman out of Ontonogon, gave the entrepreneur an idea to add a smoked fish shop as a side business. There were similar shops scattered all along Highway 2 stretching across the northern coast of Lake Michigan. Fred decided there must be some demand to keep so many afloat, so he went to the bank for more money. When all was said and done, the fish shop did pull in a few additional dollars, but nothing to get too excited over.

Wentworth was in dire need of income to support his family. He sat on the town council with three other Jessup citizens and listened to Gene Steubens paint his dreams for their future. Fred had been influential in helping to bring the Rutt'n Buck Festival to fruition. They were really banking on bringing in more tourists this year. And Steubens, after three years, came through with the golf resort that would certainly be a boost to the local economy. Although things were looking up, there still remained the matter of a heavy bank note. Extensions were hard to come by for small business owners.

Gene Steubens had an unexplainable power over the people of Jessup and Fred Wentworth knew it. He did not wish to get on the Mayor's wrong side.

"I don't know, Gene." Although Fred was as interested in making a buck as anyone else, he was also a man of high principles. He wanted no part of a plan that might inflict harm upon another, nor did he wish to be forced into making a decision under duress.

The Mayor, sensing that he was losing the man's interest, changed his tactics. *These beatniks are so easy to manipulate,* he gloated to himself. "I've got something you may like, Freddy." Steubens did his best to portray a soft, kind-hearted soul who actually cared. "Rachel Perkins has no income at the moment ... correct? Sure, she can sell the station, but heck, that place is so run down that she most likely won't get a decent price for it. Charlie still owed a sizeable sum for that new rig he bought." It didn't seem to bother Wentworth that the Mayor had personal knowledge of Charlie Perkins' financial standing. The politician was smooth and cunning. Steubens knew how to influence and he was close to bagging his goat. "How do you think poor Rachel is going to survive up here, Freddy? Yes, the ladies will keep bringing pot-roasts and casseroles, but that won't last forever. She owes money just like you, me, and nearly everyone else in this town. Remember what we spoke about earlier?"

The storeowner nodded his head slowly, still displaying some reluctance for what the Mayor was proposing.

"We've got a means of bringing people into our town to spend money. It's an attraction that will make them stop on the way to the ski resorts and snowmobile trails. Hell, it's no Eiffel Tower, but it's a start, and it's all we have at the moment. You'll be happy, the people of Jessup will be happy, and we can cut Rachel Perkins in on the pie. I'm only doing what's best for my constituents," he lied. The Mayor waved his hand toward the store's large window facing the street. "Picture that bear standing there in the window and just watch the curiosity seekers flock into your store. Hey, charge them a quarter to see the damn thing if you want. I don't care." The Mayor figured that may have been pushing matters a little, but the hook had been set and he was ready to land the fish. Steubens could now see the dollar signs reflecting in Wentworth's eyes.

"Ross ain't gonna like it much, Gene."

The Mayor withdrew his thick arm from the man's shoulder and frowned. Only with numbers could he succeed. "Then we're just going to have to take care of Sheriff Ross Pickett."

His statement caused Wentworth to give him a look of concern. "What do you mean, Gene? What do you mean *take care of him*?"

Steubens relaxed and smiled coolly. "Ross Pickett is a good man, Fred. I've never doubted that since the day I met him. And let me add that he has served the community well. But the world is passing him by. His methods are outdated and he is not in tune with the real world any longer. Pickett is a dinosaur."

"Come on, Gene. Ross is good to everyone in town. He's a smart man."

"Yes, yes, I know he is. What I'm trying to say is, I just think that perhaps he's burned out. Maybe it's time for him to step down and let someone younger, someone with more enthusiasm take over."

"I don't know, Gene," continued Wentworth. "I really like Ross. He's always been really good to me."

The Mayor felt as though he was losing the man's ear again. "Okay, Fred. I didn't want to bring this up, but I feel it necessary. You know about Ross' past ... how he used to indulge?" Steubens brought his cupped hand to his face and acted as if he were taking a drink.

"Sure, but he doesn't any ..."

"I know you don't think he does, but you've witnessed his unorthodox outbursts, just like today in the street. He nearly crucified me out there this morning in front of the whole town. I just don't think he's very stable right now. Look at how he handled this bear ordeal. Ross had no business hunting down the animal like that."

Fred appeared surprised by the angle the Mayor was taking, but he allowed him to continue without interruption.

"Don't get me wrong, Fred, I'm glad he did it the same as you. But the important question is ... *why did Ross do it*? He went over the edge is why. He allowed his ego to control his actions. He disregarded the law completely. I checked for myself." It had really been a guess on the Mayor's part, but it sounded sensible enough, and he could convince others of the same. "Ross Pickett is burned out, and we can't have a Sheriff creating his own laws. That will lead to utter chaos, my friend."

Steubens paused as he eyed the councilman carefully. He could see that the bug implanted in the man's ear was taking hold. The seed of doubt was flowering.

"Here's what I want to do, Fred. I want you to go gather the other members of the council, say tomorrow evening around seven, over to the Hall. Let's just sit down and discuss the matter like gentlemen. I'm not saying we're going to do anything drastic. I just think it's important to bring everything out in the open so that a proper decision can be made regarding his future in Jessup." Steubens waited anxiously for the response.

"Okay, Gene. I'll call the boys."

Outstanding!

***

Sergeant Berkowski huddled his pupils around the television screen. He had extracted the tape from the video camera and inserted it into a cassette recorder that was already hooked up to the T.V. The officers eagerly anticipated what they hoped to be a major break in the case. When all was ready, the Sergeant depressed the 'play' button and stepped back. The screen was blank at first, so Berkowski fast-forwarded the tape with a cordless remote until a picture appeared. The visual was black and white, and somewhat broken from overuse. Every few seconds, a fuzzy line would throw the picture into complete disarray. The back of the storeowner's head was visible, but nothing else. There was no sound to accompany the film, but that was not their concern at the moment. They needed an I.D. Movement in the upper left portion of the screen suddenly caught their attention.

"There!" Johanson pointed his finger to a man in coveralls. He appeared at the counter holding some groceries. The man casually placed the goods down on the counter and then turned to walk to another aisle, still in range of the camera. The victim cleverly stepped out of view to allow the camera full view of the store.

"Is he black?" asked Godson.

"Looks like it," answered the Sergeant. The distortion made it difficult to point out the obvious. He began to wonder if this film would provide any conclusive evidence at all.

"Here he comes again." It was Deputy Tom Jamison's turn to narrate. "That man sure as hell is black." A sudden, clear spot in the film provided a clean shot of the customer's dark skin.

"Yeah," replied the Sergeant. The picture went fuzzy again, but the Troopers continued to watch as the man set what looked to be a case of beer on the counter, along with some other items. He then proceeded to reach around behind his back for something, possibly a wallet ... or a gun. Berkowski studied what little expression he could make out. The customer appeared pleasant enough. *Hell,* thought the Sergeant, *this might not even be our suspect.* He thought about fast-forwarding, but decided against it. Then something strange happened. The storeowner turned sideways as if he was watching something. The customer appeared to be focused on the same thing out of their field of view. "What are they doing?" Berkowski voiced his puzzlement.

"The T.V.," answered Jamison. "It was on when we found him. They're both watching it."

"Interesting. Anyone recognize this guy?" Nobody responded to the Sergeant's question. Berkowski studied the customer carefully, watching for some form of reaction. The man briefly turned away from the television and looked toward the window, and that's when the storeowner made his move.

"Look at that!" Johanson pointed to the screen. "He's reaching under the counter."

The victim hoisted a large handgun.

"There's the .44," chimed in Godson.

The customer then turned his attention back to the storeowner who held the gun at his head. *If only we had dialogue,* thought Berkowski. The customer appeared to be truly shocked by what was happening as he raised his hands over his head. He seemed to be talking to the storeowner ... perhaps pleading with him. They watched as the man behind the counter made the 911 call. Without warning, he spun around violently. The gun recoiled as he fell. The customer fell to the ground as well, gripping the side of his head. Both men were now absent from the video. The four police officers were huddled around the small monitor as if they were watching a Hollywood drama unfold. The door opened and another black man entered the picture. He immediately ducked low to the ground.

"There's the second shot from the victim," said Godson.

They watched as the newcomer reached over the divider and emptied his clip into the floor on the other side. It was all so surreal, thought the Sergeant. Someone was dying on that video, but he couldn't feel any emotion. The second black man then turned, apparently to his companion. A small object sailed into his outstretched hands.

"That must be the .32," exclaimed Johanson.

The police officers looked on as the man with the gun then stood, peered over the counter, and emptied the clip of the second gun into the victim. *End of story for him,* thought Berkowski. The shooter knelt down again to his buddy, then after a few moments they both rose to their feet. The wounded man was holding his ear, and appeared to be in pain. He was definitely hit. He went to the other side of the counter and picked up the phone. After placing it against his good ear, he pulled the cord from the wall. The men then fled the scene with the groceries. Berkowski watched carefully making sure they didn't raid the cash register in the process. In fact, it seemed to be the furthest thing from their minds.

"Rewind to where the shooter comes in," said Samantha Godson.

"Why's that?" asked the Sergeant.

"I just want to check something out."

Berkowski did as he was asked and replayed the shooting a second time.

"That's him!" shouted the female officer.

"Who?"

"The fugitive from downstate. I'm sure of it."

"Have you seen his picture?" inquired the Sergeant.

"Yes. My husband and I were watching Jeopardy last night and the show was interrupted with a break-in from the local network. They put the guy's mug up on the screen. I'm sure it's him."

"Hey, Berky, what station was the set turned to?" asked Johanson.

The Sergeant tried to recall. He had turned it to channel three to operate the VCR. "Seven ... I think," he finally answered. "Yeah, seven ... I'm positive."

"What time did this all go down?"

"About seven-thirty."

"I'll be darned! He was watching Jeopardy, too!" said Godson. "We were watching the same friggin channel."

"Okay, then," continued Johanson, "we have a storeowner who happens to recognize a wanted fugitive. He pulls a gun to apprehend him and his partner. He gets shot, but manages to shoot one of them in the process."

"You got it, Mike!" boomed Godson.

"That would explain why they didn't take the money." Berkowski leaned back against the wall. "But why were they so interested in all those groceries?"

"Heck, they were hungry," added Johanson. "Munchies for the road."

"No, I don't buy that. If you're grabbing snacks for a road trip, you don't buy three or four loaves of bread and a few pounds of meat. I don't think they would buy beer either if they were smart. Why take the chance?" Berkowski had read the report on the incident down state. It had been a well-conceived plan. No, these guys knew what they were doing.

"What are you thinking, Berky?" asked Godson.

"I'm thinking that these two men are holed up somewhere waiting for the storm to blow over. They have to know that the law will be all over hell looking for them, especially now."

"Yes, but remember, these guys didn't know they were on camera." Godson was playing Devil's advocate.

"No, I think they're digging their heels in deep. There's a lot of space up here to effectively disappear. Mike?"

"Yes, sir." The Trooper snapped to attention.

"I want you to have the lab enhance this tape and try to get some decent photos printed up. We know who the shooter is, but not the partner. Sammy?" He turned to his female officer.

"Yes, Berky?"

"I want you to put this on the wire. Let the southern boys know their two fugitives are on the move up here. They're going to want that info A.S.A.P. Get this out to every law enforcement unit in the U.P. Probably wouldn't hurt to include Wisconsin, and even border security. They may have decided to move on out of Michigan. I doubt it, though. Get that picture and fingerprints of the unknown assailant into the bank and see if we can find a match. We may have a rap sheet somewhere. The man's wounded on the right side of his head. If he's in the general public, he shouldn't be too hard to spot."

"Gottcha, Sarge." Godson walked out of the building with haste in her step. This was a big moment in her career. This was big for all of them.

Berkowski stayed behind with the others. "Guys, these two men are obviously very dangerous. If they feel threatened, they will not hesitate to kill." The remaining officers nodded in agreement. "We don't need rookies out there pulling any John Wayne bullshit. You get word out that if these two are located, do not proceed without backup. Got it!"

"Yes, sir!" Both answered in unison. Berkowski then picked up the phone and dialed his home number. He told his wife that he would not be home for dinner that night. It was going to be another long shift.

***

With his hunger greatly subdued, Ross' western omelet went virtually untouched. Chuck had gulped down a heaping stack of French toast while Maggie slowly worked on a bowl of baked oatmeal covered with blueberries. There had been little time for conversation during breakfast. Ross was incessantly hazed by inquiries about his hunt in the Amen.

There was an unusually large crowd in Arlene's that morning. A number of people had decided to take time off work to see the killer bear for themselves. For the most part, the Sheriff just sat back and requested that the curious patrons allow him to finish his breakfast in peace. The growing tremor inside his head was sure to evolve into a real brain-buster if he didn't do something to remedy the stress. He silently watched Chuck spoon up a dribble of syrup and then slurp it down.

A few years ago he would have known exactly what to do in order to shut out that cruel and relentless world. *But things are better now. Aren't they?* Ross closed his eyes for a moment. *Old ghosts.* Maggie and Chuck were the crutches he needed to power through. It just seemed that the low points were beginning to frequent him again much too often. Ross thoughtlessly picked at his food with no intention on eating it.

Maggie began to see the same behavior that he had displayed earlier in the morning. "What's wrong, hon?" She began to caress his arm with gentle fingers. The memories of his bout with alcohol abuse were very fresh in her head. She could see that he was upset, and that made her nervous.

Ross lifted his head and gazed at her with a plastic smile. "Nothing, Maggs. Just not hungry I guess." His eyes returned to the full plate of food.

"It looks like a little more than nothing to me, Ross." Maggie knew that he was now lying. The *tell* was that Ross couldn't maintain eye contact with her.

Ross remembered Ray Jackson telling him once that he should never let a woman get to know him that well. That was when Eevie was still alive. Like Maggie, his former wife was also very skilled at translating his thoughts. "Really, Maggs," he finally responded, "I'm all right. Just tired is all." That part was not a lie. For some reason, he felt as though things were not well in his life at the moment. He found himself to be exhausted from the nagging stress. It was a complete turnaround of how he had felt earlier that morning.

"Okay, hon, if you say so. Maybe later we can go home and get you all rested up." Her line was followed by one of her seductive winks after making sure that her son was looking in another direction.

"You got yourself a deal, babe." An afternoon session might just hit the spot. If nothing else, just lying in bed and falling asleep in her arms might be just what he needed.

"Hey, Ross?" asked Chuck. "How 'bout getting out and doing some bird hunting this afternoon." Coach gave us the day off, and Mike Caldwell and I were thinking about rousting some pats. He and his dad got four yesterday morning, and five cocks, too. I guess his dog is a real stud."

"I don't think so. Not today anyways. Too much to clean up here in town. Maybe we can get out tomorrow." Ross did not particularly relish the idea of returning to the woods just yet. There were too many tragic memories fresh in his head. And he *did* need time to rest.

"Suit yourself, old man. I'll let Mike know that it'll just be the two of us." The boy dropped his spoon onto his plate with a loud clank. He then wiped his mouth with a crumpled napkin.

Ross was suddenly bothered by an uneasy notion. "Where you two planning on hunting today, Chuck?" he asked, showing more interest in the boy's plans.

"Mike wants to hit the edge of the swamp near Curtiss Road. We may even duck down into that spot on Townsend and plug a few squirrels if we don't get any birds."

The thought of those menacing rodents sent a familiar chill down Ross' spine. He had nearly forgotten about them. He couldn't explain the odd sense of clairvoyance, but he didn't feel right about Chuck stomping around the Amen. *Why am I so paranoid?*

The Sheriff delicately presented another option for the young hunter. "Tell you what, Chuck. There's a spread out on McKenzie," *well away from the Amen* is what he didn't say. "It has a nice stand of poplar. Barney Riley told me he went out there last fall and it was loaded with birds. He said they cleaned up." *Take the bait, boy.* "There's also a nice narrow strip of swamp out there that two guys can easily push. It's only about thirty yards wide. Grouse up the *ying-yang.*" He waited for the response.

"Cool, where is it?"

Thank God, thought Ross. He then proceeded to map out the location on an unused napkin.

Maggie observed the conversation. She noted the visible sign of relief when Chuck accepted the alternative plan. It was now obvious to her that something was indeed wrong. She did not comment in front of her son. That would come later when they were alone together.

"Sheriff!" The high-pitched squeal came from the front door. Ross turned his head along with everyone else in the room as Sharon Cooper danced over to his table. She held a piece of paper in her hand. "I've got a message for you, Ross. Hi Maggie. Hi Chucky." The dispatcher patted the boy's head. Chuck recoiled slightly, blushing with embarrassment.

"What is it, Sharon?" asked Ross.

"Let's see," she squinted at the writing on the piece of paper. "Dr. Flemming called form the Coroner's office. Yuck!" She stuck out her tongue in a childish display of distaste. "It's the Appleton

Office. He wants to speak with you or something. I don't know. He was kind of weird. Well, here's his number." She handed it over to the Sheriff. "Gotta run. Bye Maggie. Bye Chucky."

Before they could return the farewells, Sharon was prancing back towards the door, stopping along the way to say '*howdy*' to those she recognized. Chuck stared intently at her bouncing chest the entire way. Ross excused himself from the table to use the payphone next to the restroom. After depositing thirty-five cents, he dialed the scribbled number and listened as the call was picked up after the first ring.

"Pathology ... this is Flemming."

The Sheriff noted a feminine quality in the man's voice. "Doctor, I'm Ross Pickett, Sheriff of Jessup. I was told that you wanted to speak to me." Ross covered his left ear with the palm of his free hand to drown out the noise of the busy restaurant.

"Oh yes, Sheriff. Thanks for returning my call. We've examined the remains of Mr. Charles Perkins and there are some matters that I would like to discuss with you in private if that would be possible." The Doctor was all business. There was no charm in his voice.

What now? Why does everything have to be done in person? "What matters are you referring to, Doctor? I've seen the remains for myself, and believe me when I tell you, that I don't care to go through that again." Ross felt the queasiness build as he recalled the sound of his boot stepping in Charlie's intestines. It would live with him for the rest of his life.

"Okay, Sheriff, I'll lay it on the line for you. We have strong evidence suggesting that Mr. Perkins' death may *not* have been caused by a bear. Now, before you hit the roof," he quickly interjected before Ross could react, "I did say ... *may* not have been caused by a bear. I would like you to come on down here so I can explain myself in further detail."

"I'm on my way." Ross slammed the receiver home without allowing the Doctor to utter another word. *Oh God, what the hell is happening?* He rubbed the bridge of his nose.

***

"Old Jasper's gonna shit his britches when he sees dis haul, eh," croaked Frank Jones as he loaded the big buck's head and cape next to that of the smaller 8-point. The bear hide was bundled up in a corner of the truck's bed.

"One ting's sure, eh. Dey's gonna pay plenty fer dat skin. Dem were da best dawgs we ever owned," added Jesse.

"We can always git more dawgs, Jess. But I figure we gotta bout three grand worth of goods here. And dat's jus our cut." Frank pulled the tarp down over the carcasses and ratcheted down the straps.

"Hey, you see how dat Sherf was lookin down on us today? I'd like ta put a slug inta his thick skull. He ain't gonna let dat town buy dat bear from us. You jus watch and see." Jesse Jones spat a stream of tobacco juice to the ground. His mouth worked the cud of Redman like it was a large piece of bubble gum.

"Don't be worrying bout dat Sherf. Dat fat-ass Mayor'll fix em. We gonna git da cash alrighty." Frank was much more convinced than his younger brother.

"I'd still like ta put a slug into his sorry ass." The two brothers climbed into the truck and drove away from their little junkyard. A beagle yelped from its pen as they left to deliver the goods to their business associate in Escanaba.

***

Walter Hadley inadvertently gouged his customer's scalp when the stranger strolled into the shop.

"Gosh darnit, Walt! What are you doing up there?"

"Sorry, Ben." The barber apologized and then tossed the comb into a tub of sterilizing fluid. He proceeded to gently rub Ben Tucker's head to ease his pain. "Does that feel better, you old fart?" His eyes remained on the newcomer who was nonchalantly hanging a leather jacket on the coat rack.

The woodworker was also surveying the stranger with a close eye. He acted as if he were just one of the guys preparing to join in on their ritualistic chit-chat. He was a young man who wasn't much into personal grooming in the eyes of the two Jessup elders. His face showed a good three-day growth of whiskers and his clothes resembled those of a construction worker coming off a site at the end of a long day.

"Afternoon gents," said the stranger with a cordial smile.

"Afternoon," replied the barber with a nod. Although Walt was fairly certain he'd never seen the man before, there was a familiar look about him. It was possible that he was one of Ted Newhouser's men working out at Hideaway Pines. "Passing through?" he asked politely.

"Well ... not really. I guess you could say I'm working. I'm actually a journalist from a Montana outdoor magazine ... working on a little piece in your neck of the woods."

"Montana?" Ben Tucker leaned back against the head rest of the vintage Koken chair. He jerked his head slightly when the barber covered his face with a steamy towel. He spoke again with a muffled voice. "I'm going out there next fall after mule deer with a few buddies. I've heard it is some beautiful country."

"Sure is," answered the man who had been effectively meshing into the small community for a few days. Now, after a few minutes of meaningless chatter, he had befriended two more locals who might possibly shed more light on the real reason he was there. The stranger was beginning to enjoy the Rockwellesque setting inside the barbershop, with the friendly barber wearing the stereotypical white smock, and the large padded chair gleaming with chrome trim. It was small-town U.S.A. in all its glory. The only thing missing to complete the canvas was a checkerboard, and maybe a Coca Cola sign. It reminded him of his childhood.

"So what kind of article are you writing?" questioned the curious barber as he swiped the razor across a thick leather belt. Walt Hadley then proceeded to work away at his customer's spotty beard. Ben closed his eyes and listened.

"I'm writing about the black bear population in North America," continued the man. "My magazine is sending me around the country in an effort to get a grasp on current numbers."

"You've certainly come to the right place, sir. We have plenty, especially in the Amen." After a few quick touch-ups on the sideburns, Walt picked up a towel, draped it over his shoulder, and used the loose end to wipe away the smudges of lather. "Smooth as a baby's butt, Benny. That will be eight dollars."

"You crooked old sonuvagun. Raised your rates again, didn't you?" Tucker feigned his protest to the fifty cent increase.

"Have to make a living, my friend." Both men laughed together. Tucker removed two fives from his wallet and told the barber to keep the change.

"Are either of you bear hunters?" questioned the journalist.

Ben sat down in a vacant chair. He had no place to go, so he decided to pass some time looking at a few of the shop's outdated magazines. He had already delivered a box of carvings to Fred Wentworth who sold them on consignment at the Five and Dime. It was an enjoyable hobby ... woodworking. He didn't ask much for the hand-carved items, just enough to keep his tool supply in order and a bottle of bourbon for his hot toddies. The woodworker looked up from the June edition of Time. "Not me, son. Can't see much use in bear hunting." He found it odd that the journalist wasn't toting any form of writing material.

"Haven't hunted bear in ... ohhhh," the barber hesitated as he struggled to recall his last hunt. His eyes wandered to the ceiling as if the answer might be found somewhere in the drywall. "My Lordy ... must have been twenty years. When did old Jack Watts die?" The barber turned to his friend.

"1979 ... nineteen years ago. Just bought himself a new car down in Appleton. I remember because he'd been itching to give me a ride. It was my first fall up here in Jessup. Pretty little thing, that Mustang." Tucker's eyes did not sway from the picture of Tyra Banks on the cover of the previous year's Swimsuit edition. He replaced the Time magazine when he noticed the Sports Illustrated lying face down.

"Yup ... was '79 alright. I shot that big boar I got on my wall about two weeks before Jack disappeared. Was a damn shame ... a good man he was. But that's what you get for flirting with the Amen, brother." The barber turned his attention to the newcomer. "You need a trim today?" He dusted off the remnants from Ben's head off the chair.

"You bet." The younger man sauntered over to the open seat. As he sat, he couldn't help but think about what the barber had just said. Once again, the Amen Swamp had popped up into conversation with a member of the Jessup community. The intrigue was building. Walt secured the bib snuggly around his neck.

Tucker spoke up from across the room. "So you're writing about bears?"

"That's right. I'm anxious to scope out the land around here, maybe get some pictures with a little luck."

"You know, we had quite a little incident right her in Jessup. A couple of people from town got killed by a big black." The barber was almost prideful that it had occurred in his town.

"I heard." The stranger perked up a bit in the chair. He had been waiting for this topic to work its way into the conversation. "Sounds like you had a mean one."

"Wasn't just an ordinary bear," added Walt as he began snipping around the customer's ears. "That one was a demon."

"That's right, son," chimed in Ben Tucker. "Straight from the Amen. That purgatory don't treat trespassers too kindly." He leaned forward as he spoke, eyeing the stranger with a quirky grin.

He could now see the conspiracy forming. The stranger fought the urge to return the cagey smile. Although it was a poor attempt to invoke fear in the outsider, there was a reason for the game that these two men were replaying on his behalf. He decided to play along as though he were the naïve child. "I've heard some others speak of this swamp ... the Amen. What could be so prophetic about one swamp?"

"Ain't just a swamp, boy," smirked the barber. "The Amen is haunted ground. Has been for years."

He detected a subtle wink from the man holding the magazine. It was directed to the co-conspirator behind the chair.

"Heard them spirits myself once," said Tucker. "Curl your hair when you're out there all alone. That's one place I'll never set foot in."

"Jack Watts weren't smart enough to stay clear of the Amen. Look what happened to him," continued the barber as he began to work the stranger's bangs.

If he didn't know any better, he would have guessed that they were reading from a script. The man figured that he was not the first to sit in that chair and experience the well-rehearsed performance. "You say this Watts disappeared? Was he ever found?"

"Nope," was the quick reply from Tucker. "Never will be either. Wasn't the first to meet his end in the Amen, my boy. Won't be the last."

"There've been others?"

"Sure enough. Dummies ... all of them," continued the woodworker. "Got no business going in there. I don't care how big the deer get. Ain't worth selling your soul."

And then Walter Hadley recited a very interesting rhyme.

The spirits cry with haunting verse,
Warning men of Amen's curse,
Smart is he who walks away,
And lives to breathe another day.

If you will the courage,
To face the demons within,
Then pray with pure heart,
The journey ends with Amen.

***

The needle on the speedometer hovered between seventy and seventy-five as the Tahoe breezed down the two-lane road. Maggie had asked to accompany Ross for two reasons. First, she wanted to get Chuck's high school conferences out of the way. But more importantly, she was uncomfortable with Ross' conduct. He had clammed up tight after their hasty departure from Arlene's, and the earnest look in his eyes was worrisome. Maggie couldn't stand these episodes of '*no talk, just walk.*' She finally confronted him directly.

"What's on your mind, Ross? What's bothering you?"

The Sheriff did not answer her for a long minute. "Huh?" he finally said, as though the questions had not been understood. "Oh ... it's nothing, Maggs, really." He would not look at her. He gave her a soft pat on her thigh for reassurance. Ross could not look into her eyes. He was lying, something he had sworn that he would never do to her. He could not share the doubts that were swirling through his scattered head. He was just too confused.

"Damn it, Ross!" she protested. "This is me, Maggie. I saw you talking on that phone, and I watched you talk Chuck out of going near that swamp. You never talked to Barney Riley, did you? You don't want Chuck going near that swamp, do you? Now what the hell is going on?" Her efforts to break through his steel barrier were hopeless.

"Nothing's wrong. Believe me." Ross stole a quick glance at her face. Her eyes displayed the hurt ... the feeling of being betrayed.

"Fine! Sit here and rot in your own little hell, Ross! Shut everybody out! But one of these days you're going to fall through the ice and there won't be anybody there to pull you out."

Maggie made a clear affirmation that she was extremely pissed. And rightly so, he figured. He knew that she was correct in so many ways, but he could not confide in her now ... not yet. Silence was the only rebuttal that he could offer. The silence lasted until they drove into the Appleton city limits.

Ross dropped Maggie off at the high school and told her that his appointment shouldn't take more than an hour. She left the vehicle without a word and then stormed off. He knew that it was not going to be an easy hole to crawl out of.

***

Fred Wentworth, the long-time president of Jessup's diminutive town council, had called the special meeting at the request of Gene Steubens. The two retirees of the group, Frank Peterson and Paul Keegle, met Fred and the Mayor at the little round table in Town Hall. Keegle had been sweeping out the garage by order of his wife, so he was more than happy to have an excuse to put away the dust pan. Frank Peterson had been on his way to Appleton to pick up a few groceries when the president contacted him.

Pete Wilkerson, on the other hand, was not a member of the retired and relaxed population of Jessup. He had been wrapped up in his duties as Operations Manager at Eckardly Tool and Die when Fred phoned him. His irritation from the interruption was obvious when he entered the meeting room where the others patiently awaited his arrival. Steubens had changed the time for the gathering from seven, as originally planned, to three-thirty. Gene had dinner plans with the developers from the resort later that evening, but he did not relinquish that information to his fellow councilmembers. He wanted to get the ball rolling on his anti-Ross Pickett campaign as soon as possible.

"Damn it, Gene. You know some of us do have jobs during the day. What's so important that you have to call me out of the office during business hours?" Wilkerson put his hands on his hips waiting for the response.

The deceitful politician smiled at the disgruntled councilmember in an attempt to put him at ease. He realized that Wilkerson was the only sitting member possessing some semblance of a brain. He would have to be handled delicately. "I'm very sorry to disturb your work, Pete, but something important has developed and will require urgent discussion and resolution. Please, Pete, take a seat so that we can get started. We should be able to get you back to work shortly." Steubens gestured his outstretched hand to the open chair.

Wilkerson looked about the room at the other faces. He sat down next to Fred Wentworth, loosened the tie around his thin neck, and leaned back. Jessup's Town Hall was an older building, constructed in 1936. The structure was in desperate need of repairs, but the town's lack of funding had slowed progress in that department. During the previous summer, the council did manage to scrape together enough cash to have the exterior painted. Simple maintenance jobs were typically assumed by volunteers utilizing personal skills for the good of the town. Other than the Mayoral office and the quarters for the small police force, general use of the building was sparse. The council would meet about twice a month to discuss trivial topics like who would chair the committee for the festival, or why the speed limit on Main Street should be lowered to twenty miles per hour from twenty-five. Every now and then a group of couples would gather for a euchre tournament, or the ladies would organize a bake sale for one charity or another. It was all part of their small-town culture.

When Gene Steubens entered the picture, the council meetings took on an entirely new personality. His unique visions captivated the men and gave more purpose to their positions. Steubens had a rare knack for gaining trust and loyalty by listening to opposing views with deep sincerity. His forte was the ability to manipulate disapproval into acceptance. Steubens had used his tenacity to convince the council that Hideaway Pines was going to put Jessup on the map. He preached how the entire town would soon be praising the council. Things were happening in Jessup, and the small group of men sitting around that table played an influential role in its success.

"Gentlemen," began the Mayor, "first off, I'd like to thank you all for coming on such short notice. Especially you, Pete. I do know how busy you are." Wilkerson gave a brisk nod in acceptance of the apology. "As I'm sure you are aware, this gracious little town of ours has faced an extraordinary sequence of events over the past few days. Our community has been victimized by the tragic deaths of three men and an innocent boy." Steubens stopped to make sure all eyes were on him. Each councilmember was listening closely to his sermon. "The culprit, a monstrous black bear, quite possibly the largest ever taken in the State of Michigan. Although we must take sufficient time to mourn our losses and provide support for our grieving citizens, we must also look ahead to the future of Jessup." The Mayor stood up from his cushy seat at the head of the table. The spotlight was on and it was time for the show. He knew that this particular acting job was going to require one of his best efforts, especially with Pete Wilkerson in the crowd. The Operations Manager studied him like a Broadway critic.

Steubens and Wilkerson had experienced their differences in the past, but they did respect each other. Other than the educated Operations Manager, the other councilmen were pushovers compared to the real-life juries he had faced in darker times. Steubens continued his dialog. "We have a golden opportunity, gentlemen, and it's time to cash in. I firmly believe that this bear of ours is going to make us a whole lot of money." It was better to speak at their level. Cash was always king.

"What are you talking about, Gene? How is the bear going to make money? Last I heard, the thing was dead." Frank Peterson and Paul Keegle each chuckled quietly at Wilkerson's joke. Pete had not yet been made aware of the Mayor's plans.

Undisturbed by the interruption, Steubens maintained a warm smile on his round face and went on as if the comment had gone unnoticed. "It's all very simple, Pete. I've already explained it to the other gentlemen here. I've taken the liberty of contracting the Jones brothers to have the murderous animal mounted. After the task is complete, we will place the creature on display to draw in the curiosity-seekers wishing to see the man-eater for themselves. I can assure you that this will be a profitable endeavor." Steubens eyed Wilkerson closely, trying to get a fix on the man's thoughts. He had already convinced the other three men prior to the official gathering.

"Hold on a second, Gene." Wilkerson's voice rose slightly. "You know that any issues involving town funding call for a majority vote from the council."

"Pete, I have already spoken with everyone but you and we are in agreement that this is an excellent opportunity for Jessup."

Wilkerson sighed heavily, and then started again. "Okay, Gene, let's say that this is a good idea. How much money are we talking about investing?" He put his hands to the sides of his head and made quotation gestures when he said the word '*investing.*' Aside from the perpetual role of Devil's advocate at most council meetings, Pete Wilkerson was also the town treasurer, and a stingy one at that. He was well aware of what was in the till.

"Peter, the beauty of this is that we are not going to have to invest a great deal of money at all," continued the ever-optimistic Mayor. "I've settled on a suitable figure with the brothers."

"What's your definition of *suitable*?" Wilkerson was growing more cynical about the Mayor's scheme.

Steubens stalled a moment. He was expecting a negative reaction when the actual figure was released; however, he was also counting on the skeptic to eventually fall in line with the rest of the council. "Frank Jones says that the taxidermy fee for the bear will be somewhere in the neighborhood of five thousand dollars." He watched as the treasurer's eyes opened a little wider. "On top of that, they would like, or rather demand, two thousand as compensation for the loss of their dogs, as well as their own personal efforts."

"Seven thousand dollars! Where the hell do you intend to get that much cash, Gene?"

Frank Peterson, Paul Keegle and Fred Wentworth remained silent through the debate. Their heads darted from one end of the table to the other like spectators at a tennis match. Neither wished to speak up or take one side over the other. Each was content in allowing the Mayor and the treasurer to settle their quarrel. Whatever they agreed to would certainly be fine with them.

"We do have the money, Pete," continued the Mayor calmly.

"Where? Where do you see ..." Wilkerson then paused after understanding the direction the Mayor was taking. "No way,

Gene. You're not touching the festival funds, or the restoration fund for that matter. That money has been ear-marked for specific purposes."

"Ira Wall did say that the furnace could kick the bucket any day, Gene," interjected Paul Keegle, much to the surprise of both Steubens and Wilkerson. The Mayor gave him a funny look as if to say, *shut the fuck up and let me do the talking*. Keegle sank back in his chair and looked downward, realizing his mistake.

"I understand your concerns, Pete. Believe me when I say that. We're going to have to make some very important decisions. These are decisions that could change the face of our town forever."

"I'm sorry, Gene, but we're not on the same bus. How the heck is a stuffed bear going to make up for that amount of cash? What if we need that money for an emergency? What then?" Wilkerson sat and shook his head, shocked by the ineptitude of his peers.

"I'm not going to lie to you, Pete." Steubens plopped down in his chair. It was time to ease the growing tension. "This is an investment that is not void of any risk. But I firmly believe that the risk involved is very small in comparison to the rewards that could be realized. Hell, we're already seeing benefits from the golf resort. This would be just another means of attracting *Joe Civilian* to Jessup so that he can spend his hard-earned money in our town ... in our businesses. I don't want tourists passing us by and driving right on down to Appleton when we have something that deserves their dollar right here." Steubens had gently hammered his fist down on the table. He did not want to come across as being too overbearing. Wilkerson's expression had slightly changed. The door to possibility had been cracked. He was bending. It was time to go in for the kill. The Mayor went on, quoting traffic studies performed by the Hideaway Pines survey crew. He tossed out unemployment numbers, inflation figures, any form of measurement that would enforce his idealistic philosophy to enhance the wealth of their community. Gene Steubens would not allow public complacency to block his path for progress.

***

The Pathology Lab was located in the rear of the Appleton Medical Center. Appleton was kind of a crossroads where a flip of a coin might determine which direction a patient might travel for more specialized treatment. Ross parked the truck and entered the office where he was greeted by a cute African-American woman.

"May I help you, sir?"

Ross thought she would have been a good candidate for a tooth-paste commercial. A bright smile lit up her smooth face, and her warm personality was comforting. "Yes, maam, I'm here to see Dr. Flemming." Ross half expected the Doctor to pop out of nowhere just as the feisty Dr. Blake had done up in Houghton. The receptionist issued directions to the office, two doors down the hall to the left. He thanked her and proceeded.

The Doctor opened the door on the second knock.

"Sheriff Pickett, Doctor." Ross offered his hand and the man took it loosely in his own.

"Brian Flemming. Thank you for coming down."

The femininity was prominent in the man's voice, which made Ross question his sexuality. But Flemming did not fit the stereotype. He was somewhere in his late twenties to early thirties and had an athletic build with very muscular arms. The Doctor stood only about an inch shorter than the Sheriff. His face had a full beard and his eyes peered through a pair of coke-bottle lenses that rested crookedly on the bridge of his nose. The former ball player sized up his counterpart, thinking that he would make a good tight end, given his stature. The Doctor wore loose fitting green scrubs with the short sleeves rolled up over his biceps.

"I think we should get right down to business, Sheriff."

The man certainly wasn't one for small talk. That had been evident on the phone. Ross hoped that it meant this would be a short visit.

"If you feel up to it, I would like for us to review the remains."

Oh shit! Ross was thankful that he had lost his appetite before breakfast. *Thank you, Gene Steubens.*

The well-conditioned Doctor led him into a sterile lab with white, ceramic tile walls. There was an odor in the air unlike that of a regular hospital. A large examination table with a shiny, stainless steel top was planted firmly in the middle of the room. Lying on top of the table was a black body bag that even the casual observer could tell did not contain an entire human body. Ross' stomach began to roll again when he realized that it contained Charlie Perkins, or rather what was left of him.

"Please put this on, Sheriff." Flemming handed him a small face mask with an elastic band that resembled a painter's mask. "The odor in here can be a little overwhelming at first if you're not used to it."

Ross tried to prepare himself mentally for the presentation. Flemming methodically unzipped the bag. Ross quickly secured the mask around his mouth with two hands. He kept his distance as if he were being exposed to a leper. The Doctor folded away the flaps of plastic and withdrew the severed limb, minus the sleeve with Charlie's initials. Ross' nose began to detect a foul aroma building. The air seemed to thicken as the Doctor laid the rigid arm on the table. The appendage was a pale, bluish color. The stiff fingers were extended like those of a department store mannequin. Ross studied the severed region of the upper arm. It was decorated with strands of loose hanging flesh. The Sheriff gagged, bringing his hand to his mouth. He began to sweat.

"Don't worry," said the Doctor, sensing the uneasiness in his visitor. "You'll get used to it."

Ross envisioned a sadistic grin under the Doctor's mask.

"Could you step over here please?" continued Flemming. He nodded to a space at his side, next to the table.

Ross approached apprehensively, as if the arm might come to life and reach out to him. "Please relax. I can assure you that it won't bite." Flemming was reading his thoughts. He'd witnessed the expressions of many first timers to the lab. He found their actions amusing when seeing a corpse for the first time. He couldn't understand why others weren't as fascinated as he was in discovering how the human body ticked.

"Alright, Doctor," Ross said, finding the courage to continue. "Let's get this over with before you have to examine me."

Flemming giggled quietly at the Sheriff's dry humor. "You wouldn't be the first, sir. Okay, down to business. As I indicated on the phone, we have reason to believe that this may not have been a bear attack. There are a few anomalies that should be considered before the paperwork is signed."

"Look, Doctor, I saw the damn bear that did this. It was a *big* boy, let me tell you. And it did kill two of my people while we were out chasing it."

The Doctor appeared surprised by the Sheriff's comment. He had not heard of more deaths. "Well," he continued after a moment of silent reflection, "I can only apply my expertise to that which is presented to me. Unfortunately, I can't comment on evidence that I have not yet seen. Please ... listen to what I have to say. You can then draw your own conclusions." Flemming stared at Ross and waited for his acceptance of the terms.

"Okay, your floor." Ross readjusted his mask. Oddly enough, he found that he was getting used to the odor.

"Good. Now then, when we first heard that it was a possible bear encounter we looked for the obvious signs ... specifically, bite marks. The limb, as you can see, has no such marks. There are no punctures to the skin ... nothing. Strike one, if you will." Flemming grasped the appendage and slowly rotated it as he spoke. "Next," he continued, "we searched for damage to the skin resulting from a mauling, including the exposed area here." The Doctor meticulously probed the shredded flesh with a dull, stainless steel instrument. "Again, we find no such marks. Strike two. Finally, we looked for clues as to how the limb became detached from the body, precisely, whether or not it was severed. Now this is where things get a little cloudy." The Doctor lifted the arm and pointed the instrument to the rounded end of the protruding white bone.

The joint reminded Ross of a turkey drumstick.

"As you can see, Sheriff, the cartilage around the humerus here has not been compromised in any way. Had the bear bitten through this area of the arm, this bone would have been crushed, or at least damaged in some way. There are no bone fragments from the humerus. It is completely intact with no fractures. We have a clean separation from the body. Even a sharp blade would have created definitive markings, especially in the tissue. The flesh around the arm has clearly been torn, not cut. I think it's safe to say that the victim's arms was neither bitten nor severed from the body."

Ross sensed that there was a bizarre conclusion materializing. The Doctor was speaking plain enough English, and was making valid points. Regardless, he could not yet paint his own portrait of what happened. "Okay, Doctor, you've got me. How the hell did the arm separate from the body? It didn't just fall off."

"Sheriff," Flemming paused, searching for the proper words to form his response, "I believe that the limb was torn from the body." The Doctor fell silent, allowing time for the visitor to absorb the new information.

Ross could not speak. He was utterly dumbfounded. *Christ,* he thought. *How the hell could a bear tear off an arm? Why would a bear tear an arm off?*

Dr. Flemming noticed the confusion in Ross' face, so he presented the additional evidence to prove his theory. "Look here, Sheriff, at the upper portion of the arm. Do you see this darkened area on the surface of the skin?"

Ross nodded after noticing the purplish markings.

"Those marks," added Flemming, "are bruises caused from broken blood vessels. This happens when there is enough applied pressure to produce a rupture. I believe that whatever caused the separation gripped the man's arm here." Flemming grasped Ross' upper arm with one hand. With his free hand he clutched Ross' shoulder blade and made a soft tugging motion. "It then gripped him around the shoulder like this, pulling the body apart."

Ross was so consumed with the reenactment that he paid no attention to the fact that the Doctor had not taken off his gloves before touching him. "Why don't you think a bear could have done that?" He couldn't comprehend what the doctor was suggesting. "Like I said before, this was a big friggin bear." He wanted to convince Flemming that it had been the bear.

"Anything's possible, Sheriff. It's just not likely."

Ross backed up a step, looking away from Charlie Perkins' arm. "I'm sorry. I guess that I'm just not as convinced as you are." And he really wasn't sold on the theory. There had to be a simpler explanation.

"Alright," continued the pathologist, "let's examine what evidence we do have." Flemming held up the arm once again. It was now just an ordinary object, like a prop from a school play. "These bruises covering the bicep and triceps regions are deep, and encircle the entire limb. My best guess is that it was held in this fashion." He grasped the upper arm with his own gloved hand.

Ross could still see the large bruises protruding well outside his fingers.

"As I'm sure you're aware, bears have paws and are not really capable of grasping something the size of a man's arm, and pulling with much force. In my opinion," said the Doctor, "I'd have to say that this was gripped by a much larger, hand-like vice with a great deal of power. As you can see from the bruised skin, it would have to be three or four times the size of my own. And I have big hands."

"Could the bear have sat on the arm or something ... then by grabbing the body ..." Ross tried his best to imitate two paws clutching an invisible object.

"Yes, that is still a possibility that I have considered. But I believe the bruises would have been larger yet. It would still require a pulling motion to reach this end. A bear's gripping capabilities are extremely limited."

Ross just stood there, shaking his head. It was all so unbelievable.

"Of course, I haven't actually seen the animal that you've described," continued the Doctor," but even a full sized grizzly would have trouble pulling this off."

Ross sat down on a round stool with rollers and rested his back against a wall. He had to ask the question that he did not especially want answered. "Okay, Doc, let's assume that you are correct in your assessment." *Go ahead and ask, buddy,* he told himself quietly. "If a bear didn't kill this man, then what the hell did?" Ross asked the serious question, intent on receiving an equally serious response.

Dr. Flemming loosened his mask and folded his muscular arms across his chest. He sensed the anticipation in the Sheriff. "All that I can say for sure is that a bear *may* not have been the assailant. You see, my field is one of scientific, deductive reasoning that calls for a bit of speculation from time to time. There have been cases where our conclusions have been proven to be totally off base. But my job is to construct a puzzle with the number of pieces available to me."

"I understand that," said Ross, "but you still haven't answered my question." He was growing impatient with the man. He now leaned forward on his stool and glared up at the young Doctor.

"There is another possibility." Flemming stalled a minute, hesitant to elaborate.

"And that is ..."

"Homicide." The Doctor waited for the reaction.

Ross unintentionally toppled the stool as he sprang to his feet. "Murder! Jesus Christ!" He tugged at his hair with both hands. "Do you actually think that another human being could have done that? It's insane!"

"Easy, Sheriff. Just a possibility," continued the Doctor without changing his tone. He held up both hands in an effort to calm the Sheriff. "Personally, I doubt that a single man could have done this. But two or three ... maybe."

"You know, I just don't get it. You yourself said that there were no lacerations in the tissue. And I don't know any man alive who could tear another man's arm off." *Why would someone tear a man's arm off!* "No," proclaimed Ross assuredly. "Not murder, out of the question. That's just too damned crazy." He watched Flemming nod in agreement. He was too agreeable for the Sheriff's liking. Ross wondered then what he was up to.

"I can see your angle ... and I agree to a certain point," said Flemming.

"Then why the hell did you just go there?" Ross was curt with the man. He didn't care to be led around by his balls.

"I just wanted to see your reaction before I throw out another crazy suggestion."

Ross leaned up against the wall one more time and folded his arms. He had no idea what the strange man was getting at. He sure as hell had an odd approach to making a point. But at least he was honest.

Flemming walked to his side and looked him straight in the eyes. "Please don't think I'm crazy, Sheriff, but we may want to consider the existence of an entirely different life-form. Something out of the ordinary, not indigenous to this region."

Ross now expected the Doctor's face to explode with laughter. A joke played on the unsuspecting fool from Jessup. It would be something to tell his buddies about at the Friday night card game. Or better yet, maybe his buddies were in the next room preparing to storm in and surround him with an onslaught of hilarity. But there was no raillery in the man's demeanor. He just stood there in front of him and stared with eyes that were deathly serious.

Ross knew then that he was not the butt of a perverted prank, but rather the target of an inquiry that warranted a direct and honest response. He suddenly felt uncomfortable in the man's presence, and frightened by the realization that he had shared those exact same thoughts derived from what his own eyes had witnessed in recent days. Ned Crosby's terrified face came back to him ... the horrid screams ... the reference to a '*monster*.'

Ross felt emotionally drained. "Doctor?" he asked softly. "What do you mean by another life-form? What kind of animal could do this?"

"I don't know, Sheriff. But in my professional opinion, it was something other than a bear. It was something with ... hands." He hesitated a moment, held up his own hands and then continued as he opened and closed them. "Like a man's hand."

Ross felt as if he were falling into a black hole from which there was no escape. Images of demons were now looming in his head ... and then Ray Jackson began to laugh.

"Sheriff?" Flemming grabbed the slightly taller man's shoulder. "For your town's sake as well as your own, I will classify this as a bear attack. No questions asked." He waited for Ross' signal of approval.

The Sheriff slowly nodded his head, as if a puppeteer were pulling his strings. He didn't really understand the significance of the Doctor's synopsis. It couldn't be so easy as a simple stroke of a pen, end of story. But he couldn't go running around screaming about some man-eating beast stalking the Amen Swamp. People would panic, that is, if they didn't think he'd gone completely off the deep end. Ross battled with his internal feelings, ignoring the Doctor who continued to study him. *Why can't I just wake up, and there would be Eevie stroking my hair, and ... It was a bear, goddammit!* He had seen with his own eyes how the animal had nearly torn his best friend in half. There had to be a logical explanation as to what happened to Charlie's arm.

There was only one course of action for him to take. The Sheriff wasn't sure if he was more afraid of the town that would crucify him for this sort of craziness, or of the possibility that some mysterious creature might be lurking in the Amen Swamp. He couldn't deal with another death. Ross felt like a coward hiding from a reality that had yet to expose itself, but his choice had been made. “Sign it,” he said. Although he sounded firm with the decision, his conscience was in turmoil.

“Very well, Sheriff. I hope you can appreciate why I wanted to speak with you in person.”

“Yes, and thank you.” Ross appeared as if he were the victim of some ruthless torture. *Please, God,* he thought as he left the building, *don’t let me regret this.*

***

“Are we in agreement then, gentlemen?” Gene Steubens waited for a response from the four men sitting before him. Fred Wentworth, Frank Peterson and Paul Keegle each nodded their heads in approval of the Mayor’s plan. But it was Wilkerson who was the focal point of Steubens’ concern. He alone was the key to success for this mission. The Mayor watched carefully as the treasurer stared down to his folded hands like a man in deep thought. That was not a positive sign. Finally, the skeptical treasurer raised his head and nodded.

“Okay, Gene. We’ll give it a shot. But I want receipts for every damn transaction that takes place. I don’t trust those Jones boys as far as I can throw them.” Like everyone else in town, Pete Wilkerson knew Frank and Jesse’s reputation well.

“Excellent! Gentlemen, you have done your community a great service. I thank you for your support.” Steubens quietly rejoiced in his ability to manipulate. He had won again.

Wilkerson spoke up. “I also think that it would be a good idea if we kept the source of funding and the amount being allocated inside this room. I don’t care to be tar and feathered if this doesn’t work out.”

“I don’t foresee a problem with that. Men?” Steubens looked to the others and they nodded in agreement. “Don’t worry about a thing, Pete.” continued Steubens. In a few months, the people of Jessup will be licking the dirt you walk on.” Even Pete Wilkerson found humor in the Mayor’s premonition.

“I still don’t think Ross Pickett is going to be too happy about all this, Gene.” Fred Wentworth’s weak statement drew a harsh stare from the Mayor. His jovial mood quickly deflated. That nerve had been touched.

Steubens composed himself, bypassing the urge to publicly chastise the Sheriff. He realized that an outburst might result in losing any ground already gained. He began speaking calmly, measuring each word as though he were being graded on enunciation. “That’s one more topic that I would like to discuss with you men before we adjourn for the evening.” They were all fond of the Sheriff. They respected Ross Pickett, and that could be a problem. But there could be only two sides of this matter with no go-between. He would require total support if he was to succeed in achieving his goals. Sheriff Ross Pickett would have to be cast out of the picture for good.

“It seems our esteemed Sheriff,” he began again, “is in heavy opposition to our plan. I’m sure that he will rant and rave and do everything in his power to defeat our efforts to help this town.” His objective now was to somehow pit the council against the Sheriff, and vice versa. “The problem with Ross Pickett is that he is an elected official and he feels that this gives him accountability to no one. That is where he is gravely mistaken.” The four men watched curiously, all wondering what the Mayor was proposing. “The town charter clearly states that should the council deem the elected official to be derelict in his duties, the council has the authority to terminate the official altogether with a majority vote.” Steubens noted the frowns on the faces around the table. Be he could work over that hump. *Control,* he thought, *always maintain control.* “Now I don’t want you to think that I want Ross Pickett fired,” he lied. “In fact, I think that the Sheriff has done a fine job for us. But I also believe that he is greatly overstepping his boundaries and needs to be told that we have the power to pull the plug if need be.”

“You gonna tell that to big Ross, Gene?” joked Wilkerson.

“No, Pete. I don’t think *big Ross* cares too much for me right now. Frank, I’d like you to talk to him.” He turned to the older councilman. “You seem to be closer to him than anyone else at this table.” Steubens knew that Peterson was the perfect stool for the task. Ross couldn’t get too angry at the retired old man with his happy-go-lucky smile. And if he did, then that would just play into the Mayor’s hand.

“I don’t know, Gene.” Frank shied away from the idea while focusing on a broken fingernail on his wrinkled hand.

"It would sure be a big help to all of us, Frank. Just talk to him. Settle him down some. Tell him that what we're doing is a good thing."

At last, Frank Peterson raised his head and nodded slowly, giving into the Mayor's pleas. "Okay," he said dejectedly. "I'll try, but I ain't lookin forward to it. That's for sure."

***

Ross watched from the Tahoe as Maggie charged through the back door of their home. The return drive from Appleton had dragged on for what seemed like an eternity. Not a word was uttered by either passenger. Ross still could not find the strength to confide in her. He needed more time to think through his dilemma. His mind continuously wandered to those haunting images. Though he tried again and again to convince himself that the bear's demise would be the end, the doubts kept exploding in his head like popcorn kernels over a hot flame.

What if there was something out in that swamp? He was responsible for protecting the people of Jessup. His conscience could not allow him to avoid the unknown. The bow hunters would be out in full force in a week's time, filling the remote hunting camps surrounding the Amen. Whatever actions he took would have to be discreet. The last thing he needed was a wave of embellished rumors circulating through town.

Ross devised a plan. The safety of those living or hunting in and around the Amen would be his first priority. He would mock up a story for his Deputy, telling him that the DNR wanted to crack down on poachers. He and Mark would then monitor the backroads on a regular schedule. This prompted an idea to go in front of the town council and request extra help for the hunting season. He knew a few boys from Jessup who would be more than happy to lend a hand. More eyes out there would make his job easier and lighten his worries in the process.

Ross ambled slowly toward the house. As he looked to the trees that rose up the steep ridge, he wondered if there really was something out there, possibly looking down on him at that very moment. He pointlessly kicked some loose stones on the gravel drive. Suddenly, Chuck burst through the door with a shotgun in one hand and an orange vest in the other.

"Hey, Ross! Boy, mom sure is pissed about something. And I thought my grades were pretty good this semester."

"I don't think it's your grades," replied Ross with a tight grin. He knew that he was treading in deep water with Maggie.

The teenager seemed to catch on to the hidden message. "Well, I'm heading over to Mike's right now. That offer still stands if you want to come along and knock down a few birds." Chuck hoisted the twenty-gauge that Ross had given him for his sixteenth birthday. The Sheriff took in a deep breath of fresh autumn air. The sweet smell of the pines, coupled with the drying leaves of the hardwoods had a soothing effect. There was no invasive odor of death.

Ross gave the boy a quick look over. He sure as hell didn't want Chuck running around out there by himself. And now wasn't a particularly good time to face Maggie. He knew that a confrontation would not benefit either party. She needed both time and space to simmer down some. "Okay, Chuck. But only if we hit that stretch of poplar I told you about earlier." Inside, Ross hoped that they would truly find some birds that evening so he wouldn't look the fool he was.

"Just point the way, old man," said the eager teen.

Ross went into the house. He was almost creeping so Maggie wouldn't detect him. He collected his hunting gear from the front closet; a Browning Citori and a vest similar to Chuck's. As he filled the elastic slots of the game vest with number sixes, he noticed a box of rifled slugs lying on the top shelf. He stared at the box for a moment.

"Precautions," Ross told himself as he took the slugs and placed it in the front pocket of his jeans.

***

Tyrone Pullman pulled back the gauze wrapping and examined the wound with the aid of a small, dirty mirror that was tacked up on the wall. He grimaced at the sight of the torn cartilage. He soaked a cotton ball with some peroxide and carefully blotted the exposed area. There was an immediate stab of pain. "Fuck!"

"What up, Tye?" Gerald turned away from the old black and white television set. He had been glued to the thing all day. His stumpy legs stretched out across the ragged cushions of the sofa sleeper. There was a scattering of empty beer cans on the floor.

"My fucking ear is what's up!" cursed Tyrone.

"Don't be trippin, homes."

Fuck you, Gerald.

"Hey, Tye, maybe we should think about pulling out tonight."

Tyrone turned and faced his partner, wondering if he was pulling his leg. Tyrone had watched Gerald drink beer all day, and when Gerald drank, his mind became a bold adversary to common sense. Alcohol coupled with pure boredom was a dangerous combination. Tyrone was also unhappy about Gerald's frivolous eating habits. He had made no effort to conserve what little rations they had. A full loaf of bread and half of the sandwich meat had already been consumed. They could not be seen in public. He had to assume that the police knew that he was wounded, and a black man with a missing ear would not be too hard to spot. He casually strolled over to the faucet and filled a glass with water. He took a big swig to chase two Extra-Strength Tylenol that were also found in the medicine cabinet. The water had a heavy taste of iron. He then walked across the room and sat next to Gerald on the sofa. The rusty springs squeaked.

"Gerald," said Tyrone calmly, "I don't think it would be smart for us to get on the road just yet."

"They don't know who the fuck we is." Gerald spoke matter-of-factly, and continued to stare at the T.V.

"We don't know that. For all we know, the cops could have our pictures nailed up on every telephone pole from here to Chicago."

"They might have my picture, Tye, but where the fuck are they gonna get yours? You're a clean-ass pussy."

Gerald had meant the shot to be a dig, but in Tyrone's mind being a *clean-ass pussy* meant that he had done things the right way ... the smart way. "I don't know, man. A lot of them stores have cameras. We had to get out of there awful quick. It just ain't worth the risk."

Gerald hesitated a moment, contemplating his partner's opinion. But his mind was clouded by liquid courage. "Fuck that. There weren't no cameras in that cracker's store." He continued to focus his attention on the T.V. where an old episode of M.A.S.H. was playing. "I say we get the fuck outta here tonight. If you wanna stay, go ahead." He crossed his arms in a gesture of stern commitment.

There was no rationale in Gerald's behavior. The idea had transitioned from simple suggestion to solidified intent. Tyrone became uneasy, thinking of the ramifications if the two were to drive off into the night into unfamiliar territory. Although Gerald had technically saved his life, he felt no sense of allegiance toward the man. It was time for Tyrone to look out for Tyrone. Once again, Gerald proved that he was not qualified for tactical maneuvering. Tyrone's plan had been to wait out the storm for a few weeks, hoping that the owners of the cabin did not decide to show up for a weekend getaway. They were well-equipped to deal with that situation should the need arise. *No,* he thought, *we can't leave now.* They would be sitting ducks out in the open. He decided to give Gerald just one last chance to redeem himself. Tyrone owed his partner that much leniency. But he would not put up with any more of his irresponsible bullshit.

"I really think we need to stay put, G. Let's just sit tight for a week or two. Make the cops think we split, and then slip out in the night." He spoke with a delicate calm to try and drive sense into the man. But there was no swaying Gerald Johnson once his mind was set.

"Fuck you, Tye. I say I'm goin tonight and that's it. If you wanna stay, then fuck you." Gerald still would not look away from the T.V. His words were cold and sharp.

Tyrone Pullman sat back in the sofa knowing what he now had to do. He despised Gerald Johnson, sitting on that couch playing the bad-ass gangster. *You ain't taking me down with you, motherfucker,* thought Tyrone. He stared at his long-time business associate knowing that their relationship had just reached its conclusion. There was a side to Tyrone that felt sorry for the separation. After all, they had grown up together in the slums of Flint. They also rose together to a level of respect. But there was also a more pragmatic voice telling him that this day was inevitable. Though brash in his lead role, Gerald Johnson had proven too often that he was careless. Their future would be short-lived if Gerald remained at the helm dictating their direction. Tyrone did not wish to be collateral damage when Gerald's luck ran out.

Tyrone stood up and casually walked across the floor to his coveralls that were hanging on a coat rack. He wanted the object concealed in the front pocket of his garment ... his safety net.

"Where you goin?" The question arose from the couch.

"I'm going for some fresh air," answered Tyrone, continuing on toward the far side of the room.

"Close the door behind you then. It's cold outside."

Tyrone reached the coveralls and pulled them off the hook that had once been a deer antler. He looked back over his shoulder to Gerald who was laughing at some beer commercial involving small dogs and a mouse. *Fuck you, G.* Tyrone slowly reached for that front pocket, keeping his eyes fixed on his partner the entire time. It would be quick and simple. He wouldn't feel a thing. *And if he did, well fuck it.* He turned away. Tyrone's hand reached the pocket and slipped inside. There was nothing there.

"Lookin for something, Tye?" There was sarcasm in Gerald's inquiry.

Tyrone's heart began to beat faster. He turned to confront his partner. Gerald stood before him holding the .32 that he had kept hidden throughout their journey. *How did he...?* Then he remembered ... the store. Tyrone forgot that he had tossed the weapon to Gerald. It was a deadly mistake on his part. Gerald pointed the gun at his friend's head with a crazy smile plastered on his dark face. He appeared to be enjoying himself. Tyrone didn't know whether he should play dumb or just tell him to go ahead and shoot so that this misery would end.

"Looking for this, Tye?" Gerald wiggled the pistol in a bantering manner.

"What the fuck you doin, G?" Tyrone raised his arms in defense, acting naïve to the situation.

Gerald's face turned to stone with a menacing look in his eyes. He was sweating. The gun shook in his unsteady hand. "Don't fuck with me, Tyrone!" he yelled. "You were gonna cap me, motherfucker!"

"Gerald, put the gun down ... please. I don't know what the fuck you're talking 'bout." Tyrone took a step forward, but stopped when the unstable man before him cocked the hammer.

"Don't you fucking move, Tye. I saved your ass and you're gonna cap me? You motherfucker!" Gerald's voice continued to rise in disgust.

This was not a fitting end, thought Tyrone. With all of the shit he had put up with over the years, and now he was going to die while cooped up in some redneck's cabin in the middle of nowhere. He would have preferred to be hit back home in Flint. Back where his life had meant something. Back where his death would have been meaningful. But then something unexpected and strange happened. Gerald lowered his arm that held the gun. He turned away. Tyrone glanced quickly to the Klashnikov at the doorway, wondering whether or not he would have time to reach it.

"I don't understand you, Tye. With all the shit we been through together, how could you do me, man?" Gerald's voice was breaking. The alcohol was toying with his emotions.

Tyrone remained still. The last thing he wanted to do was provoke the man. When Gerald raised the gun a second time, Tyrone closed his eyes and threw up his arms to ward off any incoming rounds that were about to be discharged. *I'm going to die now,* he thought. He started thinking of his mother who he hadn't seen in years. His body shook with fear as he wondered what death would feel like.

But the gun did not fire. There were no bullets ripping through his body. He began to think that perhaps he was already dead, and that death had been painless. Tyrone forced his eyes open. Gerald was coming at him, holding the gun at full extension, but not in a firing position. His finger was off the trigger.

"I don't think you can do it, Tye. Here! Take this fucking gun." Gerald grabbed Tyrone's quivering hand and placed the gun inside his palm. He then forced Tyrone's fingers to close around it.

Tyrone could only stand there in silence, stunned by Gerald's actions ... unsure as to what he should do.

"You're my best friend in this whole fucking world, Tye." Gerald sounded as if he were on the verge of tears. "We growed up together in the hood, man. We fought our way to the top. You want to fucking kill me after all we done together? You wouldn't be here if it weren't for me."

Tyrone stared at his friend. He was now battling his own feelings that were indecisively swaying from one difficult decision to the next. He felt the gun firmly in his grip. His finger roamed the rounded steel of the trigger guard.

"We can make it, Tye," continued Gerald, pleading with his friend. "We can get outta here and hole up in Chi-town. In a month, we'll be back in Flint, running things again. We're a team, Tye, you and me."

Gerald's words sealed his fate. There was no going back home for Gerald Johnson. Only on his own did Tyrone have a chance. His partner could not comprehend the simple fact that he could never step foot in Flint, Michigan again. Regardless of how hard Tyrone pressed, in the end, Gerald would not listen. *Always Gerald's way or no way,* thought Tyrone to himself as he cocked the hammer back.

Gerald's ears heard the clicking sound. He gazed into Tyrone's eyes with a playful grin. Tyrone raised the weapon and extended it to within a foot of his childhood friend's face. He blocked out all feeling and pulled the trigger. The gun recoiled slightly in his hand as the bullet made a dime-sized hole in Gerald's forehead. Tyrone watched his friend stumble, but he didn't fall. Gerald kept looking into his eyes with disbelief. A small rivulet of dark blood trickled from the tiny wound, running down the dying man's face. Gerald's body wavered as his eyes rolled back in their sockets. Tyrone fired three more shots, this time into the heart. Gerald clutched his chest, dropped to his knees, and then fell face first onto the hard wooden floor. He was dead.

Tyrone hovered over his fallen friend's body for a good five minutes, assessing the logic of his actions. Unlike those other occasions where he had been forced to kill, this experience was different. Never before had it been someone so important in his life. They had been like brothers once. But business was business, and deep down, Tyrone thought that wherever Gerald was now, he would understand. Tyrone was now alone. Only he could determine his fate from there on out.

***

It was nine o'clock and Maggie still had not spoken to him. She appeared even more upset that he had run away from the brewing argument earlier in the day. Maggie had been in the process of leaving for the Inn when Ross and Chuck pulled into the drive that evening. She did not stop to say hello or exhibit any form of facial expression that would tip him off to her disposition. Her shunning body language was evidence enough, and it pained him to no end. Ross did not like to see her that way. He hoped that she would at least call to check on him later in the night. Now there was only silence in the home. He was alone.

Chuck turned right around and left to hook up with a few of his buddies. He said something about a movie in Appleton ... something about a vampire killing other vampires. Before spilling into the recliner, Ross made one call to the office and spoke with Mark. He relayed his plan to beef up their patrolling efforts. The Deputy was excited at the prospect of nailing some bad guys. In the meantime, Ross inwardly prayed that the Amen Swamp would remain dormant.

As he fiddled with the remote, he noticed a spec of blood on his thumbnail. The boys had done quite well that afternoon, downing four grouse and three woodcock. When he first stepped out of the truck, a sense of paranoia swept over him. He felt that something was stalking him, toying with his psyche. In his heart, he knew that there was something else out there. The pathologist's words hounded him with visions of supernatural beings lurking in the trees. Ross had not fired a single shot all afternoon. He decided to load slugs in both barrels of his over-under. Instead of watching for birds, he found himself searching the undergrowth for hidden eyes. Whenever a particularly dense section stood before them, he would bolt ahead of the small hunting party to flush anything that might by lying in wait. Fortunately, there had been plenty of game, allowing his paranoid antics to go unnoticed. Internally, he was uneasy about being in the outdoors, particularly with Chuck at his side.

The regular Monday Night Football commentators were performing their pre-game analysis when he clicked on the television set. The Lions were in Buffalo. Ross needed a good football game to escape the real world, if only for a few short hours. The cordless phone rang beside the Sheriff's chair. Ross hesitated before picking it up, wondering if it was Maggie on the other end. He had not yet thought about what he should say.

"Hello, this is Ross."

""Hi, Ross, Frank Peterson here. Uh ... how you doin tonight?"

The Sheriff recognized the soft voice of his older friend. He immediately detected some apprehension in the man. "Just fine, Frank. Getting ready to watch the ball game."

"Oh, yeah ... hopefully the Lions can get it together this year."

The caller's voice trailed off as he spoke. There was something else on his mind. Ross concluded that Frank Peterson did not call about the football game. "What can I do for you, Frank?" He muted the T.V.

"Well, Ross ... uh ... I ... really don't know ... uh ... how to say this. Ross ... uh ..."

The man was sputtering horribly. "Okay, Frank, what's bothering you?" *Something's wrong,* he thought.

"Well, Ross ... you see, the council had a meeting ... today. It was a special meeting. You see ... uh ... Gene put together this ... uh, plan. We were hoping ... for your support."

Shit! That little bastard was going ahead with his goddamned scheme. Ross closed his eyes and was pinching the bridge of his nose with his thumb and forefinger, as if the action would somehow make the phone call go away. He could just hang up. "He's actually going to do it, Frank? He's going to put that bear on display?" The Sheriff kept his cool, even though the steam was surging inside him. The Mayor was playing his puppets yet again. But Ross couldn't blame them too much ... except for Pete. Wilkerson was a sharp cookie. *Why would he get mixed up in this?*

"Is Pete in on this too, Frank?" He started massaging his throbbing temple.

"Yes, Ross. We all are. You have to understand. It's for the good of the town."

"I know, Frank, and we're all going to get rich and all that bullshit. I've heard it before." Ross began to wonder why it was Frank Peterson calling him at such a late hour. *There has to be something else,* he concluded. *Steubens has another fire burning.* The other end of the line was silent. "You there, Frank?"

"Yeah, Ross, I'm here," replied the quiet councilman.

"What's up? Why did you really call me?"

"Ross, Gene seems to think that you're going to do your best to block this plan. Gene also says, and I know that it won't come to this, but ... the ... council has the power to take away your badge ... if necessary." Frank Peterson fell silent a second time, wondering if he had just lost a friend.

A threat! Ross was fuming. *The son-of-a-bitch is threatening me.* It was not Frank Peterson who he was upset with, but rather the man who was holding the reins. A part of him wanted to take his badge and shove it right up the Mayor's ass. But now was not the time to overreact. Ross forced himself to settle down. He had things to take care of ... people to protect. The Amen Swamp weighed too heavy on his conscience. But how could he cower in the face of such an insensitive act? How could he drive down Main Street and see that bear propped up in a window when he could have done something to prevent it. *Jesus! What will Rachel Perkins think?* He mulled over his options, knowing all too well that he was wedged between a rock and a hard place. His life just seemed to be getting more complex with each passing second.

"I guess you got me hog-tied, Frank," said the disappointed Sheriff. "I won't stop you if that's what you want to do. But I will not condone your little escapade, either." Ross tried his best to instill a sense of guilt into the caller.

"Really, Ross, Gene says it will work out for the best. If only you'd just ..."

Ross hung up before Frank Peterson could make his futile attempt at self-justification. Now he truly did feel as though he were on an island.

***

Berkowski's paperwork was finally finished when the clock on his desk chimed twice to signal that it was two in the morning. He rubbed his tired eyes, sitting in the command post that was nearly deserted. As he looked up he noticed Samantha Godson hanging up her phone in the cubicle outside his glassed office. The MSP veteran pushed himself up out of his chair and opened the door.

"How's it going, Sam?" asked the elder Trooper.

Godson had been busy on the phone with other posts throughout the State. She swiveled around and tilted back in her chair. She then put her hand to her mouth and yawned, a sign that she, too, was exhausted from the day's work. "I think we've got just about everyone on notice, Berk."

"Any I.D. yet on number two?" he asked, referring to the unknown assailant who was wounded at the crime scene.

"No, Sergeant. No prints in the computer ... nothing. It's like he doesn't even exist."

"What do the boys down south think?"

"Johnson, the known fugitive, is from Flint. Flint P.D. is turning the city over right now, checking out their informants. Last I heard, they were aware that this Johnson character was dealing with an associate whose identity is unknown to this point. They're flagging pictures all over the city trying to get a name on our guy. They seem to think it might be Johnson's partner." She let out another yawn.

"Well, not much we can do about it right now. The word's out. Why don't you get out of here? It's been a long day."

"You can say that again. Just one more call to make."

"Where's that?" asked the Sergeant.

"So," she continued, "I've been looking at the map. Come here and I'll show you something." Godson motioned the Sergeant to her desk. He took three steps and rested his hands beside the State map spread out in front of the Trooper. "Flint P.D. says that Johnson is one of their top dogs in the drug trade down there. He's got connections as far as Florida all along the I-75 coke train."

Berkowski was very familiar with the reference that Godson had made. I-75 stretched from Sault Ste. Marie clear down to southern Florida and was a notorious route for illicit drug activity. Early on in his career, Berkowski had been involved in a few joint operations with both the F.B.I. and Homeland Security.

"When he was sprung from the prison van yesterday," continued Godson, "the dragnet concentrated on all routes leading out of the State to the south. The thought process was that they would be fleeing to a large metropolitan area, like Cincinnati, or maybe even Atlanta, somewhere down there ... far away from local media. That's why they were so stunned to learn that he was identified way the heck up here in no-man's land."

"So the question is ... why did they come north instead of taking a more familiar route to the south?" The picture was unclear in Berkowski's mind, but Godson's excitement told him that she was onto something. The Sergeant felt a great deal of pride when he witnessed a subordinate breaking a case.

"Okay, let's start down here between Mason and Jackson where the prison van was attacked." Godson pinpointed the approximate location with her finger and held it in place. "The fugitives most likely drove up 27 and jumped onto 75 at Grayling." She traced the path slowly with her finger. "They managed to cross the bridge and then head west. Now we have to consider why they took this northern route when they were expected to head south."

"What about relatives, Sam?" inquired the Sergeant. It was a shot in the dark, but possible.

Godson gave him somewhat of a silly look. "Not likely, sir. Regardless, that has already been checked out. Flint says there are no known relatives to Johnson living in these parts that they are aware of."

"Okay, what's your best guess? Why would they come through our neck of the woods?"

"Well, it's just a theory." She paused.

"Go ahead, Sam, deal your cards," pressed Berkowski.

"Okay," she continued with enthusiasm, "these are city boys, right?" The Sergeant nodded. "Like Flint P.D. said, they're probably heading to a populated area so they can blend in. They aren't the type to be living off the land. So if they're heading west across the U.P., I'd bet my next paycheck that our fugitives are trying to make their way to Milwaukee, or even Chicago." She traced her finger right off the edge of the map and down to where she thought the two cities to be located.

Berkowski straightened and tugged at the base of his chin with two fingers, examining the evidence before him. It was a decent point.

"Berky," added Godson, "I really think these guys are smart and knew that the southern routes would be heavily watched. As it appears, nobody thought they'd head north. And this is a darn good way to get to either of those cities without drawing much attention."

"So if what you're saying is true, we'd better concentrate on the western half of the U.P. Can't see them heading to Canada. They would be sitting ducks at the bridge."

"My feeling exactly. That's why I've been contacting every town west of St. Ignace to keep their eyes open."

"Yes," continued Berkowski, nodding his approval. "They won't chance crossing the Mackinaw Bridge a second time unless they suddenly got stupid. It's too risky. Their only real alternative is to head west. More ways to get out."

"I've got one more call to make and then the net's complete. Everyone has faxes with Johnson's picture I.D. I can't see them getting out of Michigan without somebody spotting them. If they do, Wisconsin has a line on them as well."

"What about the medical community?" Berkowski raised another important point. "One of them is wounded and may require medical care."

"Already done, sir. All medical facilities between here and Green Bay have been notified."

"That's excellent work, Sam." Berkowski gave her a sharp pat on the back. She smiled, embarrassed by the compliment. But she was proud of herself, too. "Where's the last call going?"

"Jessup," she said. "It's just northwest of us."

"Jessup?" It was Berkowski's turn to smile. "I know the Sheriff up there. Ross Pickett. Good man. He's a former C.O. from St. Ignace. Tell him I said hey."

"Will do, sir."

"Then go home and get some rest. We have a lot of bird-doggin in front of us tomorrow."

Just as Godson was ready to heed her Sergeant's advice, the phone rang on her desk. She punched the proper line with her finger and brought the receiver to her ear. Berkowski turned and headed back toward his office.

"Godson here, may I help you? Yeah ... really ... really ... Great! Spelling?" Berkowski turned his head and watched her scribble down something on a notepad. "Thank you for getting back to us so soon. Great work. Okay ... Seeya." Samantha Godson extended her legs sending her chair rolling backwards. She looked up to her superior with a big grin.

"What's got you all pumped up?" questioned Berkowski.

"We have a name."

CHAPTER NINE

The stereo in the small off-campus apartment vibrated to the tune from Hank Williams Jr. Alejandro "Alex" Chavez accompanied the singer with his own off-key rendition. "Why don't ya tell me Hank, whyyyyy do you drink? Whyyyyy do you roll smoke? Whyyyyy must you live out the da ... da... da ... da."

"Come on Al. Turn that country shit down," protested Trevor Musgrave. "The phone's ringing!" He bounced up off the couch and walked to the kitchen.

Alex set his beer down on the scarred surface of a coffee table that he had recently procured from a garage sale for a measly five bucks. He reached over to the CD player and tweaked the knob to quiet the music. A pouting frown crossed his face as he offered his middle finger to his roommate.

Trevor smiled at the gesture, then clutched his crotch and playfully thrust his hips forward. "Eat me." He picked up the ringing phone. "Hello? Hey, babe, how's it goin? Cool! Alright ... see you in bit." Trevor hung up after the brief conversation. "Yes!" he cried aloud, raising his fist to the ceiling. He looked as if he had just won a game on a last second jumper.

Alex propped himself up on one elbow and looked at him curiously. "What up, bro?"

Trevor strutted across the floor and then collapsed onto the couch beside his roommate. "That was Brenda, my man, and she said we are a 'go' with her uncle's cabin for the opener. It will be two fun-filled days of huntin and srumpin. Yes!" The raised fist gesture was repeated.

"Awe, Trev." Alex's face had suddenly lost its glow. "I thought you said that it was just going to be us." He was truly disappointed by the idea of girls ruining the outdoor experience that he had looked forward to for so long.

"We will, my man. We will. Come on, Al, give me some skin. This will be a riot." Trevor extended his open hand and Alex Chavez reluctantly slapped it. "Relax, and just picture this in your mind." He placed one hand around his roommate's slumping shoulders as he took his free hand and painted an invisible setting in the room before them. "You and me out in the woods, stalking monster bucks, dragging them back to a warm cabin. And then jumping into bed with a nice warm babe after a few beers to top off the evening." Trevor reached down to the small refrigerator and extracted two ice-cold cans of Milwaukee's Best, the beer of choice for students on a budget. He popped both tops and then handed one to Alex, who was still not satisfied with the new arrangements for the opening weekend hunt. "A toast," continued Trevor as he raised his can. "You and me ... killing bucks from a tree."

Alex hoisted his drink and clanked it against his friend's. He brought the beer to his lips and took a long swig. It tasted good. There was nothing in the world like a cold beer, he thought. And maybe Trevor was right. How bad could it be? "Okay, Trev," he finally said. "But we'd better see some horns this year. That place we hunted last year was a shit-hole." During the previous season, the college seniors had spent a number of mornings and evenings on a piece of nearby state land, and the only wildlife that Alex had encountered was a menacing porcupine that persistently dropped bark on his head. He eventually dispatched the animal with a fieldtip.

"Take it easy, Al. Brenda's uncle's place is some primo hunting land. He's got about eighty acres that borders this gigantic swamp. She said her uncle got a twelve-point last year with a rifle, and two of her cousins bagged nice eight-points with bows."

Alex could clearly see the excitement glowing in his roommate's eyes, and he began to feel that familiar twitch of anticipation himself. *What the hell,* he thought. *Maybe it would be okay to have Kayla along.* Although she had no interest in watching him kill *'poor defenseless animals'*, she was a warm body to cuddle up with.

Trevor Musgrave and Alex Chavez had been roommates, as well as best of friends, from the first day that each set foot on the campus of Northern Michigan University in Marquette. Although their personalities and backgrounds were at opposite ends of the spectrum, they had managed to establish a tight bond. Their relationship was a solid argument for opposites attracting. Trevor was a charismatic youth from Green Bay, Wisconsin, who felt that a student's success in college should be graded on how many beers could be consumed at a frat party before puking. His father and uncle partnered a fruitful Ford dealership back in Green Bay. His destiny was to one day join the family business regardless of the framework that college would provide. His goal was to have as much fun in four years as humanly possible before the family took him back.

Alex Chavez, on the other hand, had experienced nothing but harsh reality in life. He was raised by a single mother, along with four brothers and sisters, in a poverty-stricken section of Muskegon, Michigan. Their possessions were small in comparison to most, but the Chavez family exhibited a strong sense of togetherness. It was a trait instilled in them by Maria Chavez whose primary concern was to ensure that they remained off the streets and away from those who preyed upon the less fortunate. Maria worked three mediocre, low-paying jobs to satisfy her children's everyday needs. Being a single mother with little spare time, she was forced to trust in her eldest son Alex to care for his younger siblings. Alex was the father-figure in the family. He would see his brothers and sisters off to school in the mornings while his mother was working at the dry cleaners. Alex would then walk them home in the afternoons when Maria was bussing tables at a local restaurant. Alex had been approached numerous times by local gang members, but he wanted no part of that lifestyle. Alex had bigger and better plans for himself. He wanted to go to college and become somebody. He looked forward to someday escaping the imprisonment of the inner city for good.

Alex was an average student when it came to books and classrooms. He carried B's and C's throughout most of his high school career. His ability to apply common sense took over where his studies lagged. Alex made the most important decision in his life when he enlisted in the Army after his seventeenth birthday. The GI Bill allowed him to enter college upon graduation from high school. He was comfortable with the idea of studying first, and then paying back his debt by serving his country. Alex attended a mini boot camp in the summer before his first year at Northern. It served as a primer for the soldier-to-be, and he loved it.

The young Hispanic was immediately labeled a '*leader*' by his superiors. His knack to pick up on military strategies impressed the brass. When offered the opportunity for more advanced training at a base in North Carolina, Alex jumped at the chance. While there, he was educated in hand-to-hand combat, as well as how to use some of the latest technology in military weaponry. But it was the field training that Alex enjoyed the most. On mock maneuvers, he was taught to blend with his environment and use his wits to out-think the enemy. He had no qualms about covering himself in mud in order to advance on unsuspecting sentries. Eventually, he was offered the opportunity to join the ROTC program on NMU's campus, provided his grades were raised to an acceptable level. Afterwards, there existed the real possibility of becoming an officer.

Alex buckled down, driven by a work ethic that Maria Chavez had tried so hard to teach him. He worked his tail off, spending hours engrossed in his books. He would will himself to absorb the information. The learning process was slow, but his grade point did rise to the required level. Alex Chavez was shorter than most of his peers, standing only five feet six inches tall. He developed a passion for physical conditioning during his boot camp experience. He religiously practiced an arduous regimen of physical exercise that focused on muscle toning and cardio endurance. He would rise at five in the morning and jog eight miles. Four times a week, he would spend time in the campus weight room. The football coach had once attempted to recruit the cadet with the idea of transforming him into a running back. But Alex had politely declined the offer, keeping his own personal goals at the forefront.

Alex Chavez maintained his close relationship with his family despite the distance that separated them. He would spend at least one hour every weekend on the phone relaying campus stories to his mother. His brothers and sisters would all sit around Maria Chavez as she spoke with her son, each patiently awaiting their turn to chat with their older brother. It was hard for Alex to be so far away from his siblings, and he often worried about them falling into the wrong crowd without his guidance. But Maria would always ease his anxiety by assuring him that they were all very proud of him and his accomplishments, and how the younger ones were already eager to follow in his footsteps.

Trevor Musgrave was much taller than his roommate. In high school, Trevor had been a second team, all-state quarterback on the football team, as well as an honorable mention all-city forward on the basketball team. Three years of junk food and beer binging had taken its toll on his once lean body. A slight spare tire had been added to his mid-section. Trevor had been an avid deer hunter throughout his life. He introduced his roommate to the sport during the fall season of their freshman year. To Alex, just the opportunity to adorn himself in full camo and spend time in the outdoors was enough to stimulate interest. When he downed a spike-horn on opening morning with a borrowed rifle, the addiction was immediate. Even the bloody process of gutting the animal was exhilarating.

The following year, Trevor taught Alex how to handle a compound bow. After just one day of intense practice, the student had become quite proficient with the weapon. Even Trevor was amazed with how easy shooting had come to Alex. A paper plate at forty yards was no match for him. The two roommates would pack up on weekends in the month of October when Alex was free from his ROTC responsibilities. They would camp out in the remote woodlands of northern Michigan, drinking beer at night and waiting for whitetails while in their tree stands during the day. Although Alex had yet to score a kill with the bow, he thrived on the outdoor experience in the company of his friend. Bow-hunting required greater skill and patience, which in turn spawned discipline. One could not merely shoot wildly into the brush at a passing deer. The shot had to be carefully calculated so that the effort wouldn't result in either a miss or a maimed animal.

In the summer before his senior year of college, Alex had saved enough money from a part-time job at a local convenience store to purchase his own bow. After the Browning was fully equipped with an over-draw, lighted sights, quiver, silencers, broadheads, and carbon arrows, he had nearly six hundred dollars invested. Alex had anxiously waited for the upcoming season, honing his shooting skills to perfection. With this year's opener falling on a Saturday, he hoped to finally receive the return on his investment.

The two college seniors initially planned on spending the opener at the Musgrave family camp in Ironwood. When Brenda,

Trevor's latest girlfriend, offered her uncle's spread as an alternative, it was too good to pass up. However, a slight glitch had developed in their plans. Brenda and Kayla, Alex's female friend, wanted to accompany the two hunters. Alex had been dating Kayla Johnson since the end of his last semester at Northern. Trevor and Brenda took it upon themselves to set the couple up, and the two had hit it off from the get-go.

Kayla Johnson was a beautiful girl with a good head on her shoulders. Like Alex, she too had high personal expectations. Kayla was from the Marquette area and had hopes of transferring into the engineering program at Michigan Tech. She was an all A student who was very serious about her studies. Alex and Kayla had a comfortable relationship with neither expecting too much from the other. Both knew that their paths might take them in different directions one day. They were both extremely shy about outwardly expressing their feelings for fear of frightening the other away. Never was the future a topic of conversation when they were together. Things were too good in the present to worry about what might be. Alex would be starting his service in the Army in the coming summer, and Kayla would be transferring to Houghton. They would deal with matters when that time eventually arrived.

"Hey, Al, I'm heading out. You gonna come over and see Kayla tonight?" Trevor drained the remainder of the Milwaukee's Best and belched loudly. He picked up his leather jacket that was sprawled across the kitchen table and draped it over his shoulder. Trevor had been spending most of his nights with his girlfriend. Unlike Kayla, Brenda Pierson was a stereotypical blond, flighty and somewhat light-headed. The two partiers made a fitting pair, each having a flair for fun and excitement.

Brenda's dizziness tended to press on Alex's nerves. He found that he could not spend a great deal of time in her presence without getting the urge to leave. He often wondered how Kayla could put with her antics.

"Can't tonight, Trev," replied Alex as he stood and headed to his bedroom. "Got a Calc test in the morning." His grade had slipped a bit in his Calculus class and he needed a decent mark on the coming exam to bring it up. It was going to be a long night of cramming.

"Ten-four, little buddy. But I know for a fact that you're not going to be concentrating too much on math tonight. You'll be dreaming of the big one walking into your shooting lane. Two more weeks. Yes!" Trevor shot an imaginary arrow at an invisible deer. "See ya tomorrow." And he left.

As Alex sat down on his small bed and opened the thick text book, he soon realized that his roommate had been correct with his assumption. The anticipation of opening morning swelled inside him. He thought about walking over to his closet just to make sure that his bow was properly prepared, but decided against it. *Discipline,* he thought to himself, while reverting his attention back to the text book. *I can have fun later.*

***

The smooth, gentle current was displaced only for a brief moment as the leader draped across the cool water. The fly floated masterfully through the air, allowing the breeze to guide it, until settling into the targeted hole on the opposite side of the tributary. The fisherman patiently waited for the predator to mark its prey. He scanned the clear water, searching for the elusive rainbow that had hit so hard only seconds ago. He knew it was a nice one.

Then, just as the fly was about to float out of the deep hole and into the current, the water broke with an enormous splash. The trout's tubular body soared high above the waterline with its colors glistening in the afternoon sun. The angler pulled the line tight and set the hook. His rod doubled over as the big fish made its run downstream. He applied pressure to the spinning reel with his free hand, knowing that he would be forced to utilize all of his skills if he was going to land this one.

The angler maneuvered his large frame down the tricky bank, stepping over the maze of treacherous rocks and logs. A wrong step could easily result in a broken ankle. Following a few intense minutes, the fight in the fish began to ease, allowing him an opportunity to bring in some line. He could feel the trout tiring as he brought it closer to shore. It was within ten feet... and then five. His right arm groped for the net attached to his wader belt. He prayed it would be spacious enough to accommodate his trophy. The fish was a wall-hanger for sure, bigger than any he'd caught in his lifetime. It was at least a four pounder. As he continued to bring the fish in, he envisioned it displayed above the fireplace, reliving the tale to visitors who happened by.

Just as the excited fisherman stepped into the water to net the rainbow, the fish discovered its second wind and made a final dash to freedom. The reel spun again, this time catching him off guard. The line shot downstream, angling between two rocks protruding from the rapid current. He raised the rod above his head in a futile attempt to work the taut line around the obstacles. It snapped with a loud twang as soon as it brushed against the jagged edges. The trophy was lost.

Ross visually followed the water until it wrapped around a bend downstream. There would be no conversational piece over his mantel after all. He slowly reeled in the remaining guideline and then tied if off at the base of the fly rod. He worked his way back upstream to where the battle began, questioning his actions. Ross jumped up onto the raised bank and sat in the blades of grass that knifed through the fresh layer of snow. He always made a point to interrogate himself after losing an animal or a fish. It was the mark of a true sportsman to learn from a mistake made in the field. And when the lost objective was as beautiful as the one that he had just come so close to netting, it made the *'what if'* questions that much more painful to answer. He laid back and reflected on what might have been.

The Sheriff took a deep breath of the fresh, northern air and closed his eyes. For the first time in what seemed an eternity, he felt at peace with himself. Jessup had managed to slip back into its normal state of obscurity. And as the days passed without incident, his nagging doubts were fading with them. Although time stood still for a few eventful days, most of those whose lives had been touched in one way or another were managing to move on. Rachel Perkins packed up her belongings a week after her husband's funeral and moved downstate to stay with her mother in Brighton. Ross recalled the distraught woman's face as she drove out of town. It was most likely the last time he would lay eyes on her. There would be no reason for Rachel Perkins to return to Jessup. *Too many old ghosts.*

Amy Jennings, Seth's widow, had also left town, but under different circumstances. She had been escorted up north to Houghton immediately following the double funeral for Seth and

Bobby. Amy Jennings would be spending a few months under observation. The news of her husband's death had not devastated her nearly to the extent as that of her only son's. It had been a gut-wrenching period for the Sheriff of Jessup, attending funerals and attempting to ease the pain of the survivors. Everyone was affected by the town's losses in some way. He could see it in their faces when he walked up and down Main Street.

Then the letters came, hundreds of them, mostly *'bunny huggers'* from across the Midwestern states. Lovells had sensationalized the story in the Detroit News and portrayed the Sheriff as a blood-thirsty maniac who had *'murdered'* a poor, defenseless creature as if it were some evil fiend with a blackened heart from a children's storybook tale. Even the DNR, under pressure from the Capital, felt obligated to send an officer to question Ross, just as Ray Jackson had predicted prior to their adventure. Ross was infuriated by the sweeping allegations. However, much to his delight, the DNR boy turned out to be a local and fully understood what had gone down in Jessup. He even went so far as to congratulate Ross for a job well done before he left town ... off the record of course. And then, as happens with most trying experiences involving pain and suffering, time proved to be the only cure. Although those brutal memories would be forever etched in the Sheriff's memory for as long as his heart continued to beat, he now felt that he was strong enough to look forward to the future and concentrate on the more important aspects of life ... like family.

It had taken a few days for Ross to re-establish credibility with Maggie. He had finally worked up enough nerve to share what he had been feeling. He told her about the doubts that had been haunting him after finding Charlie Perkins, as well as the anxiety derived from a personal fear that something of the paranormal had come into existence outside the Jessup community. He realized how crazy he must have sounded, but the peculiarities had been just too damn convincing to push aside. Maggie had listened to him, seeing the sincerity in his eyes. She did not laugh when he presented her the idea of some creature, unknown to man, dwelling in the Amen Swamp. She consoled her man, understood his internal dilemma, and comforted his fears. If he hadn't opened up to Maggie, Ross knew that his bottled-up tension might have ultimately destroyed him. Although he appeared fit on the outside, his mental constitution had been in turmoil. Maggie had been there yet again to pull him free from that pit of irreversible despair. She was his life ... his Savior. Maggie and Chuck Barnes were his future.

Another significant factor that played a role in the Sheriff's emotional recovery was Gene Steubens' ability to stay clear of him. Ross, in fact, had not spoken with the illustrious Mayor since the uncomfortable scene at the steps of Town Hall where the bear hide had been displayed for the masses. He figured that it was probably for the best. Any day that passed without the autocrat's presence was a day that was truly blessed in the Sheriff's eyes. Most of Steubens' time as of late was dedicated to the developers of the new resort, a place where Ross had no intention of ever visiting if he could help it. While there were some who saw the project as a potential goldmine, Ross viewed Hideaway Pines from a different perspective. He cringed every time he drove by the valley he once hunted, now invaded by giant landmovers. In his mind, *that* was an act of undue aggression warranting an investigation. It was the destruction of a beautiful tract of land. The *ignorant bitch* who had been quoted in Lovells' article should have been concentrating her ire there.

Ross opened his eyes after his moment of Zen had been shattered by the thoughts of the animal rights activists from Lansing. He sat up and opened the lid to his creel to check on the three brookies that failed to escape his flies that afternoon. It would make for a nice dinner ... trout wrapped in foil with lemon and butter, and then tossed on the grill for about fifteen minutes. What proved to be one of the easiest meals to prepare was also one of the most delectable treats to ever tempt his taste buds. It was time to get home and clean his catch. He selfishly hoped that Maggie and Chuck had plans for the evening. That would mean more fillets for him.

Ross had taken the entire Friday off for some much needed rest and relaxation. There was no better cure for a case of the nine-to-five blues than an afternoon in the company of a babbling brook and a few hungry trout. There was a feeling of satisfaction as he hoisted himself up off the snowy ground. He packed up his belongings scattered on the ground and began his ascent up the steep incline of the ridge to where his Tahoe was parked.

Mark Bennington was pulling duty back in town, freeing Ross to do as he pleased for the day. The other matter continuing to make headlines still fiddled around in his head. The cold-blooded murder of a storeowner only thirty miles southeast of Jessup had sent the law enforcement community into a frenzied manhunt for two fugitives from downstate. MSP had made a call to his office the day after the crime. Ross witnessed the story unfolding on T.V. with the rest of rural America from the comfort of his living room. There were updates coming in daily as both media and police agencies hounded the countryside for clues as to where the fugitives might have gone. MSP was under the assumption that they were hiding out somewhere in the Upper Peninsula, possibly in some tucked away hunting camp. All agencies were asked to beef up patrolling efforts both in and around their areas of jurisdiction for precautionary measures. He and Mark spent time checking out the remote homesteads, spreading word to those who lived in the boonies. There were too many hunting camps around the Jessup community for just two men to cover on their own. And Ross didn't dare split apart from his subordinate, knowing that Mark was no match for two dangerous criminals.

The manhunt had been a Godsend really. It afforded Ross a reasonable excuse to venture out into the back country to search for the nemesis of his personal nightmares and dispel those haunting doubts that were plaguing him. Ross was hesitant to believe that the two fugitives had remained in the U.P. They didn't appear to be the type, a judgement ascertained from the pictures shown on the television. Regardless, he and his Deputy continued patrolling just in case. And as the days turned into weeks, with no fugitives or monsters exposing themselves to the general public, the monkey began to slowly climb down from the Sheriff's back.

Contrary to what he initially believed, the Rutt'n Buck Festival had been just what the town needed to get back on its feet. Ross found himself amazed at the numbers that showed for the annual event. The bake sale was bigger than ever, taking in an estimated fifteen hundred dollars for charity. The only downfall to the entire weekend was the cancellation of the softball tournament. The weather would not cooperate with the boys of summer who tried to stretch their season for one final outing. Ross was somewhat thankful for the cancellation. Some guys from Appleton had asked him to fill in on their team for a few games. The Sheriff was not keen on the prospect of playing ball in four inches of snow, but he would have, just to show the guys that he could still hang. And Chucky's girl, Jenna Pierson, was named *'Queen Doe'* in the pageant. He was as proud as a struttin buck, Ross thought as he smiled. The boy had chased Jenna's float like a puppy trailing a child dropping cookie crumbs all the way down Main Street during the big parade. Maggie's business had taken a slight hit over the weekend with most of her regulars visiting the beer tent instead. But the temporary lull allowed her time to rest, especially with the opener so near. Business would be booming soon enough when more hunters began to trickle in.

Things were apparently back to normal for Ross Pickett and the people of Jessup, Michigan. He could go on being Sheriff. Other than the two fugitives who were still on the lam, there wouldn't be much to look forward to, aside from hanging a nice deer on his buck pole. Ross reckoned that if the criminals were occupying a camp, it wouldn't take long for someone to flush them out. He climbed out of his waders and stepped into his boots. As he was opening the door, a squirrel began to chatter high above his head. He quickly turned on his heels, reaching for the sidearm that had become a permanent fixture to his belt. A chilling sensation riveted through his body as he remembered that day in the swamp.

Ross shook his head as he stared at the surrounding trees. The squirrel's bickering ceased. He looked skyward one last time, and then turned away. *Old ghosts,* he thought to himself. It was just another old ghost from a very dark closet. *It's over.*

***

The yearling ambled into the clearing, occasionally stopping to paw at the fallen leaves blanketing the ground. The deer would drop its head and retrieve the exposed acorns underneath the lone oak one by one, working the food in its mouth as though it were chewing on a sticky piece of caramel. Even though the animal stood only thirty yards away, the increasing snowfall combined with the dimming light made it difficult for the man holding the rifle to pick out its shape. He rested the barrel of the weapon against the trunk of a tree, holding the front site on the middle of the animal's body. He was new to this activity and wasn't quite sure where the shot should be placed. His finger switched the safety to the "off" position and then curled around the trigger. The deer scented the breeze and looked in his direction, still standing broadside. Its tail flickered nervously.

The tranquility of the evening exploded with four rapid shots from the Klashnikov. The deer flipped violently onto its back while the legs kicked at the air. It made a high-pitched blatting sound, like a small child wreathing in pain.

Tyrone Pullman leaned away from the tree, somewhat surprised that he had managed to hit the deer. It was his first, and probably not his last. He glanced around, fearing that the gunfire had reached someone's ears. His eyes surveyed the trees, anticipating a police car to come barreling through at any moment.

"Don't be so fucking paranoid," he told himself out loud. Tyrone understood the reality of his somber predicament. His life was no longer what it once was. The fugitive had secluded himself to the remote cabin for nearly two weeks, and the stock of canned foods was nearly gone. He was grateful that the owner of the encampment had found it necessary to maintain an ample supply. The preserved meats were the first to go, lasting for only a few days. Earlier that morning, he had feasted on the last container of pears that was barely enough to satisfy a growing appetite. He could feel himself losing weight. Although he had a growing urge to visit a store, Tyrone knew that it was too soon.

Gerald would not have endured the rustic living conditions. His partner may have been able to suffer for a day or two, but Gerald would have eventually insisted they leave. It was another point of reassurance for a heavy conscience. After killing his longtime friend, Tyrone dragged the body into the woods only to discover the frozen ground prevented him from digging a proper grave. Gerald's final resting place was little more than a slight indentation in the earth with a layer of leaves and sticks to seal his coffin.

Tyrone Pullman was now sentenced to live each day in solitude, like a hermit whose survival was contingent upon food harvested from the land. Since he knew nothing of that lifestyle, he was compulsed to learn ... or starve. On the day that Tyrone disposed of Gerald's body, he sat in front of the television waiting for the evening news to air. When he saw his own face displayed on the screen, he was overcome with horror. There he was, a picture from the store, standing side by side with convicted murderer Gerald Johnson. They were Michigan's two most wanted criminals with their faces now appearing in every home across the Midwest. His fear about a surveillance camera was accurate. And who was it that scoffed at the idea? Gerald Johnson. It took just two days for the cops to put a name to his picture, no doubt the result of their ruthless shakedown efforts back home in Flint.

In the days that followed, Tyrone often thought about home as he spent his time guarding the drive that snaked through the forest to his hideaway. He questioned where his home now was since he couldn't return to Flint. His only real chance for freedom would be to run ... far away. Tyrone understood that he couldn't survive much longer in his current environment. He didn't know *how* to survive. He was living in the cabin on borrowed time. The owners could show up at any moment, and then there would be more killing.

The animal's dying cries subsided and its body stopped jerking. Tyrone walked up to the deer. He watched as it lay on the cold ground, taking in air with weakening breaths. The dark eyes stared forward, not blinking as small snowflakes landed on their moist surfaces. Tyrone knelt down to the deer and ran his hand across the large hole just behind the shoulder. He felt the chest cavity rising and falling. There was nobody within earshot with whom he could express his guilt. Tyrone had killed men before, in cold blood. But never had he taken the life of an animal. He felt as though he had somehow shattered an icon of innocence. The deer looked so much smaller than when he first noticed it meandering into the clearing. He felt no pride in his feat, but he had been forced to kill it ... to survive. There was nothing else to eat.

Tyrone withdrew a large knife encased in a leather sheath from the front pocket of his coveralls, another useful item left behind by his new landlord. The wind was beginning to pick up and the temperature was falling. The rookie hunter freed the blade from it protective cover and then proceeded to cut away at one of the hind quarters. He had no idea how to field-dress the animal. Tyrone was only concerned with one thing, and that was putting food in his belly.

The knife cut easily through the tender meat of the leg. When he reached the bone, the penetration stopped. He continued to cut around the area, searching for weak spots in the joint. Different colored fluids seemed to come out of its body. His hands were warm and slippery, covered in the animal's blood. Tyrone flipped the deer on his back and made a deep incision. His blade lacerated the stomach, creating a hissing sound as trapped gasses escaped into the air. He brought his hand to his mouth to try and cover the awful stench. After turning his head away for a brief moment to taste some fresh air, Tyrone set aside the knife and grasped the slender leg of the deer with both hands. He stood upright and then began to twist the limb in every imaginable angle. Finally, after rotating it in three complete circles, the leg broke free. Tyrone stumbled backwards, nearly tripping over a dormant mound of earth that had once been inhabited by a colony of ants. He stood in the clearing alone, holding the animal's hind quarter like some prehistoric cave dweller.

***

Chuck Barnes had been soaring in the clouds for a full two weeks. The football team won five in a row and was ranked eighth in the State's Class D polls. Aside from the team's success, Chuck's individual numbers were outstanding. Six touchdown passes with an average of two hundred and twenty-five yards per game was beginning to bring some attention from the scouting community. He'd already received letters from Central Michigan, Saginaw Valley, Grand Valley and Northern. All were in-state universities that were anxious to land the home-grown prospect. Chuck Barnes, however, had much higher goals. His dream of one day rushing through the tunnel of Michigan Stadium wearing the maize and blue overshadowed any thoughts of playing elsewhere. Chuck was determined to make Michigan football a reality, and anyone who knew him understood that he was not one to underachieve.

The teenager was on his way to pick up Jenna, his steady for the past three months. Jenna Pierson was the prettiest girl in school in the eyes of the young adolescent. They hooked up at a party over the summer and had been together ever since. He was the star of the football team and she was captain of the cheerleading squad, a fitting pair for any American campus. Although the two had never engaged in sexual intercourse, it wasn't for lack of trying on Chuck's part. Jenna was a smart girl who was not about to take any stupid chances. She would appease her hormone driven boyfriend to some degree, but the homerun ball was not in her immediate plans. In a way, Chuck was glad that Jenna wouldn't *'put out.'* Her purity made her special, and he was beginning to wish that their relationship would last beyond high school.

The Appleton Marauders were playing Escanaba that night, a game that would pit two undefeated teams against each other. Chuck had been looking forward to the match-up since the beginning of the season. Escanaba was ranked fifth in the same class, and had beaten up on Appleton for three straight years. But that was before Chuck Barnes had evolved. The contest would be a nasty grudge match between two extremely bitter rivals.

Since the cheerleaders were required to show up at about the same time as the players on game nights, Chuck and Jenna always rode together. Chuck was feeling invincible. His pride swelled whenever he took that stroll from the parking lot to the lockerroom wearing his maroon and gold varsity jacket while holding his girl's hand. Then, Jenna would turn to him and lay on a nice wet kiss for luck.

Chuck eased the rusty Escort into the Pierson's driveway. He could hear the high pitch of the new fuel pump that Ross had helped him install the week before. His present mode of transportation was no eye catcher, but it did serve its purpose. He purchased the vehicle with money earned from washing dishes at the Inn for his mom.

The Piersons lived in a large ranch-style home with an in-ground pool in the backyard. Henry Pierson, Jenna's father, was a banker in Appleton and made a good living for his family of five. Chuck grinned at a flashing vision of Jenna lounging around the pool in her string bikini at the family barbecues. She was nicely developed for her age. Chuck had even caught Ross looking on occasion, but he kept it to himself, knowing that his future stepfather would be utterly embarrassed. And his mom probably wouldn't care too much either.

As the Escort rolled to a stop behind Mr. Pierson's Park Avenue, Jenna came bouncing out of the front door to greet him. She had a huge smile on her petite face. Chuck could see her father standing in the doorway. He felt obligated to get out and say *'hi.'*

"Hey, baby!" Jenna embraced him as he stepped out of the car. She gave Chuck a kiss that in his mind was a little too sloppy to be displaying in front of her father. But Chuck knew Henry Pierson adored him. They were always sitting down and discussing the team.

"Hey, Jen," replied Chuck, pulling back slightly from his excited girl.

"Chuck, my boy. How are we today?" It was Mr. Pierson calling from the front door.

"Fine, sir," he responded as a polite boyfriend would.

"Big game tonight, son. Are we going to kick some Escanaba butt on that field?" Jenna's father winked at the quarterback.

"You're going to see the biggest butt-whoopin this side of the bridge, Mr. Pierson," said Chuck confidently.

"That's the spirit. Good luck. The wife and I will be there cheering you on. Love you, Jenna. See you tonight." And with that, Henry Pierson walked back inside.

Chuck was in awe of how high school football could affect so many. The spirit enhanced by a winning program molded the smaller communities surrounding Appleton into one fiery bandwagon. On game days, there wasn't a car in town that didn't fly a flag with the school colors. Businesses closed early so workers could make the opening kick-off. Football was religion in those parts. If students didn't play on the team, they participated in the band. If they didn't play in the band, they were on the Varsity Club, planning events and creating lavish banners. And if they didn't participate in those activities, they were at the games exhibiting a frenzied spirit as though their own lives were held in the balance. Chuck's role as starting quarterback was the most glorifying of all, but he could also be the goat. There was always pressure on his shoulders.

"I've got some good news, babe," said Jenna as she cuddled up to Chuck inside the Escort. She leaned over and flung her arms around the young athlete's neck. After a quick peek towards the door to ensure that her father was no longer present, she gave him another long kiss. As she withdrew her tongue, there was a conniving look on her face.

"What's this all about, Jen? I've got a big game tonight and you're trying to drain me." Chuck's hormones were humming.

"You are gonna love this, Chucky. I was talking to my cousin Brenda up at Northern earlier today. She's going to be spending the weekend with some friends at my uncle's hunting cabin. She said we could come out for the weekend if we wanted."

"Well ... I don't know. This weekend is the bow opener. Ross and I were going to hunt together. He'd be kind of disappointed if I bailed on him." It was not Ross that worried Chuck. He had been chomping at the bit waiting for this weekend to arrive, and he didn't particularly care to spend it with a bunch of college kids he didn't know.

"Well, I guess you don't want to hunt her uncle's land then," teased Jenna. She knew his weak points all too well.

"Yeah right, like you're going to let me go out and hunt while you're cooped up in some run-down shack with no heat." Chuck was well aware of how females like Jenna handled camping without the comforts of home. It would ultimately amass into one giant bitch session.

"Well, mister smarty pants, it just so happens that Brenda is bringing her boyfriend and his roommate. And they are both big deer hunters. So it won't be just a bunch of whining girls after all, huh?"

"Really!" Chuck's temperament changed with the new revelation. He had never seen her uncle's hunting camp, but he'd heard stories of the bucks they had taken there. Big ones! "What about your uncle's family? How come they won't be there for the opener?"

"Hah!" she howled, as she studied her fingernails to make sure the recent paint job was clean and even. "My aunt Peg decided to schedule a trip to Vegas this weekend. She's making Uncle Joe tag along, and boy is he pissed. You should have heard him talking to my dad. I was on the other side of the room and I could hear him screaming through the phone."

Chuck could not fault the man for being upset. He would have felt the same way had his opener been taken away from him.

But how would he convince his mom to let him go for an entire weekend? She could be quite possessive with him. Chuck knew that she meant well, but he was in high school and needed some freedom. It would be better to manufacture a story than tell her that he wanted to shack up with his girlfriend. He didn't figure that Ross would care too much, but it was difficult for Ross to keep secrets from his mom, or so he thought.

"I don't think my mom's going to let me to be honest, Jen." Chuck sulked in the driver seat.

"What you're mom doesn't know won't hurt her." Jenna had been reading his thoughts. She, too, would have to concoct a scenario that would allow her to get away for a few days. "You can tell Maggie and Ross that you're going to spend the weekend with some friends ... like Mike Fuller and his brother Joey," said Jenna excitedly, as if she had found the cure for parental interference. "Don't they usually camp near Nisula somewhere?"

Jenna was right. Chuck had hunted with the Fullers before, so his mom wouldn't suspect anything. Mike and Joey would be roughing it on State land in tents, an unpleasant thought with the cold weather. "What the hell. Let's do it!" This was out of character for Jenna, and Chuck began to wonder if she had ulterior motives.

"Goody!" shrieked the elated cheerleader. "I'll tell my parents that I'm going to St. Ignace with Doris. They shouldn't ask too many questions."

"You know, Jen, your uncle's cabin is right on the Amen, the same swamp where that bear lived." Chuck seldom missed an opportunity to tease. To him, girls were all made from the same fabric, scared of every little creepy crawler. He recalled how she had jumped up onto her parents' kitchen table a few weeks back at the sight of a little mouse that had scampered across the floor by her feet.

"Oh, they shot that bad old bear," she replied matter-of-factly. "And I personally don't plan on walking around in any swamp. You're the one who should be worried." She gave Chuck a *'ha-ha'* smirk and fastened her seatbelt.

Chuck silently thought about what she had said. He then started to recall those verses that grown-ups would use to torment the kids when they were younger. The old men would sit on the benches along Main Street, passing the time waiting for an innocent little boy to happen by, and then ...

A man is a man,
When entering its lair,
Be aware poor soul,
For life is unfair.

Look to the trees,
That smother your path,
And prepare your soul,
For Amen's wrath.

If you will the courage,
To face the demons within,
Then pray with pure heart,
The journey ends with Amen.

The rhyme pulled from his childhood memory bank caused the boy to shudder. He also remembered the terrible nightmares hatched from the legends surrounding the Amen Swamp. *Nonsense!* Those tales were for gullible little kids who were naïve enough to believe in such things.

Chuck drove away from the Pierson home with Jenna at his side. There were much more important things to mull over at the moment, like preparing the lie for his mother whose trust he was about to compromise. Although he did feel guilty, the idea of spending an entire weekend with Jenna in a remote cabin was too tempting. But it was time to start getting his head mentally prepared for the coming game. He could ill afford to lose his concentration now with all that was riding on the confrontation with Escanaba. These were games that could make or break the careers of young athletes with ambitions. He didn't want to let down the town.

***

Gene Steubens felt like he was on top of the world. He stood at the crest of the tallest ridge in the county, gazing down into the open path of freshly churned earth that would soon be the seventeenth fairway of *The Diamond* at Hideaway Pines. Steubens was not a golfer himself, but he could still envision the beauty the place would one day define. And he was the inspiration ... the mastermind for the development that would bring financial security to his humble community. Gene Steubens would be an icon to the people of Jessup, much like old Zachariah had been in his time.

The Mayor felt a rush of accomplishment as he admired the scenery. The bulldozers and graders had just shut down for the day, and the construction workers were gradually moving off-site. Their trucks and cars formed a single line on the road leading west out to the main highway.

"Not much to look at now, Gene, but when we get this puppy finished you'll be very impressed," said Ted Newhouser, the lead contractor on the project.

"Nonsense, Teddy, this is magnificent. I may have to take up golf after all." Steubens performed a mock swing with an invisible club. His thick waist did not afford him much flexibility. "Do you think it will be ready for play by the end of summer?"

Newhouser looked over the expansive construction site from beyond the Jeep. He then peered to the sky from where the snowflakes were falling. His face was shadowed with a look of concern. "Don't know, Gene," he finally answered. "The weather may stop us earlier than expected. There's not much we can do with frozen ground and piled snow."

"Hmmm," mumbled the Mayor. That was not a good sign. Steubens was not a very patient man and he began to wonder how patient his partners would be.

"But," continued the contractor, "we'll have the clubhouse finished this winter, and probably a few condos as well. Who knows, we may even have some cross-country ski trails open by February." Newhouser shrugged.

"Excellent, Ted. This is truly going to be a diamond for Jessup." The Mayor's confidence was invigorated. "Have all of the holes been roughed out?" He turned to the taller man.

"The Diamond is close. We are having some problems getting our equipment through the swamp course. That is one wet piece of ground, but we'll get it done. You can count on that." Newhouser shot him a quick wink.

"Can I see it?" asked Steubens. He wanted to be included in every detail. After all, it was *his* project.

"Sure, Gene, hop in. I'll take you down."

"We'll have to make it quick. I've got a game to catch tonight." Steubens considered it necessary to be present at all community events, even if it was in Appleton. Tonight's crowd would be standing room only. His time would be spent wandering through the raucous spectators, showing his face to the voters. He could care less about the outcome.

The two men got into the Jeep and drove down the steep incline of the service road to the main trail at the base of the ridge. Newhouser turned on the headlights. The light was fading for the evening.

***

Maggie turned off the stove and poured the pot of hot coffee into her thermos. It was going to be a chilly night. She was excited because this would be her first opportunity to see Chuck play this year. Maggie observed Ross turning off the six o'clock news. He was fiddling with a zipper that was sticking. He was a sight to see on game days, experiencing the same nervous anticipation as the kids who played the game. But this was a special night. Unbeknownst to Chuck, Ross had enticed a friend from the athletic department at the University of Wisconsin to make the trip over to see her son play. They had kept it quiet from Chuck for fear that it might affect his performance on the field.

"Hey, Maggs, come on. We don't have a lot of time here." Now Ross was fidgeting by the back door. He was anxious to get a decent seat in the bleachers.

Maggie laughed. He looked like a child awaiting his chance to sit on Santa's lap at the mall. "Oh, you hold on. We've got plenty of time, grandpa." Ross reminded Maggie of her own father who lived for the Friday night gridiron battles. He would bundle up his young daughter and tote her off to the games regardless of weather conditions. It was a pleasant memory.

"You just better be careful who you're calling grandpa, missy. I just might come over there and swat you on the rear," joked the Sheriff.

Maggie screwed the cap on the thermos and slipped into her goose down parka. As she went to grab her purse there was a knock on the door. "I'll get it," she said.

"Now who the hell is that?" asked Ross, perturbed that they might be delayed even further. Ross went to the bedroom to retrieve his wallet.

Maggie walked over to the door and opened it. There was a stranger standing outside. He was a serious looking man with a rough face. He wore an unzipped, leather jacket with faded blue jeans. Underneath the coat, Maggie noticed an emblem embroidered on a gray sweatshirt. It appeared to be a footprint with some writing above it.

When the man saw the occupant open the door, his expression lightened. He bowed to greet the lady of the house. "Good evening, ma'am. Sorry to bother you, but I'm looking for Sheriff Ross Pickett."

"May I say who is calling? Maggie was somewhat bothered that she did not know the man.

"Absolutely. May name is David LaFontaine. I have some business to discuss with Mr. Pickett." The man eyed the heavy coat and the thermos in Maggie's hand. "I see you're on your way out. I assure you that I won't take much of his time." He smiled again. It was a soothing smile that put Maggie at ease.

"Of course," she finally said. "Please, come in." Mr. LaFontaine stepped inside as Maggie held the door open. His hands remained behind his back. He searched the interior of the home as if he were looking for something. "Ross! It's for you, hon!" called Maggie as she led the caller to the kitchen.

Ross appeared a few seconds later. As the stranger turned to greet him, the Sheriff remembered the familiar face. *Where have I seen him before?* Then it dawned on him. It was that day on Main Street, just before he had it out with Steubens. He wore the same coat and jeans. The beard may have been somewhat shorter then, but everything else fell in line. Ross stole a quick peek out the kitchen window and saw the VW van parked next to the Tahoe.

The man displayed a gentle smile when the Sheriff made his appearance. "Ah," he said. "You must be Sheriff Pickett." He extended his hand to complete the greeting.

"Yes, sir, that's right. I don't believe I've had the pleasure," said Ross as he shook the stranger's hand. Maggie propped her hind end up on the kitchen counter. Visitors were a rarity in her home, especially ones with new faces.

"Yes, of course. My name is Dave LaFontaine."

"Ross Pickett. It's nice to meet you, David. What can I do for you?" The man certainly was cordial, thought Ross. There didn't appear to be any pressing emergency, but for some unexplainable reason Ross felt uneasy in his presence.

"Again," continued LaFontaine, "I sincerely apologize for intruding on you like this. As I told your wife, I'll make my visit brief."

Maggie winked at Ross from the side after the '*wife*' remark, but Ross did not pay any attention, nor did he correct the man.

"Can we have a word ... privately?" asked the visitor, motioning to Maggie.

"No problem," she responded, taking the not so subtle hint. "I've got some laundry to fold before we go. Call me when you're ready, hon." Maggie slid down off the counter and disappeared down the hallway.

Ross wondered whether or not she had been offended by what he considered to be a rude gesture by the man. "Okay, Mr. LaFontaine. Have a seat." Both men sat down at the kitchen table and faced each other from opposite ends. "Now what can I do for you?"

"First, please call me David. I'm not one for formality."

"Very well," said Ross, "David it is. You may call me Ross. You know, I've seen you before, two weeks ago ... in town."

"Yes, of course. And I remember you as well. That was quite a day for your people." LaFontaine folded his hands on the table. He seemed very relaxed.

"You're telling me," continued Ross. "As I recall, the tags on your van out there are from Montana. What brings you so far from home, David? Are you after some northern Michigan whitetail?" Ross was beginning to enjoy the man's company. LaFontaine had a pleasant disposition about him. He made him feel as though they had been friends for years. The uneasiness that Ross had felt earlier had dissipated.

"I'm actually from Bluff Ridge, Montana. It's a small town in the northwestern corner of the state. And you are correct. I *am* a long ways from home." LaFontaine leaned back in his chair. When he moved, his leather jacket fell open and exposed the emblem on his sweatshirt. It was an outline of a footprint with the word "*Existence*" imprinted above. Ross cocked his head as he tried to decipher the symbol's meaning.

David observed how his host's eyes were focused on his chest. His ploy had worked. The polite smile slowly faded. "I see you've noticed my shirt," he said.

"Huh?" Ross was caught off guard by the comment, and a little embarrassed. "Oh ... yes. Kind of strange. What does it mean?"

"Well ... I guess you could say it's the reason I'm here."

Ross' eyes reverted back to LaFontaine's face. There was a noticeable change to the man's expression. The Sheriff felt a nerve twitch in his neck.

"Ross ..." he trailed off for a few seconds as if he were searching for the appropriate words to rationalize his purpose. He began again. "I belong to an organization. It's a very small band of people dedicated to the study of the paranormal."

Ross straightened in his chair. "Paranormal?" He smirked at the man. "What the heck is so paranormal around here?" And then the Amen Swamp resurrected itself in his mind, along with his discussion with Dr. Flemming in Appleton. Those old ghosts were beginning to reappear. Ross forced himself to remain calm. "What sort of paranormal things are you referring to, David? Ghosts?" Although it sounded foolish, that was exactly what Ross had been thinking. Only his *ghosts* were not spirits haunting old houses.

LaFontaine sensed that he had touched on something and that the Sheriff had ideas of his own. He decided to play his cards. "Well, Ross," he continued carefully, "my focus is in a field that is quite the opposite of the supernatural, or spirit world if you will. I prefer to concentrate my efforts on more incarnate beings. I have spent the last seven years of my life exploring the phenomenon of a man-like creature existing in some of the more remote regions of the world, including right here in the continental U.S.A."

Ross' muscles tightened. "What do you mean by a ... a man-like creature?" he asked with a break in his voice. He was beginning to wish that Maggie had not opened the door to let him in.

"Okay." LaFontaine hesitated again before plodding on. "Let's be blunt, Ross. There's no sense in beating around the bush." He gave the Sheriff a hard stare.

Ross gazed right back at him, wondering what he was about to hear. He shifted his weight in the chair as the visitor continued.

"I am on the trail of ... well ... Sasquatch." LaFontaine called it out, as if he were saying *moose* ... or *raccoon*.

Ross gave him a funny look, and then produced a nervous laugh. "Sasquatch! What the hell is a ...?" He fell silent before he could finish the question.

"*Bigfoot*, Ross. The Abominable Snowman ... Yeti ... Skunk Ape ... Sasquatch." Rather than pausing to allow the proclamation to set in, LaFontaine felt it appropriate to lay it all on the line. "My organization is funded by some very affluent people who believe that these creatures do exist."

Ross' eyeballs were now wide in their sockets. He was floored, thinking that he had allowed a certifiable *whacko* into his home. He wanted to laugh. He wanted to throw him out on his ass. But as Ross studied LaFontaine, there was nothing but chilling sincerity chiseled into his face. The hairs on the back of Ross' neck were standing on end.

"I ... I'm sorry, David, but I don't understand. How ... what does this have to do with Jessup?" But Ross did understand the correlation. His nightmares were coming true. He knew exactly why this man was in his home. *A bear! It was a goddamned bear!* But his internal argument was losing credibility. The doubts had returned and his inner peace had been shattered in a matter of minutes.

"Ross," LaFontaine calmly reached across the table and placed his hand gently on the Sheriff's forearm. "I know what you may be thinking right now, but please, let me explain myself before you jump to any conclusions or have me put into a straightjacket." He offered a soft smile to try and sooth Ross.

You have no fucking idea what's going through my head, thought the Sheriff. He pulled away from the man. He really wanted to just get away and forget that the conversation ever started. Ross buried his face in his hands, knowing that he had to stay. He prayed that David LaFontaine truly was some whacked out freak in the process of playing a sadistic trick.

"Mr. LaFontaine," began Ross slowly with a sigh, "you're talking about Bigfoot now. I mean ... what the hell brings you to Jessup?" Ross did not want to believe, nor did he wish to be persuaded, but he continued to listen as David LaFontaine proceeded to explain how he had followed the bread crumbs.

The unconventional sleuth told Ross about how his organization's web page was used to gather information on alleged sightings across North America. The site was built with the intent that people would reveal information of personal encounters. Experience taught him how to distinguish between the ludicrous and the possible. Most, of course, were of the first variety, and LaFontaine admitted as much. He talked about how he would concentrate his efforts on areas where there were growing trends in activity. When such a zone was located, he and a few members of his team would then sift through additional data and weed out the shams. There were no certainties in his line of work. No human being had ever obtained that one piece of concrete evidence supporting the existence of the elusive mammals. It was mainly a game of subjective reasoning. But if they did feel that sufficient evidence existed to warrant further analysis, he or another of his peers would personally visit the site to perform a more comprehensive audit. In seven years he had only encountered three valid findings, none of which resulted in a sighting by a team member. And all occurred in the western-most regions of the United States.

David further explained how the *Existence* website had been created with a Q&A forum. Team members would respond to thousands of inquiries from web browsers searching for their own truths. It was here where he began to take an interest in northern Michigan. A man from Chicago recounted an incident he had while traveling through the Upper Peninsula with his family in early September ... only a few weeks prior. Initially, the man had been reluctant to reveal much information while asking about the Bigfoot creatures. But as they conversed in the chat room, he eventually opened up. Apparently, his two young children had been traumatized by what was written off as a bear encounter during a stop along the road. The man willingly expressed his ignorance of bears or any other form of wildlife, but from what his wife claimed to have seen, coupled with the fact that his boys had spent every night thereafter in the security of their parents' bed, he was driven to find more answers. LaFontaine told Ross that he believed the man to be genuine, so he decided to investigate in greater detail.

The Bigfoot hunter garnered a tally of clippings from newspapers in western U.P. towns, none of which had been picked up by the major wires. He was able to locate the story from Houghton describing his web-site visitor's ordeal. According to hospital personnel who treated the boys, they would awake screaming in the night in fear of being kidnapped by some horrific *monster*. Had LaFontaine not been in contact with the father prior to seeing that piece, he would have written it off as a child's vivid imagination and not looked twice. But he now had a tie to the story. According to the mother, she had witnessed the animal *run* across the road on two legs. That alone was enough to categorize the incident as a "possible."

Knowing that he would need further proof to justify a trip, LaFontaine continued his search. He found an article from the Ontonogon Herald describing how a couple of hikers had been harassed during the night by an animal. The husband and wife team claimed that the creature had cleverly untied a rope securing their food stores in a tree to keep out of reach of bears. After ravishing a cooler and two backpacks, the creature then circled their tent for two full hours, growling at its inhabitants. The campers said that they dared not confront the thing, fearing for their safety. They could only wait out the siege together. A statement that jumped out at LaFontaine was how they told of a rancid stench that came and went with the animal's presence. Peculiar odors seemed to be a common occurrence with most up close and personal Bigfoot sightings. And according to the article, both campers were in tune with the outdoors, and respected members of their community. They had no reason to fabricate a lie. The incident took place about fifteen miles northwest of Jessup.

LaFontaine continued to sift through local papers and did discover a few other interesting stories. Two men canoeing on the Ontonogon River encountered an animal in the water that appeared to be hunting or fishing. It was two hundred yards away, but they could see that it was standing upright on two legs. As they floated closer, the creature raised its head and then bolted into the bush on the bank ... again, on two legs. Both men were also experienced outdoorsmen and believed that they had not seen a bear.

Feeling that he was onto something solid, LaFontaine made a few calls, one being to the hospital in Houghton where the two young boys had been treated. He spoke with a nurse who relayed a story of another man who experienced a peculiar run-in with a bear. According to the nurse, the man had hit the animal with his car and then died the following day from heart failure in the hospital. When David asked why she thought it had been such a strange case, the nurse gave him the details of how the man died ... how he had suffered from horrible hallucinations ... how he claimed to have seen a *monster*. When asked where the man was from, she told him ... *Jessup*. The two young boys had seen a *monster* as well, at least in their own minds. At that point, LaFontaine was getting excited. These weren't people claiming that a creature had chucked corncobs at them. These were people, all strangers, who experienced something extraordinary to the extent that all were traumatized.

The trend had gained enough traction to warrant a trip. LaFontaine packed up his VW and drove straight through the night to Michigan's Upper Peninsula. His first stop was Jessup. He learned of the *'Man Killing Bear'* on the day he arrived in town. LaFontaine watched the people gawking over the carcass. Though impressive, he had questions. David first read in the Appleton News how the animal had supposedly slain and devoured a man from the small town. The article went on to state how the Sheriff had led a hunting party into a large swamp and destroyed the animal while suffering two more casualties in the process. Being born and raised in Montana, LaFontaine knew that black bears rarely attacked and killed humans, especially on multiple occasions. Only when provoked or threatened might they resort to such aggressive behavior. Black bears were ordinarily shy animals. But David also revealed that he had never heard of a Bigfoot creature becoming physically confrontational with a human. When LaFontaine located Jessup on the state map, he saw that it was only a few miles from where the incident with the two young boys took place. The town was actually the epicenter of where the phenomenon was unfolding.

His next step was to contact the Coroner who performed the autopsy on the man allegedly killed by the bear. The Doctor had been surprisingly candid with his information regarding the case, one that apparently was speckled with holes. He surrendered his theory on the man's arm being torn from his body. He talked about how the bruising that, in his mind, was created by a very large *hand-like* object. At the end of their lengthy conversation, the Doctor expressed how Jessup's Sheriff had been extremely bothered by his findings. LaFontaine had found a definite *possible* at this point. It was much more inviting than some of the other wild goose chases he'd been on.

While in Jessup, LaFontaine began to mingle amongst the people. He knew that his best source for information would be the local grapevine, so he knocked on doors portraying the role of a journalist who was documenting the Michigan black bear population in the U.P. And the locals were very eager to spill local gossip and answer his questions. He found Peter Brummeister who told of two big bears that had broken into his henhouse and slaughtered his birds. Mr. Brummeister said that he had even gotten a couple of shots off at the thieves. "Big sonsabitches" were the exact words he used. LaFontaine asked him how he knew they were bears after noticing the thick glasses covering his eyes. The man answered ... "What the hell else would they be, sonny!" And they both laughed together. But LaFontaine had another theory, one that he would keep to himself.

He also spoke with the local mail carrier who told how she had been attacked by poachers. Birdie McIntosh explained how she had stopped to watch a large whitetail buck in the path of her Jeep, and how the animal had been bleeding from a large gash in its side. She told him how it mysteriously disappeared as she was preparing to snap a picture. When asked if she had seen the poachers, she told him how she had to hurry out of there because they were throwing large tree limbs at her vehicle, and that her husband was still very upset by the unclaimed damage. But the mail courier also said that her husband was a "Mister Lazy Pants" and needed to get up out of his chair in front of that '*darn idiot box.*' They both laughed together.

LaFontaine found the local folklore surrounding the Amen Swamp to be especially intriguing. He listened as the Jessup elders spoke of the legends associated with the enormous tract of land.

Some men enter,
All men fear,
The spirits watching,
As the damned draw near.

If you will the courage,
To face the demons within,
Then pray with pure heart,
The journey ends with Amen.

He first heard the chant while getting a haircut in the local barbershop, a hotspot for town chatter. He knew that the locals were just being mischievous in their futile attempts to frighten the newcomer, but LaFontaine was deeply engrossed with the symbolism in the verses. He heard similar versions from nearly every man, woman, and child he interviewed, as if they were all connected by this one common thread ... the Amen Swamp. For whatever reason, the Amen held everyone's attention, and David was beginning to form visions of his own. What had they meant by "the spirits within?" One man, a firefighter who helped battle a sweeping fire during the previous summer, told of a horrific cry from some creature one night. It was unlike any he'd ever heard before ... like a *banshee.* Every interview seemed to validate that something unusual was happening in and around the Amen Swamp ... something that might bring him closer to the proof he diligently pursued. David LaFontaine began to feel that his quest to discover a humanoid being living in the wilds of North America was coming to fruition.

***

Sergeant Jack Berkowski looked down at his cluttered desk. "What a mess," he groaned. He was looking at a collage off roadmaps, photos, police reports, and arrest records. Nothing had helped him track down his two fugitives. They managed to disappear off the face of the earth without a trace. "Where are you guys?" he asked himself as he stared at the two pictures. Over the past two weeks, Berkowski memorized every line, every out of place hair, every intricate detail in the photos. He had coordinated a massive manhunt that failed to expose even the slightest of clues.

As far as MSP was concerned, the fugitives had already crossed into Wisconsin. They were presumed to be in Chicago, probably holed up in some crack house on the south side. But the Sergeant couldn't accept that conclusion just yet. Twenty-five years of experience told him that their logic was too easy to embrace. He had a feeling that the men were still close, hiding out in one of the thousands of secluded hunting camps in the middle of nowhere. And locating them would be next to impossible. Unfortunately, he didn't have the manpower to check them all, and additional resources were not readily available. There were shacks out in that country that hadn't been inhabited for years. The only hope for a break in the case would be for someone to happen upon them and not get murdered in the process. With the arrival of the archery deer season, there would be a lot of hunters taking to the woods. Hopefully they would catch a break.

Jack Berkowski decided that it was time to give up for the evening and head home. There was nothing more to be done tonight. The next shift was already drifting into the barracks. The Sergeant picked up his notepad off the desk and quickly reviewed the scribbled notes that would be used to update the fresh staff. He would return in the morning and trudge through the same materials again.

***

Ross let go a long, vexing sigh when the visitor concluded his fascinating lecture. *Unbelievable,* he thought as he glared with a straight face into the eyes of the man sitting across the table. Ross deliberated over the doubts that had hounded him following the bear incident. He had not heard of the two boys who were allegedly attacked by a bear, or the campers from Ontonogon ... or the canoers for that matter. In those parts, folks generally stuck with their local papers. He didn't quite know what to make of those stories. Birdie McIntosh and Pete Brummeister both bragged about their encounters in town, but there was never mention of any *monsters*. Ross never connected the two with *his* bear. He wondered if they really did fit together. Could there be a creature stalking the Amen? *No, Ross! It's nonsense!* It was lunacy. But then he recalled that day in the Amen, with Chuck and Mark at Crosby's wreck. It was the smell ... like a rotting corpse. *Could it be?*

David LaFontaine detected the Sheriff's inner turmoil, as if he were engaged in a game of tug of war with himself. Judging by the man's willingness to hear him through, David also assumed that he had similar theories. The investigator always did his homework before making these wild allegations, and he was very confident that the Amen Swamp was worth pursuing. He'd been wrong before, but never with the amount of evidence that had been uncovered both in and around Jessup. Albeit much of it was circumstantial, and maybe even coincidental, but intuition told him that continued focus on that swamp could produce a historic discovery. David needed Ross' help to have any chance of achieving success. The Sheriff had to be convinced beyond a reasonable doubt that *his* creature did exist.

"Ross," continued LaFontaine, breaking the uncomfortable silence, "before jumping to any conclusions, allow me to explain another part of my theory."

Ross' chin dropped into his sweating palms as he nodded and allowed the man to proceed.

"I have researched the topography surrounding your town," began David again. "It's quite remarkable really. That swamp is enormous, and from what I've heard from your people, it's quite impenetrable in spots. Under ordinary circumstances I would say that it would be unlikely for such an animal to exist in Michigan given the size of your state's population. It's probably already crossed your mind that with all of the deer hunters out in the fall, why hasn't anyone ever run across a Bigfoot or Sasquatch before?"

Ross perked up slightly. He actually hadn't thought about that argument. It was a logical point. In fact, he recalled reading somewhere that Michigan had the second largest army in the world, next to China, during the firearm deer season. But then he wondered why LaFontaine would bring it up when it could totally dispel his theory altogether. The Sheriff's face expressed his cynicism.

LaFontaine went on. "It's something that I've mulled over for quite some time. But when I look on the map and see how large that swamp is, I can't help but feel that a life-form could go undetected by man. If it is as dense as your people say, then why not?" He threw his hands up in the air and smiled, again attempting to ease the building tension. "Let me ask you, Ross, do many people actually hunt that swamp? I'm talking about the inner core."

Ross pictured the Amen in his mind. One of the eerie chants filtered into his head. "No, David. There may be a few, but not too many at all." Only the Jones brothers might attempt it. It would take a week just to haul a deer out.

"That's exactly what I found. Now, let's assume that our creature, or creatures, were living in that swamp. Why would we be experiencing these encounters now? Why would they wander so dangerously close to civilization?"

Ross thought that LaFontaine was acting as if they were on the same page. He had not yet reached that place. "Look, David. I don't know the answer to your question if that's what you're looking for. You obviously have an idea, so please share it with me." Ross was growing a little testy. Too much had been levied on his shoulders to remain placid. He hoped that Maggie wouldn't stumble into the conversation.

"Okay, Ross. Look ... again, I've done my research here. There was a significant fire last summer that started somewhere in that swamp. The firefighting community said it was impossible to battle from the ground because of the location. Let's say that these creatures lived there and were driven out, thus sending them closer to civilization ... or at least civilization as defined by those who live in the Upper Peninsula. And let's say that as their terrain deteriorated, they were forced to occupy common territory with man. Now you have a suitable scenario for an encounter. Chickens start disappearing ... a run-in with a motorist ... a chance sighting by a little boy. It makes perfect sense."

It did make sense. *The man is good*, thought Ross. However, there was one very important link missing from his chain of evidence. "Okay, David, if what you're telling me is true, then why would it kill? I mean ... if your creature existed for so long, why all of a sudden would it ... they ... attack a man ... and eat him?" The idea was sickening.

"That's where I get stuck in the mud, Ross. I don't know the answer to that question." LaFontaine folded his hands and shrugged his shoulders.

"Ross!" It was Maggie calling from the bedroom. "Sorry, but we have to get moving!"

The Sheriff checked his watch. They had forty-five minutes until game time. The stands would be filling up fast. "I'm sorry, David, but we've got a football game to catch." He stood.

LaFontaine followed suit. "May we talk again soon? I hope that I haven't worn out my welcome. I know this is a lot to take in."

Ross studied him closely. *Is this really my job?* He thought about contacting the DNR, but they would most likely laugh him off the phone. *Come see the monster of Jessup!* Even Ross almost chuckled at the thought. But this was no laughing matter. He needed time to think about his next move, or if he even believed Mr. LaFontaine. *Christ, the bow opener.* "Where will you be staying, David?" asked Ross.

"Well, I've been sleeping out of my van mostly. I've been driving down to the State Park to take showers when my armpits get a little ripe." He giggled, but the attempt at humor went unnoticed.

"Why don't you shack up at the Jessup Inn back in town. I think Maggie said she had an extra room available. She owns the place. They'll take care of you. We can talk again tomorrow at my office ... say around ten?"

"Excellent, Sheriff. I really do appreciate your time, and I know that this has been a lot to throw at you all at once. But I firmly believe that this is worth looking into."

Ross sighed again. Whether or not he believed the man did not change the fact that a *potential* danger did require immediate attention. After shaking hands, Ross escorted him to the door and watched him drive off from the kitchen window. His thirst was beginning to grow. Ross' nerves were begging to be soothed. *Something to take the edge off ...*

"Is he gone, hon?" Maggie walked into the kitchen and placed her hands on his shoulders. "What's got you all tightened up?" She could feel the stiffness.

"Just the game, Maggs," responded Ross, still staring out the window into the trees across the road. *What is out there?*

"What did that man want?" Maggie began massaging his neck.

He couldn't tell her the truth. He couldn't tell anyone. "Oh, he was just an old friend of Charlie Perkins," he lied. "Just wanted to know how he died, I guess." *So do I,* he thought.

***

The northern Michigan sky was crystal clear that evening. Stars sparkled against the dark background as a three-quarter moon had begun its ascent to join them. It was the third quarter and Appleton was hanging onto a six point lead. Chuck Barnes felt the adrenaline rushing through his veins as he eyed the coach signaling in the play. The Marauders were on Escanaba's thirty-two yard line and looking at second and one. *Deep ball,* thought the quarterback, anxiously knowing that they could easily pick up the first down in the next two plays. His uniform showed signs of a grueling clash between the rivals. It was a perfect night with a fast turf, and Chuck Barnes was on his game. He had already amassed two hundred and sixty-three yards passing, along with forty-nine yards on the ground. Anyone watching would certainly have been impressed with his stats to that point. But there was more at stake. Bragging rights for an entire year were riding on this game.

The crowd roared in anticipation of the next play. The rivalry between the two teams had been festering for twelve months and it was time for payback. The Coach finally sent in the play. Chuck's eyes lit up when he deciphered the second-string quarterback's hand signals. He huddled the team together.

"Dewey K, one Mary Molly, slant right on three!" he called. For whatever reason, coach enjoyed inserting names, possibly from relatives or other acquaintances, into his signal calling. The boys clapped their hands in unison and then trudged up to the line of scrimmage. The linemen took to their stances. Chuck could hear the defense calling out the receivers. They were in man coverage. When he saw the injured corner on Benny Farmer, the quarterback barked out the audible.

"Check, check, check ... J, Shelly 4! Reed, one Mary Gail! Blue thirty!" After Benny split wide right, the tight end slowly jogged down the left side of the line of scrimmage. When he was set, Chuck called for the snap.

Jerry Wilson slammed the ball into his hands. Chuck drifted back and faked the hand-off to Terry Donley who was charging up the gut. The linebackers took the bait. Chuck bootlegged right, keeping his eyes on Benny streaking toward the end zone with the corner trying to keep pace. He could hear the lineman grunting and fighting for position in the pits. *Now, Benny!* The receiver, as if reading Chuck's thought, cut toward the corner of the end zone. The quarterback planted his back foot and tossed a perfect spiral. He watched as the football sailed through the air and into the outstretched hands of his wide receiver. The referee raised his hands. Touchdown! Half of the crowd erupted as the pep band fired up the Appleton fight song. Chuck raced to the end zone and vaulted into the pile of celebrating teammates.

***

"There he is, Chuck! Throw it! Throw it!" Ross stood with the rest of the people as the boy released the ball. His eyes followed the flight of the pigskin until Benny Farmer snatched it out of the air. "Alright, Chucky!" *Beautiful,* he thought. *Goddamned beautiful!* Maggie embraced him. Ross looked over her head to Vince Hobson, his buddy from Wisconsin. "Not bad, huh Vinny?" he cried with a beaming smile over the raucous crowd.

"And he's only a junior?" inquired Hobson.

"That's right. Pretty darn smart one at that."

"The boy has a tremendous arm, Ross. He's definitely got potential. I think coach might be interested."

Ross was ecstatic, knowing that his friend would not mislead him. They had played together back in the old days. And now Chuck might have a career ahead of him at a big-time program. "Well, Vinny, you've got a lot of heavy persuading ahead of you. He's got his mind set on Michigan." He laughed.

"We'll see, buddy. We'll see who wins in Ann Arbor this year. He may have second thoughts after he's seen the team we're putting together. We may just have the best line in the country when all is said and done."

It doesn't get any better than this, thought Ross. He held Maggie tighter. His earlier experience with LaFontaine was temporarily set aside. He would deal with that later. Ross was enjoying the moment, watching his future stepson play ball. He looked down toward the field where the home team was whooping it up, slapping hands and patting each other on the rear. It brought back so many wonderful memories from his youth.

"Ross?" Maggie peered up into his eyes. "How much do you love me?" It was one of those questions that preceded a request. Hobson looked away from the couple and concentrated on the kickoff.

"What do you need, Maggs?"

"How about some popcorn? I'm kind of hungry." She displayed her best puppy dog eyes, knowing that he couldn't resist her charm.

"Alright, master. Anything for you," he joked. Hobson also put in an order. As Ross sidestepped his way down the bleachers, he received a number of congratulatory gestures for Chuck's performance. He answered each one, gleaming with pride. When he finally reached the base of the bleachers, he made his way toward the concession stand that was experiencing a flood of fans following the break in action. After he slipped into line, he heard a familiar voice call out from behind.

"Sheriff!"

Oh shit! Not now, he thought. His night had been going so well. Ross slowly turned and met Gene Steubens who was huddled with Fred Wentworth and Frank Peterson.

Ross nodded his head toward the men, acknowledging their names. "Gene ... Fred ... Frank."

"That boy is incredible, Ross," said the cocky little Mayor. "You must be very proud of him."

"Thanks, Gene. I am." Ross spoke softly ... politely. He noticed Frank Peterson staring off in another direction, avoiding eye contact.

The Sheriff could not pass up the chance. "I haven't heard much from you lately, Frank. Been busy?"

"Huh ... ah, yeah," he responded awkwardly. "You know ... my wife has been getting the house ready for winter and all." Peterson would still not look Ross in the eye.

"Sheriff," continued Steubens, "I would just like to take this opportunity to personally thank you for quietly allowing the council to proceed with our plans for Jessup's future. I know how distressed you were following your personal ordeal with our animal, but I can see that you have now overcome your anxieties for the betterment of our community. Thank you, sir." He stuck out his hand.

Un-fucking-believable! Steubens was speaking to him as if he had experienced some sort of mental breakdown and was on the road to recovery. Ross really wanted to punch the little bastard right in front of everyone. He wanted to put him on his ass and spit in his face. Steubens was relentless in his struggle to augment his power. Ross would never become one of his pawns.

"Is there something wrong, Sheriff?" Steubens asked the question with a smirk, knowing that he was effectively provoking the man. "Perhaps you are still not enamored by our attempts to make Jessup a better place." He was now playing the crowd. A few others had gathered around the men to listen in on the conversation.

Ross suddenly felt trapped. He knew that Steubens was baiting him. *To hell with him,* he thought. Ross turned his back on the Mayor without saying a word.

"Sheriff? Sheriff?" Steubens raised his boisterous voice so that the onlookers could take notice. "I am speaking to you, Sheriff!" He reached out and tugged on Ross' elbow just as the stands erupted from the play on the field.

***

Chuck jogged onto the turf after the defense recovered the fumble on Escanaba's twenty-two yard line. *Just one more score and it's over,* he thought. *Come on coach, let's go for the jugular.* Coach Baker was aggressive and did not like to sit on a lead by hammering the ball on the ground. When the play was signaled in, a large smile stretched across the quarterback's face. *That's it coach, let's bury these cocksuckers!* It was a play they had worked on in the off-season. Chuck gathered his offense ten yards behind the line of scrimmage. The guys were eager to score again. He knew their next play would seal Escanaba's fate.

"Shut up, guys! Listen!" He was the leader of the squad and was respected by all, including the seniors. Their success rested on his shoulders. "B, Mary T, dash blue split 80, on two." They all clapped in unison. Chuck fastened his chinstrap and crouched down behind the center. He called the cadence over the loud crowd. Finally, he felt the ball slam into his hands and then dropped back into the pocket. Out of the corner of his eye, he saw Benny Farmer drifting over for the toss. Chuck turned and lateraled the ball to the reversing receiver. The defense followed. Chuck then drifted out towards the empty side of the field. He heard someone from the opposite bench yell for the defense to watch the quarterback. Benny stopped on the far sideline and looked back toward Chuck. He then threw a high, wobbly ball that floated. *Awwwww shit,* thought the quarterback as he helplessly watched the ball coming toward him. The defense would have time to react.

As Chuck looked the ball into his waiting hands, the safety had been building up a full head of steam on his target. Chuck didn't have a chance. The violent collision caused the ball to pop free. His head was jolted backward. The last thing he felt before passing out was a sharp pain in his right shoulder.

***

Ross turned and swatted the Mayor's arm to the side. He just wanted to be left alone, but the man kept insisting on inciting an arousal. "Keep your goddamn hands off me, Steubens!" Everyone in the concession line now turned and faced him. He ignored them. "If you ever touch me again," he continued, "I'll pop you in the eye!"

Steubens was momentarily taken aback by the Sheriff's outburst. After surveying the curious onlookers, he realized that this was a perfect opportunity. "Sheriff, I certainly don't think there's any need to be physical here." The Mayor remained calm, inviting Ross into his trap.

"Oh shut up!" His anger grew with each breath. He was losing control. "You and your partners in crime there just go on and run this town with your sick little ideas. But if you come near me, I'll flatten your fat ass!"

Keep going, Sheriff, thought Steubens. The hook was firmly embedded in Ross' lip. He was displaying the irrational behavior right in plain sight for all to see. His imbalance had been exposed. The Mayor had to maintain his own composure if he was to play this out. "I'm sorry, Ross. Please calm down. I just wanted to thank you." Steubens spoke up loud enough for all to hear. He reached towards Ross' arm a second time. Ross grabbed the outstretched limb and shoved it away, this time with a little more force. Steubens made sure the crowd believed the shove to be a little more forceful than it really was. By his own power, he fell backwards to the ground. He lay at the Sheriff's feet, acting dazed as if he had truly been injured in the skirmish.

"Oh get up, you little fool." Ross knew that he hadn't pushed the man hard enough to knock him down. Steubens had played him to perfection. He looked into the astonished sets of eyes watching him. Some scowled. Mothers turned their children's heads. He had been duped into an altercation by a very cunning adversary.

"Ross!" It was a familiar voice calling from the field. Henry Pierson, Jenna's father, waived towards him. "Chuck's down!"

Those two words stung his ears ... *Chuck's down!* He jumped over the Mayor's body and fought his way to the fence. As he looked out onto the field he could see a player lying flat on his back, and he wasn't moving. Ross jumped the fence and ran out to where the training staff was examining the boy. Coach Baker was trying to prevent the rest of the team from crowding around too close.

"What happened?" asked Ross as he knelt down.

"Didn't you see the hit? Damn, it was a killer." One of the assistant coaches had used a poor choice of words.

"Is he okay?" Ross had not yet detected any movement. The EMS team arrived with a stretcher. One of them broke out some smelling salts and waived it in front of the boy's nose. His eyes opened and blinked a few times.

"Ross?" It was Maggie running up behind him. "What's wrong with my baby?" An eerie hush had befallen the crowd.

Ross turned and clutched the boy's mother. She was crying. "It's okay, Maggs. Let them work."

Chuck turned his head from side to side. He opened his eyes a little wider trying to focus. "Dad?" He was muttering incoherently. "You there, Dad?"

Ross knelt back down next to the boy. Maggie picked up his hand and caressed it gently. "It's okay, boy. You're going to be okay." A tear formed in the corner of his eye.

Chuck turned and focused on Ross. As he moved his body, he winced.

Ross could feel the pain written in Chuck's face. It was the same pain that he had felt thirty years ago when he blew out his knee. A promising career had ended that day. He prayed that Chuck would not suffer the same fate.

"Chuck! Chuck!" It was one of the paramedics trying to get his attention. "Can you hear me, Chuck?" He shined a light in the boy's eyes, one at a time.

"Yeah, I can hear you," he replied weakly.

"Can you feel your fingers and toes?"

"Yeah." Chuck tried to move, but his attempt was suppressed by the paramedic. "Oh, God ... my shoulder is on fire."

"Easy now, son," said the emergency responder. "Just lay there and let us do our job."

Ross watched helplessly as the two paramedics attended to him. They retrieved a backboard for precautionary measures and secured his arm with athletic tape. Chuck was quickly regaining consciousness, which was a good sign. After applying a collar, they carefully slipped the board underneath and loaded him into the ambulance. Ross and Maggie followed close behind in the Tahoe.

***

The fire flickered aimlessly, sending an occasional stray spark into the protective screen. Tyrone Pullman watched the flames dance off the half-burned pieces of birch, listening to the sharp snaps and cracks. He tried desperately to avoid thinking about the hunger pains in his gargling stomach. He felt imprisoned like a caged animal. At times, Tyrone thought about turning himself in, thinking that Jackson Prison couldn't be nearly as awful. At the very least, he would have someone to talk to, and decent food on his dinner plate. His head ached as he teetered on the brink of starvation. Although he was eating, he wasn't getting the balanced diet that the human body needed to sustain. He was living day to day, with no guarantee of the next.

Tyrone lifted his weak body from the rickety recliner. It was time to eat again. As much as he despised the strong, gamey taste of the venison, he would force himself to consume it for lack of other options. The fugitive opened the cabin door with the large hunting knife in hand and stepped out onto the porch. The partial hind quarter lay on the ground outside. It sickened him just to look at the stiff hunk of meat encased with dried blood. But he *had* to eat. There was no other alternative if he was to remain a free man. And freedom was the most precious commodity of all. But was he free?

In the days that passed for the now recluse hermit, he began talking to himself as though he were having conversations with others. Sometimes he pretended there was someone else to break up the monotony ... like Gerald, or Billy, or J.C. Tyrone would ask questions, request advice, relive stories from his recent past. He would laugh and joke with his make-believe companions as a tangent from his perpetual solitude. The inactivity was torturous.

Tyrone leaned down and proceeded to slice off a sizeable steak. "Time for chow," he said sarcastically in a futile attempt to add light to the situation. He filleted off the dry, outer crust and flung it into some weeds. Tyrone noticed that the discarded remnants from the previous day had disappeared. He took a moment to search the trees, wondering what sort of animal had made a visit in the night. The fugitive then draped the slab of meat over his forearm as a waiter would carry a napkin, and then lumbered back inside. After washing off the blood in the sink, he tossed the meat into a frying pan over a burner on the gas stove. Tyrone sat and listened as the steak sizzled and smoked. That awful stench of wild game filled the cabin once again. He allowed his mind to wander from the reality of his predicament. He remembered running the streets back home in Flint with his friends. He recalled playing ball at the neighborhood park as a kid when innocence was taken for granted. Images of a single mother popped into his head and a tear rolled down his cheek. The meat continued to hiss.

***

The female cautiously advanced through the scarred undergrowth of the place where she had once been welcome. She could still scent the charred remains from the great inferno that had threatened the clan not so long ago. The memories were clear in her head. Not all had had escaped the intense heat of the flames. It was the juveniles that suffered most, becoming disoriented from the black smoke and noisy machines over the trees. The clan had been forced to move quickly. Some were left behind as their screams of agony resounded over the crackling of the burning pine.

She could scent the others in the breeze. The female chose to enter the lair with the winds in her face to avoid detection. It was a tactical maneuver. She did not want the males to discover her presence before knowing their exact location. She was taking a great risk, but the decision had been made out of desperation. She did not wish to continue her reclusive existence. The female had things that she could teach the clan. She had experienced much in her journey into the domain of the weaker, hairless ones. If she could persuade them to follow, she would teach them how to hunt and feast upon the new source of food that was plentiful outside the boundaries of the lair.

As the female approached the small clearing she observed the other females huddled together on the dampened ground. She watched them pick through each other's hair as they sat in tight circles in search of ticks and other bugs swarming on their bodies. It was a common cleansing ritual. The juveniles remained fairly close to their mothers. They were practicing their hunting skills. They would stalk one another in the thicker brush and then pounce in a playful manner. They were training for the next season when they would be old enough to hunt with the pack. The female envisioned herself in the group of adults watching her own juvenile from a distance. The pains in her heart remained strong.

There was only one male present in the lair. The female eyed him closely, careful to remain hidden until she felt the moment right to make her presence known. The male was chivvying a female in heat. He would approach from the rear and attempt to pin her arms behind her back. The targeted female protested in the customary fashion. She would not allow him easy access. The male grunted his disapproval whenever she escaped his clutches, but he persisted until the female finally gave in to his advances. When the mating had ended, he released her and drifted off into the trees. The ripe female returned to the group of mothers and took her place in the cleansing line. She would give birth to her juvenile when the days grew warm again.

Seeing that the sentry had left, the female stepped through the brush and grunted quietly to alert the others. She saw their startled faces as heads turned. The juveniles scattered from the playground and darted to the protection of their mothers. It had taken the young ones only a short time to forget. The adults, though apprehensive at first, began to rise from their crouched positions. There were snorts of caution as they searched the trees for the males. They realized how serious the punishment would be if the males discovered that the shunned one had returned. It was not in the nature of the females to hold such contempt for another of their own kind. The oldest adult was the first to approach her, walking slowly to maintain a sense of calm within the group.

The female watched the elder advance. She remained alert for danger that could erupt at any moment. Slowly, the others came to her with their unsure juveniles clinging tightly to their backsides. The females gathered around her, vocalizing their happiness and scenting her hide for clues as to where she had been. She was overcome with relief thinking that she had been accepted as a clan member again. She purred softly as anxious hands sifted through her fur.

The roar from the tree line quickly dispersed the frightened crowd, and she was alone again. The females scattered to find cover. The newcomer crouched into a defensive position and peered at the males returning from their successful hunt. They broke out of the brush and immediately surrounded her. The female could see the hatred in their eyes. The leader that was bigger than the rest, made an opening in the circle so that he could enter. His graying fur was stained red from the bloody deer hanging over his shoulder. He glanced over to the elder female and gave her a menacing growl. His anger was noted by all members of the clan. He was displeased with them for allowing the expelled one back into the lair. He snatched the deer off his shoulder and flung it through the air, striking the elder female hard in the back. She let out a whimper and cowered to the ground. She would not feast at the next meal.

The male then reverted his attention back to the one that had been cast out. He reared back and unleashed a ferocious cry. The other males jumped around, thumping their chests with massive hands and shoving each other with incredible force. The female was cornered. She knew then that there would be no second chances. They would kill her. There was only one course of action for her to take if she were to survive. She erected herself and thrust out her heaving chest. Her rage began to boil. Her muscles tensed. She planted her back foot against a log and curled back her lips to reveal her sharp fangs. She waited for the opportunity.

When the male reared back a second time, she charged. Even though the male outweighed her by two hundred pounds, the female's momentum sent the leader sprawling backwards. She pumped her legs, driving him farther and farther. The others looked on in silent shock. This was something new to them. She kept going, her shoulder buried in his chest, driving him backwards until they both slammed hard into a thick tree trunk. She heard the air expel from the male's lungs. He doubled over, fighting to breathe. Her head shot down towards his vulnerable neck. The female's teeth sank deep into flesh and clenched together like a vise. The male cried out in pain. He flopped on the ground as the determined one rode his back. Her teeth sank deeper and deeper, penetrating the thick hide. She tasted the warm blood flowing through her mouth.

The male tried to reach around and grasp his attacker, but her hold was too strong, her positioning superior. The male's efforts were beginning to weaken. The clan drew closer. Finally, there was no more movement in their leader's body. The female's jaws clenched tighter until the cracking of bone was heard by all.

***

It was two in the morning when the trio returned home. Maggie opened the door while Ross helped Chuck into the house. The boy was still a little groggy from the vicious hit, but he was going to be okay according to the ER Doctor. Chuck had suffered a concussion, and Maggie and Ross were told to periodically check on him in the night.

Chuck was devastated after suffering a serious injury that could potentially alter his life path forever. To top matters off, they later learned that Appleton ended up losing the game by three points. The quarterback felt guilty, as though he had let his team and his community down. He played the *'what if'* scenarios over and over in his head. *What if it had been a better pass? What if he had let the ball fall to the ground rather than catch it?*

The Doctor's diagnosis showed that Chuck had torn the bicep muscle of his throwing arm. It was an injury that would sideline him for the remainder of the season. They were referred to an Orthopedic Surgeon who could determine the extent of the damage and whether or not surgery would be necessary. Everything that he had worked for had been negated with one regretful play.

Ross followed the teenager into his room and helped him out of the remnants of his uniform. "Feeling okay, buddy?" he asked as he lifted the jersey over his tender shoulder.

Chuck cringed slightly. "Yeah, I'm okay. It's just that ..." His voice trailed off into silence.

"What's wrong, Chuck?" Ross saw the emotion building. He knew there was a lot going on in the boy's head. He remembered having those same thoughts once. But Chuck was young and had a better than average chance of healing properly. He would be back next year if Ross had to rehab him twenty-four hours a day. He would do it because he loved the kid.

"It's ... it's just that ... this really sucks!"

Chuck began to cry, which triggered a chain reaction in Ross, as well as Maggie who had been listening in from outside the bedroom door. Ross embraced the boy as best he could without irritating the shoulder. It felt good to hold him. Chuck needed a father, and Ross was filling that void that had been missing in his life for too long.

***

The headlights from the Dodge Durango illuminated the temporary sign marking the entrance to the Hideaway Pines Golf Resort. The truck sped through the gate and swerved onto the narrow service road. Chet Manko and Jerry White were returning from a long night of drinking at the Jessup Inn. They were both slated to work a ten hour shift on Sunday, and that meant double-time pay. The two young men were heavy equipment specialists for Newhouser Construction. Chet hired on with Newhouser in August after a lengthy stint in Sault Ste. Marie. Jerry, on the other hand, was a rookie on the big landmovers, but he quickly established himself as a fine operator. They were both single with a taste for partying.

"Slow down, you drunk bastard!" Jerry cried out while holding onto the support handle over his window.

"Watch this!" Chet punched the gas and fishtailed around a tight corner that was more appropriately suited for golf carts. Low-hanging branches swiped at the windshield as the speeding truck weaved through the grounds.

"Damn!" Jerry was all smiles. The two roared together, both exhilarated by the alcohol-induced excitement of the ride. Their open beers sloshed onto the leather seats. When a can was emptied, it was tossed to the back with the others that were rolling around freely. Chet displayed little concern that his thirty thousand dollar truck was getting trashed. It had been one wild night. With deadlines staring them in the face, the men had been working twelve to fourteen hour shifts with little time to blow off steam. They were two of the best in the business, and the boss knew it. Ted Newhouser had cleared the path for the eighteenth fairway on the *Amen Basin* earlier that afternoon. With a much-deserved "well done," Ted handed each two hundred bucks and sent them off to have some fun. Boys would be boys, and these young studs needed to burn some energy.

"Hey, Chet! Let's do the mountain. What do you say?"

Chet Manko eyed his partner as the truck skidded sideways across the paved path before coming to a screeching halt. The *mountain* that Jerry had referred to was the steep incline between the eighteenth green of *Amen Basin* and the high plateau where the clubhouse was being built. The workers on site had labeled the hill while wagering money on the abilities of their vehicles to make it all the way to the top. Only one lucky man had succeeded in the challenge to date. Had Chet Manko not been drinking that night, he probably would have thought twice about attempting the climb with his expensive SUV. But not tonight. He was primed and ready.

"There she blows!" howled Jerry as the Durango rolled to the base of the bluff. Chet stared up the precipitous track with both hands tightly clenching the steering wheel. He saw the tire tracks from days past when others had taken the dare. The task was not about money for the young construction worker. Chet was shooting for a boost in his ego, something that his co-workers would talk about for days on end. It was his moment in the sun.

"Watch this baby ride the mountain!" Chet yelled with a hoot. He activated the front axle with the 4WD-high button and floored the gas pedal. Both men produced a loud "yahoo" as the nose of the Durango rose in front of them. The wheels gripped for traction and the truck began to climb. Jerry was laughing hysterically, encouraging his partner to keep going. Chet concentrated on maintaining a straight line, knowing that one wrong slip could send them sideways and possibly rolling all the way to the bottom. But he didn't care. He was charged by alcohol and adrenaline. He was going to the top.

The Durango's progress began to slow at about the halfway point. "Come on you piece of shit!" screamed the driver. Chet pumped the accelerator to prevent the tires from burying into the loose earth. At about the three-quarter mark the truck was no longer making progress. It was then obvious to the driver that his attempt at conquering the *mountain* had failed.

"I knew it, asshole!" teased the passenger. "This truck couldn't climb a fucking hard-on." Jerry continued to laugh.

"Yeah, go on. Why don't you bring your mighty Cavalier out here and see how high you get, dickhead." Accepting defeat, Chet shifted into reverse and began the tricky roll back to the bottom. Once the Durango leveled out on the flat surface at the base of the hill, he headed off to where Jerry's Chevy was parked a short distance away. They would have gone straight to Appleton after their visit to the Inn that night, but Jerry had forgotten his cellular in the glove compartment. Chet tried to persuade his friend that the phone would be fine until Sunday. After all, it was rare that people could get a signal anyway. But Jerry was insistent that they pick it up tonight before one of those *crazy, toothless* locals got their hands on it. Besides, he had been waiting for a call from his brother in Newberry who was expecting a baby at any hour.

The headlights lit up the well-traveled Cavalier sitting by its lonesome just off the service drive. The eyes from a moping opossum glowed in a tree just beyond.

"When you going to get rid of that thing?" inquired Chet, referring to the beater that Jerry drove. "You make enough money, you cheap sonuvabitch." Chet often razed his buddy about his jalopy and the part it played in his inability to pick up babes.

"I have to piss," said the passenger. When Chet pulled up alongside the car, Jerry got out, walked around the front and disappeared into the trees. Chet's eyes followed the opossum as it scampered down the base of the tree and wandered off into the brush. After a few minutes passed, the driver rolled down his window.

"Come on," called Chet from the Durango. "Drain your pecker and let's get out of here!" There was no response. Chet then began to scan the side mirrors, thinking that Jerry was trying to sneak around from behind and scare him. "I see you!" he yelled, trying to put a quick halt to the hoax. But he didn't see his friend. "Ain't gonna work, Jer!" There was still no response. Chet opened the door and stepped out. With only a short-sleeve Polo separating his skin from the freezing temperatures, he crossed his arms and shivered. His teeth chattered slightly.

"Come on, Jerry! I'm starting to get pissed over here!" Chet heard a rustling in the trees where Jerry had walked in. At first, he thought it was the opossum making its way through the underbrush. But as the noise persisted beyond the glare of the headlights, he realized that it was something else ... something bigger.

Jerry White's face was buried in the chest of the massive creature. His eyes bulged as the suffocating arms slowly squeezed the life out of him. He could hear the fading voice of his friend only yards away. There was no air in his lungs to produce a warning sound. The course hair on the beast's thick hide made his skin bleed. His arms and legs dangled as the pressure increased.

Jerry hadn't seen the creature that was now killing him. He had been standing alone, urinating when he was violently snatched up off the ground. The monster's arm sealed his mouth until his lungs were completely void of any oxygen. His legs kicked for only a minute until his brain was deprived of the air it needed to function. As he listened to the pounding heartbeat of the creature, he felt its grip tighten one last time and then his back broke. His body was expelled to the ground.

Chet Manko heard an odd sound emanating from the forest beyond the shine of the headlights. It was a hissing, wheezing sound, like someone was squeezing the air out of a ball. And then a distinct "thump!"

"Jerry?" Chet's voice was uncertain as he called out. "Come on, man. Let's go." He listened. Above the howling winds that rippled the leaves overhead, there was something else. It was a low, ominous growl from behind the curtain of trees and brush. As Chet stepped back, he heard movement. He stopped. The movement stopped. Chet retreated another step toward the Durango. The rustling sound was repeated as if someone or something was mimicking his motions. A couple of coyotes howled eerily in the distance. He now stood at the side of the truck. Chet contemplated making a dash for the interior of the Durango, but his body wouldn't cooperate. He was scared.

The growling diminished, and Chet began to wonder if he had just imagined it. He placed his hands on his hips, still shaking from the cold. Common sense was beginning to return. Jerry was playing him. He was sure of it. Chet figured that he looked like quite the idiot in his friend's eyes.

"Alright, Jerry," he called to the trees. "You got me, buddy. Now let's get the hell out of here. I'm freezing my ass off." Chet turned toward the Durango. He smiled. "Not bad, Jerry. Not bad at all. You know you had me going there for a ..."

When Chet turned to jaw at his friend, it was coming at him, black as the night around it. The creature let out an earth-shattering roar as it hoisted a massive hand and swiped at the man. Chet felt the claws slice through his side as he spun and toppled to the ground. He screamed as he grabbed for the bleeding wound with his left hand. He felt a rib protruding from the open gash. Chet turned his head as a second thunderous cry erupted. He then saw the giant foot rise high over his head, but he managed to roll away just as the creature slammed it down. The ground seemed to tremble around him.

The creature cried in anger after missing its target. Chet kept his left hand over the wound and continued to roll ... over and over. When he reached the Durango, he kicked his feet and pushed himself underneath. The pain in his side was excruciating. He screamed as the exposed rib dug into the ground. His eyes were wide with horror and shock. Blood streamed through his hand.

The construction worker was beginning to feel dizzy. As he lay on his stomach, he gazed out at the two legs standing upright next to the truck like it was waiting for him to try and escape. His eyes focused on the feet ... the toes. It had toes!

"What the fuck are you!" cried Chet. "Leave me alone, you ..." his voice broke into a gurgled cough. The salty taste of blood trickled through his mouth.

Suddenly, the truck began to rock back and forth, compressing the man underneath. The growl began to grow as the beast exerted its incredible strength. Chet felt his right shoulder dislocate from its socket with a sickening "pop!" He moaned from the agonizing pain. His scalp tore open when metal compacted him against the hard ground. Blood now covered his face and blanketed his fading eyes. As the end neared, so did the torturous hammering on his body. Chet thought he heard footsteps circling the Durango, but for some reason he didn't care anymore. He was numb, unable to feel the pain that had seized him only seconds earlier.

There was pressure around his right leg. He did not resist as the creature yanked him out from underneath the truck. His head bounced off the trailer hitch when he was hoisted upside down into the air. He dangled in the monster's grasp ... barely alive. Then, for a brief moment, Chet Manko felt free as though he were flying through the air. When he hit the tree, his neck snapped.

The creature retrieved its two kills and vanished into the swamp.

CHAPTER TEN

When Ross walked into his office that Saturday morning he felt as if his world was one of those inflated moonwalks that children play in at fairs ... bouncing up and down in all directions with no consistency from one moment to the next. Whenever you tried to coordinate a bounce on a particular course, someone would come along and send you off-kilter. It was getting to the point where he began to expect something to happen before it actually did.

Yesterday had been quite eventful. First, LaFontaine, the *Bigfoot* hunter barged into his home with fantasies about a two-legged, man-like creature stalking the Amen Swamp. But as much as Ross had attempted to laugh off the idea, his fears continued to fester inside him. His mind was milling about in a thousand different directions, searching for a truth that he could not comprehend. His lack of sleep that night had been partially due to concern over Chuck's injury. In reality, his thoughts during the early morning hours diverted back to the Amen Swamp and what might exist there.

David LaFontaine patiently waited for the Sheriff's arrival. He had been in the office for a good hour before Ross finally showed. Mark Bennington came in early and filled the stranger in on what happened at the football game. LaFontaine stood and greeted the man as he walked through the door. "Sheriff, it's good to see you again. I'll understand if you would like to reschedule."

"No, David. Please, have a seat." Ross' shoulders sagged as though they were tied to one hundred pound dumbbells. It was obvious to both Mark and David that he was a worn man. He appeared old. His hair was uncombed. His clothes were wrinkled.

Ross sank down into the chair behind his desk and took a deep breath. *What do I do now?* he asked himself. *I've got a goddamned Bigfoot hunter sitting across from me.* He stared at the stranger as though he were trying to decipher the meaning of a Monet at an art gallery.

"Is there something on your mind, Ross?" inquired LaFontaine.

"No, just a rough night is all." Ross shook his head and prepared himself for the discussion.

"Sounds like it. Is your boy going to be okay?" LaFontaine acted truly concerned with Chuck's condition.

"Yes, and thank you," replied Ross graciously. "I take it you've met my Deputy here?" He gestured toward Mark, wondering just how much LaFontaine had already revealed to the youngster. Mark was not good for keeping secrets.

"Yes, of course. He was just filling me in on where the big bucks will be this year." LaFontaine produced a clever smile. It was obviously a ruse to keep the Deputy out of their little game.

"Ross?" It was Mark speaking up for the first time. "What happened between you and the Mayor last night?"

LaFontaine looked on, puzzled by the question.

"It was nothing important. Just forget it." That was the best answer Ross could provide.

"Well, I heard Gene talking with Fred and Art this morning over to Arlene's. He was mentioning your name."

That piece of information was interesting, but Ross quickly skirted the issue. There were more important matters at hand, like LaFontaine's monster. It was time to get rid of his Deputy who was still unaware of what the two men had discussed the night before.

"Mark," said Ross, "why don't you go out and patrol around the neighborhood for a while. I've got some business with Mr. LaFontaine." He stared deeply into David's eyes. *What do you really want from me?* he wondered.

"Sure thing, Ross. See you later. Nice meeting you, David."

LaFontaine shook his hand, and Mark was gone.

"Well then, David, it's just you and me." Ross leaned forward.

"Just you and me, Ross." David imitated the Sheriff's movement.

"What the hell do we do now?" The Sheriff raised his eyebrows. He really had no idea what this man was proposing.

Whether or not there was the need for a plan in the first place still remained unclear.

"By the way, thanks for the tip on the Inn. It felt good to get a hot shower and a good night's sleep on a real bed."

Ross did notice that David was wearing a new pair of jeans, but he still had on the same shirt with the footprint. Ross nodded and allowed him to continue while he silently deliberated over whether he was speaking to a member of some silly cult.

"Okay, Ross. One thing that I can't understand is why we haven't heard of any strange encounters over the past two weeks. We have to ask ourselves what this means."

"How about that your theory is for *shit* for starters." Ross was a little too curt with his response. It was not his intention. "I'm sorry. What I mean is, maybe you really *have* been chasing a ghost."

"Believe me, Ross I've pondered that question for days. But my gut instinct tells me *no*. I firmly believe that we've got something here that's worth investigating."

"What do you propose we do then, David? I can't just take off and go Bigfoot hunting at the drop of a hat. I've got a job to do." He smirked at the thought. *Bigfoot hunting. Who would believe it?*

LaFontaine held up his palms. "Yes, I understand. Let me tell you what I would like to do. If you could provide me with a little more detailed information of your experiences to date ... like with the Crosby gentleman ... and your mechanic ... maybe some ideas as to where to look. All I really want to do is go out on my own at this point and peek around. I'll be searching for clues ... tracks ... anything."

"Tracks?" Ross tilted his head to the side.

"Yeah, look for the obvious. Here, I've got something to show you." LaFontaine reached into a duffle bag hidden beneath his chair. He withdrew an enormous plaster casting of a footprint.

Ross figured it to be twice the size of his own foot, and he was a size fourteen. "Where the hell did you get that thing?" inquired the Sheriff.

"Oregon, and it's the real deal."

***

Moods in Jessup had taken a drastic turn when Saturday morning rolled around. Appleton had lost the big game and those once high expectations were deflated. There would be no vengeance with their mighty adversary. With the star player out for the year, a long run in the playoffs dwindled to a faint whisper. The woes of the Appleton Marauders were felt by all who lived in those communities supporting the school. It was little things like football that could create such a tightly bonded society lacking much common ground in other areas. It was a shared grief, similar to that which was felt when members of their community had fallen only two weeks prior. Their despondency, however, would fade with the passing of time. As the days stretched into weeks, the people of Jessup began to focus their attention on another piece of common ground ... deer hunting. The opener was now only days away, and after plunging to the fathoms of despair following the Friday night debacle, they had a means for ascending to a higher plateau.

The first mark of the season was the sign in Fred Wentworth's window declaring that the Big Buck Contest was off and running. It seemed to grow in popularity every year as more and more sportsmen coughed up the ten dollar entry fee to bet on their skills. Last year paid out twenty-four hundred dollars to Frank Jones, although there was some argument as to the authenticity of his prize. Frank's buck had been a nice ten-point, but people would joke that its pupils were dilated from the bright beam of a spotlight. Arlene's was taking in larger crowds. Eager men and women stretched their morning meals just a little longer to brag about their secret stands in the woods. Most of the northern inhabitants appeared happier once the long awaited season finally made its grand entrance. And this year promised to be something special. Forecasters were calling for a nice tracking snow on Saturday, and possibly more on Sunday. Light flurries were already filtering down from the gray skies.

Gene Steubens danced through the doors of Town Hall, feeling as if this would be his day to finally achieve that overdue victory. Ross Pickett was on his way out. How could the others dispense his claims about the Sheriff's erratic behavior that was so unbecoming of a law enforcement officer? Pickett had made his own bed, and now he was going to sleep in it. His second chances were all used up.

"Good morning, gentlemen." Steubens greeted his council and then sat down in his designated seat at the head of the table. "Fine day, isn't it?"

They all nodded in agreement. Even Pete Wilkerson, who would forever be skeptical of the Mayor's good moods, acknowledged the greeting.

"I think you all know why I've called this meeting, so why don't we just get down to business."

"I guess I'm not privy to your reasons, Gene. Please explain, for my sake," responded Wilkerson.

Steubens wasted little time in bringing the issue to the table. He did not want a long debate for fear of swaying decisions that had already been manipulated. "Okay, Pete," he continued, "the bottom line is that I believe it's time to relieve Ross Pickett of his responsibilities as Sheriff." He eyed the councilmember whose expression failed to change.

"Ahhhh ... I thought we already discussed this matter a few weeks ago. Has something happened that I'm not aware of?"

"Bet your sweet caboose, Pete. We have an unstable Sheriff. Just ask Frank and Fred here." Steubens leaned back, crossed his arms over his belly and requested that his witnesses take over. "Go ahead boys. Fill Pete in on the details."

It was Frank Peterson who spoke up first. "Gene's right, Pete. I saw it for myself. He pushed Gene right to the ground in front of a lot of people."

"I saw it too, Pete. Wouldn't have believed it if I didn't see it with my own eyes." Wentworth added his two cents. "I think Ross may have a problem or something."

Wilkerson examined the two men closely. He did not want to get caught up in the Mayor's little conspiracy. He realized how vindictive Steubens could be when someone crossed him. Pete had never personally experienced any problems with Ross Pickett. They were friends. Ross was everyone's friend. But for one reason or another, Steubens had labeled him an enemy. "Why don't *you* tell me what happened, Gene?"

Steubens squirmed in his chair until finally coming to an erect position. "We were at the ballgame on Friday night. I was discussing some business with these gentlemen here when I saw

Ross in line at the concession stand. Well ... when I thanked him for allowing us to pursue our plan with the bear, he became uncontrollably irate. I was not attempting to provoke an argument. He just flew off the handle."

"Off the handle, Pete," said Wentworth. "Completely off the handle. Threw Gene right to the ground in front of everyone."

Steubens gave him a look as if to say, *that's enough, you idiot... let me handle this.* He then turned back to Wilkerson. "As Mayor, I will not allow a man in his current state of mind to roam our streets wearing a badge and a gun."

"Oh come off it, Gene. We're not talking about some lunatic who's about to go off on a rampaging shooting spree." Wilkerson chucked. "Ross may get bent out of shape now and again, but I think that he does it in the best interest of the town."

"No, Pete. Enough is enough," continued the Mayor. "All we need is a majority vote. Now you are either for us or against us. I make the motion that, by the power of the Jessup town charter, Ross Pickett be relieved of his duty as Sheriff and that Mark Bennington replace him as interim Sheriff until the next election." *Bennington would be much easier to manipulate,* thought Steubens. He glanced over to Frank Peterson, who in turn looked to Pete Wilkerson.

"It's for Ross' own good, Pete. I think that maybe he needs a rest. I ... I second the motion." Frank then turned away as if he were embarrassed by his action.

"Alright," added Steubens, "all those in favor say aye."

Fred, Frank and Art reluctantly raised their hands while Pete Wilkerson's arms remained at his side.

"This is a sham, Gene. It's a goddamned sham. And I refuse to be a part of it."

"Your opinion is duly noted, Pete. The motion has been passed. Ross Pickett will step down as Sheriff and Mark Bennington will assume his duties until the next election." Gene nodded his head in triumph. His work was done.

"There's one more thing, Gene." Wilkerson had a cynical grin on his face. He was disgusted with his Mayor. "Who is going to tell Ross?" he asked.

"Why, Frank of course." Steubens answered without hesitation. Peterson, in the meantime, stared up at him in shock. It was quite obvious that he was afraid of a confrontation.

"Uh, I don't think ... I don't think I could do it, Gene," he said quietly.

"Oh nonsense, Frank. You and Ross are pals. He'll understand," said the Mayor.

Pete Wilkerson felt even more distaste for the man who led his town. Always sending someone else to do his dirty work. "Forget it, Frank," he said with eyes focused directly on Steubens. "I'll tell, Ross myself. And I'll be sure to tell him how the vote went."

***

The old Jeep's seasoned motor sputtered three or four times before roaring to life. Birdie McIntosh punched the accelerator and the vehicle lurched forward as she let loose on the clutch. The mail courier had just delivered to her last customer of the day and she was eager to get home and cuddle up on the couch under a warm blanket. *A cup of spiked coffee would hit the spot just nice as pie,* she thought to herself. Birdie's fancy was a cup of java with a jigger of Jack Daniels to ease the bite from the frigid afternoons. The weather was turning colder in the north. Dark clouds rolled across the horizon like tumbleweeds. The growing westerly winds rocked the Jeep as she drove down the road.

"Not gonna be fit fer walking tonight," she proclaimed to herself. Birdie had been pushing her husband to pick his duff up off his chair and get out of the house for some exercise. Doctor Bensen had warned them at the last physical about his rising blood pressure. *Such a lazy old fart,* she fumed. Her husband would sit around watching talk shows and soap operas all day. *Trash T.V. is what that is,* she chided inwardly. It was all just another disgusting display of the country's crumbling moral fiber. Birdie shook her bundled head in disgust. A dribble of brown spit speckled with bits of tobacco hung from her numbed lip. She was cold.

"Darn heater," she cursed while staring down the vacuous road. "Gotta git that dang thing fixed, Bird. I ain't gonna put up with this crap all winter." The mail courier didn't dislike the cold U.P. winters. She just didn't favor the abrupt transition. It could be eighty degrees one day, and then dump five inches of snow the next. Those radical changes were enough to spur a cough in the healthiest of people. Birdie could handle the sub-zero temperatures so long as she had the proper time to adjust. *A little help from a working heater certainly wouldn't hurt matters,* she thought. *I'll have to call Charlie Perkins and ...*

"Oh, Lordy!" cried Birdie, remembering the recent fate of the town's mechanic. "What an awful mess." It had been such an eventful two weeks for Jessup. Rachel Perkins had been such a dear friend. Birdie spent a great deal of time consoling the widow following Charlie's passing. Birdie tried to persuade Rachel not to leave town, but the anguish had been too great. She packed up her belongings and moved downstate to be with family. Birdie really hoped that the two of them would stay in touch, but reality would most likely keep Rachel away from Jessup for good. There were just too many painful memories.

Birdie refused to believe that bear story. No bear would attack a man the size of Charlie Perkins unless provoked. And Charlie knew enough not to meddle with a Michigan black. Birdie knew the animals as well as anyone in the area, including those dirty old Jones brothers. She had cleverly devised her own little theory on the matter.

"Bet your bottom dollar it was the same crew of roughnecks who scared me off that buck the other day." That's what she told Mabel Sanders over a slice of her blue-ribbon banana bread. The dent on the hood served as a harsh reminder of her terrifying ordeal with the violators. "Those same men were probably looting Ned Crosby's shack when Charlie showed up with the old man's car. Caught them in the act he did, and they kilt him for it plain as day," she fussed to her friend.

"Do you really think so, Birdie? Do you think they would murder poor Charlie just like that?" asked Mabel.

"Darn tootin they would. And I'll bet you a silver dollar it was them Jones boys too. Rats!" she scolded. "Nothing but disgusting rats!"

And that's how another rumor would sprout legs. There always had to be a controversial angle to spice up their simple lives. The Mayor had been quite persistent with the original hypothesis as told by Mark Bennington that morning after Ned Crosby had been killed. After all, there was incontestable proof that the animal was a man-killer after what happened to Seth Jennings and his young son, Bobby. Birdie was still not convinced that the two were related. In Birdie's mind, her poachers had slaughtered poor Charlie in an awful attempt to cover their own tracks. She knew there were some real nasties living in those backwoods.

"Poor dear Charlie," she moaned to herself. "Such a nice man." It was such a loss to the community. Birdie shuddered, forcing the visions of his mutilated remains from her drifting mind.

The Jeep turned onto Bear's Den Highway and rolled by the familiar little pond at the edge of the swamp. Although two weeks had already passed, the place still made her nervous. It had been a harrowing experience that she would not soon forget. As she had done every working day thereafter, Birdie searched both sides of the graveled road with attentive eyes for anything out of the ordinary. She only wished that she could have seen the faces of the attackers that banged up her vehicle. And to make matters worse, her employer failed to offer any form of compensation for the needed repairs. She would be forced to file a claim with her own insurance carrier and pay the two hundred dollar deductible out of her own pocket. At some point she would get the Jeep over to the Appleton Body Shop to have the dents pounded out. Lord knew her husband wasn't going to lift a finger to help.

"Damned idiots," she said aloud, directing her thoughts once again to those ruthless poachers. She saw the spot where the buck had disappeared that day. One of the large branches still lay on the side of the road. She stared at the thick tree limb as the Jeep crept by. Birdie tried to mentally picture someone plucking it off the ground and tossing it through the air. "Impossible," she barked. It was just too darn big. "No way did a man pick that thing up and ..."

Suddenly, without warning, a tremendous force caused Birdie's head to slam into the driver side window. The Jeep rocked high on its left two wheels. Her heavily padded hood prevented the broken shards of glass from cutting into her scalp. In her dazed state, she could feel the right side of the Jeep rising higher and higher off the ground. Birdie clutched the steering wheel and pulled her body between the seats. There was no time to cry for help or make sense of what was happening. She watched helplessly through the window as the ground drew closer to her astonished face. It was going to roll. There was nothing to do but await the inevitable.

But the rising sensation slowed until ceasing altogether. Birdie struggled to stop her body from sliding down further towards the driver door, realizing that any added momentum would carry the Jeep right over. She jammed her right foot underneath the parking brake to stabilize her position. After a few nervous seconds of creaking and moaning, as if the Jeep were unsure as to which way it should fall, it finally rocked back in the other direction and crashed down on all four wheels once again. The bouncy landing jolted the occupant and sent her sprawling across the passenger seat. The round knob on the gearshift plunged into her backside causing a surge of pain. She groaned.

Birdie laid awkwardly across the two bucketed seats staring up at the ceiling when the Jeep came to rest in the middle of the road. She was overtaken by a strong feeling of déjà vu. She tilted her muddled head back and noticed that the door handle had been punched inward only inches from her face. Her initial reaction was that she had been hit by another vehicle, and that meant somebody else might be hurt.

"Oh dear," she shrieked, praying that her intuition was wrong. Birdie grabbed the steering wheel and pulled herself up to a sitting position back onto the driver seat. The deep contusion in her back pulsated. After taking a few seconds to gather her wits, she looked around for the other vehicle. She cursed herself for allowing her mind to wander while driving. But there were no signs of another truck or car in any direction. Flurries began to whip through the air as the winds intensified. The left side of her face grew numb. That's when she realized that the window was missing entirely. Her head had completed shattered it. *Funny,* she thought. *It didn't hurt a lick.* She examined the top of her head with a quick peek in the rearview mirror. There was no visible damage. Other than a few tears in the fabric, Birdie determined that her scalp was unscathed. The broken heater had been a blessing after all.

She then looked back toward the caved in passenger door. "My Lordy!" She had no idea what could have hit her. She didn't see or hear a thing. Aside from the gusting wind, all was quiet on Bear's Den Highway. The Jeep sat motionless. Birdie figured that she had better move it before someone else came along and walloped her. Having assured herself that there was no other vehicle in the general proximity, she reached for the key. Birdie began to think that she had been the victim of a hit and run and her temper began to flare.

"Insensitive thugs," she scowled. "Leaving me by my lonesome, not knowing if I was hurt. Heck, I could have been lying here bleeding to death." She turned the key in the ignition and prepared to head straight into town and report the incident to the Sheriff. Ross would know what to do, she decided.

The motor sputtered as always, and much to Birdie's surprise it came to life. But when the Jeep began to advance down the road, she heard the annoying sound of metal scraping against one of the tires. Birdie grimaced as she forced the Jeep a little further. The grinding became much more pronounced. She could feel the vibrations through the steering column.

"Gosh darnit," she blasted. Now she was furious. Birdie stopped the vehicle and put an end to the irritating clamor. Careful to avoid the shattered glass particles, she eased open the door and stepped out onto the road while fighting the agonizing pains that continued to shoot up her backside. She reached around her waist and gently massaged the tender area. The mail courier then limped around the front and examined the outer structure for damage. The left two wheels appeared to be intact. There were no problems with the axles that she could see. Birdie crossed her arms and brushed the cold off her shoulders. When she rounded the front to the opposite side she could see right away that the Jeep would not be going anywhere soon under its own power. The right front tire was bent inward at an odd angle, and the front quarter panel was pinned against the rubber. The tire would blow if she tried to drive it. The beleaguered lady bent down and gave the fender a good yank in an attempt to pry it away, but it wouldn't budge.

"Umph!" she grunted after another pull, this time with a little more emphasis. The pain in her back flared again. "Oh, darn you!" She stood upright and kicked the non-cooperative piece of metal. As her boot bounced backwards she noticed the passenger door. "Crimminy!" she gasped bringing a hand to her mouth. There was a massive indentation in the door that would need more than a simple pound-out job at the body shop. Birdie walked over and ran her fingers over the misshapen steel.

Strange, she thought. *The paint isn't peeled a lick.* If another vehicle had hit her, surely there would have been paint damage. Her eyes gazed into the swamp at the far side of the road. A verse from the old incantation burst into her thoughts without invitation.

When brave men wallow,
They will follow,
As darkness nears,
The demons appear.

If you will the courage,
To face the demons within,
Then pray with pure heart,
The journey ends with Amen.

Birdie was suddenly frightened. She detected something in the breeze ... something awful. The foul stench invaded her nose like rotting catfish.

***

The female favored her throbbing shoulder as she ducked out of sight. She had second-guessed her decision to attack, but the opportunity was there ... tormenting her. It felt good to release her penned-up rage on the machine. She had silenced it for good. It would never kill again. She watched as the hairless one left its protection. It was vulnerable in the open. The female had been on the verge of retreating back into the sheltering confines of the swamp when the unmistakable noise alerted her perked ears. Remnants from the previous night's feeding still clung to her powerful hands that were parting two small pines to clear a visible line of sight. It had been a good night of hunting. Two more of the murderous creatures had been easily destroyed. Her vengeance had been further satisfied.

The female had made the effort to return and seek the forgiveness of the clan, but when the leader confronted her with his show of superiority, she was forced to retaliate. That inner fury played to her advantage when she made her charge on the unsuspecting aggressor. The other members of the clan could only watch in disbelief as she took the life of their leader in a stunning display of savagery. And afterwards, when the leader breathed no more, they had crowded around him and repeatedly hoisted the lifeless arms, much like she had done with her dead juvenile not so long ago. They took turns licking the wounds on the neck, whimpering like the weak, hairless creatures that she had desperately tried to expose. The female tried to approach the others in an attempt to amend her irreversible action, but they would not receive her. She knew then that her life as a member of the clan had forever ended. Even the females discarded her unavailing pleas for mercy. She broke the most sacred code that had governed the unblemished society for generations. They would now condemn her with lethal resolve. It was not generally in their nature. Only the leader could condone such action against a lawbreaker. But there was no leader now, and it would be some time before a dominant male accepted the role.

The conduct of the clan let her know that it was time to move on. She could no longer exist in or near the lair. If she did return and a dominant male had been established, she would not cheat death a second time. She was a threat to their existence and they would not hesitate to destroy. With a cry of despair, the female had sprinted out of the lair and into the depths of the great swamp. She did not look back. She would not return again. She knew how to survive. She would hunt ... and kill ... and satisfy the hunger for the creatures that caused her quandary.

The female ducked behind a dense patch of foliage and watched as the machine made its way toward her position. She had been situated high on a bank above the road with no avenue for escape. The female kept still, and watched. She had learned much from these hairless creatures in her solitary journeys outside the perimeter of the swamp. She learned that they were very weak in small numbers. More importantly, she learned that their hunting skills were far inferior to her own. They required the smaller four-legged animals to hunt for them. But above all else, she learned that their flesh was gratifying. If only the clan would have listened.

The advancing machine appeared to slow. The female could see the hairless one cowering inside. She watched its frail eyes. They were searching for something. Perhaps she had waited too late in the daylight hours to retreat back into the swamp. She began to wonder what the clan would think if they knew of her recent activities. They would not approve. But they had exiled her to live out her years in painful seclusion. And for that, she despised them all. The anger exposed itself again as she allowed her emotions to control her body. Her thoughts drifted back to the juvenile, how she had given birth to the young male, and how she had traveled away from the lair to teach. She thought of the untimely death ... the slaughter ... the hairless creature that had deprived the female of her motherhood. The anger evolved into rage as she eyed the crawling machine on the road below. They were the ones to blame. They would all be punished for her misfortune.

The female's powerful legs sprang into motion before she had time to fully design a plan of attack. Hatred was her burning fuel. She was now acting strictly on a passion to kill. Her magnificent body broke through the brush and vaulted onto the road below. When she hit the flat surface, she crouched and lunged at the unsuspecting machine. She felt the strong shell give as she engaged. The female immediately felt the pain knife through her lead shoulder. She backed away from the attack and retreated to the pines. The machine fell back to the earth, but it was now quiet. After a few anxious moments, the hairless creature emerged into the open. A squirrel began to bark high overhead.

***

Birdie turned to face the impetuous chatter emitted from the small creature in the tree. Of all the animals on God's green earth, there was only one that made her skin crawl ... squirrels! She hated all of them and that's all there was to it. It was their ability to disrupt a peaceful afternoon with their senseless prattle. She peered skyward to the branch that held the nasty little rodent. The terrible smell continued to linger heavy in the air. She figured that it had to be roadkill, perhaps the remains of the deer she had seen weeks before. Birdie brought her hand to her mouth to fend off the stench. She then looked back to the swamp.

"Oh stop scaring yourself, Bird," she told herself. "I'll just walk on down the road a bit and ..."

The attack came without warning. Birdie felt her rib cage being crushed as a thousand pounds of animal flesh came pummeling down on top of her. Her tongue was forced from her mouth while she gasped for air. She was pinned against the surface of the road. She could feel the warm breath against the skin of her bared neck. Birdie could not move. She lay paralyzed beneath the creature. With tears in her eyes, she was able to slowly turn her head sideways, scraping her cheek on the gravel, still unable to breathe. She was beginning to feel faint. Through blurred eyes, she saw the face with its exposed, yellow fangs as it bore down on her skull.

***

Ross and Maggie held hands as they followed the relieved teenager through the doors of the medical building. Chuck Barnes was all smiles after receiving nothing but good news that afternoon. Even though there was a tear in his right bicep muscle, the Orthopedic Surgeon claimed there was not enough damage to warrant a surgical procedure. The Doctor originally speculated that there may have been some minor displacement between the bicep and the rotator cuff, but the MRI produced negative results on all accounts. There would be a lengthy healing and rehabilitation period, but Chuck should be back in uniform by the next fall for his senior season. That was all that the boy needed to hear.

It was the best news that had been laid on Ross' ears in a month. He could see that Chuck was still somewhat despondent about standing on the sidelines for the remainder of the season, especially after such a quick start. But he also knew that the boy would one day realize how fortunate he'd been to escape a more serious conclusion to his football career.

"How about some ice cream?" yelled Chuck with a skip in his step. "Come on, Ross. You're buying."

Ross smiled at the boy. He gripped Maggie's warm hand even tighter. He truly felt that they were a family. He loved them both very much. Maggie leaned over and snuggled her cheek against his shoulder. "You're on, Chuck," responded Ross. "I'm buying."

After a quick visit to the town's Dairy Queen that was about a week away from shutting its doors for the season, the trio piled into the Tahoe and headed back to Jessup. The trip home was much more relaxing than the ride up when all three had sat silently with nervous anticipation. A lot had been riding on that MRI. But now there was jubilation, at least for Maggie and Chuck. Regardless of how hard Ross tried to grasp the moment, he found his happiness consumed by his own consternation. He was about to embark on an investigation into a phenomenon that might hold a reality better left unveiled.

As the Tahoe passed a slow-moving semi, Ross' mind drifted back to his meeting with LaFontaine earlier in the day. He recalled how David had placed the casting of that footprint in his hands. The man certainly had little doubt about the authenticity of the find. But it was all so crazy. If a band of those ... creatures did exist, he wondered how they might have gone undetected in the Upper Peninsula. *And why Jessup?* he wondered. There were certainly other towns scattered along the border of the Amen Swamp.

Amen had become a chilling curse. He remembered the squirrels at Ned Crosby's crash site that day. He recalled his paranoia that they were being watched. He wondered what might have happened had he and Chuck stayed a few minutes longer. Would they have come face to face with the being that David was describing? His mind was suddenly bombarded with verses from the surreal dirge that had become as much a part of Jessup lore as Zachariah Jessup himself.

Evil spirits, evil spells,
Haunt the damned in Amen hell,
Unaware is he who goes,
And harvests hell's own bleeding rose.

The demon's eye,
Will follow his move,
An eye for an eye,
Is the Devil's ruse.

If you will the courage,
To face the demons within,
Then pray with pure heart,
The journey ends with Amen.

The blaring horn from the approaching car awoke Ross from his trance. He steered hard to the right and back into the proper lane. The angered man in the passing car displayed his middle finger along with a few choice words for the daydreaming driver of the police vehicle.

"Ross!" protested Maggie as she grasped the dash. "What the heck is the matter with you?"

The Sheriff shook his head, infuriated at himself. He damn near killed them all. "Nothing, Maggs. Sorry." He looked at her and smiled apologetically. "Just got a little sidetracked is all."

"Geez, Ross!" chimed in Chuck from the back seat. "And I was worried about this shoulder ending my career."

Ross acknowledged the joke with a fake snicker. The distractions in his life were growing. He would not be at peace until there was closure to this mess. He would not be whole again until the Amen's mysteries were unraveled.

***

"Damn, Tyrone! You look like shit! Gerald Johnson cackled at his slumping chum who was massaging his throbbing forehead with very shaky hands.

"Get away from me Gerald!" Tyrone shook his disoriented head in an attempt to dispel the hallucination, but his former partner would not concede to the desperate pleas.

Gerald laughed, clasping his jiggling belly with pale hands. Tyrone buried his face under a pillow.

"Oh come on, Tye. It's me, homes. In the flesh. Take a look."

Tyrone cautiously slid the pillow down below his glazed eyes. He stared in disbelief as Gerald Johnson stood before him as if the past two weeks had been a figment of his imagination. *Maybe it was a dream,* he thought. But the image hovering over him was too real, as was the burning pain from the infection in his ear.

"What's the matter, Tye? Ain't you ever seen a dead brother before?" Gerald burst into a loud spasm of laughter. His skin was pale, as if the blood had drained from every vein and artery. There were bare spots on his scalp where chunks of hair had fallen out. His clothes were ragged from exposure to the elements. Tyrone watched in horror as green fluids spurted from the small bullet hole in his forehead. The corpse giggled as slime covered his gaunt face. Gerald's tongue slithered out the side of his mouth like a serpent and started lapping up the wretched fluid.

"Damn, this is fine eatin, Tye," said Gerald as he cock-danced around the small room. His chest was covered with puss that seeped from the three holes around his inert heart. The cabin reeked of decaying flesh.

Tyrone gagged. He doubled over and vomited on the couch. The gamey taste of the venison sent him into a seemingly irreversible fit of dry heaves. He slowly raised his spinning head once the contents of his stomach were completely discarded. "You're dead, goddammit!" He felt faint. Tyrone looked up to face his partner. He was now peering down on him with cold, black eyes.

"You're next, Tye," said Gerald with the wicked look of the damned. His rotting lips curled back and revealed a bevy of sharp, jagged daggers for teeth. "You killed me, motherfucker. You did this to me, Tye."

Tyrone Pullman screamed as the ghost leaned closer to his trembling face. He could smell the stink on his breath. Then Gerald whispered, "You gonna die, motherfucker." His arm reached for Tyrone's wrist.

"Nooooooo!" Tyrone sobbed. He plunged his face back into the protection of the pillow. A cloud of dust exploded around his head. "Get away from me!" *This is not happening,* he cried inwardly. *Gerald is dead! I killed him! I'm losing my fucking mind!*

Tyrone wanted to run ... to escape. He wanted to be home in Flint. He wanted to talk to people, to hold someone. He wanted his mother. He needed a fucking salad instead of the fucking animals whose carcasses littered the front porch. He yearned for the smokestacks of the auto factories. *If they found me, then so what? Fuck it!* If he were to continue living like this, he would ultimately surrender the final thread of sanity remaining in his frail head. He found himself praying for the safety of the walls in Jackson Prison. He wouldn't have to face the corpse of Gerald Johnson.

As the internal tirade unfolded in Tyrone Pullman's baffled thoughts, the image of his former partner began to fade. But before it completely vanished, Tyrone heard him utter a warning.

"I'll be back, Tye. I'll be back, and I'm taking you with me." The laughter trailed off into total silence.

Tyrone pushed himself up off the sofa. He needed air. He had to think. He had to get out of that place. As he turned to run, his left foot slipped in the pool of vomit. Tyrone felt himself falling. There was nothing within reach that he could grab to regain his balance. His foot slid underneath the couch and caused his knee to turn in an awkward position. He was knocked unconscious when his head hit the floor.

***

The temperatures dropped even further as the afternoon stretched on, but Gene Steubens didn't care. He could have been wearing cotton briefs and it wouldn't have bothered him in the least. The Mayor strolled down Main Street like a man who had just matched all six numbers in the Big Game Lottery. Ross Pickett would no longer block his path to prosperity. It was time to swear in the new Sheriff, that moppet Mark Bennington.

Gene expected a short period of opposition before the town finally settled down after the council's decision. After all, Ross Pickett was popular within the community. But the compounding evidence of the man's instability could not be overlooked. Traffic was now moving in an orderly fashion for the egotistical Mayor.

Steubens saw Ted Newhouser's Jeep approaching down the main vein of Jessup. He waved to the driver and summoned him to pull alongside the curb. Newhouser returned the gesture and did as instructed. He parked the vehicle and rolled down the window.

"Teddy, my boy, how is life in the pits?" The Mayor shook the man's hand.

"Not so good, Gene." Newhouser looked dismayed by something.

"What's up, Ted? Something wrong?" Steubens expressed his genuine concern. If Newhouser was upset, then that meant there could be something wrong with the project.

"I'm missing my two best heavy equipment operators. Christ, it's really slowing us down today. I came into town to see if they might be around somewhere." He casually scanned both sides of the street.

"What do you mean by *missing*, Ted? Have you checked their hotel?" Steubens was well aware that many of the young construction workers were staying in Appleton.

"Yeah, I've checked all over hell and back. It's just not like these two to go off and disappear like this. They didn't show up yesterday either." He sighed heavily from the stress of being the boss.

"Is there anything I can do?"

"Naw, I just wanted to check out the town. It's the damnedest thing, too."

"What's that, Ted?" Steubens raised a brow.

"Both of their vehicles are still out at the site. Nobody's seen hide nor hair of them since Friday night." Newhouser was scratching the side of his cheek, displaying his puzzlement.

The Mayor watched as the contractor worked out a kink in his neck. The man looked tired ... and worried. "Well, Ted, they probably hooked up with a couple of females and shacked up somewhere for the weekend. They'll show up soon enough. You'll see." He gave an encouraging smile.

The contractor's face lightened just a touch. "You're probably right. They're going to have hell to pay when they do return. I can assure you of that." Newhouser was a fair boss as long as his employees were able to get the job done and were up front when problems arose. But not showing up for work miffed him to no end. He didn't know whether to feel concerned because of their absence, or pissed that they had failed to report their whereabouts to anyone. He shook his head again. "Well, I've got to get back. I'll see you later."

"Alright, Teddy. You go and build yourself a golf course." Steubens patted the man on the forearm and watched him perform a U-turn in the street. Newhouser then drove out of Jessup back in the direction of Hideaway Pines.

***

It was six-thirty when Ross entered the village limits. The darkening skies threatened a snowfall that was not due to arrive for another few days. There were a few people walking the dimly-lit streets, but most were secure in the comfort of their warm homes and businesses on that cold evening. The Sheriff had gone home as intended following the lengthy visit to Houghton. There was a message on the answering machine from Pete Wilkerson requesting a meeting at the office around seven. Ross tried phoning the councilman, but his wife told him that Pete had already left for town. Ross thought it was strange for Pete to want to meet with him so late.

As he deliberated over the message, Ross remembered how Frank Peterson had previously been commissioned with the deed of telling him to get off the Mayor's back after their confrontation over the bear fiasco. He then began to wonder if the purpose of this meeting was somehow linked to his actions at the football game. *But why send Pete?* he thought. *Wilkerson wouldn't play foot soldier for that asshole, Steubens, would he?* Ross began to feel the acid build up in his stomach.

When he stopped in front of Town Hall, he noticed Wilkerson's Grand Marquis parked in front of the squad car. The Deputy wasn't scheduled to work. In fact, Mark Bennington had been adamant about getting Monday off to take care of some personal business, so Ross obliged the request. So why was Mark at this meeting as well?

The Sheriff walked into the office and saw both men sitting and chatting with one another. The talking stopped abruptly when he made his presence known. Mark had been sitting at the Sheriff's desk, but when he saw Ross enter, he quickly hopped up off the seat and skirted around the front to make room for his mentor.

"Hey, Ross." Mark greeted the cautious Sheriff, but would not look him directly in the eyes.

Ross studied his body language carefully ... the fidgeting hands ... the shuffling feet. He was definitely bothered. The Sheriff concluded that something was indeed wrong. And Mark wasn't wearing the uniform assigned to him by the town. That was an oddity in itself and spelled *trouble.*

"Ross." Pete Wilkerson stood from his chair and extended his hand.

"How-do, Pete? I see you two have been discussing some important matters," said the Sheriff with a sarcastic tone. Wilkerson looked at him as if he truly did not understand the point. Mark, in the meantime, continued to stare off into a corner with his head held low. "What's going on, Pete? What can I do for you tonight?" Ross slowly walked around the desk and eased himself into the office chair. He cupped his hands around the back of his head, prepared to hear what compelling news the man was there to reveal. Wilkerson chose to remain standing.

"Okay, Ross. Jigs up, huh?" A weak smile crossed the councilman's lips. "Originally, I didn't want to be the man to bring this to you," he continued, "but I felt you would rather hear it from me than any of the others. Anyway, I think you know who I'm referring to."

Ross acknowledged the statement with a nod. He now had a pretty good idea where this conversation was headed. It was obviously a council move of some kind ... a political ploy by Steubens.

"Ross, I'm going to be blunt with you. There was a motion at our meeting today. The motion was that you should be removed from your position by power of the council for one bullshit reason or another, and that Mark here fill in as Sheriff until the next election."

On the inside, Ross' chest felt as though it were caving. A large lump swelled in his throat. It had been the football game after all. *That fucking little asshole!* Ross' inability to maintain his self-control had sealed his fate. He was stunned. There was so much at stake. He maintained his composure on the outside and kept his eyes transfixed on Pete Wilkerson. Ross held a stupid grin on his face to cover his swirling sentiments. "Is it necessary for me to ask who made the motion, Pete?" The question did not require a response.

"No, Ross, I don't think that would be necessary. You know damn well who made the motion."

He was still puzzled as to why it was Pete Wilkerson telling him instead of Frank Peterson. He never figured this man to be one of Steubens' stiffs. Judging by the man's demeanor, Ross figured that Pete had other feelings on the matter. All Ross had ever tried to do was his goddamned job. And now they were crucifying him for being baited into a confrontation that had obviously been embellished by Steubens. "Why are you here, Pete," he finally asked. He wanted to be sure of the man's stance.

"I'm here because I wanted you to know that the vote was three to one." Wilkerson acted disgusted with what he had just said. He broke eye contact with the ex-Sheriff, bowing his head toward the ground. "I'm sorry, Ross. I really am. I wanted no part of this bullshit move by Steubens and I wanted you to know that."

Mark Bennington continued to dawdle away from the difficult conversation. He felt guilty for the part of him that was happy with his sudden promotion. But Ross was going to get out of the game before long anyways. He tried to find a positive spin on the latest development. A more suitable transition would have been preferred. Mark looked up in astonishment when he heard his friend burst out laughing. Ross did not show the bitterness that bubbled inside him.

"Well I'll be goddamned. That's it then, Pete." Ross raised his hands and stood up from his chair. "Mark, let me be the first to congratulate you on your new position. May you have much more success with the badge than I did." He tried not to display too much sarcasm. The Deputy was innocent in all this, or so he hoped. But Ross was enraged beyond comprehension. Those idiots had no right to oust him from the seat to which the people of Jessup had elected him. His thoughts then wandered to David LaFontaine. How could Ross reveal what he knew to Mark? It would just bolster Steubens' case that he was a raving lunatic. Ross couldn't do that to Maggie and Chuck. He was now on his own island with no authority whatsoever to make decisions on behalf of the town. What if something were to happen down the road ... if somebody else was killed? How could he deal with the guilt of staying silent when he had a moral obligation to expose the facts? But there were no facts, other than a footprint that David LaFontaine claimed to have been discovered in a place over a thousand miles away.

Ross Pickett began to feel the thirst that would allow him to escape the reality that just would not relinquish its grip. The old ghosts were very lucid in his troubled head. He could feel the soothing effects of the whiskey running through his veins. He could take a drive down to McKrueter's and pick up a pint ... and ... *Shut up!* He condemned his lack of internal fortitude. Ross cursed himself again for allowing his soul to weaken. But as the old ghosts continued to plague him, he found it more and more difficult to climb back up the ladder.

Mark and Pete were quiet as Ross thought the matter through. There was nothing he could say that could lighten the mood in the room. The councilman watched him closely when he began chuckling after learning that he had been fired. Wilkerson began to wonder if maybe there *was* a problem that the man had to deal with.

Ross strolled over to the new Sheriff after settling down. "Mark, I'm sorry. Really ... congratulations. I'm happy for you."

A look of relief came over Mark's face. "Thanks, Ross." He was still very uneasy with the situation. He could not look the man in the eye, embarrassed by the fact that he was taking his job. Mark had never dreamed that anything like this would ever happen in Jessup. It just wasn't right. The awkward moment was interrupted by the ringing phone. All three men stared at it like an alien article with no known significance.

Sensing the incertitude in his young friend, Ross provided some encouragement. Mark would need all of the help that he could give. "Go ahead, Mark. It's your ship now." It was a difficult statement to make, but Ross held strong and expressed confidence in the boy. He actually felt sorry for him.

Mark picked up the phone while the others listened in. "Sheriff's ..." Mark hesitated and directed his eyes to Ross who in turn nodded for him to continue. "Sheriff's office. Hey, Phil ... yeah ... yeah ... okay ... maybe she stopped off at someone's ... okay ... are you sure ... okay. I'll get on it and let you know." He hung up the phone, noticeably disturbed by the call.

"What is it, Mark?"

"That was Phil McIntosh. He said that Birdie hasn't been home. He sounded worried." Mark rubbed his chin, contemplating his next move.

"Oh, she's probably tied up with Mabel Sanders or someone else on her route. You know Birdie, always an ear for good gossip." Ross tried to put him at ease.

Mark glanced to Ross. "Yeah I know, but Phil said they were supposed to go down to Appleton for dinner tonight. They were meeting some friends there. I better go and check this out. Wanna come?" He looked over to Pete Wilkerson who had been silently observing.

The councilman just shrugged his shoulders. "I really don't think there's anything in the town charter that says the ex-Sheriff can't ride with the acting Sheriff." He offered a sly smile while picturing Steubens' face if he saw the two riding together.

Ross considered the offer for a brief minute, but then declined. If Mark Bennington was going to be successful, then it was time for him to grow up. He tried to be as pleasant as humanly possible under the circumstances, even though he realized the new Sheriff lacked the proper tools and training for the position. He was just a kid. But if they wanted Mark Bennington for a Sheriff, then they could have him. *Fuck all of them!* Steubens now had his puppet and could pull the strings whenever he got out of line. His repugnance for the Mayor grew with each fleeting picture of the man's chubby face. *Fuck you, Steubens! Ross Pickett is done!*

He took the badge from its leather sheath and placed it into the reluctant hands of the new Sheriff. Ross then said his good-byes and left the office, unsure of where he should go. The *old ghost* was stirring.

***

"That's awesome news," said Jenna Pierson into the phone after learning of her boyfriend's fate.

"The Doctor said that I'll be as good as new by next fall. I've got a whole year to get ready." Chuck was sprawled out on his bed. He glanced over to the Joe Montana poster on the wall. *Some day,* he thought.

"So are we good for Friday?" she asked.

"Yup. I asked my mom just a few minutes ago. Good timing, too. She'd give me just about anything I wanted right now. Feels guilty I guess." He laughed.

"Great! I'm good, too. Doris has the story all worked out."

As Chuck thought about the upcoming weekend excursion, his mind began to drift in another direction. It was something that he hadn't yet considered. He sighed.

"What's wrong, babe?" Jenna sensed the change in his tone.

"Well," continued the side-lined athlete, "with all that's been going on, I completely forgot about hunting this weekend." He sounded depressed.

"Oh, baby, I'm sorry. There's no way you can shoot, is there?"

"No, I'm down for the year. Shit!"

Jenna could only think of one thing that might cheer her man up. "Well, I guess you'll just have to spend more time with me then. You know, my uncle's cabin does have three bedrooms."

The teenage boy perked up when he realized what Jenna might be proposing.

***

David LaFontaine sat on the soft, squeaky mattress. He could hear the ruckus in the tavern below through the thin walls. He listened to the clanging glasses and the boisterous voices of men and women having a good time. David shut his tired eyes and placed the pillow over his head in a futile attempt to drown out the clamor.

It had been a long day of investigative work for the Bigfoot hunter. Following his meeting with the Sheriff, LaFontaine had traveled to the large swamp. He walked a few miles on the bordering roads in search of possible crossing patterns. If his creature was alive somewhere in the Amen, then David figured he could pick up a print or two at a point where it may have ascended into the highlands. His diligence went unrewarded that day, but David LaFontaine was accustomed to a slow grind. He understood that time was on his side. As long as the funding continued to flow, he would eventually have his prize.

David often contemplated what he would actually do if he were to prove the existence. Fame and fortune might follow if he were to expose a new species to the world. But achieving stardom could have its price. By presenting a find of such incredible importance, he could also jeopardize its very existence. Could man coexist with the legendary creatures of North America? His personal belief was that they probably *have* coexisted for centuries. How would humanity deal with concrete proof? He wondered how the species might react to discovery. If his intuition were correct, his creature was a highly intelligent, societal life-form whose evolution took a different turn than that of its human cousin. A threatened man could be very dangerous, but a threatened species could lead to all-out annihilation of the competitive entity.

Those questions would have to be put on the back burner for now. There was no need for answers until he succeeded in his quest. David finally managed to drift off to sleep.

***

Mark Bennington returned to the squad car following his visit with Mabel Sanders. The elderly widow explained how Birdie had stopped a few hours earlier for a piece of banana bread and then went on about her business. A few crumbs still stuck to the side of the newly appointed Sheriff's mouth from the slice that had been forced upon him. He could not resist the kind woman's gentle charm.

Since Mabel's home would have been the mail courier's final stop, Mark decided to head back into town after questioning nearly twenty people who might have seen her making the daily rounds. All of them had received their mail, but none knew of her whereabouts. *Wow!* thought Mark. It was a real missing person. This was serious police business. He was conducting his first investigation on his first day as Sheriff. Mark felt important, and looked forward to garnering more respect from the community. The Sheriff stuck out his chest a bit further as he turned onto Bear's Den Highway.

The flurries were intensifying that autumn evening. Mark was bundled in his parka. He made sure that his new badge was securely affixed to the outer breast pocket and very visible before he left. He was anxious to inform Sharon Cooper of his newly acquired status. He looked forward to the generous reward that she would eagerly supply. *Maybe tomorrow,* he thought. He could give himself the night off and take Sharon out two-tracking. Mark had hoped that his mistress would be working tonight, but it was Ruth Childs' shift. *Tomorrow,* he decided. They hadn't been together for an entire week and his wild oats required some sowing.

About two miles from Mabel's, Mark noticed a reflection in the road ahead. He slowed, fearing that it was an animal crossing down into the swamp. As the car rolled closer, the shape of the Jeep materialized. He had lived in Jessup long enough to recognize that it belonged to Birdie McIntosh. Mark surveyed the inanimate vehicle for any form of hidden life. It appeared as lifeless as the all-encompassing night around it.

The Sheriff flicked on the side-mounted spotlight to get a better look. "Gosh!" he gasped after noticing the large dent in the passenger side door. It was pushed in a good ten inches. Mark had enough experience to see that this was an accident scene. But where was Birdie?

"Hmmm, let's just get a looksee at this mess." Mark stepped out into the cold night with his flashlight in hand and walked up to the silent Jeep. It looked like someone had given it a good belt. He examined the damaged area around the door. From where he was standing he could see no evidence of broken glass or chipped paint ... or anything else that would indicate the inclusion of a second vehicle. The Sheriff flipped the hood over his head to shield him from the chilly air. He sauntered around the front end, guided by the beam of his flashlight. As he reached the opposite side, he saw the sparkling glass in the road. He followed his light to the driver's window. It had been shattered outward. *What does this mean?* he asked himself. He leaned closer to the window and illuminated the interior, checking for blood or possible signs of a struggle. It was empty. Then he saw Birdy's purse lying on the floor. "That's odd," he said aloud, knowing that she wouldn't just up and leave without her personal belongings.

Mark began to run the scenarios through his head just like Ross had taught him. *Birdie's driving up the road ... someone buffaloes her good ... the Jeep is immobilized ... the second driver gives her a lift ... or Birdie has to hike it back to town.* It sounded simple enough, but there was still the matter of her purse. He opened the door to check one more thing. When he leaned around the other side of the steering wheel he saw the keys still in the ignition. *Why would she leave her keys and her purse?*

Mark turned suddenly. There was movement in the trees behind him. His right hand instinctively unsnapped the restraint over his sidearm. He directed the flashlight's beam along the tree line of the swamp. He heard the sound again, this time farther to his left. He scanned the pine boughs carefully, searching for the source. The wind made listening difficult. Mark found himself wishing that Ross was by his side. He felt alone out there. The Amen Swamp! He knew of the legends. Men went in and never returned. Mark never really believed in the fables told by the old-timers, but he had never been so close ... by himself ... at night. He began to feel that creepy sensation that he had experienced as a child when older brothers ruthlessly threatened to leave him in the Amen for the monsters. He recalled the nightmares ... the screaming. He remembered the verses.

Venture forward,
The curse is true,
If you dare continue,
Death haunts you.

If you will the courage,
To face the demons within,
Then pray with pure heart,
The journey ends with Amen.

The sound of footsteps made him jump out of his self-induced trance. It was just beyond the tree line, coming toward him. Mark drew his revolver and aimed. His other hand gripped the shaking flashlight. He cocked the hammer and prepared to shoot. It was coming through ...

Bang! The shot echoed as the animal darted into the open. The deer spun around and then fell to the ground. Mark watched in horror as it struggled to regain its feet.

"Shit!" he yelled, knowing that he had made an unforgivable mistake. He discharged his weapon without identifying the target. Luckily it had just been a deer and not Birdie McIntosh. But what if it had been Birdie ... and she had seen him ... and was coming out to ... *Damn! Stupid! How could I be so damn stupid!* He continued to condemn himself as the deer finally picked itself up off the ground. Mark could see the blood draining from the wound. He prayed that the animal would live. The deer limped away and disappeared back into the cover of the swamp.

Mark Bennington trudged back to the squad car. He sat down on the cold vinyl seat, disgusted by his behavior. He now was glad that he had been by himself. If someone had witnessed his actions, he wouldn't be wearing the badge for long. He stared at the Jeep on the road, feeling like a failure. He knew then that he needed Ross regardless of what the council had done to him. Mark retrieved the mike and called in the report to Ruth Childs.

***

Ross stood nervously in front of the counter, staring at the assortment displayed on the far wall. His body trembled. His face was pale. His eyes danced off each mesmerizing label, searching for the one medicine that would put him at ease. His tongue thirsted. He had succumbed to his weakness. With all of the positives existing in his life, only the negative now commanded his actions. He had given up. Ross Pickett had failed.

"What can I do for you, Ross?" Fred McKrueter walked out of the meat cooler and instantly recognized the familiar face. He wore a white apron, stained with blood from the cuts he had been preparing. He smiled warmly at the customer.

Ross turned and looked at the man as if he had never seen him before. He was in a different world ... an abyss where only the damned could exist. The town had turned on him and he had nothing left to give.

McKrueter noticed the odd look about his friend. He saw him examining the bottles of alcohol that were uniformly stacked behind the counter. "Is something wrong, Ross?" The storeowner asked the question with concern in his voice.

"I need a bottle." Ross hesitated and peered back at the alluring beverages. He didn't care which one. Any of them would fulfill the purpose he was searching for. "Give me a bottle of Jack ... a pint." There was nothing congenial about his mannerisms. He just wanted to purchase his salvation and run.

McKrueter approached the customer. He was well aware of Ross' rocky history with alcohol. He'd seen the man at his worst when he used to come in for a night of binging. There was a time when Ross had been his best, and worst, customer. It was Jim Beam back in those days, and typically a fifth at a time. He could clearly see that there was something eating away at his friend. He didn't feel right about allowing the Sheriff to make the purchase. "Ross?" Fred spoke gently as he tried to get a feel for the man's problem. "If there's something wrong, you can ..."

Ross quickly cut him off. "I just want a goddamn bottle, Fred! Now please ... give me a pint of Jack and let me be." *Just a pint,* he thought.

McKrueter reluctantly did as ordered and retrieved the bottle from the wall. He rang up the sale on the register. Ross handed him a ten dollar bill and told him to keep the change. Fred watched as he exited the store in a rush. No "thank you" or "good bye." He was gone, leaving Fred holding the bill in his hand. The store owner then picked up the phone and dialed the number for the Jessup Inn. Regardless of what Ross might think, Fred determined that he was in need of some help.

***

The female's body went rigid as the report of the gunshot sounded through the trees. It was close. Her hand released the appendage that she had been feeding on. She raised her head high and took in deep breaths through her nostrils. She could only detect the remains of the hairless creature strewn about the swamp floor around her. The female understood the danger represented by the gunshot. She had witnessed how effective their weapons could be. She remembered how they destroyed the large bear. But it had taken three of them to finish off the animal that was not even half her size.

The female resisted the urge to further investigate the disturbance. Although her gut was full from the recent meal, her compulsion to kill remained the driving force of her existence. But there would be another time. She was still learning from the hairless creatures. She slowly retreated deeper into the swamp, leaving the remains of Birdie McIntosh to be consumed by the scavengers. She would return soon and continue her quest for vengeance.

***

The Tahoe rolled to a stop on the dark, deserted road just a mile outside of Jessup. Ross figured that he probably had no right in keeping the police vehicle owned by the town. *Screw it,* he thought. *Screw all of them.* He had to get home somehow. If they wanted their truck bad enough, they would just have to come and get it.

After shifting into park, he stared down at the pint sitting on the seat beside him. *My new partner,* he mused. Ross snatched up the bottle and pressed it firmly against his sweating forehead. He closed his eyes so tight that he began to feel pain from the pressure. *What are you doing, Ross?* He shook his confused head and gradually opened his eyes, gazing at the hypnotizing brown contents of the glass container. How could something so frivolous have such everlasting effects? He watched the liquid sloshing around like ripples in a lonely trout stream. *It was just liquid ... nothing more.*

His right hand grasped the cap and began to twist. He felt the paper seal break. He watched the cap spin in slow motion, taking forever to separate from the short, stubby neck. Finally, it pulled free and the sweet aroma filtered out. Ross inhaled, feeling the intoxicating fragrance as it seeped into his lungs. He felt his muscles relaxing ... his nerves settling. He anxiously awaited the freedom. The bottle moved toward his thirsting lips. He visualized the liquid entering his bloodstream and numbing his raging head.

The moment of truth was rudely interrupted by the radio. "Ross, this is Ruth. Can you hear me, Ross?" The bottle stopped just before making contact with his mouth. His eyes glanced to the radio. He did not want to answer it. He didn't have to answer it. Mark was the Sheriff now. "Go to hell," he cursed.

"Ross? If you can hear me I need to talk to you. Mark needs help. Birdie McIntosh's Jeep was found banged up on Bear's Den Highway and she's nowhere to be seen. Come on, Ross." The radio went silent.

His eyes moved back and forth between the radio and the bottle that he continued to hold close to his face. He thought about Ruth's words. Bear's Den Highway. The road paralleled the Amen Swamp. Birdie was missing. "Oh, Christ, what have I done?" Ross started thinking about Maggie and Chuck, and what they would think of him. Maggie wouldn't speak to him. She couldn't take the stress of seeing him devoured by the ghosts that she had battled so hard to save him from. He had betrayed her trust ... again.

Ross opened the door and stumbled out of the truck. He could not feel the cold wind whipping against his skin. Enthralled with animosity for his soul that had become so weak under pressure, he raised the bottle and flung it to the ground. The pint exploded upon impact, showering the road with Jack Daniels and glass.

"Goddamn you!" he screamed, cursing the bottle as though it were a living being that had just assaulted him. "Get the fuck out of my life! I don't need you!" Ross continued to cry out. He released the penned up emotion ... his hatred for Gene Steubens ... the old ghosts ... the bottle. He let it all go like a wild animal released from capture. It was a turning point with a choice between life and death, and Ross Pickett chose life. He opted for happiness with Maggie and Chuck.

Ross felt as if he had been reincarnated for the second time in life. Although one battle may have been won on that dreary autumn night, he also realized that a war continued. It was a conflict that would require all of his senses if he were to succeed. He could not afford to allow Gene Steubens to dictate his sanity now.

Ross jumped back into the Tahoe and picked up the microphone.

"Hey, Ruthy. This is Ross. What's up?" He glanced into the rearview mirror at his disheveled face. He needed to clean up his act.

After a brief moment of hesitation, Ruth finally answered. "Hi, Ross. Thank goodness you're there. Mark would like you to stop by the office. He needs your help."

Ross agreed to meet the new Sheriff. He needed to be a part of this investigation. He just hoped that he could be resilient enough to face the enigma that was the Amen Swamp.

***

Trooper Samantha Godson was sitting at her desk when the call came in. She and a few other rookies had been rotating shifts due to the absence of Ray Jackson who was on the mend. The injured Trooper wasn't expected back for another few months. She didn't know all of the details surrounding his accident, just that there had been a bear involved. He seemed like a nice enough fellow around the barrack. The senior Trooper had helped her out on a few occasions at the range.

The call came from the Sheriff of Jessup, but the name didn't coincide with the man she had talked to only a few weeks earlier. It had been Russ Pickard, or something along those lines. The man on the phone identified himself as Mark Bennington, and he was reporting a missing person. He relayed how Mrs. Birdie McIntosh had been the town's mail courier, and how he had discovered her abandoned Jeep on Bear's Den Highway, a few miles outside the village limits. Sam Godson thought it odd how the Sheriff had referred to the woman in the past tense as if he were under the impression that foul play might be involved. The man sounded young and excitable. She told him to calm down and take a deep breath. As first, he appeared offended by the suggestion, perhaps because she was a woman. When he did manage to quiet, she was able to jot down the details on her notepad. When he finished, she told the Sheriff that an officer would be dispatched right away.

***

"What's going on, Mark?" Ross had just entered the office. His Deputy ... the Sheriff, looked troubled sitting at his new desk. There was a State Trooper who introduced himself as Danny Baldwin from the Appleton Post.

"This is a weird one, Ross. I really need you, man."

Mark Bennington had a blank expression on his face. Ross remembered having a similar look back in college when he attempted to pass Calculus. That experience hadn't ended very well either. Mark looked tired. "Okay," said Ross, "anything I can do to help. Now what's this about Birdie?" He sat down where his Deputy used to station himself. It felt odd.

"She's gone, Ross. I don't know where the heck she could be. Nobody's seen her since this afternoon." Mark then explained how he found her Jeep out on Bear's Den Highway. He described the damage to the door and the busted out window. He left out the part about the deer. "What do you think, Ross?" he asked when finished with his summation.

"Don't know. I mean, what's the worst case scenario? Yes, it's possible that we may have foul play, but I doubt it. And I wouldn't recommend bringing that notion to Phil McIntosh's attention just yet." Mark nodded his approval. Ross was composed as he offered suggestions to his protégé, but in the back of his mind he was painting another story, one that directly involved the Amen Swamp. He was terrified by the thought that the victim list may have increased by one that day. It was beginning to happen again. After two peaceful weeks, perhaps it was another emergence. He would have to get in touch with David and let him know about this.

"Mark," Ross continued, "I don't believe it's necessary to become overly anxious here. It's very possible that Birdie may have been picked up and given a ride." *But to where?* he asked himself. He placed his exhausted arms in his lap and initiated a wrestling match between his two thumbs as he pondered the situation. Ross wanted to tell Mark what he knew. He had an obligation to tell the acting Sheriff everything, but his conscience held him at bay. After all, he had no real proof that his doubts, or LaFontaine's claims, were valid. It might just force Mark to send him on his merry way.

"Well, gentlemen," added the Trooper who had been listening intently, "I would like to inspect the vehicle if you don't mind, before it gets hauled in."

He was right. They might gain a better perspective if there were multiple sets of eyes surveying the evidence. "Mind if I tag along, Mark?" He made the request out of respect for the boy. Ross wanted to assure Mark that he had confidence in him.

"Honestly, Ross, I was really hoping you would." Mark looked relieved.

The duo took the Tahoe out to Bear's Den Highway while the Trooper followed. It would be a long night for all.

CHAPTER ELEVEN

Maggie had been waiting impatiently when he arrived home in the early morning hours. Much to Ross' surprise, she embraced him as soon as he walked through the door. There were tears in her eyes. Maggie explained how Fred McKrueter had called her at the Inn and told her about the liquor, and Ross' insolent behavior. She told him how furious she had been. At one point, Maggie said that she had gone so far as to pack a suitcase. But as the night dragged on, Maggie had time to think. She discovered that her love for him was too great to just throw it all away because of one setback. After hearing that he had been terminated from his position during the Mayor's brief visit to the Jessup Inn earlier in the night, Maggie Barnes realized that she was now the only possession that really mattered in his life. She swore to herself that she would never give up, regardless of the challenges that life bestowed upon them.

It was noon when Maggie nudged her man and woke him up from his dreamless sleep. As he caressed her soft face, Ross wondered how he could ever have allowed himself to grow so weak. Had he gone ahead and taken that drink, he could have lost her forever.

When he did get home, Ross explained the sequence of events that had nearly led him to resurrect his old ghost. Ross loved her more than ever and vowed never to cause pain in her life again. He hoped that he could live up to that promise.

Another day had arrived and Ross felt like it was a new beginning for their relationship. He wanted to stay in bed with Maggie, but he knew that this day would not be an easy one. There was still the matter of Birdie McIntosh's mysterious disappearance, and Mark Bennington was in over his head. He had to be there for him, just in case.

"That LaFontaine guy called you this morning, Ross. I didn't want to wake you." Maggie softly brushed the hair off his forehead as she lay down beside him. "How come he's here, Ross?" Maggie knew that he had been holding something back, but she hadn't pressed too hard.

The question felt like a knife being driven through his heart. He wanted to tell her, but he just couldn't bring himself to do it. But neither could he continue to lie. There had to be a happy median.

"Maggie," he started, "I'm going to tell you something important and I do not want you to ask any more questions." He massaged her smooth shoulder. He was prepping her for a condition that would be difficult to accept. Maggie's face showed her confusion. She was somewhat hurt by the evasive tactic. But it was necessary, at least for the time being.

"Please don't start this," she pleaded. "Not now." She pulled away from him ever so slightly. Ross reached out and grasped both of her shoulders.

"Maggs, I love you more than anything in this world. I would give my own life for you. But please ... please promise me that you won't ask any more questions right now. It's very important."

Maggie stared at him and saw the pain in his eyes. "Okay, Ross," she conceded. "Have it your way. But I don't like it one bit."

Ross relaxed and gave her the brief explanation that he promised. "David LaFontaine is in Jessup performing an investigation that I must be a part of. It is imperative, in my opinion, that this is not leaked to the general population. I have to go with him and it could mean some long hours away from home. And that's all I can tell you for now. Do you understand?"

"But what about ...?"

"Maggie, please, I'm begging you." He interrupted her.

She studied him closely, despaired that he would not share all with her. But this was a start. Although she shook her head '*no*', her mouth uttered something else. "Okay, Ross. But promise me that you are not putting yourself in any danger." She watched him carefully for anything that would indicate a lie.

"I promise, Maggs." He offered a soothing smile. "Everything will work out. Just give me a few days." Although he did bend the truth a bit, Ross was proud of himself for at least giving her that much. He couldn't keep everything from her.

Maggie could have insisted on more, but she didn't. That told Ross she had faith in him.

***

Mark Bennington sat in his office with his feet propped up on the desk, awaiting the arrival of his friend. Gene Steubens strolled in with Ted Newhouser at his side. Mark nearly toppled over in his chair when the door opened. He quickly straightened himself and greeted the two men.

"Mark, my boy, how did your first day as Sheriff go?" Steubens spoke to him in his typical animated fashion.

"Fine, sir, except for ... except ... for Birdie McIntosh that is." He fumbled for his words like the intimidated child he was.

"Any news yet on what might have happened, boy? We've got a number of concerned citizens around town."

"No sir," continued the Sheriff, "the State Police have been checking into some things, but nothing important to speak of." Mark grimaced, wondering if the Mayor had expected more information than he was able to provide.

"Hmmm," continued Steubens, "this doesn't look good for us, Mark. We need to get some answers fast." He rubbed his second and third chins together as if he were in deep thought.

"Ross should be coming in soon, and we're going to ..."

"What!" stammered the Mayor. "What the hell do you mean by that?" He glared at the Sheriff.

"Well, I thought we might need a little help, and Ross is ..." Mark tried to interject his logic, but the Mayor continued to interrupt.

"Nonsense! He is not to be allowed anywhere near this building, do you understand me?" Steubens stared hard into his new Sheriff's face. This was not what he planned. He needed to get a handle on the boy, and fast.

"Darnit, Gene," responded Mark, "Ross is a good man. And I really need ..."

Bennington was cut off again. "I don't care, Deputy ... Sheriff! I said no and that's it!" Steubens crossed his determined arms. Mark suddenly saw Ross appear through the open door. Steubens hadn't yet detected his presence. "We've had enough of Ross Pickett. He's an unstable drunk and a menace to this town."

Mark nearly laughed when Ross knocked on the door frame and caused Steubens to jump from the unexpected intrusion.

"Afternoon, gents," said the newcomer with a wide grin. "Ain't it a beautiful day today?"

"Ah ... and what ... what the hell are you doing here?" Steubens tried to maintain his haughtiness before the group, but his jumbling speech revealed that he was nervous.

Best thing to do with a bully is to call him out. That was a life lesson taught many years ago. "Oh shut up, Gene. You can't do jack to me anymore and you know it." Ross continued to smile as he brushed past the aggravated man. He half-expected Steubens to flop to the floor. "Good morning, Ted. How's the project going?"

Even Newhouser had to smile, but when he remembered his real purpose for being there, his face turned serious. "Not so good, Ross. We've got a little problem of our own that we're trying to deal with."

Ross turned and looked at the man. "What sort of problem, Ted?" Steubens had clammed up. For what must have been the first time in his life, he could not extract a single word from his endless vocabulary.

Ted Newhouser went on to explain how his two operators had disappeared. He displayed real concern for their well-being. Newhouser had already contacted both families and nobody had heard a word.

There it was, staring him in the face again. The Amen would not release its grip on him. Ross' eyebrows curled inward as he peered at Newhouser with his own worrisome look. "Where exactly were their vehicles found, Ted?"

"At the site. Both were abandoned. Right off the main service drive around the Amen Basin course."

How long can I keep this from Mark? Ross felt that he needed to hook up with LaFontaine right away and get out to those places.

"Mark?" Ross walked up to the acting Sheriff.

Steubens tried to intervene. "Now wait just a minute ..."

"Shut the hell up, Gene. And I mean it." Ross peered down at the much shorter man and gave him a stern *'try me'* look.

"Bennington, I want you to arrest this man right now!" The Mayor's face turned two shades of red. He was unaccustomed to such disrespect. He was furious.

Much to Gene Steubens' dismay, Mark finally got the courage to step out of his box and side with his former mentor. "Like Ross said, Gene, just shut up. We've got business here. Now get the hell out of my office before I throw *you* in jail for obstruction." The release gave him a feeling of empowerment, and it was fantastic.

Steubens, on the other hand, could not produce a response. He stood in shock of the mutiny that was taking place before him.

Ross wanted to applaud the boy's bravery. "Relax, Gene," he said. "I'm leaving anyways."

"You are?" Mark certainly didn't want to be left alone with the town's Mayor. But he was feeling more self-confidence.

"Yeah, I've got some business with LaFontaine. You let me know if anything happens. Okay?" The Sheriff nodded. Ross turned to Newhouser. "Ted, do you have any qualms about me taking a look around Hideaway Pines with a friend of mine?"

Newhouser shook his head. He was eager to solve the mystery that had befallen his crew. "Absolutely not! Please, be my guest. And let me know if you find anything."

***

Tyrone Pullman was sweating profusely in the mid-afternoon sun. His body ached from the long hike through the forest. He had achieved success yet again and harvested more food for the table. The past few weeks had molded him into a survivalist. But the hermit's lonesome existence was taking its toll, and strange thoughts were now undulating through his troubled head. The hunter dragged the deer to the front porch and piled it on top of the others, no longer bothered by the stench of the decaying carcasses.

"Yeah, there you go, Mr. Deer. You just sit right there while I goes and gets my knife." Tyrone now prattled with the dead animals as if they were dinner guests. He spoke to the walls and conversed with the fireplace. Tyrone talked to anything with which his impaired imagination would allow him to have a dialog. And sometimes those objects would speak back. When the television picture went out a few days earlier, he lost the last piece of contact with the civilized world outside. His sanity was plummeting with each passing day.

Tyrone opened the door and peeked cautiously inside. "Gerald? I'm home, G. Brought us some dinner." Although he had not yet experienced a second coming of his dead compadre, Tyrone still spoke to him on a daily basis. If his spirit was listening in, he hoped that his continuous efforts to communicate would ease the tension should Gerald decide to reappear.

Once assured that Gerald Johnson was not in the general vicinity, he entered his home. Tyrone unslung his rifle and leaned it up against the wall. He turned to the deer head over the fireplace. "Let's see, Mr. Deer. What should we have for dinner tonight? What? You think?" He smiled. "Hey! That's a great idea. We haven't had deer ass since ...when was it?" He paused as if waiting for a response. "Yesterday, you say? You know I think you're right?" He smiled as if he were satisfied that an important decision had been resolved. "How about a nice steak, Mr. Deer? Great! I'll get cookin." Tyrone began to whistle a tune as he casually walked over to the counter and retrieved the dulled knife that had seen more than its share of use in recent history.

As Tyrone returned to the open door, he heard a humming sound emerging from the trees. He cocked his head and tried to identify the source. It was subtle at first, but as the noise drew nearer, he knew that it could only be one thing. As he looked into the woods he started to see movement. It was a truck making its way up the path to the cabin. Tyrone turned and faced the deer head, this time with a cagey grin on his thinning face. "Well look what we gots here, Mr. Deer. Company! And I haven't even cleaned up yet. How about you tidy things while I go on out and say howdy to our friends?" Tyrone turned back to the door. There was no sense of urgency in his actions ... no thoughts of how to escape. He simply strolled to the table by the window, picked up the Glock, and stuffed it in the rear of his pants. "Be right back, Mr. Deer," he said as he walked out the door.

***

Wayne Samuels was in his sixteenth year with the Northern Michigan Power Company. He had witnessed some pretty crazy things while on the job, but never before had he laid eyes upon a sight so bizarre as the one standing before him.

"What the hell do we have here?" He looked over the strange black man who was grinning from ear to ear. He was waving to Samuels like a long lost cousin. Samuels studied the stranger carefully, unsure as to whether or not he should turn around. His supervisor gave him the order earlier in the afternoon to check out the cabin after the owner complained of an unexpected electric bill. The man from Newberry claimed that the place had been shut up tight for eleven months. The camp was only used during the firearm deer season that was more than a month away yet. Samuels had a fairly good idea of what he was facing.

"Goddamn squatters," he muttered. Every so often, NMP utility workers would run across a vagrant holed up in one of these remote camps. Samuels recalled one occasion where a buddy had discovered an entire family. They were often migrant workers transitioning between harvest seasons, or others who just plain fell on hard times and had no place to go. The secluded cabins were easy enough to access. All it typically took was a swift kick on the door. Personally, Wayne Samuels despised the type. Any man who couldn't put in a decent day of work to earn an honest dollar was worthless in his mind.

The strange man continued to wave. He looked friendly enough, but there was something in his eyes that bothered the utility worker. He had seen the deer lying on the porch and he certainly didn't figure the man to be an early season bow hunter. It was common practice for squatters to kill wild game. Samuels was apprehensive about approaching the man. With dead animals lying about, there was sure to be some sort of weapon on the premises. The smart move would have been to contact the Sheriff and have the vagrant hauled off. But the NMP worker enjoyed intimidating these criminals with both his size and authoritative presence. He wanted to have some fun with this one.

***

"Afternoon, sir. Ain't it a fine day?" Tyrone continued with his pleasantries. He had not seen another human being in weeks, and he was not about to let this opportunity slip through his grasp.

Samuels hesitated a moment. He scanned the man from head to toe, searching for that hidden weapon. Inwardly, he scrutinized the battered coveralls that were stained with blood that was both new and old. Samuels figured the man must have been there for some time. When he finally mustered enough gumption to continue toward him, his nose picked up the foul odor that permeated from the man's unbathed body. It was a pungent mixture of body odor and aging blood. Samuels crinkled his nose in disgust. "Okay, son. Now what's going on here?"

"Well," answered Pullman, "I was just about ready to fix me and my homeboys some grub and look who shows up?" A broad smile stretched across his face exposing his discolored teeth. "I swear, ain't that just like you to not call ahead. Well, no bother. We got plenty."

Samuels watched as the man gestured to the deer carcasses. It was then that the utility worker realized he was dealing with a lunatic. "You got some friends with you, son?" he asked carefully as he glanced to the open doorway.

"Yes sir I do. Mr. Deer is inside tidying up the place right now." Pullman placed his hands on his hips and continued to grin at the newcomer.

Samuels was dumbfounded. He hadn't detected any other activity in the general vicinity. It was possible that there were others in the trees, perhaps watching them right now. "Mr. Deer?" he finally questioned. "Where is ..." And then he realized. This guy was speaking to the dead animals. Confronting him had been the wrong move. It was time for Wayne Samuels to quietly back out of the situation and get some help. He was in over his head.

"Look here, son. I'm going to go get my friend, Mr. Sheriff, because I think he's hungry, too." Samuels spoke slowly and gently as if he were speaking to his six year-old-son. He turned and began walking back to the truck. "You just wait right here," he said with his back turned to the squatter. "I'll be back in a spiff." His hasty retreat was abruptly halted when he heard the man speak up from behind.

"Ohhhhhh, Mr. Utility Man. Yoo-hoo."

Samuels swiveled to face the vagrant, thinking that he would have to put one final scare in the man. His machismo quickly subsided when he saw the handgun being pointed in his direction. The utility man's hands began to tremble as he raised them slowly into the air, not sure of what he should say or do next.

"Now why did you have to go and get all official and shit? All I did was offer my company and some fine food." Pullman acted as though he was truly put out by his visitor's standoffish attitude, but he continued to smile.

Samuels watched as the man flopped the gun from side to side with his finger on the trigger. He tried to remain calm. "Listen ... sir ... I don't want no trouble. I ... I ... I'm just ... doing my job." Samuels stuttered. He was terrified.

"Oh relax, Mr. Utility Man. I just wants us to be friends. Now why don't you put your hands down and come on up here for some eats."

The man was completely off his rocker. The first thing that came to mind was *drugs*. He acted so peculiar, like he sincerely believed that he had a dinner guest for the evening. Samuels had no choice but to play along. One wrong move and he would be a dead man. "Okay, sir," he answered, now attempting to act the part. "You know, I am kind of hungry."

"Well ain't that fine and dandy. Come on up here." Tyrone Pullman waived his guest up to the porch.

***

The sun had just peeked through the swollen clouds when the Ford Taurus left the Marquette city limits bearing west on Route 41. The car, a loaner from Musgrave Auto World, was loaded to the hilt. Both boys had vehemently protested the bulky bags belonging to the girls who insisted they were full of nothing but necessities. They barely had room enough for the hunting equipment, the purpose for the trip. When Trevor sat on the trunk to lock it in place, Alex cringed at the pressure being applied to his bow.

Brenda and Kayla chattered aimlessly in the back seat. Each was dressed more appropriately for a ski trip to Aspen than an outing in the boonies of northern Michigan. A Coleman cooler stocked with two cases of beer separated the girls like an oversized armrest. Two reserve cases were stored away in the trunk. All four passengers held an open container. They would carefully check in all directions for signs of police before stealing a quick drink.

"Hey, Alex." Trevor whispered to his friend, just loud enough to be heard over the Guns and Roses song on the radio, but not loud enough for the girls to pick it up from the back seat. "Check this out." He handed his roommate a folded newspaper clipping from the Detroit News that a friend had given him a few weeks earlier.

Alex took the paper, and as he unfolded the edges the headline jumped out at him. He silently read the article.

Man-Eating Bear Stalks UP Town

The peaceful community of Jessup, Michigan, a town barely noticeable on many State maps, was stricken by an unsuspecting form of violence. An abnormally large black bear, turned vicious for reasons unknown, brutally attacked and killed three men and one teenager. All of the victims were residents of Jessup. Witnesses claim that the animal's live weight may have exceeded eight hundred pounds, which would have shattered the State record by nearly two hundred pounds. "This is highly unusual for a Michigan black," said an official from the Department of Natural Resources district office in Crystal Falls. After the gruesome discovery of one victim who had been partially devoured during the murderous rampage, the animal was ultimately hunted down and destroyed by four men with the aid of tracking dogs. The hunting party consisted of Jessup's own Sheriff, Ross Pickett, a State Trooper from the Appleton outpost, and two local outdoorsmen. Trooper Ray Jackson was seriously injured in the chase and has declined comment. Frank Jones, who accompanied the officers with his brother Jesse, stated, "It was one down and dirty brawl out there." Jones also took credit for firing the fatal shot as the bear was charging on Sheriff Pickett. In an interview, the Sheriff expressed doubts as to whether or not his party had found the true culprit. He later recanted his statement and claimed that they had indeed succeeded. Gene Steubens, Mayor of Jessup, was quoted as saying, "This is an incredible tragedy for our tightly bonded community, but we are strong and we shall rebuild our lives." Mayor Steubens went on to say that the town has made plans to have a taxidermist mount the bear and place it on display as a monument to those who perished. HUFAR (Humans for Animal Rights) out of Lansing is currently formulating an official letter of protest to both the DNR and the Governor's Office for the actions taken in Jessup. HUFAR Spokesperson Diane Lang commented, "Those men should be prosecuted for extreme dereliction of duty. Another innocent creature is meaninglessly destroyed." None of the victims' relatives would comment on these allegations.

Winston Lovells/ Detroit News

"Wow!" exclaimed Alex after finishing the piece. There was a small picture of the bear's hide draped across some steps centered next to the article. "That must have been one nasty animal. Where is that town anyways?"

"About six miles from where we'll be hunting," responded Trevor, glancing into the rearview mirror to make sure the girls hadn't picked up on the conversation.

"Well, so what. They got the thing."

"Did they now?" questioned the playful driver. "Didn't you read what the Sheriff said?"

"Oh bullshit! It was eight hundred pounds, man. It had to be the bear. Everyone else thought it was." Alex gazed out at the passing scenery. "Besides, six miles is a long way, Trev."

“Dude!” Trevor began to laugh. “It’s not like they bagged it at the Post Office. They got it in the swamp that just happens to back up against our hunting retreat for the weekend.” Trevor was trying to create a stir in his friend. He saw that his attempts were working.

Alex felt a twitch of uncertainty. He didn’t know too much about bears, only that they were big. He also understood that there were many in the U.P., and he’d even talked to people who’d seen them not far from campus. He didn’t realize they could be so dangerous. The article portrayed this animal to be some kind of monster. His imagination began to wander, piecing together scenarios where he might encounter one. What would he do? Could they climb trees?

Brenda picked up on the tail end of the conversation from the back seat. She leaned forward and began to massage her boyfriend’s neck, reaching around both sides of the head rest. “What are you two studs talking about?” She blew a large bubble with the gum in her mouth.

“Well ...” Trevor paused, unsure as to whether or not the girls really needed the tidbit of information that he had just passed along to Alex. He decided that inciting a little scare might bring her a little closer to him that night. He winked at his observant roommate. “There was a bear that killed a few people down by your uncle’s place a few weeks ago.”

Alex handed the article back so the girls could read it for themselves. Brenda withdrew her hands from the driver’s relaxed neck and flattened the paper out on top of the cooler. Alex, in the meantime, returned to staring out the window at the snow-covered ground, mentally calculating where a lethal shot would be placed on a bear. He silently thought about their ability to climb trees.

“Oh ... my ... God! I’m not stepping foot outside that cabin.” Brenda’s overly exaggerated reaction humored the two young men.

Kayla, with a much more rational head atop her shoulders, was not as moved. A sardonic smile broke on her bright red lips. “Oh, Brenda, it’s just a little ole bear. They are as scared of you as you are of them.” She mimicked a mother lecturing an adolescent. In a way, that was exactly what she was doing. Although she loved her best friend dearly, Kayla knew that if she yelled in the blonde's ear, her own voice might echo back three or four times.

"Little!" cried Trevor as he reached back for another cold brew. "I'd say that eight hundred pounds is anything but little."

"Oh, Trevor, grow up." Kayla loved debating with the likes of Trevor Musgrave. "I've lived up here all my life and I've seen bears before. They're completely harmless." At times, Kayla could not see how Alex put up with his roommate's '*live fast – take chances*' outlook on life. She loathed how Trevor would often goad her man into doing things that were alien to his nature. Alex was so timid and innocent.

Kayla had known for some time that she was in love with Alex Chavez. But his future was in the military. It was the life he wanted, with no distractions. That inevitable day when they would part ways was approaching much quicker than she had hoped. Kayla often considered voicing her true feelings, but decided against it out of fear that the truth might drive Alex away before the school year ended. She would be patient and remain hopeful that he would someday change his perspective on their relationship.

"Trevor, you're just trying to scare me," whined his girlfriend. She gave the instigator a harmless pat on the top of his head.

Kayla smiled at her simpleton roommate, a girl whose sole ambition in college was to obtain a *MRS* degree. In her mind, Brenda and Trevor were perfect for each other. The thought of the two of them with a house full of senseless blonde children scampering about nearly caused her to giggle out loud.

***

Wayne Samuels' startled eyes gazed down at the plate in front of him. He had been immobilized. His hands were tied behind his back and his fingers were beginning to numb from the lack of circulation.

"Well go on, Mr. Utility Man," said the host, motioning to the raw hunk of deer meat.

"I can't. It's not cooked." Samuels swallowed hard. Sweat was draining from every orifice on his body. He stared at the slab of venison. It sat in a pool of blood, riddled with brown and white hairs from the animal.

"Oh, come on now. Me and Mr. Deer there made it special for you."

Samuels looked up at the old mount over the fireplace, wondering what kind of life this man had been living in that place. He turned his attention back to his captor. "Please, I've got a family. I've got a kid."

"Fuck you and your family!" The captor kicked the table and exploded from his seat. His expression instantly changed to that of a wild man. "I had a family, too, motherfucker! And where are they now!" He reached around his backside and withdrew the pistol.

Wayne Samuels continued to tremble. "I ... I'm sorry. I'll eat it." He was quick to give in to the weapon pointed directly at his forehead from only two feet away. He chastised himself for not attempting to overtake the man when he had a chance. He cursed his rationale to approach him in the first place. If only he had turned around and gone on home. He would be eating dinner with his family.

The black man seemed to simmer down. The smile returned to his face as if the last ten seconds had never happened. He pulled his chair back and sat. "Well, that's more like it. I just hate to waste fine food." He set the gun on the table and waited for his guest to partake in the prepared feast.

"I can't ... move my hands." Samuels thought that if the man would release his hands, then maybe he could reach for the gun. But he also knew that he could ill afford to set him off a second time.

"Oh, you don't need hands, Mr. Utility Man. Just use your mouth like this." The man then bent over and picked up a piece of meat from his own plate in his teeth like a dog.

Samuels watched in horror as the man chewed the raw venison. Blood trickled from the corners of his mouth. He then swallowed and let out a hefty burp.

"Now that's some fine eatin. Your turn. Remember, Mr. Deer gets awful mad when someone don't be appreciating his cookin."

The NMP employee had no choice but to follow the instructions. He closed his eyes and bobbed his face around the surface of the table until he located the plate that had not been washed in weeks. He grabbed the steak in his mouth and tasted the blood circulating through his teeth as he chewed the raw flesh. The strands of hair tickled his sickened tongue.

"Come on now. Take it down like a good boy." The black man was watching him with anxious anticipation, as if he were waiting for a food critic's rendition of his signature dish.

Samuels swallowed, and then opened his eyes. The sweat continued to flow. He could feel his body shaking ... his insides churning. He willed himself to hold in the meat, but those efforts were hopeless. The eruption in his throat sent the contents of his stomach onto the table. He began to sob. "I'm sorry! I can't do it! I just can't ..." His voice trailed off into silence.

"Why you ungrateful motherfucker!" The man's temper flared. Samuels watched as he stood and picked up the gun. There was no time to beg for mercy. The man aimed and shot. The first slug hit the prisoner in the left cheek. His head was thrust backward. Samuels cried out in pain, but his words were gargled from blood and pieces of teeth. The NMP employee looked up in time to see the man take aim again. The second slug exploded his nose and ripped through his brain cavity before exiting the back of his cranium.

***

"Did you hear that? Ross stopped and held up his right arm motioning for his companion to stop. He thought there was a faint "pop" off in the distance.

"Hear what?" LaFontaine looked to the trees descending into the swamp.

Ross stood still for a moment, trying to listen above the howling winds that had been building once again all afternoon. He turned back to his new partner and shrugged. "It was nothing, I guess." He brought up his hands to shield the snow from hitting his face and began walking towards the two vehicles. LaFontaine followed.

"So these are the cars?" asked David.

"That's what Newhouser, the contractor said," replied Ross.

"This snow isn't going to help our cause." LaFontaine sighed heavily. If his creature had been here, there would be nothing to show for it.

"Let's have a look anyway, David." Ross first stepped around the Cavalier, examining the vehicle's outer structure. He didn't know exactly what he was looking for, just something out of the ordinary. He tried the driver side door, but it was locked. Ross then walked over to the Durango. Unlike the Cavalier, the door on the truck was open. He immediately smelled the acrid aroma of stale beer. There were a number of empty cans scattered about the floor. "Looks like our boys were doing a little partying." Ross had to raise his voice even higher over an especially strong gust. LaFontaine was at the tree line kneeling on the ground.

Ross continued his examination of the Durango. The keys were in the ignition. Nobody in their right mind would leave the keys lying around like that, especially with such a costly truck. It wasn't making sense. He was beginning to get an uneasy feeling again.

Young men, old men,
All men same,
Enter Amen,
Seeking fame.

Vanishing souls,
Never found,
Sought their fate,
On Amen ground.

If you will the courage,
To face the demons within,
Then pray with pure heart,
The journey ends with Amen.

"Ross! What's the matter?" LaFontaine had sneaked up from behind and tugged on the larger man's coat.

Pickett shook away the cluttered thoughts. "Nothing, just daydreaming is all." He turned around, ashamed by his lack of focus.

"Did you find anything of interest?" David looked at him with an anticipative expression.

"Keys still in the ignition," responded Ross. "Kind of strange."

"Let me look at something." David moved past the ex-Sheriff and peered inside the Durango. "Did you notice that the dome light isn't on with the door open?" He asked the question with his back turned.

"No," answered Ross, somewhat befuddled.

"Yeah," continued LaFontaine, "the lights were left on. Battery is dead." He spun around and faced his partner. "That's kind of weird, huh?"

"Damn, David. What the hell is going on here? What happened to those two boys?" Ross' anxiety was growing with the grim scenario taking shape.

"Your guess is as good as mine, but I don't think the authorities are going to rule out the possibility that something bad happened to them. It doesn't look good at all."

Ross stared off into the swamp only yards away. *What the hell is out there?*

***

Only twelve unopened cans remained in the cooler by the time the Taurus rolled to a stop in front of the cabin. The eighty mile journey had taken over two hours because of the frequent pee-stops impeding their progress. Trevor repeatedly ribbed the girls for their lack of bladder control. By the trip's end, all four passengers had tied on a decent buzz. Brenda, especially, was feeling no pain as she nearly fell while exiting the stuffy car.

Trevor's erratic driving caused Alex and Kayla to become more than a little nervous at times. At one point, the driver had blatantly swerved to the shoulder, intent on splattering a raccoon that was in the wrong place at the wrong time. Trevor broke off the vehicular assault when Kayla cried out her objection.

"Oh ... my ... God!" Brenda finally discovered her stability and looked over the building that would be her home for the next two days. It was Brenda's first visit to her uncle's hunting cabin, and after the first impression, would probably be her last.

"Yuck," added Kayla as she stood at her friend's side.

"Cool!" boomed Trevor, with the exact opposite reaction. He was more than impressed. "Check this place out!"

The structure might have been labeled a cabin in the most primitive sense of the word. It was little more than a square shack, loosely fabricated with aged wood and rusty nails, similar to a fort built by adventurous children on summer vacation. Four walls, each thirty feet in length, sat atop a wooden, uneven foundation that had been laid many years ago. A battered, tin roof served as protection from the outside elements. Alex followed an electrical line from the top of the structure to a leaning pole in the yard. At least they would have power. That would keep the girls a bit more comfortable while he and Trevor were doing what they came to do.

Brenda stomped through the snow up to the front door. "I hope there isn't just one big room inside," she pouted as she inserted the key into the rusty padlock. She had to kick the door twice to break the tight wedge in the warped frame. Trevor brushed past her and darted into the darkness of the interior. He reached along the wall until he located a switch. Brenda's fear of a slumber party arrangement was dismissed when the light clicked on. The cabin was actually split into four sections. The middle room, where the hunters likely spent the majority of their time, had two large sofas that looked as if they had been purchased in two different decades. There was a long picnic table in desperate need of a paint job for dining purposes. Water was supplied by a hand pump at a porcelain sink stained from the heavy iron content. Two shelves colored in a dull, yellow paint from another era were attached to the wall above the sink. Each held a misfit assortment of dishes, glasses, pots and pans. An antique wood-burning stove was nestled in a corner. There was an ample supply of kindling in a basket close by.

Alex was relieved when he saw the thermostat on the wall. He figured that it was a recent improvement to the building. He brushed the snow from his feet on the doormat that had a faded "Welcome" message. It was clear to him that the owners of the property were more enamored with hunting than they were with keeping the place clean. He studied the two large deer heads on the far wall. They were nice racks, certainly worthy of being shown and talked about. The cabin also held about ten smaller European mounts scattered about, also worthy of bragging rights in his mind. Five additional racks that were smaller yet, were displayed on plaques. He guessed that they probably belonged to younger hunters.

Kayla settled down into one of the enormous couches built for at least four full-sized men. Its cushions were checkered and torn, exposing large pieces of foam padding. A tall spring protruding from the backrest made a soft twanging noise when she plucked at it with her fingers. Brenda sat down in the other couch that was lacking much of its upholstery. The elbows of her snow-white turtleneck showed patches of dust when she raised her arms to stretch. She sprang from her sitting position after noticing the filth and quickly brushed it off.

"Gross! This place is sooooo gross!" protested the blonde.

"You picked the wrong color, babe," clucked Trevor, amused by his girlfriend's anguish.

There were three doors inside the cabin. Trevor walked over to one and opened it. Inside was a cramped sleeping quarter holding two twin-sized bunkbeds. He found similar setups behind the other two doors.

"Trev, hon, where's the bathroom? I have to pee." Brenda twirled around on her toes, searching for the elusive fourth door that would lead to the restroom. There was no fourth door.

"Outside and to the right," laughed her boyfriend, pointing to the entrance. "It's one authentic, nineteenth century outhouse."

"Oh great! I have to pee in a hole. This really sucks," she whimpered.

"Come on, Bren. I've got to go, too." Kayla led her depressed friend outside.

Trevor nudged Alex as they joined in the center of the living room. "Can you believe that shit, girls will even go to the outhouse together."

"I think we're in for a lot of bitching this weekend," responded Alex. "They're going to get bored real quick." He hated the idea of the girls ruining his weekend. He wanted to hunt.

"They'll get used to it," said the ever-positive Trevor Musgrave. "Just keep the beer flowing. At least we were smart enough to bring the boombox." Trevor performed his best moonwalk impression across the floor. His shoes left a path in the thin layer of dust that had collected over months of inactivity.

"Well, we'd better get that heat on," said Alex with a smirk. "It's going to get pretty cold tonight, and these walls won't keep us any too warm. We should head out and set up the stands before dark."

CHAPTER TWELVE

Tyrone Pullman stared at the corpse slumped across the table. His body was shaking uncontrollably. The fugitive held the Glock firmly in his hand with his finger on the trigger. *What have I done*? he begged of himself. "What the fuck am I becoming?" This time he screamed out loud and clenched his eyes shut.

After the second bullet took the life of his prisoner, Tyrone had been slapped with a sudden dose of reality. He felt as if he had lost a full year of his life. When he awoke from his hypnotic state, he found that he was holding the gun and looking at a dead man with his hands bound behind his back ... and he didn't remember any of it. His head was cluttered with vague memories, but he couldn't piece them together to harvest any sense of what had just occurred.

Tyrone Pullman began to cry. He was completely drained. There was no longer any sanity in that place. He did not want to continue living like a wild animal. He wanted to be free of his self-imposed prison. His right arm slowly raised the weapon toward his head, gripping it tightly with both hands. He pressed the barrel against his forehead, prepared to end the nightmare. He would be with his mama again.

Tyrone cried out, compelling himself to find the strength to follow through and pull the trigger. His soul would be liberated. He yelled again, but his finger would not flinch. He thought of Gerald and how he had stolen his freedom. Still, his finger would not move.

"Do it, homes. Come on, pussy!"

Tyrone turned and saw his dead friend peering down at him from the ceiling. He glared into the eyes of the floating corpse. Tyrone's grip on the Glock loosened. "Ger ... Gerald?" He blinked a few times to try and wash the vision from his sight. But Gerald continued to loom overhead, smiling at him ... taunting him.

"That's right, Tye. In the flesh ... or should I say, pieces of flesh." Gerald ripped open his shirt and exposed his decaying chest cavity. No longer were there just three bullet holes grouped around his heart. It was one cavernous pit filled with shredded, green skin and infected intestines. The ghostly apparition reached into the void and extracted a slimy, dark object that pulsated between his fingers. It was his heart, blackened by death. Tyrone looked away as Gerald squeezed the organ. Three lead slugs squirmed out of the sloppy holes and dropped to the floor below, each producing ann ear shattering "plink!"

"I told you I'd be back, Tye. I told you." The tormenting continued.

Tyrone stared down the cylinder of the 9mm. There would be salvation in that tiny hole. His eyelids sagged. He felt a drunken sensation overtaking his body.

"I told you that I was taking you with me, Tye. So giddy-up and let's ride." Gerald began to laugh uncontrollably.

One little pull of a tiny piece of metal, thought the distraught man. *It would all be over with one little pull.*

"Do it, motherfucker!" yelled Gerald with anger in his voice.

Tyrone suddenly perked up. His eyes opened wide. Gerald's hands burst into snapping flames that reached out to him. Gerald began to laugh louder, clutching what little belly he had left while spinning in circles. Tyrone became hypnotized by the aerial display as he listened to the spirit continue to cry out. "You better do it, nigger! I'm taking you with me!"

A passing bald eagle screeched loudly over the trees outside. The distraction through the open door caused Tyrone to shake his head and take notice. He peered out the window and into the clearing. A brilliant ray of sunlight illuminated the snowflakes falling from the sky, transforming the world into a scape that was pure and serene. He focused on the heavenly sight, forgetting the things that had made his life a living hell. The magical snow danced like fairies in the gusting wind, extending to him an avenue ... a means for redemption.

Tyrone began to slip from the stupor as he deliberated what was happening. For the first time in nearly two weeks, his brain and eyes began to work in unison. When he turned and looked at the hallucination, his head was already working the puzzle. *It was Gerald Johnson! That's all! Just Gerald-fucking Johnson!* Gerald was still trying to lead him through that same unforgiving, misguided inferno. And Tyrone's feeble mind had allowed it to happen again, just as he had done back in Flint. Even in death, Gerald continued to *'be the man.'* Maybe his damnation was to rot in an afterlife that was neither heaven nor hell, and plague the lives of those who he had made so miserable in his worthless excuse for a life.

Tyrone found the ability to smile. He lowered the gun and rested it on the table. He felt his muscles loosen. "Go fuck yourself, Gerald," he said casually.

"What you doin, Tye? I said I'm takin you with me. So do it!" There was now frustration in the imagined voice.

"Shut the fuck up. You done, homes. Look at yourself ... all fucked up and shit. Damn, G! You stink." Tyrone stood up, stuffed the Glock into his coveralls, and walked to the door.

"Get back here, Tyrone Pullman! Get back ..." The pleas of Gerald Johnson faded as Tyrone left the cabin for the final time. He picked up the Klashnikov leaning against the wall, walked outside and headed to the truck. Gerald Johnson was dead. Tyrone Pullman was alive.

***

"What is this, some kind of joke?"

"No, Ray. This is far from it," responded Ross into the phone. He looked to David LaFontaine who was perched atop the kitchen counter. Ross gave the man a nervous smile. He did not want to involve Ray Jackson again, but they needed help. LaFontaine protested the idea to inform the Trooper about what they had been doing for the past few days, but Ross insisted on bringing someone else into the mix. Ray was someone who could back them up if necessary.

"Wow, buddy. I mean ... what can I say?" Jackson struggled for words.

Ross detected the indecisiveness in the silence that followed. "Ray, something is going on up here. It's something bad, and I can't really do shit about it without any resources to back me up." He almost expected his friend to hang up. Ross knew that he was asking an awful lot of the man.

"Well, I don't really know if there's much I can do, brother. I'm still pretty gimped up."

"Yeah, I know. I guess I'm just trying to get a little advice from an old cop." Ross chuckled slightly, trying to soften the conversation.

"Ross, I know what they did to you up there, but have you considered filling in your new Sheriff ... on what you are ...?" He hesitated. "What the hell *are* you doing?"

Ross rubbed his temple. It had become a common tick in recent weeks. He knew then that he wasn't going to get anywhere with his friend. They would have to go it alone. "Listen, Ray," he continued, "I know it sounds crazy, but from what I've seen so far, something is in that swamp. Something is killing our people."

"Hold on, Ross. Hold on now, Haas." Jackson now sounded a bit confused. "Now why do you think this ... this whatever it is, is killing people? Have you found more bodies?"

"Well, no, we haven't yet. But we've got everything but bodies. Abandoned cars, missing persons. The list keeps getting longer." Ross watched LaFontaine ease down off the counter and reach into the cupboard for a glass. "What will it take to convince people that we have a problem?" The frustration was growing again.

"I'm sorry to say this, buddy, but I'm not that convinced from what you've told me. Have you thought about maybe taking a break? Get out of Jessup for a while. Take Maggie and just ..."

"Goddammit, Ray!" Ross cut him off. David nearly dropped the glass that he had been filling with water. "Are you listening to me? Do you think I'm a fucking lunatic, too?" Ross was getting over-emotional. The stress was building. He had no right to unleash on his friend.

"Come on, Ross. What am I going to do?" begged the Trooper. "Do you want me to go down to the station and put together a ... a Bigfoot task force? Do you know how crazy that sounds?" Ray offered a nervy giggle. "I want to retire some day."

"Forget it, Ray. Just forget I called." Ross hung up the phone. He was upset with his longtime friend for not having more faith in him. When the phone began to ring, he just watched it.

"Do you want me to get that?" asked LaFontaine after taking a swig of water.

"No," answered Ross. "It's Jackson. To hell with him."

"What do we do now, partner?"

"I have no clue, David." Ross rubbed his temple again.

***

"Pick up the damn phone, Ross. Come on ... come on. Shit!" Jackson finally slammed the receiver down after the tenth ring. "Goddammit!" he cursed out loud.

"Ray? What's wrong, dear?" Carol Jackson waltzed into the living room holding a sheet of freshly baked cookies. "Who was on the phone?" she asked.

"Ohhhh, it was Ross. That sonuvabitch!"

"Ray! Why are talking like that?"

Why am I talking like this? thought the recovering Trooper. He winced at the pain shooting through his shoulder as he turned to face his wife. "I don't know, Carol. I'm sorry. It's just that Ross is starting to bother me a little, that's all."

"Well calm down. You know what the Doctor said. You can't let your blood pressure get too high." She smiled sweetly and returned to the kitchen.

Ray sat and glanced at the newspaper article spread out across the coffee table. It was the piece from the Detroit News that someone from the Post had sent over with an apple pie. He looked at the bear's hide in the picture, thinking back to that day in the swamp when he had nearly lost his life. He wondered how Ross could have any possible doubts about that animal. It *was* a monster. But then he remembered what the man had tried to express to him on the steps of the cabin after he found the town's mechanic. Ray remembered seeing the fear and uncertainty in his friend's eyes. But what Ross was proposing was utter nonsense. He felt remorse for his reaction, but there was nothing else he could do to help ... or was there?

Ray Jackson leaned back on the sofa and closed his eyes. Images of the bear returned to him when he finally found sleep.

***

The eighty-acre tract of land was far better than Alex or Trevor had anticipated. Two-thirds of the property consisted of high ridges and hollows with varying degrees of cover. It was great for rifles, but difficult to get close with a bow. The remaining third descended down into a dense cedar swamp that both hunters knew would be crawling with whitetails. The two young men found numerous game trails winding in and out of the thick swamp like a confusing city highway system. Although rubs were plentiful where the bucks had shed their velvet, they failed to locate any scrapes. It was too early for the rut. It would be a few weeks yet before the bucks would begin their mating rituals, hounding the does in heat like horny college boys.

Regardless, the abundance of deer sign was euphoric. There was nothing like the opener of any season. He reveled in that first taste of the brisk fall air numbing the cheeks, the anticipation of a deer appearing from behind a tree at any moment, the excitement of hearing a twig snap as the sun began to cast its shadows on the dawn. To Alex, deer hunting was as close to an orgasm than anything he'd ever experienced, other than the real thing of course. Ever since Trevor had introduced him to the sport, the young Hispanic became obsessed. Whitetails were such beautiful creatures, graceful in appearance, yet powerful in their uncanny ability to overcome and adapt. Alex had read somewhere that the species inhabited every county in the State, which was incredible considering some of the more industrialized communities in southern Michigan.

During their search for suitable sites to hang stands, Alex and Trevor jumped three deer bedded on a ridge. Although they couldn't make out horns, seeing the white flags bounding off into a thicket aroused their excitement even further. Alex located an area to his liking at the base of the ridge where the deer had been spooked. They stopped and surveyed the conditions. Trails leading in and out of the swamp showed signs of heavy deer traffic. Alex found a good-sized pine with a bare spot near its midsection, an obvious sign that someone else had once used the tree for a stand. The opening offered clear shooting lanes in nearly every direction. Trevor wandered on alone farther up the ridge.

"This is the spot," said Alex to himself. He set the folding platform on the ground and then proceeded to screw in his first step. Once the other seven were securely in place, Alex shimmied up the tree to where the skirt of branches began. He was able to climb freely from that point on.

When the stand was finally secured around the thick trunk, Alex sat down on the padded seat and studied the shooting lanes.

The main trail entering the swamp was directly in front of him. That's where he assumed a shot would most likely develop. On his left, he could shoot another trail paralleling the swamp. His right side was blocked by the branches of another tree, but any deer coming from that direction would either enter the swamp on the trail in front or continue along the base of the ridge. Either way, he should get a shot. It was perfect in Alex's mind. Now all he needed was for that elusive monster to walk by in the morning to complete the experience.

Trevor returned after positioning his own stand in a very similar tree only a hundred yards down the ridge. Together they made their way back to the cabin. Both hunters were so confident that a twenty dollar wager was placed for the first buck of the season.

"It would be nice if this snow sticks," commented Trevor as they reached the summit of the ridge. "It'll be harder to track my buck tomorrow in that swamp if it doesn't." He spoke with arrogant conviction, insinuating that he would soon be twenty dollars richer.

"Well, while you're tracking your maimed deer," added Alex, "I'll have mine tagged and bagged right where I drop it." The male bonding continued until they returned to camp. The snow began to fall again, settling on the inch already on the ground.

"My baaaaaby!" Brenda came stumbling out the door with a beer sloshing over the brim of a mug held loosely in her hand. She bumbled up to the arriving boys and then tackled Trevor. She kissed him passionately while straddling his body. "Miss me?" she asked after coming up for air.

"Yeah, Bren," said Trevor. "I hope you saved some beer for us," he kidded.

She giggled, tweaking her nose against his.

Alex smiled at the pair rolling around on the white ground. He continued on toward the cabin.

"Did you big men have a nice walk in the woods?" Kayla appeared in the doorway with an inviting look on her face.

Alex went to her and offered a quick peck on her lips. "Hi, babe." The smell of alcohol was heavy on her breath. As he was about to enter, she embraced him, pressing her breasts tightly against his chest. Alex was surprised by her behavior. He was unaccustomed to the outward display of emotion in the presence of others. But the warmth of her body felt good, and he held her tight.

A soft moan escaped Kayla's lips. She buried her head into his neck and began nibbling at his cold flesh. "God, Alex, I love ... I mean ... I ..."

Alex's body tensed after hearing her utter that word, unsure of how he should react. She tried to rephrase the statement, but the word just sailed off her tongue. It was the beer talking. Kayla scolded herself for being such an imbecile. Brenda had been daring her to keep pace all afternoon, and like a total fool, she accepted the challenge. Her head was in a fog. She did not want to pull away and see the rejection in his eyes.

"I like you too, Kayla," he finally said. Alex relaxed, knowing that she had been tipping beers for a good part of the day. But he questioned whether Kayla had meant what she said. Would that be so bad? Alex gazed into Kayla's wondering eyes. A single tear rolled down her reddened cheek. She looked so helpless to him. A ray of fading sunlight glimmered off the crystalized snowflakes that fell in her hair. She shivered gently from the cold air as if her beckoning face yearned for forgiveness. Alex had never before known true love, but if it was something that could make him feel like he did right then, then perhaps it wasn't such a bad thing. He smiled warmly and brushed away a few long strands of hair.

"I'm sorry, Alex. I ... I didn't mean ..." Kayla fumbled for words as more tears welled up in her eyes.

Alex realized her agony and held her close. "It's okay, babe. I know." He questioned himself for exhibiting such a frail sense of commitment, but he was frightened. His plans for the future were set in stone. Kayla had a good life ahead of her.

"Come on you guys. Geeeez! Let's go into town and get some chow." Trevor was giving Brenda an unsteady piggyback ride. She swatted his rump to encourage more speed.

Alex and Kayla turned and laughed simultaneously at the two stooges making a spectacle. Alex wiped away the tears on her cheek with the cuff of his shirt. "Hungry?" he asked.

"Yeah," she replied. "Let's go." She snuggled against him.

***

The female had made her way out of the swamp yet again. Her stomach was empty and she needed to feast. Had the hairless ones not satisfied her so much, then perhaps her crusade would have eventually waned. But the taste of their meat was as enticing as the look in their eyes before she killed them. She would continue to hunt them with the same skills learned for purposes of evading. They were not strong animals that required tactical planning. They did not run like the deer, or swim like the fish. They wandered aimlessly about in an environment not suited for their being.

The female followed the game trail deep into the forest. There was little scent in the air to spark much interest. She did not wish to settle for another source of food and revert back to the ways of the clan. The female would pursue until her hunger was satisfied.

Her ears detected a soft hum in the distance. She jumped off the game trail and listened as the noise drew nearer. She recognized the pitch. The female waited for the arrival of her prey.

***

"Where are you taking me, Sheriff?"

Mark Bennington smiled. It felt good to hear the title attached to his name. He was an important man now in Jessup. He looked over to Sharon Cooper in the passenger seat. "Just a special spot of mine."

"I've never been two-tracking with a Sheriff before. Are you gonna handcuff me?" she asked in her youthful style.

"Only if you're good, Sharon." Mark had been looking forward to this little outing since he first attached the new badge to his shirt. He hadn't been with Sharon for over a week and his loins were ready to explode.

He steered the squad car down the winding trail, deeper into the forest. The snow continued to fall outside. The wipers worked frantically to push away the flakes clinging to the windshield. Before the two-track began to ascend up a narrow ridge, Mark pulled off to the side. He shut off the engine, but left the radio tuned to the soft-rock station from Escanaba. The mood was set. Mark knew that he probably should have stayed back in town, but there was only so much he could do. Besides, the Troopers were now involved.

"Aren't we going to get a little cold?" asked Sharon. "Why don't you leave the heater on?" She crossed her arms and shivered a bit.

Mark watched her breasts compress beneath the heavy sweater. He was hungry. He reached over and pulled her face to his. Their lips joined and tongues began to explore. Mark wrapped his arms tightly around her slim waist and hoisted her onto his lap. Her back arched as his cold hand slipped underneath her clothing and massaged her bare skin.

***

The female slowly advanced on the machine. The strong scent pierced her flaring nose. She ducked from tree to tree, conforming to the shadowy silhouettes of the forest. The falling snow stuck to her hide, camouflaging her presence even more. She was only fifteen yards away. She surveyed the target sitting dormant on the white ground. Then, she heard a sound. It was a whimper. The female froze, searching for danger that may have gone undetected. The machine began to rock as the noises from inside its hollow shell intensified. She stepped closer.

***

Sharon Cooper's palms were firmly affixed to the roof as she quickened her gyrations above the Sheriff's naked torso. She shrieked with every motion of her body. His hands grasped the flesh of her buttocks, pulling her closer, tightening the gap between them. Her head shook from side to side as she readied herself for the nearing explosion.

Sharon's eyes opened as she rode him. She watched his face straining with pleasure. She did not observe the sinister eyes that were peering at them through the window. The night air instantly engulfed them both as shattered glass sprayed over their bodies. For a brief moment, Mark thought that Sharon might have inadvertently kicked out the window. But reality turned to terror when his head was pinned against the headrest by the powerful arm of the unseen creature outside. Mark could neither see nor breathe as thick hair covered his face. Its wretched stench was sickening. Mark feverishly fought to push the appendage away, but he was no match for its overpowering strength.

Then, the arm slowly began to retract back towards the window. The course hairs scraped against his cheek. As the arm moved, so did Sharon. Her legs flailed. Her blood-curdling screams intensified. Mark managed to duck his head and free himself. Sharon groped for something ... anything to grasp as she was pulled closer to the open window. Mark's terrified eyes watched as the beast's arm wrapped around her midsection. He grabbed for her arms and tugged with all of his might.

Sharon pleaded with him to save her. "Mark," she cried. "Don't let go! Please don't let it ..." Sharon Cooper made one final attempt to reach out to him before her body folded through the window with a sickening *crack* and disappeared into the night.

Mark's body went numb with shock. "Oh God!" he cried, mortified by what he had just witnessed. After a moment of indecisiveness, Mark's ears detected a crunching sound coming from outside the window. He stared out into the darkness, unable to move. Then, a black silhouette began to emerge. As it neared, the shape materialized. Mark's body shook uncontrollably as the creature's head filled the open window. Its eyes studied him. The lower jaw moved up and down as if it were chewing on a piece of jerky. The foul smell filled the interior of the car. The creature then expelled an object from his mouth. Sharon Cooper's crushed thumb landed in his lap. Mark Bennington screamed. He fumbled to turn the key in the ignition.

Sensing that its prey was trying to escape, the creature plunged its arm into the car. Mark cried out in pain as claws sliced into his thigh. Blood spurted from the fresh wound and covered his face. As the engine came to life, he grasped the gear shift and thrust it into drive. The monster roared and yanked him toward the window. Just as Mark Bennington was in the process of being dragged across the bench seat, he slammed his left foot down on the accelerator. The cruiser impacted the tree on the opposite side of the trail. Mark was instantly pinned against the seat by the two inflating airbags. He couldn't move. His body grew weak from the mortal gash in his femoral artery. He was bleeding out.

The Sheriff's hand frantically searched underneath the front seat for his revolver. His eyes were growing heavy. His fingers touched the leather holster and he was able to unsnap the guard. The radio continued to play an Air Supply melody. Mark battled the urge to sleep and hoisted the .357, jerking it through the narrow space between the airbag and his body.

There was a warm breeze against the skin on his face. He slowly raised his head and found himself looking into the bloodied face of the beast that now was only a few inches from his own. Its putrid breath flowed into his gasping lungs. Mark's head swayed as he lifted the gun. His thumb cocked back the hammer. Terror had somehow transitioned into total relaxation. In his cloudy mind, he knew that he was dying. But his last duty as Sheriff would be to kill his murderer.

Mark aimed the weapon at the curious face before him. But as his finger sought the small trigger, Mark Bennington's eyes closed in permanent slumber. The gun fell to the floor and discharged a round into the steering column.

***

The two-man investigative team had stopped working for the evening. Ross dropped David off at the Inn and then drove home to an empty house. He settled into his La-Z-Boy and pondered the day's events with the aid of the remote control. Following the fruitless phone call to Ray Jackson, the two men continued their search near the area where Birdie McIntosh's Jeep had been abandoned. Her disappearance was now in the hands of MSP who had nothing to go on. No sign ... nothing. She was just gone. And Mark Bennington was as about as much help as a one-armed bartender. Ross knew the truth was out there somewhere, just out of his reach.

He was exhausted. Still adorned in his Carhartt jacket, he looked around the room. He scanned the pictures of Maggie and Chuck over the fireplace. *Maybe I should just take off,* he thought. *Just like Ray had suggested. Get away from this place.* It wasn't like he had a job to hold him back. He thought about quietly living out his days hunting and fishing, and no longer involving himself in the problems of others.

Ross couldn't blame Ray Jackson for dodging his accusations. Ray was a firm believer in acting on cold, hard facts rather than speculation. Ross felt guilty for hanging up on his long-time buddy. Once again, he hadn't been able to control his flaring temper. But there was one thing for which Ross was grateful. The thirst had not returned during that moment of defeat.

As he stared at a picture of Chuck sitting proudly with his first buck, Ross suddenly remembered that the boy had gone off camping for the weekend with some of his schoolmates. He'd forgotten about Chuck's plans for the opener. The boy mentioned that they were heading up near Ontonogon, a good distance from the Amen. He relaxed a bit after mentally calculating the distance. He decided the boy was far enough out of harm's way. Neither he nor Maggie could say *'no'* to the kid after all he'd been through. Chuck Barnes would be fine. Ross figured that he was busy draining a few beers next to a campfire. He did feel bad that the boy would miss the bow season. But a part of him was glad, too.

Ross closed his eyes. His thoughts drifted back to the Amen.

The black pit summons,
On Amen's floor,
Lost are the damned,
For evermore.

Charmed is he,
With arrogant will,
There is no mercy,
For whom it kills.

If you will the courage,
To face the demons within.
Then pray with pure heart,
The journey ends with Amen.

***

As the Escort neared the cabin in the small clearing, Chuck was quick to notice the lack of light in the windows. The place was deserted. He did, however, observe the fresh tire tracks in the snow. At least someone had been there.

"I wonder where everyone is?" asked Jenna.

"They've been here," responded Chuck. "I can see the tracks."

Jenna began to pout a bit, thinking that her cousin had dissed them. She had really been looking forward to the weekend.

Chuck suggested they check the door. "Maybe they left a note or something."

The two high school sweethearts got out of the car and walked hand-in-hand to the front door. Sure enough, there was a piece of paper tacked up to the trim. Jenna retrieved the note off the nail and read it in the light from the headlights. "Oh, it looks like they went into town. They went to get something to eat and have a few drinks."

Chuck eyed her with a look of concern. There was only one place local to eat and drink at that time of night ... the Jessup Inn. "Nice," he said. "What if they start talking and someone overhears the conversation?" He then relaxed in knowing that his mom had never met Jenna's cousin. But there was still a chance.

"Come on, Chucky. The door's open." Jenna led him by his good arm into the cabin. She reached around the corner and flicked on the light.

***

The Jessup Inn packed in more than its usual Friday night regulars on the eve of the bow-hunting opener. Cars lined the snow-blanketed street outside as out-of-towners congregated with locals to reminisce about hunts of old and to plan strategies for the coming days. Hunters decked out in jeans and flannels over-indulged in mass quantities of beer and liquor to celebrate the much anticipated arrival of their favorite season. Opening day was an event unlike any. It was a time when differences were set aside and conversations were monopolized by bragging bouts over mythical bucks that either did or did not evade the flight of the hunter's sharp broadhead. Nearly every patron had a story to tell, boasting of his or her skills and knowledge of the whitetail deer. The noise level from the tumultuous crowd grew at a steady pace as harmless, alcohol-induced buzzes evolved into total inebriation. Half of those present would not see the sun rise in the morning, but they didn't care. The shared release of life's tensions was all that really mattered.

The four college coeds had just received their half-pound burgers at a round table tucked away in a corner underneath a taxidermy mount of two fighting bucks. Each had a tall schooner of beer at the ready. Alex and Trevor laughed aloud when the girls lit into the meaty sandwiches. There was a glob of fresh ketchup affixed to Brenda's chin when she pulled the sandwich away from her mouth.

"Geez, girl, get you some of that," hounded her boyfriend. She gave him a look of aggravation before chomping off another healthy bite.

"Trev!" shouted Alex over the crowd. "Are you going to pop a doe if you see one tomorrow?" The question had not yet been discussed, but it was certainly a worthwhile topic.

"Hell no!" Trevor's response was immediate and firm. He appeared somewhat astonished by the notion of taking a doe. Although regulations in Michigan allowed hunters to harvest an antlerless deer during the early bow season, his chosen quest was to wait out a buck. "I'm going for Bullwinkle," he crowed, referring to the nickname he attached to that once-in-a-lifetime animal that had yet to cross his path. "I smelled him out there today, Alex. I smelled his piss all around my tree." Trevor raised his glass as if gesturing a toast and then took a long pull.

"Gross!" objected Brenda as she spit out a mouthful of chewed burger onto her plate.

"To Bullwinkle then." Alex hoisted his own schooner and joined his roommate in the tribute. "May he smell your morning farts and wander into my kill zone."

"In your dream, burrito-breath. Just have that twenty-spot ready to hand over around noon tomorrow." The boys clanked their glasses together and a wave of beer sloshed onto the table.

"You guys are unbelievable." Kayla decided to cut in on the conversation. "I don't know how you could even think about killing some poor, defenseless creature like that. They're so beautiful."

"It's easy, baby," said Alex. "You just point and shoot." He and Trevor slapped palms.

Kayla was unimpressed by their bravado. She had been raised in the northern country and had always been around hunters. Kayla's father tried to spark an interest with her when she was in high school. That was the first and last time she would ever witness the slaughtering of a wild animal. She found herself deeply saddened by the death of the whitetail her father had taken, that only moments before had been breathing the same air flowing through her own lungs. Kayla Johnson did not venture out on any more hunting trips after that experience.

Alex detected the change in his girl's behavior and quickly retracted his last statement. A frown was etched across her rosy face. He knew that Kayla was drunk, and alcohol tended to over-inflate emotions. He proceeded to try and comfort her before getting himself into too much trouble.

"Listen, Kayla. I didn't mean that the way it sounded. Trev and I don't just hunt for the sake of killing. We hunt for the food, babe. Hell, we're college kids without money." *Or at least I am*, he didn't say. "It's a great, inexpensive way of putting meat in the freezer." He caressed her wrist. "Now you take your burger there," he continued, pointing to her empty plate smudged with grease. "You know that the cow didn't volunteer his body for your dinner plate. If you want to see something cruel, go to a slaughterhouse. At least the deer has a chance out there in the woods, especially with a dummy like me chasing him." He tried to instill a little humor into the conversation, but it wasn't working.

"I know. But it just seems wrong." Kayla folded her arms across her chest and stared dejectedly to the floor.

"The way I see it," added Alex, "I'd rather kill what I eat than have someone else do it for me. I think there's more meaning in it that way. Look at it like growing your own garden ... you take what you need and that's all." Alex sat up a little straighter, proud of the analogy. "Besides, wild game is a lot healthier for the body."

"I know, Alex. It's just the beer talking, I guess." *Just like earlier when I said the 'L' word,* she thought. "Don't mind me," she muttered. Kayla took his hand and began rubbing his calloused fingers.

"Hey, you've got a right to your own opinion. I'm just expressing mine. You don't have to like it. That's what I adore about you. You have a mind of your own and I respect that."

His words caused Kayla to look up and smile with hidden hope.

Alex's heart fluttered as he returned the gaze into her innocent eyes. She was so beautiful and strong. He began to sense that maybe he actually did love this woman.

"Would you get a load of these two? Blah ... blah ... blah!"

Leave it to Trevor to ruin a good moment, thought Alex.

"I think I'm going to cry," whined his roommate with his typical insensitive self. He tugged on a passing waitress' apron and ordered a round of Cuervo.

***

The Chevy pickup loomed silently at the side of the road only thirty yards from the entrance to the Shell station. The pump area was well lit for customers. Tyrone studied the setting carefully, watching for any concealed threat that could ruin his plan. He had driven the two-tracks and country roads without a clue as to where he was or what direction he was taking. When he finally found a hardtop, he followed until it brought him to the outskirts of a small town. He made one pass along the main artery and was surprised by the lack of activity. Other than a bar at the opposite end, which appeared to be doing quite well, the rest of the town was asleep.

He waited patiently in his hidden spot, studying the traffic patterns. But there was really nothing to study ... no cars ... no people. More importantly, there was no evidence of a police presence. It was too easy. Ahead, he could see the street lamps through the falling snow lining the empty corridor of Main Street. He glanced at his watch. It was ten-thirty. *Damn,* he thought, *where is everyone?* It was Friday night and no sign of life. Back home in Flint, he would have been primping himself for a night on the streets with his homeboys, a memory of days that seemed so far away.

Tyrone understood that he was taking a risk. He considered breaking into another cabin or home, but the thought of some redneck with a loaded shotgun dispelled that idea altogether. He figured that most people up there had a loaded gun by their door, which wasn't all that dissimilar to Flint, albeit for different purposes. This gas station would be easy pickings if he played his cards right. Just in and out ... nobody knows nothing. He was desperate.

The fugitive pulled the stocking cap down over his wounded ear to cover the bandage. He started the truck, put it in gear, and started rolling ahead to the entrance. He searched in all directions for any sign of oncoming headlights. A strong feeling of Deja-vu swept over him, but this time Gerald Johnson was not there to fuck things up.

He turned into the parking lot and drove on past the pumps. There was only one attendant visible through the window. It was a man, probably in his late thirties. Tyrone performed a U-turn so that the front of the truck was facing the road. He left the motor running. He was not proud of what he was about to do, but it was necessary if he was to have a chance. His mother always told him that sometimes you had to claw and scratch in order to survive in the world. But that advice did not involve murdering innocent people. Tyrone got out of the cab and strolled to the door. He held the 9mm firmly at his side. The Klashnikov remained in the truck.

The door opened to the sound of jingling bells ... another feeling of Deja vu. The man behind the counter glanced over to the arriving customer with a pleasant smile.

"Evening, sir. How are we tonight?" asked the worker.

The man was quite the opposite of the last storekeeper he encountered. Tyrone found himself wishing that he and Gerald had happened upon this store instead. Things would sure have been different. But Gerald would still be alive, and who really knows what would have gone down.

Tyrone returned the man's smile and walked calmly toward the back of the building after grabbing a small basket for groceries.

"Up hunting this weekend?" The man spoke up from behind, raising his voice to the customer walking further away.

"Huh?" Tyrone turned. "Oh yeah ... hunting ... rabbits. Me and some friends." He continued to return the man's grin, trying not to let on that he was lying.

"Rabbits you say? Hmmmm, I don't know of too many folks huntin rabbits this time of year, especially with deer season comin in." The man looked somewhat confused.

"Yeah, well," continued Tyrone, "you know us black folk. We like our rabbit." It was the only retort to cross his mind, and he hoped that it hadn't sounded too foolish. Tyrone continued on toward the back of the building. He stopped periodically to pick a food item off the shelf. He grabbed bread, candy bars, and chips. He visited the cooler for milk, juice, and sandwich meats. His choices were random, yet premeditated. He needed supplies that would keep him going. Tyrone could taste the contents of the basket through the touch of his fingers. His mouth watered.

When he determined that all of the essentials were in his possession, the customer returned to the front counter where the attendant waited patiently by the register. His basket was so overloaded that he had to hold a few items in place with his free arm to prevent them from spilling out onto the floor. He watched the man behind the counter closely. The eyes seemed to question his wide assortment of products. When Tyrone finally reached the counter, he set the basket down gently.

"Somebody's a little hungry tonight, eh?" joked the man, unaware that he was about to become another statistic.

"You right about that," answered the customer. Tyrone did not want to kill him. He was nice enough. He probably had a family and was just trying to make ends meet. But Tyrone's focus now had to be about himself and his own survival. It was all that mattered. His mama would understand.

"Could you get me one of those lottery tickets?" Tyrone's conscience told him to do it in the back. He didn't want the man to experience the agony of realizing that he was going to die.

"Sure, what game we playing?"

"What you got over there?" Tyrone pointed to the wall of lottery ticket dispensers.

"Let's see." The man turned his back and began to read aloud the choices. "Okay, we've got Big Buck ... Instant Millions ... Cash in a Flash ..."

Tyrone pulled the gun from his pocket, aimed it directly to the center of the man's head and pulled the trigger. When the weapon discharged he saw the blood spray against the back wall. The body dropped to the floor. He hadn't felt a thing. Tyrone returned the 9mm to his pocket and seized his groceries from the counter. On his way out, he grabbed a case of beer on display by the doorway. Although he thirsted for something a little stronger, the Miller Lite would do.

***

Peter Brummeister crept down Main Street, irritated by his wife's insistence that he run the late night errand. The rheumatism in her knuckles had flared and she wanted some Ibuprofen to ease the pain.

"Why the heck couldn't ya git some earlier," he cursed when he walked out the door. *Damn woman was always forgetting something.*

Peter was half-tempted to stop at the Jessup Inn for a quick beer. When he drove by the building on the south end of town, he saw a few cars belonging to some of the old cronies. He always enjoyed having a cold one with the boys. But the Inn was pretty busy with the bow-hunting crowd in for the opener, and he didn't want to upset Mildred any more than he had to. He'd never hear the end of it.

The lights of the Shell station beamed to the north. As he approached the station he saw a man exiting the building with an armful of groceries. He watched the man climb into a Chevy, much nicer than the '73 that he had been driving for so many years.

***

When Tyrone slammed the door shut the headlights from the truck pulling into the lot blinded his eyes. "Damn!" He instinctively retrieved the handgun from his pocket and rolled down the window. It was another problem to deal with. He shifted into drive and eased his truck forward. Tyrone then reached out the window with his left hand and waved to the other truck, motioning for the other driver to pull alongside. He held both the 9mm and the steering wheel with his right.

The other driver did just as Tyrone had planned and rolled up parallel to him. He watched carefully as the window slowly went down. It was an elderly man with an inquisitive sneer.

"Good evening, sir," said Tyrone in a friendly manner. He nodded his head as a greeting for his next victim. "Could you please tell me where Dexter Street is?" The name was pulled from out of nowhere.

The man appeared puzzled. "Never heard of it," he replied in a gruff voice.

Tyrone instantly disliked the ignorant tone in the response, sensing that the man was most likely agitated by the color of his dark skin. He did not feel any guilt for killing this one. Tyrone brought the 9mm around with his right arm and shoved it out the window. The gun spit out a continuous barrage of fire into the other cab. Tyrone watched the old man's body jerk as the slugs tore through his skin and riddled his insides. By the time the chamber was empty, the old man was a bloody mess slumped across the steering wheel. The truck began to roll forward with nobody to guide it. Tyrone followed the vehicle's path with his eyes. He suddenly realized that it was headed directly into the pumps.

"Fuck!" He jammed his foot down on the accelerator. The rear wheels squealed as the Chevy spun out of the lot. In the rearview mirror, Tyrone observed the driverless truck crashing into the pump closest to the building. Fuel flowed across the pavement. Then a thought crossed Tyrone's mind. Why leave evidence? He brought his Chevy to a stop, shifted into reverse, and then proceeded to back up. The old man's truck was propped securely atop the pump spewing fuel. Tyrone inserted a new clip into his gun, chambered a round, and then fired a single shot into the saturated pavement. The asphalt ignited and a streak of fire raced toward the main flow from the pump. Tyrone sped off down the road, quickly putting distance between him and the gas station.

He saw the flames shooting skyward in the mirror, changing darkness into daylight for a few seconds. The flash was followed by a thunderous explosion. The Chevy was rocked by a shockwave, but continued onward. The town would be busy putting out a fire while Tyrone Pullman made his way out of Michigan.

He reached across the seat and picked up a package of sliced ham. He ripped open the plastic with his teeth and shoved the tasty meat into his mouth. He devoured the ham in three bites, savoring the salty flavor.

***

Wally Keifert pedaled his Schwinn vigorously down the gravel shoulder. He was over an hour late, but Chad Foley had just traded him a Mark McGuire rookie card for a 1997 Ken Griffey Jr. *What a fool,* thought the boy as he pulled the orange cap over his ears. He couldn't wait to show it to his brother. Wally had been collecting baseball cards for three years, and at age twelve, he realized a good deal when he saw one. He already had three hundred and fifty in his collection, some with excellent potential.

Although the negotiations had lasted for over two hours, Wally was the victor when the deal was finally sealed. The McGuire card was his, and he would one day reap its great rewards. It was only a matter of time, he figured, before the big St. Louis slugger topped Marris' homerun mark. The tongue-lashing waiting at home was well worth the prize. It was a cold, dark night, one in which he would ordinarily have stayed home and touched up on his Sega skills. But tonight he would instead be basking in the glory of his latest acquisition.

Wally was wishing that he had been dropped off versus taking his bike. It was becoming difficult to ride with the snow. As he rode past the dark forest, he suddenly felt a chill that wasn't induced by the frigid temperatures. He recalled the story that spread earlier in the week during recess. Kathy Whitaker and Todd Ballinger, two classmates from Appleton Elementary, claimed to have actually seen Ned Crosby's ghost hovering through the trees just outside of town ... right before nightfall. It was later learned that a boy from Iron Mountain had disappeared after the old goon had been killed by that monster. The kid's parents found two empty shoes covered in blood. And inside one of the shoes was the little boy's pinky finger with bite marks. Wally envisioned the troll's face, with his yellowish fangs and blood dripping from his mouth. He began to wonder if what the high school kids were saying was true ... that Mr. Crosby was coming back to settle matters with those who made fun of him for so many years.

The twelve-year-old's legs began to pump faster as the flurries in the air grew stronger. He began to see shapes in the trees ... monsters just waiting for him to stop so that they could devour him. He began to breathe harder, sensing that the ghost was on his heels ... chasing him. Wally Keifert did not want to look back as his imagination ran amuck.

The boy didn't begin to relax until he saw the first few lights of town. He coasted down a small hill to relieve the aching muscles in his legs from the short sprint. As he skirted a bend in the road, he could now see the lights of the Shell station ahead. There were two trucks in the lot sitting side by side. When he briefly turned around to check his backside for pursuing monsters one last time, Wally thought he heard something ... a popping noise. But it was muffled by the thick wool hat covering his ears. When he looked forward toward the Shell station, one of the trucks was racing out into the street with its tires squealing. The other was slowly rolling. Wally's bike skidded to a halt when he saw it ram straight into the pumps. Gas sprayed everywhere. Then the other truck stopped in the street and backed up. He saw a flash inside the cab, and then the parking lot caught on fire. When the pumps exploded, Wally Keifert was knocked to the ground. As he lay in the loose gravel at the side of the road, mesmerized by what he had just witnessed, he watched the big blue truck roar right past him.

***

"All right, Trev," said Alex. "It's time to go. We've had enough for tonight." He had been ready to leave for over an hour, but his roommate kept insisting on one more round for luck. The girls were listless in their drunken stupors, and were pleading to be carried out by the less-affected boys.

"Okay, okay, just don't let me hear you argue the next time I tell you I can drink your ass under the table." Trevor scooted his chair out into the aisle and clutched Brenda's arm. "Let's go, babe. We're outta here."

The four college students stood in unison and began their slow weave toward the exit. A hearty gathering of hunters still engrossed in their drinking and storytelling, remained to close the place down.

Gene Steubens was indulging in a bit of small talk with a group from Illinois near the L-shaped bar. The men, all struggling for balance, were huddled around the shorter man like a football team awaiting the play from their coach. Steubens was in rare form, putting on one of his flamboyant selling jobs. He was an expert at planting the seed of curiosity, and this particular piece of bait was the town's most recent prize.

As Trevor Musgrave led his crew past the throng, his ears could not help but pick up on the conversation. He paused and listened in on the little man's spiel. Alex prodded him toward the door, but Trevor stood his ground. He was already lured into the Mayor's net.

"The black bears just don't get that big in this state, mister," stammered one of the out-of-towners.

"Well, this one sure as hell did, young man. Eight hundred pounds and change!" roared Steubens so that his voice could be heard by all in the general vicinity.

Trevor found himself amused by the man's carnivalish appearance. He wore a white dress shirt with a bright, red bow tie and suspenders to match. He was definitely out of place in present company, but he was holding their attention with magnificent prowess.

"You can see it for yourselves in about three months," he continued. "We'll have it on display for anyone to see down at the Five and Dime ... fangs, claws, the whole nine yards."

"I don't know. I've hunted black bears in this state for a long time ... Canada, too. I've never come across anything that big." The doubtful one shook his head, not yet convinced by the Mayor's allegations.

"Ya might grow balls dat big too if ya was inta eatin people, mista." The group of men turned to the newcomer who had just perched himself up on a stool at the bar.

Trevor eyed the rough looking character closely. He figured him to be a local. The story was about to get even better.

Jesse Jones ordered a shot of Beam and a beer from the woman behind the bar and then swiveled to face the others. He stared at the men through two grim eyes embedded in a face overlaid with skin seasoned from the outdoors. He resembled no other patron, clad in a faded camo field jacket and ragged blue jeans with grease stains. His crooked grin mocked the onlookers, with their Eddie Bauer clothing and their snobby *know-it-all* dispositions. He downed the shot, and then took a long swig from his mug.

"Ahhhhh, Mr. Jones." The Mayor appeared elated by the man's arrival.

"Trevor, come on," begged Brenda, tugging on his arm.

"Just a sec. I want to hear this." He ignored her groan of disapproval as the little man introduced the hardened woodsman.

"Gentlemen, I'd like you to meet our distinguished Jesse Jones, one of the men who hunted down the murderous creature and slayed it, saving our town from certain catastrophe. Ask him for yourselves." Steubens made a wide swooping motion with his hand as he bowed and offered the floor to the new storyteller.

Jesse gave the Mayor a subtle smirk, drained the remainder of his beer, and then began to retell the tale as he had done over a hundred times in recent weeks. He left out no details for the attentive audience, describing every ensuing shot in the Amen Swamp.

Even Alex had been drawn into the story when the local took over. His mind began to size up that kill zone on a black bear once again.

"Had killer eyes, dat one did. It was im or us out dare. Bastard kilt two of da best damned dawgs ever run bear, too." He spoke with a menacing squint in his eyes.

"And Jesse fired the fatal blow, boys," added the Mayor.

"Nawwwww. Wuz Frank who got em. Blowed his head off wit dat 300 mag of his. Dat bear wuz after us even when it wuz dead. He wuz a devil all right."

"How big was it, Mr. Jones?" asked the man who had continuously questioned the legitimacy of the Mayor's claims.

Jesse looked at him hard, daring the man to doubt his words. "Bout eight, eight-fifty live weight."

The hesitant out-of-towner turned away. The intimidation was reflected in his facial expression. His peers were murmuring amongst themselves, amazed by the mere possibility that such an animal could exist in Michigan.

Trevor Musgrave was not so impressed. He thought the tale was more exaggeration than truth, and better suited for a campfire setting. The college senior could not resist the temptation to chime in.

"Mr. Jones?" he asked. "I read that article in The Detroit News about your bear. The reporter made it sound like your town Sheriff was not completely convinced that you killed the right animal. There are quite a few bears up here. How can you be so sure that your bear was the one doing all of the killing?" Trevor imitated a prosecuting attorney breaking down a defendant on the witness stand.

Jesse turned and looked at the provocative youngster. His left eyebrow raised a tad as he studied the boy. The men surrounding him nodded their heads in agreement with the inquiry.

Alex, who stood behind his roommate, rolled his eyes. His friend was drunk, and that generally resulted in obnoxious behavior. Alex could see the fury written in the local's eyes, as if he were sizing up Trevor mentally, preparing to knock him upside his wavering head. The two of them were heavily outnumbered. *Shut up, Trev,* he said to himself. *Not tonight.*

"Well, *boy*," said Jesse Jones, stressing the word '*boy*,' "I'd have to say dat da Sherf don't know shit. If it wasn't fer ma brother Frank, he'd be da one gittin himself stuffed tonight." The rebuttal drew a round of laughter and cheers from the crowd of observers. "Besides," he continued, "ma dawgs picked up dat scent right where ole Charlie Perkins bought it. Day don't stray from one track to da next once dare noses is set. Dem were some fine damn dawgs, boy."

Trevor's mind worked vigorously to form an argument that would refute the man's testimony. He did not like to be beaten by the likes of the beatnik who was currently patronizing him. Surprisingly enough, it was another member of the crowd who rescued him from humiliation.

Reggie Stillwater, a resident of Appleton who was camping just north of town with some friends from Escanaba, had also listened in on the conversation. He had some personal knowledge of the tragedy in Jessup through a network of acquaintances in the Appleton State Police Post. The one underlying mystery that had yet to be uncovered was that there was no body.

"Excuse me, Mr. Jones, but if your dogs picked up the trail where the man was killed, wouldn't they have come across the body that was dragged from the scene?"

The crowd now looked to Jesse, awaiting his response to a question that required an answer.

Alex thought him to resemble a cornered animal searching for a path to freedom. The fat, little man next to him was also perplexed by the inquisition.

After an uncomfortable pause, Jesse finally spoke up. "All I know is dat we tracked dat bastard from da damn doorstep. I don't know what da fuck happened to ole Charlie. Probably buried along da way. Bear's do dat you know." Jesse's voice reflected his aggravation from the intrusion on his floor time.

"Now you don't go listening to all of that gibberish that's being spread around, my good friends." It was Steubens jumping in to maintain control of the situation. "The killer has been defeated," he boasted loudly, "and if you wish to see the monster for yourselves, come back in a few months. We'll give you a good showing."

Alex, having lost interest in the bar gossip, was bent on getting Trevor out of the establishment before he stepped on the wrong person's toes. He finally nudged his roommate hard enough to start him moving toward the door. Besides, he was anxious to get back to the cabin and spend some alone time with Kayla.

"That redneck asshole don't know shit," protested Trevor as Alex pushed him into the street.

"Jesus, Trev. Now is not the time or place to be picking fights." By the looks of the local inside, he was probably packing a blade somewhere on his body. Alex was not worried for his own safety. He could have handled the man, knife or no knife. He's been trained for it. But Trevor, with liquid courage guiding his brain, could get messed up if he wasn't careful.

Alex Chavez was just opening the door to the Taurus when the crisp popping sounds erupted. It took only a second for the trained soldier to recognize the noise as gunfire.

Trevor turned in the direction of the disturbance. "What the hell was ..."

"Gun," replied Alex before his roommate could finish. He stood in the light of a lone street lamp and stared down the road. It was close. There was something wrong.

The girls pulled themselves out of the back seat of the car.

"What's going on, Alex?" asked Kayla, snuggling up to him.

As Alex was about to answer, the entire town seemed to light up. An enormous fireball burst into the sky. The four students looked on in shock. Silence was short-lived when the explosion shook the ground.

***

"Ross?"

"Yeah, Maggs. What's up?" He rubbed his sleepy eyes. It was the phone waking him yet again. He seriously considered pulling the cord from the wall.

"Something's happened, hon. There's been an explosion."

Ross' eyes opened a little wider. "What do you mean? What explosion?" He leaned forward, concentrating on the receiver in his hand.

"The Shell station, Ross, it's on fire. Maybe you should come down here."

What the hell can I do? he thought to himself. He had no right to be snooping around, although he did still have the Tahoe at his disposal. Jessup's fearless leader had not yet summoned enough courage to look him in the eyes and demand its return. Ross thought that it was a little childish on his part, but he didn't care. He planned to drop it off on Monday morning regardless.

"Ross? Did you hear me?" Maggie spoke loudly. There was a lot of background noise.

"Is Mark there yet?" Ross sifted his hand through his uncombed hair. He felt like a mess. The sleep had been nice, and he wasn't the Sheriff anymore.

"No, Ross. Nobody's seen him since this afternoon. There are a few Troopers up the road, but that's about it. You really should come on down."

Ross sighed. Even though it wasn't his job, Mark probably could use a hand. He owed him that much. The new Sheriff was green, and they certainly had their share of unsolved mysteries to deal with. In the very least, he could see what was going on. The Troopers would be doing most of the digging anyway.

"All right, Maggs. I'll come down and take a look."

"Thanks, love. I'll see you in a bit." Ross snickered as a notion crossed his mind. He could send Steubens an invoice for his personal time.

***

Jack Berkowski and Mike Johanson looked on as an army of exhausted firefighters battled the blaze. Three tankers had already been summoned to the scene. Men and women alike worked frantically to douse the flames that consumed the small building. They had already managed to cap the pumps. The two Troopers, along with three other units, had been questioning potential witnesses for twenty minutes. A young boy on a bicycle was able to shed some light on what happened. The local youngster had been riding home when he claimed to have seen a man in a blue, Chevy truck racing down the road after the explosion.

"Sir?"

The Sergeant turned to address the voice that arose from behind. The young Hispanic boy's hair was cropped tight ... military style. "Yes, son," answered Berkowski, "what can I do for you?"

"Sir," continued the boy, "my name is Alex Chavez. My friends and I were just coming out of the bar when the station blew up." He motioned to the three other kids huddled together a short distance away.

Berkowski could smell the alcohol on his breath, and he could see very clearly that the others were a little tipsy by their body movements. But now was not the time for a lecture on drinking and driving. "Do you know anything about what happened here, son?"

"Maybe," continued Alex, "before the explosion I heard gunshots ... small arms fire coming from this direction."

Berkowski immediately perked up. This was new information and definitely worth noting. "What makes you say that? I mean, how do you know you heard gunshots?" He had to confirm the boy's credibility.

"I'm in the Army, sir. R.O.T.C. up in Marquette. I've been to basics and have had some advanced training. I know gunfire when I hear it."

Berkowski studied the kid. He was correct with his earlier assessment based on the haircut. "How many shots did you hear?" he asked.

"Ten ... eleven ... couldn't really keep count. But it was definitely a handgun ... semiautomatic."

The Sergeant wrote down the information with cold hands and thanked the boy for his input. After getting his name and where he was staying, he sent him on his way. Berkowski did tell him to be careful on the roads.

***

By the time Ross pulled into town the fire had been extinguished. After locating an open space along the buzzing street, he took a moment to watch the firemen. They were covered with soot as they picked through the rubble that was once the Shell station. He recognized a number of local volunteers working the sight.

"Damn," he whispered as he turned off the engine. Once outside, he walked over to the remaining crowd of spectators. Gene Steubens was buddying up to Fred Wentworth and a few other men when Pickett arrived. The Mayor pretended not to see the ex-Sheriff and ducked away quietly. It was probably for the best, Ross figured. He was not up for a bickering session tonight.

"Hey, Ross." David LaFontaine was amongst the crowd of onlookers. He motioned Ross over.

"What's up, David?" Ross kept his eyes on the firemen as he approached his new friend.

"Big mess, huh? When the tanks blew, I swear it shook the whole town. Just about knocked me out of bed."

LaFontaine acted a little too excited for Ross' liking. The youthfulness was evident in his eyes ... like a boy at a fireworks show. But Ross could see right away that another tragedy had occurred. Although he did not recognize the burned out truck, he knew that its occupant or occupants could not have survived. His speculation was proven accurate when he saw two firemen loading a charred body into a bag.

Ross stood by David's side for a few minutes before deciding to take a closer look. He recognized one of the Troopers in the parking lot. He ducked under the caution tape. "Jack!"

Berkowski pivoted when he heard his name. He saw the big man approaching with a friendly smile on his face. "Hey, big Ross. How's it going?" The two men shook hands.

"What do we have here?" Ross turned his attention once again to the mess in front of them.

"Don't know for sure, Sheriff. Hey, ain't you kind of underdressed tonight?"

Ross smiled again. The man hadn't heard of his recent demotion. "Naw," he answered, "it's a long story. So what do you think happened? Drunk driver?"

"Well, we've got a body in the truck. We're not sure about the store just yet, but there was someone working the shift and he hasn't yet been accounted for. A kid on a bike says he saw a blue pickup hightailing it out of town after the explosion. There's something else that's interesting, though." Berkowski paused and turned to Ross. "A young military kid was coming out of the bar and claimed that he heard gunshots. If that's the case, then I'd say we might have a robbery-homicide on our hands."

"Damn." Ross looked into the crowd. "You haven't seen the local officer on duty around have you?" Mark was nowhere to be seen.

"Nope, just us Troopers ... and a few of your people over there."

"Sergeant!" Both men turned toward the burned building as another officer called out to them. "We've got another one!"

Ross followed Berkowski to where three firemen were hauling out another body bag. The Trooper who had beckoned the Sergeant was a woman.

"What do you have, Sammy?" questioned the senior Trooper.

"It's a male. Hard to tell how old. There's really not much to look at. The coroner will have some work to do."

Ross thought the female Trooper looked a little green in the face. He guessed that it was probably her first burn victim.

"Sammy," said Berkowski, "this is Ross Pickett, the Sheriff here in Jessup."

"Yeah," she answered, "I spoke to you on the phone a few days ago about a woman who disappeared." She eyed him curiously, wondering why the other man had said that he was the Sheriff.

Ross understood the inquisitive look and finally explained that he no longer held the position. The job had been bequeathed to his former Deputy, Mark Bennington, the one who had made the call to Appleton.

"Well, that's a damn shame," said Berkowski. Although they weren't great friends, he genuinely liked Ross Pickett. They'd gone hunting a few times after being introduced by Ray Jackson.

"Yeah, oh well. What can I do?" Ross shrugged his shoulders. It was all he could say at the moment.

Berkowski motioned for the firemen to carry the bag over to an awaiting ambulance, but Ross stopped them. "Do you mind if I have a look, Jack?"

"No, be my guest."

Ross bent over the bag and undid the zipper. As the material separated he caught wind of the awful stench of burned flesh. Holding his breath in, he pulled away the flaps to expose part of the body. "Ayeee!" He swallowed hard and then quickly covered his mouth. The outer clothing had been burned completely away. The victim's mouth was open with the lips peeled back, as if it were calling out to him. Ross noticed that a sizeable chunk of the skull was missing.

"Looks like he took one in the back of the head, Jack," said the ex-Sheriff as he hoisted himself back up to his feet.

"Well I'll be a ... would you look at that." Berkowski leaned over and saw the evidence for himself. Samantha Godson peeked over his shoulder.

"You might find similar wounds in the other one at the pump."

"Do you think it's them, Berky?" Godson raised the question that the Sergeant had already considered. His two fugitives were still in the area.

***

Chuck Barnes and Jenna Pierson had cocooned themselves in the warm, oversized sleeping bag. They held each other tight, listening to mellow tunes on the radio. A candle, the only source of light, flickered on the coffee table next to the sofa, adding a romantic aura to the room. Chuck nestled his head against his girl and whiffed the coconut fragrance of her hair. The closeness of their bodies was arousing his compulsion to go farther. He slowly slipped his good arm around the back of her shirt.

"What do think you're doing?" she whispered. Jenna rolled toward him and inadvertently nudged his injured shoulder. Chuck winced from the sudden rush of pain. "I'm sorry. I almost forgot about your ..."

"It's okay, Jen," he replied as he pulled his hand free of her shirt.

"Oh no it's not okay. I'm such a klutz. Will you forgive me?" She then carefully wrapped her arms around his waist and pulled him closer. When she kissed him the pain was forgotten. Jenna was offering herself. It would be the first time for both of them.

As Chuck's hand began to explore again, he heard something outside. It was a creaking sound. He pulled back to listen. "Did you hear that?" he asked his girlfriend.

Jenna opened her eyes, looking frustrated by the interruption. "Hear what? I didn't hear any ..."

"That," he said after the noise was repeated. It sounded like a footstep. "I think someone's outside."

"Who could it be?" Jenna now sounded nervous. "I didn't hear a car pull in."

Chuck began to wriggle his way out of the sleeping bag, careful to avoid moving his right arm that hung in the sling. When he eventually freed his entire body, he stood up.

"Chuck, just stay here," pleaded his girlfriend.

"Don't worry. I better check this out." He crept silently in his socks toward the door. Seeing the two compound bows stacked on the recliner, Chuck picked up an arrow from one of the quivers. When he reached the door, he hesitated. The pronounced creaking sound continued ... right outside. Something was definitely there.

"Chuck, don't! Please!" Jenna continued to plead with him.

Chuck turned and placed his finger on his lips trying to get her to quiet down. The teenager was intent on exposing the source of the noise. Just as he reached for the doorknob, it began to turn ... slowly ... on its own. Chuck's heart began to race. It was coming inside. He raised the arrow over his head, prepared to thrust it into the intruder.

Chuck was suddenly knocked backward by the surging door. He cried out in pain when it swung open and made contact with his shoulder. Trevor Musgrave's drunken head stuck through the gap.

"Boo!"

There was a chorus of laughter outside.

***

The truck fishtailed sideways at a junction between the crossing two-tracks. He just kept going, farther and farther into the middle of nowhere. Tyrone Pullman had absolutely no idea where he was or how he had gotten there. There had been no time to calculate direction.

The fugitive ventured onto the first available two-track after passing a speeding police cruiser heading in the opposite direction. There would be more where that one came from. The hunt was on again and Tyrone found himself living the part of the desperate prey. He had no alternative but to veer away from the main roads where the cops would be concentrating their search efforts.

"Motherfucker!" he cursed as the rear end of the Chevy slid off the trail. Tyrone was jolted against the door when the bed scraped up against a tree, but the truck kept moving forward. The driver was able to straighten the wheel and continue down the slick track. "Gotta be more careful, homes," he said to himself. The snow created hazardous conditions, and this was the last place he could afford to get stranded. The fugitive slowed a bit after noticing that his rear taillight was no longer working. While penetrating the forest, he debated the motive for making the hit on the store. But he needed food ... good American food for his journey. To *where* was yet to be determined. He couldn't allow a witness to tie him to the area. He would now be forced to improvise as his plight progressed. Regretfully, Tyrone decided that his best bet was to hole up a second time for at least a couple more days. He could stand it now that he had proper nourishment. What Tyrone Pullman didn't know was that many of the hunting camps in the U.P. were now occupied.

Two deer darted to the center of the trail. Tyrone slammed his left foot on the brake, sending the truck into an irreversible skid. When the vehicle finally nestled to a stop, the two does scampered off to safety. Tyrone buried his head in the steering wheel. He then relaxed and collapsed across the bench seat. He was tired of running. He wanted his life again. His thoughts turned to the man he killed at the old cabin where Gerald Johnson had relentlessly haunted him. In a way, that man had been a Godsend. He thought about how close he had come to purchasing that non-refundable ticket to insanity. One more day in that hellish pit and he quite possibly could have lost himself forever. Murder bestowed an awakening effect, like accidently stepping on a rusty nail with a bare foot.

Tyrone gagged at the idea of choking down another bite of deer meat. His gamey diet had depleted his energy and clogged his bowels. His clothes fit much looser than when the adventure first began. After a few meditative minutes, he slowly regained his composure. He wondered what he could have done differently in life. What other avenue was there? Somewhere down the line, something had gone terribly wrong that generated a partnership with Gerald.

The fugitive reached down to the floor of the truck and picked up a Hershey bar. He had nearly forgotten about his precious stash, the incentive for his desperate actions. He tore away the wrapping and devoured the candy. The delicious chocolate electrified his tongue and had a settling effect on his agitated nerves. He grabbed a can of Miller Lite and a bag of Doritos. The food made him feel closer to home.

When finished with his quick meal, Tyrone sighed deeply as if he had just finished a Thanksgiving dinner at his Uncle Ben's house. He rolled down the window and allowed the fresh air to flow through the cab. It was cool and invigorating. He was actually beginning to feel better.

"I ain't never gonna let you in my head again," he said referring to his dead friend.

Acting like a new man who had just been saved, Tyrone decided that it was time to move on. If nothing else, he still had his freedom, and his life. It was now time to find shelter for the night. He wanted a bed. Tyrone reached for the ignition, but just as he was ready to turn the key, he heard a faint, but familiar '*thumping*' noise. He listened quietly as the noise came closer.

"What the hell is that?" he whispered to himself. The soft '*thumping*' became louder and louder, until finally evolving into a wicked vibration that swayed the trees around him. "Oh Jesus!" cried the fugitive. Tyrone instinctively ducked as the chopper passed directly overhead. He watched in horror as a powerful ray of light blazed down from the heavens.

***

Frank Powell was watching the tail end of the LSU-Florida State game when the call came in. A part of him was angry that he would be unable to see the final quarter of the Friday night special edition of college football. LSU had just come back from a twenty-one point deficit, and it was going to be one helluva fourth. Frank Powell, however, was a professional and would carry out his duty as ordered. Besides, he loved to fly, especially at night. When it came to piloting, he was the best in the business.

Powell was currently in his fifth year as a member of the Michigan State Police Air Corp. Carrying over the many talents learned while serving in the United States Army, the thirty-five-year-old bachelor gained the reputation as one of the most capable pilots in the Upper Peninsula. He was good and everyone knew it, including Frank Powell.

The pilot had been born and raised in Newberry. After receiving an honorable discharge, he knew that his calling was to return home. Although jobs downstate paid more than those in the north, he found the exhilaration of skirting the treetops at someone else's expense to be compensation enough. As a pilot in the Upper Peninsula, he was primarily summoned for search and rescue missions when misguided civilians lost their way in the expanse of the Michigan wilderness. Plucking campers and hunters from helpless situations was fulfilling, but the real action came with the forest fires. Frank had saved the asses of many ground humpers in his time.

He and his co-pilot, Mario Delvechio, also a former military man, were dispatched to Jessup, only a five minute flight from the airfield. The mission was to seek out a blue Chevy pickup that had taken a westerly heading. Two suspects were wanted in connection with a double homicide.

"Nice night to fly," yelled Delvechio as he hopped up onto the skid of the Bell JetRanger.

"It's an awesome night to fly, Vech," answered the pilot, taking a moment to gaze up to the dark skies. Actually it was quite the opposite of perfect, but any opportunity to fly was just fine with him.

The two men settled into the chopper. Powell fired up the engine while the co-pilot sang through the pre-flight checklist.

***

Tyrone Pullman could not force his body to move. The menacing helicopter hovered directly overhead. The sound of the rotors pounded his eardrums. “Leave me the fuck alone!” he screamed at the ceiling of the truck, but his cries were drowned out by the suffocating noise. He then heard those dreaded words.

“Hold your position! This is the police! Do not move!”

Tyrone was trapped with nowhere to go. How had they found him in the middle of nowhere? “Fuck it,” he declared decisively. “If you gonna take me, then you gonna have to earn me.” He was sick of running.

When the fugitive opened the door and stepped out, the helicopter reacted. The chopper performed a complete 180-degree turn, keeping its nose and spotlight aimed at him on the ground below.

“Hold your position!” repeated the voice from the sky. “Turn around and place your hands on the truck or you will be fired upon.”

Tyrone did not yield to the bluff. They could not possibly shoot at him, or so he hoped. His only option was to try and disable the machine long enough to give him time to escape. There were probably a hundred cops converging on his location. He looked up at the blinding light and smiled. Then, Tyrone Pullman opened the toolbox in the back of the truck.

***

The two Troopers had been in the air for twenty minutes. Frank Powell was skillfully finessing the treetops just as the Army Corps had trained him to do. Although his craft did not possess the same capabilities as the AH-64 Apache, Frank still enjoyed the way the JetRanger handled. When it came to commercial helicopters, the Bell product was second to none. The Allison 250-C20J engine kicked out over 420 horsepower, and with a light load, the pilot could push the chopper close to 140 miles per hour. Delvechio was accustomed to his partner’s daring behavior behind the stick. Powell’s hard banking at excess speeds was arousing for him as well.

"We're coming up on our search site, Vech. Better activate the eye," said the pilot as he slowed the charging bird. He was referring to the Flir Systems gimbaled sensor attached to the nose. The infrared camera was used to detect heat sources on the ground when visibility was low. The *'eye,'* as it was called in the profession, was a basketball sized sphere with a 2x electrical optical zoom scanning process. It was capable of providing a complete hemispherical coverage with a 360-degree rotation.

The Air Team's job was to search the endless miles of two-tracks cutting through the forests to the west of Jessup. The cruisers would be effectively scouring the main roads. When the *'eye'* was activated, Delvechio attached the night vision goggles to his helmet. The outline of the treetops soon came into focus. He could see the landscape against an eerie green backdrop. Mario immediately detected five objects on the deck with an orange glow ... body heat.

"Anything down there?" asked the pilot as he pulled into the proper search speed. Moving too fast could nullify the effects of the infrared system.

"A few animals. Probably deer."

"We're looking for two men, buddy. Let's not be doing any sightseeing up here tonight."

Delvechio laughed under his breath. Powell could be such a cocky SOB. "You just do the flying, old timer. Let me do the rest."

"Old timer!" objected the pilot. "You're only a few months behind me, little brother. Be careful who you're calling old. I might just ..."

"Hold it, Frank." Delvechio cut his partner's jab short. "I think I have something here."

Powell slowed the JetRanger to a crawl, allowing Delvechio time to scope out the object that had drawn his attention. "What is it?" he asked as he looked out his side window. He could see nothing through the darkness.

The co-pilot trained his eyes on the large, glowing blemish directly beneath them. "Don't know for sure," he answered, "but it looks big."

"By itself?"

"Yeah, it's just standing there like it doesn't even see us."

"Deer?" asked Powell.

"Don't think so. Too big. Jesus, what the hell is that?"

"Bear maybe?" That was the last guess that the pilot could offer.

"A bear would be running his ass off by now," said Delvechio. He zoomed in on the alien creature. It was definitely standing, but it was too large to be a man. He tweaked the joystick that controlled the camera and scanned the surrounding area. There was another source of heat to the north. "Let's let this one go for a second, Frank. There's something else at your two o'clock."

Powell eased the helicopter to the north, waiting for further instructions.

"Hundred yards, hold your heading. Looks like it could be a vehicle." Delvechio watched intently as Powell steered him closer. The orange blip began to take shape. "Fifty yards, hold your heading." He could now see the outline of the truck against the snow-covered ground. The engine was still hot. He guessed that it had just been shut off. And there was one solitary life form with it. "Okay, Frank, we may have something here. But I'm only detecting one person. Let's check it out anyway."

***

The female remembered the sound emerging from the sky. She had seen many of the flying machines during the warm season when the fires had threatened her clan. As the machine came closer, the female began to wonder if it was searching for her. She felt panic at first, but she was in her element. They could not spot her underneath the canopy of trees. She understood how to blend with the environment.

When the machine slowed to a stop directly over her position, the female began to question her decision to remain in place. She continued to stand completely still, thinking that she had underestimated its capabilities. She then thought that it might be bluffing. It was a familiar tactic. Provoke movement from the hidden prey. Allow the hunted to compromise its position and then attack. The female remained anchored to the trunk of the large tree, camouflaged by the thick branches. She prepared herself for a fight.

Then, the machine slowly drifted away. Her intuition had been correct. It did not see her after all. She watched as it floated over the tops of the trees toward the one she had been stalking. She cautiously followed.

***

"You ready?" asked the pilot.

"Just a sec." Delvechio took one last look to make sure they were in position. Neither the vehicle nor the occupant had made a move. He wondered whether or not that was a good sign. The goggles were removed as he reached for the control to the spotlight.

"Light it up, Vech," ordered Powell.

Mario flicked the switch and activated the powerful beam. The truck immediately came into view. It was blue, but it only had one occupant. Delvechio wondered if the other hit on the Flir a short distance away was the partner.

"Okay, Vech, ask the occupant to please step out of the vehicle ... and be polite."

The co-pilot did as he was told and ordered the man via the loudspeaker to exit the truck. Powell, in the meantime, reported their location to dispatch. For a moment it appeared as though nothing was going to happen. Both Troopers expected the suspect to bolt, especially if it was the truck they were seeking. Then, the door swung open and a black man stepped out.

"What the heck do we have here?" questioned the pilot.

"Did they say anything about the suspects being black?" asked Delvechio.

"Nope, just that there was a blue pickup involved."

As the two Troopers surveyed the situation, the man on the ground turned towards the truck and opened the tool box.

"What the hell is that idiot doing? I don't like the looks of this, Vech."

The co-pilot ordered the man to cease and place his hands against the truck. He even tried a little intimidation by claiming that they would fire if he failed to comply. It was a fabrication that often proved quite effective. Only in the movies did they really take shots from choppers.

"Holy shit!" cried Powell, but his reaction was too late. He heard the distinct pinging sounds of bullets slicing through the helicopter's underbelly. When he tried to bank away he felt the stick tighten in his hands. The machine tilted hard to the port side. "Christ! She's spilling something, Vech! I can't control her! Hang on, buddy! We're going down!" Powell fought the stick as the helicopter began to spin in circles. They were plummeting hard toward the trees. He was too engrossed with the task at hand to notice that his partner was slumped over in his seat, gutted from a round that had ripped through his rectum and exited through his chest. Mario Delvechio had been killed instantly.

Powell knew that he could not save his ship. Rounds from the automatic rifle continued to pepper the chopper. With no suitable LZ in sight, he had only one opportunity to save their lives. He had to go for the shooter on the ground below and hope for the best.

Just when he thought he was going to miss his target, he amassed all of his strength and yanked the hard stick to the right. The JetRanger leaned one final time and then collided with the truck. As the rotors snapped against the tall pines lining the trail, shards of metal whistled through the air. Powell felt something give in his back at the point of impact. After a terrible grinding sound, the chopper rolled off the vehicle and wedged upside down against two trees. Powell hung loosely in the pilot seat, unable to move his legs. The pain in his back was unbearable.

***

Tyrone Pullman could not believe his eyes. He had actually done it. The Chopper jerked and sputtered in the night sky. It then started falling. He dove into the cover of some nearby trees as the machine crashed into his truck. A four foot hunk of metal from the rotor imbedded itself into the trunk only four inches above his head.

"Yeah, fuck you!" he yelled in triumph when silence returned to the forest. He had beaten the odds again. He was surviving. He surveyed the heaping remains of the helicopter like a hunter admiring his trophy. But as the adrenaline rush began to wear off, so did his moment of glory. He saw what was left of the truck, his only means of escape. Reality now found him stranded in a place where he did not belong. He was alone. His body shivered from the cold that was quickly penetrating his sweat-soaked clothing.

With rifle in hand, Tyrone jogged over to the flattened truck. He reached through a narrow crevice leading to the caved-in toolbox and extracted a bandoleer holding ten clips for the Klashnikov. Tyrone stole one last look at the disabled helicopter. He then turned and ran off. With no current plan to guide him, his best bet was to just keep moving until an opportunity presented itself. Tyrone had to keep his body in motion in order to stay warm. He would continue to improvise.

***

Frank Powell was suspended upside down. The rush of blood created an intense headache. The pain in his back worsened with each breath. Snow blew into the cockpit through the shattered window. He fumbled with the latch to his safety belt, but it would not release. Powell battled the urge to panic, knowing that he had suffered a serious injury to his spinal column. His legs dangled to the sides as if they were performing the splits in an inverted position. He wanted to cry out, but he didn't. Powell took a deep breath ... or as deep as his pain would allow. *Okay,* he told himself, *remain calm.* He was alive, and that's all that mattered right now. Help was on the way. They were able to call in their location prior to going down.

"Vech," he whispered weakly. "Vech?" There was no response. He slowly rolled his head to the side and saw his partner's limp body. A stream of blood drained from the exit hole in his chest.

"Oh Jesus, Vech!" This time he did cry out. Mario Delvechio, his partner and friend for three years, was dead. He turned his head away, wondering how he had screwed up. Maybe if he had been higher, or rolled the opposite way. Powell then noticed the mike hanging loosely from the radio. He raised his arm and reached out, but it was too far away. He brought his arm back to his side and prayed for help to arrive soon. He was beginning to feel nauseous.

When the pilot opened his eyes after a few minutes, he heard a twig, or branch, snap somewhere outside the cockpit. He hadn't detected any squad cars pulling in. And then a thought came to him. The fugitive! Had he returned to finish the job? Now he did begin to panic. He had no means of defending himself. They weren't required to carry a weapon when they flew. Frank Powell was a sitting duck. He could hear the footsteps now ... coming closer toward the open window. The blowing snow made visibility poor.

"Who's out there!" he called to the darkness. "Stop or I'll shoot!" Still, the footsteps came closer. Another branch snapped. The bluff had fallen on deaf ears. "Stop right now or I will fire!" It was a final attempt to stop the advance. Every time he spoke, the pain exploded in his back. Powell's eyes strained to see through the darkness. With his side of the helicopter leaning at a downward angle, he could only make out a few tree trunks. Then, two of those tree trunks began to move. He watched in horror as the thick *legs* walked toward the chopper ... one lengthy stride after another. The pilot's body began to shake as his imagination drew pictures of the creature attached to those legs. Ten yards ... five yards. When they finally reached the chopper he could now hear its heavy breathing. An awful smell filled the cockpit. The pilot stared down at two massive, hairy feet directly beneath him. He counted the toes ... ten of them ... each tipped with a black, crusted nail. Powell's head began to roll from side to side. His world was spinning in circles.

The helicopter suddenly began to shift. As the craft moved, so did his body in the belt that harnessed him. He screamed from the intolerable pain in his back. It felt as though someone were twisting his spine. Powell's legs were now hanging in his face. The added pressure against his chest made it even more difficult to breathe, but he kept his eyes on the beast outside. Slowly, the helicopter began to rise off the ground as if someone had placed a jack underneath it. His eyes followed the line of the legs to the torso ... to the chest ... the wide neck. And then ... the face! Frank Powell screamed again as the massive hand surged through the open space and wrapped around his head.

***

Tyrone stopped in his tracks when he heard the muffled roar over the winds. It seemed close, but yet it wasn't. He spun around and searched the trail with frightened eyes. There was nothing there. He looked to the trees on both sides to see if anything or anyone was following. Fingers caressed a fresh clip in the bandoleer hanging over his shoulder. The extra ammunition added a false sense of security to whatever lay ahead for him.

The fugitive's lack of movement for even the shortest period was causing his body temperature to drop. He was out of breath after the two hundred yard dash from the truck. His stamina had deteriorated greatly over the past few weeks. He gasped for breath, wondering if what he had heard was just in his head. There were a number of things that had been playing in his thoughts ... some real and some not. Tyrone was having a hard time distinguishing between the two. But the sound was something that he'd never heard before. Tyrone shook off the notion. He forced himself to believe that it had been a figment of his imagination, most likely the wind in the trees. He had to keep his wits about him.

After a short period of rest, Tyrone continued down the trail at a much slower pace.

CHAPTER THIRTEEN

The demonic wolves had returned to the woman's side like pets protecting their master's flanks. Two sets of fiery eyes glowered at him as he retreated. A bloody froth formed in their mouths. He tried to call out to her ... to say her name. But words would not come. He could not speak as some unseen force strangled his vocal chords. The four-legged beasts slithered on their bellies. They backed him up against the cliff with their jaws feverishly chomping, preparing to feast. He turned and peered hopelessly into the bottomless gorge from which there was no escape. The woman followed her pets closer.

Why is she doing this to me? He had loved this woman with all of his heart. They had a life together. He could not see her hooded face, but he knew who she was ... who she had been. But still, she persisted in tormenting him from her purgatory. Methodically, she raised her bony arm and pointed at his heaving chest. The wolves looked up to her, awaiting the command. And then she spoke, with a voice unlike that which he remembered. He knew that voice from ...

It waits for you,
In black of night,
There is no mercy,
To ease your plight.

Beg salvation,
Repent your deed,
Or lose your soul,
To Satan's weed.

If you will the courage,
To face the demons within,
Then pray with pure heart,
The journey ends with Amen.

The woman's raspy chant spawned hunger in the devil dogs. They snarled and snapped at the air. With a flick of her wrist, the winds blew and the ground trembled. He was losing his balance. And then, as one powerful gust arose from the pits of hell, the shroud was blown from her head. He stared in disbelief at the woman's face ... the one who he did not expect to see. It was not Eevie beneath the black cloak. It was ... it was his Maggie.

She looked at him with burning eyes, despising him for existing. *But it couldn't be her*, he thought. Her open mouth revealed jagged, rotten teeth. She looked to the wolves and smiled. They appeared to return the gesture, knowing that her next command would give them pleasure. She raised her pointed finger a second time and shrieked.

"Kill him!"

Both animals vaulted from the ground ... one high and the other low. He felt a searing pain as teeth sank deep into his calf. He could not cry out. The other beast lunged and locked its jaws around his neck. It twisted and pulled, suffocating the life from his feeble body. The ground beneath him began to squirm. He looked down in horror to see that he was standing on a bed of vipers. He stumbled backward and fell farther and farther into the abyss. As light turned into darkness, he could see the woman at the top of the cliff laughing.

"Ross! Ross!"

He opened his eyes and saw her. The scream that followed was real. His body trembled.

"Ross!" cried Maggie again. "What's gotten into you?" She reached for his shoulder, but he pulled away. He looked at her as if she were a stranger. "What's the matter?"

Maggie had witnessed his rough nights before, but she never mentioned it to Ross for fear that it might embarrass him. She had heard him cry out the name of his former wife. A part of her was jealous that she was still in his thoughts, but she had come to the realization that Ross would always love the woman he married. She couldn't blame him for that. He was an emotional man who kept his feelings locked away. Ross had gone through hell following Eevie's death, and Maggie had been there for him. She would always be there for him.

Ross did not shun her second attempt to reach out. She began to caress his shoulder, feeling the tightness. "Are you okay, hon?"

His muscles finally relaxed as the real world came into focus. It was Maggie Barnes sitting next to him and not some horrifying apparition from one of his nightmares. He smiled at her as he shook off the troubling visions from his sleep.

"Yeah, Maggs," said Ross gently. "I'm just fine. A bad dream I guess." He leaned over and kissed her cheek. She wrapped her arms around his neck and held him close.

***

The sun was casting its first rays on the morning of October 1st, the opening day of the Michigan bowhunting season. Alex Chavez's senses were sharp as he sat in his stand awaiting the trophy that had visited him in his sleep every night for the past few months. There was barely a breeze to cover even the slightest of noises. The swamp was deathly quiet. Alex had been sitting motionless in the stand for over an hour. Although the temperature was beginning to rise, it was still bitterly cold. The fabric of his facemask could not contain the steam from his breath.

The hunter allowed his thoughts to wander to take his mind off the chill penetrating his fleece pullover. It had been an eventful evening for the college kids. First, it was Trevor's foolish antics with the local redneck at the bar, and then the explosion, which they later heard had killed two people. When the group made it back to the cabin, Trevor was insistent on scaring the hell out of Brenda's cousin. Alex smiled, recalling her boyfriend's fall when his roommate burst through the door. It took a while for him to get over the gag, but he did eventually loosen up. And boy did they drink. The two teenagers were passed out in less than an hour. Brenda thwarted Trevor's plan to cover them with shaving cream.

Alex had been somewhat disappointed when Kayla passed out in his arms before they could have a little alone time. He was forced to listen quietly as the headboard banged against the wall in the next room. When the alarm clock sounded at four-thirty A.M., Trevor was dead to the world. Alex had to drag his naked body from the bed and splash cold water on his moping face. After a few slugs of piping hot coffee, he was a new man and ready to hunt some whitetail.

It doesn't get any better than this, thought Alex Chavez as he watched a black squirrel peek out of its nest high in the tree above him. The moon had descended over the horizon and the swamp began to wake up. Alex shifted his weight slightly to alleviate a cramp. As he moved, the metal stand creaked. He winced, knowing that anything within a hundred yards would have heard the disruption. Although subtle to human ears, the noise was an explosion in the animal world. *Shit!* he cursed to himself. What a great way to screw up a perfect setup.

He listened for the sound of deer scampering off to safety. Nothing happened. He began to wonder if Trevor had heard his blunder. *Man would he be pissed,* he thought. He would never hear the end of it either. Alex relaxed and leaned back against the trunk of the tree, but before his thoughts drifted off again, a twig snapped.

The hunter's heart picked up a beat as he surveyed the trail leading into his shooting lane at the base of the ridge. His mind raced with possibilities. This time the metal stand remained quiet. Another twig snapped. It was an animal ... coming his way. With his legs properly positioned, he attached the release to the string with his right hand. A lone owl hooted off in the distance, and then a squirrel began to bark. The forest was alive.

Alex took short, controlled breaths, keeping his eyes focused on that trail. He saw a flash of movement ... a flicker of white. It was a tail ... a whitetail. He could feel his heart pounding against the inner wall of his chest. Alex watched anxiously through the branches as the deer cautiously skirted the edge of the swamp. The sunlight glistened off a bone-white antler. It was a buck! Though it wasn't a big deer, it was still a buck. *My first rack with a bow,* he hoped. This would be his chance. Alex waited patiently until the animal was out of sight behind a tree before drawing. He no longer felt the cold air. When the deer meandered into the shooting lane, he placed the fifteen yard pin just behind the shoulder. He couldn't have asked for a better opportunity. His conscience battled with the fact that it was only a four-point, but his yearning to make his first kill with the bow was overwhelming.

As Alex's finger touched the trigger on the release, his peripheral vision detected more movement off to his left. He hesitated on the shot and stole a quick peek through the trees. The buck's rack was bigger than any he'd ever seen in the wild. The tines rose high above its gray head. Alex watched as the small fork-horn looked back to check out the larger deer. It then pranced through the shooting lane and on down the trail. That opportunity was gone, but the risk was deserving of the potential reward. It took all the energy that he could muster to maintain the draw. He struggled to hold the string steady. The buck ducked its head into the shooting lane and exposed the full trophy atop its head. Alex counted the eight perfect, chocolate-colored tines, none of which were shorter than ten inches. It had at least an eighteen inch inside spread. The deer lifted its head and scented the air. *Come on,* urged Alex, coaxing the animal in his mind to step forward.

Then, as if the deer were heeding his command, it took a step into the shooting lane only fifteen yards away. Alex tightened the muscles in his arms to steady the shaking pin on its broad shoulder. When he released the arrow, the buck instinctively ducked. But its evasive maneuver was in vein. The arrow slammed hard into its side. Alex felt a sense of relief when he saw the blood flowing from the open wound. His eyes followed the animal's path as it darted up the ridge behind him and stopped. He became a little worried when it started back in his direction ... walking as if nothing had happened. He then began to question the accuracy of the shot, wondering if he had hit it too far back.

Alex couldn't let him get into the swamp. He pulled another arrow from the quiver and knocked it in place. The buck walked directly underneath his stand and started for the thick cover. Alex drew the string back and took quick aim. But before he released the second arrow, the buck stopped. It staggered a bit, and then fell over dead. Alex Chavez was a virgin no more. His body began to shake uncontrollably.

"Alex!" The cry came from the direction of Trevor's stand.

***

Reggie Stillwater was suffering the consequences of a long, first night of deer camp. He had been in his stand for two lengthy hours as a jackhammer ran rampant in his throbbing head. His eyes would periodically close. When he reopened them he would find himself leaning dangerously close to the rail of the climber, staring at the twenty-foot drop to the ground. Every so often he would adjust the safety harness to ensure that it was snug around his shoulders, just in case.

What Reggie really wanted to do was shimmy down the tall oak and pass out. But if any of his buddies were to find him ... well, that was out of the question on opening day. It was sacrilegious to miss the opener for the rifle and bow openers regardless of physical or mental state.

"Why do I do this to myself?" he whispered to himself. Every year the same ... booze it up at the Jessup Inn and then stumble back to camp. He had been up sixty bucks in the burn game before the trip into town, but by the time the cards were put away for the evening he was at least fifty in the hole. For the last seven years, they had been hunting state land near Jessup. Only once had a member of their camp succeeded in shooting a deer. Stocking up the freezer with venison was not their purpose for the pilgrimage to the Michigan wilderness. It provided five men who graduated college together an opportunity to catch up and tighten their bond. And if one of them happened to get a buck in the process, then it would just be another reason to celebrate.

Reggie reached into his fanny pack for a plastic bag of essentials. He withdrew three Extra-Strength Tylenol tablets and popped them into his mouth that felt as though it had been stuffed with cotton balls. He then loosened the cap on his canteen and took a few swigs of water. He thought how nice it would be to have a warm bed. Sleeping on folding cots got old in a hurry. It was times like this when he really appreciated the comforts of home and family. He was cold, thirsty, and tired. But the hunter also understood that he had better relish this moment of quiet solitude because as soon as the boys gathered for lunch, the booze would begin to flow for the second go-around.

The hunter closed his eyes and tried to think away the brutal headache. A noise startled him. It was a shuffling sound beyond his line of sight, just behind a thick patch of briars. A high-pitched growl, like that of a small dog emerged from the brush. Another growl erupted with a slightly different pitch. Although

Reggie had never seen a coyote in the wild before, he'd often heard them howling in the night.

The first coyote darted into the clearing and then stopped to look around. It was carrying something in its mouth. The object looked to be a piece of meat ... possibly a rabbit. The second animal copied the pattern of the first, nipping at its tail as if it were trying to slow its progress. Reggie studied the animals. The pleasant distraction gave him a short reprieve from his hangover. Both coyotes had thick, mangy hides. Each mouth was stained red, indicating that the kill was fresh and the battle for the final bite was ongoing. The animal holding the remains of the rabbit crouched low to the ground and growled viciously at the challenger. The second coyote then lit into the first, snapping its teeth. Both animals rolled on the ground, unaware of the hunter watching from above.

Reggie could not resist the chance to bag a coyote. He would be king of the camp for a good day or two, unless of course someone was to accidently kill a buck. He rose to his feet and drew back the string on his Matthews. He placed the first pin on the back of the coyote holding the rabbit and waited for the shot. The animals decided to take a break from the scuffle. They stood snout-to-snout, staring at one another, baring teeth. Reggie released the string. He watched the wobbly flight of the arrow until it hit the target squarely in the spine, dropping it instantly. Reggie was stunned that he had made the shot. The other animal disappeared in seconds into the forest.

Anxious to inspect his prize, the jubilant hunter swiftly maneuvered his climber down the straight trunk of the tree. He hopped off the base and walked over to the dead animal that lay sprawled out on all fours in the snow. Blood drained from the fatal wound down both sides of its hunched back.

"The guys aren't going to believe this," said Reggie, knowing that he had just scored big in the eyes of his peers. It was damn near as exhilarating as shooting a buck, at least from what he imagined it would be like. He could have the hide tanned and the head mounted like a bearskin rug.

With a prideful smile, Reggie Stillwater stood over his trophy like a conquering Napoleon. As he was bending down to grab the rear legs for the drag back to camp, he noticed the hunk of meat still protruding from its mouth. Reggie raised his boot and kicked the side of the coyote's head. The meat fell free and rolled into the snow. Reggie felt a sudden eruption in his stomach as he stared in shock at the exposed object. He doubled over and vomited. The human hand lay motionless next to the fresh puddle of regurgitated breakfast.

***

Alex could hear his roommate's heavy breathing from fifty yards away. He purposefully ignored Trevor's pleas for help, anticipating the look on his face when he saw the big buck. Alex judged Trevor must have shot the four-point that continued down the trail. The hunter's heart was still racing from the adrenaline rush. He couldn't wait to parade his prize.

"Jesus, Al! Didn't you hear me calling?" Trevor popped up over a short rise. Alex just sat and smiled at his buddy who struggled to drag his deer across a troublesome log. "You know ... a little help ... would be appreciated," said Trevor, attempting to catch his breath. His face was cherry red and dripping with sweat. Trevor hesitated when he saw the queer look on his friend's face. "What the hell are you grinning at?"

"Just admiring a real set of horns," said Alex proudly.

Trevor hauled the small buck down the embankment. "What are you talking about?" He then saw the eight-point lying next to the fresh gut pile. "Holy shit! Holy shit!" Trevor raced over and knelt down next to the much larger animal. He hoisted the rack in his hands. "I don't believe it!" he roared. "This is a monster!"

"I can't believe you shot that dinky thing there," chided Alex as he slapped his friend on the shoulder. "I just couldn't bring myself to do it when he passed right in front of me."

"Oh don't give me that crap. Man, I can't believe you got this big bastard. You have to mount it, Al."

"I know, Trev. I'll sell my car if I have to." Alex had already been thinking about where he was going to get the funds.

The two friends then sat together and shared in the moment. The long drag back to the cabin would be welcome exercise.

***

Maggie poured a cup of hot coffee and placed it in front of Ross who was mulling over the morning sports page.

"Are you going out with LaFontaine again?" she asked with some skepticism.

Ross looked up and saw her pouting expression. "Yeah, Maggs. I'll probably be out most of the day." When he saw her wrinkled forehead he knew that she was upset. *Better nip this one in the bud,* he thought as he stroked her hand. "Don't worry, babe. I'll be home by dark. I promise." He offered a confident smile and retuned his attention to the newspaper. As he listened to her walk off without a word, Ross hoped for a quick end to the charade. Maggie would not let on verbally, but he could feel the tension building again between them. *Just a while longer, Maggs,* he said to himself silently as he looked to the empty hallway leading to the bedroom.

Ross straightened up when he heard a vehicle pull into the driveway. He stood and peered out the kitchen window. It was a blue Ford Explorer with Pete Wilkerson behind the wheel. The councilman parked behind the Tahoe and strolled up to the door. Ross opened it before he could ring the bell.

"Morning, Pete. What brings you out this way?" Ross thought the man appeared worried. His smile was phony.

"We need to talk, Ross. I'm sorry to bother you, but this is important."

"Come on in, councilman. We can chat in the kitchen." The presence of the unexpected visitor triggered a nervous reaction in the ex-Sheriff. Something was wrong. He led Wilkerson to the table and offered him a chair that was graciously accepted. Maggie had returned from the bedroom.

"Good morning, Pete," she said with a load of laundry in her hands.

"Hi, Maggie. Good to see you again."

Ross noticed the lack of eye contact from the visitor. Maggie set the dirty clothes down on the counter. She was not going to allow them any privacy ... not this time. Ross thought he would be pressing his luck by making such a demand.

"What brings you out here, Pete?" asked Maggie, inserting herself into the conversation.

"Well, I've got some bad news." Wilkerson took a deep breath before continuing. "Mark Bennington's squad car was found earlier this morning by some hunters out on the Benson Track about five miles in."

Ross pictured the approximate location in his head. The Benson Track was an old logging trail that ran through the Chiahawah State Forest just outside of Jessup. It was a popular route for hunters in the fall and snowmobilers in the winter. It was a picturesque trail, winding along a number of high ridges bordering the ... the Amen. *Oh God!* Ross' face wilted from a premonition that Pete Wilkerson was about to unveil some horrific news.

"Anyways," continued the councilman, "the car was a mess. It was smashed against a tree." He shook his head. "Evidently, there was blood everywhere. That's what I gathered from the Troopers investigating the scene."

"What about Mark?" asked Ross abruptly. *Christ, why didn't I tell the kid?*

Wilkerson looked him in the eyes. "I don't know, Ross. He wasn't there. He was ... just gone."

"What the hell do you mean he was just gone?" Ross' voice was elevating, but he was not angry with the man at his table. He could only be mad with his own selfish motives to hide what he knew.

"Just like I said, Ross ... he's gone. They didn't find a body ... nothing. The State Police really think something happened to him. I guess the car looked like it was assaulted and a struggle ensued."

"Oh Jesus." Ross buried his face in his hands. Maggie came around and gently rubbed his back. "What was Mark doing out there?" he asked.

"It appears he had company."

"Who?" Ross allowed his hands to fall to his unshaven chin. "Who would Mark have been riding with out *there*?" Now he was truly confused.

"Well, it sounds like Mark may have been having a little fling with Sharon Cooper." Pete acted uncomfortable that he had to reveal that information. He wasn't one for spreading rumors.

"Sharon? You've got to be kidding! How did you come by that conclusion?" Ross had never suspected. Mark had a wife ... and kids. *That stupid bastard!*

"The police found evidence that a female had been in the car ... a bra ... a pair of ...," Pete hesitated and looked up to Maggie, unsure as to whether or not he should continue. But he did anyway. "They found a pair of women's underwear. When they questioned his wife, she was the one who popped the name."

Ross couldn't believe what he was hearing. *Mark Bennington and Sharon Cooper together ... and now they were missing ... or dead?* He had a sinking feeling in his stomach that had become all too familiar. His guilt was agonizing.

"There's something else, Ross." Pete Wilkerson then went on to share what happened with the police chopper. MSP was in the process of combing the countryside for the wanted men who were now being tied to the shooting downstate a few weeks ago. The hunt for the cop-killers was now their priority. He further explained the discovery of the cabin where it was thought the men had holed up for a while. A utility worker was found murdered, execution-style.

It was all so surreal how his tiny, shithole of a town could suddenly be hit with such a plague of absurdity. Jessup was suddenly in turmoil and he was right smack in the middle of it. *But it wasn't Jessup*, he thought. *It was that goddamned swamp!*

The end is coming,
Death is near,
Follow the path,
Suppress your fear.

If you will the courage,
To face the demons within,
Then pray with pure heart,
The journey ends with Amen.

"Ross?" The councilman interrupted his reflection.

"Sorry, Pete. Just a lot to jaw on I guess," he answered slowly.

"I convened the council this morning to discuss Mark's disappearance and what actions we should take in light of recent events." The statement caused Ross to raise an eyebrow.

Wilkerson continued. "We took a vote and it was nearly unanimous." The councilman gave him a little smirk.

"What kind of vote, Pete?" Now it was Ross' turn to give a hard stare.

"This town needs a police presence to stay in touch with what's going on around here. We need a Sheriff, Ross. We would like to reinstate you."

Ross Pickett had mixed emotions about Wilkerson's offer. He still felt a tremendous amount of resentment to how his termination had been handled. He then began thinking about David LaFontaine and his wild quest. If there actually was something stalking the Amen, he would be much better suited to help if he held the position. He glanced up to Pete. "You said nearly unanimous. Need I ask who voted '*nay*' on the issue?"

"No, Ross. You need not ask. You damn well know who it was, but it doesn't matter. The Mayor has only so much power. It didn't take much persuading to make the rest of the boys see the light."

Ross suppressed his urge to smile as he visualized Steubens hollering at the council for siding against him. He gave them credit for standing up to the prick. But a smile did not cross his face. There was nothing funny about what had happened and the job he now had to execute. "Alright, Pete. I'll do it."

"That's great, Ross. Here ... you'll need this." Wilkerson took a badge out of his coat pocket and slid it across the table. "I think we can bypass the swearing in ceremony."

Ross felt Maggie's hands tighten on his shoulders. His thoughts shifted to the fugitives running loose in the U.P. He was apprehensive about Chuck being away from home. Although Ontonogon was a hike from Jessup, it was impossible to predict where desperate men would go. He wanted him home.

"Maggie?" Ross turned and faced her. "Would you do me a huge favor and call Paul Fuller. Ask him if he would go get Chuck and his boys and bring them in."

"I will, Ross." Maggie knew right away why he was asking. She did not want him out there either.

***

The snow had already begun to melt when Tyrone Pullman awoke from his dreamless sleep. Sunshine filtered through the large, bay window and warmed his skin. It was a soothing feeling, like taking a warm bath after returning home from a long, wintry day of sledding in the park. They were pleasant images of a faded childhood. But those days were long removed. He would never see his hometown again.

Tyrone clumsily rolled out of bed. His legs ached from the hike. He rubbed the sleep from his eyes and surveyed the spacious room around him. It was a comfortable place. The decor displayed a woman's touch with soft colors and frilly draperies. When his eyes spotted the AK-47 nestled against a rocking chair, the memory of how he had come to be in that place returned to him.

The fugitive trotted out to the living room. The four bodies were still there ... a grim reminder of his seemingly unsalvageable plight. His boot slipped on a few of the spent casings on the carpeted floor. He looked down from the blood-stained walls and peered into the dead eyes of his latest victims. It was two grown men with two young boys ... a father-son outing brutally interrupted by a stranger who had no business being there. He wondered what they had been thinking when he burst through the door uninvited ... the shock ... the pain ... the blood. The boys had screamed for their fathers as he unleashed the barrage of lead. Tyrone Pullman had lost all respect for human life. He felt nothing for them. He had become a machine, not unlike his former partner. He was turning into the very thing that he despised. But he had to go on. He had to live.

Tyrone decided against disposing of the bodies. He was not planning on extending his stay. It was more important for him to conserve his strength now. After retrieving a leftover hunk of ham and some cheese from the refrigerator, he returned to the bedroom to live out the remainder of the day. He would rest until nightfall, and then continue his expedition in the car parked outside.

***

"Goddammit! I tell you, Ted, I'm going to bring that no good sonuvabitch down if it's the last thing I do!" Gene Steubens let loose his ire at the contractor's expense. The Mayor's ego had taken a heavy beating that morning. He couldn't believe that the council had actually reinstated Ross Pickett after all he'd done to discredit the man. *And for what?* he asked himself. *Because that idiot kid disappeared.* But that was his fault. Steubens was kicking himself for not going out and finding someone who knew what the hell he was doing. Instead, he had promoted a zit-faced punk whose hero in life was the very man the Mayor spurned.

"I think you're over-reacting a bit, Gene. It sounds like the council had to make a move, and Ross was available." Ted Newhouser didn't understand the erratic behavior of his business associate. Ross Pickett *was* a good man. He had been surprised when they took away his badge.

Steubens' scowl relayed his animosity. "Over-react my ass!" he cried. "That man will not rest until he sees this town crumble from boredom." He hesitated, and then pointed his chunky forefinger at the contractor's chest. "And you can bet the farm, Ted that I will not rest until he is put in his place."

Newhouser was becoming irritated with the man who seemed to have a one-track mind. The contractor had more important things to worry about. He was still minus two heavy equipment operators. "I really don't have time for this, Gene. If you want to scream and holler about one of your own little schemes running astray, then you go ahead. I'll see you later." Newhouser turned and left the office.

Steubens watched him get into his Jeep and drive off. He sensed that he was losing control. The pains from those earlier failures in life were beginning to haunt him once again.

"No!" he said firmly, sitting alone in his small office. "I will not let them drive me out again. This is my town!" Steubens hammered his fist on top of the expensive oak desk. His mind began to click. As he gazed out his window overlooking Main Street, he saw the Tahoe drive on by. It was Pickett, and he had the stranger with him.

***

The crime scene was nearly scrubbed by the time Ross and David arrived. The car had already been hauled down to the lab in Appleton to be dissected by the experts. Ross pulled up next to a cruiser with State Police markings. He saw Jack Berkowski performing some magic with a measuring tape. There were only two other Troopers on site.

"What's up, Jack?" Ross walked over to the Sergeant with LaFontaine in tow. The officer turned to greet the duo.

"Morning, Ross. We've got to stop meeting like this." It was a shallow attempt at humor, but Berkowski was exhausted and he was finding it difficult to think straight. He had been up nearly all night. The Sergeant knew that this would be a difficult situation for Ross to manage given that he knew the apparent victims.

"Find anything yet?" The Sheriff surveyed the scene. There was a pile of broken glass just off the two-track. A large chunk of bark was missing from a tree on the opposite side. It reminded him of Ned Crosby's wreck.

"Not really. I wish we had more personnel on hand to help out, but most of the Troopers are looking for the guys who shot down the chopper last night. Not too far from here either." Berkowski shook his head in disgust. "I knew both of those guys."

"I know how you feel, Jack." He too had lost something that could not be replaced.

The Sergeant frowned when he saw his friend's frustration. "I'm sorry about your Deputy," he finally said.

"Don't sweat it, Jack. Let's just try to find out what happened." Ross introduced David. He did not expound on why the two were teaming together. "Is there any chance this could be related to the chopper incident?"

Berkowski rubbed his chin and looked to the treetops as if he were in deep thought. "You know, one might think so," he said after a minute. "But from what we've gathered so far, I really doubt it. The helicopter was brought down with a 7.62 ... probably an AK. It must have been an automatic from the patterns in the metal. There were casings everywhere. But here ...?" His eyes searched the accident scene. "Not a thing. No spent casings ... no bullet holes ... nothing. I would say that we're dealing with an entirely different animal."

Ross cringed when his friend uttered the word that was not meant to be taken literally. "I don't mean to nose, Jack, but how exactly did your two men die?" Ross didn't know why he asked the question. It just rolled off his tongue.

"Well," continued the officer, "it appeared that the co-pilot died from a gunshot wound. A round penetrated the underside of the chopper. These bastards used armor-piercing ammo." He looked disgusted by the idea.

"And the pilot?" asked Ross.

"Decapitated in the crash," answered the Sergeant. He winced, remembering the sight of the pilot's head found beyond the wreckage. "They crashed the chopper into the truck driven by the assailants. The pilot must have died on impact.

"The fugitives, what happened to them?" Ross needed to know what they would be facing out there.

"Don't know. It looks like they moved out on foot. We brought dogs in this morning to try and pick up a scent. The handlers couldn't get them out last night because they were at some inner-state competition over in Green Bay of all places. Can you believe that crap?" Berkowski kicked at the snow. "Nice timing, huh? From what I've been hearing on the radio, they're not picking much up. That snow last night wiped the place clean. Same as this area here."

Ross studied the Sergeant. He understood his frustration. Berkowski was a dedicated Trooper who had a tight bond with the men and women on his force. "Well, Jack, they can't be too far. You guys should be able to find them," he added with encouragement.

"I hope so, Ross. We've got everybody pulling double-duty today."

After the Sergeant brought them up to speed, Ross and David decided to take a look around for themselves. Berkowski felt slightly ashamed for the lack of resources delegated to the scene. The brass did have their priorities, and this was not it.

Ross' fist inclination was to head toward the swamp that he judged to be about two hundred yards to the west. He and David set out through the woods to look for clues as to how and why Mark Bennington and Sharon Cooper vanished.

***

After stuffing another load of dirty laundry into the washing machine, Maggie returned to the kitchen to make her call to the Fullers. Peggy answered on the second ring.

"Hi, Peggy, it's Maggie."

"Hey, Maggie," answered the woman with a pronounced hoarseness in her voice.

"Oh, are you feeling okay?" asked the caller sympathetically. "You sound like you have a cold."

Peggy Fuller proceeded to hack out a phlegmy cough into the phone. "The whole family has the crud. The boys have been up all night. They're miserable. They were devastated when I told them that they couldn't go hunting this weekend. You know how they have a one-track mind when it comes to hunting."

Maggie dropped the towel that she had been folding. "What do you mean? The boys are up in Ontonogon ... with Chuck."

"Sorry, dear, but Mike and Joey are home for the weekend. Is something wrong?" Peggy Fuller detected as much from the few seconds of silence that followed her question.

Maggie's mind was racing in another direction. If Chuck wasn't with the Fullers, then where was he? "Uh, sorry Peg. I ... ah ... have to go. Hope you feel better soon." She hung up the phone without allowing the person at the other end to respond. Maggie felt as though something valuable had just ripped from her possession. It was not like Chuck to pull a stunt like that. She was worried, especially in light of what they learned from Pete Wilkerson's visit earlier that morning. The distraught mother picked up the phone again and dialed the Pierson's home. Maggie was not angry. She was frightened.

***

The two men hiked through the forest examining everything in their path. There were at least three inches of fresh snow cloaking the ground. The odds of finding a track were slim to none. With the rising temperatures, Ross figured they would be walking on pine needles and leaves by day's end. As he weaved through the timber, a sense of urgency began to cultivate inside him. Something was telling him that their every move was being watched, and studied. It was as if a ghostly presence was waiting for them to draw nearer to the Amen Swamp.

The weight on Ross' shoulders was overwhelming. Although his eyes searched, his mind drifted. He placed blame on himself for the recent tragedies ... Ned Crosby, Charlie Perkins, Seth and

Bobbie Jennings, Birdie ... and now Mark Bennington and Sharon Cooper. The names revolved in his head on a carousel that seemed to pick up speed with each rotation. Ross thoughtlessly snapped a small branch off a dying elm and rolled it between his palms. He wondered what someone looking in from the outside might think of his actions at that very moment. *Insanity,* he told himself. Nothing made sense anymore.

He glanced up and squinted at the sun. The weatherman from Iron Mountain said that it was supposed to reach fifty by mid-afternoon. He prayed that the warmer temperatures would keep some of the hunters out of the woods, but it wasn't likely for an opening day. Still, the deer would be less likely to move.

Just as Ross was about to suggest they venture further north away from the swamp, David yelled from a crouched position some thirty yards to his right. "Over here, Ross!"

The Sheriff made his way through the brush that separated them. "What is it?" he asked while bending down over his partner's shoulder for a closer look.

"Take a look at this." LaFontaine held up three dark strands of hair, each approximately eight inches in length. He pointed to a few more pinched behind a thick slab of bark.

Ross studied the specimen in David's open palm. He'd seen similar hair ... on the fender of Ned Crosby's car. But there were bears all over the area. What could be so different about this particular sample? *Wait a minute,* he thought, as an idea popped into his head. *Could Ned possibly have...?"* Ross shook off the notion, realizing how absurd it was.

"Have you ever seen anything that might resemble these?" asked David as he shoved the specimen closer to the Sheriff's face. He felt that Ross was holding something back.

"I ... ah ... I can't really say. Why do you ask?" Ross knew he did a poor job of concealing his suspicions.

After a curious look, David continued. "Let me show you something." He reached into the side pocket of his leather jacket and brought out a plastic cylinder. He then popped off the cap and dumped the contents into Ross' open hand. It didn't take a genius to mark the strong similarities between the strands in his hand and the ones just plucked from the side of the tree at the doorstep of the Amen Swamp.

"Where did you get those?" questioned Ross. His eyes moved between David's hand and his own, studying the hairs carefully.

"Oregon ... Pacific Northwest. What you have there is the genuine article, just like that plaster cast I showed you." David LaFontaine's face beamed as if he had just struck gold. In the young man's mind, that was exactly what happened.

"How can you be so sure?" Ross wanted to believe that David LaFontaine was a fraud ... a nutcase pulling the prank of all pranks. But the more time he spent with the man, the more truth began to unfold. They were getting close to something.

David sensed his partner's apprehension and explained how his specimen had been found by a couple of Bigfoot hunters in northern Oregon. They were sent to a P.O. Box in Montana listed on his organization's website. After sending it off for further analysis to a member of the science staff at Washington State University, who by the way was also a believer, it was determined that the hairs were not synonymous with any mammal indigenous to North America.

"What else could it be?" asked David. "I know there's always the possibility that someone's trying to pull the wool over our eyes. Believe me, we've been hit by all kinds of fakes. But when you believe in something as passionately as we do, Ross, you sometimes have to rely on a little faith to lead you to the promised land."

The Sheriff handed the strands of hair back to David and stood upright. "I have seen those before," he finally said. Ross glanced nervously down a ridge feeding into the Amen. "I'm sure of it." He then enlightened David on his discovery of Ned Crosby's car and how he had found the chunk of hairy flesh on the front fender. The frightening possibility was now difficult to dispel. He dissected the scenario in his mind. Crosby was out in some nasty weather, driving home from a night of heavy drinking. He then hits something crossing the road. He remembered the old man's terrified eyes. "The Devil," said Ned. "The Devil is coming." Ned Crosby knew what bears looked like. Ross shuddered, knowing that Ned may very well have come face to face with the creature they were after. *Do I really believe this?*

"David," continued Ross, "theoretically, let's say that there *was* a creature and that it had been wounded somehow. Wouldn't this rampage over the past few weeks make a helluva lot more sense?" Ross glanced to his partner. "I mean ... just like a bear ... a wounded bear that is. Christ, who knows what it could do."

"That's a very interesting theory. My God, do you think ...?" LaFontaine jumped to his feet. The adrenaline was pumping in the excited young man. "Do you realize the significance of this find?"

"I'm afraid I don't see the *significance*, David." Ross understood the possibilities, but this small piece of evidence didn't exactly spell '*Bigfoot*' in his mind. He didn't know if it was his law enforcement training, or just his conscience not wanting to believe that such a beast actually existed.

"We have proof of contact, Ross. Man, I've got to send for help on this one." LaFontaine walked in a tight circle, planning his strategy. "We have never had this type of connection before. This is incredible." He stared up into the taller man's eyes. "Do you still have that sample from the accident?"

"Yeah, at least I think so. I put it in the pocket of my jacket." Ross hadn't worn the garment since that day when this whole mess began. He knew that Maggie wouldn't have touched it. He also suspected that it was smelling a little ripe by now.

"We've got to see if we have a true match, Ross," said David anxiously.

***

Samantha Godson hung up the phone, somewhat confused by the call. She had just talked to a Mr. Gene Steubens who claimed to be the Mayor of Jessup, the town a few miles to the north that had been experiencing more than its share of drama. Although Godson had never heard of the man, she had no reason to doubt his credibility, especially after he provided a number where he could be reached for further questions. Mr. Steubens made some interesting allegations tying the presence of a stranger in his town to the recent disappearance of a Jessup mail courier.

"Coincidence? Maybe," he told her, "but this gentleman is an odd one, and I would consider it a personal favor if your people could check him out." Steubens informed her that the '*vagrant,*' David LaFontaine, had arrived from Montana shortly before Birdie McIntosh vanished. Godson remembered taking the call on the night of the disappearance. This new information certainly warranted further investigation. Steubens even claimed to have heard rumors from some members of his community that this LaFontaine had been stalking the local playground. Godson informed the Mayor that she would check it out. She also relayed to him that they had been extremely busy in light of other events. After taking a few seconds to review her notes, the Trooper walked over to the computer terminal and performed a search. She punched in the name, as well as the plate number that the caller had graciously provided.

***

Tyrone Pullman heard the vehicle pull up to the cabin. He slid off the bed and picked the Glock up off the nightstand. Keeping his body low to the floor, he moved to a shaded corner and then slowly rose to his feet. He immediately saw the cruiser's inactive flashers through the part in the blinds. He shouldn't have stayed there. It was stupid. But he was so tired.

Tyrone saw a flash of blue move across the window. It was a cop's hat. The officer was checking out the exterior of the building ... looking for him. The officer appeared again, this time peering inside. Tyrone watched his eyes searching the interior of the room. Suddenly, there was a knock on the door. *Two cops!*

"I ain't goin without a fight," he whispered. The Trooper at the front door knocked harder the second time. Tyrone slowly raised the Glock and aimed at the face in the window from his position in the shadows. When he fired, the face disappeared. Tyrone darted to the front room. When he turned the corner, he raised the 9mm and emptied the clip, drawing a well-aimed line from one side of the door to the next. He then dove across the slick wooden floor on his belly and grabbed the Klashnikov propped up against the wall.

Tyrone realized that if either cop were still alive, there would be a call for help. He cautiously raised his head and peeked out the bottom corner of the window with one eye. He caught a quick glimpse of a man dragging himself around the front of the squad car, leaving a red trail in the snow behind him. Tyrone angled his head with his cheek pressed firmly against the wall and scanned the outer edge of the building toward the side bedroom. He saw the motionless torso of a body lying on its back. He had to make a move on the other one before he reached the radio. The fugitive slid up the wall. He racked a round into the chamber of the rifle and then turned. The butt of the weapon shattered the glass in the window. Cold air filled the room. Two shots from the Trooper's handgun zipped through the opening, one breaking the porcelain lamp on the far side of the room. Three more shots rang out. A slug made a hole in the wall directly between his legs. Tyrone suddenly felt vulnerable. It was now or never.

With the rifle raised to his shoulder, the fugitive pivoted to the window and began plinking the cruiser with rapid, semi-automatic fire. He watched through iron sights as the rounds tore away at the metal shell of the car and ripped into the fabric of the seats inside. When the chamber was empty, Tyrone quickly discarded the clip and slammed in a fresh one. As he readied the gun for a second volley, he gazed through the smoke for signs of life. There was a sharp squawking sound. *The radio!*

***

Ross detected that something was bothering Jack Berkowski the moment he and David stepped back through the trees. The Sergeant stood with a Trooper at each side, sternly eyeing the duo as they approached.

"Jesus, Jack. What's got your goat?" questioned the Sheriff. He smiled at his friend. Berkowski did not reciprocate. His face told Ross that something was wrong.

"I hate to do this to you, Ross, but I'm going to have to take Mr. LaFontaine down to Appleton. It appears your friend has an outstanding bench warrant in Montana." The Sergeant motioned for his two subordinates to take David into custody.

"Oh, come on," protested LaFontaine as if he had been expecting this. He did not resist when the handcuffs were slapped on his wrists. He stared solemnly at the snow-covered ground.

"What is this, some kind of joke?" exclaimed Ross. "Come on, Jack, this guy's with me. You can't just ..."

"Forget it," interjected David before the Sheriff could finish.

Ross gazed into David's eyes, stunned by what was happening. He saw the embarrassment written on the man's face. "What's going on, David? What the hell is this all about?"

"Mr. LaFontaine," answered the Sergeant on the prisoner's behalf, "decided not to show up for a court date on an assault and battery charge. His hometown authorities are requesting his company as soon as the paperwork can be shuffled. It turns out that your friend here has quite the little rap sheet."

"What do you mean, Jack? What rap sheet?" The Sheriff suddenly felt as though the world were caving in around him. His reality had been turned upside down.

"Ross," interrupted David, "I had a few run-ins with the law when I was younger ... much younger. Nothing big. Just nickel and dime stuff."

His case was presented a little too matter-of-factly for Ross' liking.

"This thing the Sergeant is referring to," continued David, "it's just a big misunderstanding ... really it is."

"I don't know how they look at things in Montana, young man," said the Trooper gruffly, "but here in Michigan we don't take too kindly to assaults on police officers."

"A police officer!" Ross' anger was duly noted in the tone of his voice. He looked to David for quick answers.

"It's not as bad as it sounds, Ross. You've got to believe me," pleaded LaFontaine, trying desperately to reclaim his credibility.

"And the drug charges?" added Berkowski, driving a stake into the cornered man's defense. "I believe it was possession with intent to sell, and I'm not talking about a little weed."

"Jesus Christ!" roared Ross. A familiar throbbing had managed to return to his head. "How could I have been so fucking stupid," he cursed. Ross watched David struggle for words that would redeem the apparent miscues of his secret life. But the man had no answers.

After a brief moment of silence, David finally spoke up. "Like I said, Ross, I was young. I did some stupid things that I'm not proud of, but I paid my dues, man."

He wanted to slug the man in the face. Ross was ashamed of himself. He had been used by a two-bit hack with a helluva sales pitch. The Sheriff ran his fingers through his hair and turned toward the Sergeant. "Can we at least have a word in private, Jack? Please?"

"Ross, we've got to get him to Appleton. There is something else that you might find interesting."

"What? What do you mean by that?" asked the Sheriff. *How much more could there be?*

"Your Mayor phoned the post and told one of our duty officers that your friend might be linked to the disappearance of your mail courier. We'd like to ask him a few questions regarding his sudden presence in the area."

"That's a bunch of bullshit," clamored David, surprised by the accusation. "I don't know what the hell you're trying to do to me, but that's a load of crap."

"Well, we're still going to ask a few questions, son," added the Sergeant in response.

Ross kept quiet as he studied LaFontaine's face carefully, contemplating what Berkowski had just suggested. He didn't want to believe it, but the Sergeant had touched on something that had never crossed his mind ... something that was very plausible. Then again, it was Steubens who made the call. *That bastard's getting back at me,* he thought.

"You don't believe him ... do you Ross?" David noticed how his friend had been looking at him and quickly attempted to disconnect the circumstantial evidence. "No way, Ross, don't you even start to believe any of that bunk."

The Sheriff turned again to the Sergeant. "Please, Jack, I would like to have a few words ... privately. I wouldn't ask if I didn't think it was important."

Berkowski frowned, and then looked to his two sidekicks. He reluctantly nodded his approval. The Troopers released the prisoner and allowed him to walk freely to the Sheriff. Their hands rested on holstered weapons.

Ross turned his back to the officers and stared hard at David. "What the fuck is going on?" he whispered angrily.

"I know what you're thinking, Ross, but ..."

"You have no goddamned idea what's going through my mind right now!" Ross' face turned bright red with his rising temper. Never before had he been so furious with a man, not even with Gene Steubens. The urge to take a swing presented itself again. He looked into the smaller man's cowering eyes. "Now you level with me, David. Are you legit, or have you been yanking my chain these past few weeks?"

"Everything I've told you has been on the up and up, Ross. My organization ... the website ... the strands of hair we found out there ... it's all real. Bigfoot *is* real. My God, you can't actually think that I made this shit up ... can you?"

Ross looked away. A part of him said to get out while there was still time, but another side of him wanted to believe in the man. "I don't know, David," he said while shaking his head. "I just don't know anymore." He felt so deflated, as if the air had been sucked from his lungs. He was tired. Ross glanced toward the Troopers. Jack Berkowski was speaking to one of his men while holding a watchful eye on the prisoner. Ross then turned back to David, who had quickly evolved into a distant stranger. The doubts in his head were staggering. He envisioned the people of Jessup laughing behind his back, mocking their Sheriff. And then he saw Steubens' face grinning from ear to ear with each *'I told you so'* uttered from his greasy lips. *'Look at the Bigfoot hunter,'* they would say.

Fuck David LaFontaine, Ross declared to himself. *Fuck your goddamned monster*. "Goodbye, David." Ross turned his back on the man and began to walk away. "Get him out of here, Jack." His mind was set. He was finished with David LaFontaine.

David reached awkwardly with his cuffed hands into his coat pocket and withdrew the specimen that the two had discovered on their walk. "Ross! Wait!"

The Sheriff hesitated, keeping his back turned to the man.

LaFontaine sprinted up to him, inspiring the Troopers to take a precautionary step in his direction. "Please, Ross. Take this. Just check it out for yourself. See if they match." David stuffed the plastic bag into Ross' pocket. "Please, Ross. You owe me that much."

"I don't owe you shit. I don't even know who the hell you are."

***

Chuck Barnes sat in envy of the two college boys. He watched as they proudly admired their opening day prizes hanging from the buck pole. Each held an open beer in celebration of their success. He wanted to be standing there with them. But instead, he felt like an invalid unable to partake in the one thing he loved more than football.

"What's the matter, Chucky?" Jenna noticed his brooding behavior and stumbled up to him. To bypass the morning hangover, the girls had insisted on opening a few beers for breakfast while Alex and Trevor were off in the woods. It didn't take much to get the buzz going again.

Chuck smiled. Jenna was a sight when she was drunk. "Nothing," he replied. "I guess I was just wishing I could have been out there this morning."

"Awwwww, Chucky. I'm sorry. I thought you'd rather be here with me." The cheerleader snuggled up tight against his chest and gave him a quick peck on the lips.

Chuck's stomach still groaned from his overindulgence the night before. Alex and Trevor kept daring him to keep pace, which proved to be a costly mistake. After Jenna passed out, Chuck had spent a good hour on his knees outside the cabin puking in the snow. He had a rough time getting to sleep with the room spinning in his head. Chuck could not bring himself to sniff a beer at the moment. He would wait it out until evening.

"So what do you think of this big bastard, Chuck?" Trevor had his paw wrapped around the larger rack.

"Not bad," answered the teenager. "He's got a beauty there."

"Not bad, my ass! This is a goddamned Bullwinkle." Trevor Musgrave turned to the proud owner of the trophy. "Alex," he bellowed, "you *are* the man!" He then reached into his pocket and took out a crumpled twenty dollar bill. Trevor snatched his roommate's hand and slapped the money into his open palm. "By the power invested in me, I hereby dub you the *Great Hunter of the North*." He took his beer and sloshed it over Alex's hair as if he were anointing him.

Alex Chavez was too giddy to stop him. He didn't care. He was too consumed in anticipation of the drive home when he would be parading his buck to the world atop the car.

***

The Sheriff gunned the Tahoe down the Benson Track. His grip was firm on the steering wheel as he finessed the truck down the winding trail. He had to be careful, knowing there were archers out there. He had already passed a number of cars and trucks parked along the way.

Ross had been on his way to Jessup when the call came over the radio. Jack Berkowski had requested a ride in while the other two Troopers were transporting David LaFontaine down to Appleton. The Sergeant was going to meet up with Samantha Godson at Arlene's for a quick lunch before getting back on the road to continue their search for the fugitives. The dispatcher relayed the message that two Troopers were under fire. The young officer who made the call reported that he had been wounded and that his partner was down. After communication broke off, a nearby hunter made a 911 call and reported that he heard a number of gunshots. Since Pickett and Berkowski were so close, the Sheriff was more than willing to offer his services. He had no pressing matters in Jessup, especially after the uncloaking of his partner's true identity. Ross was trying his best to remove the face of David LaFontaine from his head. As far as the Sheriff was concerned, he was just another ghost.

Ross figured that they were within five miles when he wheeled the Tahoe onto the two-track. He gathered there were at least ten other cruisers in route from the chatter on the radio. It appeared that the two fugitives had finally been flushed and the Troopers were securing the net. The diversion offered a much-needed distraction from the Amen Swamp.

The Sheriff saw the first *'No Trespassing'* sign marking the line between the public lands and the private encampments. A large stretch of the Benson Track split through a bevy of hunt clubs, most of which contained a form of living quarters. It was an ideal place to hide out for men on the run, unless they stumbled into the wrong hunting party.

"We should be getting close, Jack." Ross stole a quick glance to his passenger who wasn't as familiar with the area. He could see that his friend was worried at the possibility of another tragic discovery.

The Sergeant unsnapped the harness on his holster and drew his semi-automatic. "Take it easy, Ross. We could run into anything up here."

Both men kept alert eyes forward, searching for the cruiser that had made the distress call. As the Tahoe leveled out at the peak of a steep incline, the two lawmen saw the car parked at the base of a little bluff next to a plush cottage. When he saw that the cruiser was the only vehicle in sight, Berkowski realized they were too late. He then saw the bodies.

"Oh Jesus," muttered the Sergeant as Ross brought the vehicle to a stop. Both men hopped out with weapons pointed to the open doorway. Berkowski motioned for Ross to sweep towards the left while he scurried in a crouched position to the right. Jack scrambled up to the Trooper lying on his back outside the bedroom window. There was a sizable hole in the dead man's temple. The snow on the ground underneath his head was saturated with blood. Berkowski bent down and placed his finger on the man's cold neck, knowing that he would not find a pulse.

Ross, in the meantime, crawled up to the Trooper lying behind the car. He had suffered numerous hits to his legs and chest. Ross too checked for a pulse, keeping his eyes glued to the open door. The cruiser had been ripped to shreds by what appeared to be a high caliber weapon. The Sheriff glanced toward Berkowski who was peeking through the open window. When the Sergeant turned, he signaled for Ross to converge on the door. The two men sprinted to the building with their heads low to the ground. When they met, Berkowski then dove through the doorway and rolled to the left. Ross followed, hearing the sirens off in the distance.

***

The female knew that she had been careless for staying in the high ground so long. She was vulnerable. Arrogance had jeopardized her safety. The scent of the hairless creatures seemed strong in all directions. She began to wonder if they were hunting her again. But she did not hear the dogs.

After her successful kill during the dark hours, the female had feasted yet again on the flesh of the hairless ones. With her stomach full, she had become indolent and decided to rest before returning to the cover of the swamp. The images of her juvenile's bloodied body did not haunt her sleep that night. Consequently, she did not wake before the sun ascended into the sky. Perhaps she had been removed from the clan too long, causing her senses to weaken. Her deviate behavior was inconsistent with the ways of her species. She growled softly in disgust of herself for being so reckless. The growl was slightly enhanced at the thought of the ones who had banished her.

The female lifted her nose. There were hairless ones close to where she lay. But she dared not move. If she attempted to retreat now she would leave evidence of her presence. The snow was now her worst enemy. The female remained calm and waited. She would let them come to her.

***

Jesse Jones studied the evidence like a well-seasoned detective. His eye picked up the red speck next to the fresh track. He kneeled and scooped it up in the palm of his bare hand. It wasn't much, but it *was* blood. He knew that he hit the animal. He heard the *'thwack.'* But the arrow must have glanced off an unseen twig, diverting it from its intended path. Jesse guessed that it must have struck the deer in the front shoulder, accounting for the lack of blood. The buck then carried the arrow for some thirty yards before it was able to pull it free. They didn't bleed as much when bone was involved.

The hunter contemplated as to whether or not he should pursue the animal, guessing that it would live to see another day. Tracking a small six-point was hardly worth wasting an entire morning. But, after mulling it over, he decided to give it a couple hundred yards at least. There was, after all, a slim chance that he could sneak up on the animal and get another shot. Jesse Jones worked like a panther. Though the forest floor, with its crunchy snow, was not conducive to still hunting, he was able to advance with remarkable stealth. He would skirt the pines, using the ground padded with needles to bypass any obstructions that might compromise his position. After a few delicate steps, he would stop to listen ... and watch. Jesse Jones, like his brother Frank, became one with the animals when he traipsed across God's green earth. He was at the top of the food chain.

A disturbance in the trees caused Jesse to stop. He tuned his ears to the frequency of the forest and listened. Something shuffled ... possibly a deer. It had not yet been spooked. He would have heard it crashing off. Jesse checked the wind that was blowing in his face. He had the advantage. He knocked an arrow and gripped his bow tightly. He had stalked deer a thousand times before and took great pride in his abilities.

Jesse took two quiet steps forward. Suddenly, he heard a *'thump,'* like a deer stomping the ground to alert others of impending danger. For a moment, the hunter thought he had finally been detected. Experience taught him to remain completely still ... just in case. A deer's behavior was difficult to predict. A squirrel overhead began to chatter from its leafy nest. Jesse got down on all fours and slithered beneath the pine boughs. The challenge of the silent stalk was exhilarating, testing his skills against a wary adversary.

***

The female scowled in silence at the bothersome creature marking her presence. The rodents in the trees continued to side with the hairless ones. She felt trapped. Her only comfort was in knowing that the hairless ones were not aware of the bothersome warning signals. It proved to be an advantage to her as well. The squirrels alerted her of their presence.

She tediously swiveled her enormous head and surveyed the forest. One of the hairless beasts was very close. She could smell its foul odor, even from upwind.

Just then a deer scampered into a small gap in the wall of pines before her. The female saw blood trickling from a small wound. Sensing danger, the four-legged animal skidded to a stop with its front hooves planted firmly in the soil beneath the snow. The female patiently waited while the deer bobbed its head in an attempt to ascertain the curious figure hunched against the tree. When the creature stomped its hoof and snorted, the female did not move. She knew the game well.

Suddenly, a crisp noise arose from the thicket. The female watched the object sail through the air until it stuck the animal in the clearing. The deer made an attempt to escape. It stumbled forward a few steps and then fell to the ground. The female looked on as the hairless one appeared from its hidden position, holding the weapon in its hands. The female had learned something new from this opponent.

***

Jesse watched the buck fall after the perfect shot hit just behind the shoulder, straight through the heart. The hunter's mouth stretched into a wide grin. He was filled with that familiar wave of excitement. He slowly rose to his feet, knocking another arrow just in case. But he knew the buck wasn't going anywhere. He was too good.

As Jesse crept into the clearing, he caught wind of a strange, rank smell. His first impression was that he had gut-shot the deer and opened up the belly. But as he closed the distance he saw that the shot had been pure. He then noticed the squirrels. One turned into five, and then twenty. Jesse looked up into the tall branches of the pines. He turned in circles, not knowing what to make of it. The chattering intensified, needling his eardrums.

"Shut da fuck up!" The woodsman screamed at the top of his lungs, unable to bear another high-pitched bark. But as Jesse cried out with his eyes affixed to the trees overhead, he lost his balance and stumbled over the outstretched legs of his dead buck. When he tumbled to the earth, his head slammed hard into a rock hidden beneath the snow.

Jesse moaned in agony. The back of his head felt like it was on fire. When he opened his eyes, his vision was blurred. "Awww shit," he groaned softly. As he tried to move, the beating in his head grew. He eased himself back into a lying position and closed his eyes, allowing time for the cobwebs to clear. While he laid there beside the buck, he listened to the silence in the trees around him. Jesse looked up after realizing that the squirrels were now quiet. He stared up into the branches overhead, blinded by the bright sunshine.

"Now where did dem bastards all go?" he asked himself. As he gazed skyward, a hulking silhouette appeared above him. He brought up his left hand to block out the glare. "Frank? Dat you?"

CHAPTER FOURTEEN

An exhausted and frustrated man entered the empty house. Ross Pickett could not shake the bitter feeling plaguing him since the sudden departure of David LaFontaine ... *'Bigfoot Hunter.'* A sarcastic sneer crossed his face as he envisioned the title that the man from Montana had bestowed upon himself. *A goddamned Bigfoot in Jessup, Michigan. What an ass I've been,* he thought.

Throughout the drive home, Ross searched deep into his soul and attempted to find meaning in the past two weeks ... the fugitives ... the killings ... the disappearances ... the hunt in the Amen. He wanted the nightmare to end. He wanted his old life back. He had spent close to an hour consoling Jack Berkowski who had also lost people close to him. So many lives had been altered in such a short period of time.

David LaFontaine continued to fester in his head. The Sheriff pulled out a chair at the kitchen table and sat down. He rolled his head from side to side to stretch out the cramping muscles in his neck. He then buried his face in his filthy hands. He needed sleep, void of the unforgiving ghosts. He needed Maggie.

After locating the two bodies earlier in the day, Ross and Jack, and a swarm of pissed off Troopers, continued the search for the wanted fugitives. He could see the frustration and anger in their faces. MSP had their own ghosts to deal with, but those ghosts were very real. The Troopers were rooting out every hunting camp within a ten mile radius with nothing to show for their efforts. Ross witnessed the flared tempers. Four of their own had fallen to the hands of ruthless criminals, and they would not stop until they had vengeance. Ross figured that once found, the fugitives would not live to see a jury trial. Their fate had been predetermined by their actions.

Ross truly felt sorry for the Troopers. He understood death more than most. It was coming to everyone's doorstep at some point in time, but it was the unseen arrivals that led to so much confusion and pain. He wondered what road his life would have taken had Eevie not been seized from him.

It was Jack Berkowski who finally ordered Ross to return to Jessup. The Sheriff would have preferred to stay in their company and keep his mind off of David LaFontaine and the Amen Swamp. But the Sergeant insisted that Ross would be more useful in town if the fugitives decided to wander that way. It made sense. His job was to protect his town. He should have protected Mark Bennington, and Sharon Cooper, and Birdie McIntosh.

Ross left the search and made a quick stop home to shower and wash away the dirt on his body, as well as the haze that filled his head.

The winds blow through,
The screams grow loud,
The dead are cursed,
And never found.

Amen beckons,
The proud and brave,
Come seek the cedar,
That marks your grave.

If you will the courage,
To face the demons within,
Then pray with pure heart,
The journey ends with Amen.

He did not intentionally summon the words. The ghost would not relinquish its hold. Ross wondered what journey he was taking ... what demon awaited.

He remembered the plastic bag that David had forcefully inserted into his pocket. The Sheriff hesitated at first, but then reached in and extracted the specimen. He stared at the long, black strands of hair through the clear plastic, trying desperately to mentally attach them to the hide of a bear. The Amen Swamp loomed in his thoughts. "Is this really necessary?" he asked out loud. But Ross knew that he had to be sure.

The Sheriff walked into the foyer and stared at the parka that he was wearing on that first night when his world had seemingly changed forever. His hand slowly reached into the pocket for the piece of flesh. He felt the course hair and dried tissue between his fingers. He immediately smelled the decay when he pulled it out.

Ross reluctantly returned to the kitchen table and laid the old specimen next to the new. He examined each with a scientific eye. Though similar in color, they were different in other ways. The hairs from Crosby's car were shorter and not as course. The specimens from the Benson Track were frayed and exhibited signs of graying, as if it had come from a more mature animal. Witnessing those differences provided the Sheriff with a delicate sense of confirmation. The hairs had come from two different animals. David LaFontaine was wrong. The Bigfoot hunter was a fraud.

When the phone on the counter started ringing, Ross stuffed both specimens into the plastic bag and tossed them into the garbage can.

***

Frank Jones heard his brother cry out. It was unlike him to create so much noise when he knew that Frank was still in a tree. He would have been far less understanding had there been deer moving around him that morning. As it turned out, the hunter had not seen an animal after four hours of sitting, and he was ready to throw in the towel.

When he arrived at Jesse's empty stand, Frank saw the tracks leading to the north. He also noticed the scant blood trail. He judged that his brother made a poor shot on the animal.

"Stupid ass," he quirked, "I told ya dat tree don't have shit fer shootin lanes." Frank would take the opportunity to rib his brother a bit when he caught up with him. The deer's track wasn't all that impressive. Frank guessed it was a small buck. The Jones brothers were not too picky when it came to hunting. Their goal was to fill the freezer, and the small deer would be tender. They rarely tagged the animals anyways.

As Frank followed the track, he couldn't help but sense an odd ambiance about the forest. Nothing moved. There was no sound. He recalled similar circumstances in the swamp while they had been hunting the bear. Frank was not one to fear nature, but there was something in the air that agitated him ... like a presence amidst the pines.

Jesse's tracks were not difficult to follow. Frank approached quietly in case his brother was involved in an active stalk. He saw the spots in the snow where his younger brother crept on hands and knees, and the disturbed pine needles where he walked to cover his steps. Frank followed suit. Ahead, he could make out a well-lit break in the cover. As he neared the clearing, he saw the buck lying dead on the ground. Jesse was nowhere to be seen. Frank casually walked up to the animal. He saw the kill-shot behind the front shoulder of the six-point. Jesse's bow rested in the snow next to the deer. It wasn't good practice to place the expensive piece of equipment in snow like that.

Frank examined the perimeter of the clearing. Jesse was not the type to leave a fresh kill *and* his bow, and just walk off. The buck had not yet been gutted, and the boot tracks mysteriously stopped. It was as if he had disappeared into thin air. His eyes suddenly picked up on another patch of red snow. It didn't conform to where the buck had been shot or where it fell. Paranoia overcame the elder Jones brother.

"Jesse!" Frank's call went unanswered. He scratched his head, perplexed by what could have happened. It wasn't making any sense. Frank then noticed the path of displaced snow leading away from the clearing and into the trees. It looked as if someone had taken a branch and swept away at the ground ... to hide tracks. Frank knelt down and placed his bow on top of the dead buck. He then withdrew the .44 Magnum from his shoulder harness. He often carried the sidearm for coyotes and other menacing critters.

***

The melting snow created havoc on the narrow two-track. On one occasion Tyrone was forced to get out and jam some sticks underneath the tires for traction when they got buried in the soft mud. He found himself wishing for the four-by-four that was put out of commission by the helicopter the night before. Cops would be looking for him under every rock once they discovered that two of their own had been killed. But he was not about to give up so easily in his pursuit of freedom. He would fight the battle until the bitter end, regardless of the outcome he was destined to face.

As the fugitive drove the trails in search of a means to escape, he noticed a number of vehicles abandoned along the way. He was in a precarious position. If someone should see him passing by, there was no telling what might happen. And he couldn't risk firing his weapon. It would only alert others of his whereabouts. Tyrone had to keep moving forward and hope for the best. The Klashnikov rested close to his side if he was forced to defend himself.

As the driver's thoughts diverted from the trail ahead, he did not see the large root protruding from the ground. When the front tires hit the obstacle, the nose of the car bounced upward. The rear end began to slide. As Tyrone punched the gas and turned the wheel, the car careened out of control. He watched helplessly as the front end met a tree. His head was thrust backward when the airbag exploded in his face.

"Fuck me!" he cried after the car came to an abrupt stop. He opened the door and fell out face first in the soupy mud. When he stood, he heard the loud hissing sound coming from the engine. Steam billowed into the sky.

"Fuck you!" he cursed. He kicked the door from his laying position.

***

Frank Jones kept his eyes glued to the trees ahead. He did not call out to his brother. He sensed that something had gone terribly wrong. He derived as much from the drops of blood that speckled the trail he was now following. Frank gripped the .44 firmly with both hands ... ready to fire. He tried to picture in his head what might have happened. His best guess was that Jesse had somehow managed to get himself into a scuffle with another hunter, possibly over the buck. That would have explained his yell.

"Goddamned flatlanders," he whispered under his breath. Frank abhorred the ones who invaded the north woods in their fancy hunting getups and expensive toys. He had his share of run-ins over the years. But he didn't figure that his brother could have been bested by one of them.

Frank felt no emotion in knowing that Jesse might very well be dead. He had been raised to be tough as nails. His father imbedded a stern disposition in his boys and would not allow them passion in a world that showed no mercy. Frank Jones also lived by the creed ... *an eye for an eye. You fuck wit me and I'll fuck wit you.* He tried his damnedest to suppress the anger boiling in his black heart.

Frank stopped for a moment and stared down the trail. Whoever had created it made quite an effort to conceal tracks. It didn't add up why someone would expend so much energy to haul off a body. Then, as Frank continued to examine the path closer, he saw something that made the hairs on his neck stand on end. He first saw the limb that had been used as the makeshift broom. Beyond the discarded branch was a track unlike any he'd ever seen. Frank crept over and knelt down quietly. He placed his humbled hand into the deep indentation.

From heel to toe it was over twenty inches in length. He brought his hand to his chin and tugged at the scraggly beard while sizing up the creature in his head. Frank counted the toes ... five of them. But it wasn't a man, and it sure as hell wasn't a bear. He suddenly felt a drop of moisture explode on his arm, a catch of snow melting in the tree overhead. Oddly, it didn't feel cold against his bare skin. It was warm. As he brought his hand up to wipe it away, he saw the bright red coloring. *Blood!* Frank rolled back his head and looked up. Jesse's mangled body was bent over a swaying limb twenty feet off the ground. Frank only knew that it was his brother from the clothes on his back.

***

The town was uncharacteristically deserted for a Saturday afternoon. Ross expected more pedestrians to be strolling the sidewalks with the milder temperatures. The peak of the tourist season had long since passed, but there were always enough locals meandering about the small businesses that lined Main Street.

"Must be the opener," he said to himself as he drove the Tahoe up alongside the curb in front of the Jessup Inn. With the absence of vehicles in Maggie's parking lot, he figured that the hunters were sticking to their stands. Ross knew the rooms were full for the weekend as they always were that time of year. He certainly couldn't blame them for staying outdoors. On the drive in, Ross thought about taking a day or two at the end of the week and get out himself. He could use the solitude. The demons had all but subsided from LaFontaine's absurd theories.

It was Maggie who phoned him. Evidently Chuck had not gone up to Ontonogon with the Fuller boys after all, and she was worried for his safety. Maggie knew of the manhunt currently in progress. She witnessed the steady stream of State Police cars zipping in and out of Jessup all morning. Ross convinced her that there was nothing to fret about. Chuck was a good kid and knew enough to stay away from trouble. To appease her, Ross said that he would check things out when he arrived in town. His best guess was that the teenager had decided to shack up with his girl somewhere for the weekend.

"Hey, Maggs," he said as he broke through the swinging doors to the Inn. Maggie was behind the counter polishing silverware. He could see that she was still not comfortable with not knowing where her son was. What mother would be?

"Have you heard anything, Ross?" She walked around the end of the bar to meet him.

"I haven't looked into it yet," he answered. "But I'll work on it now." He offered a comforting smile to let her know that everything would be okay. *And it would be okay*, he convinced himself.

"It's just not knowing that bugs the hell out of me. Chuck has never done this type of thing before." Maggie placed her arms around his waist and nuzzled her chin into his chest.

"Did the Piersons get back to you yet?" Maggie told him over the phone that she had already tried Jenna's parents. They weren't home at the time so she left a message.

"Not yet. I'm going to tan that boy's hide when I get ahold of him." Again, her motherly instincts took over. Chucky meant more than anything else in the world, including the man she held.

Then, as if on cue, the phone behind the bar started ringing. Maggie let go of her grasp on Ross and quickly pranced around the counter to answer.

"Jessup Inn, may I help you? Hi, Henry ... okay ... did she go? Did you? She wasn't with them then? Do you think they are there? I can ... but ... okay. I'll ask him." Maggie covered the mouthpiece with her hand and turned to Ross. "It's Henry

Pierson. They found out that Jenna went to his brother's hunting camp off of Rylander Road for the weekend. He thinks that Chuck probably hooked up with them.

Ross knew *of* Ted Pierson's camp, but he didn't really know where it was exactly. There were only a handful of camps out that way so he didn't figure it would be too difficult to find. "Does he want me to take a look?" Ross thought it would be better if he were the one to pick up the kids. Henry Pierson was a conservative Baptist who was very strict in his ways. He reminded Ross of Eevie's father. Although it might be a good lesson for Chuck.

"Would you, hon? He's tied up in the office and it really looks like they might be there." Maggie gave him a beggar's stare.

"Tell Henry I've got a few things to wrap up here in town, but I'll get after them as soon as I'm done."

"Thanks, babe." Maggie turned her attention back to the phone and told Henry Pierson that Ross would fetch the kids.

***

Tyrone Pullman tried his best to maintain the brisk pace through the woods, but he was beginning to tire. He stayed well away from the trail, knowing that the cops would be centering their attention there. The fugitive had no other recourse but to pick a direction and go. He did not know where he was, the direction he was traveling, the time of day, or even the day of the week. He was lost in a foreign land, but he kept moving. He continued to survive.

As Tyrone's legs pushed his body forward, he thought of how his plan to drive north had seemed so simple at the time it was conceived. *Avoid the open areas to the south*, he thought. Who in their right mind would think that two *brothers* from Flint would attempt a break through the Upper Peninsula? *It had been a good plan*, he said silently to himself as another branch whipped across his cheek. He knew what he should have done from the beginning. He should have capped the man who was the source of all misery in his wasted life.

A wailing siren in the distance caused the fugitive to stop. He listened as the high-pitched noise got louder, and then gradually faded. He knew there would be more. They wouldn't stop hounding him until he was dead. Tyrone despised those who pressed him as if he were merely an animal. But he also felt confident in knowing that he had bested them at every opportunity so far. Tyrone set off again. He would have to find shelter and food soon.

It was a familiar voice that caused him to stop again. He turned, holding the rifle at the ready against his shoulder. There was nobody there. He listened above the afternoon breeze. Although faint, there had been a voice calling out his name.

"Who's there?" he called. He turned to his left after hearing a subtle sound. "I'll shoot!" he yelled. But there was no answer. He stared into the trees, seeing nothing but shadows.

"Tyroooooooooone!" The fugitive's eyes opened wide with terror as the voice descended from the treetops. He looked up nervously. The swaying limbs resembled arms reaching down to him. "Tyroooooooooone!" It called to him again.

"Who's there?" cried the confused man. His aim darted from side to side as he tried to locate a target.

"I came back for you, Tye," called the distant voice.

"Gerald?" Tyrone's body began to shake. His partner *had* returned, just has he said he would do.

"Told you I'd come back, Tye."

"Leave me alone, Gerald! You're dead!" Tyrone screamed, but the voice of his former partner continued to harass him.

"Time to come with me, Tye." The voice grew louder, as if Gerald was right next to him.

Tyrone turned and ran. "You dead! You are fucking dead!" He repeated those words over and over as he busted through the undergrowth of the forest, trying to escape the haunting presence that had returned to challenge his sanity. He forced himself to believe that it was the stress of his plight toying with his delicate psyche. *Gerald is dead!* The voice continued to trail him, so he ran faster.

***

"I don't give a damn what those dogs are doing," said Jack Berkowski, "I want them up here now! You got that?" He slammed the mike to the floor of the squad car in frustration. Of all the times, the Canine Unit had their dogs after some lost hunters over sixty miles away. It was bad enough not having them last night, and now some genius decided that he had to assign the Unit elsewhere. The Sergeant vowed to have someone's ass over this fuck-up.

Sam Godson glanced over to her supervisor. "Good timing huh, sir," she said with a smirk.

"I tell you what, Sammy, there are some real pieces of work out there. You would think that someone would have the sense to know that with a couple of murderers running free up here, we might have some need for the dogs."

"I know what you mean, but we'll find them." She turned her attention back to the two-track."

"Yeah, Sam, we'll find them." Berkowski's response expressed his lack of confidence. He was running on fumes and beginning to feel his age. *This sort of work is for the young bucks*, he told himself as he gazed out the window at the passing trees. Five more years and he would be kicking back in his boat with a fishing pole in one hand and a cold beer in the other ... hopefully in the Keys. Those days couldn't arrive fast enough for the seasoned veteran. But the Sergeant also knew that it was his responsibility to set an example for the younger generation. He would not allow his drive to be slowed by age.

"Where do you really think these guys have disappeared to?" asked Godson, sensing the uneasiness in the man sitting in the passenger seat.

"I don't know, Sam." He answered as if he were lost in deep thought. "There's a lot of space up here. But what concerns me most are the hunters. If we don't catch up with them soon, I'm afraid someone else is going to get hurt."

"We'll get them, Berk." Sam Godson turned on the wipers to swipe away at the chunks of mud that splashed onto the windshield.

***

The lean woodsman took another deliberate step and then stopped to listen. The breeze had subsided and was no longer masking his movement. The forest was unusually quiet for the time of day. Even the birds had mysteriously vanished from their mid-afternoon roosts. Years of hardened experience in the Upper Peninsula told him that something was amiss.

Frank Jones understood that he was on to an animal of enormous size. He marveled at the stride that he guessed to be twice as long as his own. He saw where bark had been displaced on trees well above his own reach. But Frank Jones vowed to find it ... and kill it. He feared nothing in the northern woods. His .44 was the hand of discipline that would render punishment for the heinous crime. Frank had found himself wishing for the bigger bored rifle, but there was no time to retrieve it. The track was fresh and he was getting closer. The Ruger Super Blackhawk would suffice his needs that day.

A sudden disturbance in the bush ahead made him freeze every muscle. He held his body completely still. Only his eyes moved from side to side, scanning the narrow crevices between the branches for the elusive predator. The track had taken him to a thicket on the outskirts of the Amen Swamp. The cover was thick enough to shroud an elephant. But it also concealed the hunter's advance. Frank couldn't risk a blind shot. The noise would drive his prey away and eliminate his chance for vengeance. The creature was retreating into the protection of the cedars. If he allowed it to reach the Amen, he would lose it. He approached the thicket, gauging each step with careful precision.

While holding the .44 in his right hand, he brought up his left and started to pull away at the tangle of branches and vines standing in his path. Entering the thicket was the only way to flush what awaited inside. Frank stepped through the barrier that seemed to swallow him up. He was amazed at how such a creature could navigate with such apparent ease. Stalking was near impossible as he was forced to pick his way through the maze of crisscrossing limbs, one foot after another, his eyes alert for movement. Branches snapped at his backside. He continued moving forward, holding the Ruger in front of his body ... ready for that first vital shot. He willed his heartbeat to slow into a slow murmur. He was close.

The hunter concentrated his eyes on where to place his next step as he snaked through an awkward patch of thistles. The explosion of noise came without warning from five feet away. He raised the powerful handgun and instantaneously fired two quick shots without looking. It came right at him, passing within inches of his ducking head. The .44 followed the sound with flames shooting out the end of the barrel. As the echoes from the gunfire faded, Frank Jones look up and watched the grouse disappear in the trees.

***

After an inconsequential hour of office time, Ross decided that it was time to go after the kids. There was nothing for him to do there but sit and think. Maggie had already called three times just to see if he had left. He sensed her growing agitation. Maggie would not relax until she knew her boy was safe.

The Sheriff had been following the ongoing manhunt on the scanner. MSP had yet to find their two fugitives, but the constant chatter made it clear that they were not about to relax their efforts. Although his spirits had risen to a manageable level, Ross still felt grief from the latest losses to his community, Mark Bennington and Sharon Cooper. Two young lives were snuffed out forever. Regardless of the circumstances that brought them together, it was still tragic. Absent from his conscience, however, was the heavy sense of guilt. Ross convinced himself that guilt was for those who had something to hide, and he no longer held a lie that could cause suffering to the people he protected. David LaFontaine was a fraud who would never manipulate the small-town Sheriff again.

While in his office, Ross thought about Mark Bennington's disappearance. It had to be linked somehow to the assault on the helicopter and the deaths of the two policemen. The car was found too close to the crime scenes to disregard the correlation. It was Jack Berkowski's intuition that the two were unrelated that bothered him. So what if there were no cartridges found around the vehicle. One could certainly kill a man without a gun. And then again, there was another possibility that he did not discuss with the Sergeant. Perhaps Mark and Sharon had falsified the evidence to make it look like a crime had been committed so that they could run off together to start a new life. They were both immature enough to try and pull off a stunt like that. *Now that made sense*, he told himself as he glanced out the window into the near-empty street.

When the recently widowed Mildred Brummeister rode by as a passenger in a late model car, his thoughts reverted back to the manhunt. If he was guilty of anything, it was for not paying more attention to what MSP had been up to. There he was, off gallivanting across the Upper Peninsula with a goddamned Bigfoot hunter by his side. His actions had been both idiotic and embarrassing. The fugitives from downstate were very real and had committed terrible crimes. The coincidence between Birdie McIntosh's vanishing and their presence could not be disregarded. He envisioned the mail courier out on the backroads confronting the wanted men. They wouldn't allow an eye witness to escape, and that made them all the more dangerous. Even the State Police were now thinking along those lines. And as for David LaFontaine, Ross couldn't see him as a killer regardless of what Berkowski might think. *A nutjob ... yes ... but not a murderer.*

Ross broke away from his quiet meditation when he saw the familiar Ford Ranger pulling up along the curb outside. The sight of Ray Jackson's face was a breath of fresh air. He quickly hopped up out of his chair and ran outside to greet his long-time friend.

"Ray, I never thought I'd be so glad to see you," said the Sheriff with an apprehensive smile. He hoped that his friend had forgiven him for his boorish behavior. He watched the Trooper carefully slide his body out of the small cab with his arm secured tightly to his waist. The only difference between Ray's bandage and Chuck's was the bulky padding protecting the stitches where the bear had affixed its jaws. Jackson's gold tooth sparkled as he returned his buddy's grin.

"Ain't you a sight for sore eyes. I've been sitting on my ass wondering what the hell happened to you up here."

"Damn, Ray, I'm so sorry about all of that BS I threw in your lap. I was just ..."

"Don't sweat it, Sheriff." Ray interrupted the apology. "Don't mean a thing."

Ross walked up to the Trooper and shook his hand. He hadn't talked to Ray since the day he made the phone call from his kitchen ... with LaFontaine. "So what brings you up this way," he asked.

"Man, Ross, I couldn't take another day on that couch. That wife of mine was driving me up a wall." But then Ray's face turned serious. "I'm sorry about Mark," he proclaimed solemnly. "Jack gave me a call this morning. He thought you could use a little cheering up."

"Thanks. I'd just like to get to the bottom of this before someone else gets hurt. I hope to God that your boys catch up with those punks before too long."

"You can bet on that, Haas." Jackson gave the Sheriff a supportive pat on the back. Although he did not mention it to his friend, his real reason for driving up to Jessup was to help the boys out by covering some ground himself. Nearly every off-duty cop within four counties had volunteered their time to aid in the search. Overtime was not an issue. They wanted justice.

Jackson didn't particularly want to ask the next question, but he felt it necessary to see where Ross was at mentally. "Is there anything else that I should know about?" Berkowski had also informed him about Ross' companion from Montana and how they hauled him in for the open charges. Ray was well aware of Ross' background and wanted to see for himself how it had affected him.

"What do you mean, Ray?" Ross acted confused by the inquiry.

"You know ... any *monsters* still running rampant in your neck of the woods?" Jackson tried to hide his sarcasm, but his friend's story had been utterly ridiculous.

"Ohhhhh ... sorry about that. It was all a big mistake that I would just rather forget if you don't mind." Ross grimaced, embarrassed by what Ray must have thought of him when he told him what they were up to.

"Can I assume then that we have bypassed those theories and moved on to greener pastures?" Jackson wanted to be sure there was nothing else on his friend's mind. He felt guilty for lacking faith in the man, but he remembered the bad days.

"Everything has been worked out, Ray," assured Ross as he thoughtlessly kicked away at a few loose pebbles on the sidewalk.

"Glad to hear it, buddy. Damn glad to hear it!" Jackson placed his good arm around the man's shoulder. "We got to get out and do some fishing before the weather sets in."

The Sheriff looked into the friendly face. "You got it, Ray." Then a notion crossed his mind. "Hey, how would you like to take a drive?"

Before Jackson could answer, they were interrupted by the whining engine of a speeding pickup. Both men quickly turned and faced the vehicle barreling down Main Street. Seeing that the middle-aged driver was adorned in camo, Ross guessed he may have just come in from the morning hunt. When the driver saw them standing next to the Tahoe with police markings, he swerved their way and came to a screeching stop.

"What the hell is this guy up to?" Ross watched the man reach for something on the front seat. He then jumped out of the truck holding the unidentified object wrapped in a red bandana.

"Watch yourself, Ross. I don't like the looks of this." Jackson lowered his good hand to where his sidearm was ordinarily attached to his belt. There were too many crazies in the world to think it might be otherwise. The gun wasn't there. He scolded himself for leaving it in the truck.

"Are you the police?" asked the stranger. He was out of breath and sweating profusely.

The man appeared tense to Ross. Beneath the five o'clock shadow, his skin was pale ... as if he were frightened.

"Yes sir, I'm Sheriff Pickett. Are you okay?" Ross expressed his concern, trying to settle the man down.

The newcomer dropped the object from his hands that he no longer wished to hold. He stared down at it, as if it were infected with some form of plague. "My ... my ... name is Reggie Stillwater. I ... I found it ... this morning." He pointed to the object.

Ross studied him closely. He noticed his quaking body. He was terrified. The Sheriff's own inner fears suddenly began to resurface. He tried desperately to dismiss them. *Old ghosts!*

It was Ray Jackson who knelt down and slowly folded away the corners of the bandana. When the last corner flopped to the side, both men stared at the shocking sight. There was a human hand lying at their feet. Ross recognized the wedding band still attached to the ring finger.

***

The female immediately halted her retreat when the noise erupted from behind. The hair on her thick neck bristled at the sharp report of the weapon. It was close. The female lifted her head as high as she could extend and sniffed the air. Her eyes searched for danger.

The creature snarled in frustration at the unfavorable conditions. The air was warm and there were little to no winds to carry scent to her nostrils. But the female now understood that she was being hunted. She heard the strange, high-pitched sounds on and off again. They would approach from the distance, grow louder, and then drift off. She began to feel as if they were driving her, perhaps to a trap at the boundaries of her lair. Though they did not pose an immediate threat, the female was nervous. She was out of her domain and anxious to find sanctuary in the land that would protect her.

After detecting no movement, she started off again with more haste in her step. She could not risk waiting. The hardwoods were too thin and did not supply enough cover. She would lead the hairless one into the lowlands where she would have the advantage. If it chose to follow, she would kill it.

CHAPTER FIFTEEN

Alex Chavez stood at the window, cherishing the sight of his buck hanging on the pole outside. The setting sun illuminated the antlers, creating a phosphorescent aura about them. It was a feeling unlike any he'd ever felt, and one that he hoped to experience again.

"Look at you," said his roommate as he accompanied Alex with a beer in hand. "Feels pretty damn good, don't it?"

"It's unbelievable," answered the young Hispanic, keeping his eyes on his trophy. "It's like I don't ever want this day to end." His heart continued to race with excitement.

"I know, Al, but don't worry. There will be more hunts and more bucks. I can't say you'll ever top that one out there, but it's fun to dream." Trevor slapped him on the back. "I've got to use the shitter." And with that profound statement, Trevor left his friend and walked outside.

Chuck Barnes, in the meantime, was curled up on the couch next to his girlfriend who was half in the bag. There was a growing stack of empties adorning the coffee table in front of the couple. It had taken time for the effects from the previous night's party to flush through his system, but Chuck had now joined in with the rest of the group and was feeling pretty good. After a rough start to his relationship with the two college boys, he had come to like them more and more as the afternoon wore on. They all shared common interests, especially Trevor who talked football with him for a good portion of the day. Chuck was thankful that Jenna had persuaded him to come along. It felt good to get away from the typical high school crowd. He felt older.

"Oh, Chucky," muttered Jenna. "I feel like I'm floating." She had a dazed look on her face as she swayed back and forth in her sitting position.

"Better take it easy, babe," he responded. "Let's try to not pass out tonight and enjoy some time together." Chuck was really looking forward to the evening hours.

"You never told me how good looking your man was, Jen." It was Brenda stumbling up to the sofa and plopping down next to them. "I think he's just the cutest little thing in the world." She playfully pinched Chuck's cheek. He pulled away and scooted closer to his girlfriend.

"Well he's all mine, and you can't have him," responded the cheerleading captain of Appleton High as she placed her protective arms around his neck.

***

The man watched from his hidden position in the tree line as the figure walked across the yard and entered the small, shed-like building. Tyrone Pullman was cold. The temperature was quickly falling as the sun fell from the sky. He needed warmth or he would freeze. He would have preferred to keep looking for an uninhabited cabin, but he was running out of options. From what he could see through the window, there was a group of kids inside. There were at least five ... maybe six ... not much younger than he was. Tyrone saw the deer hanging from the pole in the clearing. The memory of the gamey venison sickened him. He fought back the urge to vomit.

"Looks good, don't it Tye?"

Tyrone looked up, wondering if he'd ever be alone again.

"Go on, Tye and get you some of that pussy in there. Been a while, hasn't it?"

"Shut up, Gerald. Do you want them to hear us?"

"Whatcha gonna do, Tye? You gonna shoot them all, you sick motherfucker." The voice then began to laugh.

"I said shut up!" Tyrone's voice rose in frustration. He was being provoked. Gerald Johnson would not rest until Tyrone joined his lost soul in the world for the damned. It was becoming more difficult to keep from plunging into total insanity. He shut his eyes tight and tried to think away that haunting voice. He was at least thankful that it was now only a voice. After a few moments, he opened them and looked to the darkening sky. "Gerald?" he whispered. "Where you at?" Finally, there was no response. Tyrone turned his attention back to the clearing.

There was a car parked in front of the door. He thought about just jacking it and moving on. But if he was going to chance a break tonight, he could not leave witnesses. Tyrone decided that he would be better off lying low for a little while and getting something to eat. He assumed that the kids had food. He also decided to keep them alive as bargaining chips should the police show up. Besides, gunfire would attract attention.

He made his move, following the backdrop of trees, circling the clearing toward the shed. He would have to take that one first. When he was out of view of the windows, Tyrone cut across the open ground and slowly approached the small building. He could hear the kid shuffling around inside. Tyrone wondered what he was doing in there, or more importantly, if he had a weapon. He pointed the barrel of the Klashnikov directly at the narrow door. He cringed when his foot made a crunching sound as he stepped down on a patch of iced over snow. It did not go unnoticed.

"Oh boy, someone's trying to scare me." The voice inside was over-exaggerated.

Tyrone glanced toward the cabin's door to assure himself that nobody else had heard the disturbance. He could hear music. That was good.

"Bren? Is that you?"

Tyrone reached for the latch, keeping the nose of the rifle up. He then swung the door open.

"What the fuck are you ...?" The boy stopped in mid-sentence when he saw the military-style rifle pointed at him.

Tyrone brought a finger to his lips, motioning for him to stay quiet. He gave the boy a grim stare as if to say ... *'you will die if you don't shut up.'* His hostage got the message and stayed silent. Tyrone studied the white boy who was sitting with his pants pulled down around his ankles. The smell inside enlightened him as to what the shed was for. He had heard about outhouses, but he had never actually seen one.

The captor then motioned for the kid to stand. He did as he was told, pulling up his pants and then stepping outside. Tyrone then nudged him in the back with the barrel of the rifle, pushing him toward the cabin. It was time to make his presence known to the others inside.

***

The hunter's pace slowed with the fading light. It became more difficult to make out the track. The snow had all but disappeared from the day's sun, leaving little sign to follow. He was spending too much time on hands and knees searching for those indentations in the earth. Frank found where the creature had stopped when it must have heard him discharge his gun. He continued to chastise himself for the unforgiveable error. The woodsman took notice of how its pace had quickened by the longer strides. It knew he was there, and it was fleeing. Frank now realized that he was losing ground. Without a flashlight, he would be completely out of luck when total darkness set in.

He erected his gangly body after examining the latest track. It was time to make a decision. He could either continue on this level with little hope of catching up to his prey, or he could make a move to head it off. The experienced hunter knew its destination. Though the creature had attempted to throw him off track by changing its pattern, his brother's killer was heading for the Amen Swamp. Frank had to get there first.

There were no second thoughts about returning to Jessup and caring for the body. He knew that his brother would understand. Jesse would have done the same for him. Their father had taught them that there was no sense in carrying on about the dead. Frank left the trail and headed west. He wanted to be ready when the beast showed itself.

***

"Hey, Trev!" yelled Alex. "What's the matter, you having problems with your colon again?" He ribbed his roommate after noticing the serious look on his face when he walked through the door.

"Leave my baby alone," added Brenda as she glided across the floor toward him. She stopped suddenly when the second man entered carrying the gun.

"Everybody get the fuck over there!" barked the black man as he motioned for them all to huddle near the larger of the two couches. When Alex took a step in the wrong direction, the intruder responded by placing the nose of the rifle against his head. "You make one wrong move, motherfucker, and I'll blow your fucking head off!"

"Easy now," said Alex as he hoisted his hands into the air. He tried his best to remain calm. The soldier had been trained on how to deal with these scenarios. The girls, on the other hand, were hysterical. Alex had to silence them before the man became too agitated. The invader's eyes displayed desperation, a dangerous emotion to aggravate. Alex slowly stepped backwards in retreat toward the couch. He sat down next to Kayla who hugged him tightly. He could feel her body shaking. But Alex stayed calm. He would not take a chance until he fully understood the situation and an opportunity presented itself.

The man was jittery in his movements. He clutched Trevor's collar, holding him in place as his eyes searched frantically about the room. As the aim of his weapon passed over their heads, the hostages instinctively ducked ... everyone but Alex.

The soldier knew better than to make any sudden movements that might instigate aggression. "Take it easy, Kayla ... all of you. It will be okay."

"Shut the fuck up!" cried the man. "I'll shoot all of you, motherfuckers!"

"Sorry, sir. I apologize." Again, Alex held up his hands, calmly requesting forgiveness from his captor. He then saw something in Trevor's eyes that terrified him. As his roommate stood with his back turned to the intruder, he began to make some odd gestures with his eyes. *Oh no*, thought Alex. *Don't you do it*. But Alex's inner pleas were not successfully transmitted. Trevor turned suddenly and attempted to grab hold of the rifle. His reaction was too slow, a product of an afternoon of drinking. The man batted his groping hands away and hit Trevor squarely in the middle of his head with the butt of the gun. Trevor dropped to the floor, cursing all the way down.

"Goddammit!" screamed Alex's roommate.

The soldier could not move. He would jeopardize the safety of the others if ...

"You fucking asshole!" continued Trevor.

"Trevor, stop!" pleaded Brenda. Her hands covered her open mouth. "Please stop."

"Shut the fuck up! All of you!" screamed the black man as he aimed the AK-47 at the back of Trevor's head.

The alcohol, coupled with what was now a moderate concussion, prevented Trevor Musgrave from making an intelligent decision that would save his life. He turned his head around and peered up with a glazed look. He then uttered the words that would seal his fate. "Go fuck yourself."

The coeds watched in horror as the rifle jumped in the man's hands. Trevor Musgrave slumped to the floor. His arms and legs twitched like an epileptic as a gurgling sound escaped his dying lips. A pool of blood expanded around his head. The girls screamed while Chuck Barnes leaned forward and vomited on the floor.

***

The Sheriff had already checked two of the hunting camps on Rylander Road. Both were occupied, but not by the group he was looking for. A familiar sensation was beginning to creep back into his body. He could not discard the vision of Mark Bennington's severed hand lying at his feet. He tried desperately to invent scenarios for the couple's disappearance, but the new, disturbing evidence manifested what he had feared all along. Mark Bennington *was* dead, and he was certain that Sharon had met the same fate. But he still did not know how or why.

After the hunter presented the discovery, Ross felt an urgent need to find Chuck. He reported the find to the State Police in Appleton and then told the man to stay put until a Trooper arrived. Now he was searching for his future son with Ray Jackson, praying like hell that the kid was okay. Ross was upset with himself for not going after him right away.

"Is there something bothering you, buddy?" Jackson was not comfortable with the driver's silence. He saw how the hunter's discovery had upset Ross back in town, and rightly so. The reality of the moment was catching up to his friend.

"Yeah, Ray," he answered finally. "I'm okay." The Sheriff continued to stare down Rylander Road that was barely a road at all. He knew where the trail ultimately led and began to wonder if that was his destiny all along. He wanted to believe that his Deputy had been gunned down and then dragged off into the woods where the scavengers did their damage. He wanted to believe that it was the doing of the fugitives. But there was a frightening resurgence of a not so old ghost. David LaFontaine's objective began to loom in his thoughts like a freight train ready to burst through a paper wall.

"Ross, would you please share with me what's going on in that head of yours?"

"Look, Ray," Ross glanced over to his friend. "I'm just not comfortable with Chuck being out here. That's all ... really." He turned his attention back to the road, knowing that he had made a feeble attempt to conceal his latest lie. Ray Jackson would not understand. He couldn't explain his anxiety to himself. Ross Pickett just wanted it all to end.

The Sheriff noticed how the terrain was now making a gradual descent into the lowlands. The hardwoods were giving way to thickening conifers. The Amen Swamp loomed ahead.

***

The muffled noise was distant, yet it was just loud enough to be detected by her sensitive ears. The female could not ascertain the direction from which it came. She had been moving too fast ... another careless act. She stopped briefly and listened to the forest. There was nothing to be heard but the strengthening breeze whirling around her body.

She found comfort when darkness finally fell from the sky. The female now held the advantage. In her retreat, she made the decision to make a stand once the edge of the lair was reached. If there was a hairless one following, she would destroy it. Her stomach began to hunger.

As she took a step, her attentive ears picked up a new sound ... a cry of pain. This time the female honed in on the direction of its source. It was a hairless one crying out between her position and the domain she sought. She lifted her head and inhaled deeply. The hairless ones were close.

***

Alex Chavez could do nothing but sit and listen to the quiet whimpers of the three girls as their captor continued to intimidate them. He felt helpless. His eyes looked to the corpse on the floor. Trevor was dead, and he had done nothing to stop it. He worked over the scenario again and again in his jumbled mind, trying to justify his inability to react. He felt tremendous guilt for not saving his friend's life. All of his training and knowledge had been ineffective when he needed it most. But Alex Chavez swore to redeem himself for the sake of the others. He would protect with his life if need be. He waited for the opportunity. He vowed to kill the murderer for taking the life of his closest friend.

"What the fuck you looking at!" The man saw the expression on the young Hispanic's face. He read the boy's thoughts and understood his intent. "You want to kill me, don't you?" he asked. The man rose slightly from his sitting position and teased the prisoner by pointing the rifle at him. The movement of the gun incited a stir in the girls. "Ya'll don't even know who the fuck I am ... where I'm from. You hate this brother, don't you?"

The soldier held his emotions in check. He would not allow himself to be baited into providing an excuse. "I'm sorry, sir," he answered calmly. "I don't know who you are. I just don't want to die." Alex tried to insert guilt into the equation. It was a psychological tactic. He wanted to make the man realize that there were consequences for actions. Showing the murderer any form of respect made his stomach churn, but it was necessary. He alone was their only hope for survival. They would all be killed eventually. Alex began to forge a point of vulnerability. "I'm sorry," he said as he broke off eye contact. Alex directed his attention to Kayla who continued to tremble. There was shock in her eyes.

"Don't be gettin no crazy ideas, asshole." The man turned and looked out the window as if he were expecting someone. "I won't feel no guilt bout killin you." His voice trailed off as if his mind was somewhere else.

Alex sensed a slight change in the man's demeanor. He appeared to be tiring. He had no idea how this man had come to be in his current predicament, but Alex guessed he was on the run. He wondered what would happen if those pursuing suddenly showed up at the doorstep. An idea surged in his head, but he had to make sure that the man with the gun was in a more pacified state.

"Sir?" asked Alex. "Can I please make a small request?" He was cautious not to look him in the eye when he turned.

"What the fuck you want now?" The man's tone was now more conversational.

Alex noted the wearied response and began to feel that his opportunity was brewing. "Would you please allow me to put him," he nodded toward Trevor's body, "in the other room. It would be much easier on the girls." Alex spoke with a soothing tongue. He sagged his shoulders and allowed his head to swagger to the side so that he appeared fatigued and weak. His mind, in the meantime, calculated how and where he would take the man.

The captor stared at him for a few tense seconds. He looked to the body on the floor and then over to the girls who were huddled together beneath a heavy blanket. All of them stared blankly into space, avoiding the grisly sight in front of them. "Alright," he said quietly. "Move his dead ass into one of those rooms." He motioned toward the three open doorways. Before Alex could move, the fugitive straightened up in his chair. "Wait a minute, homes." He stood up and walked to each door, inspecting the rooms for weapons. When he stopped at the room where Alex and Kayla had been sleeping, his face turned serious. He knelt down, holding his aim on the five coeds, and grabbed something off the floor. When he swung the bow and quiver around the door frame, Alex's first thought was that he would be the next victim.

"You weren't planning on sticking me with no arrow now, were you?"

Alex shifted his body away from the others on the couch in case the man did decide to take a shot. "No sir," he answered. "It's just my bow. We were hunting this weekend. I barely know how to shoot the thing," he lied.

The black man eyed him closely, as if he were considering ending his life right there and then. He then strolled across the floor to the front door, opened it, and tossed the weapon outside. He did the same with Trevor's bow that was leaning up against the wall next to the doorway. "There," he said after slamming the door shut. "Now you go ahead and git him the hell out of here." He stepped back to put some space between them.

The soldier slowly lifted himself up off the sofa. He felt Kayla tug at his arm.

"No, Alex. Stay ... please." She pleaded with a broken voice.

Alex gently smiled at her. "It's okay, Kayla. I'm just going to move Trev. That's all." A lump formed in his throat as he turned to the man holding the weapon.

"If you try any shit, I'll kill your bitch first."

Alex nodded. He heard Kayla's pronounced gasp from behind. He would have to be extremely careful. When he reached Trevor's body, he grabbed both arms and proceeded to drag him across the floor. Brenda began to cry when she saw the streak of blood left behind. When the soldier reached the bedroom, he was surprised that their captor had not followed. He slid the body around the wall. Keeping his rear in plain sight for the man outside, Alex then bent over so that he concealed his torso behind the wall. As he pulled the corpse into the room with his left hand, his right reached into the duffle bag and withdrew the buck knife. He carefully removed the weapon from its sheath and slid it up his sleeve. When the body was clear, Alex stepped back out into the living room and shut the door behind him. He looked up to the man who was studying him closely.

"Thank you, sir," said Alex politely.

"Don't be giving me that *sir* bullshit. Sit yo ass back down on that couch."

Alex did as he was told.

"*Do it, Tye. Shoot the mothafuckers.*"

Tyrone Pullman looked frantically about the room for the source of the voice. *You ain't gonna get to me Gerald*, he told himself. *I ain't gonna let you drag me down.*

"*Come on, Tye, be a man for once.*"

"Shut the fuck up, Gerald! Leave me alone!" Tyrone screamed out loud at the ceiling. When he turned toward his prisoners on the couch, he could see the confusion in their eyes. They looked at him as if he was crazy. He wondered if they were right. Without saying another word, Tyrone walked over to the recliner and plopped down. He was exhausted.

***

"Sorry about disturbing you this evening. Let us know if you see anything." Ross politely shook the man's hand.

"No problem, Sheriff. Hope you find them before the snow gets too bad." The owner of the cabin then went inside and shut the door.

Ray Jackson had suffered the silent treatment long enough. Ross was becoming more aloof with each failed stop. There was something pressing on his friend's mind and it was time for him to reveal what exactly that was. "What is wrong with you, Ross?" The Trooper drilled the Sheriff as they both got back into the vehicle. The recipient of the question would not acknowledge. He was in his own world, sealed away in a tight vault. "Ross!" This time Ray shouted.

The Sheriff turned. "What?"

"I said, what the hell is wrong with you?"

"What ... what do you mean? Nothing ... is wrong." Ross turned away and started the truck, eluding his friend's glare. He looked ahead as the snowflakes began to trickle down from the sky.

"I've had it with you, Ross. If you're not going to share whatever it is you're thinking, then take me back to Jessup. What has got you so absorbed in yourself?" Jackson would not allow him to escape this confrontation.

"Don't start, Ray. Please ... just let me work this out." Ross' response was barely a whisper. He had just checked the fifth camp on Rylander Road, and still no Chuck. The reawakened nemesis was now thoroughly entrenched in his twisted thoughts. He scanned the trees and brush along the side of the road as the Tahoe carried them closer to the place he dreaded. His eyes tried desperately to penetrate the wall of darkness for the silhouette of truth. Ross was no longer dismissing David LaFontaine's theories. The idea that some malicious force existed out there would not surrender its hold on him. He didn't know whether the sight of Mark Bennington's severed hand jolted him with reality, or drove him from it.

"Ross!" boomed the Trooper after his friend avoided the issue.

"Huh? What?"

"Jesus H. Christ! Stop this fucking truck now!" Jackson had enough.

The Sheriff did as his friend requested. When the Tahoe came to a halt, the driver slammed the gear in park, opened his door, and stepped out into the cold, snowy elements. Ross walked off the trail, keeping his back to Ray Jackson, and stared off into the night.

The Trooper followed his lead and circled the truck. "Come on, Ross. It's me, Ray. Enough of this bullshit. Talk to me, man."

Jackson begged to be let in. He now knew that there was a deeper, driving force behind the detached behavior.

"Why is it so hard to believe, Ray? You tell me." Ross spoke above the winds, feeling the cold snowflakes biting his cheeks.

"What are you talking about?" Even though Jackson now stood by his side, Ross continued to avoid eye contact. "Why is *what* so hard to believe? Tell me." Ray toned down his aggression, sensing that Ross was about to expose his burden. He could see something odd in the man's eyes. His friend was frightened, but by what?

The Sheriff turned with a beseeching look on his face. Ray Jackson recognized the expression. It was the same front that the Sheriff had exhibited when he met up with him at Ned Crosby's place.

"Something's out there, Ray," proclaimed Ross. "I don't know how I know ... but I know. It's something evil. I didn't want to believe it."

"What the hell are you ...?" Jackson hesitated after he connected the dots and saw where Ross was heading. He didn't like it. "Are you referring to your ... *monster* ... a Bigfoot?" He brought it out in the open so Ross could hear the word for himself. Perhaps then he would see the insanity of his delusions.

"Why not, Ray? What's so crazy about the idea? You tell me ... right now!" His melancholy tone was rising ... not because of his doubtful companion's conduct, but because he knew it all along. And he had done nothing but try to dissuade himself from believing. Since that night when he sat on Ned Crosby's porch with Charlie Perkins' entrails clinging to his boots, he knew there was something in that swamp, and he did nothing. What he needed more than anything now was for his best friend to have faith in him.

Jackson looked him hard in the face. His buddy had lost his grip on reality and was teetering dangerously close to schizophrenia. When he placed his hand on Ross' shoulder, the Sheriff pulled away.

"Goddammit, Ray! Why can't you just listen to me for once and see the facts!"

"Okay, Ross," said Jackson calmly. "Tell me the facts and I will listen."

"Oh cut the condescending bullshit. Don't stand there and patronize me like I'm some fucking imbecile!"

"Okay, no bullshit!" Jackson was frustrated, but for different reasons. "You've obviously got some major problem here, so tell me what these facts are," he demanded.

"Christ, Ray. Ned Crosby ... Charlie Perkins ... Mark ... what the hell happened to them? And don't tell me it was a bear." His tone softened as he walked off a few paces down the two-track. *It wasn't a bear*, he told himself. *It wasn't a bear*.

"Hey," continued the Trooper, "I know you've had a lot of shit to deal with over the past few weeks, but listen to me ... please." Now it was Ray speaking in a more controlled voice. He was pleased that they were now communicating.

The Sheriff turned and allowed the Trooper to speak ... to justify the deaths and resolve his anxiety.

"Maybe it wasn't a bear," said Ray. "I'll give you that." Ross nodded. Jackson held up his good hand like a cop stopping traffic. "What about the two fugitives, Ross? These are some bad boys that have done some nasty things."

"No!" Ross was steadfast in his response. "I don't buy that, and I don't think you do either."

"Okay, Ross. Now it's your turn to refute."

"Because men don't go around mutilating other men like that! Goddammit! You saw for yourself!" The hostility surged again. He was getting nowhere with Ray Jackson.

"Believe me when I tell you, buddy, that men are very capable of such godawful atrocities." Jackson had firsthand experience. "I've seen it," he continued. "I lived it, man."

"No, Ray. Don't compare what's happening in my town to what you saw in your war." As he shook his head, Ross stretched out his arm and pointed a sharp finger. "No way, Ray. Different times, man. Different ..."

Ross Pickett suddenly fell silent as the roar echoed in the distance. Ray Jackson's eyes opened wide.

***

Alex studied the man closely. He used his peripheral vision, careful to avoid direct eye contact that could spook him. He noted how the man would unknowingly close his weary eyes and then slump in the recliner. They would quickly reopen after the error was realized. He was tiring and becoming more vulnerable as the seconds ticked by. Alex couldn't wait much longer. The man was unstable. He had cried out for no apparent reason, yelling at something or someone that only he could see. He would look about the room every so often, acting paranoid as if he was being watched. If the intruder decided that it was time to leave, it would then be too late. There would be no witnesses left behind to give testament to the crime.

Alex Chavez was confident that his opportunity was close at hand. When the man closed his eyes yet again, he reopened them, this time as wide as they could stretch. He shook his head vigorously to shake out the cobwebs. After rising to his feet, he started off across the wooden floor toward the tiny kitchen area without muttering a word. When he lumbered by, Alex noted how loosely the rifle was held in his right hand with the barrel pointed to the ground. Alex had already concluded that the man was a righty when he witnessed him discharging the weapon when he murdered Trevor. He would have to shift the gun to his other hand. That would give him an additional second, an eternity for the act that he was about to attempt.

The young soldier calculated the hit zone in his head, measuring both time and distance required for a successful assault. He deliberately extended both legs to stretch out his tight muscles. When he assured himself that they were in proper working order, he curled his right foot back against the face of the sofa in such a position that would allow him to push off and propel his body forward. He slowly shifted his weight to the edge of the cushion. When the man observed his movements, Alex acted as if he were trying to work out a cramp in his back.

When the man reached the stained sink, he bent over and worked the hand pump to access water from the well. As the cool liquid gushed from the spout, he pulled a dish towel off a hook, dampened it thoroughly, and then draped it around his neck. The man tilted his head back and stared at the ceiling for a brief moment. The cool water seemed to revive his senses.

Alex straightened his arm and cupped his hand. He allowed the concealed knife to slide down his sleeve and into his open palm. As he looked up, he saw something in Chuck Barnes' eyes that he didn't like. The teenager gave him a short nod as if he were insinuating that he was prepared to assist. Alex responded silently with a curt shake of his head. He mouthed the word *'no'* to make sure the boy understood that he was not to intervene. Chuck seemed to acknowledge that he did understand, or so Alex hoped. The disabled football player shifted his weight forward regardless.

The man was returning to the recliner. He continued to hold the rifle neglectfully in the wrong hand. *This is it*, thought Alex to himself, knowing that he would be risking the lives of his friends. There was always the chance that help would arrive, but the situation could worsen if the man grew more desperate. *No*, he told himself, *I've got to do it now*. The next few seconds would determine whether they would all live or die that night.

When the man passed by again, he turned his head ever so slightly in the opposite direction toward the far wall. Alex rotated the knife in his hand and propelled himself off the couch. Kayla shrieked from behind. The man turned, but not before the attacking soldier closed the distance. Alex's fingers wrapped securely around the barrel of the rifle before the man could swing it around and take aim. Alex then thrust the knife toward his chest. The man shifted when he saw the weapon and tried to knock it away with his free hand. Alex plunged the blade into the meat of his shoulder. The man cried out in pain. Alex pivoted his body and knocked his opponent's legs out from underneath him with a sweeping leg whip to the back of his knees. The soldier purposely fell with him, careful not to allow him to regain control of the gun.

The girls screamed in the background as the struggle ensued. Alex caught a quick glimpse of Chuck jumping off the sofa, but he could not concern himself with the boy now. His priority was to get the weapon out of the man's hands. The opponent was powerful, but he was no match for the professional. Alex could feel the man weakening as they rolled on the floor together. Then, Alex shoved his elbow into the man's neck and pinned his head down. He had him. When their eyes met, the soldier applied more pressure, cutting off oxygen to the man's brain. Alex could now sense that Chuck Barnes was standing over them. He was holding something in his hands.

"Alex!" shouted Chuck. "Alex! Move!"

"Chuck, no!" Jenna called out from the couch. Alex could hear her sobs.

"Watch out for Alex!" It was now Kayla trying to draw Chuck's attention.

Alex wanted to turn his head, but he was too involved with neutralizing the man beneath him who was nearly unconscious. Suddenly, the knife fell free of the man's shoulder sending a spurt of blood from the wound into Alex's eyes. He was momentarily blinded by the stinging sensation. *Just a few more seconds*, thought Alex as he kept his firm hold.

With a desperate burst of energy, the man rolled. The young soldier felt a strange pressure in his side. He screamed in agony when he realized that he had been stuck with an arrow. As he moved, the blades on the broadhead sliced deeper. Alex's strength quickly faded. His elbow slipped off the man's throat, allowing him to breathe again.

***

When Frank Jones broke into the clearing, he heard the screams. They were coming from inside the cabin. Frank was only sixty yards away, but he could barely see through the window. The storm arrived without warning, rolling over the northern landscape. Using his free hand to block the flakes from his eyes, Frank approached to within thirty yards of the structure until he was finally able to see some activity. There were two girls jumping up and down hysterically. Their attention was directed to something on the floor that he couldn't see. A young boy then emerged. He appeared to be holding and arrow.

"What da fuck is dis?" he asked himself. He could hear the high-pitched screams from the females. The boy with the arrow was yelling. As Frank continued his curious stare, the boy hoisted the arrow and thrust it downward.

Frank Jones had never thought himself to be the hero type. He now had a critical decision to make. If he were to succeed in cutting off Jesse's murderer at the edge of the swamp, he would have to keep moving. The Amen was just a few hundred yards out.

"Fuck it!" he decided. "I ain't got no business wit dem." But before he turned to pursue his prey, he saw a black man stand up, and he was holding a rifle.

***

At the onset of the assault, Chuck immediately darted across the room and retrieved the arrow that was resting across the tines of an old rack hanging on the wall. He yelled for Alex to move to the side so he could stab the man. When he thought the college student was finally clear, the teenager brought the weapon down with all of his strength. Unable to grasp the arrow with both hands, his hold had been too weak to properly control it and he struck Alex by mistake. Chuck stood over the wrestling men, horrified by what he had done. Before he could react, the man pushed Alex away and sprang to his feet. He rammed his foot into Chuck's knee, sending him crashing to the floor. Alex wiggled in pain. The man hoisted the rifle and backed up toward the window. Blood poured from the wound in his shoulder. All three girls cried in the background.

The captor staggered from side to side, weak from the strenuous battle. He turned his head and surveyed the damage to his shoulder. His shirt was soaked in blood. Chuck and Alex both remained on the floor, agonizing over their own injuries.

As Alex looked up to see his fate unravel, the man's face stretched into a wide grin.

"You wanna fuck with me!" he shouted. He stared up to the ceiling as if there was someone there. "Watch this, Gerald! All these motherfuckers gonna die now!" With a deranged look, he centered his attention on Kayla. "Like I said, you stupid fucker, your bitch gonna die first."

The disabled soldier could only watch in horror as the man brought the rifle up to his shoulder and aimed at his girlfriend. "Noooooooo!" cried Alex. The man's boot landed squarely in the middle of his back. As the soldier fought to breathe, he heard the safety click off. "Nooooooo!" he called again.

"Alex!" screamed Kayla. She covered her face with trembling hands in an attempt to shun death.

Suddenly, Alex heard a thunderous *boom!* His first thought was that the man had ended the life of the woman he loved. But when he looked up, the murderer was staring down in shock at an enormous hole in the middle of his chest.

"Gerald?" sputtered their captor as he stumbled backward. "Fuck, Gerald ... I ... been shot." He brought up a hand to cover the flow of blood.

Boom! An identical hole appeared above the first causing the man to jerk. Alex ducked his head from the spray of blood and tissue. The AK-47 discharged a round, splintering a truss above the girls' heads. The man fell backwards, shattering the remaining glass in the window.

***

The Tahoe sped through the forest. All four tires worked in unison to grip the slick earth. The black October sky was now dumping snowflakes the size of dimes. The inch of white powder that had accumulated over the past twenty minutes made for terrible driving conditions. Visibility was poor, yet Ross continued to push on.

Ray Jackson fidgeted in his seat, unnerved by both the hazardous ride and the noise that they had heard moments before. The cry was followed by a single gunshot. Although Ray found it difficult to determine direction, Ross was adamant that they would find the source at the end of the trail.

He looked into Ross' wild eyes, unsure of what he should say. Ray had been up close and personal with a bear, and he knew very well that what they heard was no bear. Ross was now on a frantic mission to find his boy.

"Ross?" asked the Trooper nervously as the big truck fishtailed around a bend. The rear end brushed up against some overhanging tree-limbs. Jackson held onto the handle above his window to steady himself. "I don't know what that thing was, but I've got a bad taste in my mouth." Jackson was much more in tune with his friend's recent neurotic behavior.

"Try to climb over the seat, Ray." The driver gave the order without pulling his eyes from the trail. "There's a rifle back there. See if you can reach it." The .30-06 had become a permanent fixture of the Tahoe since his activities with David LaFontaine first began. He hoped that he would have an opportunity to use it. Ross reached up to his shoulder pocket and felt for the single bullet. It was something he did every hunting season ... a token of luck ... just in case. It was a tradition passed down from his grandfather.

Without a word, the big Trooper managed to scale the bench seat. "Shit!" muttered Jackson as he fell into the rear. He felt the sutures pulling in his shoulder. The gauze moistened as his wounds began to bleed. Disregarding the pain, Ray reached into the back and retrieved the case holding the Remington.

"Check the clip," said Ross as he maneuvered another turn in the road. "It should be full."

Ray did as he was told. He opened the plastic hard case, popped the clip out of the rifle and pushed down on the exposed cartridge. It didn't budge. "It's full."

"There's a second one in the case. Get that one, too."

Without warning, a strong gust of wind caused a wave of snow to fly from the trees and engulf the racing truck. Unable to see through the windshield, Ross tweaked the wheel slightly, guessing the pattern of the road. His foot pumped the brake. When the cloud finally cleared, the driver saw that he had greatly misjudged his turn.

"Hang on, Ray!" Before he could correct the error, the Tahoe glided off the trail and slammed into a stand of young birch. The upper half of Ray Jackson's body spilled back into the front seat. Ross heard the sheared stumps ripping away at the underbelly of the truck. When they finally came to a stop, the Sheriff rammed his elbow into the door out of frustration. The engine was dead. Ross turned the key in the ignition. The only response was a discomforting grinding sound.

The Trooper was struggling to untwist his body when Ross opened the door. He stepped out into the night, leaving Jackson to fend for himself. Ray kicked his legs over the headrest and scooted out behind his friend.

"Goddammit!" cursed Ross.

"Easy, buddy," said Ray as he turned and opened the rear door. He took out the rifle that was lying on the floor and snapped in the clip. The second clip had fallen somewhere beneath the seat.

"Give me the rifle, Ray," said the Sheriff impatiently.

Jackson hesitated before handing over the weapon. The Sheriff looked like he was ready to sprint into the unknown.

Experience taught the Trooper that running blindly into a fight was dangerous. “Hold on a sec. Let’s think this through first.”

“Give me the gun, Ray!” Ross glared at his friend like a man possessed. He had to find Chuck.

“Ross, wait,” pleaded Jackson, attempting to force some sense into him. “If we go running around like hellfire down that road, we don’t know what we’ll find, or what’s waiting for us.” Jackson spoke cautiously. He had to calm his friend down a few notches. “Let’s just settle a minute.”

At first, Ross’ eyes burned with hatred at the indecisive man who was preventing him from confronting his destiny. But then common sense slowly came back into focus. Ray was right. He nodded and assured him that he was now in control.

Sensing the change, Ray returned the nod and finally handed over the .30-06.

“Take this, Ray.” Ross pulled his .357 from its leather holster and placed it in the Trooper’s hand. He then racked a round into the chamber and the two men set out down Rylander Road on foot.

***

Alex stared in disbelief at the dangling legs of the body arched backward over the windowsill. He was unable to compute what had just happened. There was no sound in his ears but the isolated rhythm of his heart. Blood and sticky strands of flesh clung to his face. It felt like warm oatmeal. A faint voice began to penetrate the wall of silence. Someone was saying his name. The volume of the voice progressively grew until he was able to distinguish who it was. As he turned to see Kayla’s face, the pain in his side flared.

“Alex!” Kayla swooped down beside her boyfriend. “Oh my God!” she cried when her hand slipped in the pool of blood.

The soldier looked into Kayla’s weeping eyes. He tried his best to yield a smile. “I’m ... okay.” His words lacked strength. Every twitching muscle caused the blades to cut away at more flesh in his side. He had to get the arrow out before it hit something vital. Gathering all of his energy, Alex stretched out his arm to Chuck. “Take ... my hand,” he sputtered. “Pull me up.” There was someone else outside with a gun, and not knowing who that person was made Alex nervous. He had to make himself mobile should he be needed to defend again.

"I'm sorry, Alex. I'm so sorry," implored the teenager as he grabbed the outstretched hand.

"Forget it. Now ... pull me up." Alex was careful to keep the protruding arrow parallel to the floor.

When Chuck Barnes hauled Alex into a sitting position, the soldier then thrust his body backward until the end of the arrow met the wall. As he forced his body further back, the broadhead moved forward until it broke through the flesh six inches from his belly button. Alex held back the temptation to scream. Perspiration flowed from his forehead. His body quivered from the pain. All three girls turned their heads from the bloody mess on his abdomen. With a shaking hand, he reached up and slowly twisted the broadhead free of the shaft. He then rolled onto his side.

Alex took three deep breaths and then looked to Chuck. "Okay," he said in a hoarse voice, "I want you to pull it out."

"But, Alex," protested the teenager, unsure if he was capable of following through with the crude surgical procedure, "I can't just ... I mean."

"Do it, Chuck!" Alex's vision was blurred. His consciousness began to fade.

Chuck bent down and grasped the shaft. "Ready?" he asked.

"Oh God, Alex, don't do it," pleaded Kayla.

Alex paid her no attention. He untucked his shirt from his waist and stuffed a wad of material into his mouth. With his teeth clenched, he then nodded.

As Chuck pulled, the soldier's cry was drowned out by the roar of the creature outside the window.

***

The October storm was now attacking the north with tremendous ferocity. The towering pines wrestled like gladiators, fighting for supremacy in the narrow spaces separating them. Lashing winds carried branches and debris to the forest floor. Animals sought safe havens to escape the threatening squall. Rabbits burrowed into holes, whitetails dashed into their thickets

... and the female continued on to the boundaries of her lair where she would make her stand.

The weather was favorable. It would now be easier to slip down into the dense wetland. But the storm did present its dangers. Her senses were dulled. The female could not find scent in the swirling winds, nor could her eyes bore through the curtain of snow. But her ears continued to detect a strange cry. It was the same sound that the hairless ones made as they were killed. The female was now confronted with a curiosity to see what caused panic in her enemy.

She found her way closer to the source of the noise. Her progress had been slowed, but she maintained a steady pace. Her hands swiped away at the pine boughs, breaking trail through the dense foliage. The noises grew more pronounced with each step. When a brief lull in the storm allowed her eyes to see more clearly, the female observed a source of light through the web of branches. She hunkered down and crept closer until the clearing came into full view. Before the snows grew heavy again, she saw the dwelling.

When the flash of light exploded from the yard, the female ducked into cover. Her eyes searched until locking in on the solitary figure off to the side. Another flash preceded the second loud noise. She looked to the dwelling where another hairless one fell into the opening. The female was confused by this new revelation, unsure as to what her next action should be. She had just witnessed one of the hairless creatures destroy one of its own kind for reasons that she did not comprehend. Her thoughts drifted back to the clan and to her own close call with death at the hands of the alpha male. But that was because she had broken their laws and was not worthy to live amongst them ... for the sake of their survival. Desperation forced her to defend herself and further break those laws.

As she stared at the hairless one in the clearing, the hatred infiltrated her instinctive senses like a plaguing illness. She would not retreat from ensuing danger. The female arose from the ground like a hulking phantom and broke through the safety of the trees.

***

Frank Jones looked on as the second shot found its mark just below the first. He was somewhat surprised that his aim had been so accurate given the elements. Narrowing his eyelids to block the blowing snow, he centered his aim for a third shot. Before pulling the trigger, the man crashed backward through the window. He was done. The rifle fell from his grip and landed in the yard.

The woodsman stood still, studying his target to make sure that he wasn't going to move again. The others inside were silent. Frank found himself questioning his motive for intervening when he had been so close to fulfilling his objective. He had just killed a man. He would now have to answer to the police. There would be questions about why he was there in the first place. And he would have to surrender the location of Jesse's remains. Frank thought about turning and running ... escaping into the trees. But that would send the wrong message to the authorities. He cursed himself for getting involved. He was now forced to stay put. Vengeance for his brother's death was lost ... at least for now.

The elder Jones brother approached the cabin. He continued to hold the gun in firing position because he still wasn't sure what was going on inside. Where there was one, there might be more. His eyes surveyed the body at the window only twenty yards away. He saw the two hand-sized holes in the man's chest where the .44 slugs exited. When he was ten yards from the window he could see movement inside. He saw the boy who had held the arrow ... and the girls. Just as Frank Jones was about to call out and make them aware of his presence, he heard a subtle sound that was inconsistent with the resonance of the storm. Only a man with his keen senses would have detected the snow compressed beneath the weight of a foot.

Keeping his body moving forward, Frank cocked the hammer on the .44. Whatever made the sound was directly behind him. He couldn't explain the impulse, but something told him that it was not a man advancing on him. It was the creature that had murdered his brother, and now it had found him. There were four live rounds in the .44. He would fall to the ground and then aim for center mass. The snow crunched again, this time much closer.

Frank Jones dove to his right and rolled. When he settled on his back he swung the weapon around to fire. Just as he made out the massive shape bearing down on him, his arm was pinned by a tremendous force. His hand went numb when his forearm snapped. Frank's legs kicked wildly at the mammoth appendage that would not release him. A terrifying roar erupted. Pain then ripped through his abdomen and he felt himself rising into the air. Frank stared in horror as he was drawn to the gaping jaws of the beast. The blades imbedded in his belly clenched together, squeezing his organs. Before the teeth clamped down on his exposed neck, Frank Jones pulled the trigger and discharged a single round into the ground. The .44 fell from his hand. He gazed into the human-like eyes before its teeth tightened around his throat and tore out his windpipe.

***

"What ... what ... was that?" Kayla's trepidation was felt by all as they looked to the dark window. None of them wanted to know what was now lurking outside the feeble protection of the cabin walls.

Only Alex had sense enough to act. He forced his body into motion and rose to his feet. The spine-chilling roar was followed by a man's scream, and then a gunshot. Something else had entered the fray. If Alex was to put up a defense, he had to stop the flow of blood from his wound.

"Chuck, get me that scarf on the hanger by the door." Alex took control like the leader he was. His orders were whispered so as not to alarm whatever it was outside. Using his hand, he signaled for the others to hunch down to the floor and remain quiet. He then crept over to the wall and turned off the light. The room fell into total darkness. The only thing he could hear above the storm was the hushed whimpers.

Chuck brought the scarf to the soldier without a word. Alex winced as he knotted the fabric around his midsection. Assuring himself that the bandage had been adequately applied, he lightly massaged the area around each wound. Although the scarf was moist, he was satisfied that the blood flow had been effectively minimized. He could not afford to lose more strength now. He had to remain sharp.

"Okay," he whispered to the group huddled close behind him. "We back up to the far wall." His eyes had acclimated to the lack of light and he could see the terror written in Kayla's eyes. They were all scared. He was scared. The cry they had heard outside was unimaginable. Alex gently caressed Kayla's neck and smiled to let her know that she would be okay. She clutched his arm and held it tight. Alex then turned to Chuck. "Can you quietly ... try to find a weapon?" He motioned to the small kitchen area.

"What ... what weapon?" questioned the frightened boy.

"Anything," answered Alex. "A knife ... fork ... anything." He watched as Chuck slithered across the floor toward the place where the utensils were kept. Alex then moved to the window. He had to see what they were up against. Kayla would not release her grip.

"No, Alex ... please stay with me."

He turned to her, once again trying his best to smile under the circumstances. "It's okay. I'm just going to take a quick look. I'm not going to let anything happen to you." *At all cost*, he told himself. He would protect them with his life.

With a forceful tug, Alex pulled free and crawled across the floor toward the window. Every movement caused a surge of fire in his side. He fought through it, focusing only on the window.

When he reached the two legs dangling in the opening, snow spit against his face. He placed his hands on the thighs of the fresh corpse and pulled himself up. Holding his eyes just above the man's crotch, he peered out into the clearing. As he surveyed the yard, he trained his eyes on a dark silhouette rising high above the ground. Alex studied the object closely, measuring its girth. It was closer than the tree line, yet it was not part of the clearing as he remembered it. Then it moved ... coming closer to the cabin ... *walking* closer to the cabin. When the two-legged shape materialized thirty yards out, Alex began to tremble. He was unable to pull himself away. He was frozen in a hypnotic trance, unable to grasp in his mind what was coming at him. He watched the legs ... the strides. The arms were swinging. The face was hidden beneath the black cloak of hair.

The fulminating growl jerked the young soldier from his stupor. The creature attacked. Alex fell backward to the floor. The wound in his side no longer burdened his ability to move. He heard the girls scrambling to the far wall with panicked screams. After a loud smacking sound in the window, he looked up expecting to see death staring back at him. But it was not the monster. Had he not become so accustomed to death, he might have been sickened by the sight of the headless body wedged in the frame on top of the black man.

"Alex!" cried Kayla, now in absolute hysterics. Brenda and Jenna kept her from running to him as they too cried out in fear of what they could not see.

"Stay back!" ordered Alex as he turned away from the gruesome scene. He rolled onto his stomach to push himself up off the floor. The creature bellowed again just above the clogged opening above his head. He then felt a wash of cold air infiltrating the room. One of the bodies landed on his back. As he struggled to brush the corpse away, his arm scraped across the protruding spinal column. He tried to dig his heels into the floor to scoot himself away from the window, but the blood made for a slick surface. His feet moved, but his body didn't. A flash of dark fur wrapped around his leg. Alex screamed in defiance as the powerful hand pulled him closer to the window. He kicked wildly at the arm. He looked up and then saw the face of the creature glaring down on him. Its black, leathery face was not unlike a man's. He could see its wide nostrils, almost apelike, flaring. The teeth were bared. He could do nothing to thwart its strength.

Adrenaline continued to pump his legs. Suddenly, Chuck blew past him and thrust a steak knife into the thick forearm. The creature howled in pain and released its grip. The arm withdrew from the window. Alex was momentarily free. With the teenager's help, he climbed to his feet and sprinted across the room into Kayla's arms.

Alex's sanctuary was brutally shattered when the wall next to the open window began to buckle as if it were being struck by a wrecking ball. Through the darkness, he watched as the wooden slats bowed inward with each mighty blow from the beast's fists.

"Make it stop!" begged Kayla. "Please make it stop!"

"It's breaking through, Alex!" yelled Chuck who was now holding a long meat fork.

Alex knew that if the thing broke through, they had nothing to stop it. He had to make a move. The wood was beginning to splinter as the creature continued its fierce assault. He didn't have much time. It roared again, and with one massive rap, a piece of the wall gave way. Alex walked in a tight circle, working a plan in his disoriented head. *Outnumbered ... enemy attacking.* The others looked on as the soldier formulated his strategy.

"Diversion!" he exclaimed out loud. Alex fell to his knees and ran his hand between the grooves of the wooden slats. "Chuck!" he called. "Throw me the fire stoker!"

The teenager stared at him in disbelief, caught up in his own sense of helplessness.

"Damn it, Chuck! Get the fucking stoker! Now!"

Chuck Barnes snapped to attention. He quickly searched the room until he located the object that Alex had requested. The hole in the wall grew bigger as the creature continued to pound. When it subsided for a moment, Alex looked to the opening and saw the eye peering in at them ... studying them. The creature cried out again with rage and continued the drubbing. Alex figured they had about three minutes before it completely caved. When Chuck handed him the fireplace tool, he rammed it between two slats and began to pry up the floor boards. He heard the squealing of rusty nails pulling free. The first six-foot board was awkward, but when he finally broke it loose, the others came much easier.

"Alex?" asked Chuck. "What are you doing?"

The soldier paid no attention to him. He had a plan, but time was short. The second board came free, and then the third. Satisfied that there was ample room, Alex then poked his head into the opening. He reached down with his arm into the dark space. He couldn't touch the ground. "Alright," he told the others, "everyone get in."

"But why ..." Chuck started to ask.

"No time, get in ... everyone!"

"Alex," sobbed Kayla, "I can't move.

He went to the girl and pulled her toward the narrow gap in the floor. There was no time to provide comfort. He now had to wash all emotion from his body. "Brenda, help her down."

Jenna was the first to scamper into the black hole. Alex was impressed that she hadn't asked any questions. He figured that she was also overwhelmed with shock. Brenda followed, holding on to Kayla's outstretched arm, and then Chuck. When they were all clear and out of sight, Alex threw the loose planks over the opening. He would be the diversion.

Alex picked up his bloodied hunting knife and then dragged the second sofa over the boards. He could hear Kayla's muffled screams below. He could only pray that the others would settle her down to give him time. Just then, the wall gave way. A thundering roar filled the room.

***

Ross could not wait for his companion who had fallen behind. The Trooper fought to keep pace, but he had been out of commission for too long. Ross turned around and backpedaled for a few steps. Jackson, who was now barely visible, stopped and was doubled over trying to catch his wind.

"Ray?" called the Sheriff.

The Trooper waved him on. "Go on!" he yelled.

That was all the coaxing Ross needed. The cold steel of the .30-06 burned in his hand, but he didn't care. He needed to get to Chuck. Ross could hear the chilling cries of the beast above the winds. It grew louder as he made his way down the trail. He could almost see it taking shape in his mind at the end of a long, suffocating tunnel. He ran as hard as his legs could take him, exerting every ounce of strength that his body could muster.

Death seeks he,
Who touches fear,
And sees the face,
Of Satan's peer.

Nearer the lair,
It invites you in,
No turning back,
From fatal sin.

If you will the courage,
To face the demons within,
Then pray with pure heart,
The journey ends with Amen.

He screamed aloud to try and block out the chaotic verses spinning in his head. He prayed that he wasn't too late. Ross envisioned Chuck's body, mangled and shredded, his guts strewn about like those of Charlie Perkins. What would Maggie think of him when he had known all along? He shook away the horrid thought. He ran even harder toward the nightmare that awaited him. His foot slipped on a hidden root, causing him to fall headfirst into a cloud of white dust.

***

Alex's feet were glued to the floor when the creature blasted through the remaining remnants of wood holding the wall in place. He watched as it slowly, almost cautiously, ducked beneath the low ceiling. As it entered the room, Alex could hear its deep, labored breathing, like an idling motor waiting to be throttled. Its back was hunched over, yet its head was still just inches below the ceiling that was ten feet from the floor. He watched as it looked about the room with its face hidden in the blackness of skin and hair. It was only fifteen feet away. He dared not flinch. His heart pounded uncontrollably in his chest.

The soldier held his breath when the beast took a step in his direction. The floorboards moaned under the weight of its mass. Alex gripped the knife tightly in his hand, prepared for a fight that he had no hope of winning. It stopped when a growing murmur emerged from beneath the floor. The foul odor filled his nostrils, causing him to cringe. He watched as it honed in on the source of the high-pitched squeals. The creature grunted loudly, as if it were trying to spook its prey from its place of hiding. The menacing sounds caused Kayla to become more hysterical and her screams grew louder. Alex thought he could hear Chuck trying to comfort her. The creature looked directly to the sofa covering the crawlspace. Although he couldn't see its eyes, Alex sensed that it was confused. When it turned to approach the couch, the soldier silently slipped into the bedroom where his belongings were stashed. He could hear the creature moving in the main room.

Alex stepped over Trevor's body and felt for the fanny pack next to his duffel bag. After securing it in his hands, he then picked his fleece jacket off a hook and snuck over to the window. He carefully unlatched the lock. The glass moaned when he pushed up the pane. The creature heard him. It was coming toward the bedroom. Alex tossed the fanny pack and fleece through the opening, hoisted himself up onto the ledge and slithered out into the cold night air.

Once his feet were planted firmly on the frozen ground, Alex turned and peered back through the opening. He could only see darkness. Without looking, he bent down, retrieved the fanny pack and then snapped it around his waist. “Hey!” he shouted, while slipping into the jacket. “Over here!” The ruse was answered be a ferocious growl that seemed to cause the entire building to vibrate. He could hear all of the girls now screaming in the crawl space. “Over here!” he called again. The creature charged through the cabin, busting up anything in its path. Its body slammed into the furniture and walls. Alex sensed the increasing anger as it battled to find a target. “I’m over here, goddammit!” He continued to taunt the creature, calling through the open window while using himself as live bait. Then, as if it had managed to disappear altogether, there was no sound ... no heavy breathing or weighted steps ... nothing.

Alex squinted his eyes, trying to penetrate the dark interior of the bedroom. He began to think that the creature had tried to flank him. He quickly checked both sides. A subtle shuffling noise, like a gliding mop, drew his attention back to the window. The gap in the doorway was darker than before. It was filled by an immense shadow. It was the creature ... watching him with its head ducked in an awkward position inside the room.

“Come on, you fucker!” Alex’s heart continued to race with both anticipation and fear. There was no second guessing his strategy now. He was all in. “Come on,” he whispered. “Come and get me.”

Suddenly, the creature roared again, squeezed through the doorway and vaulted forward. Alex backed up and fell to the ground as the massive arm rifled through the window. The claws were inches from his face, straining to rip into his body. The wall buckled against the tremendous force, but it held the charge in check. The creature cried out in frustration and withdrew its hand.

Alex rolled and sprang to his feet. The first step to his plan had worked to perfection, but the second phase would now determine his fate. The soldier sprinted around the corner of the building and into the clearing just beyond the front door. He frantically searched the ground for the weapon that was now covered with snow. Inside the cabin, he heard the thing making its way back to the opening in the wall. Alex wanted the rifle, but it was too close to take a chance. There was no time. He began to kick away at the snow in the general area where he thought the black man had tossed his bow. His boot struck a basketball-sized object. When it rolled over, he saw the face staring up at him with open eyes. Alex turned away, unaffected by the gruesome sight of Frank Jones' head. He had to find the weapon. Just when the panic began to set in, his boot touched something solid. He looked down and saw the cam of his compound bow rising out of the small drift.

The soldier's hand plunged into white powder and grasped the weapon. He brushed away the snow and then popped an arrow out of the quiver. He raised his head when the shrill scream erupted from inside the cabin walls. It was one of the girls! It was Kayla! Alex knocked the arrow and ran to the hole in the side of the building. He wasn't prepared for what he then witnessed. The sofa had been tossed to the side. The creature was bent over the exposed pit, reaching for a victim. The arm extracted a struggling body up through the crawlspace. It had Kayla!

"Noooooooo!" screamed Alex. The creature pivoted in the darkness and glared at the silhouette standing at the opening. It roared in fierce defiance. Kayla threw weak, ineffective jabs at the beast as it plucked her off the ground.

"Alex!" she called. Her voice was wavering, losing strength as she writhed in its clutches.

He heard the sickening sound of claws penetrating skin and bone. Kayla screamed louder as its hold tightened.

Alex drew back the string and brought the bow to full draw. He leveled the sight on the center of the creature's back and released. The monster bellowed in pain as the broadhead sank deep into its shoulder. The arrow had sailed high. Alex watched as it flung Kayla across the room. She landed hard against the far wall and fell to the floor in silence. "Kayla!" he cried. Alex wanted to go to her. The creature that was desperately trying to locate the arrow imbedded in its back blocked his path. He had to lure it away.

"Hey!" he called. "Come on, bitch!" Alex backed up as it turned toward him, snarling with nasty distaste from the harm he had caused. He ran when it started to advance. Alex continued to scream at the top of his lungs in order to draw it from the cabin.

He ran to the edge of the tree line, looking back to make sure he was being followed. Behind him, the creature tore through the wall and exploded into the clearing. It continued to roar with uncontrolled fury. His plan was working. Alex stopped and watched as it lifted its mighty head and scented the swirling winds. *Come on,* he told himself. *Follow me.*

Then, as if his thoughts had transcended across the clearing, it looked up and gazed directly at him. Alex could barely define its outline in the storm, but he knew that it could see him. "Come on!" he yelled again. It cried out in anger and started across the clearing with the arrow still protruding from its thick hide. Alex turned and ran into the trees. He would now have to rely on every resource he could find, and a lot of luck. His job now was to ensure the survival of the others ... at all costs.

CHAPTER SIXTEEN

When Maggie Barnes walked out of the office and into the street, she was overcome with despair. She felt that something was terribly wrong ... that her son was in danger. Ross was nowhere to be seen, and she hadn't talked to him for hours. Maggie decided to leave the Inn and try to locate him. She repeatedly tried to raise him on the radio with no success. The buzzing static only added to her anxiety.

Maggie gazed up into the gloomy sky, watching the snowflakes zipping through the glare of the streetlights. The weatherman from Channel Seven had said on the six o'clock news that the storm would pass to the north. She cursed the man's erroneous forecast as though he could have personally prevented the squall from moving into the Jessup area.

The distressed woman stood alone on the sidewalk, unsure as to what her next step should be. Maggie couldn't stand idle knowing that Ross and Chuck could be in trouble. *Rylander Road*, she said to herself, recalling her conversation with Henry Pierson. It was the only place that came to mind.

"What are you doing out here, Maggie?"

The voice came from behind. She turned to see Art Conley approaching. He looked like an Eskimo, donning a heavy, down-filled parka with a fur-lined hood.

"I'm looking for Ross, Art. Have you seen him?" She tried to smile, but couldn't.

"No, Maggie. I haven't seen him since this morning." Conley studied her closely. He could see the uncertainty in her eyes. "Is everything okay?" he asked.

"I guess so, Art," she lied. "I guess everything is fine."

Conley softly patted her on the shoulder. "That was something about Mark, huh?"

Maggie turned abruptly and looked at him. "What do you mean? What about Mark?" She hadn't heard anything. The afternoon crowd had been small. Most were staying home or in their camps because of the weather.

"That hunter, Maggie." Art Conley spoke as though he was surprised that she was not aware of what had happened. After all, news does travel fast in a small town. "That guy who found Mark's hand."

Maggie gasped and covered her mouth. "What do you mean ... Mark's hand?"

"Oh geez, Maggie," responded Conley, suddenly wishing that he hadn't brought up the topic. But he couldn't stop now. Maggie would demand that he tell her everything, or at least all that he knew. He revealed the remainder of the story to her. "Mark's hand ... his severed hand ... was found out on the Benson Track this morning by a hunter. He brought it in and showed it to Ross. Wendy Murphy said she saw the whole thing. Ross and that Trooper friend of his took off right away."

"Do you know where they went, Art?"

"I don't know. Probably out to where that guy found it." Conley bowed his head. "Poor boy," he said. "Mark was a good egg, too."

***

"This shit is getting nasty," exclaimed Jack Berkowski.

"It's going to be tough finding anyone tonight," replied Godson. "We might want to think about getting back on the hardtop." She was struggling to keep the car on what little trail she could see. The snow had nearly wiped out all traces of the two-track. It felt as though she were merely driving through the forest, picking her way between the trees.

"Damn it, Sam, they have to be out here somewhere." The Sergeant's frustration had reached its peak. There hadn't been any word from anyone. The suspects disappeared into thin air ... again. The only moment of hope came when a unit stopped two men in a blue Ford pickup over an hour ago. When one of them jumped out and bolted into the woods, a number of units converged on the scene. After the suspect was apprehended, they found that it was only a scared kid who had been on probation.

He and his brother had evidently been doing some road-beering and toking on a joint. What the reporting officer failed to report was that the boys were white.

"Let's get out of this mess before we have to hike it out," declared Berkowski in defeat.

Just as Godson began to turn around, the dispatcher's voice sputtered on the radio. The Troopers listened to the reports of shots fired in the vicinity of Rylander Road. All units were to respond.

"Do you know where Rylander Road is, Sarge?" asked the driver.

"Kind of. I believe it's north. Let's get back to the main road and go from there."

***

Ross' chest was heaving when he saw the break in the trees. The snow had let off a bit and he was able to see more clearly. He first noticed the rear of the Taurus. When he rounded the last of the trees, he found himself standing in front of a small cabin. He stopped to catch his breath.

"Oh Christ!" he cried after seeing the obliterated wall. It reminded him of Ned Crosby's door ... shattered to bits. "Chuck!" he called to the dark building. "Chuck!" There was no response. Ross steadied his rifle and stormed up to the structure. His only mission was to find his boy. There were no lights. He stopped suddenly when his eyes detected the body in the window. As he walked closer he saw that it was a black man, bent backward out the window. Ross began to think that his worst fear had been realized. Chucky had been ...

A faint noise emerged from inside. It was a person calling his name. "Chuck!" yelled Ross again.

"Ross! Under here!"

The response was hushed, as if it was from another room. But he recognized the voice. It was Chuck! The Sheriff sprang through the gaping entrance, paying no attention to the lifeless corpse in the window. Unable to see in the darkness, he felt along the wall. When he located a switch, he flicked on the lights and illuminated the room. His jaw dropped. There was blood everywhere. The furniture was torn and battered. He saw the body of a young girl lying against the far wall. Then he saw the headless body just inside the window. But it wasn't anyone he recognized.

"Chuck, where are you?" cried the desperate Sheriff.

"Down here, Ross," came the reply from beneath the floor.

Ross raced to the gap in the boards. When he reached it, Chuck's head popped out. He saw the relief written on the boy's face. Ross grabbed his free hand and hauled him out. He then pulled him close and held him tight, as though he had not seen him in years. He never wanted to let the boy go again. Chuck reciprocated, holding him with the same commitment. His body convulsed as he sobbed in Ross' chest.

"It's okay," said Ross warmly, fighting back his own tears. "I've got you now."

"I ... I ... I thought we were going to die," said the boy.

The Sheriff cupped his hand behind Chuck's head. "I know, but it's okay now. Everything's okay."

Ross allowed the teenager to finally pull away. He watched him wipe the tears away on this sleeve. Ross then noticed the other two girls climbing out of the hole. Jenna was followed by a young lady he didn't recognize. Both were dazed, their bodies were shivering. Faces displayed a torturous experience that Ross could not begin to comprehend. They were all in shock.

"Kayla!" The girl behind Jenna wailed when she saw her friend lying on the floor. "Oh, Kayla!"

Chuck embraced Jenna while Ross laid down his weapon and went to the one who was injured. "What happened here?" he asked while kneeling down beside the girl. The side of her head was soaked with blood, but she was breathing. There were also gashes in her side. He gently slid one hand under her head and brushed the matted hair from her face.

"I ... I don't know what it was," said Chuck. "It was a ... a thing ... a monster," stuttered the boy.

Ross turned and peered up into his face. His own hands began to tremble. "What do you mean ... a monster?" But he knew very well what the boy had meant.

***

The pain in her shoulder flared. Her acrimonious cries echoed through the forest with damning ferocity. The female charged through the trees with reckless abandon, committing herself to the destruction of the hairless one who had caused her injury. Her deadly claws sliced through the undergrowth like a combine through a cornfield, allowing nothing to stand between her and the satisfaction she sought.

The female had tried hopelessly to extract the slender stick from her back. Her attempts only worsened the situation when the arrow snapped off, leaving the knifing pain inside her. She could feel blood saturating her hide. But what drove the female more than her bitter hatred was the frustration that she had allowed herself to be bettered by one of those weak creatures. She wondered how she would now appear in the eyes of the clan. She roared in revolt of their neglectful ways, angered by their unwillingness to accept her. She was alone.

The female focused her thoughts on her one objective as she pushed herself forward. She would hunt the hairless one, kill it, and prove her superiority in the domain where they did not belong. Hunger no longer played a role in her actions. Only the kill would satisfy her now. She stopped and listened for the sounds of her fleeing prey.

***

Alex Chavez heard the cries of his relentless pursuer. They sounded like war drums preceding an assault on a defenseless enemy. His legs pumped through the burdensome snow. He pressed one hand against the seeping wound in his side while the other gripped his only means of defense. His eyes picked out obstacles like fine-tuned radar, sending signals to his brain to duck and avoid. He hurdled over logs and weaved through trees. Still, he was repeatedly slapped by those unseen branches that came out of nowhere. He was at war and the enemy was gaining.

Alex worked his strategy as he ran. Knowing that the terrain was too open to outpace the closing creature, he headed toward the lowlands that would provide cover. If he could make the swamp, he could find a more suitable place to hide, or in all probability, make a stand. Alex was now a soldier in a battle for his life. Though his enemy was not a human threatening the sanctity of his country's constitution, it was a being that endangered humanity. He discarded his heartfelt sorrow for

Kayla, no longer wondering whether she was alive or dead. The distraction would lead to failure.

When the slope of the ground began its descent to the swamp, Alex slowed his progress. He was careful to maintain his footing on the slippery earth. The relentless bellowing of the wounded beast grew louder, informing him that he was not moving fast enough. He passed the tree where a lifetime ago he had spent a quiet morning in nature's glory. But now he faced the other side of nature's volatile personality ... her grotesque wickedness.

Once he reached the bottom of the ridge, a wall of cedars stood before him. The storm front had seemingly passed and the forest had submerged into an eerie quiet. A break in the clouds overhead allowed the full moon to beam through. The light sparkling off the white ground gave him a false sense of security. He looked up to the top of the ridge. Less than a hundred yards away he saw it ... standing on its two legs ... watching him. He gasped at the sheer size of the body. It was the first time he had actually seen the creature in full form standing upright. It reared back and unleashed a horrible cry. Alex turned and ran into the Amen Swamp.

***

Ross walked through the doorway and out into the clearing. He stared up at the sky and was somewhat lifted by the brilliant showing of stars. The thought of what he had to do next quickly dispelled the momentary high. Chuck was safe, but his nemesis still existed. It was time to face his fear. He found himself wishing for David LaFontaine. Instead, he would go alone into the demon's lair with four rounds in his .30-06. He looked up into the heavens a second time and closed his eyes.

"Give me some help, Eevie. For Maggie and Chuck ... please be with me."

"Ross!"

The Sheriff turned as Ray Jackson lumbered up from the two-track. Chuck, Jenna and Brenda were loading their injured friend into the snow-covered Taurus. They were preparing to take her to Appleton. The Trooper passed by the kids and worked his way up to his friend. His eyes danced between the body in the window and the caved in wall.

"What the hell happened?" asked the Trooper, trying to interpret the scene in his head.

"There's one of your suspects, Ray," answered the Sheriff quietly, "present and accounted for." He held his own eyes on the tracks leading to the trees.

"What the hell happened here," questioned Ray again. "How did that ..." His voice was silenced when his eyes followed Ross' stare down to the tracks in the snow. Jackson cautiously approached the prints as if they might jump up and bite him. "Damn," he whispered quietly as he measured the print against the size of his own boot. "What is it, Ross? Bear?"

Ross had to chuckle from his friend's remark. "I could only wish, Ray."

"You mean that LaFontaine character was right?" Jackson then looked up to him after noticing the flashlight in his hand. "Uhhhhhh, what you planning on doing with that, Haas?" He had a pretty good idea.

"I'm going after it, Ray. There's a boy out there running for his life. I'm going to hunt this thing down and kill it." There was no hesitation in his voice. He was determined, and neither Ray Jackson nor all the Troopers in the world would keep him from his destiny.

"Ross, please don't," pleaded Chuck from behind. "This thing is not ... not ... it's a monster. You can't do it by yourself." Chuck was crying again.

The Sheriff looked to the boy and saw him shaking with fear. It was fear of losing a father. He tried to smile, but couldn't. He wanted to heed the advice and take him home to Maggie. But this was his opportunity to silence those old ghosts forever. *This is the way it was meant to be,* he affirmed.

"Kid's right, Ross. This ain't right and you know it," added Jackson.

"Cut the shit, Ray!" barked the Sheriff, angered by his friend's opposition. "I'm gonna do this and the only way you can stop me is if you pull that trigger and shoot me dead."

"Please, Ross. Please don't ... don't do it," pleaded Chuck over and over again.

Ross could hear the concern in his voice. He knew that Chucky loved him. But that was why he had to do this. He fought back temptation. "No, Chuck." He placed his hands on the young boy's shoulders. "Please understand, I've got to go. I'm sorry." He pulled back, clicked on the flashlight and started off toward the trees.

"Wait a second, buddy. If you gonna go and get yourself killed, then I'm coming along to watch." Jackson trudged off after him.

Ross turned and smiled politely at his friend. "Sorry, Ray," he answered. "I appreciate the offer, but you'll slow me down. I need you to get those kids out of here." Off in the distance they all heard the creature roar. Kayla screamed.

"Go on!" yelled Ross sternly. "Get them out of here!" With that, he turned and ran off into the night.

The others looked on as his flashlight disappeared in the trees beyond the clearing.

***

The enormous figure stopped after entering the opening, unaware of the hidden eyes that followed its movements. The head swiveled from side to side, searching the undergrowth for his unseen presence. It lifted its broad nose skyward and inhaled deeply, holding in the air to taste the scent of its prey. Alex Chavez controlled his body with his mind, fighting the urge to shiver from the layer of black muck. He barely breathed while he fixated his universe on a single hair at the center of the creature's exposed back ... his target.

Chavez eyed the enemy before him, unaffected by its terrifying appearance. He allowed the menacing growls to pass through his ears. Fear was a distraction that was of no use to the soldier. He was only concerned with the target ... that single hair on its back. He did not think about Trevor Musgrave, the roommate he would never see again, or his love for Kayla. He watched that solitary hair.

Alex slowly emerged from behind the deadfall with the bow in hand. The distance was twenty-five yards to that single hair. His moment had arrived. The ambush was set with the target in the kill zone. The creature continued to scent the subtler breeze. It inspected the tracks leading to the other side of the clearing. Unbeknownst to Alex Chavez, he had used its own tactic against it ... backtracking to the deadfall. It was a lesson that had been taught by instructors under similar circumstances, yet from different worlds. The goal for both species here was survival. The soldier had submerged himself into a deep swamp pit to cover his human odor.

Alex placed his fingers on the string. His mind washed away the numbing pain from the cold. The only variance surging in his thoughts was that he was unaccustomed to shooting without a release. But he'd taken those shots before at targets much smaller than the one before him. Experience told him to compensate slightly to the left. He raised the bow and drew. As he pulled back, the cam creaked ever so slightly, but loud enough to be heard. It pivoted with incredible finesse, crouched and ready for the unexpected. Its movement detracted from the archer's concentration because his point of focus had been altered. He held his breath, still hidden in the breakup of the fallen tree. The creature glared directly at Alex, but it did not see him. He held the draw, aiming the arrow through a narrow opening between branches, straining to maintain a steady arm. The creature was producing low, guttural growling sounds, informing the beings of the forest that it was prepared to kill. The rancid stench was even stronger as it drifted to his nose yet again. His eyes watered.

After an excruciating thirty second standoff, Alex realized that he could no longer hold the draw. With his energy depleted, he had to release or risk a wild shot. Slowly, he moved the pin until it was steadied on the beast's chest. *Aim small, miss small,* he told himself. The creature spotted the movement and unleashed another horrendous cry that seemed to shake the trees around him. The string slipped through his fingers. He watched the arrow sail. The creature's eyes zeroed in on the propellant as it flew from the brush. It sprang to the side just before the shaft sank into the same shoulder that still held the first broadhead.

The soldier stood in awe of the creature's frantic struggle to grasp the exposed shaft in its back. The ground seemed to tremble from its massive feet as it cried out in contempt of the pain that he had inflicted. Flailing claws carved off pine boughs as if they were nothing but flimsy toothpicks. Alex quickly took out another arrow from the quiver and knocked it in place. He drew back again just as the beast turned to face him. It now realized the source of its agony and snarled with cruel intention. Its muscles flexed in preparation for the charge.

"This one's for you, Kayla," he whispered as he released the string. At the sound of the *'twang'*, the creature dove to the swamp floor. The archer watched in frustration as the arrow flew over its head and ricocheted off a branch. Knowing that he would not have enough time to get off another shot, Alex turned and sprinted into the darkness of the swamp. The beast crashed through the trees close behind.

***

Maggie saw a flicker of light on the trail ahead. She had been following the single set of tire tracks down Rylander Road hoping they would lead her to Ross and Chuck. Every cabin she passed with no sign of the Sheriff's Tahoe augmented her worries. She could do nothing but continue on ... and pray.

As she rounded a curve, a large lump swelled in her throat. She saw the Tahoe off the road along with another car she didn't recognize. The front end of the truck was wedged against a tree. Her initial thought was that Ross had been in an accident and was hurt. As she drove closer, she then saw Chuck standing with some others.

Maggie parked her vehicle, got out, and dashed over to the small group of onlookers. She was startled to see Ray Jackson get out of the Tahoe. Before uttering a word, she looked around to identify the people standing there. Ross was not one of them. "What's going on, Ray? Where's Ross?" she asked desperately.

"Mom!" Chuck flew into her arms.

Maggie was surprised by his outpouring of emotion. She gently pushed him away. "What happened, Chuck?"

"Maggie," piped in the Trooper, "something's happened. I just radioed for backup. Help should be on the way."

"What ... what happened? Tell me where Ross is," she demanded.

"Okay, Maggie," continued Ray as he winced at the pain from his reopened wound. He was going to need some quick medical attention as well. "The truth is, these kids had a run-in with one of our fugitives back there."

"Oh God, Chuck, are you alright?" She took her son's hand and patted it.

"Yeah, mom, I'm fine now." The boy suddenly lost his composure and collapsed into his mother's arms. "I'm sorry, mom. I'm so sorry." He wept, clinging to her body like a toddler, not wanting to let go.

Tears formed in Maggie's eyes. "Please tell me where Ross is?" she asked as she looked over to Ray Jackson. "Is he ... is he dead?" Saying that word felt as if a heavy brick had landed on her.

"No, Maggie." Ray attempted a smile, but was unsuccessful.

She could see that he was hiding something. He would not look her in the eyes. "Goddammit, Ray! Where the hell is he?"

"Ross' monster is real, Maggie, and he's gone after it." Ray couldn't believe what he was saying, but there was no denying the truth now. A siren blared in the distance.

***

Brave souls follow the enticing path,
Find remorse in Amen's wrath,
Spirits await your arrival there,
All eyes follow you into its lair.

Welcome he who seeks his fame,
Turn back now or bask in shame,
Call the damned their souls to sell,
Hear the toll of Amen's bell.

If you will the courage,
To face the demons within,
Then pray with pure heart,
The journey ends with Amen.

It was easier for the Sheriff to move through the snow. He ran in the prints of both beast and boy that had already broken trail. He was headed to a place that he had sworn to avoid. Ross battled his inner fears, suppressing the desire to run from those haunting demons that would now scribe his future. His testimony to life would be written on this night in the Amen Swamp. Destiny had been there all along, nipping at his conscience like a hungry mosquito.

Ross stood as a martyr before the alluring cedars at Amen's gate, readying himself for the fight against the evil presence hidden within. He could hear the surreal cries of the creature not far in the distance calling out its invitation. Memories of those he had loved both past and present circulated in his thoughts. They were his purpose in life and would give him strength. Ross took a deep breath and exhaled the frigid air. When the cloud of steam dissipated around his head, he gathered his senses and entered the forbidden domain of the Amen Swamp.

***

The young soldier was running for his life, muscling his way through the dense cover. Vines and branches reached out to him like tentacles of an octopus, and he was the struggling fish attempting to escape its clutches. He could feel his legs and arms weakening from the continuous strain as he fought to penetrate deeper into the swamp. Thorns lashed his exposed face. He could hear the creature closing the gap. It thrashed about in a wild frenzy. Alex could not believe how it could move so easily in such difficult terrain. He was ducking and avoiding, while the beast was plowing through whatever lay in its path. His confidence deteriorated as he listened to the creature getting closer.

The fleeing soldier cringed as he brushed against a jagged branch that snagged the makeshift bandage around his waist. He could feel the warm blood now saturating his fatigues that were already drenched from swamp water and snow. The wound in his side was widening. Blood and sweat were now hindering his vision, but he pushed onward. The only survival skill he was now utilizing was to run.

The creature was so close that Alex could feel the breeze from the parting trees flushing against the nape of his neck. While he was forced to duck underneath the cedars, the beast merely ran over them. Its swiping claws were inches from the flesh on his back. The stench of its body smothered his nose. As he focused his eyes forward, he found himself heading for a bastion of thick pines that horseshoed around him in an impervious trap. He had nowhere to turn. Then, he saw the narrowest of gaps in the wall of green. The soldier shot toward it. Alex's feet left the ground and he lunged for freedom. He pulled the bow tight to his chest and closed his eyes. His tucked body blasted through the maze of receding limbs. When he exited the other side, he plunged headfirst into a wave of icy water.

Alex was overcome by total silence as he floated weightlessly in the depths of the Ontonogon River. The heinous world above had transformed into pure tranquility. His body gently rolled with the steady current, giving him a wondrous sensation of flying. When he opened his eyes he was blinded by total darkness, but he was at peace. For a few precious seconds, Alex Chavez thought he had died and his soul was being lifted to the heavens. He relaxed his aching muscles, overwhelmed by the harmonious state. He glided like a bird with outstretched arms, soaring high above the clouds overlooking the hell below. His buoyant feet bounced lightly off the rocky bottom.

A burgeoning pain slowly oozed into his body. His exposed skin began to burn. When the pressure grew in his chest and lungs, he then realized that he needed to breathe. Alex shook his head when his brain relayed the message that he was still alive. He planted his feet on the river bottom and pushed himself upward toward the light. His head broke the river's surface and he sucked in oxygen, replacing stale air with fresh. He was alive, and incredibly rejuvenated.

The moment of exultation quickly mutated to harsh reality as the familiar cry of hell's relentless angel tickled his ears again. He allowed his body to sink back down into the freezing water as he kept his eyes just above the surface. Alex slowly turned and surveyed the riverbank. It was standing fifty yards upstream, looking in the wrong direction. He read the creature's mood in its body language. It howled in frustration, jumping up and down like a demented lunatic, swatting away large chunks of rotted bark from a defenseless tree. The soldier's lips curled into an insidious grin. *Fuck you and your mother*, he chided silently.

Alex continued to drift with the current away from the beast. He also knew that prolonged exposure to the water would be dangerous. As he studied the creature, he noticed its reluctance to enter the river. An idea began to unfold in his head. The soldier had a new strategy. He had three arrows still in his quiver. If he could put the river between them as a buffer he should be able to get off at least one or two decent shots. When the water became shallow enough to touch bottom, he gradually made his way to the opposite bank, careful to stay low. He found it odd that he had not yet been detected, but he would take the good fortune and use it to his advantage.

Once the bank was reached, Alex slid through the greasy muck. The dirt felt good, as if he were back in basics, on maneuvers in the peak of a thunderstorm. He held the bow high so as not to contaminate its fine-tuned mechanisms. He wasn't sure what kind of effect the water would have on it. The archer understood that the slightest deviation could offset its functionality. Alex crawled up into the tall swamp grass and began to slink his way back upstream. He did not look up for fear that it might alert the creature. He gauged his direction by the sound of the flowing water and the echoing screams it carried. He crept closer with cunning skill, molding his body to the contour of the soft earth. He savored the bitter taste of the muck as it gritted between his teeth. The creature's tantrums grew louder with each passing yard. He could hear the splashes as it threw large objects into the water.

When Alex felt as if he were even with the creature's position on the opposite bank, he slowly poked his head above the slender blades. It was there, directly across from him, now searching both directions of the river. It had settled down to some degree, as if it were pondering its own strategy. Alex felt a sense of calm as he watched the giant man-like figure milling about. He calculated the distance to be forty yards, give or take a few. He would have to lure it closer, once again using himself as live bait. When it turned away, Alex slowly rose to his feet and knocked an arrow.

"Hey!" The creature crouched into a defensive position as the soldier cried out again. "Remember me, asshole!" Alex saw it lock in on his silhouette. The creature reared back and let loose another roar. But Alex was now immune to its antics. He waited for it to make a move.

Alex could hear the loud thumping as the beast beat its powerful fists against its own chest. He could see the shaft sticking out of its shoulder. But the creature did not appear to be affected. Then, with extraordinary quickness it leapt into the river. The displaced water caused a wave to spill over the river bank in front of the surprised boy. It had covered ten yards in a single bound. The creature stood in waist deep water that had been well over Alex Chavez's head only moments before. But it did not advance. It just stood there, unsure about what it should do next.

Alex burst out of the swamp grass and screamed at the creature. “Come on!” It was now fully illuminated by the moon. Alex could see the hatred in its eyes. Its face was that of an animal, yet it was similar to a man’s. It roared again and took another step toward him. Alex lifted the bow and began to draw, but with the muck still caked on his fingers he could not maintain his hold. The string slid through his grasp and catapulted the arrow in a harmless looping flight until it fell well short of the approaching target. Alex quickly wiped the sludge from his hand onto his pant leg. He tried desperately to suppress the panic that was now building. He still had time. In one smooth motion he snatched another arrow from the quiver and rested it gently on the overdraw. Alex took a deep breath, knowing he now only had one shot at this. The creature was twenty yards and closing. He drew back the string a second time and placed the twenty-yard pin where he thought its heart to be. The animal stopped like it learned from its earlier experience with his weapon.

“Die, you bastard,” he whispered as he let go of the string. At the sound of the release, the creature turned sideways and dove into the water ... like a person. Alex could not follow the arrow’s path. In the blink of an eye, the enormous figure had completely disappeared beneath the surface of the river.

Now he shook with terror, unsure of what he had just witnessed. The velocity of its reaction was implausible. It had thought through the equation and evaded the threat. It was there ... and then it wasn’t. But he couldn’t stand around and wait for the outcome. For all he knew, the creature could swim. Alex had been fooled into thinking that it was afraid of the water. He suddenly felt defenseless. There were no weaknesses to its existence. It was the ultimate predator and it was after him. He turned and ran again. What little hope he had was lost. Alex Chavez had no clue where he was. He could only go as far as his body would take him ... or until he finally succumbed to the certain death that followed. Another howl erupted from the river behind.

***

The Sheriff brought the discolored catch of snow to his face. The clearing looked as though a herd of buffalo had passed through. The trampled ground was littered with freshly gouged chunks of bark. When he first saw the blood his initial reaction was that he had been too late and the boy had lost his race. But when he noticed the clump of hair lying atop the snow, he knew otherwise. Ross heard the commotion from a few hundred yards out and detected the anguish in the creature's cries as if it had been wounded. He reveled in the thought that it was suffering. He also knew that a maimed animal could be even more unpredictable.

Ross followed the trail deeper into the Amen. The wild screams were loud and distant, but he could feel its presence around him. There were no other animals roaming the night. All had escaped the path of terror that systematically drew him in. He continued to follow the prints left behind from the boots of a boy and the enormous feet of a monster. The blood from the wound seemed to dissipate to just a few spurts here and there. His thoughts diverted to David LaFontaine and the creature he described during their time together. Having not yet seen it, the image that Ross drew in his mind incited chills.

As the hunter ducked underneath a limb, his foot nearly slid out from under him in a slick spot under the snow. It felt like a root, but gave under the weight of his body. Ross bent down for a closer look and discovered the broken shaft of the arrow. "Oh Christ," he whispered. The kid was trying to kill it with a bow. Ross discarded the piece of arrow and began to run faster, praying that he could catch up in time. With each labored step, he knew that his odds were diminishing. With the flashlight off and his eyes adjusted, the swamp was aglow from the bright moonlight gleaming off the fresh snow. Ross peered up into the clear northern sky convincing himself that one of the stars was his former wife looking down on him. "Show me the way, Eevie."

He switched his rifle back and forth between hands, trying his best to keep the scope clear. His legs were covered in slimy muck to his knees. His socks made squishing sounds in his soaked boots. *Four shots,* he told himself, wondering if it would be enough.

As Ross broke through a heavily tangled cluster of trees, his feet slipped out from underneath him. He slid on his butt down the steep embankment and into the murky waters of the river below. He planted his feet firmly on the bottom and held his balance, managing to prevent the gun from going under.

"Shit," he cursed quietly. The water was up to his waist. He turned around and sized up the bank. There was no way to get back up it. Retrieving his flashlight from his coat pocket, Ross clicked on the beam and searched the far side. He saw the tracks leading out of the water. "Shit," he said again, realizing that he was now forced to cross. Ross held the gun high above his head with straight arms. He then began to walk toward the opposite shore. As he continued further out into the river, the bottom dropped out. When he reached the middle, only his two arms remained above the waterline. He held his breath until his head finally broke the surface near the other side. When he slogged out of the Ontonogon, his entire body shook terribly. Ross rubbed his arms and shoulders to fend off the freezing cold that had penetrated his bones. There was something now preventing his legs from going on.

For the first time since he embarked on his charge into the Amen, Ross Pickett felt absolute fear. As he stood and shivered on the quiet riverbank, his spirit plummeted. He was afraid, as though he had just awakened from a nightmare only to be thrust into another of much greater proportions with no means of escape. It was the sudden realization that he was vulnerable to the elements. Death was glaring down at him.

"I can't do it!" he cried, falling to his knees. "I can't go on like this." The grown man was reduced to a weeping child as he released the Remington and laid on the ground. He curled his body into a ball on a clump of moss. "Oh God, I can't do this." His voice grew silent as he stared with swollen eyes into a dimming world around him. He had reached a breaking point. His body ached from exposure and he was slipping into a great void.

I'm sorry, Maggie, he said to himself. *I'm so sorry.* When the tear rolled across the bridge of his nose, Ross read aloud the final verse with no remorse.

"If you will the courage,
To face the demons within,
Then pray with pure heart,

The journey ends with Amen."

***

Ray Jackson did not feel comfortable until the third cruiser pulled into the clearing. Satisfied that there was enough manpower in the immediate area, he stashed the .357 in the rear pant line of his jeans.

"Is that him?" asked Jack Berkowski, jogging up from behind.

Ray turned and shook the Sergeant's hand. "Good to see you too, Berky. Yeah, that's him all right."

"Thank God it's finally over," declared the newcomer with a heavy sigh. He began to walk toward the body in the window. Berkowski had not yet noticed the human head in the yard.

"That ain't exactly true, sir," said Jackson.

The Sergeant turned and faced his fellow Trooper. "We already found the other one, Ray. A couple of hunters found the body this afternoon. The word just came through. Looks like this one," he motioned to the corpse with a nod, "couldn't live with the other. Killed his own partner. From what I heard, the coyotes had their way with him."

Ray cringed at the ugly thought. "Seems to be a lot of that going around," he said while turning away. "But that's not what I meant."

Berkowski had an inquisitive expression on his face. "What do you mean?"

"See that hole there?"

The Sergeant glanced to the building. He hadn't even considered it until then. "Now that you mention it, what the hell did that?"

"Take a look-see down by your foot," said Ray in a ghoulish manner that somewhat bothered his co-worker.

Berkowski did as Jackson asked. His eyes widened when he saw the track in the snow. "Holy hell! What in the name of Jesus is that?"

"*That* is what tore the hell out of the cabin. And *that* is what Ross Pickett is now chasing somewhere out there." Ray pointed toward the trees. Both Troopers stopped their conversation when they noticed Maggie approaching.

"What's going on, Ray? Why isn't anyone looking for him? Why are you all just standing around?" She was frantic in her pleas.

"We're doing everything we can, Maggie," answered Ray calmly. "But first, the crime scene needs to be secured."

"Crime scene! Damn it, Ray, that man is dead! Ross is alive and he needs help!" She brought her hands up to cover her reddening face.

Ray slid his good arm around her back. "Don't you go worrying about Ole Ross now. He can take care of himself." She looked up into his eyes like a young child trying to find hope. She was crying. He smiled. "I would hate to be that ... that animal right now." That slight hesitation made her sink back into his chest. The Trooper kicked himself for the mistake. But he didn't know how to describe the creature as portrayed by the youngsters. Even though they hadn't actually seen the thing, their illusions painted a horrid picture. He read the terror in their faces. It was too much to believe, but it *was* real. Jackson was angry at himself for not having more faith in his friend. Maggie was right. They couldn't just stand around while Ross was out there alone.

"We need air support, Berk," proclaimed Jackson with sudden swagger. "I want a helicopter scouring that swamp in ten." He could feel Maggie perking up as he laid out his orders. "I want a search and rescue team assembled in thirty, ready to get out into that swamp. We're going after him, Berk, and I don't care how many stripes you got on your shoulder." Although his commands were firm, Ray winked to his boss to let him know that his inappropriate behavior was for the sake of the woman.

Berkowski offered a touch of a smile to relay his understanding. "Okay, Ray. We'll get that Sheriff of yours." He trotted off toward his car.

"Thanks, Ray," said Maggie with more tears in her eyes. "Thank you so much."

***

With the bow strewn over his shoulder, the soldier scaled the rising pine like a coon fleeing a hound. His hands and feet worked in unison, pulling and pushing his body higher above the ground. His muscles burned as he struggled against total exhaustion. What had once been a carefully planned strategy had changed to all out desperation. His last gasp for salvation would depend on the creature's willingness or ability to follow in the trees.

Alex figured he had about an eighty yard head start when he heard the cries from the river. It wasn't much of a comfort zone. This new idea had been introduced solely by accident when he misjudged a vault over a sloping log. He found himself flat on his back, gazing skyward to the canopy of trees. Outrunning the pursuer was senseless. He now saw his only chance for survival. He could rest there, and pray that the creature was not limber enough to climb after him, or powerful enough to bring down a tree altogether.

Not until he reached a height of twenty feet did Alex begin to slow his ascent. When he stopped at twenty-five, he looked down to judge the length of the creature's arms. If he were to move higher he would sacrifice stability in the thinning limbs. His current position would have to do.

Alex could hear the large animal slowly approaching through the brush. His ears distinguished the ominous growls growing louder. Alex did not knock his remaining arrow, nor did he free it from the quiver. The soldier took a deep breath, closed his eyes and took control of his feelings. He allowed the panic to retreat from his body. The self-control that had been lost in the moment of utter helplessness had once again been recovered. Alex Chavez became the soldier he was trained to be.

When the creature finally came into view, Alex wrestled with the temptation to climb higher. Though he felt exposed in the high perch, he did not move. He assured himself that he was beyond its reach and there were plenty of branches in between to thwart an assault. The beast followed his tracks until they disappeared at the base of the pine. Alex watched as its head scanned the swamp. As he looked closer he saw that it was scenting the air, trying to pinpoint direction. He could hear its heavy breathing as if it were fighting its own fatigue. Alex then noticed the limp when it took a couple of steps. The dark spots left in the oversized tracks could only be one thing ... blood. Its tenacity was missing. The actions were deliberate and almost ... weak. For a few victorious seconds, Alex Chavez thought that his arrow may have found its mark back at the river and the creature *was* dying.

The young soldier seized the rare opportunity to scrutinize his adversary for potential weakness. It was his turn to learn. But, even with his body camouflaged amidst the boughs in the pine, it was the inevasible scent that surrendered his location. The black face peered up into the branches. Its nose guided the two demonic eyes. Alex stared into the face. The creature knew he was there, but it could not make him out against the thick trunk. He could see its neck muscles tighten, preparing to initiate another attack. He listened as the oxygen circulated through its nose, taking in his odor.

Suddenly, the creature propelled its head upward. Alex felt the fetid breath engulfing his body as a thunderclap shook the tree. The roar was deafening. He tried with all of his will to keep his body pinned to the trunk. There was nowhere for him to go. With a slight turn of his head he saw the enormous body leap off the ground. Claws shredded the bark just beneath his feet as gravity pulled them back down to earth. The beast jumped a second time ... and then a third, but still it could not reach high enough. The tree shook terribly each time contact was made. Overcome by frustration, the creature started picking up objects off the ground and throwing them randomly into the branches above. It then grasped the trunk with both hands and began to rock the pine vigorously. The tree swayed back and forth like a flimsy flagpole. Alex marveled at its sheer power.

The creature then grunted as it leveraged its body against the tree in a final effort to bring him down. Alex looked up after hearing a sharp *'crack'* above him. He rotated his body just as the crown of the pine came toppling down past his head. Another few inches and it would have taken him down with it.

And then, as if the *'off'* switch had been toggled, the creature ceased its crazed assault. Alex studied the strange behavior. It looked upward one last time before concentrating its attention on the surrounding swamp. And that's when Alex realized that he had not been seen at all. The creature had only been trying to provoke a response, an old but effective ploy, just as it had done back at the cabin. But Alex was now on to its strategy and knew enough to hold his ground. The creature sensed that he was close, but it could not see him through the network of branches. It offered the soldier a small feeling of triumph as he watched it hobble off into the swamp.

Alex unzipped the fanny pack around his waist. With frozen fingers, he withdrew one of the hand warmers inside and rubbed it between his palms. The plastic packet immediately warmed against his bare skin. He reached into his pack again and found a Hershey Bar for some much needed energy. Alex quietly unwrapped the chocolate and ate, keeping his eyes alerted to the ground. As the soldier relaxed, his mind began to work a new strategy. He was a machine and would not let down his guard until he was safe in the arms of Kay ...

Alex shrugged off the thought of his girlfriend. He had to stay focused. He had to stay in the game.

***

Come lay with her in shallow grave,
Close your eyes to Satan's slave,
Grow tired and sleep, the end is near,
Let go the ones who hold you dear.

He willed the courage,
To face the demons within,
Now he prays with pure heart,
His journey ends with Amen.

The sound of the distant voice drifted into his ears. It was like the muffled melody of a music box buried deep in the bottom drawer of a dresser. It would reach a crescendo, and then hush to barely a whisper as if it were trying to break through some translucent barrier. His eyes opened just a fraction of an inch. There was a brilliant light hovering high above. A voice was calling out to him ... using his name. It was someone he knew ... a woman. He opened his eyes wider and watched as the light danced off the trees until it settled on the white ground a short stretch away. He looked on in a daze as the fairy-like apparition slowly began to emerge into the shape of a person. A golden halo of stars circled the head of the angel coming to harvest his soul. Ross Pickett did not fear the woman. There was an overwhelming peace about her. He welcomed her arrival.

"Hello, Ross."

A tear formed in his eye. It was Eevie. *She* was the angel who had come for him. They would be together again. "Eevie?" The name that he had longed to use escaped his trembling lips. He stared into the eyes of the woman whom he had loved so dearly.

"Yes, Ross," answered the angel, "it's me."

"I've missed you so much. Oh God I've missed you." The tears steadily flowed down his frozen cheeks. He no longer felt the flogging cold. There was only warmth in his heart. He picked his head up off the mossy pillow.

"I know, Ross," said the angel, "and I have missed you."

Ross felt his body slowly rising as she used her holy powers to bring him closer. The heavenly winds slipped underneath his arms and hoisted him up until his feet no longer touched the earth. Ross closed his eyes and embraced the fulfilling sensation. He had finally found his destiny. There was no more pain as he made the transition into the afterworld where he would spend an eternity with his wife. When he opened his eyes he was looking directly into her tender face, just as he remembered it. Her smile warmed his soul.

"I'm so sorry, Eevie. I ... I failed your trust." He bowed his head in shame. The hand of the spirit touched his chin and raised his head back up.

"Poor Ross," she said soothingly. "You have been through so much. You are more of a man than you will ever know. But your time is not yet finished in this world."

Ross looked at her, not understanding the meaning in her words.

She smiled again as she read his confusion. She knew him too well. "Do not feel shame, dear Ross. Never have you broken your trust in me. Only your faith in yourself will heal your wounds."

"But Eevie," he pleaded, "I can't go on without you. I have no strength left to ..."

"You have found the same love that we once shared," she replied. "You have found purpose in life. I have watched you, Ross Pickett. I have always been with you ... in your heart." Eevie placed her hand on his chest. "And I will never leave you. But now you must be strong for there is too much at stake. You have found love again, and fathered a child who is like you in so many ways."

"But I'm so tired," he protested, once again looking down to the ground. She was asking too much of him.

"You are such a gentle man, Ross, but you are also naïve. Do you think that Maggie was merely a coincidence?"

Ross looked up into her eyes. "Do you mean ..."

"She is a wonderful woman. Do not lose faith in yourself for the sake of all who love you. There is so much to live for."

"You don't understand." He tried to express his doubt, but he could not find the proper words to do so. She just continued to smile and urge him to continue living.

"It is time for me to leave, Ross." Her hand pulled away and she began to glow with more vividness. Her image rose toward the stars.

"Eevie, wait! You can't just leave me here." He called out to her, begging her to stay. He needed her strength.

"Just remember this, my love," said the angel as she drifted up toward the heavens, "the spirit that haunts you is only a rogue. Do not condemn all for the sins of one. It is you who will decide their fate. Seek out your demon, Ross, and live the life that the creator has bestowed upon you." And with that final word, Evelyn Pickett was gone.

Ross opened his eyes as the steady rumble rolled through his aching head. The sweeping cold over his wet skin made him shiver uncontrollably. Without moving, he surveyed the swamp around him. There were no brilliant lights. The angel was gone, but he was very much alive.

The echoing roar invaded his ears again. The demon was close. The horrendous cries brought him out of his repose. It was the Devil that drove Eevie away and left him alone in the hell that was the Amen Swamp. The pain and darkness made Ross believe that his heavenly encounter had been nothing more than a figment of his dulled imagination. *But it was so real,* he thought to himself. Eevie had spoken to him, and touched his face. There was another eruption in the trees a hundred yards out. Ross looked in the general direction. His mind was filled with questions and fears. And then, as if he had suddenly been slapped in the face, her words came back to him. *No,* he said to himself, *she was real.* Eevie had not come to take him away, but rather to save him from his own self-pity. He did have too much to live for. If he were to give up now, he would betray Eevie who continued to love him even in death.

"I will not give up," he said confidently as his eyes searched the stars. She was up there, in the sky, watching after him. He could feel her strength. His heart beat with more fervor. Gone was the cold sensation that death delivered. He was alive and ready to face his demon. He became filled with passion, no longer plagued by anguish and guilt.

Ross stood up and stared into the swamp. He listened to the animal's closing screams. "Thank you, Eevie," he whispered. He bent down and picked up the rifle.

***

The female's thigh throbbed as she moved. She circled the area where she knew her prey was in hiding, but she could not flush it. The blood continued to flow from the multiple wounds on her body, depleting her energy with each arduous stride. She cried out her frustration, but there was no prey to excite. Her vision was blurred and her once superior senses were dulled. She fought to find motivation in the anger that had driven her. Her mind returned to the night when the horror first began, when she had lost her motherhood and the right to live with her own species. She remembered her time with the young one, teaching the lessons of survival within the boundaries of the lair. The female could not accept that she was at fault. It was the hairless ones who prevented her from raising a juvenile with the life that it was meant to live.

She stopped and scented the breeze, searching for the putrid stench of her hated adversary. The smell was in the air, but from where she did not know. Her head was too muddled. Her wounds were severe, but she would not retreat. Her kind was not accustomed to surrendering regardless of how inevitable defeat might seem. She would fight the enemy as long as there was breath in her lungs. If she were to die that night, her last act in life would be to kill the ones who cheated her from the motherhood she so badly wanted.

The sudden surge of the familiar scent made her turn to face the prevailing wind. She forced herself to forget the pain in her body. Once again, she detected the hairless creature, only this time from behind. The scent was not fading as she would have expected. It was growing stronger. The enemy was approaching *her*. The female curled back her lips and ran her tongue over her teeth, anticipating the slaughter. She longed to see the terror in the eyes of the creature that dared to trespass in her domain.

***

The Sheriff crept through the tightness of the trees, careful not to brush against the branches and generate sound. He could not compromise his position. Still-hunting in such difficult terrain was nearly impossible for a man of his size. His finger was affixed to the safety of the Remington, ready to switch it off for a snap shot. He now found confidence in believing that an angel was guiding him.

Ross' boot sank into a shallow sinkhole. As he pulled his foot free of the muck there was a pronounced sucking sound. He stood completely still, listening for a reaction. The swamp was deathly quiet. The moon continued to shine brightly in the sky overhead. In his mind, Eevie was showing him the path of truth. The creature had stopped its clamorous bellowing and fell silent to blend with the night. Every crunching step in the snow was magnified tenfold. What concerned him most was that he was traveling upwind and would be alerting the animal of his presence.

As Ross slid through a narrow crevasse between the trunks of two small pines, a sudden movement ahead caught his attention. He leaned back against the larger of the two trees and froze. Through the branches, he could see something moving in his direction ... something big. He could not control his heart from beating faster in his chest. But the feeling was different than that of an approaching buck on opening morning of rifle season. The intentions of both man and beast were identical ... to destroy the other. Only one would survive.

Ross quietly raised the .30-06 and rested the stock on a limb at chin level. He slowly adjusted the magnification on the scope and brought the reticle to his eye. The Leupold collected the light from the moon and allowed Ross to see with amazing clarity. He scanned the trees until he found the dark object. It was the first time he had laid eyes on the creature ... the *Bigfoot.* He saw the massive legs ... walking upright through the brush. The rest of its body gradually materialized into David LaFontaine's frightening prophecy ... a man-like creature... a legend from a faraway world.

He moved his hand up again and increased the magnification of the lens. Ross would not pull the trigger until he had a clear shot. There were too many obstructions between him and his target. With only a 150-grain bullet, he was doubtful that it would penetrate the thick cover. *Four rounds*, he thought to himself. He had to make each of them count. He moved the crosshairs up the length of the enormous body. He saw the chest ... the bosom. It was a female. As he watched the creature walking closer through the trees, he began to wonder what had driven it to lash out in such a violent rage. Why now when it had probably lived in the Amen for only God knew how long.

When the scope zeroed in on the head, Ross finally witnessed for himself the true demon of the Amen Swamp. The face was covered by black skin, scarred from surviving in the wild. But its characteristics were not that of an animal. An unsettling feeling washed over him as he watched the facial expression ... as if it possessed cognitive abilities. Ross began to wonder if the creature actually *was* some form of man that had taken a different turn in its evolutionary cycle. He contemplated whether killing it might actually be wrong in the eyes of the creator. Ross shook off the disturbing idea after remembering that it was Eevie, his angel, who had told him to seek out his demon.

Suddenly, the creature stopped its approach and stared directly at the trees where Ross was hiding. It was only fifty yards away. He could see the head clearly above a large deadfall. The cavernous mouth opened wide and produced a horrible roar into the night. The gun began to shake in Ross' hands. But as he looked closer, he saw a new manifestation on the weathered face. It was not wild rage written in its eyes. It appeared as though the creature was experiencing a pain that Ross was now beginning to understand.

He centered the crosshairs on its broad nose. When he clicked off the safety, he saw the creature's pointed ears perk. But it did not retreat from the sharp noise, as if it too had a destiny to fulfill. His finger probed the trigger. *This is a killer,* Ross assured himself. He could not allow it to live and continue destroying. *You are not a man. You are a fucking animal.* The Sheriff took a deep breath and held it in. When his aim steadied, he fired. Ross watched anxiously through the scope for the beast to fall from his bullet. It disappeared below the deadfall at the sound of the shot. Ross was confident that he had hit the creature. He waited in the trees just in case.

Without warning, the beast exploded through the brush, lunging toward him. It howled in anger. The bullet had missed. He laid the crosshairs on its chest as it burst into the open. His body shook with fear. He touched off another shot, yet still the creature continued to come ... unharmed. *It can't be!* he thought. But a terrible fear had been realized. The thing couldn't be killed. It *was* the Devil. Ross started to run. From behind, he heard the creature in close pursuit.

***

The soldier whittled away at the branch. With the folding bonesaw from his fanny pack, he had cut the heavy limb from the tree and was now converting it into a weapon. He was cold sitting in the tree. The branches provided little protection against the night air. He had remained dormant too long and was now suffering the consequences. It was time to attempt his escape.

Satisfied with the sharp point at the end of his spear, Alex returned his tools to his fanny pack and then carefully began the tricky climb down. Once on the ground, he planned to backtrack his route, hoping that the misguided creature had continued to hunt in the opposite direction. There would be plenty of tracks to lead him through the snow.

When he reached the base of the tree, Alex snatched up the bow in one hand and the homemade spear in the other. He pitted one end of his new weapon against the tree and leaned against the shaft to ensure that it was fit. The branch barely moved under the force of his weight. Alex stole one last glance to the creature's tracks leading off into the trees in the opposite direction and then turned to run. After a fifty-yard sprint, he stopped suddenly at the eruption of gunfire in front of him.

***

As he ran for his life, Ross dissected the errant shot in his head. He was certain there had not been a branch to deflect the bullet. He jumped over a pit of black water and darted into a thick patch of sawgrass on a heading toward the river. A log appeared from out of nowhere and caught his boot. When he fell, the rifle slipped from his hands and bounced off the dead wood.

"The scope!" he cried, now recognizing the grave error. The gun had been tossed around like a hot potato all day. It had to be the reason for the misses. The scope had been bumped and knocked off center.

Ross looked up in time to see the dark object coming at him. He dove for the rifle and rolled onto his back. Without aiming, he brought up the gun and fired into the beast only fifteen feet away. The creature erected itself and squealed with pain as a patch of hair exploded from its midsection. It backed up a few steps and wobbled slightly. Ross sprang to his feet and ran again, his boots slipping and sliding on the soft mud below the snow. He looked over his shoulder. Although slowed by the fresh wound, the creature continued the chase. But it was not the invincible demon. It bled and it cried ... just like a man. Ross ran as fast as he could, evading the many obstacles standing in his path. The longer strides of the beast allowed it to close the gap again.

The Sheriff stopped abruptly when he found himself standing in front of the river. He turned to face the attacker just as it flattened an innocent cedar at the edge of the clearing. The creature hesitated when it saw him, as if it were surprised that he was no longer fleeing. One of its hands covered the bleeding hole in its abdomen. Its broad chest heaved while it struggled to breathe. Ross had one final chance for a clean shot. He sank the stock of the rifle into his shoulder and aimed, this time utilizing the peep sights below the offset scope. Sensing danger, the beast hunched low to the ground and shot toward him like a charging rhino, dragging its knuckles for support. With the vitals no longer exposed, his only shot was the head. He waited until it was twenty feet away and then pulled the trigger for the final time. A shrill scream followed the explosion of the gun. The creature dived head first into the ground, plowing through the snow like a derailed train.

The Sheriff stared at the mammoth head lying motionless at his feet. A chill crept up his spine as he mentally sized up the outstretched body. Its girth was unimaginable. He looked at its hands ... the fingers. He could not move. His entire life had come down to this one defining moment in the Amen Swamp. Then, he fell to a knee and bowed his head, thankful for the protection that he had received from above.

It was a strangled noise that made Ross look up. There was movement in the animal. He instinctively aimed the unloaded Remington at the creature's head and stood up. It's back rose ... and then fell. There was a strained sigh as if it had just expelled its last breath. Ross took a step toward the river behind him, but as he turned to check his distance to the bank he felt pressure around his right ankle. When he looked back, the beast then reached out with its other paw and grasped his left leg. Both feet were yanked out from underneath him. He hit the ground hard.

Ross screamed at the top of his lungs, now overcome with panic. He tried to kick, but the creature would not release its stingy grip on his shackled legs. He could feel its claws sinking into his calves. Ross raised the gun and hammered it down on one of the massive forearms. The creature was too strong and would not disengage. He could now see its face, displaying a terrifying savagery as it pulled him closer. A sinister growl was uttered from its frothy mouth. Maintaining its firm hold, the monster struggled to its feet. It raised its head and howled as if it were letting the swamp know that it was the master of all that dwelled there.

Ross knew then that he had been defeated. The pain in his legs was excruciating as he was pulled from the swamp floor and hoisted upside down. He could hear the jaws snapping as it prepared to end his misery. "Eevie!" he cried, praying for a quick and merciful deliverance. The blood rushing to his head made him feel woozy. Suddenly, the world around him seemed to rotate. When his head flopped back to the center of his shoulders and his vision cleared, Ross found himself staring directly into the eyes of the Amen's demon. He was suspended above the ground, held by claws that had now impaled his sides. He could not pull his eyes away from the face of the being that was about to kill him. He wanted to understand it.

The stench of its foul breath was sickening. He saw the caked blood and the rotten flesh from old kills littering the hair lining its chin. But there was something in the eyes. It was the same expression that he observed through the scope. It studied him, as if it too were trying to ascertain a deeper understanding.

Ross then made a profound connection in the rhyme that had been tormenting him. "*You* are the spirit," he whispered, recalling the tale of the hunter from years past who had been left for dead but had somehow managed to crawl out. He remembered the stories the firemen told of the strange cries from the Amen. His thoughts drifted to Dr. Flemming and how he had presented the possibility of an alien presence. "*You* are the demon," he muttered again.

Find the demon that rules the dark,
Hear the cries of the Devil's lark,
Amen's prize cannot be sought,
Your soul is the prize for which you fought.

If you will the courage,
To face the demons within,
Then pray with pure heart,
The journey ends with Amen.

"Amen!" shouted Ross in his increasingly drunken state. He had no other recourse but to finalize the rhyme and end the mystery of the Amen Swamp. "Amen! Amen! Amen!"

The creature's narrow eyes widened, puzzled by the conduct of its defeated prey. Ross' consciousness faded as life-giving blood continued to drain from his wounds. The gashes in his sides widened as the creature gripped him tighter, but there was no pain as he prepared himself for death. He was no longer fearful, knowing that Eevie would not allow him to suffer. She would take him from this place. He closed his eyes and waited for salvation.

There was a sudden whoosh of air, like a passing missile followed by a loud *'thwack.'* Ross felt the claws clench tighter still, and then the creature's body went rigid. When he opened his eyes he saw a broadhead protruding from the middle of the thick neck just inches from his own face. He looked into its eyes and watched them roll back in their sockets. A gurgling noise escaped its lips as blood flowed from both corners of its mouth.

Ross felt himself falling. When he landed on his back, he stared up and saw the creature teetering back and forth like a tree succumbing to a lumberjack's axe. Another cry erupted in the swamp ... from a smaller creature. The monster arched its back as the spear was thrust into its torso. It let out a high-pitched squeal. Ross forced his eyes to remain open. When the creature wheeled around he saw the boy riding its back while hacking away at its hide with what appeared to be a small knife.

"Run!" yelled the boy who the Sheriff did not recognize. "Get out of here!"

But Ross could not move. To run would be futile. He calmly lay down and watched like an impartial spectator. Sleep was close at hand.

In a final act of desperation, the creature reached back and snared Alex Chavez. The soldier was tossed through the air until he landed just a few feet from Ross' legs. The Sheriff clawed his way over to the unconscious boy. He sat beside him and gazed into his face. He was too young to be caught up in this battle.

The beast, in the meantime, laboriously stumbled over to the two humans.

"What's the matter?" Ross joked with cocky arrogance. "Gotta backache, you big fucking ... bitch."

The creature's body jerked as it stood over him, fighting to live for just one more second to satisfy its evil existence. Ross then remembered the extra shell permanently stored in the sleeve pocket of his parka ... the lucky *'just in case'* bullet. He had a fifth round. Ross reached for the zipper. It was there! He grabbed the bullet with two fingers and then reached for the Remington. Sensing that something was amiss, the demon slammed its foot hard into the earth beside his arm. Ross paid no attention. He slid the round into the chamber and brought the rifle to his shoulder. He heard the boy whimper beside him. Alex awoke just as the creature gathered its last thread of strength and raised its foot high into the air, ready to crush the life out of both of them. But before the foot came down on them, the massive body went limp and toppled to the ground. The demon of the Amen Swamp was dead.

"Oh, Jesus," whispered the boy as he coddled up to the Sheriff. And then he cried, releasing the emotion that only a soldier could understand in the aftermath of an intense battle.

Ross laid the rifle down and hugged him. "It's over," he said with his strength quickly diminishing. "What do you say we get out of here? I think you're going to have to give me a hand." He offered a weak smile.

As they both scooted away from the corpse at their feet, Ross felt the boy's fingernails sink into his arm. "What's ...?" The question was quickly answered before he could finish. When he followed the boy's blank stare to the edge of the clearing, his own body stiffened. Standing at the broken tree line was a black silhouette, larger than the one they had just killed. Both of them sat on the ground like a pair of garden ornaments, unable to make their bodies work. They were both experiencing the horrid realization that all of their efforts, every inflicted wound, had been in vain.

Ross watched the figure take a step toward them, and then stop. It did not charge, nor did it roar with the unharnessed ferocity of its predecessor. It just looked at the two of them as if sizing up its next meal. But he still had one shot remaining in his rifle. Very carefully, he picked up the weapon and shielded the boy with his body. *At least one of us will have a chance*, he thought with remorse, knowing that he lacked the strength to run. He raised the gun and aimed ... and waited. But still, the creature did not advance. Ross then detected movement off to his right. Keeping the gun pointed at the first target, he turned his head slightly. Another creature stepped into the clearing ... and then two more. Now there were four, all captivated by the sight of the corpse.

Ross could hear the boy's excited breathing. "Alright ... move back," he whispered. Together, they slid backwards toward the river. If they could sneak into the water, then maybe they would have a chance. At least the boy could make it. Ross doubted he had the stamina to make it to the other side. Ross saw a fifth creature sneak out behind the first ... and then a sixth ... meticulously converging on their prey.

"Be ... behind us," stuttered the boy with fear in his voice.

Ross turned and saw five more shapes on the opposite bank cutting off their only avenue for escape. They were trapped ...

helpless against a superior predator. They were now facing a hoard of demons that were scrutinizing their every action. There was not one spirit in the Amen ... there were many, perhaps hundreds. Ross then began to think that he was the one that did not belong in this land, and he would ultimately be punished for intruding on their private sanctuary.

Guessing the remainder of his life would most likely be measured in seconds, he thought of one final thing that he could do. If nothing else, he could spare the boy from a brutal death. There was one bullet left. Ross turned to the kid, hating himself for what he was about to propose. “My name is Ross Pickett, son. I don’t believe I’ve had the pleasure.” He smiled in an attempt to set the boy at ease.

“My ... my name is Alex ... Chavez.”

“Well, Alex,” continued Ross, fighting the pain in his sides, “we sure have raised some hell out here, haven’t we?” He watched as a tear rolled down the boy’s cheek. *Goddammit, Ross,* he scolded.

“Yeah ... we have.” Alex stole a quick glance to the creatures on their side of the river. They were closer. He then detected the solemn frown on Ross’ face. “You’re bleeding pretty bad, sir.” Alex placed his hand over the Sheriff’s wound.

Ross pushed his hand away, chuckling and wincing at the same time. “Never mind that, Alex. I think our ... I mean ... I mean it ain’t lookin too good for us.” His face turned grim as he laid the cards on the table. “I’ve got one round in this rifle, Alex,” he said with a weakened voice. “One of us doesn’t have to go through with this.”

“Well, I don’t ...” And then Alex Chavez understood. He looked down to the rifle in Ross’ trembling hands.

“I sure as hell can’t make it out of here, Alex. So if you want ... I’ll ... what I mean is ...” Ross looked away, unable to face the young boy’s eyes.

“Alright,” said Alex Chavez.

Ross watched him nod with sad approval. The boy then clenched his eyes shut, took the barrel of the rifle in his hand and brought it up underneath his chin.

“I’m so sorry for all this, Alex. Oh God, I’m so sorry.”

“It’s ... it’s okay, Ross,” he replied bravely. Alex Chavez then said *‘good-bye’* to Kayla Johnson in his heart.

The Sheriff clicked off the safety. All he had to do was pull the trigger and the boy would be spared the agony. He delicately touched the short, metal curvature that would end his life ... and give him life. He peered into the distraught face, trembling with fear of the unknown. *So brave*, thought Ross. But he couldn't do it. He couldn't end the boy's life. Ross switched the safety back on and rolled away, looking up into the heavens.

Alex opened his eyes and saw the older man shielding his own sobbing face with bloody hands.

"I'm sorry, Alex ... I can't do it. I can't do it!" The Sheriff's voice rose out of frustration.

Alex scooted over and wrapped his arms around him. "Don't sweat it," he said calmly. "Whatever happens ... happens."

Suddenly, there was a noise from the group of creatures on the far side of the river. Ross and Alex now awaited their pending demise. The other creatures joined in one by one, until they were all partaking in some choreographed ritual. Ross and Alex watched with growing tension, each wondering how their deaths would be delivered.

But then something strange happened as the largest of the group broke from the pack and walked up to the body of the one they had killed. Ross stared into its eyes, figuring that this was the leader. He pointed the rifle at its chest, ready to fire before the deadly claws could swipe down on him. But much to his surprise, the creature did not attack, nor did its body language suggest that it would. It looked into Ross's eyes, and then ... nodded off toward the edge of the clearing.

The Sheriff sat on the ground, confused by what he was witnessing. The beast began to grunt and wave at them, as if it were prodding them to leave.

"I ... I ... think ... it wants us to leave," whispered Alex into his ear.

Ross heard the shock in the boy's voice, much like his own. He felt Alex slide his arms underneath his armpits and then help him to his feet. "Come on, Ross. Let's go." He began to move Ross toward the trees.

"The rifle," responded the Sheriff. "We can't leave it."

"Forget it, sir," said Alex. "Leave it."

As Alex helped him to the edge of the clearing, Ross looked back, wanting to comprehend what he was seeing. He needed to understand. He forced the boy to stop so that he too could experience what no man had ever seen before. The creatures converged on the center of the clearing. Their demeanor was morose, as if they were grieving the loss of a loved one. A lone squirrel barked in a tree above. Two of the creatures stooped down and picked up the legs, while two more were assigned to the torso. Together, they carried the fallen one ... *the Rogue* ... back to their home in the Amen Swamp.

Ross began to see a clearer picture as he watched the last one disappear into the trees. These swamp-dwellers were not a murdering band of savages. They were a species of living, thinking beings ... an ancient tribe existing in their own civilized fraternity that humanity could neither understand nor accept. *They* were the spirits of the Amen ... the focal point for legends and rhymes shared by generations.

Ross remembered Eevie's words ... "*do not condemn all for the sins of one. The demon you seek is only a rogue.*" *Perhaps it was a rogue*, he thought while staring at the empty clearing. Maybe it was an outcast that, for whatever reason, had found Man to be criminal and negligent in his ways. It was Man who caused it to lash out, not in a violent unjust rage, but in self-defense for fear that its own existence was in jeopardy.

The Sheriff suddenly faced an insurmountable impasse, just as David LaFontaine had predicted. Exposing the species would result in certain extinction. Man could not live in such close proximity with what could only be perceived as a dangerous competitor. The creatures would ultimately be killed off, simply out of fear.

The Sheriff's eyes grew heavy as he shifted his weight to Alex's shoulder.

"Are you okay, sir?" asked the boy.

"I'm fine," said Ross, and then he passed out. His nightmare was over.

CHAPTER SEVENTEEN

"We've been up here for an hour ... we're not going to find anything tonight ... recommend we wait until morning."

"Roger that, Eagle-one ... hold for confirmation."

The radio went silent as the dispatcher awaited her next order. Jack Berkowski looked over to Jackson. "It's too thick, Ray. They can't see through those trees. I'm sorry, but ..."

"Just a while longer," pleaded Maggie Barnes. "Please, Ray."

"What about infrared, Sarge?" Jackson knew that he was grasping at straws.

"This bird isn't equipped, Ray. The Flir was in the chopper that went down last night. All they have is their eyes. I understand we had to try, but ..."

"Don't you do it," cried Maggie. "Don't you give up on Ross."

Ray held her close. "Come on, Berk. He's alone out there. Just a little longer ... please." It was Jackson's turn to plead.

"Sorry, buddy, but all we can do now is hope that our patrol can find them." A small squad had departed just a few minutes earlier following the trail into the Amen. Berkowski turned his attention back to the radio. "Eagle-one, this is Berkowski ... return home ... repeat ... return home, over."

"That's a rodge, Berk. Eagle-one out."

Maggie's body wilted as she slid down Ray Jackson's oversized frame and dropped to her knees, weeping uncontrollably. The Trooper knelt down next to her.

"Listen, Maggie, maybe you should go home and be with your son."

She peered up angrily into his eyes. "Don't you think for a second that I'm going anywhere. You all might just go ahead and give up ... but I'm ... I'm not." She collapsed in his chest, overcome with grief.

"Hey, Berk!" The pilot's voice suddenly squawked with excitement.

The Sergeant picked up the mike. Ray and Maggie looked up to him, each feeling a glimmer of hope. "Go ahead, Eagle-one."

"I've got something ... on the ground. I think ... it is! I've got a small fire in a clearing. Going in for a closer look."

Ray hoisted Maggie to her feet. They waited impatiently for confirmation. "Is it them?" asked Maggie.

"Can you see anything?" questioned the Sergeant into the mike.

"Yes!" exclaimed the co-pilot. "I've got them in the spotlight! It's them! They're alive!"

"I'll be damned," said Berkowski to nobody in particular. He leaned on the roof of the squad car and sighed. Maggie and Ray embraced.

***

Alex stoked the fire with any dry object he could find. He first lit a cord of rope to start the blaze. He then added the fanny pack with all of its contents ... anything to produce warmth. Ross was rapidly fading, but Alex could not leave him to die alone. Disregarding his own wounds, Alex took off his shirt and applied a tourniquet around his new friend's waist. *Nobody gets left behind*, he said to himself.

The soldier recognized the soft '*whumping*' sound the moment it touched his eardrums. He'd heard it a hundred times before ... choppers charging in for an extraction. He searched the sky as the noise grew louder. And then he saw the light ... off to the north ... coming their way. Alex picked up his flashlight and frantically waved it at the approaching helicopter. He watched as it rushed over the clearing like a fleeting wisp of optimism. Just when he thought that his signal had not been seen, the chopper performed a hard bank. It was coming back! "He sees us!" yelled Alex exuberantly. "Ross!" He turned to the man lying on the ground. "They're here, Ross! They're here!"

The Sheriff opened his eyes and gazed up into the sky, blinded by the bright light from the heavens. The angel of mercy had returned to claim him. "Amen," he whispered with pure heart. "Amen."

***

The eyes of the dominant male at the rear of the hunting party followed the machine's lights as it flew off into the night. Though he marveled at its great powers, he understood the peril that now faced his species. As the new leader, the others would look to him for wisdom. He could see fear in the movements of the other males as they carried the fallen one back to the lair. It was fear for what lay ahead in their unwritten future.

It was the leader's decision to seek out the female and allow her back into the protection of the clan. It had been a difficult choice, but one of necessity for the sake of their survival. And now they had been compromised. The hairless creatures had inferior skills, but their numbers were great. He could easily have destroyed the two creatures at the clearing and proved his superiority. But what end would that have achieved? More would come in time. Every generation was properly schooled on the destructive ways of the hairless ones; the way they killed for no reason, the way they devastated the earth with their machines. And now they would come for the clan ... to destroy them. His kind had acted in similar fashion at various times throughout their history. There was a rogue in every generation. The male obtained his new role because of the intelligence he possessed. He understood what must be done and he knew that the others would follow out of respect for his position. It was time for the clan to move on and find another lair where there were no hairless ones to jeopardize their existence. They would find a place where they could do the one thing that came natural to them ... survive.

***

The earth vibrated horribly around him. When he looked up and recognized the boy staring down on him, Ross smiled. They had made it. He was teetering in and out of consciousness as the helicopter rushed its passengers up to Houghton.

"You had me kind of scared back there," said Alex. The boy's face showed his relief. "I thought I had lost you, buddy," he continued.

"Don't think yourself so lucky," whispered the Sheriff barely loud enough to be heard. He stared into the boy's gritty face, soiled by mud and blood from the Amen Swamp. He prayed that

Alex Chavez would understand what he now felt compelled to ask of him. "Do me a favor, son." Alex would have to play along. They were the only ones who had actually seen the creature clearly enough to recognize what it really was. Ross felt obligated to allow the species a chance to live the way God intended.

"Anything, Ross. Name it."

The Sheriff fought his way up on one elbow. "Ohhhhh, God," he cried as the pain flared in his side. There was a man in blue coveralls beside him rubbing some ointment on his wounds. He leaned over to Alex's ear and whispered. "What we saw out there, Alex ... a bear. It was a bear ... not ... a ... not a ... " He tried to clear the fog in his head as he struggled to speak.

The boy looked at him curiously. "What do you mean? What bear, Ross?"

"Please, Alex." His voice began to fade again. "Between us ... a bear ... please." The Sheriff collapsed on the gurney. Alex covered him with a blanket while the paramedic continued to apply first aide.

EPILOGUE

ROGUE BEAR SLAIN IN U.P. TOWN

In a dramatic turn of events, a rogue bear was finally hunted down and destroyed in a western U.P. town this week. Two weeks ago, this paper reported how the Sheriff of Jessup, Michigan, Ross Pickett, along with three other hunters, tracked down and killed a black bear that allegedly attacked and caused the deaths of three members of the Jessup community. As Pickett conveyed in an interview following the first hunt, the bear was not the true culprit. After several disappearances in the Jessup area in the weeks that followed, alleged victims of the killer bear, the Sheriff was finally able to seek out and kill the guilty animal without assistance from the Department of Natural Resources, the branch of State government designated to deal with such problems. Pickett has refused further comment and is currently recovering from serious wounds received during his encounter with the bear. The story unfolded when a group of college students from Marquette were being held hostage by Tyrone Pullman, the man who police believe masterminded the escape of convicted murderer Gerald Johnson while in route to Jackson Prison to serve out a life sentence. The two fugitives then fled to the U.P. and holed up in various hunting camps in the remote wilderness leaving a trail of victims in their wake. State Police discovered that Johnson was ultimately killed by Pullman. They now believe that Pullman's reason for freeing his partner was to silence him and

> avoid his own implication in the murders of a Lansing Police Officer and his family in Potterville, Michigan. Sources revealed that the DNR has promised a full investigation into the activities of Sheriff Pickett. HUFAR (Humans for Animal Rights) spokeswoman Diane Lang, who spoke up against Sheriff Pickett after the first incident, has labeled the man's actions to be a travesty of justice and complete dereliction of duty. Gene Steubens, Mayor of Jessup, was quoted as saying that Ross Pickett has served the community well, but that his inappropriate actions will be investigated thoroughly by the city council. Sources close to Sheriff Pickett have stated that he is now contemplating retirement.
>
> Winston Lovells / Detroit News

"It's amazing what people will say to get their names in print," said Ross as he folded the newspaper. He laid it on the table next to his bed. "Was there a reason you had me read this, Maggie?"

"I thought the last line of the article was rather intriguing," she answered playfully, as she lay next to him on the narrow mattress.

"Yeah, and I wonder who that *source* close to the Sheriff was?" He gave her a cynical look.

"What matters is that we're together now, babe. It's over." She snuggled up tight against him and kissed his cheek.

Ross carefully manipulated the tubes in his arms and wrapped her up. "It's over, Maggs." The love he felt for the woman was never stronger, and he would be with her always.

"Hello?" Ross and Maggie turned as the boy's head peeked through the doorway. "Can we come in?" Alex Chavez and a girl that Ross did not recognize strolled into the room.

"Aren't we a couple of beat-up bastards," laughed Ross when he observed the bandages adorning Alex's body. The young man had one arm around the girl's shoulder for support, while the other was wrapped around his backside to hold the drafty hospital gown in place. The girl's shoulder was in a sling, and there was a deep bruise on her forehead. But she appeared to be at peace, considering the traumatic experience.

"Hi, Ross. I want you to meet someone. This is Kayla Johnson ... my fiancé." The young coeds looked at each other and smiled.

"Well congratulations, Alex." The Sheriff then turned to the young woman at the boy's side. "It's a pleasure to meet you, Kayla." He took her outstretched hand and gently kissed it with dry lips. "You've got quite a man there."

"I know," she answered. "I've always known." After two days of rest and a few lengthy sessions with a psychologist, Kayla had beaten her severe state of shock. The moment of shared terror had established a remarkable bond between all of them. Under ordinary circumstances their worlds never would have met.

"When we get out of here, Ross, I'm going to buy you a beer," proclaimed Alex.

"Make it a Coke and you've got a deal." As far as Ross Pickett was concerned the old ghosts had been laid to rest. With the help of an angel, he had his life back. He would do everything within his power to see that he was worthy of his salvation.

When Maggie and his two visitors left him for the evening, Ross had time to deliberate over his experience in the Amen Swamp. Missing from his thoughts were the rhymes that prophesied the large tract of land and the spirits that lay within. Alex Chavez's silence allowed him peace in knowing that the species they encountered together would now have a fair chance. They were not demons. Ross was grateful for Ray Jackson's understanding, too. The Troopers who were at the cabin that night saw the tracks for themselves, and their questions warranted immediate answers. But with Ray's help, Ross was able to persuade them that a low-key approach to the ordeal was better than initiating an all-out panic. The last thing they needed was for people to start their own crusades.

In time there was always the possibility the secret would be revealed. But these creatures possessed a sophisticated intelligence that gave them the ability to learn and adapt, perhaps more so than Man.

There would be only one other human being with whom he would share his story. The only person in the world who could be trusted with the truth was the man from Montana, David LaFontaine. Ross owed him that much. David had dedicated his life in pursuit of a myth. He would understand Ross' motives.

Do not condemn all for the sins of one. The demon you seek is only a rogue. Eevie had been right. His angel had shown him the path. The rogue was no more and the Amen was at peace.

THE END

Made in the USA
Middletown, DE
03 September 2021

47525135R10308